SMOKE EATERS

ALSO BY CHRISTINE ANDREAE

Trail of Murder
A Small Target
Grizzly

SMOKE EATERS

Christine Andreae

THOMAS DUNNE BOOKS
ST. MARTIN'S MINOTAUR
NEW YORK

THOMAS DUNNE BOOKS.
An imprint of St. Martin's Press.

Library of Congress Cataloging-in-Publication Data

Andreae, Christine.
Smoke eaters: a thriller / Christine Andreae.—1st ed.
p. cm.
ISBN 0-312-25206-4
1. Women fire fighters—Montana—Fiction. I. Title.

PS3551.N4134 S65 2000
813'.54—dc21 99-054818

First Edition: March 2000

10 9 8 7 6 5 4 3 2 1

To my editor, Ruth Cavin, who encouraged me to reach;
and to my agent, Jane Chelius, who helped me find the way.
With love.

Burning to death on a mountainside is dying at least three times. First, considerably ahead of the fire, you reach the verge of death in your boots and your legs; next, as you fail, you sink back in the region of strange gases and red and blue darts where there is no oxygen and here you die in your lungs; then you sink in prayer into the main fire that consumes, and if you are Catholic about all that remains of you is your cross.

—Norman Maclean, *Young Men and Fire*

Acknowledgments

If writing is a solitary business, researching a novel is not. I am grateful to many, many people, both in the world of wild fire and in law enforcement, for their stories and their expert advice. At the top of my thank-you list is Candace Gregory, a firefighter whose experience on command teams inspired this tale and who patiently and painstakingly answered a two-year stream of my questions. Special thanks also to Tim Eldridge, former smoke jumper, for his insights and enthusiastic support.

For hours of conversation and instruction on everything from fire forensics, to fire camp food service, to FBI profiling, thanks to Douglas Lannon, Ted Putnam, Bob Meuchels, Leslie Anderson, Doug Raeburn, Mark and Betsy Gerlach, Dave Needler, Hal Nelson, Beverly Adams, Jeanne Bibler, Ward McKay, and Richard Ault.

Thanks to my friends Harry Pagapan, Suzanne Kilgore, and Anna Collins for their (yet again!) attentive readings. Thanks to Joe McGreevy for last-minute advice.

And thanks to my husband, Andy, my companion in research, my best critic.

Part I

THE DRAGON

1

06 June 9:32p   Directory C:*.*

It started last September, after the Fletcher Canyon Fire. The last crews had been demobed, I had folded up our tent, the caterer did a Last Supper thing, surf and turf at three o'clock in the afternoon. We happy few. We band of brothers. We were all supposed to stand up and sing Hail to Logistics. Going out I got stuck behind a U.S. West communications rig, ate its dust for twenty miles with a rubber string of langouste stuck in my top molar, hit hardtop and stopped off at the first place I came to: a dive in the middle of nowhere. Log front, broken neon sign, cabins out back under the pines, inside packed with groundpounders making up for lost time. The road was lined with vehicles on both sides.

She was with a hotshot crew, four or five of them, in red T-shirts. Red with a dragon that looked like a squirrel on the back. If every other jerk in this business thinks he's got the Great American Novel waiting up his ass, every tenth jerk thinks he's some kind of Rembrandt. She wasn't wearing the artwork. She was wearing a sleeveless undershirt and no bra. You could tell right off she was no groupie. The undershirt was white cotton with tiny little ribs in it and on the back it was stained pink where she'd taken a hit from retardant. You could see it made her cocky, not that she didn't have the right. Her Nomex jeans were baggy, bunched around her waist with a web belt, like, don't give me no shit, bud. Her body had a hard little strut to it. She had the shirt stretched down into her jeans and the front of it was wet, and so was her hair, one of her pals had slopped beer all over her, and you could see her nipples, small and dark through the wet white cotton. Her tits were nothing to write home about, but she acted like they were. Her eyes were beer-blurry, someone said they'd been demobed that morning.

Well, I got in there at eighteen hundred. I lost count of the beers, but after a while, the place began to thin out. She stayed. She did an arm-wrestling number at the end of the bar with a college kid from Minnesota. You could see tufts of dark hair under her arms. She won. She was stronger than she looked and the kid was slobbering. He passed out and she came over and took the stool next to me. Hey, she said, her voice slightly hoarse.

Hey, I said back. I lifted my bottle. Join me?

Who are you? she said. She squinted, then said, Don't tell me. You're a camp slug.

I raised an eyebrow. I wasn't wearing anything she could ID. No badge, no cap, I'd changed into a polo shirt. I hadn't bothered to change out of the olive-drab jeans, but there was no way she could have known I was overhead.

She reached over and with two firm fingers drew a slow line along the top of my thigh. Your Nomex is unsullied, she said. Diction like a queen. You like it, don't you? she said.

I'm thinking, oh shit. Like what? I said, casual.

Wearing your Nomex. She grinned and the sinking feeling stopped, just was gone, and then, Christ! I felt a stab, a jolt—like, long time no feel! I couldn't believe it!

She looks at me amused and cocky at the same time, like she knows exactly what's happening with me.

You like fire, she says.

I respect fire, I tell her.

Hey, we all got respect for the Dragon, she says. But with you it's more than that. With you, it's different.

You can tell.

I can tell, she says. I'm a witch.

As in Wicked Witch of the West?

She corrects me: As in Fire Witch.

I'm wondering how drunk she is, how reliable my resurrection is. I ask her if she wants a beer. She says she doesn't think so. I drain mine and put the empty on the bartop between us. I say, You got a name, Fire Witch?

Cat.

Sounds familiar. Not wonderful, but she gets it. She peers at me, checking to see if it was intentional. So to speak, I say.

She laughs, then chokes and coughs up black shit into a blue Kleenex. She looks at it. "Fucking smoke." Then she laughs again.

I was feeling dry. I nod at the bartender and he plunks down another cold brown bottle streaming icy water. I close my hand around it and she touches me again, presses two fingers just above my knee, presses hard. "Don't drink it," she says and she pulls a book of matches out of her jeans, holds them up like a magician about to perform. I'm still feeling where she pressed her fingers into my knee. She swivels around so the bartender's at her back, straightens her spine, opens up her knees, there I am, sitting pretty.

Watch, she says. She lights a match, meets my eyes and moves the flame under her chin. Yellow light flickering on her throat. She stretches her neck like a dancer, then elegantly draws the match down and circles her right breast with it. She holds it against her nipple, smiles, then with a quick flourish, shakes out the flame, drops the match in my fucking beer. She flashes the book of matches at me.

How about you light the next one? she says.

I got the key to one of the cabins from the bartender. I ask him how much.

No charge, he says. You guys worked hard, you deserve a good night's sleep. He winks. Jesus! I was so turned on, I was embarrassed to walk to the door. Outside, it was still light, only eight o'clock, and the acrid smell of ash, pushed down the mountain by cooling air, hung over the cabins. There was one narrow little window over the bed. Abracadabra time. We went through her book of matches, shiny maroon cover, from a bar off Higgins Avenue. Small world, she was from Missoula too, but the coincidence wasn't a big deal, it just felt normal, like it was meant to be and I don't mean like in some cheap little song. It was as if something had shifted and we were moving on another plane of existence, everything was meshing, it all worked, I had this clarity. Margaret's inept fumblings, her pathetic attempts, all that discreet maneuvering to get me "to see someone," it didn't matter, none of it mattered at all. Tires crunched outside on the gravel and she worked her magic. She *was* a witch! I was six years old and forty-six at the same time. We ran out of matches and I had to get dressed and go back to the bar and bum a pack off the locals who were celebrating their pathetic windfalls, some guy with a dozer making megabucks off us, another bragging about three thousand ham sandwiches he'd sold us at five bucks each.

Matches worked best. We tried her Bic, yellow mini number she had, disposable, but it wasn't the same. Matches

06 June 10:04p   Directory C:*.*

Shit. Margaret came in. I exited so fast I almost lost this. Next time I'll just switch screens. Saved this under CAT, got to come up with something safer. I imagine Margaret squinting at the menu. CAT?

I can't believe she's doing this to me! The bitch lit a fire in my head all right, but I'm not plucking any silver apples of the moon or golden apples either. Road apples is more like it. Here I am sinking in shit and Margaret comes in and puts her hand on my shoulder. What are you working on, hon?

Go to bed, I tell her, I'll be up in a bit. She wouldn't leave. Maybe her estrogen was kicking in. What, I say, you want me to come up and diddle you?

She didn't. Where was I? Matches. Strips of cardboard dipped in sulfur. They consume themselves, a one-of-a-kind event that leaves only a residue of ash. Matches equalize. Both the one worshiped and the worshiper feel the sting of flame. The match releases its wave of heat, the flame bites her skin, my fingers. We're connected by a line of fire, a sacred radius. The radius may move, like the needle of a compass, but it's indelible. *She is still connected to me.* She doesn't know it, but she is.

We drew a magic circle. A square in a circle, futon on the floor

under the windows. The floor had just been refinished after the last tenant, so we put mayonnaise lids under the candles. A magic circle of fire. We had two whole days together, candles burning the whole time. Shit came out that I'd forgotten. We were both crying. You're healing, she said. She sucked on a jay, sucked on me. You're incredible, she said. You really are a fire god.

07 June 8:45a   Directory C:*.*

Never made it upstairs last night. Crashed in the den, woke up on the carpet—no hangover! But on the way into work, I'm seeing the needle of a compass. A fire-licked needle against the darkness, something out of William Blake, but it's moving, gently swinging back and forth. A radius isn't static. I got her on my car phone. Male voice answers: Hang on. Real casual. Maybe it's one of her brothers-in-fire, a warrior pal fucking her brains out, thinks he's something else. Then she comes on. Cat? I tell her about how we're a moving radius. I can hear myself telling her. She says, Are you stoned?

Listen carefully, she says. Call me again and I won't call your wife, I'll call this geek I know at the paper and give him a Pulitzer on sexual harassment and Smokey Bear. You'll make our president look like a saint. She hangs up. I almost rear-ended a fucking Volvo in front of me, had to stop at MacD's to get it together. Went into the men's, locked myself in a stall, started blubbering, talk about your head in your underpants, Jesus Christ, I had them stuffed in my mouth trying to keep it down. She's not going to get away with this. I can tell you that. I can tell you that right now.

10 July 2.19a   Directory C:*.*

What's amazing is, no one notices. They say, Looking good, lost your love handles, ha-ha. This afternoon, tried it with this whore, big blond girl. Bought a bunch of wintergreen candles, it was that or carnation, they were out of unscented, and took her to the

Twilite Motel out Fourth Street. She was game. Problem was, her bush was blond and kind of scraggly and without glasses it was hard to see where it was and she got a little singed and freaked out about it and I let her have it. She claimed I'd broken her nose and I had to give her two extra bills to shut her up. All that wintergreen, the place stank like a locker room. No way she's going to report it. It was an accident. What's she going to say, this trick burned my bush? I'd like to see the cops' faces! Besides, she hasn't got a clue who I am.

2

Mattie McCulloch caught her first glimpse of the Justice Peak Fire as she sped over the crest of the Continental Divide and rolled down toward the Sophia River Valley. On either side of the highway, naked hills lay brown and sere under a sharp blue Montana sky, but in the distance ahead, a soft afternoon haze hung over the valley. Through the windshield of her Forest Service–issue Jeep Cherokee, she scanned a pale blue wall of mountains and picked out four—no, five—slender ribbons of smoke. Another driver might have missed them. The ribbons were thin and white, randomly spaced but slanted at the same oblique angle. Like multiple offerings of incense, they streamed dreamily up out of the ridges' folds into a smudge of cinnamon-colored sky. The Justice Peak Fire. *Her* fire. A bright blade of anticipation pierced the brown tangle of her nervousness. *Finally*, three years after she had qualified for high command, the boys in Boise had let her off the bench. The call had come that morning. They were giving her the Justice. One of the big ones. Seventeen hundred troops. A million dollars a day. When she hung up, tears of relief had welled in her eyes. It was as if an eighty-pound pack had been lifted off her shoulders. She had not realized the daily weight of her frustration. She felt light, flooded with a rush of sunlit warmth. She had done it. She had wriggled through a crack in the Forest Service's famous glass ceiling—not without lacerations and splinters, but the miraculous balm of victory had eased the puckering and festering. She had not been prepared for the sensuousness of success, the lazy opulence of it: a kind of glowing golden ball she could evoke and bathe in at will. She was in the club, a brand-new fire general rolling to the rescue, windows open, a hot road-wind batting her face. She wished her mother were still alive. She wished her tough, beautiful, wise-cracking mother could see her now.

Mattie had come out of her mother's womb fighting, her tiny fists quivering, her flailing arms and legs hard as sticks. When the wet strands across her scalp dried, Kate McCullough saw that the wisps were bright orange. "A redhead!" she exclaimed in maternal delight. "Where did that come from?" But no one on either side of the family could remember red hair. "My little foundling," Kate used to coo.

Growing up, Mattie had enjoyed the distinction of her hair, a striking red-gold color that drew compliments from strangers in stores. What she did not enjoy was the general assumption that a volatile temper came with her hair. As far as she could see, her temper was no worse than any of her friends' and was measurably better than her older sister Harriet's. Harrie flew into fits for no reason at all.

By the time Mattie was a teenager, she had squashed all signs of temper. Stoic by nature, she had learned that a blank stare could be as effective as a punch in the mouth—and got her into less trouble. Her hair, however, remained untamed. She wore it long and unbraided. At track meets (she had a shelf full of trophies for the 880) her hair would stream out behind her like a fiery mane. She was tall, but not willowy. Her shoulders were broad, her torso sturdy, her white thighs solid and muscular, but when she ran, her body almost seemed to float. The sight of her moving up through the pack for her final sprint home would bring spectators to their feet. Chin leading, face frighteningly pale, she looked like a goddess flying to her fate. Her mother, who attended every race, would feel a lump rise in her throat and have to stop cheering.

She married young, against her parents' better judgment. Her husband was a smoke jumper, one of the glamour boys of the business, and when he left her not long after the birth of their baby, she cut off the shining treasure of her long hair. From time to time, she would think seriously about letting it grow, but then would lose patience. Now, in her forties, it was still efficiently short and still bright enough to turn heads. She glanced in the rearview mirror of her Cherokee and wished there had been time for a trim.

Her assignment was to take over command of the Justice from an old-school, seat-of-the-pants warrior named Owen Kingman, who spat out words like "consensus" and "diversity" as if they were poison. Mattie was not surprised to learn that he had badly bungled the aftermath of a racial incident at base camp. There had been a nasty fight. A white crew, a hotshot team from Kentucky called the Dixie Dogs, had burned a six-foot-high cross—"All in fun," they claimed later. An Afro-American crew out of L.A. had responded with knives. Three of the white hotshots had been cut. Kingman sent the black team packing. The black team's supervisor called in the NAACP and the ACLU, who immediately held a press conference. Since it was August, a time when politics go on hold and news editors across the country resort to shots of children playing with hoses, the rumble at the Justice (the very name of the fire was a headline writer's dream) suddenly hit the national news. Forty-eight hours after the story broke, the Forest Service removed both the Dixie Dogs and Incident Commander Owen Kingman from the fire. As a public act of contrition, they designated Matilda Mary McCulloch as Kingman's replacement.

She had no problem with being launched off a penitential springboard. What rankled was the administrator's cluelessness. One of the new breed of politically correct bureaucrats, he paid lip service to equal rights without *getting* it. "Feelings are still running pretty high," he had said. "It's right up your

alley. We want you to go in there, pour oil on the waters, unruffle the feathers." His voice was plummy, confidential, as if he were bestowing a secret gift. In point of fact, conflict resolution was not one of her strengths. She had worked under a number of commanders who were far better "feather smoothers" than she was—men who actually enjoyed exploring the nooks and crannies of disputes. But she had held her tongue. "I appreciate the opportunity," she had said evenly and sensed his disappointment. Clearly he had wanted her to jump up and down.

How could the man be so dim? Forget his sexist assumption that she, as a woman, was a natural peacemaker. Simply in terms of strategy, assigning her to the Justice was far more likely to stimulate conflict than resolve it. Educating the troops about racial tolerance was one thing. Taking over an interagency command team was another. Kingman's chieftains had battled fires together all over the country, season after season. Like any command team, they would have bonded, not only with one another, but with their leader. Whatever Kingman's faults and failings, they would hardly welcome a politically correct outsider—male or female. Being female, and a female with a reputation for being a stickler, made it even trickier.

She felt as if she were driving into a lions' den. On either side of her, the tawny hills with their long curves and drought-starved hollows had the look of haunches ready to pounce. She accelerated past a lone pickup and glanced at the driver. Under a spanking-new straw cowboy hat, his face was old. She remembered the appointment she had made with her chiropractor for her father. She had made it without telling him—he was hostile to doctors in general—and she had been planning to take him herself that afternoon. She flipped open her cell phone and punched the self-dial number for home.

She was surprised to get through. The phone had been ringing off the hook ever since the news of his daughter's appointment had broken and Jack McCulloch, relishing his

own fifteen minutes of fame, had invited everyone who called, friends and reporters alike, over to the house, where he plied them with cold beer and stories unprintable in a family newspaper.

The phone rang six times.

Finally Jack picked up. "Yeah?" he barked.

"Dad?"

"Oh, it's you. You there?"

"Not yet. I'm still under way."

"So how's it feel to make Forest Service history?"

"I feel like throwing up. Since you asked."

For a minute he said nothing, as if gauging the seriousness of her answer. "You can handle it."

"Do you know Ned Voyle?"

"No. I don't think so."

"Government engineer. Based in Missoula." She was always surprised by the number of people her father knew, but this time there was no match.

"He's on the team at the Justice," she went on. "Head of Plans." Planning was the section responsible for developing attack strategies. She had crossed paths with Ned Voyle at previous fires—though she doubted he would remember her. A tall, lean man with the narrow face of a Norman lord and the arrogance to match, Voyle had been more into building his own fiefdom than teamwork. "He qualified as a Type One IC the year before I did," she told her father. "He was the logical one to take over from Kingman."

She could hear Jack digesting the situation. Impatient, she burst out, "Voyle's not exactly going to see my arrival as 'relief.' "

"You can handle it," her father repeated firmly.

It was what he always said. And for some unknown reason, she had always believed him. Suddenly she was moved. "I never could have done it without you, Dad. All those years you supported us, Jimmy and me—"

"He called," Jack announced abruptly.

"Jimmy called?" She perked up. She had not seen her son since the beginning of the summer. It was his second season with the Millville Hotshots—her old outfit—and thanks to the drought that had parched the mountain states, he and his crew had been on the go since May. His calls home were few and far between.

"He left a message on the machine," Jack informed her. "I had to make a run down to the store."

"What did he say?"

"He says he's at the Justice."

"The Justice? They're at my fire?"

"That's what he said. Wait a sec." She heard a series of clicks. Her father swore at the answering machine.

"Push rewind, Dad."

"Hold your horses." She heard a long whir and some more clicks. On the machine, a pleasant female voice said: "Mr. McCulloch? I'm with *Cosmopolitan* magazine and we're working on a feature on men who—" *Click*.

"Men who *what?*"

"You want to hear the boy or not?"

Then Jimmy's voice crackled in her ear. "Hey, Mom, Jack. Sorry I haven't called in sooner—"

"Can you hear it okay?" interrupted her father.

"Not when you're talking!"

"It's as loud as it goes."

Jimmy was saying, ". . . finished mopping up in the Sawtooth and then they sent us over to the Frontiers. The Justice. A real bear. We've been busting our hump for a week and she's still only sixty percent contained." He hesitated. "I hear Mom's got her heart's desire. Way to go, Mom."

Was there a grudging note in his voice? Her relationship with Jimmy was not a cozy one. Ever since his adolescence, she had the sense of not being able to get it right. Every other thing she said seemed to irritate him—though she had no idea why. A psychologist friend had suggested that Jim blamed her for the breakup of her marriage, for depriving him of a father.

But that struck her as too facile. She suspected their discomfort with each other went deeper than a circumstance of his childhood; a clash of individual genes, perhaps, or some primordial constraint between mothers and sons.

"So," Jimmy concluded lamely, "maybe I'll see you here."

She caught the fatigue in his voice. Was his lack of enthusiasm at the attainment of her "heart's desire" nothing more than exhaustion? She wondered how long his crew had been without a break. Federal work/rest ratios specified one hour off for every two hours on, but when things heated up, the regulations tended to get pushed aside. She pictured her son in his Nomex—the fire fighter's uniform of flame-resistant fabric—egg-yolk yellow shirt, olive-drab jeans. Back on her desk at her office she had a snapshot of him taken out on the fire line, and now, as she heard his voice played back, the image hit her with the force of a punch: soot-streaked shirt, sweat-soaked bandanna around his neck, a manly stubble on his nineteen-year-old jaw, a proud grin. She felt her heart buckle with love. He was all right. He was strong and healthy, liked by his friends, cherished by his family. She had not failed. She simply couldn't talk to him.

Jack clicked off the machine. "Is that it?" she asked.

"You want me to play it again?"

"No, that's okay," she decided, moving on. "Listen, I made an appointment for you with my chiropractor at five-thirty this evening. I was planning to come home early and take you over there."

He said nothing.

"Dad, you can hardly walk. At least give it a try. Doris can take X rays, she's got great hands; maybe she can do something for you."

"Doris?"

"Dr. Doris." She gave her father directions to the office. It sounded as if he was paying attention. She felt encouraged. "You'll go?"

"I'll have my secretary check my calendar."

It was a joke. She let it go. At least he hadn't flat out refused. "Did your secretary schedule the *Cosmo* woman?" she bantered.

"That's not till tomorrow."

"You're kidding."

"No."

She blinked. He wasn't kidding?

"She said she wanted to explore the sex appeal of men who nurture outstanding women," her father volunteered.

"Explore the what?"

"Maybe she said virility."

"You're going to let her interview you?"

"For a start," he said lecherously.

She took a breath. "Another reason to see Dr. Doris, Dad. It might smooth out your moves."

3

Jack McCulloch replaced the receiver on his desk, erased his grandson's message, then gingerly lowered himself into the swivel chair. Whatever was wrong with his lower back, it wasn't getting any better. He had barely made it to the phone in time to pick up his daughter's call. He remembered the beer he had left out on the porch. To hell with it. He rummaged through the rolltop's cubbyholes for his bottle of extra-strength over-the-counter painkillers, shook out four tablets and swallowed them dry. The house felt suddenly empty. The last of his visitors had left just before Mattie's call.

Jack was seventy-four, a retired independent contractor. In the early fifties, he had purchased twenty acres of Douglas fir in one of the canyons south of Missoula and built a low-slung log house out of timber he and his wife had felled themselves. Since then, their road had been developed: a miniature golf course marked the turnoff from the highway, and along the creek, cul-de-sacs of boxy new "Colonials" sat looking inward, like wagons in a defensive circle. The McCulloch house, however, was protected by the old fir trees. The wide window in Jack's den looked across a lawn to trees now grown giant. Despite the lawn's drought-brittle grass and the gray road dust on the trees' lower boughs, the property had a secluded, alpine feel. Although downtown was only ten minutes away, the view from his den made it easy to indulge in the illusion that his world had not changed.

But of course it had. Earlier that day, he had pulled out his albums for a reporter. Gazing at his old Kodaks, he had to fight the urge to describe his long-ago fires as gifts from paradise. The brittle, ivory-bordered snapshots showed smooth-faced, firm-chested young men posing in dungarees and felt hats. There were crosscut saws in the pictures and walk-in canvas tents and tiny prop planes fixed in a glossy sepia sky. Fifty years ago, there had been no fire-resistant clothes, no chain saws, no computers to model fire behavior, no cell phones and pagers, no drug deals and undercover cops in the camps—and no women.

He reached to the stack of *Missoulians* he had bought that morning, picked up the top copy, and read the front-page feature yet another time. The piece ran under a color file photo of Mattie in her hard hat and a headline that read:

FIRE GENERAL SMASHES GLASS CEILING.

> AP—As wildfires rage across the West destroying thousands of acres of pristine forests and threatening private vacation homes, firefighter Matilda M. McCulloch has blazed the way to the top of the Forest Service's chain of command. McCulloch is the first woman to be designated Incident Commander of a federally fielded fire team.
>
> She will take over the management of the Justice Peak Fire which was ignited by a lightning strike in the mountains of southwestern Montana. After smoke jumpers failed to control the blaze, they were evacuated by helicopter and ground troops were deployed. The fire has been marked by racial strife and cross-burnings.
>
> McCulloch underwent command training at Marana, the Forest Service's elite leadership college outside Tucson. The school's rigorous curriculum is taught by a faculty of veteran firefighters. The top course, known in the trade as "Generalship,"

has a failure rate of close to forty percent. Three years ago, McCulloch graduated second from the top of the Generalship course.

Born into a family of firefighters, McCulloch began her career with the Forest Service clearing brush with a seasonal crew. At that time, women crew members were not allowed near a fire line unless they were delivering lunch sacks.

After receiving a BA in Forestry from the University of Montana, Missoula, she went to work for the Forest Service as a clerk-typist. In 1978, she spent her first summer on the fire line with a BLM crew in Oregon. She joined the Millville (Montana) Hotshots in 1982. After completing her MA in Forestry, McCulloch was appointed Fire Management Officer for the Lolo Ranger District.

Her ground-level firefighting experience includes stints as a strike-team leader and division supervisor. To qualify as a Type 1 Incident Commander, McCulloch spent eight fire seasons on Type 1 command teams working in two different capacities, Chief of Operations and Chief of Planning.

McCulloch has been the recipient of ten Forest Service awards for "outstanding performance."

The story, Jack reflected, was more accurate than most. Only one cross had been burned, and the protests had come from outside organizations, not from the ranks, but at least this time the reporter had gotten his daughter's credentials straight.

Marana. An old army facility in the middle of a desert. In the fifties and sixties, the CIA had used it as a base for secret air operations in Indochina. Then the Forest Service had captured a piece of it. Jack remembered how Mattie had come home shaken after her final session in the course. A classmate—a big burly guy, she'd said—had dropped dead of a heart attack during a computer-simulated fire. It was one of the few times he could remember that she'd accepted a beer from him. She'd become softer, sleepy before she half finished it, but no more forthcoming. A month later he heard the details from one of the trainers, an old-timer named Hal Pfeiffer.

"We kept turning up the screws," Hal told him. "We were trying to get this guy to delegate and all of a sudden he turns gray and falls onto the floor. We're at the consoles, our mouths hanging open. Your gal doesn't turn a hair. She calls the medics and starts CPR. The ambulance comes, we're all standing around wringing our hands, and before they get the guy out of there, she's back in her chair, working the game."

The story of his daughter's cool made Jack uneasy. But when he confronted her with it, she gave a dismissive little snort. "I thought it was part of the scenario, a test." He didn't know whether to believe her or not. The force of her ambition worried him.

Jack took his scissors from a coffee can full of pencils and ballpoints and clipped the article to send to Harriet, his older girl, who had a husband and a family of her own up in Seattle. He clipped a second copy for the family scrapbook and felt the welcoming burn of the pills he had swallowed. They were beginning to kick in. He leaned back in his chair and gazed up at the framed photograph on the wall beside his desk.

It was a studio portrait of Kate, his wife, posing with the two girls. Kate was wearing a dress he didn't remember and a forced smile. She sat with one arm around Harriet, who was leaning into her thigh, and her other arm locked around Mattie, the baby, who was squirming in her lap. Kate had never liked the picture. ("I look like an old stick," she used to complain.) But he liked the formality of it, the way the lighting caught the folds of their skirts, the soft shine on their neatly combed hair.

He had been missing his wife all day. She would have been

jubilant on their daughter's behalf. He could almost hear her saying "I told you so."

For two summers during World War II, before her marriage to Jack McCulloch, Katherine Haggerty had joined an all-woman crew of firefighters in California. She saw the work as a temporary lark, part of the war effort, and when the war ended she had not questioned the wisdom or necessity of turning her fire job over to the returning warriors. She was working toward her nursing degree and looking forward to using it. What she did resent, however, was the way the same "boys" patronized her. As if she had belonged to a crew of starlets posing with Pulaskis—the firefighter's combination hoe-ax—to boost wartime morale. As if all their blisters and aching backs and numbing fatigue counted for nothing.

Years later, in the mid-seventies, when the Bureau of Land Management in Alaska fielded its first all-female fire crew, Kate McCulloch felt vindicated. Some years after that, while she was locked in mortal combat with her cancer, the news that women had been allowed to join helitack crews triggered a brief remission. During this spell, she encouraged Mattie's divorce from her smoke-jumper husband (a bad apple if there ever was one) and had welcomed her daughter home with her baby boy. Mattie had long dreamed of a career in fire management and her mother urged her to reach for it, to go for her master's.

Kate McCulloch died on a clear, cold January morning. A month and ten days later, her husband saw her in a dream. Jack was not one to remember his dreams—he claimed he never had them. But this dream was inescapable. He did not so much "see" his dead wife, as step into the wholeness of their life together. She was surprisingly, buoyantly alive and well. She was wearing a white satin wedding dress—though, in fact, they had been married in suits before a justice of the peace. She wore no gauzy fluff of veil, but her nurse's cap set at a jaunty angle. The neckline of her dress was cut to expose her left breast, older than her face, and leaking milk. "It's going to waste," she told him. He woke up.

During the battle for her life, at age fifty-three, Kate had undergone a double mastectomy. Jack had wept when he saw her after the surgery, but she had been cavalier about the loss. "When I was growing up," she joked, "I wanted to be a boy." She paused, her eyes flashing, then delivered the punch line: "Be careful what you wish for!"

The dream had startled Jack. But it stayed with him and he found an odd, almost sexual comfort in it. He remembered how Kate had delighted in her own dreams, which had come regularly and, as she used to quip, "in living Technicolor." (He imagined Charlton Heston and a cast of thousands behind her sleeping brow.) Jack tried to decipher his dream as she might have done and, in doing so, felt her familiar presence. The dream was a puzzle, like the interlocking twists of steel she used to put in his Christmas stocking. Gradually, he worked out a solution.

One evening as Mattie was feeding Jimmy his supper in his high chair in the kitchen, Jack came home from a job site. He took a beer from the refrigerator, leaned back against the counter, and observed his daughter and his grandson. He noticed that the pages of the textbook open in Mattie's lap were spotted with orange-colored sauce from Jimmy's canned ravioli. "You got a test tonight?" he asked.

Mattie pushed her hand through her shorn crop of bright copper hair. "Just a quiz," she answered. "Eat up," she said to Jimmy.

"I was talking to your sister Harriet," Jack said.

Mattie looked up. Usually he said "Harrie." "Is everything okay?" She tried to keep her voice casual, but since her mother's death, she was braced for disaster.

"Yeah."

Harrie hadn't called the house—at least not today. "When did she call?"

"I called her."

"Oh?" *What was going on?*

Jack considered his beer. "I was thinking." He took a swallow. "I mean, if you're serious about wanting into the fire business."

"Yes?"

"I talked to a guy who thought he could get you a place on a hotshot crew. It might be a good move for you."

Mattie stared. "What about the office?" During the day, she worked for her father managing the phones and the paperwork—a job that allowed her to mind Jimmy at the same time. On her school nights, Jack sat for his grandson.

Impatiently Jack dismissed the office. "You'd have to get yourself back in shape," he warned. "Harrie said she'd send Beth Ann down here to help out with Jimmy."

Beth Ann was Harrie's eleven-year-old daughter—Mattie's niece. Mattie was dumbfounded. "Leave Jimmy alone with Beth Ann?"

"I'm not going anywhere," he said indignantly. "Between the two of us, we ought to be able to handle him."

Jimmy dropped his plate of ravioli onto the floor.

"Jimmy!" she exclaimed in annoyance.

"Looks like he's finished," Jack observed. He stooped, picked up the baby dish and deposited it in the sink.

"I want to get down," said Jimmy.

"Here you go, big fella." Jack lifted him out of the chair.

"But the summer's your busiest time. What about the business?"

"It'll keep."

"Dad." She let out a happy, nervous laugh. "I don't believe this! Are you sure?"

Jack did not want to tell her about his dream. He did not want it to evaporate in the telling. "Your mother would have wanted it," he said brusquely.

Mattie wet a paper towel at the sink, wiped Jimmy's face and hands under protest. She kissed his damp cheek, hugged him hard, and let him go. Then she picked up a sponge and, down on her hands and knees, swiped at the spilled sauce. She stopped and looked up at her father. "I'll give you thirty seconds to take it back."

"You want to give it a try, go ahead. Harrie said she'd come down with the others for a week in August."

"Beth Ann wants to spend the summer baby-sitting Jimmy? Did you talk to her?"

"I did."

Mattie was leery. "How much did you offer to pay her?"

"I told her I'd get her a horse."

4

29 Aug 2:40p   Directory C:*.*

She's here! Cat's here at the Justice! I saw her, saw her in the food line, goddamn her twisted little soul to hell! At first I wasn't sure, she's cut her hair off, all her long hair. I didn't say anything to her but she saw me, she saw me all right! This was about eleven-thirty this morning. One of my minions passed me the word that the kitchen had just gotten in some forbidden fruit (Diet Pepsi this time, instead of Coke) so a couple of us went over to stock up before the rabble sucked them all up. Lunch was just starting and there she was standing in the salad bar line in her fucking team T-shirt, the red one I'd seen on her pals in the bar. I felt like I'd been stabbed, her back was to me, but it was the way she was standing, the cock of her hip . . . Of course I'd been wrong before, like that time in the supermarket, and I didn't want to make an ass out of myself *here* of all places; I've learned the hard way that you have to be careful with those protean types! The tighter you hold on to them, the more they change shapes. So of course just when I'm not thinking about the little witch-bitch for the first time in months, she appears in her natural form!

But at that point I wasn't sure, so I walked around behind the drinks table and told the kitchen cons to fish all the Pepsi out of the ice tub for us, then I grab the first one and stroll around to the front, like I'm standing guard during a panty raid. Everyone's getting a big kick out it, but she's still got her back to me, she's doing a number on this asshole pilot. The rest of her crew's back down the line, meek as mice waiting for their slop, but she's jumped the line, she latched on to the flyboy and everyone's giving them a lot of space, no one wants to crowd Mr. Deus Ex Machina! He's got his arms crossed over his chest, like he could care less, but you can see it on his face, what she's doing to him—the slight drop of jaw, the lazy smile, the blurriness and, at the same time, the exquisite *locality* of it! *It's still there.* She's still connected to me, I don't care how many cretins she burns, it is still there. Our radius is still burning; what I know now is, you can only see it in the dark.

This is what happened. The idiot pilot glances over our way and gives me this patronizing little smirk. He says something to her, she turns and looks right at me. There I am, with my clowning cohorts, *ridi, pagliaccio*, ice-cold Pepsi dripping in hand, and just as I'm taking a swallow, she gives me this look, zap. For a second it was just the same, we were back in our circle, I could smell her, I could *taste* her, never mind the Pepsi! She smiles at me like she knows what I am thinking, like she's got the whole *irony* of it, and I wink at her.

I was thinking she'd come over, say hello, whatever. But no, the bitch turns back to Baby Face and pulls out a book of matches, no cigarette, just the matches. She lights her fucking paper match, holds it up between them, and lets it burn down. All the time she's locked on to his eyeballs. She blows it out, we don't want to scare the kid off, do we, so she blows it out, then pulls out the front of her shirt and drops it inside, frail little black twist falling between her breasts, dun-colored little tits. Nooo, my mistress's eyes are nothing like the sun!

And here I sit, trying to get it back together, bleeding all over my laptop like some sophomore who can't even keep his fucking tenses straight! I've got another goddamn meeting coming up and all I can think of is that match brushing the taut, drumlike stretch of skin between her tits. *Our* matches were *live*. High notes. Beloved scattering of red pings. I used to anoint them, watch them blister into tiny balloons. When they broke, the skin underneath was so pink, pink as dog's prick, she used to say. Now they're probably white as old pox marks. Will Baby Face touch them? Go, hey, what happened here?

She dropped the match. His eyes widened. Then she had her knee inside his. She was leaning into him, whispering something into his ear, her eyes on me; he looks over, looks at me standing there, lets out a laugh, big chummy laugh, drapes an arm over her shoulder.

I wanted to punch his face in, right then and there, and then he steers her out the line. Guess what they're having for lunch, the motherfucks. And then the line closes up and it was like they were never there. But she WAS there. Too bad for her. She's got to pay, that's all there is to it; after all, this is the *Justice!*

And on top of all that, as if I didn't have enough on my plate, we've got a pussy coming in to take over, the grapevine had it right. Darling of the media, Ms. Good Copy herself, Mattie McCulloch. Hardly a chip off the old block but at least we're spared the dose of so-called Irish charm, I never found Jack McCulloch anything but tedious. I hear McCulloch *fille* doesn't drink, a textbook control freak, they say. What's interesting is this encroaching shadow of femaleness, the leisurely dark wing overhead—as it were! The whole team's running around in circles like a bunch of blind mice. What no one understands is, McCulloch is nothing. What no one sees is the *real* fire bitch!

5

When Mattie drove into Sophia ("Gateway to the Frontier Mountains") on the afternoon of August 29, the streets were clogged with out-of-state fire trucks, local ranchers' pickups, school buses transporting fire crews, and dusty tourist RVs. Although the fire was not visible from the town, the smoke was heavy, trapping the traffic fumes under its ceiling and shrouding the storefronts in a brown twilight. Shoppers on the sidewalks wore bandit-style bandannas over their noses. Mattie, stuck behind a Corrections Department bus carrying a prison crew to the fire, watched a Huey rattle over the rooftops. It was hauling a Bambi bucket—a five-hundred-gallon sack of water scooped out of the river.

The traffic started moving again. She followed the prison bus out of town, then zipped past it on the wide scenic byway that followed the river along the east side of the Frontiers. Sightseers had parked their cars along the shoulders of the road and stood squinting into the sun at the blackened mountainside. Like a drunken god, the Justice had fallen off the ridges, reeled across the open hills, and finally lain down beside the road. In places, however, the fire had slopped over. It had twisted the guardrail and leaped across the river, down over the wide stony beaches to the other side, where it had been extinguished by dozers and hand crews.

She looked back up the mountain. Here and there, the fire had jumped random clumps of trees and brush, leaving green islands in the black. They reminded her of pieces of a jigsaw puzzle. It was as if the Justice, sweeping through in a chaotic, elemental rage, had banged a fist on a card table and sent dappled bits of foliage flying to the floor. For Mattie, the utter accident of it invariably provoked a sense of awe. There was no cause, no known scientific reason why one clump was spared and another destroyed.

At the turnoff to the incident command post, a local sheriff's deputy turned away tourists and waved engines and supply vehicles on through. Mattie waited behind a food delivery truck. She glanced at her watch. It was four-ten—sixteen-ten, she amended, switching herself on to military time. She curbed her impatience. She still had enough time to check in before the operations briefing at seventeen hundred. There was no need to jump the line—though she had no doubt her predecessor would have done so.

Past the roadblock, she followed the food truck up a paved two-lane road that wound through old-growth forest. The base camp was located halfway up the mountain at the Meander Mine Campground, a public facility named after a nearby copper mine long since defunct. In the 1940s, the Forest Service had established a ranger outpost on the site, but during the seventies, the rangers were moved to new, centralized headquarters outside the town of Sophia. Their old bunkhouse and jackleg corrals were torn down, a metal maintenance barn was built and the gravel access road widened and paved. Parking lots and campsites were cleared and the ranger station was renovated to serve as an office and residence for a seasonal camp host/manager. When the fire on Justice Peak escaped the smoke jumpers, the Forest Service had closed the Meander to the public and bused in its troops.

Fifty feet from the entrance gate, the delivery truck in front of her braked. After a laborious pause, it beeped slowly backward into the food-service area that had been set up across the road from the gate. The caterers' kitchen trailers and eating tents occupied a natural open meadow where once rangers had turned out their supply mules; where earlier in the summer, campers had photographed deer and elk grazing in the summer dusk.

As she waited for the truck, she scanned the food area for red T-shirts. Jim's crew had chosen red ones and one of the men, a promising young political cartoonist whose work had just been syndicated, had produced a fire dragon for the front of the shirts. The dragon had a dopey look, but the hotshots wore it proudly—a kind of mock-heroic statement, she supposed, though she had not explored her take on it with Jim. "Ma," he would have complained, "it's just a T-shirt."

The dinner line had already formed: a patient snake of firefighters waiting for the kitchen to start serving at sixteen-thirty. Many of the crews were fresh from the showers and in clean T-shirts, but she saw no red ones among them. Jim and his pals might be spiked out on the mountain, she reminded herself. Even if his crew *was* in base camp, the likelihood of either of them having time to exchange more than a quick hello was remote. Then, out of the corner of her eye, she caught flashes of red between the trunks of the giant ponderosa on the campground side of the road. A moving line of red shirts. Her heart quickened. Clearly a hotshot crew. Seasonal crews tended to mosey along in loose knots, but hotshots liked to march everywhere in single file and this red-shirted crew was marching double-time to dinner. Chins up, eyes forward, they jogged smartly across the road in front of her car—a crew of Apaches from Arizona.

The delivery truck cleared the road. She turned into the campground. A local volunteer posted at the entrance directed her to Check-In and handed her a Xeroxed map. Crudely drawn, the plan of the campground suggested a vital organ; a brain, perhaps. Or rather, she decided, a womb—for the lay of the land was concave, a shallow bowl. A service road ran around the bowl's lopsided rim. Inside, loops of paved drives provided access to graveled parking lots and wooded tenting areas.

She found Check-In in an air-conditioned trailer. When she introduced herself as the new IC, the men looked up from their computers with interest. They were helpful and friendly. They punched her ID number into the computer, filled out a resource card for her, added her name to their list. When she asked after the Millville crew, one of the men pulled them up on the computer. He informed her that the crew was presently off-shift and in camp, but not for long. They were scheduled to go back up on the fire line that evening.

None of the recorders asked why she wanted to know, but she sensed a strong current of curiosity rising from their worktables. Normally she would have ignored it: "Say No More Than Necessary" was a rule she had learned working in a male milieu. But the cheerful goodwill of the clerks, along with her own maternal pride, prompted her to explain. "My son's with them," she said.

They nodded approval. A freckled-faced man volunteered, "I can have him paged for you."

"No," she said. She knew Jim would not appreciate being paged. "I'll hook up with him sooner or later." She thanked them and left.

Back in her vehicle, she wondered at her own sense of relief. Had she really expected them to hurl rotten tomatoes at her?

She drove slowly around the spiraling drive, following the one-way signs and checking out the fire camp's "neighborhoods." Beyond the Check-In trailer, on the outermost northern loop of the campground, there was an "industrial park" where the incident's generators and fuel tanks had been moved in. Farther on around the loop, rows of school buses for transporting crews to the fire took up two entire parking areas. Water trucks, fire engines, flatbeds for transporting the dozers took up another.

The "residential" area was located at the southern end of the perimeter road, as far away as possible from the continual racket of the generators. In the avenues between dome tents and canvas shelters, off-duty troops played with Hackysacks and Frisbees. She slowed, looking for red T-shirts, then drove on. She would find Jim after she settled in.

The fire's "business district" had been set up in the labyrinth's inner loop: Forest Service trailers, a pair of satellite dishes, and open-air offices whose folding tables and chairs were protected by tarps strung between trees. Command Headquarters was located at the very center of the spiral in the former ranger's quarters, a 1920s-style board-and-batten chalet with a high-pitched roof and dark wood siding. Someone had planted purple petunias and dusty miller along the fieldstone foundations and there was a new wheelchair ramp—a mark of the time. In a side yard sheltered by cottonwoods, a man in Nomex was practicing his golf swing sans club. Pretty cushy, she thought, remembering all the fires she had worked out of the back of a truck.

She parked in one of the spaces in front of the chalet. The golfer pivoted and swung, then gave his shoulders an irritable shake and once again addressed the imaginary ball at his feet. Was that Voyle? She thought not. Ned Voyle was taller, thinner.

She got out of the Jeep, slung her pack over one shoulder and walked up the path. The chalet, she noted approvingly, was protected both by the screen of trees and the rise of the surrounding terrain from any view of the Justice; she knew from experience that she made better decisions when she could not see the creeping lick of flames, the thunderheads of smoke. The visual impact of a fire on the move, even seen from a safe distance, tended to prompt errors on the side of caution.

There was no one in the front room, a brightly lit office with desks and file cabinets behind a long information counter built of blond wood. Posters of wildflowers and trail maps were mounted on the wall, and shelves displayed books and postcards for sale. Mattie was pleased to see that the renovators had kept the original pine flooring. Although the wide planks had been sanded and refinished, beneath an amberlike gloss of polyurethane the pockmarks of hobnailed boots evoked the hardy ghosts of rangers past.

She left her pack propped up against the counter and walked through a passageway into the living quarters, where she found Ned Voyle and two other men glommed on to the screen of a laptop on a table in the kitchen area. In the light from an overhead fixture, Ned's bald spot gleamed beige like a polished egg. Its diameter had expanded noticeably since the last time she had seen him, but he had not attempted a comb-over. The surrounding fringe of hair was austerely clipped. A point in his favor, she conceded.

"Ned," she said, willing herself to smile.

He turned in his chair. She saw him register, a flicker in the eyes, then his narrow, bony face went blank. "Be with you in a moment." She might have been delivering pizza.

Her mouth tightened. "Take your time." Giving him permission.

He let out a snort of contempt, turned back to the computer screen. The two men looked curiously at her.

Give him a little space, she told herself. You'd be pissed if it were you. She moved into the living area, a recent addition with casement windows and vinyl tile flooring. A Scandinavian sofa, a TV, and a tweed recliner—the chair of power?—formed an inner circle around a pine coffee table littered with Styrofoam cups. Folding chairs made an outer circle. She picked up a shift report from a stack on the coffee table. The booklets were issued every twelve hours, at the start of each shift, and included everything from operational goals to cell-phone numbers. This one, the one for the shift about to end, had a cartoon on the cover. It depicted Acting Incident Commander Ned Voyle suited up in chain mail and thrusting a toy-sized lance at the Scales of Justice. The likeness was not flattering (the artist had caught Ned's weasel-like squint) but Ned had endorsed the cover with a proud ballpoint scrawl. Mattie flipped through the stack. Like a celebrity sure of his fans, he had signed every one.

She considered the three men crowded around the laptop on the kitchen table. They were silent, focused on the screen, as if monitoring strategic information. But the colors on the screen were suspiciously green. Since July, the pixels of the region's satellite fuel maps had been yellow and red. Was she interrupting a game of computer golf?

"Be back in a minute," she informed them. They ignored her. She went out to the office and took her pack into the large, handicap-accessible bathroom. She stepped out of her jeans and sneakers, exchanged her underwired bra for a metal-free sports model, and donned her fire clothes. The Nomex was as thin and freeing as pajamas. In comparison, her custom-made boots felt like anchors. She laced them up sitting on the toilet, then stood, a confident two inches taller. The boots' heels and heavy soles elevated her to the eye level of the majority of her brothers-in-arms.

At the mirror over the sink, she gave her hair a fierce brush, put on an earth-tone lipstick and considered her image. Now and again, friends would call her "stunning," as if it were a known fact, and Mattie was always a bit surprised and flattered. When she looked in the mirror, she saw a blaze of red hair, unblinking gray eyes, a straight nose with lines curving down to a thin, Irish mouth; except for the cowlicks in her hair, no irregular twists or bumps. A pleasant-enough face but, she suspected, were it not for the color of her hair, she would be invisible. She counted her skin as her best feature and was careful about the sun. In winter, it was as opaque as whole milk. Now, at the end of summer, it was a healthy beige color.

From a pocket in her pack, she fished out her Forest Service cap and pinned her new ID over the embroidered badge above the bill. Under her name, the red plastic tag read "Incident Commander." She flipped the cap over her head, snugged it down, tucked in unruly sprouts of hair. She studied herself in the mirror. She looked respectable, pulled-together. Chief, she addressed herself silently. Then she screwed up her face, squeezed it tight for several seconds, and let it go with a long, slightly shaky breath. She drew in a firmer breath and went out to claim her command.

She walked up to the three men as if she were a chum about to look over their shoulders. Ned, caught off-guard, hastily stood up, catching his chair as he twisted around to face her. The other two followed suit, blocking the computer screen like guilty schoolboys. Clearly, Ned had told them who she was.

"So," she said to Ned. "When would you like to transition?"

He perched on the edge of the table, crossed his arms over his chest, refusing to budge. "There's no big hurry. Why don't you take a look around, familiarize yourself?"

She ignored the suggestion, looked him over. "How long have you been on?"

"The last two shifts." He met her eyes and the hatred in them shocked her.

"You could use a break, then," she tried.

He didn't give an inch. "I'm fine. I've gotten in my catnaps."

"Great," she said briskly. "Then I'd appreciate it if you run the five-o'clock briefing. After that, we can tie up any loose ends at the staff meeting and I'll spell you for the night shift." She waited.

Abruptly he turned back to the laptop on the table. Under his breath, he muttered an epithet, unintelligible to her, but his pals blinked in shocked surprise. She felt a twist of shame, then the *clunk* of iron plates falling into place. "Excuse me?" she demanded coldly. She had been here before, too many times to count.

"Whatever you say. *Chief*."

His companions smirked. For one hideous paranoid second, she wondered if they had seen her posturing before the mirror.

Ned punched at the laptop's keyboard and the screen died. He turned back to her with a smug, vengeful smile that said, *On your head.*

She felt a worm of doubt beneath her armor. What if it hadn't been a golf game? How far would he go to make her look bad?

6

The olive-drab privacy flaps of the briefing tent were down on three sides; on the open side, a pair of rattling fans blew the hot evening air over rows of metal chairs borrowed from a local funeral parlor. The chairs faced a lectern and two easels. The camp's Situation Unit, which produced an average of seventy-five maps a day, had unfolded its latest map on one easel. The other one displayed the meeting's agenda, hand-lettered in blue marker, on a pad of newsprint.

The tent was full and, despite the fans, hot. A few latecomers stood in the opening at the back along with a lone reporter, the only civilian in a sea of yellow shirts. He was a squarely built man about Mattie's age wearing a rumpled white linen jacket over a black T-shirt and press tags around his neck. He stood leaning against a tent post, observing her with frank interest. His hair was sandy, graying at the temples and casually unruly. He looked fit, no softness above the belt line of his jeans. What paper was he with? Usually the reporters were younger, edgier in their movements. He looked vaguely familiar—an attractive, open face, handsomely weathered—but she thought that if she had met him before, she would have remembered. Even from a distance, there was a casual authority about his stance. For a second, she met his gaze: the intensity in his eyes gave her a small shock.

She turned her attention to her colleagues in the tent. She recognized many faces from previous fires but none of them gave her any sign of acknowledgment. The lords of fire leaned back in their chairs, waiting. Some sat with their arms folded skeptically across their chests. Others impatiently tapped their knees with rolled-up copies of the new shift report. Mattie noted that the cover was baby-girl pink—in her honor, no doubt. No cartoon, at least not yet. Only the title: "Justice Peak Fire, Night Shift," and the date.

Ned took the lectern. "Okay, folks. Let's get started. Turn your cell phones to off and your pagers to vibrate."

The latter instruction inspired someone to let out a moan of ecstasy. Someone nearby made a wisecrack. A ripple of humor spread through the tent.

Mattie kept her eyes on Ned. He smiled indulgently. In a Let's-get-this-over-with-boys tone of voice, he reiterated their objectives. Hold the fire west of the Scenic Byway. Hold the fire south of the town of Sophia. Protect structures in the Fortitude Valley area. Mitigate threats to lives and property. And so on. No surprises.

Then it was her turn. She stood up but instead of claiming the lectern, she remained at her chair and turned to face the gathering before her—all white, middle-aged males. Their faces, shaven and unshaven, shiny from the heat, showed the fatigue of long shifts and interrupted snatches of sleep. They stirred restlessly. Meetings they didn't like. A lecture on teamwork from a new IC they didn't need.

She pitched her voice to the back row. "As Ned told you, I'm Mattie McCulloch. It's an honor to be assigned to this fire with you. Thank you." She gave Ned an over-to-you nod. As she sat down, she felt the gathering relax.

Mike Robuck, the Operations chief, stood up to give his update. He was a hefty man with the rugged look of a cowboy whose meat and potatoes were beginning to catch up with him. His trademark was a spotless white Stetson which he never took off, except to exchange it for his helmet. He claimed to have stolen the Stetson from the husband of a rodeo queen whose charms he lovingly described with a cupped hand. Now, like a gunslinger tipping his hat to the schoolteacher, he touched its brim with his forefinger, acknowledging Mattie in the front row.

Positioning himself beside the fire map, he boomed, "This morning we started out on a spot up here, then dropped some hand crews in on this ridge. Divisions B and W are quiet. But on this front"—he swept his hand along a toothed line that indicated the uncontrolled edge of the fire—"Division C is still going a hundred and fifty percent. We have three crews of hotshots up there and they've been working on a twenty-four-hour rotation. However, due to the general shortage of resources"—and here a weary murmur of acknowledgement ran through the tent.

"Due to the lack of relief crews," Mike repeated firmly, "starting this shift, we're putting the 'shots on coyote tactic. Basically, we're constructing a line to tie in with Division D and hoping all the hotshot work will pay off. We've got some heavy fuels down these chutes, so we're trying to keep the fire up top where we can fight it out in the open."

Huh, Mattie thought. They had told her at Check-In that Jimmy and his crew were headed for Division C and she was not surprised to learn that Division C was the trouble area: hotshot teams were regularly deployed to the ugly spots. They had both the training and the skills to hack out a fire line—a path of bare soil—across terrain and in conditions that would put less experienced crews in danger. Nonetheless, Mattie could not help feeling a pang of maternal apprehension. Coyote tactic meant that the crews would camp out on the mountain instead of returning to the Meander at the end of the shift. Even if the regulation rest periods were observed, the longer a crew stayed on the fire line, the greater the chance of injury. Moreover, unless she caught Jim before he left, there was no telling when she would see him. It could be days before the Division C line was complete.

And she did want to see him. Not only to set eyes on him, to see how he was after the months of hard labor, but more selfishly, to have him see *her*. If a tip of Mike Robuck's white hat was as warm a public welcome as she was going to get, she wanted at least a small moment of private glory. She wanted Jim to see her as IC.

She glanced at her watch. He was probably on his way to the staging area now. There was, however, no way she could walk out of her first briefing. It was out of the question. But if no one was too long-winded, she might be able to make it over to the buses in time to say hello and good-bye.

She leaned forward in her seat for a better view of the fire map. The fire's origin on Justice Peak was marked with a circled X. From there, dry winds had pushed it down the eastern side of the mountains all the way into the Sophia River. Now it was creeping down the western ridges. On the map, it had the shape of a gigantic, wind-shredded flame. Long, chaotic tongues reached out from the sides into canyons and gulches. Around the edges of the flame, the map was sprinkled with spot fires started by embers blown over the line. Jimmy and the Millville 'shots were constructing line on the western front, below the fire's uncontained edge. As drawn on the map, the path of their line zigged and zagged like stitching on a crazy quilt.

Not a good line, she worried. Zigzags were not conducive to containment. If the terrain was too rough for a straight line, it would be better to move out the perimeter. Then she saw the circled *P*s that signified private land. Evidently, they had zigzagged to protect private property. She took a small, brand-new, spiral-bound pad from the breast pocket of her shirt and made a note. If they could not expand the line without putting ranches and vacation homes at risk, then at least they should brief the community about establishing secondary lines through the properties in question. It was too late now for a reconnaissance flight over the area. The choppers didn't fly at night, except in emergencies. She would have to wait till the morning.

She listened intently as a fire-behavior specialist discussed potential areas of spread and reviewed escape avenues for the division supervisors. "Our lines could be breached if winds go over twenty miles per hour," the man warned. "Conditions are conducive to spread. Let's put a lid on it." He sounded like a coach urging weary players to step up.

One of Ned's "boys" gave the report from Plans. The mention of evacuation plans for the Circle Seven ranch—wherever that was—evoked half-smiles. She glanced at Ned. Was his mouth twitching? It was hard to tell. She wrote "Circle 7" in her notebook and added a question mark.

The Medical Unit leader, a female registered nurse, warned against poison oak. "We're seeing some pretty severe cases. Remind your crews not to wear contaminated clothes inside their sleeping bags." The cumulative tally of injuries—from blisters to sprains—on the fire was seventy-five. Amazingly, none had been serious. The airship assigned for medevacs had not yet been utilized. "Keep up the good work," she urged the division leaders.

Then Grant Sonderdank stood up at the back of the tent. Grant was the Safety Officer. It was his job to investigate every accident on the incident—be it an ankle broken in a fall or a femoral artery severed by a chain saw. He was also required to identify all "hazardous situations" and to "stop and prevent unsafe acts." In the minds of many veterans, the Safety Officer was the most powerful man on an incident: he had the authority to shut down the entire show in the name of safety.

Like every Safety Officer in the business, Grant Sonderdank took his responsibilities seriously. He was respected for this, but not popular. In a business whose first commandment is the oxymoronic order "Fight fires aggressively but provide for safety first," the ground troops, most of whom are still young enough to consider themselves invincible, generally are inclined to err on the side of derring-do.

However, Mattie found it hard to imagine that Grant, even in youth, had ever been reckless. He was fastidious to the bone. The joke was that he'd been born with a silver

Dustbuster in his mouth. Reputedly, he once had closed down a kitchen in the middle of dinner after finding a hair in the spaghetti sauce.

"Know what the fire is doing at all times," he intoned. "Keep lookouts posted. Know your escape routes and safety zones. Be sure you keep good communications. Stay on your assigned frequencies."

The chiefs politely suppressed their yawns. Mattie, however, regarded Grant with curiosity. His features had the almost feminine cast of a movie idol from the 1930s. His dark hair was slick at the temples and he wore the bandanna like an ascot. But he lacked the vital splash and dash of a Fairbanks. Over the years, Mattie had observed him at other fires. Now, once again, she marveled that someone so handsome could be such a bore.

Grant Sonderdank glanced down at his pad. "Watch out for flaming rodents. There have been two sightings in Division C. Unconfirmed sightings," he amended. Over in a corner, someone's wisecrack triggered chuckles. Grant Sonderdank ignored them. "In addition to poison oak, dehydration has been a problem. Make sure your troops urinate every two hours," he instructed solemnly.

The chiefs looked startled. There were several muted guffaws. Mattie, despite her growing impatience to see Jim, allowed herself a smile. But Sonderdank didn't get it. He sat down.

Despite the casual feel of the meeting, Ned Voyle kept it moving briskly. To Mattie's relief, it lasted only twenty minutes. A smiling man with a fighter's blocky nose set in a round face intercepted her as she made her escape—he was the golfer she had seen outside the chalet. "Mattie," he said, extending his hand. "I'm Brian Flaherty. Your Information officer."

"Of course," she said graciously. No wonder he had looked familiar to her. Outside fire season, he ran the public relations office at the Forest Service's Regional Headquarters in downtown Missoula, and although she had always dealt with one of his underlings when she visited the office, she knew him by sight. At the Justice, both he and Grant would be working directly with her as part of her command staff.

Brian's handshake was firm and dry. "Welcome aboard." He sounded as if he meant it.

She felt a small blush of relief rise to her cheeks. "Thanks. Glad to be here."

"Have you got a minute? I've got someone here who wants to talk to you."

The reporter who had been watching her so intently from the back of the tent now stood in front of her. His eyes were blue, she saw. For the second time, she met them—and was disconcerted by the sparkle of amusement in them. "Gerald Spencer," he introduced himself.

Brian put in, "He's an author researching a book on fire."

"I'm sorry," she apologized distractedly, torn between wanting to please Brian and see Jimmy. "Can we talk another time? I'm trying to catch my son before he goes out on shift."

"No problem," Spencer assured her. "I'm here for the duration." His accent was not exactly British, but his enunciation was more precise than casual, like someone used to speaking English in Third World countries. He kept his eyes on her.

She felt a sexual buzz—how long since that had happened? She flashed him her best smile. "See you later, then," she promised.

Cutting across concentric loops of road, she hurried through the pines toward the crews' buses and wondered about Gerald Spencer. Then she glimpsed a line of red shirts and forgot him. The Millville crew was boarding their bus. She'd caught them in time.

"Hey, Chief," they greeted her.

"How's it going?"

"Excellent," they responded, but beneath their cheerful

swagger she sensed a new deference, as if her recent elevation made them shy.

The crew boss standing by the bus door looked up from his clipboard. “Hello, Mattie,” he said. He grinned. “Fancy meeting you here.”

Mattie raised a jaunty eyebrow. “Fancy.”

“Congratulations,” he said and before she could thank him, he ducked his head inside the door. “Jim,” he called. “VIP to see you!”

Through the open windows, she heard not Jim but the commotion caused as he worked his way over gear and around his boarding teammates.

“Hey, watch it.”

“Who?”

“She’s his *mom*. Where’ve you been, lardbrain?”

“Ex-*cuse* me.”

“Move your butt, will ya?”

“Hey, Jimbo, did she bring your blankie?”

“Awww.”

Someone called through a window, “Hey, Chief, how about a steak dinner for us?”

Mattie shook her head in mock gravity. “Bread and water,” she called back.

A high-spirited chorus of boos. Jim emerged from the bus, ducking his head, his face flushed. She was gratified when he embraced her in a quick, but firm hug. She squeezed back, then steered him around to the relative privacy in front of the bus.

He looked well, she decided. Thinner, tan, handsomer. Not the wild, reckless sort of handsomeness of his father, she was relieved to see. A quieter, more solid sort of good looks. She could discern the man emerging under the face of the boy. Clearly the rigors of the job agreed with him. There were dark circles under his eyes, but he seemed bright-eyed and rested, his dark hair clean, curling thickly over his ears—in need of a decent cut if he was going to wear it long. Don’t mention it, she warned herself.

"I'm glad I caught you," she said happily. "How's it going?"

"Fine, Mom. Everything okay?"

She caught an edge of impatience in his voice. And concern. "Everything's fine," she reassured him. "I just wanted to see you."

"Well, now you see me."

She looked at him.

He took a breath, as if starting over again. "So you made it."

"Yes." She waited for a conspiratorial grin, a thumbs-up of approval, but he simply stood there considering her. She felt a flash of annoyance. "What is your problem?"

"*My* problem? You're the one who hauled me off the bus."

"Jesus, Jimmy. You're my son. I wanted to see you."

"You're supposed to be the IC. If it had been Dad—"

She knew, instantly and with icy certainty, that he was not referring to his grandfather, whom he sometimes called Dad. "What?" she challenged.

He looked away.

"What?"

His eyes came back to hers. "Nothing," he said.

She felt the familiar stone wall of his will. It seemed stronger, denser than she remembered. She insisted, "Eddie wouldn't have dragged you off the bus?"

"That's not it."

She felt a wave of fury. "Oh?"

He remained silent.

She wanted to yell, "Your father deserted you when you were two!" Instead she said coldly, "Eddie didn't make IC."

Jimmy let out an exasperated breath. "What's he got to do with anything? All I meant was, a man in your position wouldn't have gotten me off the bus."

She stared at him in disbelief.

"Look, Mom," he said quickly. "Congratulations. I'm happy for you. I mean it. But you're holding up the show."

She saw that his crew had all boarded the bus. The boss was

standing by the open door, one foot on the bottom step. He saw her looking and looked the other way.

"All right," she said. "Get going." She put a hand on his shoulder (had he grown taller?), pecked at his cheek. Dutifully he pecked back. She restrained herself from saying, Be careful! He got on the bus without turning back. The crew boss gave her a casual salute, swung himself aboard, and the door swished closed.

Walking back to the ranger station, she felt bruised and obscurely ashamed. What was wrong with wanting to see her own son? And what was the matter with him? *If you were a man* . . . Didn't he *get* it? Despite all her efforts to raise a liberated male, had she hatched a dinosaur?

He's only nineteen, she consoled herself. It's in the air, part of the culture. Along with all the fire and smoke and the stink of one another's socks, we all breathe in molecules of machismo, particles of bigotry and fear. She was not immune. What made her think Jimmy would be? She glanced at her watch. Their visit had taken all of two minutes. She had meant to ask him about the cross-burnings, to get his take on the rumble. Had he witnessed either event?

She decided there was time before her staff meeting to set up her tent. Unpacking her gear was a private ritual of arrival, an announcement, as much to herself as to anyone else, that she had left her ordinary life behind and stepped into the balloon of reality called the Justice. She retrieved her pack from the ranger station and hiked through the pines to the southern end of the Meander's loops. Although the troops had only arrived in force the week before, when the Justice had been designated as a Type 1 fire, the sprawl of tents and makeshift shelters had the settled-in look of a long-term camp. Beaten paths led to the long rows of blue portable toilets, to the bank of imported pay phones at the one end of the camp, to the catered shower trailers at the other. Yards had been claimed with yellow plastic rope and hand-lettered signs boasting the crews' identities had been mounted on posts. Someone had even set up a horseshoe pitch.

She found the section staked out for the Overhead team, set up her small blue dome, rolled out her sleeping pad and, although she did not plan to use it that night, pulled her sleeping bag out of its stuffsack to fluff up. She backed out of the tent, zipped it up, and stood surveying the area. The nylon-bright colors of the tents and tarps, the flaglike lines of clothing strung out to air, and the self-congratulatory signs posted by various crews gave the camp a festive air. She caught the fragrance of dry pine needles, the pungent animal reek of nearby dirty socks, the faint chemical stink from distant toilets, the summertime aroma of charcoal and steak wafting from the kitchens across the road.

How about steak for us? someone had called from the Millville bus. Had they not had steak? she wondered.

Guiltily, she realized she had not even asked Jim how he was. What exactly had set her off? The answer came instantly, before she had even finished posing the question: the magic button had been Jim's evocation of his father, of Eddie, the shit, who had abandoned them both. For a stewardess. At the time, the fact that he had fallen for a stewardess had made it worse. Once, not long after he had moved out, Mattie had spotted them together in the supermarket. She had not seen the girl's face, only her back: dark hair to her shoulders, a tight little miniskirt, suntan nylons, white boots. Her legs were unusually long, but not shapely. Barbie-doll legs. Quickly Mattie had rolled Jimmy and her cart into the cereals aisle. There, amid the Fruit Loops and Cheerios, she had been assaulted by a fantasy of Eddie's hand between the stewardess's long, nylon-smooth legs. Out in the parking lot, she had strapped Jimmy into his car seat, flung the groceries in beside him, then goosed the car backward, smack-crash into a car waiting for her space.

She wondered if Eddie knew that she was IC here at the Justice. She tried to imagine his reaction. She realized she wanted him to be impressed—no, she wanted him to eat his heart out. The realization hit her with a dull thump. There it was again, the same old issue: My husband left me for another woman. Talk about boring! What's wrong with me? she wondered angrily. Why can't I get past it?

7

29 Aug 5:40p   Directory C:*.*

Boise just issued a Red-Flag Watch—a cold front moving down from Canada, winds gusting up to fifty miles per hour, dry lightning storms, etc. Could make things interesting up on Division C! That's where she is, Division C, I found out. Our weather guru says twenty-four to thirty-six hours, but he might just as well be looking at entrails as satellite maps. There's no telling how long she'll be up there, that depends on the fire, which depends on the weather, so it's all one big circle, surprise, surprise! What's critical is the timing. I have to be patient. It's going to happen, one way or another. Play with fire and you get burned. She's got to pay, that's all there is to it, she's going to pay, and it's not just her little fling with the flyboy, it's everything she's done to me, mother of God, when I think of all the shit I've had to wade through on her account, nobody would believe all I've had to put up with—like that business with the clothes washer. I had to call up Margaret and ask her how to work the fucking machine—and after all her mewling about an amiable separation—I couldn't believe it! I had to find an appliance store downtown and pretend I was going to buy a new one, a whole afternoon shot; it would have taken her five minutes to come over and show me!

Get your girlfriend to show you she said, but she didn't know, she was just guessing. The mouse that squeaked. Margaret never was a match for me—as it were! Poor stupid Margaret, she even offered to let me fuck her in the ass if I thought it would help my little problem, as she called it. Maybe she was trying to put me in touch with my Inner Faggot! She always did have a thing for fairies—but I can tell you there was no little problem with Cat! I keep thinking what I should have said. I should have gone up to her in line and said something, we could have found a place to do it, to make our circle—Christ, just thinking about it is killing me.

8

On her way into the chalet for her staff meeting, Mattie saw the Red-Flag Watch taped to the glass in the door. Red-Flag Watches and Warnings were not issued casually; and Mattie experienced a jagged scrape of fear as she read it. She read it again and noted the time. It had come in half an hour before, while she had been setting up her tent. *Why hadn't she been paged?* Then she remembered she was not yet officially in the loop: she had asked Ned to bring the transition papers to the meeting. She took a deep breath as she opened the door.

As she turned to enter the chalet, she saw Brian Flaherty and his reporter coming up the walk. Gerald Spencer walked with a pronounced limp, though it did not seem to slow him down. An old injury, she guessed. His linen jacket, she noticed, was loosely constructed—the sort of jacket modeled by unshaven men in dark glasses. On the writer, however, it looked more old-shoe than haute couture. She imagined it hanging on the back of an office door, a permanent fixture, perpetually on hand.

She waited for the two men to come up the steps, then the three of them went into the front office together, Brian holding the door with easy courtesy.

"Did you catch Jim?" he asked.

The fact that Brian Flaherty knew her son's name impressed her. "I did," she answered. "Of course he was thrilled to see his mother."

The men smiled.

"Is this your first fire?" she asked Spencer.

The question seemed to take him by surprise. "Uh, no," he said. He paused, then added humorously, "I've been on a fire before."

Had she made a gaffe? Should she have known that the Justice was not his first? She looked to Brian for help.

Brian frowned. "When was that?"

Spencer shook his head. "A long time ago. Nothing on this scale."

"Gerald's a war correspondent," Brian informed her. "His book on the Desert Storm fires was a Pulitzer nominee."

"My goodness! How wonderful!"

"It was," he agreed with mock sorrow. "For about five minutes. When it didn't win, my publisher immediately put it into remainder."

"It's not often we have an author of your caliber in camp," Brian said. A straight-forward statement, not at all oily. The man was clearly good at his job.

"I got pulled in by the military metaphor," Spencer told her. "Wildfire as war."

She frowned. "War is a conflict between human beings. It's not a good model for controlling fire."

The rebuke in her voice made Brian shift nervously, but Gerald Spencer was unoffended. "I'm interested in the metaphor. Why it persists. Where it fails."

"I'll be glad to help, however I can." She felt Brian relax. "We've got a staff meeting coming up now, but why don't you join us at supper?"

"I'd be delighted. Thank you." And again, that peculiar flash of expectant amusement in his eyes. Perhaps it was a writerly trick, a way of keeping his subjects off-guard. He handed her a business card. "See you later, then."

He limped toward the door. Shrapnel?

As he reached to open the door, Grant Sonderdank came through, five minutes early for the meeting. He clapped

Spencer on the shoulder. "Hey, Ger. Going to sit in with us?"

Grant's familiarity surprised her. How long had Gerald Spencer been hanging around the Justice? Then suddenly it hit her. Ger, Grant had called him. Gerry Spencer? Her jaw dropped open. She looked down at the card in her hand, then up at the man standing in the doorway.

"Wait!" she cried. In two strides, she was at the door. She grabbed hold of the author's arm, pulled him around. "You're Gerry Spencer?" she challenged.

He grinned. "Took you long enough."

"My God, I don't believe it! Gerry Spencer? The reporter lost in the woods?"

"Oregon. The Sparta Creek Fire," he confirmed.

"I don't believe this! I thought you were Jerry with a *J*—Jerry as in Jerome."

"The papers got it wrong."

She let go of his sleeve. "Good God." She shook her head, then released a great whoop of laughter.

"What?" Grant demanded. Both he and Brian looked bewildered.

Spencer, beaming with pleasure, told them, "This woman saved my life."

"A hundred years ago," Mattie said dismissively. She did not want to go into it in front of two men she barely knew, but she could not repress her delight in the sheer coincidence of the reunion. Gerry Spencer! Imagine! She felt like hugging him. Instead, she clutched his arm again, bobbed against it. She felt as light as a party balloon.

Spencer beamed with pleasure. "Twenty years ago," he corrected her. He shook his head. "You look exactly the same."

"Oh, right."

"You haven't changed. Not really." He turned to Brian and Grant. "Back in the seventies, I was working for a paper in Oregon. I got sent out on assignment to cover a wildfire in the Wallowa Mountains. I hooked up with a freelance photographer, a real wild man, and when we got there, they told us conditions were too dangerous, that they couldn't let us get close to the fire. Well, Len, the photographer, had set his sights on *National Geographic* and he bribed one of the helicopter pilots into giving us a lift up to one of the spike camps. We hopped off while he was unloading supplies, then followed an Indian crew up the side of the mountain. Len kept stopping to take pictures, and of course, we ended up lost."

Spencer's voice became somber. "There we were, black smoke boiling over the treetops, and we had nothing, no Nomex, no shelter. We hadn't even thought to bring drinking water. I was in sneakers, for Crissake." He looked at Mattie. "You saved my life."

The emotion in his voice embarrassed her. "And all because I had to pee," she joked. Then, seeing the uncertainty on his face, she gave his arm a reassuring squeeze. "It's true! It was my first year on a crew. I was working with the rearguard and I'd dropped back to pee. It was always a problem back then. The guys weren't used to having women on the crews. I knew a number of women who solved it by not drinking, but I couldn't see any sense in that."

She took a breath and looked at Grant and Brian, including them in the story. "So there I was squatting down and I look up and see these two dudes wandering out the woods. I couldn't believe my eyes. Next thing I know, the wind shifted and the fire jumped the line. A safety zone had been cleared about half a mile away, but it was pretty clear these guys weren't going to make it in time, so I deployed my shelter."

"There were three of you in it?" Brian asked. The shelters were tiny, one-person aluminum-foil pup tents. They were thinner than a firefighter's shirt, had no floor, and folded up into a four-pound case the size of a tissue box. Every groundtrooper wore one on his or her belt, and at least once a year practiced deploying it. Entrapped firefighters were supposed to shake them out, step inside, and let the fire roar over them. "Shake-and-bake," went the grim joke. Like most of the brotherhood, neither Brian nor Grant had ever had occasion to deploy one in the field.

"It was pretty cozy," she allowed.

"I've never been so terrified in my life," Spencer assured them. "It sounded like a train coming at us. Pillars of flame shot up over a hundred feet, then joined into a roaring wall. We made it up to a logging road, then Len started to run. She tackled him, made us lie down in a ditch, then she shook out this little piece of foil. The wind almost tore it out of her hands. I thought, that's what she means by *shelter*? She got her arms and legs hooked into its straps, then stood over us. I'll never forget it. She looked like Amelia Earhart about to jump, a parachute banging at her back, a look of doom on her face. I remember it in sepia," he told them. "A brownish light. The sun was a tiny copper disk over your shoulder."

He gazed at her as if reaching back through the smoke for the girl in the hard hat. She tried to remember what he had looked like and failed. "How long have you been here?" she wondered.

But Spencer was determined to finish his story. He turned to Grant and Brian. "There she stood, looming over us, and the next thing I knew, she came crashing down on top of us!" He met her eyes. "I thought I was going to die."

No one said anything.

"Did you?" Spencer asked her.

"Did I what?"

"Think you were going to die?"

She was aware of Brian and Grant. She looked at Spencer, saw pain and gentleness in his blue eyes, and made an effort to recall her state of mind at the time. "I think I was too busy trying to keep us tucked in to worry about it."

He winced.

"Of course I was scared," she protested. "It just didn't really hit me till afterwards." She paused, shifted her weight. She was ready for her meeting. "I saw you a lot in my dreams," she admitted humorously.

Spencer, however, would not let it go. "I completely lost it," he confessed to the men. "Len and I both freaked. We almost tore the damn tent to pieces trying to get the hell out of there. She had to pound our heads on the ground. Literally. She knocked Len out."

Grant and Brian looked at her.

"There was a rock under his head. I thought I'd killed him," she explained. She remembered the photographer's screams, her irritation as he fought her, her mild surprise at the force in her arms, at the silken feel of her own strength. Still, she could not recapture Gerry Spencer's youthful face. But closing her eyes for a second, she caught a distant replay of his voice. She heard again the boy's profanities in the dark, the shrill timbre of his sobs. She remembered that he had called out for his mother.

She was struck by an absurd urge to ask after his mother. Instead, she said, "I thought I was in big trouble. I thought maybe you guys would sue for damages."

As it turned out, the photographer suffered nothing more than a mild concussion. She had not broken his skull. He had passed out from fear. It was Spencer who had been hurt, his left foot and ankle badly burned. There had been no time to dig a perimeter around the shelter, or to clear away the dry tufts of grasses beneath them. As the fire raged over them, Spencer's outside leg had kicked free of the shelter and the leg of his jeans had caught on fire. It wasn't only panic that had caused him to scream for his mother. His leg was burning. Had she paid more attention, had she looked behind her, she would have discovered the source of the smoke that was choking them. She could have doused his leg with her canteen, secured the edge of the tent. As it was, she had her nose in the ground, trying to suck oxygen out of the dirt. After the fire passed, she saw the boy's blackened leg and foot. She called for help on her radio. By the time the medics got to them, he was in shock.

Spencer and the photographer had been evacuated by helicopter. She had hiked out and rejoined her crew at base camp. It wasn't till later that she realized her back had been burned. The yellow fabric of her shirt had turned orange, her skin was a dark lobster-red, and the metal hooks on her bra had melted between her shoulder blades.

She had expected a reprimand—at the least. Her foreman, a crusty old veteran, disapproved of "firefighters in petticoats," and she feared he might use the mishap against her. But when she finally faced him, he had only growled, "Next time you stumble across a pair of assholes, run the other way."

"What happened to the photographer?" Brian asked.

"Len? No idea," Spencer said. "I used to look for his byline in *National Geographic*. Never did see it."

She looked at her watch. Ned was five minutes late.

"I'm off," Spencer said. "Catch you at supper."

"Right," she said. She turned to the two officers. "Where's Ned?"

"Sulking, probably," Brian remarked. She looked at him in surprise and saw respect in his eyes, in Grant's as well. She was not sure why Gerald Spencer had chosen to unburden himself in front of them. Had he needed absolution from his fellow males? Or were they simply a buffer, passing strangers whose presence allowed him to speak of things he might not speak of to her alone? Whatever his reason for telling it, the story had impressed the two men on her staff. Sooner or later, everyone on the command team would know how, once upon a time, Mattie McCulloch had saved the life of Gerald Spencer, Famous Author.

Can't hurt, she mused as she led the way back through the office to the chalet's living quarters.

9

Mattie ignored the recliner throne and took one end of the Danish sofa. Brian plopped down on the other, closest to the TV, and sat back with one ankle crossed over his knee. Several inches of tanned shin showed between the top of his sock and the dark-olive cuff of his Nomex jeans. A country club tan? "You a golfer, Brian?" she asked.

He cocked his head in humorous disbelief. "Does my fame precede me?"

She smiled. "I saw you working on your swing as I drove up."

"That's not an invitation to tell us about your game, Flaherty," Grant said. He pulled up a folding chair.

She started the meeting without Ned Voyle. The Justice was hers, paperwork or not, and it was time to get down to work. She asked Grant to brief her on the fight between the Dixie Dogs and the crew from L.A. When he had finished, she asked, "Did Kingman put in a request for a Human Resource officer?"

"A Human Resource officer? Kingman?" Grant demanded cynically. To a commander like Owen Kingman, Human Resource specialists were frills at best and troublemakers at worst. A comparatively recent addition to command teams, the specialists—usually female—were charged with sorting out complaints of discrimination.

Which in this case, Mattie reflected, was exactly what was

needed. She made a note, then turned to Brian. "How do we sit with the town?"

Brian uncrossed his leg and sat forward, as if to keep pace with her. "Aside from the usual number of citizens threatening to sue us, we're sitting pretty. The church ladies are baking up a storm. They keep sending up chocolate-chip cookies and pies 'for the boys.' And the Chamber of Commerce loves us. They put out an official 'Fighting Justice in Sophia, Montana' T-shirt and can't keep them in stock." He paused and added humorously, "Their guy told me they've made more money off T-shirts than they see in their annual budget."

But Mattie remained firmly on track. "Who wants to sue?"

"The local chapter of Trout Unlimited is concerned about reduced water levels in the river. They're trying to get an injunction to stop us from taking water out of it. Then we've got two air quality complaints: a woman who says we've aggravated her mother's respiratory disease and a homeowner who claims we've ruined a new paint job on his house."

Mattie checked her notepad. "What about the Fortitude Valley area?"

"That's another kettle of fish. Lauren Sloan owns property in there. She's been flexing her muscle, demanding that the Forest Service keep the fire off her place—"

"Excuse me," Mattie interrupted. "Lauren Sloan? The actor?"

"One and the same."

"Huh," Mattie said. Lauren Sloan's career was marked by the versatility of her roles. She had started out in grade-B sci-fi movies and last year had won an Oscar for her performance as the mother of an incest victim. "I didn't know she had a place down here."

"Fifteen hundred acres and a brand-new nine-thousand-square-foot 'cabin,' " Brian confirmed. "Local rumor has it that the only person who's ever actually been in residence is her decorator, but, she told me she was going to get the governor to call in the National Guard."

"Oh, good," Mattie said drily.

"Our other headache in the Fortitude Valley area is the Circle Seven outfit. They aren't worried about their buildings. They're worried about losing their trees." He added humorously, "These folks like their privacy."

Grant chuckled.

Brian cleared his throat and went on in a more serious tone. "Like Sloan, they've got clout. It's come down that protecting those properties is a priority. That's what's keeping us from wrapping this baby up. Division C's in there busting their hump on a line that never should have been drawn. So far, the fire's breached it four times but the ranch refuses to evacuate. I've told them I've been working with the sheriff and that he's agreed to post deputies to prevent any looting, but they've dug their heels in. They say they are staying put."

"This is a cattle operation?"

The men smiled. "More like a commune," Brian said. "A bunch of back-to-nature types, I guess you'd call them. They're threatening to chain themselves to their trees."

"So where are you on this one?"

"Well, I went out there and they wouldn't let me in the gate. Said they would only deal with the Chief."

"Did Kingman go?"

"Owen? Naw. He said let them come see him."

Mattie sighed. "I suppose I better pay them a visit." She noted their surprise. "Unless you think it would be counterproductive," she said to Brian.

"Oh, no. On the contrary," he said quickly.

"You'll have to give me directions. I'll go right after the Plans meeting."

"What about your dinner date? With Spencer," Brian reminded.

Mattie shook her head. "I certainly hadn't expected so many celebrities. A Pulitzer nominee, an Oscar winner—what next?"

The two men smiled politely. The boss's joke. Restless, she

stood up. "Our author will have to wait," she decided. "Give the Circle Seven a call and set it up. I want to talk to the whole group." She checked her notepad. "I guess that's it. Anything else?"

They stood up. Were they avoiding her eyes?

"Okay then," she concluded.

Grant was smirking. Brian's expression was carefully pleasant. She felt a sinking sensation. Keeping her voice light, she asked, "Is there something I need to know about the Circle Seven, lads?"

Grant straightened his face.

She felt a flash of impatience. "Brian?"

"They're militia types," he said solemnly. "I hear they've got some big guns."

10

The Circle Seven ranch lay on the Folly River side of the Frontiers. Mattie took the fire road out of camp, a wide dirt track that switchbacked down the west side of the mountain. Below the turnoff to the old Meander Mine, she pulled over at a break in the trees for her first look at the fire. Behind her, a full moon hung in the smudged night sky like a tarnished brass disk. The moonlight gave the heavy air an eerie luminescence, and, seen through this transparent scrim, the fire on the northern ridges had an operatic look. The long front line burned like a magical river. Behind it, in a saddle between two peaks, a multitude of orange spot fires sent up a reddish, urban glow. The fire was a metropolis of flame, an infernal city slowly advancing through high, distant forests. She would not have been particularly surprised to hear a Wagnerian blast come through her radio.

After a quick surf through all the fire frequencies, she confined herself down to monitoring the command mode and "tac"—the tactical channel used by the crews on the line. Often the chat on "tac" would loosen up when the fire lay down at night, but tonight the talk was terse, all-business. She thought of Jimmy somewhere out there in the darkness. At least he was no longer a rookie—though she doubted his first season had been anywhere near as bad as her own, that year out in Oregon. Her new "brothers-in-arms" had never before had a woman on the crew and were openly hostile. She had never, before or since, felt so alone and miserable.

The gate to the Circle Seven ranch was located at the end of a dirt road full of potholes. The gate was a chain-link electronic affair, the kind used to protect government installations. The fencing on either side of the gate, however, was ordinary three-strand barbed wire. Perhaps the ranch was only worried about intruders in vehicles. Perhaps they had buried land mines under the barbed wire. Whatever, Brian had done his job. One of the men from the ranch was waiting for her in a new pickup gleaming darkly under a floodlight on the other side of the gate.

As if by magic, the gate shivered, then haltingly slid open. She nosed her vehicle across a cattle guard. In her rearview mirror, she saw the gate closing behind her and felt a spasm of apprehension. What if they held her hostage? Had Kingman been right to stay put at home base?

Her greeter got out of his pickup and walked toward her car carrying an AK-47. He was wearing a baseball cap, a green-and-black buffalo-check shirt whose tails flapped over the top of his thighs, and wool hiking socks with his rubber sandals. Between the tops of his socks and the bottom of his shirt, his bare legs were spindly, and dark as an Indian's.

Mattie stared through her open window. Was he wearing a bathing suit under his shirt? A bikini? He walked up to her window. Suddenly she found herself looking at his penis. He was not wearing any pants at all. "Howdy," he said. Then he saw the alarm on her face. "They didn't tell you?"

"Tell me what?"

"This is a nudist camp, ma'am."

"Oh." She stared at her steering wheel.

"Are you all right with that?" he asked.

"Uh," Mattie said stupidly.

He waited.

Mattie told the truth. "I thought maybe you were freemen."

"We pay our taxes," the man declared indignantly.

"Of course." She turned from steering wheel to window with her most charming smile and again confronted the man's penis softly nestled in a thatch of grizzled hair. She turned back to the steering wheel.

"We have the constitutional right to bear arms," he scolded her. "Same as any citizen."

Mattie did not argue.

"I'll drive you on up to the lodge in the pickup," he offered.

"If you don't mind, I'll follow. I want to stay with my vehicle."

"In that case, I'll ride with you. All nonmembers need an escort."

As he walked around to her passenger side, she cleared the front seat of the material she'd brought along: maps of the Justice fire, a Forest Service video, printed handouts. He opened the door and slid in, laying his weapon across his lap. In the light from the overhead, she saw his face was as leathery as an old turtle's. She wondered how old he was. The hair on his chest was white. She kept her focus firmly above his nipples. He shut the door, then reached across the barrel of his weapon to offer his right hand. "Dan Hanover," he said.

"Mattie McCulloch." They shook hands.

"You're the new IC?"

"That's right."

"What do you do when you aren't fighting fires?"

"I set them. I manage prescribed burns."

"So you got it covered both ways," he said dourly. "Just follow this road to the top."

She drove up through old-growth forest, her headlights bouncing off the heavy, pinkish trunks of ponderosa. She noted the dense understory of brush, the abundance of dead lodgepole pines. A fire running up this slope would be uncontrollable. Even with a favorable weather forecast, she would not want to risk laying hose through the nudists' forest.

The camp's compound had an unkempt look, as if it had been built by hippies some thirty years before. The main lodge was an unmatched pair of A-frames joined by a wide deck. Stovepipes pierced the steeply sloping roofs covered with rustic cedar shingles. Floodlights showed more shingles on the roofs of outbuildings in the surrounding trees. The collection of handmade cabins and shacks boasted free-form walls, whimsically set windows and sculpted doors, but Mattie was immune to their hobbitlike charms. The merry use of wooden shingles depressed her. The compound was a tinderbox. And they expected her to defend it?

Hanover told her where to park. She pulled in beside a van with a bumper sticker that read: "Back off, I'm a postal worker from Montana."

Through the windshield, she noted the uncut clumps of dry grasses growing around foundation posts, the dead pines listing between the buildings. "I see you have a lot of pine-bark-beetle damage," she said. "Might be a good idea to clear out the dead wood around your structures."

"We don't believe in prettifying nature," Dan Hanover said sternly. "This isn't a country club. Our emphasis is on wilderness activities."

"I can see the forest is important to your lifestyle," Mattie said diplomatically.

"You bet your sweet ass, it is. And I'll tell you right up front: we aren't going to put up with your 'let burn' policy." He opened the door on his side to get out, then changed his mind. "Almost forgot." He looked her over disapprovingly. "We have a no-clothes-in-the-compound rule."

Great, Mattie thought. She waited.

"I guess we could make an exception. Under the circumstances."

"I'd appreciate it."

"Well, come on then. Everyone's waiting in the lodge." He put his hand on the door, and again stopped. "Don't try and be polite," he advised.

"Excuse me?"

"Just have yourself a good stare and get it over with."

The nudists had gathered in the larger of the two A-frames. An old Franklin stove sitting on a curling piece of sheet metal threw out enough heat for a sauna. The room smelled of coconut oil and apples. About twenty naked men and women milled around the room drinking coffee from earthenware mugs or munching Golden Delicious. Several of the men wore automatic revolvers in black nylon shoulder holsters. All were wearing shoes of some sort—sneakers, sandals, flip-flops—and they all carried towels, as if they were headed for the showers. A blond woman wearing a cartridge belt under her wrinkled belly appeared to be packing a six-gun. Mattie stared, then looked away, then, not knowing where to look, looked back. The woman winked at her. Mattie accepted a cup of coffee from a jolly man with sunburned jowls, and thereafter kept her focus determinedly at head level.

Dan Hanover, now sans shirt and weapon, called the meeting to order. The campers spread their towels on the seats of the room's sofas and chairs, then sat down on the towels. A few limber souls folded their towels into cushions and sat cross-legged on the painted plywood floor, but mainly Mattie had the impression of creaky bones under an abundance of flesh. She started off with an eighteen-minute Forest Service video that explained the regenerative nature of wildfire. It showed bull elk grazing on luxuriant post-burn grasses, bright carpets of wildflowers between charred, but still living trees, a red squirrel nibbling on seeds released by the fire's heat from the cones of lodgepole pines. Sound bites from ecologists endorsed "friendly flames" as vital to the health of a forest.

Mattie had seen the video uncountable times, and with any other group, she would have watched their reactions in the dark. At the Circle Seven, however, she kept her eyes glued to the nudists' large, high-resolution TV screen. When the lights came on, she stood, unfolded her fire maps, taped them to the walls, and began her briefing.

"I'm afraid," she apologized, "that showing you my video at this time is like closing the barn door after that horse has escaped. There's a big difference between the natural, forest-friendly cycle of wildfire and the kind of thing we're facing tonight. Here in the Fortitude Valley, generation after generation of fire suppression has allowed debris to build up in the understory. As I pointed out to Dan, you have a lot of deadwood here that can send the fire running up into the treetops. The intensity of crown fires not only kills the trees but sterilizes the soil. Without living plants, erosion becomes a problem. The damage already done by the Justice will have a severe impact on your watershed. So it is to everyone's advantage to prevent any further spread. More immediately, however, we are concerned with the risk to your lives and the lives of our firefighters."

Her audience listened intently, their faces skeptical, and when she had finished, they asked angry questions. They were less interested in her explanations than in their own accusations—a familiar hot seat for Mattie. She began to relax. As she acknowledged their fears, her focus expanded. The bronzed bodies before her were scarcely beautiful. They were worn, bulging, sagging, deeply wrinkled bodies. She was reminded of the joke about the old streaker. As he ran naked down the street, past a pair of old women sitting out on their porch, one of the women wondered, "What on earth was that?"

"I don't know," replied the other, "but whatever it was, it needed ironing."

"I understand your concern," Mattie said for the fifth time to an irate taxpayer ranting away at the back of the room. She resisted the urge to glance at her watch. The woman with the six-gun strapped under her belly was sitting in the front row. Mattie saw that the gun was a toy, a silver cap gun in a red leather holster. A joke?

The speaker paused and Mattie jumped in. "As I've said before, we are hoping to avoid evacuation. Residences in the Fortitude Valley area have been given top priority. We're doing everything we can to protect your property."

"We're not leaving, that's all there is to it!" burst out a woman. "We'll shoot anyone who trespasses—and that includes the FBI!"

There was a murmur of approval.

"It's time for me to get back to work," Mattie announced firmly. "Thank you."

Dan Hanover stepped forward and escorted her back down to the gate.

Fat lot of good that did, she thought as she drove home. She was no closer to resolving the standoff. But after an hour with all that sunbaked flesh, she felt unusually cheerful about her own body. She thought of the woman with the toy gun. Dale Evans, circa 1958. Mattie and her sister Harriet had guns just like it. Once, she had tested the heft of its butt on her sister Harrie's head and gotten in trouble. Had her mother taken the gun away from her? Mattie didn't think so. Perhaps she had been more persuasive with her parents than she had been with the nudists.

11

Back at the Meander campground, traffic had slowed to occasional trucks, the PA system was quiet out of consideration to sleepers, and the incessant noise of the camp's generators, unnoticeable during the general hubbub of the day, now thrummed loudly on the night air. Mattie parked in the designated lot, then walked to the chalet at the center of the base's labyrinth. A ten-mile-an-hour breeze carried the dry smell of dust and ashes, and the sky above the ponderosas had a dirty rose-colored glow, as if a distant neon-lit city were polluting the horizon.

The chalet was deserted, all lights on. In the kitchen, she opened the refrigerator looking for a can of fruit juice. To cap the frustrations of the evening, she found a cache of Diet Pepsi.

Because carbonated soft drinks with caffeine had diuretic properties and thus increased the risk of dehydration, Forest Service regulations prohibited sodas for the troops. Caterers ordered sports drinks fortified with electrolytes, fruit punches, and decaffeinated ice tea sweetened with sugar and corn syrup. Now and again, however, at the behest of one fire lord or another, a caterer would bend the rules and hide a few cases of Coke or Pepsi in a shipment of Gatorade. When the soft drinks showed up in camp, they quickly disappeared.

Mattie counted twenty-two Pepsis in the refrigerator. Who was responsible? She doubted it was Grant, who was such a stickler for the rules. What about Ned? For a moment she entertained a vengeful fantasy in which she called everyone in Overhead to a special midnight meeting and kept them there till Ned Voyle confessed his sin before them all. *How to win friends and influence people.* She realized she was letting her dislike of Ned get to her. In fact, the Pepsi pig—or pigs—could have been any of several dozen people in the war room next door. She let out a small resigned sigh and helped herself to a can of apple juice. As she shut the refrigerator door, she heard footsteps out in the corridor. She turned and saw Gerald Spencer hesitating in the doorway. "Mattie?" he said.

"Oh," she said, surprised not only by the fact of his presence, but by how glad she was to see him. The anxieties and frustrations of the day ebbed; she felt suddenly buoyant. "Come on in—I'm sorry to have stood you up at dinner!"

"Is now good?"

"Now's good. Would you like something? We've got juice—and Pepsi," she added recklessly.

"Just a glass and some ice." He pulled a small silver flask from the saggy pocket of his jacket and held it up. "If you don't mind."

Fire-camp regulations forbade alcohol, but she did not feel inclined to object. Spencer was not a member of the team. He was a visitor, a distinguished writer, she reminded herself, who was writing about them. She found glasses in a cupboard—a collection of amber-colored tumblers left over from the days of Harvest Gold kitchens—but the freezer compartment's plastic ice trays had already been picked empty and not refilled. "Ice is going to be trickier."

He waved it away, twisted off the tiny cap of his flask, and poured a generous measure of gin into his glass. Mattie caught the fresh, medicinal scent of juniper. They moved out of the fluorescent glare of the kitchen into the living area, where a shaded lamp on an end table cast a softer, more intimate light. She settled on the sofa, he took the folding chair Grant had pulled up to the coffee table earlier in the evening.

Mattie watched him take a first swallow. "You're not still in Oregon, are you?" she asked.

He lowered the glass, holding it in both hands between his knees. "Mostly I'm on the move. Home base is New York. I keep an apartment there."

"And now you're into wildfires?"

He began to outline the path of his research for her. But what she really wanted to know was his take on the Justice. What had he thought of Kingman? Had he seen the rumble between the black and white crews? Even more, she wanted to swing the conversation back to their own, long-ago fire. She wanted to know about his game leg. How badly had it been burned? How long had he remained in the hospital? How long had it taken him to walk again? After the fire had been contained and her crew was on the way home, she and her foreman had detoured to an unfamiliar city where Gerry Spencer had been moved to a hospital that specialized in the treatment of burns. It had not been a satisfying visit. For fear of infection, they had not been allowed into his room. They had peered at him through a Plexiglas window. He had been asleep, doped up, his exposed leg swollen like a giant sausage that had burst through its skin. She had not been able to learn anything about his prospects from the nurses. She had left with a vague feeling of guilt.

". . . William James," he was saying. ". . . the moral equivalent of war . . ."

Did he have a wife? she wondered. Were there children? There was a weariness about him, as if he had traveled too far, seen too much, but at the same time the lines on his face were forgiving. He would not judge one's secrets, she thought. There was a sense of decency about him, an unaffected courtliness that struck her as old-fashioned—like the ancestral-looking flask he had pulled from his pocket.

Now he was citing Stephen Pyne, the wildfire historian. His face was flushed. Writerly enthusiasm? Gin? Sunburn?

"What do people call you?" she interrupted.

He broke off, confused.

"Sorry. It's just that you don't seem like a Gerry."

He smiled. "And what is a Gerry like, pray tell?"

It seemed to him that she took a long while to answer. Her face was perfectly still, her brow as smooth as a Greek goddess's. Athena, he decided. The gray-eyed warrior in a baseball cap. In the lamplight, her skin had the glow of antique marble. He suppressed the impulse to reach out and, with the side of his forefinger, trace the straight line of her nose.

She said, "I guess I'm having a hard time reconciling you with that boy coming out of the woods so long ago."

"My friends call me Spence."

"Spence," she tried. She might have been tasting a new wine. "Sounds like a boarding school name. The kind where all the boys wear ties to class."

But he was not in the mood for banter. Gin and fatigue took him deeper. He leaned forward and put his glass on the coffee table. "Mattie, you should know . . ."

"What?" Under the bill of her cap, her gray eyes were guileless.

He searched for the words. "I want you to know that you gave me a gift. That day at the fire, I looked my own death in the face and I saw that it didn't matter."

He held up a hand to still her protest. "No," he went on. "My *life* mattered, but my dying didn't." He frowned. "Clear as mud. For a wordsmith, I'm not doing very well." He let out a short laugh. "I don't remember trying to put this into words before."

He looked at her sitting on the other side of the coffee table, her long legs relaxed, crossed at the ankles, her brow creased in sympathy, and he tried again. "I think what happened was, I looked at my death and I lost my fear of dying. It's a gift I can never repay. Without that gift, I never would have spent my life studying war. I would have been too afraid of the risks, of the danger. You gave me my life's work." He paused. "Such as it is."

Suddenly embarrassed, he shifted into an ironic drawl. "You understand, that when it comes to the importance of my work, I am prey, like all writers, to delusions of grandeur."

She did not smile. He felt as if she were measuring his mettle. Her eyes were grave, worried, even. Her next question took him by surprise. "Is that a pain? I mean, owing me."

He sat back in his chair. "I don't know," he said truthfully.

She waited, her face unreadable.

"I suppose it was always a slight nagging somewhere in the back of my mind. But now, seeing you after all these years, I realize that saying 'thank you' isn't enough."

"It's enough for me."

"Your gift is beyond recompense."

"I may have saved your life," she said flatly. "But I certainly didn't give you your gift. You found it on your own."

He was polite, but disbelieving. Mattie saw that he was attached to the notion of being bowed under a heroic, unpayable obligation. A romantic, she diagnosed. Her stomach rumbled loudly. She laughed. "Sorry. I missed supper." She remembered the smell of grilled meat wafting on the late-afternoon air. "Steak night, too," she regretted.

"Every night is steak night."

"What do you mean?"

"We've had steak every night since I've been here."

"They've served steak every night?" she repeated dumbly.

"Just at the Command team tables," he allowed. "One of the perks of the job, someone said. Your Logistics chief, I think it was."

"Frank Cicero?"

"Big Italian guy," Spence said.

"Frank," she confirmed, keeping both her face and her voice in neutral. Shit, she thought.

12

30 Aug 5:51a Directory C:*.*

So much for our red flag. Nothing moving, front stalled out somewhere up above the highline. Stay alert, McCulloch ordered at this morning's briefing. She can keep her cool, you have to give her that. Everyone was twitching last night. Not that anyone would come right out and say it, but after the Watch was posted, they were spooked. The ghosts of Storm King were walking! Fourteen dead of their own stupidity and now we quake in our boots at a mere heads up.

I have to say I thought this was it, that Cat was going to join their ranks, make the supreme sacrifice herself! Not that I'm ruling out a hero's death for her. The weather geniuses haven't lowered the flag yet, the front's standing off Glacier, it could still blow through and gimme shelter, as it were, cloak me in the divine breath of Justice. Watch and wait. If this isn't it, there'll be another conjunction, another circle. I keep feeling McCulloch's a link, that if she hadn't showed up I might not have seen Cat, might not have staged the Great Pepsi raid. I could have just as easily stayed in the war room and sent one of my minions to scoop them up, as befits my station, I should add. Such a narrow little window. It opened with McCulloch's appearance—her showing up. Her *appearance* is another thing: she's got little tits like Cat, two peas in the same pod, or I should say four peas! Though McCulloch's hardly my style, butchy-looking haircut, what you can see of it under her cap, face like a cop's—doesn't give anything away. Kingman's standing order for sirloin for Overhead pissed her off, so this morning's briefing, she goes: No more special steaks, boyos.

You could have heard a pin drop on what's left of the grass inside the tent. So kiss red protein good-bye, now we eat the same as the troops and no butting ahead of them, thank you very much. Our gal Mattie, champion of the downtrodden and oppressed. Not a bad ploy, I have to give her that. The old order changeth, enter Dancing Matilda in the guise of Democrat. No one could grumble too loudly about it. She also put in a request for a gender cop—excuse me, a Human Resource Specialist. My informants tell me we're getting some Chiquita Banana—so that may be significant, another pussy in the wings! I just have to watch and wait, it's not like I don't know how, I spend my fucking life waiting on them!

13

At 7 A.M., after a virtuous breakfast of shredded bran and skim milk, Mattie headed toward the command team's helispot for a reconnaissance flight over the Justice. In a field behind the staging area where she had seen Jimmy off on his bus, she spotted her Huey, dark as a sci-fi insect. Mike Robuck, her Ops chief, stood talking to their pilot beside a fuel truck, its stainless-steel tank brushed with the rosy light of dawn, its hose connected to the Huey like an umbilical cord.

Mike was wearing his trademark white Stetson. If at thirty-five he inclined toward beefiness, at twenty-five he had been rangy and—like Mattie's smoke-jumper ex—he had radiated the aura of the chosen few. Only instead of jumping out of an airplane and parachuting a thousand feet to the fire, Mike Robuck had rappelled out of a helicopter down thirty feet of rope. He had been a member of a helitack crew, an elite Forest Service corps whose self-esteem rivaled the smoke jumpers but whose public profile was considerably lower.

The fuel truck finished feeding the Huey and pulled away. Mike, Mattie, and the pilot donned flight helmets and climbed into the chopper. Mike took the backseat, leaving the front seat next to the pilot for Mattie—a courtesy for which she was grateful. It not only allowed her the better view; it saved her the trouble of asserting rank and claiming it for herself. The helispot manager strapped them in and the pilot started up the rotors. As the Huey lifted off, Mattie had a sensation of release. The parked trucks and nylon tents became toylike and the obstacles of her job receded along with the ground. The gun-toting nudists who refused to listen became less problematic and more farcical—even her struggles with her own teammates fell into perspective. Had she really expected Ned to yield gracefully? The secret cache of Pepsis was iritating but insignificant—it affected only the camp slugs. But the nightly flaunting of sixteen-ounce New York strip steaks under the noses of Pulaski-wielding grunts was another matter. Let the mighty lords of fire pout and fuss. If they had any sense at all, they'd thank her for sparing their arteries!

At altitude, the craft hovered for a moment as if releasing a final tether to earth, then shouldered off to the west. She sat with the newest fire map in her lap and picked out the landmarks of her kingdom below—its dark peaks and rough humps, its folds of dusky forest and open swatches of golden meadow. To Mattie's right, the paved surface of the scenic byway was the color of a weathered bone. It ran up one side of the Frontier Range along the Sophia River, then turned to gravel and ran down the other side, following the course of the Folly River. The Justice Peak Fire had originated at 9,479 feet and burned down both sides of the range. On the east side, fanned by favorable winds, it had galloped all the way down to the Sophia, even crossing it in places, as Mattie had observed on the drive in.

On the western side of the Frontiers, however, the dragon was moving more leisurely, allowing crews to construct a firebreak several thousand feet above the scattered cabins and vacation homes on the lower ridges. Progress was slow. Not only was the pitch steep and the footing dangerous, but at night, falling cool air pushed smoke downslope onto the crews. For the last several nights, Grant had pulled crews off the line on account of low visibility. No one had questioned his decision. Now, in the slanting early light, Mattie saw that the draws and canyons below were still filled with cloudlike billows of smoke.

Certainly, she reflected, the Forest Service's priority of protecting private property made the fire more difficult to fight. The nudists' forest was a scary example. A safer, more cost-efficient strategy would have been to let the Justice run through it and make a stand on ground more accessible to dozers, water trucks, and hoses. Safer, saner, cheaper—and political suicide, she thought wearily.

"Division C off to your right," Mike told her through the headphones of her flight helmet.

She peered down at a bald crag jutting through a dispersing blanket of smoke. She checked the map. Below the knob, an *S* inside a circle marked a safety zone, an area cleared of fuel where the line-builders could take refuge if the fire blew up on them.

"There's a ridge below the knob," Mike said. "You can't see much, on account of the smoke, but that's where they're building line. They've got about three miles to go before they can tie in with Division D. It's pretty slow going, but the good news is I've finally sprung a C-One-thirty loose from Missoula. We'll start flying retardant runs later this morning. If our cold front will stand off for another twenty-four hours, we should be able to nail down the perimeter."

"How many crews on Division C?" Mattie asked.

"Two. Both hotshots. The Millville crew and a Seminole team from the Everglades. We're busing in an inmate crew this shift—and next rotation we should be able to add another team of 'shots." He paused. "I hear your boy's with Millville."

"Right."

"Hey, Mike," said the pilot. "We're coming up on the Garden of Eden."

Mike let out a lecherous chuckle. "Wake up, little pussies!"

The pilot shot her a quick glance.

Mattie looked out the window and spotted the nudists' compound in the distance ahead.

"We come in friendship," Mike intoned.

"I hear they've got some mighty fine-looking little sun-worshipers over there," the pilot informed him. "One unnatural blonde in particular, just as sweet as sweet can be."

"Set this crate down. I am ready."

Had the pilots been buzzing the compound? No wonder the nudists were angry. "Stay on the fire," she ordered sharply. "The Circle Seven's off-limits."

"Aw," teased the pilot. "She's no more fun than Kingman."

So Kingman had forbidden sightseeing. "We're talking about the kind of folks who worry about black helicopters," she said. "They're pretty touchy about their space. I wouldn't be surprised if they had the hardware to knock us down."

"Hey." The pilot, who had flown in Vietnam, shrugged. "Adds a tingle."

"You're killing me, mama," Mike groaned.

"Trust me. You've seen better."

They followed the perimeter south, inspecting the spot fires Mattie had seen by moonlight on her way to the nudist camp. Now, in the early-morning sunlight, the Folly River shimmered like gold lamé as it trickled around exposed sandbars and channeled through wide, stony beaches. On the tac channel, Mattie listened to Mike talking with the division supervisor below. His questions were concise and clear; his replies, though noncommittal, managed to convey reassurance. The troops trusted him. He was a professional. Never mind his locker-room mouth, his purient devotion to the pursuit of pussy.

In fact, Mattie suspected that of all the men on the Overhead team, Mike Robuck was one of the few who remained faithful to his wife. Over the years, Mattie had seen Mike and Peggy Robuck together at Forest Service functions. Peggy was a plump, brassy woman given to gold bangles and "skorts." She gave Mike back as good as she got. But their insults had a polished, almost ritualistic quality—as if they had practiced at home. Beneath their party-time patter, Mattie sensed a deep-seated deference on Mike's part, a maternal softness on Peggy's. They had been high school sweethearts, had been together almost twenty years. Mattie could not imagine either of them with someone else.

The chopper turned, skirting the point of origin below Justice Peak. Through the bubble of the windshield, a slow flood of golden sunlight filled the cockpit. Mattie focused on the charred landscape below. They were cruising back along Division C. In the warming air, the smoke had begun to lift from the canyons. Through raglike tears in the blanket, she could now see segments of the line, a thin, rule-straight seam of mineral soil hacked into the side of the ridge.

"Visibility's improving," Mike told the Division supervisor on the ground. "We ought to be able to drop off your breakfast before too long."

"We could use a dozen Pulaski," the supervisor radioed back.

"See what we can do," Mike said.

Pulaskis were the groundpounder's weapon of choice and Edward Pulaski, the inventor of the tool, had been a hero in Mattie's house. When Jimmy was little, and she was off at her night classes, Jack McCulloch had put his grandson to bed with tales of firefights past, but Jimmy's all-time favorite had been the story of how Ranger Pulaski survived the Great Fire of 1910.

"Back in the days when my father was still a young man," Jack McCulloch would begin, "the government decided to start up a Forest Service. That would have been in 1905. And one of the first rangers they hired was Edward Pulaski, a good-looking jack-of-all-trades with fighting blood in his veins. One of his ancestors had been a Polish count who came over here during the American Revolution and taught George Washington a thing or two about guerrilla tactics. Casimir was his name. Count Casimir Pulaski. Now Ed lived over in Wallace, Idaho, where he had worked as a miner before he got the job of ranger, so he knew the lay of his district like the back of his hand. But more than that, he had the heart for fire.

"Well, the summer of 1910 happened to be the worst fire season in the history of the American West. Seventy-eight men died that year—and that's more than any year since. The skies were black all the way to California, but the worst of it was up along the Divide, in the Coeur d'Alene and Lolo National Forests. Here in Missoula, evacuation trains were bringing in two thousand refugees a day.

"On the nineteenth day of August, Ed Pulaski was back in Wallace rounding up supplies. He'd just sat down to his dinner—which in those days was in the middle of the day—when someone came running over to his house with the news that a fire storm was headed toward Placer Creek, where he had a forty-five-man crew. So he got up from his dinner and rode out to Placer with a string of supplies. When he got there, the men were so glad to see the food that they paid no mind to his warning. They started cooking. They were new volunteers and most of them had no experience of fire, and what they didn't realize is, they were sitting in the eye of the storm. Then suddenly there was a great whoosh and all around them the trees exploded like furnaces. They were completely surrounded by a hundred-foot-high wall of flames. It looked like they were finished.

"But like I said, Pulaski knew the lay of the land. He dashed a can of water on an old flour sack, threw it over his head and sprinted off through the flames to check his bearings. Then he came back and had each man put his hand on the man in front of him and he led them through the burning forest to this old mine he knew about. The War Eagle mine. They all made it, all except for one fella at the back of the line. He didn't keep up and a tree fell on top of him and that was the end of him.

"So there they were, safe in the tunnel, thanks to Ed Pulaski. Well, the next thing they knew, the smoke started coming in. Everyone was coughing and choking and some of the men were seized by panic. They cried out that they were suffocating, and if they were going to die, by God, they were going to die out in the air. They started to stampede out of the tunnel, but Ed stood his ground. He knew this was their only chance, that if they ran out into the fire, they'd be cooked to cinders. He pulled out his revolver and swore he'd shoot anyone who bolted. Well, this one fella rushed him anyways, so Ed put a bullet right between his legs. And that stopped him, all right!

"Then the goddamned smoke got 'em. They all passed out and Ed fell where he stood, near the mouth of the tunnel. So after the fire burned over, the smoke began to clear in the shaft, and the men started to revive. As they stumbled out into the air, they found Ed laying beside the entrance. It looked like he was a goner. 'He's dead,' one of them said.

" 'Like hell he is,' Ed snarled. And he stood up and got back to work."

Now, whacking through the air above her son, Mattie had to wonder that the story never gave him nightmares. She remembered the anticipation on Jimmy's face as Jack approached the punch line. In a deep, bearish rumble, her father would growl, "Like hell he is!" and Jimmy would squirm with delight. With a pang, she remembered the smoothness of his skin after his bath, the warm, soapy smell of him, the way the lamplight fell on the combed grooves of his dark, wet hair. All those summers she had spent with her crew away from Jimmy, she had dreamed of baking him cookies, of teaching him to swim in the creek beside the house, to ride a bike. As much as she enjoyed life on the line, she grieved for what she was missing at home. Nonetheless, the money was good—and it was the money that kept her at it.

She had set aside a small bequest from her mother to pay for her tuition, but Eddie Sterling's child-support payments had stopped before the first year of their divorce was out. Mattie needed grocery money, baby-sitting money, money for the pediatrician. She remembered the last time she had called Eddie to beg. She had shut the door to her bedroom so her Dad couldn't hear. "Jimmy's your *son*. Don't you care?" she had hissed fiercely into the phone.

"Look, I'd like to help you out. I just don't have it."

"He needs sneakers, Eddie."

"Your dad's got plenty. Ask him."

She hung up and let out a shriek that pierced the heavy log walls. After things settled down, her father's only comment was, "Can't get blood out of a stone."

Mattie had to give him that: Jack McCulloch had never complained about money. He complained routinely that she was "spoiling the boy," but he had never asked her for a share of the rent, nor even her phone bill. The only thing he demanded was that, like the hero Edward Pulaski, she never say die. That was the moral of the firestorm story he told over and over to Jimmy: Work till you drop, and keep on going.

She had kept going. And it had worked out. Despite the bitter, three-generational quarrels, despite her aftermaths of black despair, it had all worked out. Over the years, Jimmy had shortened "Granddad" to "Dad" and his own name to "Jim." At fourteen, he went to live in Bozeman with his father and Eddie's second wife Brenda and their two children. Before the agreed-upon year was up, Jimmy called and said he wanted to come home. Mattie never asked why. She did, however, tell him that if he came home, that was it. He was home to stay. She wasn't going to have him jerking her around going back and forth.

So Jimmy came home. He volunteered nothing about his father's household, and she did not press. The following summer, she heard via the fire grapevine that Eddie's second marriage had broken up. By the time Jim was sixteen, he was going by "McCulloch," though he was still "Sterling" on his driver's license. And now he was grown up, on the edge of his own life, and they were both working the Justice. Jimmy with her old crew, the Millville 'shots, and she with the Overhead team. If the old prickliness between them was still there, the world outside them had changed. Fifteen years ago, Mattie realized, she could not have imagined she would end up as IC. Fifteen years ago it was not within the realm of female possibility.

Mattie spent the rest of the morning in the chalet's front office receiving a continuous stream of petitioners who could not or would not be satisfied by talking to anyone less than the IC. She posed for pictures with a Girl Scout troop who presented her with a dozen cases of chocolate-mint cookies for the troops. She discussed escalating costs with a self-important aide from the governor's office, fielded questions from reporters about racism and sexism in the Forest Service, and continued negotiations with the nudists by phone. She met with the State Water Conservation representative and briefed the newly arrived Human Resource specialist, a young Hispanic woman named Celia DeJesus who had flown in from Los Angeles. When Gerald Spencer appeared at the chalet at noon, she whisked him away for lunch, grateful both for his company and the chance to escape the office.

The food line was short. He took the salad bar. She indulged in a cheeseburger from the caterer's grill. She led the way to the Command team table under the light shade of a ponderosa. Although she would have preferred to lunch with him alone, to continue their explorations of the night before, she felt it more politic to join her teammates: Mike Robuck and his co-chief Pat Patrocles, Ned Voyle, Grant Sonderdank, Brian Flaherty, and at the far end of the table, Frank Cicero, the Logistics chief. Frank "the Fixer"—a soubriquet in which he took pride.

A heavyset man with olive skin and a raptorlike beak of a nose, he had the thinning, curling hair and double chin of a well-fed Roman emperor. People tended to be careful around him. Perhaps because his Silician heritage conjured up images from *The Godfather*; or perhaps because he tended to watch more than he spoke. In any case, Frank had the power to arrange most anything—from guns to butter. When she had counterordered the Command team's nightly sirloin, all he had said was, "No problem." But his stare, cold as a reptile's, had given her a shiver.

The men at the table welcomed Spence. They were flattered by his interest in their work and curious about his own. They asked questions about advances and royalties, about paperback rights and movie options, and Spence obliged them with actual numbers from his own statements—figures whose meagerness raised concerned protests from his audience, yet at the same time, Mattie felt, boosted their egos: they were out-earning a Pulitzer nominee. She was content to listen. She felt like an impresario, secure under the umbrella of her connection to him.

Then, to the surprise of the table, Frank put down his fork and announced grandly, "Here's something for your book."

"Ah!" Spence brightened. He fished his skinny reporter's notebook out of his pocket.

"This occurred only last year," Frank stated. His delivery bordered on pompous. There was a note of disdain in his voice that reminded Mattie of a Shakespearean actor condescending to common speech. "We were working a fire up at Flathead Lake, putting a line in behind one of the new developments up there, and the dragon started acting up."

Flathead Lake? Mattie wondered. She didn't remember any project fire there last year.

"One of our dozer jockeys was trapped. So Mike called in the choppers, the pilots busted their humps pulling water out of the lake and dumping it on the fire, and pretty soon our boy on the dozer's home free."

Everyone at the table watched Gerald Spencer scribbling in his notebook.

Frank Cicero continued, "Next day the troops are mopping up, and someone finds a burned piece of rubber stuck to one of the stumps. It appears to be a swim fin. These guys are thinking, Naw. But next thing they know, someone finds a mask and snorkel. Then, about a hundred yards up the mountainside, they find the body."

Frank gave a resigned shake of his head. "As it happened, one of the pilots had scooped a tourist up out of the lake and dumped him on the fire. Autopsy said he died of a heart attack."

Spence looked up, startled. He turned to Mattie for confirmation.

Mattie had heard the story before—only the way she'd heard it, the fire had been in the Everglades and the snorkeler had been scooped up out of Florida waters. The men around the table were watching her, waiting to see whether she would play along. She kept a straight face, looked around the table, then fixed on Ned. "I guess I should thank my lucky stars I wasn't the IC on *that* one," she said.

Ned stared back at her, a fleck of doubt in his eyes.

She smiled. "Imagine the paperwork."

The other men laughed their approval. Ned shrugged off the joke with a tight smile. And Mattie felt an opening. Not exactly acceptance, but a kind of unclenching around the table. It's going to be all right, she thought. It's all going to work out.

14

30 Aug 2:08p   Directory C:*.*

She's coming down, down off the line, I heard her on the fire net! Div C was on it all morning, whining about missing lunches, then I heard her, just now on one of the radios, loud and clear! She's going to hike down with her squad to pick up a load of provisions, down the Copper Creek drainage. It's perfect, it's about time, time to get it out of my *brain* and over with. Christ, I've been going around with half a hard-on all day, my nuts hurt so bad I can hardly piss. This is it, no question, it's got to be it. I was waiting for the cold front, but the weather's irrelevant. It doesn't matter. I just wasn't paying close enough attention. Attention to my own energy, the tickle of fire! The sacred lignum, talk about obvious!! I checked the dispatcher's log. One plus two equals three. So I need to get out there by fifteen hundred. One plus five equals *six*.

Part II

THE BLOWUP

INCIDENT STATUS SUMMARY

1. date	time	2. initial / update / final	3. incident name	4. Number
AUG 30	1405	update: X	JUSTICE PEAK	P11016

5. incident commander	6. jurisdiction	7. county	8. type incident	9. location	10. started
M.McCulloch	USFS	Bearjaw	WILDFIRE	SW Montana	date AUG 20 time 1900

11. cause	12. area involved	13. % contained	14. expected containment	15. est. control	16. declared controlled
LIGHTENING	7,125 acres	80%	date SEPT 1 time 2000	date *NA time *	date *NA time *

17. current threat	18. problems
Habitat, pvt property, wildlife	acess, terrain

19 est. loss	20. est. savings	21. injuries	deaths	22. line built	23. line to build
*NA	*NA	75	0	1100 CH	190 CH

24. current weather	25. predicted weather	26. cost to date	27. est. total cost
ws 6-10 temp 90 wd W/NW rh 20	ws 15-45 temp 75 wd N/NW rh 27	$2,730,000.	$5,100,000.

28. AGENCIES

29. RESOURCES	US FS		BLM		BIA		DSL		PVT		NWS		NTS				TOTALS	
kind of resource	SR	ST	SR	ST	SR	ST	SR	ST	SR	ST	SR	ST	SR	ST	SR	ST	SR	ST
ENGINES								2	2								2	2
DOZERS									2									
CREWS	14	4			5	9							1				20	13
HELICOPTERS	3				1												4	
AIR TANKERS																		
TRUCK COS.																		
RESCUE/MED.																		
WATER TENDERS									18								18	
OVERHEAD PERSONNEL	210		35		37				18		1		1					
TOTAL PERSONNEL	660		35		491				52		1		21					

30. Cooperating Agencies

National Weather Service

31. Remarks:

LINE CONSTRUCTED AROUND FIRE IS TO BE COMPLETED ON SUNDAY. MOP-UP PROGRESSING WELL ON EASTERN SIDE OF FIRE. HWY CLOSED. CAMP CREWS INCLUDED IN OVERHEAD PERSONNEL.

32. Prepared by	33. Approved by	34. Sent to DSP.R01:R01D
R. Wells	M. McCulloch	date time by

15

Wade Lowry, a squad leader with the Millville Hotshots, turned twenty-eight on August 28 at the Justice Peak Fire. He had been fighting wildland fires since he was twenty, and for the past week he had been building a line along the jagged western front of the Justice. Born under the sign of Virgo, his soft, spongy light-brown hair stood out like a 3-D halo when it was clean. Now, however, beneath his hard hat, his hair was a dark, sweaty tangle pasted to his scalp.

Wade had a wife named Greta, an eighteen-month-old baby boy, and a half-built frame house in Lolo, Montana. He and his wife were both grade-school teachers. He had started college as an economics major with the vague idea of going into mortgage banking but changed his mind after one summer as a groundpounder. The backbreaking physical labor, combined with the intense, high purpose of a combat zone, had satisfied a restlessness that he had never been inclined to name. He liked the coiled hardness of his body that came along with the grit and the blisters. He liked the way his wife liked it.

He also liked the company. He enjoyed working shoulder to shoulder with people who, it might turn out, had backpacked across China or climbed Mount Kenya. He marveled at the accomplishments of new friends who could do Bob Marley on the harmonica or quote the *Iliad* in ancient Greek. He switched majors and, over his parents' protests, began working toward certification in Special Ed. He wanted to do something that mattered. Moreover, as a teacher, he would not have to relinquish his wilderness summers.

After graduation, Wade made it into a hotshot crew and felt lucky to have the job. Fielded by the federal government, " 'shots" are known as the endurance runners of the wildfire game. Although a notch or two below "jumpers" in the glamour department, the twenty-person crews are always at the top of any commander's wish list. As a rule, they are older, more experienced, and more competitive than local crews. Wade's bunch were no exception. Since daylight, when the smoke pulled back up the mountainside and the bombers started flying in with their loads of retardant, they and a team of Seminoles from the Everglades had been racing the fire.

Both crews were working on Division C. Their assignment was to build a buffer zone between the fire licking its way down the western slopes of the Frontiers and the private property along the Folly River. Most of the trees of any size were located at the bottom of the mountain: cottonwoods bordering hayfields along the river, stands of old-growth fir and pine sheltering cabins back in the hills. Except for occasional wind-tilted ponderosa, the steep folds of the high slopes were exposed.

The fire line drawn by the Justice strategists followed these upper contours. It cut up and down across tonguelike slides of gray rock, over tawny flanks dotted with sage, through drainages jammed with head-high brush. While the C-130 dropped loads of pink retardant above them, sawyers cut the way through the drainage thickets, toppling scrubby pine, willow, and bitterbrush. Their chain saws whined like angry hornets. Working in blue exhaust, swampers carrying fuel cans wrestled the slash out of the way and tossed it downhill into the green. Behind them a line of Pulaskis and shovels raised clouds of dust as they hacked through a dense rug of duff and roots to build the line—a three-foot-wide path of naked mineral soil. As the crews moved forward, they lit fusees and set backfires to destroy all fuel above them. Below them, mop-up squads extinguished spot fires started by embers blown over the line.

At five-thirty on the morning of August 30, a Deer Lodge prison crew had hiked up from an old wagon road below to join them. At seven-thirty, a helicopter touched down on H-3, the helispot cleared for the Division, and dropped off hot breakfast for the three crews: coffee and orange juice for sixty, scrambled eggs, sausage, and hash browns in aluminum containers. The morning load included newly sharpened Pulaskis and, instead of sack lunches, the packets of emergency rations known as MREs. (Officially, the acronym stands for "Meals, Ready-to-Eat" but there are more creative versions, "Meals Rejected in Ethiopia," being among the less savage.)

Word spread quickly through the ranks. The Division supervisor, a BLM biologist named Zack Hartwig, got on the radio and learned that there had been a "miscalculation" in the kitchen. Zack extracted a promise of sack lunches by eleven. But the turkey on kaiser buns, the roast-beef-and-swiss on whole grain, the slippery little packs of mustard and mayo, the warm Gatorades and apple juice, the melting Milky Ways and Mars Bars never appeared. For close to an hour, Zack worked the radio. Overhead was apologetic and Frank Cicero himself got into the act. To no avail. A grunt over on Division A had fallen off the mountain and the chopper was hovering, waiting for the first responders to bring him out on a backboard. Frank "the Fixer" promised to make it up to them later.

Finally, at twelve-thirty, Zack Hartwig broke the news to his troops: they were stuck with MREs. The crews were hot, dirty, tired, hungry, and low on water. They complained loudly as they tore open the flat brown plastic bags. Each of the crews built their own cook fire in the burned-out safety zone designated as a lunch spot. To save water, instead of heating the sacks of spaghetti with meat sauce or rice and beans in boiling water, the crews propped them up on sticks around the edges of their fires.

Wade settled back against a rock away from the smoke of the Millville fire. He took off his hard hat. Despite the smudgy, ocher-color haze hanging over them, the air felt cool on his sweat-soaked head. A light breeze was blowing from the west. He wondered if the red-flag front was behind it. He ate his one-ounce bar of chocolate first. It was speckled with age and had the powdery taste of dried milk. Then he opened his "accessory" pack and wiped his face and hands with a pre-moistened towelette. The cool alcohol raised goose bumps on his forearms. The towelette came away black with grime. He dropped it beside the candy wrapper, then drank warm, plastic-tasting water from his second canteen. He leaned back against his rock, waiting for the water to settle in his stomach, and almost dozed off. He shook off his fatigue, kneaded a pack of "cheese spread," and squeezed it onto crackers. The crackers were tasteless but crisp. The spread, which pulsed out of the pack in a greasy ribbon, tasted more like lard than cheese. It was exactly the same shade of beige as the crackers—a perfect match.

He dropped the wrapper on his pile, picked up his pack of chicken à la king, then put it down. He picked up his maple-nut cake and read the label. Both the dessert and the entree had been packed in Mullins, South Carolina. He knew from experience that both were as beige as the cheese and crackers. He also knew that if he was going to make it through the afternoon, he would have to eat one or the other, if not both. But all morning, he'd been looking forward to a piece of fruit, preferably an orange. They'd been getting good ones in the lunch bags, juicy and seedless, sometimes still with a hint of refrigerated cool, but more usually warm, as if plucked off a sunny tree. He closed his eyes and saw blue water.

The voices of the Deer Lodge crew, off to his left, intruded.

"They call this fucking *spaghetti*?"

"Suck it up, asshole. You've sucked up worse."

"Shut the fuck up, you little piece of sissy shit."

"All right," warned a lazy voice of authority.

Wade kept his eyes closed. He wished they would shut up.

He did not like working with cons. Last year, sitting across from them at a breakfast table at a California base camp, one of them had gotten cute with a banana. He had taunted Wade with it, showing his teeth as he ate it, jiggling the exposed fruit obscenely. Wade had told him where to put it and reported him. But the memory of the malice in the man's eyes had lingered, and after that, whenever he cut up a banana for his son, he felt uneasy.

Now he was stuck on a mountainside with them, listening to them bitch. As if they, convicted criminals, were *entitled* to sandwiches dropped from helicopters that cost the taxpayers God-knows-what per minute. Not that his own crew was exactly stoic.

"Goddamn, this looks like my dog's puke!"

"You gotta dog? I didn't know you had a dog."

"My girlfriend's got a dog. Pukes on the rug."

"Take a peek at this. Look like it came out your dog's other end."

"Thanks for the metaphor, Richie."

"It's not his dog. It's his girlfriend's dog."

Only the Seminoles tended their packets without protest. Wade opened his eyes and saw them sitting together, a solid clump around their fire. Their communal bulk, their impassive faces seemed a rebuke. Wade remembered a California fire, three years ago, up above Monterey. He and his crew had been housed in a Zen Buddhist retreat house. The monks, out of gratitude, had cooked for them: vegetables from their garden, mountains of steamed rice, homemade tofu, freshly baked breads, plums and apricots off their own trees. They had eaten in a long white room cooled by turning fans. They had been served by men and women who smiled like happy hippies and the food had been some of the best he had ever eaten in his life. Nonetheless, his crewmates had bitched nonstop—especially the older ones. They kept it up until Overhead ordered a chopper to make daily drops of red meat and Coca-Cola.

The memory of those serene, monastic meals made Wade regret—and not for the first time—that he had married a woman who had no interest in cooking. When Greta came home from school, her meal of choice was two gin and diet tonics chased by a strawberry Slim Fast. Wade decided on the maple-nut cake. He had never particularly cared for maple, but at least he didn't have to cook it. The dessert slid out of its envelope, a lump of—yes, beige dough flattened into a free-form cookie that had a plastic sheen at the edges. The nuts were dots of walnuts gone soggy. Maybe he should have warmed it up. But it was no big deal. Word was that new crews were en route to relieve them. They would be back in camp for a real dinner and with yet another chunk of hazard pay on their timecards. That was one thing no one bitched about, the H-pay. Before July was out, he had already made enough to finish the addition on his house. With the baby out of their bedroom, maybe things would look up between him and Greta.

Wade began to feel perkier. He attributed it to the sugar in the cake and considered heating up his chicken entree. But Dan Mowatt, their team leader, came back from a confab with Hartwig, the Division "supe." The team leaders for the other crews had been in on it and also two liaisons—one for the Native American crew, the other for the inmates. "Okay," Dan announced wearily, and they knew it was not good news. "Listen up. Hartwig says the ETA of our replacements is uncertain. So they're busing out a load of water for us, new batteries, and some more MREs—"

There was a chorus of groans. Dan, a barrel-chested man whose handlebar mustache drooped into determined twin curls, held up his hand and the group complaint died. "Just in case we don't rotate off the mountain tonight," he finished his sentence. "They're going to make the drop below us, drive it into the end of the wagon road. We'll go down the way the Deer Lodge crew came up this morning, down along the creek—it's probably less than half a mile. A bit steep, but we figure a couple squads could bump the stuff up in about an hour."

No one jumped to volunteer. "A bit steep" was an understatement. The pitch was close to a 70-percent grade. All morning, the line-scratchers had been leaning into the mountain as they wielded their Pulaskis and the mop-up squads below had been dodging killer rocks loosed by slipping feet. Moreover, the temperature was close to ninety, each five-gallon cubee of water weighed forty pounds, and the route down the drainage was full of thick brush. Bushwhacking down and back up with a cubee in each hand was no one's idea of fun, particularly after a lunch of MREs. Wade considered his left knee. It was bothering him again. Downhill would only make it worse. Downhill was always worse.

Dan waited. Wade found the silence embarrassing. He didn't want to let the boss down. He liked Dan Mowatt and wanted his good opinion. In addition, he wanted a recommendation that would boost him up the job ladder. He had been working as a squad leader for the past two seasons and hoped, sooner or later, to qualify as a team leader. But most of all, he didn't want the Indians or the cons to think his outfit was a bunch of wusses. To hell with his knee. "We'll go," he said. He stood up.

He looked around for confirmation from the other members of his squad: Cat Carew, small, fearless, all sinew, and next to him the most senior; Jim McCulloch, a hardworking wild man whose mother—of all things—had ended up running the whole show; Richie Gower, a grumpy graduate student from Oregon and, like Jim, in his second year with the team; and rookie Pami Gustavisson, a Wisconsin farm girl and the only other woman on their crew. They avoided his glance—all except Cat. He caught a play of amusement in her olive-brown eyes. He saw no glaze of exhaustion and was annoyed that she didn't jump in. Instead, she crossed her arms and sat back to watch, as if savoring the awkwardness of the moment.

Jim McCulloch took a breath. "Okay," he said, forcing up a note of enthusiasm. He stood up and nudged Richie Gower's boot. "Okay, Gower?"

"Christ," Gower growled. He took off his glasses and wiped them on his bandanna.

"How does it work?" Pami asked. She was a big pink-and-white girl who dotted the *i* in her name with a circle. Sitting next to Cat, she looked softer and lumpier that she was: Wade was willing to bet she could buck bales all day.

"Like a bucket brigade," he explained. "We peel off into a line on the way down. The guy below you carries the stuff up to you, then you bump it to the guy above you and go back down for the next load. It's quicker and easier than having everyone make the whole trip a couple times."

She nodded. "No problem."

"Off your butt, man," Jim said to Richie.

"Oh, Mommy, do I have to?" Richie said.

Everyone stopped eating. "Yeah, you have to," Jim answered.

"You gonna spank me, maybe?" Richie needled.

Jim flushed. Wade didn't like it. The kid couldn't help his mother. "What's gonna happen," Wade drawled to Richie, "is no supper for naughty little bunnies. Guaranteed. Cat, you in?"

She gathered up the plastic debris from her lunch. "Sure," she said. She stood up, laced her fingers together and stretched her arms, curved her back, then delivered her line in a voice husky with sexuality. "You like spanking, Gower?"

"Oooh," hooted her crewmates.

Richie brightened. "With your bare hand?"

She smiled a small, sly smile that drew another chorus of hoots.

"Let's do it," Wade said firmly. Dan gave him a gruff nod of approval.

A few minutes later he cursed himself for being a brownie. The other squad to volunteer was from the Deer Lodge crew.

Five men in standard-issue yellow shirts and olive-drab jeans. In California the cons at least wore orange fire clothes. These men looked no different from any other crew. They stood together in casual stances waiting for orders. They didn't speak but their eyes followed Cat and Pami. The women, used to stares, ignored them. But suddenly their femaleness was conspicuous. It seemed to Wade that the women's banter was a notch louder, a notch more macho than usual.

Dan shook hands with the inmates' supervisor, a Bureau of State Lands man with a weather-beaten face and gray stubble on his chin. He was unarmed. He was not a guard. There were no guards on the line. The guards did their guarding on the bus, in camp. This man, the BSL supervisor, was a wildfire vet. Wade overhead him vouchsafing for his crew and was surprised by the note of pride in the older man's voice.

Then Dan handed Wade an extra handset. "You're in charge," he said, with a nod toward the inmates. "They've got one radio between them. Stay on Channel Three." Channel 3 was the Division's own private frequency. Dan glanced again at the inmates and lowered his voice. "I know their boss. He says they won't give you any trouble. But keep them together." He hesitated. "Maybe out of the girls' way."

So Dan had noticed, too. Wade felt relieved. "I was just thinking the same thing," he admitted. He paused, visualizing the relay in his head. "I'll take the middle. Put Richie at the top as lookout. Keep 'em between us."

Dan gave him a fatherly clap on his upper arm. "Good man," he said warmly. "Leave your packsacks here in the safety zone." He glanced over at the Deer Lodge crew. "I'll keep an eye on them for you."

Suddenly it didn't seem like such a chore. Halfway down wasn't so bad. His knee could manage halfway. Especially without the thirty extra pounds in his personal pack.

He briefed Cat. "I want you to take point," he said.

"Oh, goody. I get to go all the way down."

But it was not a serious grumble. Wade gave her the extra

handset. "We're on Channel Three. But first get on the fire net and tell Ops we're on our way. Make sure they've delivered. We don't want to sit around twiddling our thumbs for it."

"No, sir," she said, with mock military crispness. She keyed in the handset. "Justice Operations," she called. "Millville 'shots. Carew here."

Wade walked over to the five inmates. "I'm Lowry," he announced. "Who's on the radio?"

An inmate with a handsome, pockmarked face stepped forward. "Me," he said.

A poor man's John Travolta, Wade thought. "What's your name?"

"Hallihan."

"We're on Channel Three."

"That's what the boss man said," Hallihan said cheerfully.

"You guys are up top. Between me and Gower. That guy over there. With the glasses. Okay?"

"Okay with me," Hallihan said.

Wade walked back to Jim. The kid was studying a pale green geodetic survey map he had taken out of his personal pack. Lowry reflected that for all Jim's reputation as a madcap boozer, outside the saloon he was more of a Boy Scout than a macho man. "Be Prepared," not "Can-do," was engraved on his soul. Wade felt a protective tug of tenderness toward him.

Jim looked up from his map—a bit sheepish, as if caught cheating on a quiz. "I like to know where I am," he explained. "I picked it up coming through town."

Wade remembered they had stopped for burgers in Sophia before checking in at the Meander Campground. It seemed a long time ago. At the counter of a local greasy spoon, Wade had bought a postcard of the town's main drag and sent it off to his mom.

Jim folded up his map. "It's an old one," he said. "From 1963."

Wade shrugged. "Mountains ain't moved much since then. We'll leave our packs up here with Dan. I'm guessing Richie's a bit worse for wear, so I'm going to put him at the top with the Deer Lodge crew. I'll take the middle. You and Cat get the bottom."

"Hey. You've come to the right man. No sweat."

Wade grimaced at the boast. "Ri-i-i-ght."

Cat ambled over, with Pami in tow like a faithful blonde retriever. They were ready to move out. "The stuff's down there now," she reported. "They sent some kitchen trusty out with it. He's waiting for us in a pickup at the end of the road."

"Let Jim make the contact with the trusty," said Wade.

"You think I can't handle him?" Her voice was dangerously sweet.

"You handling him's what I'm worried about," Wade said, deadpan.

Pami let out a snort.

At thirteen hundred forty-five, the two volunteer squads left their packs in two separate piles in the safety zone and started down, single file. Dislodging stones and rocks, they plunged down through head-high brush—a brittle, dusty tangle of willows and serviceberry, rabbitbrush and alder. The afternoon breeze had stiffened enough to make every one of them alert for directional shifts, but as it was, the wind blew upslope into their faces, carrying the clean scent of the river with it. As long as it remained in the west, it would keep the fire above them off their backs.

Richie Gower stopped first, about seventy-five yards below the fire line. The rest of them continued on down. The inmates peeled off next, three of them, then Travolta Hallihan, and the Indian last, just above Wade. Wade remembered Travolta's needle scene in *Pulp Fiction* and wondered what Hallihan was in for. He dug in his heels, careful not to dislodge rocks on Jim and the two girls crashing through the brush below, then hunkered down in the hot, feathery shade of a bitterbrush. He could see nothing from his post but a nicotine-tinged sky and gray-dusted shrubs. The pale leaves reminded him of a photographic negative. He wondered if Greta had picked up his last roll from Kmart, as he'd asked. His mouth felt dry. He debated taking a swallow from his canteen.

The next thing he knew, his handset squawked. It was Cat. He realized he had fallen asleep—sound asleep. While hunkering, no less. A wonder he hadn't fallen. His knees felt numb. He rocked back onto his ass against the slope, uncranked his legs in front of him, and felt prickles of circulation. He checked his watch. He'd been asleep for over ten minutes.

"I'm bumping up some cubees to Pami," Cat reported on the radio. "Jim's on his way back down for the next load. He said the cubees and MREs were there in the bed of the truck, but no sign of the trusty."

Wade asked, "How about batteries?"

"Affirmative."

Wade felt a faint stir in his bowels. Last night's Mexican beans, he diagnosed. Maybe the trusty had gone off to take a dump. "Okay. Over."

"Wade."

"Go ahead."

"Jim said there's a case of melons. Cantaloupes."

Wade felt suddenly cheerful. "Finders keepers. Bump 'em up! Hey, Dan. You copy?"

"I copy," their leader answered from above. "Must be your just desserts."

Wade heard Richie groan.

"How many melons?" The strange voice on the handset startled Wade. Then he remembered that Hallihan, the inmate, had a radio.

Cat answered, "A sack of them, Jim said."

Richie broke in. "Wade? What she say? You guys keep breaking up."

Wade announced, "We'll divvy 'em up at the top, fair and square."

"I'm allergic to honeydew," Richie announced. "Wade, do you copy?"

"I copy. Don't wet your pants. It's *cantaloupe*." He swallowed a mouthful of saliva. "Get a move on, down there," Wade ordered. He heard the distant rattle of a Huey. Then it faded and the breeze seemed to fade with it. All of a sudden it seemed very still. Wade stood up. He could see nothing. Did he smell smoke? Or was it his own stink? He thought about the showers waiting down at base camp. He sat back down.

Once again, a squawk from his handset startled him awake. Richie—he thought it was Richie, but the transmission was garbled. He couldn't make out what he was saying. Then Dan came on, his voice terse. "Lowry. Go to the fire net."

Wade's first thought was of the melons. The trusty had reported them. He keyed his radio to the fire channel.

Dan said, "Air Ops says there's spot fire below you. A chopper reported heavy black smoke. Can you see it?"

"Negative."

Through a crackle of static, Wade heard Dan talking to the pilot. He started hiking up the side of the drainage for a look. Then he saw it, an ugly black cauldron of boiling smoke. "Something's cooking pretty good down there," he told Dan.

"Move out," Dan ordered. "Get up to the safety zone. Now."

Hurriedly, Wade switched back to Channel 3. "Cat, move up to S-One. Fire reported below us." He started hiking up the slope, then stopped. "Cat, do you copy?"

No response.

"Hallihan. Get your guys up to S-One. Cat, can you respond?"

No response.

"Can you respond?" He looked at the handset. The seriousness of the situation sank in. He plunged downhill to warn Pami, sliding on his boot heels, arms out like a snowboarder.

He heard the fire before he saw it and the noise confused

him. They said a blowup roared, roared like a locomotive, everyone said. But this was a great oceanic whoosh, the breath of a galaxy. He saw Pami running toward him, a twenty-foot-wall of orange flame behind her. She was carrying two cubees of water, one in each hand. Jesus, he thought. "Drop your load!" he screamed at her. "Deploy your shelter!"

He heard Dan calling him on the radio.

He pulled his own shelter off his belt, out of his yellow case, then keyed in Dan. "Get a bomber in here," he yelled. Horrified, he saw Pami stop. She teetered, like a tree about to fall, then crashed over backward, feet uphill.

Clutching his handset in his left hand and his silver shelter in his right, he started toward her, but the force of the fire's wind held him in place. Burning branches blew past him. He doubled over, fumbling for the red ring on his shelter. "Get us some retardant!" he shouted at the handset on the ground. "We're going to get nailed!"

16

The Justice's war room was located in a three-bay equipment barn behind the renovated chalet. The maintenance vehicles and machinery—two pickups, a tractor, brush hog, plow blade, chipper—had been moved outside and trestle tables, folding chairs, and plywood easels had been moved inside, along with portable floodlights, copiers, telephones, fax machines, and computers. Maps and charts taped around the outside walls billowed like laundry in the steady electric breeze from an industrial-sized fan.

Mattie sat at an unoccupied desk with an iced tea she had carried back from lunch with Spence and a pile of paperwork she hoped to get through before her next meeting. She read Brian's latest press release and initialed it. She was skimming the Incident Status Summary (1,100 chains of line built, 190 to go, expected containment 48 hours, cost to date $2,7 million.) when an urgent off-note in the muffled transmissions from her handset on the desk made her look up sharply. Through the workaday monotones, someone's voice rose in desperation. The fear in it was contagious. She felt the skin on the nape of her neck tighten, as if someone were leisurely drawing a blade down it. She fumbled at the radio's volume control.

". . . emergency traffic only," a base dispatcher announced crisply. The words echoed loudly off the barn's aluminum walls: around the room, a dozen handsets had been simultaneously turned up to catch the exchange.

"Can you respond?" a male voice yelled over a background roar that sounded like a waterfall. "Lowry," beseeched the voice, "talk to me, goddammit!"

Mattie was aware of a new energy passing through the war room. The blanket of after-lunch drowsiness slipped soundlessly to the floor. People began to move. There was no rush, no flurry; their movements were measured, deliberate. They left their seats, grouped around maps posted on the walls, paused to cock their heads toward their handsets.

"Air Operations to Division supervisor, request report on conditions," a voice droned over the radio.

"Fire all around us," the supervisor responded from the ground. "Three-hundred and sixty degrees, spiking up to fifty feet."

An entrapment.

"What is it?" a worried clerk at the next desk asked her.

"Sounds like a flare-up," she said, automatically employing the low-impact term. She picked up her handset and joined the cluster of people gathered in front of one of the maps on the wall.

The enlarged Xerox of the topography was overlaid with sheets of clear plastic, each marked with fire-information updates. "Where is it?" she asked.

An Operations man swept the side of his hand between the black parentheses that indicated Division C. "Up in here."

Jimmy.

The man tapped a new red dot far below the fire line, down at the base of the mountain. "One of the choppers called in this spot. It's not far from the river road. Sounds like the wind pushed it up the Copper Creek drainage over the line. There may have been multiple spots. We aren't sure yet."

Mattie looked around the room. None of the Command team was in the war room. "Where's Mike?" she asked his subordinate.

"En route to the heliport."

"Raise Voyle," she ordered. She took a slow, deep breath and strode back to her borrowed desk. She swept the papers into her briefcase, grabbed her handset, and clutching them both to her chest, made a beeline for the door. Outside, she broke into a run. A small crowd around the communications trailer parted for her.

She opened the trailer's flimsy door and squeezed inside. The narrow, air-conditioned space was packed with dispatchers and members of the Overhead team. Someone vacated a chair for her. She sat down, rested her elbows on the work surface and leaned forward, hands against her mouth, eyes closed, screening out everything around her except the disembodied voices of Division C.

The crews had deployed their shelters in the safety zone. The squad bosses had their radios in the shelters with them and she could hear them calling back and forth, choking, cursing, yelling through the thin foil to the troops deployed around them.

You can handle it!

Jones? Romano?

Keep it together!

Stay down!

Tommy, Tommy? Don't panic!

Radios crackled. She heard screams, profanities. The skin on her arms and neck crawled. Then the roar of the dragon obliterated the voices.

No one in the trailer moved. No one's eyes met. Mattie stared unseeing at the wood-grained Formica of the work surface in front of her. Air Ops reported zero visibility. This, together with gale-force winds generated by the blowup, was keeping the Hueys with their buckets at bay. A bomber pilot, ignoring regulations that forbid him to fly through smoke, made a blind pass over the fire, dumping tons of orange-red retardant on the slope below the entrapped troops.

By sixteen hundred hours, the blowup was under control. The crews crawled out of their foil tents and began taking count.

Many had burns on their backs, on their legs, hands. Several had breathed in superheated air and seared their lungs. One of the Seminole crew was unconscious: the retardant drop had dislodged a boulder the size of a TV set, which had bounced onto the man's shelter. EMTs on the scene did what they could, but on account of the smoke, they had to wait over an hour for the Medivacs.

As specified by the Incident's accident plan, Mike Robuck as Operations chief, and Grant Sonderdank as Safety officer, flew to the scene with the first responders. It was all Mattie could do not to go with them, but the accident plan ordained that she coordinate the evacuation, and Communications was the most efficient place to do it. She called the Forest Supervisor but had no firm answers for him, either on the number of casualties or the cause of the accident. News from the site came in at irregular intervals. Brian Flaherty, staffing a phone ten people away, fielded all media calls.

After the first hour, her confidence began to waver. The lack of information, the long periods of radio silence fed the communal sense of dread in the trailer. Finally, just after seventeen hundred hours, Mike keyed in. In a flat voice, he said, "We have fatalities at the scene."

The worst had happened. For a moment Mattie could see nothing. As if she had been hit over the head, the thin paneled walls of the trailer seemed to throb, echoing Mike's words. She heard herself talking. "Do we have a number?"

"Five confirmed."

"Have the victims been identified?"

"Affirmative."

She took a breath. "Mike, none of the names are to be used on the radio. Repeat: During evacuation process, the names of the fatalities will not be used on the air. Do you copy?"

"Affirmative."

"The bodies of the victims are not to be moved at this time. Do you copy?"

"I copy."

"Signing off." Slowly, she swiveled her chair around and scanned the shocked faces around her. It was as if she were seeing them through a fog. She latched on to Brian's face. "We'll need a statement for the press," she said. "No names until notification of kin. In fact, no information regarding the accident will be released without going through me. Understood?"

Brian nodded.

She spotted Ned perched on the shelflike desk that ran the length of the trailer, his arms folded across his chest, his eyes obscured by the bill of his cap. Her head still felt oddly thick, but what needed to be done was clear. It was as if her brain were a well-oiled machine operating in a slightly soupy atmosphere. "Ned," she directed, "I want you to take over here. You'll need to notify the local Sheriff. They need to be in on this. I'm going up there."

He pursed his mouth. She saw him catch Brian's eye.

"What?" she demanded.

"Are you sure you're all right?" Ned insisted.

"I'm fine," she said impatiently. Belatedly, she heard the concern in his voice. He means on account of Jimmy. "I'm fine," she repeated. "So far. Thanks." It couldn't be Jimmy.

There was nothing for Mattie, as Incident Commander, to do at the scene that she could not do as well from the base. The evacuation of the survivors was proceeding smoothly, and by the time she was airborne, the uninjured crews were in buses on their way back to base camp for debriefing and counseling. But she could not wait any longer for the names of the dead—it might be several hours before the list was confirmed and sent back to base.

She disembarked from the helicopter in the zone where the survivors had deployed their foil shelters. Mike and Grant, each with handsets in both fists, were busy with other men in Nomex. She scanned the ruined mountainside. On the blackened terrain around her, steaming boulders dripped with bloodred retardant that smelled like mildew. An upslope snag crashed to the ground, prompting a flurry of activity from the emergency mop-up crews. She saw that someone had set up a flag. A clean new American flag flying at half-mast from a pole set in a rock cairn. That was quick, she thought numbly. Where did they find the pole? The flag snapped in a stiff evening breeze. A hundred yards downhill, a man sat beside a blackened tree trunk. Someone's foil shelter had blown away and snagged on it. The man held his helmet in his hands, between his knees. His back was shaking. She realized he was crying.

She gazed on down the drainage, saw rescue workers at the bottom. They had walked in from the river road. The river itself was blocked from view by a charred hill. Which meant the fire had started behind the hill. The wind blew ashes into her face. Odd, she thought. A spot fire down there? And where were the bodies? She started hiking down.

"Chief," Grant said behind her.

She stopped and turned. "I thought I said the bodies weren't to be moved."

"They haven't been moved."

She stared at the man below her on the slope. She realized it was not a tree trunk he was sitting beside.

Grant's face looked haggard. He handed her a handwritten list. She took it, stared at it uncomprehending.

"Those are the five," he told her. "Four of the Millville crew—but your son's not on it," he added in a rush.

She felt momentarily weak with relief. Her knees sagged. She felt Grant steady her. She blinked, focused on the list. It was in alphabetical order. With a sinking heart, she recognized the names. Two women: Cat Carew and Pami Gustavisson—the rookie. She remembered Jimmy speaking of them. "Manuel Leonard?" she asked.

"One of the inmates."

Wade Lowry. The name hit her with a thump. Jim's squad

boss. Then she saw the last name and let out a cry. "But he's here!" She clutched Grant's arm. "He's here!"

"Who?" Grant demanded, his face alarmed. Mattie was doubled over, making an odd moan. "For Chrissake, Mattie, who?"

"My son!" She thrust the paper at him. "Jim Sterling!"

"Sterling?" Grant squinted at the names.

"Sterling. His father's name. On his red card." The explanation came out in gasps as if she were drowning. She saw the disbelief on Grant's face and clutched at it. "It's a mistake!"

"No, no. No mistake. My God, Mattie, I'm sorry. I didn't know . . ."

She sank down into a crouch, pressing the heels of her hands against her forehead. Grant squatted beside her, put a hand on her back. "Mattie. Is there someone you'd like me to call, someone you want with you?"

She looked up at him with anguished eyes. "Jimmy?" Her voice was wooden.

"I'm sorry." He cast around for help.

Jimmy dead? She looked downhill. It seemed to take a long time for her eyes to focus. She lifted an arm and pointed at the man sitting beside the treelike body. "Who's that?"

"Dan Mowatt. The crew boss."

She shook her head, formed the words. "Is that Jimmy? Is that my son?"

Grant shook his head. "They think he was farther down. At the bottom."

It seemed unreal. Half-formed questions sailed slowly through her head, like ships shrouded in fog. Why did I think it couldn't happen? she wondered dully. People die every day. The same way they walk out of a room. "I want to see him," she said to Grant.

"Mattie—"

She put her hands on her knees, pushed against them and stood up. "I'm going down."

"Shit, Mattie, there's nothing left to see!"

"Show me where he is."

He let out a blast of frustration and swung away, a violent reeling motion. "Goddamn it!" he swore explosively. Then he saw Mattie's startled face and pulled himself together. "Okay. All right. I'll take you down."

They stopped ten yards above the charred body. The breeze carried puffs of an unpleasant sweetish smell. She thrust one hand under her armpit in a self-protective half-hug, pressed the other hand against her nose and mouth. The arms and legs were in the air, rigid, bent at the joints. Where were his feet? She saw the head—balloonlike, no nose, no ears—and looked away. She closed her eyes. "Jimmy?" she tried. "Jim?" she amended, as if addressing him in public. She heard no answer, felt nothing at all. I must be in shock, she decided. She opened her eyes, this time careful to focus more widely. Where was his shelter? Had it been entirely incinerated?

And how had he gotten caught? It was inconceivable. He was young, strong, he knew all the lessons, old and new. He had grown up on her father's pre-shelter entrapment stories. There was the famous Pulaski story of 1910, but others as well: how Ranger Ed Thenon in the same year had saved a crew of thirty by making them lie in a creek where all the fish had boiled to death as the fire passed over; how Wagner Dodge, foreman at the Mann Gulch Fire of 1949, had survived by stepping into flames he himself had set. More important, however, were the newer lessons. After the fourteen deaths at Storm King, she and Jack and Jimmy, like every smoke eater in the business, had devoured each new piece of information.

"What happened?" she cried out. She felt Grant grip her arm. She realized she was shaking.

"Come on, Mattie. That's enough."

"Just a minute." She squeezed her eyes closed. I'm going to find out, she promised Jimmy. I'm going to find out what happened.

17

Mattie hiked back up the hill, gathering speed as she went, leaving Grant behind. The exertion stopped her shakes but the fog in her head did not lift. Through it, the sound of her huffing and puffing seemed distant, as if belonging to someone else. She pushed through the men around Mike Robuck and heard herself demand in a choked protest, "Why were they bumping up the supplies? Why didn't we drop them in?"

She saw Mike's mouth tighten. "We were short on choppers. We had one down with a mechanical, one engaged in a medical evacuation. The decision was made to keep the other three on the bucket brigade."

She felt a slow, heavy turning of her brain. Given the tactical goal of getting the Justice buttoned down before the red-flag front blew in, she could find no blame. "I see," she said. But she didn't. She looked back down the blackened pitch.

Mike said grimly, "Of course now that it's happened, they've diverted an entire fleet for us."

Grant joined them, out of breath, his face distressed. "Mike," he said. "Her son—"

Abruptly she walked away. She did not want to hear it.

A shiny new Chinook ferried Mattie back to the Meander. She issued a short statement at the outdoors press conference Brian had set up at the edge of the Command helispot. Looking out at the crush of reporters, she wondered how so many of them had gotten there so soon. Was Gerald Spencer among them? She found she wanted him to know, to know about Jimmy. They had talked about their own entrapment only last night. They hadn't been all that much older than Jimmy when it happened. More than anyone, she felt Spence would understand. Somehow, their own escape and Jim's death seemed inexorably entwined.

The man's a perfect stranger, she reminded herself as she hurried back to her post in the Communications trailer. The newly arrived Human Resource specialist, Celia DeJesus, gave her a hug. Mattie stiffened and Celia peered at her. "You coming to work?" Celia asked, but it was more of a statement than a question.

The phones rang continually. Mattie fielded calls from law enforcement agencies, State Lands directors, firefighter union representatives, fire-management scientists, mayors, and senators. Most of her callers had a political ax to grind. They embraced the accident as "one more example" of underfunding, overfunding, lack of training, lack of staffing. A minister called to say the accident was God's punishment. An environmentalist called to say it should never have happened. A psychic called to say he had foreseen it would happen. The calls seemed strangely unreal, yet she was grateful for them. They not only provided distraction from the horrifying image of her son's blackened body; they confirmed that the catastrophe had actually happened. The call she expected, however, did not come: a call from the Forest Supervisor. Why had he not called? Deep in the political crevices of her brain, sensors prickled a warning.

Celia was stationed next to Mattie. A gentle-mannered woman with large, firmly anchored breasts under her starched uniform shirt, Celia DeJesus had the dire task of notifying the families. She broke the news patiently, with a calm insistence in her slightly accented voice, and although Mattie did not speak with any of the relatives, she felt the need to listen, to hear other families being told. Celia had offered to call Jack

McCulloch as well, but Mattie felt obligated to break the news herself. She was sure her family knew about the blowup. No doubt they had followed the coverage on TV and were concerned and anxious to hear that Jimmy was all right. Her sister Harriet (probably against her father's orders) had called while she was on the phone arguing with the Forest Service Comptroller. Harriet's message was terse and trusting: "Call when you can."

But Mattie kept putting off the call, preferring to talk to strangers. At nineteen hundred hours, with a ghastly flood of guilt, she suddenly remembered that her family still did not know that Jimmy was dead. At the same time, her political sensors were beeping louder: What had Ned been up to while she had been working the phone? Had the Forest Supervisor called Ned instead of her for a report? She decided it was time to touch base with Ned. "I'll be back in bit," she told Celia.

Ned was not in the chalet. The brightly lit front office was busy, and when she went through to the living room in back, she found Brian holding a strategy conference with two of his staff members, a man and a woman, both fresh-faced and sturdy-looking. Mattie was reminded of a German operetta—perhaps it was the woman's short, shiny braids, or the way the man's pristine yellow shirt bloused under his suspenders. They sat together on the sofa, heads bent over papers on the coffee table. Seeing Mattie, they stood up. They looked uneasy, as if caught hatching a plot. Behind them, color images slid across a mute TV screen: a man lathering himself in the shower, a large bar of soap. On the coffee table, there were three cans of Pepsi among the printouts and lined pads. Was Brian the one who had been stockpiling Pepsis?

"Where's Ned?" she asked.

"Have you tried the war room?" Brian suggested. He peered at her. "How're you doing?"

How do you *think* I'm doing? she wanted to snap. "Okay," she said stiffly.

"Mrs. McCulloch?" said the man in suspenders. "I just want to say, how sorry I am—" He floundered.

Like a protective older sister, the young woman took a step forward. "Yes," she said. "We're so sorry. We didn't know Jim, I mean, not personally. But he's a hero. They all are. They all made the supreme sacrifice."

Sacrifice? Mattie looked at Brian. Was that what they'd been cooking up, a sacrificial spin? She looked at his assistants and was momentarily appalled to see tears shining in their eyes. She glanced away, caught an aerial view of charred mountainside on the TV screen behind them.

"Oh dear," murmured the woman in braids. She swooped down on the remote on the coffee table.

"No, it's okay," Mattie said. "I want to see it." She imagined Jack, sitting alone in the house, watching the tube. For the first time she felt a wobble of sorrow. How could she tell her father? What should she say? Perhaps she should let Celia make the call after all.

Brian dismissed his workers. "We'll finish this up later," he said. There was an undertone of warning in his voice, as if he were humoring a nursing-home patient.

The woman gave him the remote. "We're real sorry," she repeated to Mattie, then she and her co-worker hurried out of the room.

Mattie stood with Brian watching the coverage of the Copper Creek blowup. She saw herself ducking out from under the rotors of the Chinook that had flown her from the scene to the press conference. Then she saw herself standing on a makeshift platform in front of a bank of microphones. The wind ruffled her short hair. She looked grave and pale and androgynous. It was hard to tell her apart from the men on the platform.

Among them, she recognized the governor of Montana wearing regulation Nomex. Had he been up at the scene or were the fire clothes a political costume? The camera lingered on him. He was taller than the rest of them and more photogenic. Silver-haired and tan, he waited respectfully for her to speak, his brow wrinkled with paternal concern. A longer shot pulled back to show a giant red-and-white Chinook dwarfing the gathering on the platform, testifying to Forest Service capabilities. Beyond the chopper, fire-blackened hills and a dirty evening sky pierced with molten streaks of pink.

"Did you plan the sunset, Brian?" she asked. It came out acidly.

Brian looked startled, then quickly rallied. "Getting the Chinook was harder," he quipped, matching his tone to hers.

She saw herself reading the brief announcement Brian had composed for her. "At two P.M. this afternoon, in the Copper Creek drainage area . . ." Her voice was steady but flat. The words "tragic loss" came out of her mouth without feeling. When she finished, there was an awkward moment, as if the men on the podium were waiting for something more. She stepped back and Brian took over.

The reporters' questions were urgent, demanding, tumbling over one another at the start, then, by some mysterious consensual mechanism, falling back to allow one to shoot cleanly forth. At each sally, Brian would duck his head toward the surviving question, shielding his face with the bill of his cap, as if heading into a stiff wind. Then he would lift his head to respond.

"Where was the point of origin?" a male voice called out.

Pause. "Approximately ten miles south of Sophia on the east side of State Route Three-oh-seven."

"Can you tell us the cause?"

Another pause. Brian raised his head. "Cause has not yet been determined."

A female voice: "Is there a possibility of arson?"

Pause. One, two, Mattie counted. Head up. "Our investigators are on the scene now. As soon as cause has been determined, we will let you know."

Although at the time Brian had seemed interminably slow to answer, now watching him on the screen Mattie realized that his pauses actually lent a measure of gravitas to his stock-in-trade replies.

"Is it true that a vehicle was burned at the point of origin?"

"A Forest Service pickup was overrun at a staging area half a mile from the point of origin."

"Was the driver a victim?" someone else called out.

"We are not releasing any information about the victims until the coroner has made positive identification."

Click. The screen went blank. "Et cetera," Brian said.

Mattie let out a long breath. "You're good at it," she complimented Brian.

"It's my job," Brian said.

"All those funereal pauses."

Brian stared.

"I mean, your timing was good. Appropriate for the occasion."

He put the remote back down on the coffee table.

"I sounded like a robot," she said.

His eyes were sympathetic, but he didn't deny it.

"They'll think my heart is made of ice."

"Well," he reassured her, "they don't know Jim is a victim. Once the names are released, you can expect a tremendous outpouring of sympathy."

She felt a prickle of irritation. "Brian, I'm not going to do a mother-of-sorrows sound bite. You can take it from here. You can write me a statement if you like, but I'm not going to stand in front of the cameras again. Or give interviews."

He looked relieved. "I understand."

But did he? Did he think she was withdrawing? "Everything you put out still goes through me," she reminded him.

"Of course," he said. But his eyes were guarded. What did he know? She turned to leave.

"Have all the families been notified?" he asked. "Can I release the names?"

"Not yet." She felt a flush rising to her cheeks. "I'll let you know."

Mattie strode purposefully across the floodlit parking area but in fact she had no destination other than somewhere private to use her cell phone. She cut behind the Communications trailer and picked up a footpath that wound through the dark pillars of the pines. The night air felt like a cool hand on her brow and the path, padded with pine needles, was soft and silent underfoot.

Ma?

She stopped. Jimmy. Inside her head, not outside—she was certain about that. She listened, waiting for more, but that was it, just "Ma?" A question, distinct, familiar, as if he'd just walked into the house and, not finding her in the kitchen, had called upstairs.

Was he—his spirit, his soul—actually hovering, calling across the membrane between the living and the dead? Or was it merely a neurological trick, an echo wedging itself out from the folds of her brain?

"Peace," she said out loud. Her voice soundly oddly everyday. Peace, she prayed silently, urgently. She remembered Jim as a baby racked by colic. In her efforts to soothe him, she had felt the same edge of panic, the same tug of maternal despair.

Ahead, she saw a greenish glow through the trees. Puzzled, she walked toward it. The eerie light came from lanterns set on picnic tables. Around them, groups of firefighters sat with slumped shoulders. Others milled around weeping and hugging each other. The Critical Stress Debriefing team, she realized, had taken over a picnic area. One of the metal grills had been turned into a low, impromptu altar: dozens and dozens of candles flickered violently in the night breeze. She stopped, scanned the groups for Jimmy's friends, then, hearing voices behind her, stepped off the path and hiked upslope into the darkness above the tables.

She stopped beside an ancient ponderosa and pulled out her cell phone. She pushed the automatic dialer and listened to the beeps of her own number. The phone began to ring. Five, six times. Where was her father? Had he gone out?

Then he picked up.

"Dad? Dad, it's me, Mattie. I, uh. I—"

Jack McCulloch interrupted. "I already heard."

"You did?"

Jack said nothing. Mattie listened to his silence, straining for clues. She heard no TV in the background, no voices. "You heard about Jimmy?" she asked cautiously.

"Yeah. Poor Jimbo. The fire got him. It grabbed him and ate him all up."

Shocked, Mattie wondered if her father was drunk. Had Celia gone ahead and called her father? "Dad, who told you?"

"Someone called. One of the others." His speech wasn't slurred. But his vagueness alarmed her.

"One of the others?"

"Forget the name. Pal of Jimbo's."

"One of the Millville 'shots called you? From here?"

"He's dead, how's he gonna call? It was his dad. Nice fella, poor devil. Just wanted to touch base. Can't think of his name now. They live out two hundred, near Potomac."

"Lowry? The squad boss—his dad called you?"

"That's it. They're taking it pretty hard. You better call your sister."

"Does she know?"

"Yeah, I told her."

"Dad, I'm sorry. I couldn't call any earlier."

"It doesn't matter. Harrie's flying in tomorrow morning. What time is it?"

"You mean now?"

"Can't see my watch."

"Did I wake you up?"

"I didn't think I was asleep," Jack said.

Mattie glanced at her watch. "It's nine-fifteen."

"Eight-fifteen in Seattle."

"I'll call her now, Dad."

"I'm picking her up at the airport. We'll drive on down from there."

Mattie felt reassured. Her father sounded more like his old self. "Go to the Hotsprings Inn," she told him. "It's on the main drag in Sophia. We've got a block of rooms there reserved for the families. I'll get you each one." She paused. "You okay, Dad?" she asked. "Do you want me to get someone to come over and be with you?"

"At this time of night? What in hell for?" Jack growled.

Mattie waited.

Then, his voice more tentative, her father asked, "Where is he?"

"Up on the mountain. I gave orders not to move them until the investigation team approves release. One guy's coming in from D.C. They should all be on the scene first thing in the morning." She stopped. "I'm sorry, Dad," she apologized. "It's the only way we find out what happened. They need to see how the bodies—fell."

"Yeah. Just do your job," he instructed. He paused. "That's what he'd want."

Mattie heard him choking off a sob as he fumbled to replace the receiver. She imagined him crying in the dark of his bedroom. For a moment she listened to the hum of the dead line. She looked down at the grieving crews. The tangled press of their bodies, their stricken, upturned faces, mouths agape in soundless grief might have come off a Grecian urn. She felt as if she were looking down into a netherworld full of antique heroes. The sight moved her. She felt the sting of tears. *He's dead*, she tried. But the words struck no releasing chord. She contemplated calling her father back and decided against it. Instead she dialed her sister's number in Seattle.

Harriet was irate. At the sound of Mattie's voice, she loosed a massive buildup of anger and despair. "You never cared about this family," she raged. "You weren't there for Mom when she died and nothing's changed. All you ever cared about was yourself, about being Mrs. Big Shot. You never cared about Dad. Not the way I did. You just used him to get your way."

"Harrie."

"No, you listen to me for a change! You made him give up contracting, you took over his house, shit! All he ever talked about was you and Jimmy, *and you didn't even have the decency to call! You have no idea of the hell I've been going through . . .*"

Goodness, Mattie thought, startled by her sister's accusations. I made him give up contracting? Is that what she's thought all these years? She held her phone a couple of inches away from her ear, leaned back against the rough bark of the ponderosa, felt its scrape through her shirt as she slowly lowered herself into a squat. For several minutes she listened to Harriet's tinny blasts. She felt nothing more than mild amazement at her sister's stockpile of resentments.

Finally she managed to disengage. She folded up her phone, but remained crouched against the tree. Tentatively, as if pulling aside a curtain, she allowed herself to focus on the image of Jimmy's charred remains. There had been no nose on the blackened head, nor ears, a toothy gash for a mouth. She had recognized nothing of her son. That's Jimmy, she insisted. Still, she felt nothing.

She thought of the press conference, of the hollow-sounding statement she had read. What's wrong with me? she wondered. Certainly, her colleagues would have been much more comfortable if she had collapsed on the charred hillside. They would have lifted her up and carried her along, consoled her, taken care of her. The idea of it seemed a balm. Why couldn't she cry?

Because you don't trust them, said a small inner voice. She realized it was true: she didn't trust the knee-jerk self-interest of the entire Overhead team. Even Brian, who was the most civilized of the lot. She remembered the report that came out after the Storm King blowup. In a hundred and fifty pages of maps, graphs, photographs, statements, and sequence charts, the final analysis had spread blame around like a shotgun. The investigators had cited failures at all levels, from state management officials to the jumpers and hotshots on the scene. But someone had leaked the charge that the "can-do" attitude of the latter had "contributed significantly" to the deaths.

It was a debatable charge—one that Mattie felt was misguided. Nonetheless the media had latched on to it, taken it out of context and blown it up out of all proportion. In effect, the charge against the dead firefighters had served as a smoke screen for the bureaucrats. Mattie would not put it past Brian to try something equally creative to protect the Command team. However pleasant he had been to her, she had to remember that she was a newcomer, an outsider. If someone on the team had made a mistake, the first line of defense would be to close ranks. It would be easy enough for Brian to put a deflecting spin on the fatalities, to leak some distortion that would distract from, if not obscure, the truth. She imagined a headline: "Mother's Fire Order Kills Son."

Well, she decided, whatever happened, whoever was at fault, she would discover how and why Jimmy had died. She had not been able to protect him from the accident. But she could protect his reputation. It was the only thing left to do for him—and for her family as well. He would have wanted them to know his story. It was the only thing she could do for all of them: Find the truth.

18

At six o'clock on Friday evening, August 30, Ivan Wilkie drove the family Dodge van down a dirt lane and pulled up in front of a cabin some two hundred and fifty miles north of the Justice Peak Fire. Ivan had borrowed it from a friend in his Men's Bible Study group. Despite his first name, he had no connection to Russia. He came from a distinguished South Carolina family. His father, Beauregard Wilkie III, a graphic artist, had liked the look of a name that could be written entirely with straight lines: in block letters, IVAN WILKIE had no curves. For the same quirky reason, twenty-five years later, he gave his blessing to Ivan's marriage with LIZ.

Liz Wilkie sat in the front passenger seat of the van. Packed into the back of the van were the two Wilkie children, two friends for the children, a black Labrador, dog food, tapes for the kids' Walkmans, fishing tackle, an electric fan, inflatable swim rafts, a first aid kit, charcoal, enough groceries to last the long Labor Day weekend, and Monopoly in case it rained. Lashed to a rack on the top of the van was Ivan's brand-new canoe.

The borrowed cabin was located on the west side of Flathead Lake, and built of dark logs. It had a roof of old green asphalt shingles and twin fieldstone chimneys at either end. (There was a fireplace in the master bedroom—"Helps warm things up," Ivan's friend had said with a lecherous wink.) Red geraniums had been planted in a barrel beside the front door. Above the door, a varnished pinewood sign read THE HAVEN. Through the firs around the house, the lake glimmered invitingly.

"Is this it?" asked Liz Wilkie, not quite able to believe their good luck. She had spent all day packing their duffels, packing the coolers, packing the van, but she had been skeptical about the venture. Although she had seen her husband's friend and his wife at their church, she had never said more than hello. Moreover, despite Ivan's promise, she had not really expected him to get off from work early. She had been prepared for the worst: for Friday evening gridlock leaving town; for the children fighting in the backseat (or throwing up—her daughter's friend had announced she was prone to car sickness); for a bat-infested shack with moldy mattresses and temperamental plumbing. But here they were, on schedule, tempers all intact, at a charming lakeside cabin.

"This is it," Ivan assured his family.

Even the children were impressed. "Cool," said their son.

"Excellent!" echoed their son's friend.

The children and the Lab tumbled out of the van and ran off to inspect. Ivan and Liz smiled at each other. They got out of the van. Liz gave Ivan an excited hug. Ivan locked his arms around her and she giggled. "I put a bottle of Taittinger in under the beer," she said.

"Hmm," Ivan said.

The little girls came running back. Liz and Ivan stepped apart. "Daddy!" said their daughter. "There's a hot tub on the deck! You didn't tell us they had a hot tub! Can we go in it?" The girls hopped up and down with excitement. "Please, Daddy, please? Please, Mr. Wilkie!" they chorused.

"One thing at a time," Ivan said firmly. "First we unload." He reached inside the van for an envelope on the dash. He took out the house key his friend had given him and walked to the front door.

His wife summoned the boys. "Okay, everybody grab something," she ordered.

The key turned smoothly in the lock. The door swung open into a cool dark interior that smelled faintly of old fires and mothballs. The children crowded in behind him with bags of groceries. "It's dark in here! Where's my room? Can I have a Coke, Mrs. Wilkie? Mommy, he pushed me!"

Ivan found the light switch to the left of the refrigerator, right where his friend had said it would be. He flicked it on—and at that moment the phone started ringing.

Three hours later, Ivan was back in Missoula waiting to be briefed on the entrapment that had occurred that afternoon at the Justice Peak Fire. Wilkie worked at the Forest Service's Fire Sciences lab. By leaving his office early, he had just missed the emergency call from the Northern Region Coordination Center ordering him to conduct an on-site analysis of the protective equipment—clothing, helmets, shelters—involved in the fatalities. He tried not to think about the steak his wife was grilling without him. Her eyes had teared up when he broke the news and he knew it wasn't only for the five dead firefighters. He tried not to think about the cost of the taxi summoned from Polson to drive him back to Missoula. (He had refused Liz's offer to put the kids back in the car and drive him back herself.) And, as he waited at the airport for his assigned teammates to arrive, he tried not to think about the hot tub on the deck, about soaking with Liz after the kids were in bed, with only the sound of the lake lapping in the dark. Instead Ivan Wilkie prayed.

He prayed for the dead firefighters and for their families; he prayed for his own family and for himself. Over and over, he prayed for clarity in the grim work ahead. A fragment from one of the psalms came to him. "For my days vanish like smoke and my bones burn like logs . . ." Which one was that? What was the rest of it?

He invoked Psalm 91, one of his favorites: "He shall cover thee with his feathers, and under his wings shalt thou trust: His truth shall be thy shield."

The Big Mac he'd eaten for supper sat uneasily in his stomach. *"His truth shall be thy shield,"* he insisted. Reconstructing the truth was part of his job description. Two years ago, he had come to work at the fire lab as a trainee and assistant to a senior scientist named Ed Kinloch whose pioneering research had created the field of PPE (Personal Protective Equipment) analysis. Thus, Ivan had experience with fatal entrapments, but always with pieces of fabric salvaged from the bodies, always in the lab, and always under the direction of his boss, who enjoyed an international reputation as a forensic wizard.

In Ivan's opinion, Kinloch's reputation was wholly deserved. By examining a few scraps of burned fabric—be it aramid or foil, cotton or polyester—Kinloch could reconstruct not only the heat and rate of speed of a fire, but the wearer's escape efforts and frame of mind as well. Ivan never tired of listening to his boss's stories. Like a conjurer, he was always dazzling Ivan with facts pulled out of thin air. He would stop Ivan in the hallway and, for no apparent reason, deliver an explanation of why a tidy stack of five quarters beside the body of an entrapped dozer operator meant the victim had been standing when the fire hit. (The victim's pocket had burned out and fallen to the ground with the stack of quarters intact before the fabric burned away.) Or, in the middle of a discussion on budgetary matters, Kinloch might suddenly recall why Montana's prisoners now wore yellow and green instead of orange fire clothes (several had been killed when the pilot of a retardant bomber, flying low through smoke, mistook them for flames and unleased his load on them).

It seemed to Ivan that Ed Kinloch's brain was like an untidy, overstuffed closet: something was always falling out—an odd sneaker, an unstrung tennis racket, the missing wand of a vacuum cleaner. Twenty years of information was stored in his head. The scientist had never stopped to organize, to write it down. Over after-hours beer, he used to contemplate with some pride the loss that fire science would sustain if he went down in a plane crash.

In June, however, the Forest Service announced yet another series of cutbacks. Dr. Kinloch was given the option of early retirement and his pet research project—an improved fire shelter—was discontinued as "a frill." His department was merged with two others and Ivan, who was still working toward his doctorate in chemistry (and whose GS rating and salary was therefore lower than the illustrious Kinloch's) was put in charge of equipment analysis. The summons to the Justice Peak Fire was the first time Ivan had been called to the actual scene of a fatal entrapment.

Ivan was one of two dozen fire people who had been summoned to the investigation from various stations across the West. He was instructed to meet two others at the Missoula airport and proceed directly to the site. He had met neither of them. One was an audiovisual specialist from the Forest Service lab in Ogden, Utah. The second man was a fire investigator from the National Interagency Fire Center in Boise, Idaho. Both flights were delayed. Ivan took out his cell phone and starting making calls. He thought about calling his wife up at the cabin and decided against it. It would only make it worse.

19

30 Aug 7:41p   Directory C:*.*

It's extraordinary how such a small act of violence can generate so much peace. One strike of the match, that was all it took. One strike of the match, a thread of sulfur in the nostrils, the flame scarely visible in my cupped hands. It took two tries on account of the wind, but then I had it, had the god in my hands, kneeling like I used to for her. Love's sacred fire. To be fragrant you have to burn. To scent the whole house, you have to burn it to the ground. At night, of course, I would have seen the god's curls, yellow and orange, streaming toward her through the grass, then exploding, leaping into the pines on the other side of the hill, coming and coming and coming. I mean we're not worried about recovery time here! But it would have been slower at night. You would have had the rise in humidity to reckon with. No, it was perfect. At mid-afternoon, the fuel moisture ratios were perfect. The sunlight gave it angelic lightness. All you could see at the beginning was a mirage of heat over the sagebrush. God in the burning bush—as it were! A veil of oily smoke. Then it started running, you could hear it building up head. It took off over the hill, and then for what seemed like too long, nothing. Then the pines at the bottom of the gulch started torching. I couldn't see it from where I was, the hill was in the way. Maybe at night I would have seen more than smoke. Probably not, though; by the time it exploded up the chimney, I was out of there. I was floating. I'm still floating. Though that's not exactly it. It's like—*gnosis*. I mean, I'm talking a whole lot more than an après-fuck buzz. Been there! Though I have to say, on that level, I figured it was going to be pretty good; I'd been building up my own head all day. I waited till two o'clock. I timed it pretty well, getting there, if I do say so myself. I only had to wait a few minutes. Then I got out of the car with my little towel, one of the good ones, Irish linen with the monogram in gray, Margaret used to put them out for guests in the downstairs john—I'm just waiting for her to ask for them back! If she didn't want them in my pack, she could have shown me how to use the goddamn washing machine! What does she expect? I'm going to pack a dirty towel? They were the only ones left. So I get out of the car with my towel, all nicely ironed, like a little altar towel, and I fuck it. I'm standing there, my ass against the fender and the metal's so hot I wonder if my goddamn Nomex is going to change color on me. But it only takes a couple pumps, no more. It was okay, but no big deal, like taking a shit. Seems like it should have been more, like I *deserved* more, but what's new. I think about throwing in the towel—literally. A burnt offering. It feels right, but then I remember the arson cops. I'm thinking DNA, I'm thinking how many degrees Fahrenheit to obliterate the fucking monogram, and the numbers don't compute. The god's an old god, the oldest. Which means he hasn't the slightest interest in "justice." Just his style to throw the towel back at me. Well, two can play that game. I put it back in my pack. It's so foolproof it's almost funny. I mean, Yes, Detective, that's my towel. Yeah, I jacked off, so what? Peace and love, man. Tomorrow I'll get one of my minions to put my stuff through the laundry.

20

Having told her family about Jimmy, Mattie returned to Communications. As she came through the trailer's flimsy door, Celia, who was still at her post on the phone, swiveled in her chair and signaled her with a raised finger. "Yes, sir," Celia said into the phone. "She just came in." She hung up and told Mattie, "That was Ned. He wants us in the war room. He didn't say why."

Mattie felt a quickening under her skin, as if at long last she was about to do battle. "I expect he has something he wishes to share with us," she said dryly.

They crossed the graveled parking lot to the barn and found Ned in a huddle with his Plans people—the fire-behavior analyst, the meteorologist, the field observers. The other section chiefs were there as well: Mike Robuck of Operations, Frank Cicero from Logistics, even Ralph Jessup, head of Finance, had come out of his corner. Brian was looking through a stack of photographs on the desktop. Grant Sonderdank, his face haggard and streaked with grime, looked over Brian's shoulder. All their faces were grim—not the solemn grimness with which they had faced the TV cameras that evening. This was something else. The lords of fire looked angry. Their eyes were bloodshot, their unshaven jaws hard, their bodies tense. One of the women, a Documentation leader, blew her nose wetly into a tissue.

"Mattie," Ned said. He acknowledged Celia with a nod and waved them both forward. He seemed taller, more commanding than she remembered. The talk in the room quieted. "We've got preliminary findings on the Copper Creek accident," Ned announced.

"And?" She could feel the room listening.

"Arson." The word came out of him like a punch.

The impact of it disarmed her. It was not what she expected—though exactly what it was that she had expected from Ned she was not sure. Nonetheless, in her confusion, she experienced a small pop of clarity. She saw the blackened, rock-strewn mountainside, saw again the dusting of white ash on her boots, and, down the pitch, the figure of the Millville crew boss sitting on the ground beside the twisted remains she had mistaken for a stump. She remembered the wind in her face, blowing the stink of wet ash up the slope. "The wind was out of the wrong quarter," she said slowly.

"Right," confirmed the meteorologist. "At fourteen hundred, it was just north of west, blowing upslope toward the line. Wrong direction for a spot fire. Any embers and light-burning debris would have been blown back into the burn. As for rolling snags, none of the lookouts in Division C and B reported any slop-over."

Mattie glanced at the orthophoto map taped down on to the desktop. "Slop-over? The blowup started almost a mile away from the main fire."

The meteorologist nodded. He indicated a point below Division B. "We've got a portable station here. The data gives no indication of site-specific wind changes—or of a dry lightning strike."

"What about an area ignition?" she asked. This was an explosion of unburned gases trapped at some distance from the main front—usually in airless ravines.

The Incident's fire analyst answered brusquely, "Topography's wrong." He picked up a sheaf of 8-by-10 black-and-white photographs and handed them to her.

"Color film's not in yet, but as you can see, we've got a classic V pattern, we've got cupping on the stumble—everything indicates the origin was down by the river."

Brian handed her the stack of photographs. Mattie pulled her reading glasses out of her pocket and shuffled through the prints, pausing at an aerial shot that showed the blowup's funnel-like path. The tip of the funnel lay only a few yards off the unimproved road along the Folly River. The fire had started on a grassy embankment. The wind had pushed it into the dense ranks of lodgepole pines. Then the flames had burst out of the woods and roared up the drainage. On the photo, a white line, the wagon track off the road, ran through the stubble of the ruined pinewood. At the end of the line, a dark speck was circled in red crayon. "What's this?"

"Our supply truck," Ned said.

There were no other red circles on the pictures. Perhaps the victims lay farther up the creekbed. Mattie's eye went back to the truck. With her finger, she traced a rough triangle across the glossy surface of the photograph. The river road formed the base of the triangle. The black tip of the funnel formed one corner of the base and, a mile and a half down the road, the turnoff onto the wagon track formed the other. The track followed the creekbed up the drainage. The truck at the end of the track formed the apex of the triangle.

"By the time the fire got to the truck, it was really cooking," the fire analyst put in. "Once it got into the fine fuels, it just exploded up the chute. They wouldn't have had more than a couple minutes' warning."

"What about accelerant?" Mattie asked. "Any evidence of gasoline, kerosene?"

"Not that we can see. Tomorrow the state people are bringing in some dogs to sniff it out. But given the conditions, a match or a cigarette would have been enough."

They stared in silence at the map.

"So it could have been accidental," Celia said. "A passerby. Someone going down the road."

"Could have been," Ned confirmed. "But the driver of the pickup's unaccounted for." He paused. "He was a trusty."

"What do you mean?" Celia said sharply. As a Human Resource specialist, she had developed an acute sensitivity to the nuances of discrimination.

"I mean," Ned said coldly, "the responders found five bodies. If the trusty was trapped with the crew, there should be six." He turned to Mattie. "The sheriff's put out an APB for him. I authorized Brian to give the media a statement."

Was this what she had been waiting for? Was he telling her that he was in charge? She turned to Brian. "You can go ahead and release the victims' names as well. All the families have been notified."

Brian looked at Ned.

Ned compressed his lips. "We need to talk," he said to Mattie.

Here it comes, she thought. "Yes?" she said, challenging him.

"Privately." Without waiting for her to follow, he turned and made his way through the maze of desks to a side door in the barn's aluminum walls.

She scanned the faces around her. No one but Celia would meet her eyes. Celia's were dark and beautiful and worried. She gave Mattie a sympathetic little shrug.

Mattie followed Ned outside. They stood just beyond the rectangle of light from the door.

"Yes?" she said.

Ned cleared his throat. "It's come down from the Forest Supervisor that you're to be relieved." His long face was in shadow, but his voice gave nothing away—no hint of triumph, no grace note of compassion.

"By whom?" she heard herself ask. But she already knew the answer.

"By me."

"I'm fired? On what grounds? I didn't make any mistake!"

"No one says you did."

Not yet, she thought to herself.

"Effective immediately," Ned went on firmly. "I've got all the transition paperwork ready and your demob's in the works. You'll need to—"

A commotion inside the barn drew them both back to the doorway for a look. The governor of the state of Montana was in the war room, charging toward them through the desks. He had changed, Mattie saw, out of fire clothes into a plaid flannel shirt, twill trousers, and hiking boots. Immediately behind him trailed a uniformed deputy, an aide in a safari vest. Behind them, the Overhead team and a scurry of media people.

"Where's the IC?" demanded the governor.

Mattie and Ned stepped back into the room together. A flood of camera light dipped and swelled, dislodging truss shadows from the corrugated ceiling and sending them sliding down the metal walls. Sound booms were thrust forward.

"Ah, there you are," the governor said crossly, fixing on Mattie.

"Governor Crispin," Mattie acknowledged.

"You need to get your priorities straight, little lady," the governor scolded. He turned to the gang of reporters. "I've been besieged by calls from the families of the victims," the governor declared. "The wishes of the families are paramount. I will not stand by and allow the remains of their loved ones to be desecrated!"

The reporters' faces remained impassive. The governor turned back to Mattie. "It is absolutely essential that the wishes of the families be respected. If I didn't feel strongly about this, I wouldn't have driven all the way up here."

"What seems to be the problem, governor?" Ned asked man-to-man.

"The problem is the way you are treating those victims, those heroic young men and women who sacrificed their lives for—" The governor broke off, stumped for a moment by the nature of the sacrifice. Then he recaptured the wind of moral outrage and sailed on: "Let's be blunt about this. We're in a wilderness area here. You simply cannot let them lie out there strewn over the mountainside like so much garbage. What, in the good Lord's name, makes you think the animals are going to leave human meat alone?! For heaven's sake, man, think of the families!"

The governor stood eyeball to eyeball with Ned, waiting for his answer. Ned, however, gave Mattie an "over-to-you" nod.

You little shit, she thought. She drew in a breath and let it out. "Governor Crispin."

"Bob," he instructed.

"Bob. I gave the order that the scene was not to be disturbed. For two reasons." She paused. For a moment her mind went horrifying blank. Then the reasons floated back. "For one, the pitch is too dangerous to remove the remains at night. We don't want to risk further injuries. Secondly, we need to hear what the bodies can tell us about the fire."

Brian stepped forward and jumped in, laying it out for the press as much as for the governor. "Bob, our equipment specialists need to examine body position and the condition of protective clothing. Their analysis of the escape efforts and causes of death may help prevent future deaths."

Bob Crispin frowned.

Mattie pressed on. "There's more than science at stake here. Both OSHA and law enforcement need the scene intact. There are strong indications that the entrapment was triggered by arson. We are treating the area as a crime scene."

A rumble moved through the press. Mattie saw the governor's jaw drop, then tighten. "I doubt that you," she continued, "or the families, for that matter, would want to block the one very fragile path we have to finding out who is responsible, wittingly or unwittingly, for setting the fire."

She paused. A murmur of approval arose from the fire lords. Mattie felt the governor's bluster deflating. "There's something else." She took a breath and went on, her voice lower, but steady. "It may help you to know that my son was one of victims."

The governor leaned forward to hear, then jerked back.

"Your son? My God, I had no idea." The pain dawning in his eyes was genuine. "I'm so sorry."

Seeing the man behind the politician disarmed Mattie. "I think it hasn't hit me yet," she said.

"A terrible tragedy," he muttered, his eyes unseeing. "Terrible."

"My point is, I share the loss of the families. Perhaps it will help them to know that I made the decision not only as a professional firefighter, but as a mother."

She stopped. Once again, her mind went blank. Perhaps they are right, she thought. Perhaps I'm not fit to command.

The fire analyst spoke up. "From what we've seen of the site," he told the governor, "it's unlikely that there are any large animals left in the area, and probably no rodents or insect life either. We won't be able to calculate BTUs until the victims' Nomex is examined, but I'm guessing the fire was hot enough to effectively sterilize the drainage."

There was an awkward moment of silence. Then, to Mattie's surprise, Bob Crispin pulled her into a hug. Zap, zap, zap, went the electronic flashes. The governor released her and, in one deft movement, turned her toward the cameras, his arm protectively around her shoulders. Zap, zap.

Blinking, she held up an arm in front of her face and strode angrily out of the way. "*Brian,*" she ordered.

Brian stepped forward. "Bob, how about a few shots of you with the team here? Burning the midnight oil, as it were. Show the depth of your concern."

Mattie said to Ned, "I'll be in the chalet."

He looked blankly at her.

"*We're not finished,*" she insisted.

She called the Forest Supervisor from the front office in the chalet. When she finally got him on the line, he reiterated what Ned had told her: she was removed from command.

"I would have appreciated hearing it directly from you," she said.

He said nothing.

"I'd like to see this through," she persisted.

"I'm sorry. This is the way it is," he answered. He hung up.

She slammed down the phone. "Fuck!" she cried, startling the fresh-faced firefighter behind the counter. Anger loosened her joints, propelled her back into the living area where like a caged wolf, she paced up and down. "They can't do this to me!" she protested to the empty room. But she knew they could.

Steering herself back to a tentative calm, she went to the refrigerator. There were still a dozen or so contraband Pepsis left. She pulled out a bottle of water, unscrewed the plastic cap, and took a long pull. She could feel the coldness moving down inside her, a slow sharpness, as if she were swallowing an icicle.

She heard Ned's voice in the front office and screwed the cap back on the bottle. He came into the room.

They stood looking at each other. He scratched the back of his neck. "I don't think there's any more to say on this, Mattie."

"Yes, there is. Listen to me. *I need to be here.*"

He stiffened. "The feeling is that your loss will have a detrimental affect on your judgment."

"So what? I already gave you the fire. I'll sign it over to you. I'll take over the inquiry, you put the fire to bed."

He did not respond.

Mattie let out a violent snort of contempt. "Do you think I'm incapable of finding out what happened to my own son?"

Ned shook his head. "It's not that."

"What is it?"

"There's a lot of anger among the troops. Your presence is being seen as counterproductive."

She stared. "You mean they're blaming me?"

"This is getting us nowhere. I've got to get back to work." He turned to go.

I don't believe this, she thought. "Wait. Exactly who's

blaming me? Nobody even knows what's happened and they're blaming me?"

Ned was silent.

"Do you have children?" she asked.

In an odd trick of fatigue or shock, she saw Ned standing as if she were looking down on him: the lamplight glinted off the pale bald spot on his scalp, off the gold-rimmed reading glasses hanging around his neck. His arms were folded across his chest and his chin jutted out slightly. Then her perspective shifted back to eye level. "Just answer this one question. If it was your kid, would you pack up and go home?"

She waited. She saw Ned's shoulders soften, saw the fatigue in his eyes. "No," he admitted. "But with all due respect, the fact remains: it's not my kid. I'm sorry, Mattie. You came aboard under adverse circumstances and you did your job, I'll give you that. But I'm not going up against the Forest on this. We're walking a tightrope here, as you well know. There's too much at stake. The guidelines are clear. I can't let you stay on—in any capacity."

"I'm not leaving till I find out what happened." She said it calmly and quietly, but until the words were out of her mouth, she had not known her intention. "I'll sign the fire over to you. But I am not leaving."

Ned studied her. Mattie had the feeling that he was about to say something but thought better of it. He turned and walked out of the room.

21

Mattie looked at the plastic water bottle in her hand. She felt numb. What next? Back to the phones in Communications? What was the point? She lowered herself down to perch on the arm of the sofa and felt an acute ache fan through her lower back. She remembered that she wanted to talk to Zack Hartwig, the Millville crew's supervisor. What had he seen? What could he tell her about Jimmy?

The young clerk from the front desk nervously poked his head through the doorway. "There's someone here who says—"

"Mattie," said a voice behind him. It was Spence.

At the sight of him, she felt a constriction in her chest. "It's okay," she told the clerk and he withdrew.

"Oh, Mattie," Spence said as he came into the room, his voice full of sorrow. "I heard you telling the governor. I'm so sorry . . ." He made a small gesture of helplessness.

She saw the pity and the tenderness in his blue eyes. She could not speak. She felt her face twisting like rubber, heard a croak escape from her contorted mouth. She began to cry, ducking her head, gripping the back of a folding chair with both hands, arms rigid as locked hinges.

Spence saw the bill of her cap shaking, saw her leaning over the chair as if to push it through the floor, but he hesitated to reach out to her. Her grief struck him as fragile, somehow tentative: to touch a shoulder, to offer a tissue, might dry it up. Did he even have a clean tissue in his pocket? He remembered his father's gentlemanly square of fine white cotton, ever ready for ladies' tears, if not a child's scraped knee. Silently, he grieved not only for her loss, but his own as well, for love bungled and hopes long compromised, for friends and colleagues dead too soon.

Then she was at the sink over in the kitchen, splashing cold water on her face, blowing her nose on a paper towel. She gave him a wobbly smile and the puffiness of her face, the fuzziness of her features pierced his heart. He opened an arm, stepped toward her and she folded herself into his embrace. The pliancy of her body under her fire clothes stirred him. He pulled back below the hips. Had she noticed? A phrase floated to mind: "... the eroticism of sorrow." French? Something out of *Les Fleurs du mal*? He gave her a sympathetic pat on the shoulder, a conclusion.

She moved out of his arms. "Let's walk."

The suggestion surprised and pleased him. He felt a rush of privilege. Outside in the dark, she confided, "They've fired me." They picked up a path behind the chalet and started walking. She talked about Jimmy and the burned bodies she had seen on the slope and she talked about her colleagues and the politics of the accident. She looped and plunged, circled around, picked up one piece, left another flapping.

Spence had the feeling that her story was propelling them through the dark, pushing at their backs like a heavy wind. He lost track of time, of how many times they had passed through this clump of pine trees, skirted that parking lot, but gradually the story became his own as well as hers. He longed to tug at the hidden seams of it, to unravel long zigzags of thread, to see what came apart, what held.

"I've got to know what happened," she said, over and over.

"Let me help," he replied as many times. "I'm good at finding things out." And each time he said it, she seemed to gather a bit more strength.

He began asking questions, making a mental list of names. The first time she said "we," he felt a surge of joy.

At one point, as they circled yet again past the Supply depot, angry voices made Mattie stop. To Spence, the depot had the look of a play castle: it was surrounded by a head-high wall of cardboard cartons and lit by portable floodlights. But the guard posted at the castle's gate, a truck-sized opening fenced with orange plastic mesh, was armed. He sat in a folding metal chair, arms crossed over his chest, watching three soot-covered groundpounders confronting the supply boss on duty.

"Aw, man, come on!" one of the men pleaded, a note of desperation in his voice.

"Do you believe this?" another asked his companions. "Do you believe it?"

As Mattie listened to the scene, it seemed to Spence that she was gathering up the scattered armor of her rank, donning the authority of her generalship. Determinedly, she stepped out of the shadows under the trees into the depot's floodlit clearing. Spence followed her to the gate.

The supply boss turned at their approach. "Yes, ma'am?" he said brusquely.

"Mattie McCulloch. I'm the IC."

"Yes, ma'am. Mornin', ma'am."

"Good morning," she said, her tone severe.

The three groundpounders stepped back to give her room. Their faces were clean and recently shaven, but their eyes were red-rimmed and their fire clothes filthy. One man's boots were reinforced with duct tape. Spence guessed they were about to go back on shift, but they looked as if they had not been off long enough. At their feet, the newly sharpened blades of Pulaskis and brush hooks glinted in the floodlights.

A supply grunt brought out two rakes, added them to the pile, then gave the crew a form to sign.

The protesting groundpounder shook his head. "I'm not signing anything, not till the order's complete!" he declared angrily. His nose was running. He wiped it with a crumpled bandanna.

"What's the problem?" Mattie asked the supply boss.

"We're out of Nomex shirts," he answered. "There's been a media run on them. We issued the last one to the governor this afternoon. Flaherty's orders."

The groundpounder stepped forward. He held out his arm to show a rip in his sleeve. "They won't let me back on the line with this."

The youth's accent puzzled Mattie. "Where are you from?"

"Vermont."

The supply boss let out a little snort, shot her a what-can-you-expect look. As if Eastern firefighters made a habit of ripping their Nomex.

Mattie looked at the Vermonter. He was big and solid, over six feet tall and close to two hundred pounds. She looked at the supply boss. Size extra-large, she guessed. His fire shirt was pristine, a bright egg-yolk yellow. There were still package creases down his sleeves. "Give him yours," she ordered.

The supply boss stared. Then he moved a lump of tobacco in his cheek.

"I said, Give him yours."

Her fierceness startled them all. Spence saw the men exchange uneasy looks. The guard uncrossed his arms, casually rose to his feet. The supply boss stripped off his extra-large yellow shirt. Underneath he was wearing a T-shirt that boasted, "Firemen Have Bigger Hoses." He thrust his fire shirt at the groundpounder.

The groundpounder took it, shoved it between his knees as he hastily maneuvered out of his own fire shirt. He put on the new one, buttoned it up, and handed the old one to the supply boss. The supply boss took it. Exchange complete, they all looked at Mattie.

"Thank you," she said. "Sign it to me," she instructed the supply boss.

Back in the screen of the woods, Spence could feel the heat

off her. She pressed her fingers into the top of her head. "What's the matter with me?" she asked, her voice bewildered like a lost child's. "I could have killed him. Literally."

"You were angry. I think that's part of it," he said.

"Part of what?"

"Losing someone. Come on. Keep walking."

"There was no way he could have fit into my shirt," she fretted. "Otherwise I would have given him mine."

At three o'clock in the morning, Spence persuaded her to lie down. "At least for an hour or so," he urged. He escorted her to her tent. She knelt and slowly unzipped the nylon dome, trying not to disturb the sleepers around them. Then she stood. "Stay with me," she pleaded in a half-whisper.

The childlike worry in her voice deflated the lust that had been nudging Spence all evening. "Okay," he said.

She searched his face in the dark. "Do you mind?"

"No," he said gently.

They took off their shoes. Out of habit, Mattie set her boots outside the fly and capped them with her fire helmet, which had her name stenciled across the front. "So they can find me without waking the whole campground if something comes up," she whispered.

He did not respond.

"I haven't signed off yet!" she insisted. They crawled into the tent and lay down together on the cool, puffy nylon of her sleeping bag.

Mattie had no sensation of having fallen asleep, but she dreamed three dreams, each worse than the one before. In the first, she was working at her laptop. She wanted to exit but did not know how to use the Save function. All her work would be lost if she exited.

In the second dream, it was Christmas Eve. She was home. In the dark outside the house, the graceful boughs of the old fir trees were covered with snow. Inside, the family had gathered, the festivities were about to begin, but she had no presents. She had neglected to go shopping. It was too late to get to the malls. She had nothing to give Jimmy. Nothing to give her mother (who was still alive), or her father; nothing for her sister or her nieces.

In the third dream, it was late summer. She looked out a deep-set mullioned window and saw a funeral cortege passing by. Mourners were pulling rickety wooden carts containing the coffins of the fallen firefighters. The procession was sunlit. Bright flowers decked the coffins. As if the dead were Viking warriors, their favorite possessions were displayed among the flowers. To her horror, Jimmy was among them. But he had not been properly laid out. He was sitting up in a crude, open-sided crate. He had been wrapped in white linen bandages, knees bound against his chest in a primitive burial position. Under the bandaged face, she discerned the fine, manly angles of Jim's profile. There was no mistake. It was her son, bandaged all the way up to his forehead. Left exposed was an inch of forehead (red, red, red) and his dark hair, thick and shockingly healthy. Inexorably, the procession rolled on. But they hadn't done Jimmy properly! Why hadn't they laid him out like the others? She felt a deep maternal rage.

The dream was both insistent and unmalleable. Reruns offered no softening of the vision, no saving adjustments or resolution. The sound of her own groan pulled her out of it. She woke feeling Spence's unshaven chin on her forehead, the bone of his upper arm under her neck. The walls of the tent were dark gray in the pre-dawn twilight. She sat up.

Spence opened his eyes.

"I had a dream." She shuddered, then lay back down, worming against him for comfort.

He shifted to accommodate her. "What was it?" he asked groggily.

She rolled onto her back and told how Jimmy, bound in white linen bandages, had rolled past by her window. "What do you think that means?"

"Search me. It's your dream."

Mattie cringed, but she could not let it go. "The bandages were long strips, a kind of dirty white. Like the winding bands in a medieval painting—the ones where Jesus comes out of the tomb trailing his bandages. Or is it Lazarus? But these were wrapped tight. Like swaddling clothes."

He cleared his throat. "A dream about resurrection? Life out of death?"

"I'm not sure I believe in an afterlife."

"What was the feeling in the dream? What did you feel when you saw him bound up like that?"

"I thought it was unfair. I wanted to straighten him out." She caught a double meaning in her own words: *I wanted to straighten him out*. She felt a wave of despair. "I guess I was always trying to straighten him out," she confessed.

"I believe that's what mothers are suppose to do," he observed wryly. He extracted his arm and squinted at his watch—a vintage, steel-banded Rolex. "If you want to make the five A.M. briefing," he said, "we ought to get moving."

22

Back in Missoula, at one o'clock in the morning, Ivan Wilkie's teammate from the fire lab in Utah finally arrived in a chartered plane. His name was Addison, Pete Addison. He carried a battered-looking backpack and three aluminum suitcases full of cameras. The other man had arrived from Boise two hours before. His name was Holmes—David, not Sherlock, he had joked as they shook hands. He was a round young man with a baby face. Ivan piled the two men and their gear into his rented Honda Accord and sped south east on Interstate 90 toward Butte. His new teammates instantly fell asleep. At 4 A.M. Addison woke up as Ivan drove through the town of Sophia. Holmes woke up when they stopped at the gate of the Meander Campground.

At 5 A.M., the investigators attended the general operations briefing in the tent adjacent to the chalet. After that, it was hurry up and wait. They rushed through breakfast, made it over to the post's helispot before the sun came up, then napped on the stony ground beside a portable toilet as they waited for a helicopter to lift them up to the site of the accident. The ongoing fire, however, had first priority. At 8 A.M., Ivan lost his temper and told Air Operations to forget it, they would hike in. The men used the Johnny blues, piled into Ivan's Honda and drove down into Sophia, where they stopped for more coffee. North of town, they turned off the paved scenic byway at a police blockade. When Ivan rolled down his window to speak to a deputy, a reporter rushed up and shoved a tape recorder past the deputy in through the window, clipping Ivan on the ear in the process. Eyes smarting, Ivan rolled up the window. The three men stared straight ahead, ignoring the reporter's persistent taps on the car's windows. The trooper at the barricade was in no hurry; he moved the orange cones aside one at a time. A cluster of sightseers with video cameras dutifully recorded the officer's movements. Finally he climbed in the patrol car that was blocking the track and backed it out of the way.

Ivan gunned his Honda through the opening and sped down the gravel road, leaving a fallout of gray dust on the lenses of the tourists' cameras. To his left loomed the ravaged mountainside. Three miles down the road; he slowed as he passed a line of parked vehicles along the shoulder. A cluster of men stood in an unburned fringe of grass.

"They've got dogs," Holmes said excitedly. "They're using dogs!"

Addison, a silent, older man, grunted. "Sniffing for accelerant. Must be the point of origin."

Ivan braked. For a moment, the three men stared through the windows at the blackened knoll that screened the entrapment site from the road. Then a trooper appeared between the parked trucks and waved them on.

Another trooper guarded the turnoff to the old wagon road. This time, there were no reporters, no curious onlookers. A ranger in a Smokey the Bear hat radioed the command post for clearance. She had not been informed they were arriving by car. She went to her truck and came back with three white masks. "You might want to try these," she said.

They took the masks, left the Honda with the ranger, and went in on foot carrying cameras, measuring tapes, notebooks, and water in their day packs. They walked slowly, not speaking, through a moonscape of ruined forest. At the end of the track, they found the burned-out pickup. The heat of the fire had oxidized the Forest Service's regulation green paint, leaving the body rust-colored on the outside. The inside was black. Three of the tires had burned down to their rims and the bed of the truck had buckled and twisted away from the cab. The glass in the windshield had disappeared, but a segment of crazed rear window remained. The soft bulge of it and its opaque silvery crackle reminded Ivan of a sequinned top his wife had worn to a party last New Year's Eve.

Holmes peered through an empty window on the passenger side. "No crispy critters here," he observed cheerfully.

"They were *people,*" Ivan said. "Five *people* died in this place. They took their last breaths here, thought their last thoughts. Show a little respect."

Holmes looked at Ivan. "Sure," he said. He stepped back to allow Ivan a look. The interior was uniformly and densely black. It took Ivan's eyes a minute to adjust. Then he saw that the dashboard had burned away, leaving the blackened instruments dangling in a tangle of bare wires. The steering wheel had melted into a lopsided circle that reminded Ivan of the melting clocks in Salvador Dali's *Persistence of Memory.* He had never liked Dali. Especially the famous *Last Supper.* It made him uncomfortable, the naked breast of Christ, the intimacy of his nipples. Focus, he told himself. He saw that the upholstery on the seat was gone.

He made room for Addison, who thrust a flashlight through the window and combed the seat springs with its beam. The springs sagged onto the floor of the truck. "Looks like they've annealed," Addison said. He slid the beam up the steering column. "Keys still in the ignition."

The men walked around to the back of the truck. Flies buzzed over chunky pieces of something black strewn across the bed of the truck. No one said anything. Ivan sniffed, but the only smell was the oppressive stink of burned rubber and plastic. Addison spotted a piece on the ground. He turned it over with the toe of his boot. "Melons," he said.

"A blevie," Holmes said authoritatively.

"Looks like cantaloupe to me," Addison said.

"B-L-E-V-E," Holmes spelled. "Boiling liquid expanding vapor explosion. Happens to skulls, too. Heat just pops them open."

Ivan felt his stomach turn. Kinloch, his illustrious predecessor, had never mentioned that. "What temperature?" he asked.

"Can't remember," admitted Holmes. "I could look it up."

Addison walked over to one of his aluminum suitcases and took out a video camera.

Stepping away from the truck, Ivan noticed a lopsided spill of melted plastic containers near the tailgate. "Here's the cubees," he announced. A mat of weedy plants beneath them had been saved by leaking water. The plastic had melted before the water had had time to boil and explode. He counted container caps. "Six cubees, four feet from, truck," he wrote in his notebook.

Holmes was stuck on his BLEVEs. "If you put a bullet in someone's head," he informed Ivan, "it won't BLEVE."

Ivan wanted to punch him. Instead he announced, "I'm going on ahead, walk it through. Get an idea of the layout."

"Be our guest," said Holmes. "You're the expert."

The expert? "How many of these have you done?" Ivan asked him.

"Me? None. I figure they were scraping the barrel." He let out a nervous laugh. "Let's face it, this isn't exactly the kind of job people stand in line for."

Great, Ivan thought. He looked questioningly at Addison. "Pete? What about you?"

"I've done my share," Addison said dryly. "Go on ahead, if you like. We'll start here. With the easy shit." He took a light meter out of his pocket and held it against the rusty fender of the truck.

Ivan slipped on his mask as if he knew what he was doing and hiked up the boulder-strewn draw.

High above him, a wide ribbon of red slurry had been dumped across the slope. Like a spill of cement, it had bowed and crushed the unburned brush beneath it. Although the fire had jumped the treated area, the retardant had added crucial seconds to the escape of the firefighters at the top of the drainage.

The five firefighters lay below the retardant line. Their bodies were perfectly camouflaged, ashy black on ashy black, but Ivan had no difficulty locating them. The footsteps of the rescue workers had worn paths through the brittle remains of the charred vegetation. The exposed tracks of earth were rose-colored and had the hard, slick look of fired clay. Like a net flung against the blackened mountain, the rosy paths surrounded and connected the bodies.

A short distance below the first victim—the IC's own son, he'd been told—Ivan stopped to catch his breath. He was sweating heavily, a symptom he chose to blame on his nerves rather than his aerobic condition. The mask felt hot and damp on his face, but at least it seemed to be working. Not so bad, he thought. The body might have been a charred log. Had it not been for the paths, he would have climbed past it without notice. He spotted the remains of two cubees and sketched their position in his notebook.

Then the morning breeze shifted and the reek of roasted flesh hit him, a heavy sweetness. He gagged inside the mask. Fearful of vomiting into it, he snatched it off his face. He bent over, steadying himself with his hands on his knees, and gulped air. After a moment, he straightened up and tried the mask once more. If anything, it made it worse, trapping the stink inside it. Angrily, he threw the mask on the ground, a stark patch of white on black.

Keeping to the existing paths, he angled upwind, breathing through his mouth. "Firefighter #1," he scribbled hurriedly in his notebook. "Approx. 50 yards above pickup, in streambed." He studied the charred ground around firefighter number one. Gradually his eyes began to adjust to the absence of color. He spotted a nail clipper, then a metal disk (part of a watch?), scattered boot eyelets, the spring from a ballpoint. A squirt of interest revived him. He looked again at the remains. Now he could make out human lines: it lay on its back, slightly rolled to the left, arms and legs extended in a rigid, pugilistic attitude. There were no fingers left. Hair and facial features had burned away. "Head downhill, faceup," he noted. The rest was hard to tell. No clothing remained, only partial boot soles lying on the ground below the ends of the legs—the feet were gone.

"Over 1000 F," Ivan jotted. Suddenly, without even a warning heave, his stomach slid smoothly up and down. Staggering, he vomited, catching a corner of his notebook. He wiped the page on the leg of his jeans, then uncapped his water bottle, rinsed out his mouth, spat. He kicked ash over the mess and climbed up to firefighters number two and three.

They lay a few feet apart in the rocky streambed, about 135 yards above number one, but equally as charred. They were similar in size, both of medium build. He had been told that Pami Gustavisson and Wade Lowry had fallen together, but there was no way to tell which was which. "FF #2," he labeled the downslope body. Like firefighter number one, number two had fallen faceup and head downhill—knocked over backward by gases or heat, Ivan speculated. A blue hard hat five feet below the head had been partially melted. "Nylon straps missing—over 470 F," Ivan noted. Just to the right of the torso lay a small blackened rectangle. He recognized a shelter, still neatly packed in its PVC case.

However, a partially deployed shelter had snagged over firefighter number two's arm. The shelter's lengthwise accordion folds still were visible: patches of the foil had melted, but most of it had delaminated, leaving the cloth backing exposed. Originally white, the fire had striped it brown and black.

Ivan guessed the shelter belonged to number three, who lay above number two, facedown, perpendicular to the slope, left arm extended toward number two. Had he shaken it out only to have it blow out of his hands? or had he not gotten that far? Perhaps the heat of the fire had expanded the folds.

Like a diver about to plunge, Ivan took a gulp of air, held his breath, and bent over number two. He lifted the shelter off the rigid arm.

He was prepared for the smell, but not for the color. The shock of it staggered his brain. An explosion of yellow. Yellow Nomex. It almost knocked him over backward, the brightness of the shirt's singed forearm, the even brighter cuff, a double thickness of fabric. No glove. He made a mental note to look for it. The hand was intact, the skin violently red. Suddenly, firefighter number two was human.

Human and female. Her short, childish fingernails were painted pink.

He felt as if he should speak to her, but did not know what to say. "I'm sorry," he said, but the words sounded hollow on the stark hillside. He lowered the shelter back down over her. "Under His wings shalt thou trust," he whispered.

Nausea forgotten, he scanned the ground around her. "Partially melted water cubees by #2," he scrawled in his notebook.

coins
Skoal lid
buckle
safety pin
eyeglass frame
canteen
buttons (metal)
knife
key ring with three keys
blob melted alum.
suspender clip

Keeping his eyes on the ground, he moved several yards up the draw. Another object stopped him. A blackened rectangle, partially melted, too small for a shelter. Then he recognized it. He skipped a line in his notebook. "Handset above #3," he noted.

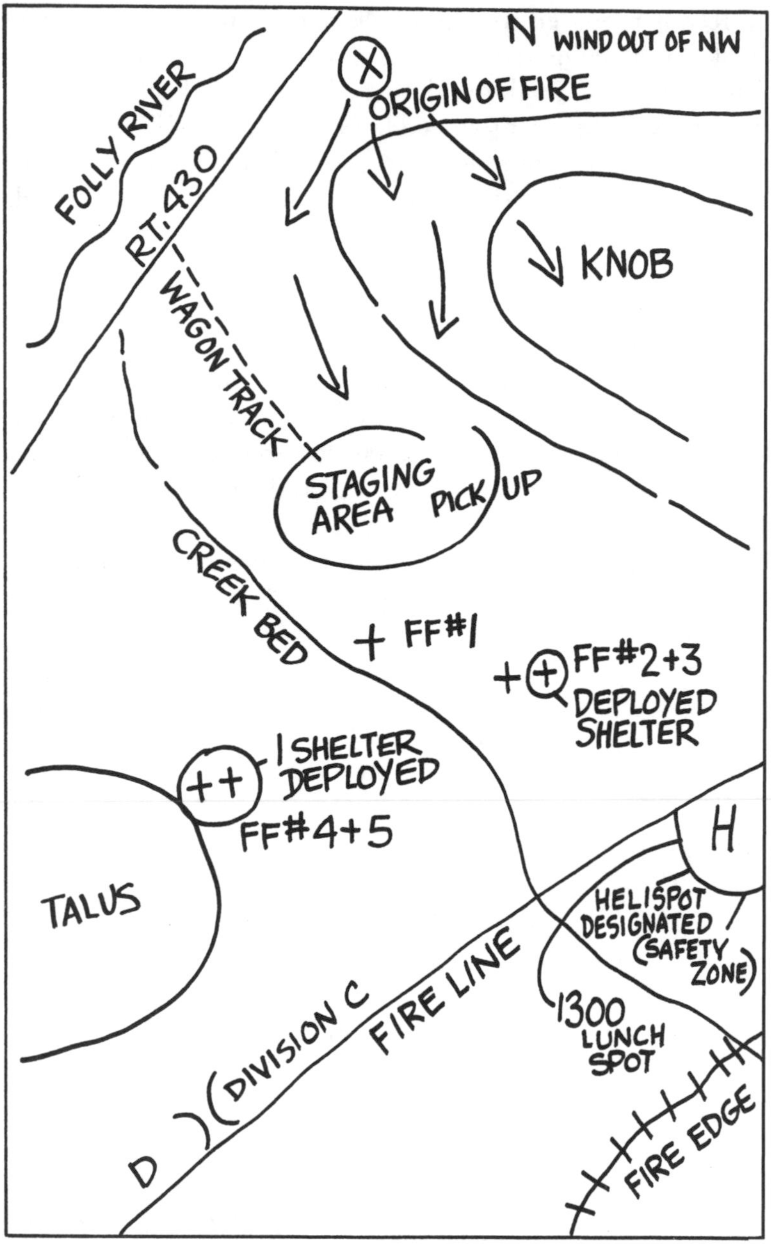

COPPER CREEK ACCIDENT/ PRELIM SKETCH/ I.W.

23

31 Aug 11:01a   Directory C:*.*

McCulloch the bitch still here; Christ, let it alone! Like take a hint. She's been bugging everyone all morning, going around with her reporter pal playing mother of sorrows, grabbing anything she can get her hot little hands on, printouts, photos, maps, you name it. Who's going to say no to her? I heard last night she made one of the guys over in Supply take off his shirt and give it to this peon. Now the troops think she's Joan of Arc all over again; well, we know what happened to her. At least the Maid knew what she was doing, she won a few battles before she got burned. McCulloch's not clean. I hear she was fucking her friend in her tent last night, moaning like a stuck pig. What do you expect? She whored her way to the top, then, when she got there, clueless. Voyle's not much better. Kingman certainly wouldn't have let them take my fax line, I don't care how many hotshit Dick Tracys were standing in line for it. The latest big clue: The arson dogs came up with my match, one of them anyways, clever beasts. Their masters have deduced from the tear that the striker of said match is right-handed! You have to wonder what the price tag on that one was. This whole thing has been blown totally out of proportion, every battle has its casualties, for the love of Christ, let's bury our dead and get on with it!

24

Once the Forest Service had determined the cause of the blowup as arson, the deaths of the five firefighters were immediately classified as homicides. The sheriff of Bearjaw County requested assistance from Helena and the state police sent in Agent Chip Zampill to head up the investigation.

Zampill had thirty-one years of law enforcement under his belt, the last ten as a state homicide cop based in Billings. He was fifty-seven years old, recently separated from his wife, and a two-pack-a-day smoker—when things were going smoothly. When things were not going smoothly, he tried to keep it to three. He lived alone in the split-level house his wife had left. (Her note explained that she'd waited fifteen years for him to fix the screen door and that was long enough.) His old bird dog, an overweight English setter with cataracts, slept on his bed. The animal farted all night long and could barely make it outside in the morning, but Chip preferred not to think about putting him down, just as he preferred not to think of himself wheezing away at the end of an oxygen tank. His father had died, inch by inch, of emphysema and heart failure. Nonetheless, Chip kept on smoking. What he gave up was going to the doctor. As he drove into the Meander Campground in the pre-dawn dark, he was already six smokes into his first pack of the day. Well, he consoled himself grimly, cigarettes or not, he'd made it longer than the five kids killed at the fire.

Chip Zampill was a logical choice to head up the investigation: in law enforcement circles, he was considered one of the state's big guns. He had broken a number of celebrated cases during his career and enjoyed a reputation as a team player who didn't use his badge to put a shine on his ego. When the call came, he had been working a tedious fraud case and he welcomed the assignment. He was not particularly surprised to get it, but he was reassured. Lately, he had been hearing noises from above about retirement. Even folks he barely knew would ask in cheery voices, "What are you going to do when you retire?" This happened for the first time when he was still in his late forties, and the notion of not working had shocked him. Now, however, he had a stock answer—a lie, in fact, but it worked. He'd grimace like a farmer checking out the sky and scratch the back of his neck. "Maybe travel a bit," he'd say. "Wouldn't mind checking out my ancestral village."

And people would light up with interest. "Really? Where's that?"

"Southern Italy," he would answer.

The village was called Zampillo. His wife, bitten by the genealogy bug after their youngest left home, had discovered it on a map. Zampillo, she informed him, meant "gush" in italian, as in a spring. Perhaps his grandfather had come from the village, perhaps not. (His wife's research on his behalf had been a passing courtesy: her real passion was her own family tree.) Nonetheless, he fantasized about a whitewashed village where men sat in the morning sun with shots of grappa, played bocce, and smoked without shame.

Chip was impressed by the efficiency of the Justice Peak Fire's Command system. By the time all the introductions and preliminary briefings were over, a thirty-foot-square tent had been set up behind Communications to accommodate the investigation. The tent was white with scalloped edges, like the tent a rich man would hire for his daughter's wedding.

When the sun rose, a swarm of workers had furnished the

tent with folding tables and chairs, pads and pens, a pair of telephones, computer hook-ups, two overhead bulbs, an insulated yellow barrel of hot coffee, and a tray of Danish pastries. The number of phones was less than ideal. Zampill had asked for three phones, one for him, one for each of the two agents working the case with him, but after questioning the installer, he let it drop. There were no extra lines. One of the phones, in fact, had been "stolen" from the Command team.

Inside the tent, the sheriff's people in their tans and the fire people in their yellow-and-green mingled with people in jeans or suits. The two other state agents assigned to the case wore sports jackets and dress slacks with hiking boots. They were both younger men, recently hired, one from the Kalispell office, the other from Helena. The Kalispell agent's name was Orr. Chip had not met him before, but he had worked one case with the Helena agent, Bruce Burton. Chip remembered nothing noteworthy about him; the case had been straightforward—they had wrapped it up within twenty-four hours.

Chip himself was wearing a baggy brown business suit and a tie with his button-down shirt. Standing by an easel holding a large pad of newsprint, he held up a marker and cleared his throat for attention. The chatter stopped. Chip loosened his tie a notch and inaugurated the workspace with his usual "We're-all-in-the-same-boat-here" pep talk. "Your job is to pull the oars, my job is to steer," he said.

If the metaphor was hackneyed, the intense energy behind it alerted his listeners. Zampill's leathery skin, the loose jowls above his blue oxford-cloth shirt collar, gave him the look of a Brooks Brothers turtle. But he clearly wasn't going to move like any turtle. Nor, if the rumors about him were true, was he afraid to stick his neck out.

"There's a mountain of information out there," he told the gathering in the tent. "We're going to bring it in while it's still stinking hot. I don't need to tell you this is a high-priority, high-profile case. For the next forty-eight, seventy-two hours, whatever it takes, we are going to be eating, drinking, and sleeping this case. You aren't going to have any time to sit and read in the shit house. I want all the information, I want it collected fast, and I want every scrap of it documented. Everything on paper, right here on the table in front of me." He stabbed the table twice with a rigid forefinger. "For interviews, I want notes *and* tapes."

He turned to the easel, and in fat blue marker, he wrote "ASSIGNMENTS" across the top. The flimsy aluminum easel quaked under his hand. The Helena agent stepped forward to steady it. "Dallas," Chip wrote.

A man named Billy Dallas had been the driver of the pickup. As soon as he had been discovered missing, Voyle had notified the sheriff's department and the sheriff had assigned a detective. The sheriff's man, who had been working the case since midnight, briefed the group.

Billy Dallas was twenty-six years old, Caucasian, clean-shaven, six feet tall in his flip-flops and 170 pounds. He had no known address. "The guy's no rocket scientist," said the detective.

Billy, who had been "passing through" the state in a converted school bus, was running a little low on both gas and money. At eleven o'clock on a Thursday morning, he had stopped at a convenience store in Great Falls, took an orange soda up to the counter, and pulled an Uzi out of his tie-dyed shoulder bag.

"Is that for real?" asked the cashier.

"You betcha," Billy assured her.

The two other customers in the store dived for cover. The frightened cashier emptied the cash drawer into Billy's shoulder bag. Billy backed out of the store, the way he'd seen it done in the movies, and tripped over the curb. He fell backward, crashing into one of the pumps and giving the cashier the opportunity to call 911. When the police arrived, he was topping off his bus: he neglected to fill the tank *before* robbing the store. Police found half an ounce of marijuana and a sampler of amphetamines inside the bus.

At Deer Lodge, Billy had worked his way up through all the necessary therapeutic groups and rehab programs into minimum security. For the past two fire seasons, he had worked "off-campus" with an inmate camp crew. He was up for parole next month. Interviews with prison officials and the other inmates on his camp crew had turned up nothing except a collective surprise that Billy had skipped out so close to parole. The sheriff's detective concluded, "Question number two is: Why did he go out on foot?"

"Do we know he left on foot?" Chip asked.

The detective looked disconcerted. "The pickup's still there," he argued.

"He might have had a ride. Did you look for tire tracks?"

The sheriff's detective hesitated uncomfortably. The answer was clearly no. "The fire made a real mess. We didn't see anything obvious."

Chip caught a smirk of contempt on the face of the Kalispell agent. What was obvious was that any evidence of tire marks or footprints left on the wagon track before the fire had swept through undoubtedly had been destroyed by the subsequent traffic of rescue workers and fire investigators. Par for the course, thought Chip. Agent Orr had yet to learn that pristine crime scenes were the exception, not the rule.

Chip glanced at the map spread out on the table behind him. "Do we know that Dallas escaped the fire?" he asked, directing the question to the Incident Commander, Ned Voyle, who was standing at the back of the tent. "How extensive was the search in the area?"

The fire people conferred among themselves. Voyle said, "The focus was on controlling the blowup and finding the missing firefighters. By the time the kitchen realized the trusty was missing, it was dark. EIT's on the scene now, but they're working on the known victims. We're under pressure from the families to have the remains processed as soon as possible."

"EIT?" Chip disliked initials.

"Emergency Investigation Team," Voyle rattled off. "We signed the investigation over to them earlier this morning."

Chip turned back to the sheriff's detective. "Keep on it," he instructed. He wrote the man's name under Billy's. Turning back to the group, he saw the face of the Kalispell agent.

"You got a problem, Agent Orr?"

Orr stiffened. "No, sir."

Clearly, Orr had expected to relieve the sheriff's man. One of the axioms of the trade was that cases are made in the first twenty-four hours. Billy Dallas was their only lead, and with each passing hour, the chances of finding him diminished.

However, in Chip Zampill's book (the one he could write if he had the time) homicide detectives, like news reporters, were only as good as their sources. If Billy Dallas had left the truck on foot, local cops knew the turf. They had the sources, and they already were seven hours into the hunt. To reassign would be a waste of precious time.

"Okay, kiddies," he said, dismissing the gathering. "Go bring the mountain to Mohammed."

No one smiled. The old man didn't look like a prophet, but he had a hard gleam in his eye. Moreover, each one of them standing there in the tent wanted to believe that he could pull miracles out of his brown serge sleeve.

To a sullen Agent Orr, Chip assigned the job of organizing an on-site search for the possible remains of Billy Dallas. "And get a couple evidence technicians down from Missoula to check out the wagon track."

"Yes, sir."

Chip assigned Bruce Burton, the Helena man, to read the Justice's preliminary report prepared for the incoming investigation team. "I want a complete witness list. I want to know what they know and what they don't know."

Behind Burton, Chip saw a pair of yellow shirts hovering. "Yeah?" he asked impatiently. Then he saw that one of them was Mattie McCulloch, the deposed IC, mother of one of the victims. She had come by his tent earlier to introduce herself.

"When you have a moment, Detective," she said, her face calm, her voice unhurried.

Chip dismissed Burton and Orr and shifted into what he thought of as his Great Ear mode.

"This may not have anything to do with anything," Mattie said, "but I thought you ought to know." She introduced Grant Sonderdank.

Chip saw a man with thin, arching eyebrows, a perfectly chiseled nose and chin, and slick black hair.

"Grant's the Safety officer here," Mattie explained. "He was one of the first responders on the scene."

Chip pulled extra chairs up to the folding table he had taken as his desk. "Have a seat." He waved a hand in the direction of the coffee urn. "Help yourselves." He slipped his hand in his pocket and found his lighter. He wanted a cigarette. He saw Mattie looking over the tray of pastries and decided against it.

Mattie took out her pocket knife and cut off a small half of an apple Danish. She wiped the blade on a paper napkin and took a bite. Grant filled a Styrofoam cup with coffee. They settled down around Chip's table.

Chip took a pad and a mini tape recorder from his briefcase and put them on the table. "With your permission," he said, "I'd like to tape this conversation."

"No problem," Grant agreed.

"Mrs. McCulloch?"

She swallowed the last mouthful of her Danish. "Please call me Mattie." She looked at the tape recorder. "I'm not officially here. I'm just, uh, trying to facilitate."

"I need all the help I can get," Chip assured her. "The tape is simply to prevent mistakes. For your protection as well as my own. I want to make sure nothing gets taken out of context." He turned on the recorder and glanced at the black digital watch on his wrist. "Today is August thirty, seven-thirty A.M., Justice Fire camp. Please state your names and addresses."

He went over their names, inquired about spelling, and wrote them down on his pad. Then he looked up expectantly.

From his lap, Grant produced the unit log. He laid it on the table in front of him for reference, then told Zampill about the fight between the two crews earlier in the week. Grant told the story economically, in the passive voice: "Racial epithets were exchanged . . . a cross was burned . . . the decision was made."

Mattie, listening with one ear, considered Chip Zampill's lined face, his faded sandy hair, his nicotine-stained fingers. There was an earthiness about his presence that reassured her. He looked like a farmer suited up and come to town for a loan. Behind his steel-rimmed glasses, his light-brown eyes were as guileless as a puddle after a storm. And every bit as opaque.

Grant finished his narrative and pulled out a folder from an olive-drab document case. "These are copies of the witness statements we took. Both on the cross-burning and the subsequent fight."

Zampill looked down at his notes. "This occurred on last Monday?

"Right." Grant leaned forward to check the log. "August twenty-six. We've got a video of the fight. I'm having copies made. You should have one later today."

Zampill nodded.

Grant then placed a pile of forms on the table. "These are copies of the medical reports on the crew injured in the fight. The damage on both sides was mostly abrasions and minor cuts, but two of the Kentucky boys were sent to the hospital in Butte for treatment of knife wounds. One was cut below the eye—he was sewn up and discharged from the emergency room. The other had surgery to repair a severed tendon in his hand. He was discharged the next day."

"Tuesday."

"That's right."

"And the blowup occurred yesterday—Friday."

"Four days after the fight," Grant confirmed. "They may not be connected."

Chip sat back in his chair. He found his disposable lighter in his pocket, turned it over and over. The plastic felt warm and smooth. "Maybe not," he agreed. He sat forward, warmed his voice up a notch. "But I appreciate you bringing it to my attention. Thanks for your time. That completes the interview."

He turned off the tape. He wanted a cigarette *very* badly. He turned to Grant. "Can you find out where the crews are now? Both of them. I want a head count. Also statements from their drivers. Where they went after leaving here, routes, times, and mileage off their bus odometers."

"Right," Grant said.

Mattie took off her cap and ran her fingers through her hair.

Chip was unprepared for the color of it—a blondish red, something out of a fairy tale, he thought—but he caught the flicker on Mattie's face. A reluctance? He watched her. "Yes?" he said.

His attentiveness disarmed her. She flipped the cap back on. "I just hate to think it was one of ours."

Chip nodded and sat back in his chair, inviting more, but he got nothing. Her mask was firmly back in place. He reached into his suit pocket and pulled out his lighter and an unopened pack of Marlboros.

"Maybe it was the trusty," Grant posed. "He could have set the fire to cover his tracks."

"Maybe." Chip tapped the pack hard on the side of his hand. He pulled the cellophane tab, opened a foil flap, tapped again. "It certainly created a diversion," he added somberly. He took out a cigarette. "Anything else?"

Grant Sonderdank stood up. "What you said about Dallas getting a lift?"

"Yes?"

"One of the guys on the Millville crew said he saw a flash before the blowup. Like the sun off a windshield, he said. I don't know if any of the others saw it."

"I'd like a copy of his statement."

"It hasn't been taken yet. That's up to the EIT. This was in conversation. Our job was to find out the facts of the case as quickly as possible," Sonderdank said sternly. He ducked his head and smoothed back his already slick hair with an open palm. Chip wondered if they still made Wildroot cream oil. "The EIT's mandate," Grant went on, "is to determine cause and to recommend correction action. They'll be taking formal statements today."

"I see," Chip said. He glanced at the cigarette in his hand, then back to Sonderdank. "What's this witness's name?"

"Richard Gower."

"I'd like to talk to him."

"He's not going anywhere," Grant said. "The fire could be cold as January but we'll be sitting here till the EIT says so."

Chip didn't wait any longer. He put the cigarette in his mouth, thumbed his lighter, and bent over the flame. Then he straightened up, tilted back his head, and took a long, luxurious pull.

25

The town of Sophia was built on a wedge of land formed by two rivers whose Indian names have long since been lost. The names bestowed in 1805 by Lewis and Clark on their way home from the Pacific were displaced some eighty years later by a mining engineer named Thomas J. Foley who gave the larger river his family name and called the smaller one after his wife Sophia. When Foley returned home to Philadelphia, his glowing prospectus of mountains riddled with copper and silver triggered a rush on the Frontiers and a boomlet town sprang up between the two rivers. Unfortunately, the mines proved less fecund than expected and Thomas Foley died of disappointment and drink. A generation later, a nearsighted cartographer in Washington, D.C., mistook the flowing copperplate *e* in Foley for an *l* and transcribed the Foley River to the Folly River—much to the satisfaction of the descendants of the original investors.

The town's only claim to scenic distinction was its handsome pair of narrow iron bridges, engineered in the 1880s to span the rivers. In the town itself, there were no fanciful miner's mansions, and although the founding fathers had optimistically laid out the main street as wide as a Parisian boulevard, it was only three blocks long. The wind-scoured paint on the wooden signs of the commercial buildings and the lack of sidewalks gave the town the movielike look of a dying cow town—as if a tumbleweed might blow down the street at high noon. On the other hand, tourists who bought hiking maps and jerky at the general store or soaked in the sulfur-scented pool at the Hotsprings Hotel were impressed by Sophia's "authentic" Western ambience and later, back in their coastal cities, they would boast to their friends about "this incredible little nowhere town" where louvered café doors banged emptily in the wind. In fact, the town's one café (open for breakfast and lunch) had an air-lock entrance whose outside door was foam-insulated metal with diamond-shaped plastic mullions crisscrossing the glass in the upper half.

On the afternoon of August 31, some twenty-four hours after the blowup, the dusty streets of Sophia were clogged with media vans with satellites on their roofs, school buses filled with sleeping groundpounders on their way home, out-of-state fire engines and water trucks, Forest Service pickups, rental compacts, state police cars, unmarked sedans bristling with antennae. At the schoolhouse, a 1920s building with a hip roof and high windows that looked to the mountains, the Forest Service's Emergency Investigation team had moved into the classrooms. Their first official meeting was closed to the public. But by hanging out in the hallways, Mattie managed to meet and exchange cards with the team's various specialists—all except Ivan Wilkie, who was still "processing" the scene on the mountain.

She bumped into Brian talking to a well-dressed couple in the stairwell. He introduced her to John and Ruth Lowry, the parents of Jim's squad boss. John Lowry, Mattie remembered, was the one who had called her father last night and inadvertently broken the news. Brian's genial face looked drawn, as if he'd dropped ten pounds in the last twenty-four hours. The Lowrys looked dazed. Mrs. Lowry, Mattie noticed, wore little gold hearts in her earlobes. It was an awkward moment; none of them knew what to say. She shared Brian's relief when the couple excused themselves. "What do they want?" she wondered.

"Same as you," Brian said evenly. "They want to know what happened."

At four-thirty, Spence pulled her outside into the school yard. He had been monitoring the radio and had just heard that the bodies of the victims were about to be evacuated. "Come on," he said, ushering her to her Jeep, "we need to get to the forensic guy before he comes off the mountain."

She stopped and flipped through the sheaf of papers she had collected and found his name on her list of EIT team leaders. "Wilkie," she said. But she made no move to get in the Jeep. Suddenly she felt depleted. She was reluctant to go back to the scene. She was not sure she could bear to see them loading Jim into the back of a van. "I really ought to go over to the hotel," she told Spence. "My father should be there by now."

"Wilkie's key. It would be good to get his first impression. Before he goes all official."

"What makes you think he's going to talk to me?"

"First come, first served."

She looked at him.

"It's his first time out of the lab, Mattie. If he's not the clam-up type, he'll need to unload."

"They sent us a novice?"

"That's what I hear."

"I don't believe this."

"It can't hurt to try," Spence pressed. "He's going to be hot and thirsty. Offer him some cold lemonade."

"Lemonade?"

"Well, what if the guy's a Mormon? You can't very well offer him a beer. So I got lemonade. Pink lemonade, no less. A rather alarming shade of pink, I should say, but at least it's cold and wet. I bought a gallon jug of it and a cooler over at the general store. I've got it on ice in the back of your Jeep."

She took off her cap and ran her fingers through her hair. "Okay," she agreed wearily. She found his enthusiasm disconcerting.

He gave her a brisk hug, then opened the Jeep's door for her. "You better drive. They'll let you through the barriers."

It was early evening when they drove back into Sophia. Spence had been right: Ivan Wilkie had been relieved to talk to them. His findings raised more questions in her mind than they answered, but the information was strangely energizing. She was anxious to get a professional take on it from her father.

The Hotsprings Hotel was a two-story log building across from a gas station at the south end of Main Street. A porchlike wooden sidewalk, complete with a hitching rail and rocking chairs, ran the length of its facade. Mattie parked in back, where a collection of small log guest cabins made a quadrangle around a bright-green lawn. The cabins looked new. Their log walls had a golden, polyurethane glow that contrasted with the dark old logs of the main building.

A sheriff's deputy had been posted at the entrance to keep the media at bay. Spence pocketed his press tags and escorted Mattie inside. The two-story lobby was as spacious as a dance hall. It had no lounge chairs and its polished pine floors were bare of rugs except for one long strip of bright green Astroturf. Like a VIP carpet, it ran from the bar area at one end of the lobby across the expanse of open floor and up a short flight of stairs to an exit to the hot-spring-filled pool. A large sign posted beside the door enumerated SPA RULES.

She found her father at the bar end, perched on one of the stools, holding forth with Celia DeJesus. He was wearing jeans and a flannel shirt. Was it the one Jimmy had given him last Christmas? She saw that Jack looked both younger and larger—as if tragedy or grief had somehow expanded him, plumped him up like a raisin marinating in liquor. But she also saw that her father was drinking beer—a good sign.

"Daddy," she said. Celia moved back to give them space.

"Mattie. So here you are." The words came out leisurely, grandly, with a soft hint of his pseudo old-sod lilt, and her heart sank.

"Yes," she said. "Finally." She leaned in to exchange a ritual kiss and saw with some relief that his eyes were still darkly sober.

She introduced Spence to both her father and to Celia.

Jack raised his beer. "What's your pleasure? Celia here refused to join me."

Mattie flashed Celia a comradely look of sympathy.

"A beer would taste good," Spence allowed.

"Mattie?" Jack offered.

"I'm fine." Then she saw the look on his face. "What I'd really like is a glass of iced tea."

Jack waved the bartender over. "One beer, one iced tea. You got iced tea?"

"Yes, sir."

"Dad," Mattie said, "we need to talk."

Tactfully, Celia started to withdraw, but at the same moment a bandy-legged man in jeans and a canvas barn coat barged in, cutting off her escape. Gossamer-soft locks of white hair floated out from his speckled scalp, but his face was hard and wrinkled as a walnut. "You Celia?" he demanded. "They said I had to talk to Celia."

"I'm Celia," she said.

He clamped his mouth shut, looked her over, then complained, "I've been waiting to see you since one o'clock this afternoon. Rusty Stanislaw. I'm here for Pami."

Pami Gustavisson, Mattie recognized. One of the victims. Ivan Wilkie said it looked as if Wade Lowry had run back into the fire to try and save her.

"Are you a relative?" Celia asked, her voice gentle.

"I'm all she had," he snapped. He whipped out a folded packet of papers from his pocket and shook them under Celia's nose. "You see this? This here's her insurance. She made it out to me and don't you let anyone tell you different. You can see she signed it right here." He unfolded the papers and tapped a signature. "I want the death certificate. They say I've got to have the death certificate to collect."

Mattie and Jack and Spencer exchanged glances, but Celia kept her eyes focused on Stanislaw. "Why don't we talk about this more privately," she suggested.

"Oh, no, you don't," he said cagily.

Celia took a breath. "Are you claiming her remains, Mr. Stanislaw?"

"That's up to you people. I can't afford no funeral. All I want is a certificate of death."

"The autopsies are being conducted tonight in Missoula," Celia informed him. "I imagine the death certificates will be signed sometime tomorrow. Are you staying here?"

"On you," he asserted, challenging her to contradict him. When she didn't, he let out a snort of contempt and walked away.

"Pity," Spence murmured.

"What?" Mattie said.

"If he was all she had."

The bartender brought their drinks. Celia gave Mattie a quick hug and left. Jack took a delicate trial sip of his beer, then remembered. "Go say hello to your sister," he ordered. "She's in the pool."

Mattie plucked up her iced tea and followed the synthetic-grass path, up the steps and outside to a large rectangular pool. Its concrete deck had been built above the street level and although the pool was screened by an eight-foot-high board fence, it was open to the darkening sky. Despite the peach-tinged charcoal clouds, Mattie felt as if she were underground in an eroding limestone cavern. The concrete aggregate had turned yellowish and the edges of the pool were crumbly. Billows of sulfuric steam rose from the surface of the water which, thanks to underwater lights, glowed a sinister jade green. Her sister Harriet and a younger woman were the only two soakers. They had taken white plastic patio chairs into the pool with them and were sitting on them, side by side, submerged up to their necks. Seen through the green water, their pale female limbs looked both twisted and bloated. They sat with their eyes closed as if enduring a liquid punishment in Dante's hell.

"Hello, Harrie," Mattie said. Given the scene, her greeting sounded absurdly pedestrian, but the only other salutation that came to mind was *Ave*, and she didn't want to risk it with Harriet.

The two women opened their eyes. "Mattie," Harriet recognized. Her voice was slow and heavy, as if the sulfuric soak had cooked her anger into a dense oil.

"How are you?"

"Okay. I think. This is Gretel."

"How do you do?" Gretel said. Her small heart-shaped face floated above the surface of the water like a talking Valentine. Mattie guessed she was in her twenties.

Harriet stirred in her underwater chair, releasing a new veil of steam. "Her husband was with Jimmy—his squad boss, in fact."

"You're Wade Lowry's wife?" Mattie asked.

"Widow," she corrected flatly.

"This is my sister, the IC," Harriet told her.

"That's what I figured," said Gretel.

"Harrie, we need to have a conference. With Dad."

Harrie expelled a long, weary sigh. "How is he?"

"Still upright."

"You go ahead. I'll be along in a minute."

Right, Mattie thought, annoyed that Harriet showed no sign of moving. She's had Dad all day, she reminded herself as she followed the emerald turf path back to the bar, but the annoyance still prickled. In the bar, someone had activated the jukebox; the Everly Brothers were on with "Wake Up Little Susie." She gathered up her father and Spence and they exited under the head of a mountain goat to the parking lot in the back of the hotel. As Jack led the way across the quadrangle of living grass, bright as the fake inside, Mattie noticed that her father's walk was almost jaunty. "You're walking better," she observed.

"I went to see your friend."

"My friend?"

"Doris Murphy."

"Doris Murphy?"

"Your chiropractor friend. I think she did me some good."

Light dawned. "Oh," Mattie said. "You mean Dr. Doris."

"She's got great hands," Jack informed Spence with a manly wink.

Jack's cabin was tiny and immaculate: the polyurethane-coated logs glistened; the narrow lanes of pine flooring around the furniture gleamed. There was a thin white coverlet on the double bed. A TV sat on the thickly varnished maple dresser, and a two-hundred-watt bulb glared in the glass-and-brass ceiling fixture. White light bounced off every hard, dust-free surface. Mattie felt as if she'd wandered into a hospital, an operating theater, to be exact.

Jack retrieved a traveler from his battered satchel which lay open on the bed like an old-fashioned medical bag. He dispensed two inches of Bourbon into both of the two glasses on the dresser, then fished out a few melting ice cubes from a little plastic bucket and slid them into the glasses. He handed one to Spence. Spence offered it to Mattie, who shook her head. The men took trial sips. Satisfied, they settled down on the end of the bed, feet on the floor, elbows on knees. Standing against the dresser, Mattie told her father what the investigators had pieced together about Jimmy's last movements.

"He was the first one down," she said. "They think he picked up a load of water out of the truck, bumped it up to the next man—I mean, person," she corrected hurriedly. "It was Cat Carew. She had one of the radios," Mattie explained, flustered by her lapse. "Jim carried two cubees up to her, then went back down for the next load while she moved them up to Pami Gustavisson. Wilkie thinks it hit him on his second trip up. He found two melted cubees below the first body. He thinks Jimmy must have dropped them and started moving uphill when he realized what was happening." She hesitated, then plunged on, keeping her voice in neutral. "Wilkie found him faceup."

Jack started and the bedsprings wobbled. "Faceup?"

"Faceup. He was on his back."

"That's not right," Jack objected. "The fire must have rolled him over—I mean, afterward."

Mattie said nothing.

"He didn't die faceup!" Jack said angrily.

Spence asked, "Why not?"

"Because he knew better," Jack snapped. "He would have gotten down on the ground below the heat. Even if there wasn't time to deploy his shelter, he would have assumed the position, facedown, arms over head—like he was trained!"

Spence looked at Mattie.

She took a breath. "They think he was running upslope at the time."

"Bullshit!" Jack made an explosive gesture and his drink and the ice in it spewed over the white bedspread. "Bullshit," he muttered as he got up to replenish his glass. Spence brushed the little cubes off the spread. They fell on the floor with a dull clatter, like small chunks of bone. "Jimmy wouldn't have panicked," Jack declared.

"He might have miscalculated," Mattie said with quiet maternal resignation. "Wilkie's hypothesis is that the fire's gases came roiling up the drainage in front of the flames. Wilkie thinks the gases came swooshing around him, rushed up his body, but in front got trapped under the visor of his helmet. He would have been blasted in the face, knocked over backward before he knew what hit him." She paused, then insisted, "His head was downhill."

Skirting Spence's knees, Jack moved around the bed to his bag and retrieved the Bourbon.

"Dad," Mattie said, "you don't need any more."

He poured two neat inches into his glass.

"Listen to me," she pleaded. "None of them were wearing their packs. They'd left them up top. He might have thought he could make it without his pack. Remember all the discussions we had after the South Canyon Fire? How those kids could have made it to the ridge top if they'd dropped their packs?" She turned to Spence. "One of the investigators calculated that the firefighters who died could have gone sixteen percent farther in the same amount of time without the weight of their packs. Jimmy checked out the math. He liked math. Remember, Dad? I brought home the report with me and you and Jimmy went over it at the kitchen table. Jimmy pulled out his calculator and started crunching the numbers—body weights, pack weight, speed of walk, degree of slope—"

Jack interrupted. "If he was going to run, he'd have run into the fire—not away from it."

Mattie compressed her lips.

Jack turned to Spence. "He should have held his breath and made a dash through it to the other side. That's how Robert Jansson survived at Mann Gulch back in '49. Ran right through a fire whirl at the bottom of the gulch. Held his breath and ran into it. He conked out for a couple seconds in the vortex, the fire had sucked out all the oxygen, see, but then he came to and got back on his feet and ran out the other side. What's-his-name wrote about it." He took a quick gulp of Bourbon.

"Norman Maclean?" Spence said.

"That's the one. He wrote about spot fires blooming like flowers in the gulch, making a garden of flowers that exploded like a lightbulb. Mixing his metaphors . . ." He voice trailed off, then returned full force. "Jimbo would have tried a dash through the flames." He shook his head. "Now I'm not saying he would have made it. But he would have tried, goddammit, I *know* he would have tried."

"Not if a mass of superheated air got him first, Dad," Mattie said sharply. "You can't see gases coming. They're invisible. The only warning may have been a hot wind picking up or a few sparks flying by overhead. Don't forget, he was hauling two cubees—that's eighty pounds of water on a nasty pitch. I've been out there. I've seen where it happened. He had to have been concentrating on his footing. His eyes would have been on the ground. If the gases rolled up the creekbed like they think, he was already down by the time the flame front came through."

"Jimbo wouldn't have panicked," Jack insisted. He took another swallow of Bourbon, then, as an afterthought, offered the bottle to Spence.

Spence shook his head. "I'm fine, Jack. Thanks."

Jack slopped another inch into his glass, then looked up at his daughter. "Did he deploy?"

"I don't know. Wilkie says he found no shelter."

Jack gave her an indignant stare. "The man's incompetent." He squared his shoulders and took a swallow. "Clearly, he's made a mistake. It wasn't Jimbo. You're telling me my Jimmy wouldn't have had his shelter with him?"

"It could have blown out of his hands. The gases could have gotten him as he tried to deploy."

"What about the case? Where was the case?"

"I don't know where the case was! I didn't ask about the case!" She saw that her father was standing perfectly still, not even a teeter, as if her outburst had stung him into paralysis. She took a long, calming breath. "It was just a preliminary survey, Dad. They'll do the equipment mapping tomorrow. We should know more tomorrow."

Jack moved. He shook his head in disgust and sat down carefully beside Spence on the end of the bed, drink in hand. He considered his glass for a long moment, then looked up at Mattie. "Did you see your sister, then?" "Yer sester," he said. His Irish had gone sodden.

"I did."

"She wants horses at the funeral."

"Horses?"

"I vote for mules. Tell your masters I vote for mules." He turned to Spence. "You want old-timey Forest Service, you use mules." He closed his eyes, retreating into memories of mule strings and canvas-wrapped packs and crosscut saws. His anesthesia of choice was beginning to take hold. He began rocking gently on the end of the bed, back and forth, a mute, stiff-spined keening for the loss of mules, the loss of his grandson, the loss of his own sweet and glorious youth.

Spence stood up, quietly put his glass down on the dresser.

"We're going now, Dad," Mattie said.

"Let me take care of this for you," Spence said, removing the glass from his cupped hands. "You don't want to spill it all over you."

Jack opened his eyes, tried to focus on Spence's face. "I didn't think it would come to this." His words were slurred. "I shoulda put a stop to it."

Spence frowned. "To what?"

He made a slight gesture with his chin toward Mattie. "Her." He closed his eyes. Slowly he fell back onto the white spread.

As they stepped outside onto the cold emerald grass, Spence asked, "What was that about?"

"Evidently he thinks it's my fault."

"The blowup? It was arson!"

"He's never approved of women in command."

Spence looked shocked. "But he supported you."

Mattie shrugged. "I'm his daughter. What else could he do?" She caught the faint, familiar strains of a big-band sound coming from the main building. She stopped to listen. The jukebox in the bar was playing "String of Pearls," one of her mother's favorites. Suddenly she was struck by a bleak insight into her mother's relationship with her father: Mary Katherine McCulloch had made her marriage work by shielding her husband from the strength of her dreams. She saw her mother's life as a long, flat plain shrouded in dim gray light. Could it be true?

"My father blames my ambition," she told Spence, and as

the words came out, she knew that much, at least, was true. "He thinks we're being punished for my hubris."

"Oh, well." Spence dismissed Jack's blame with an impatient wave. "He's in his cups."

"In vino veritas," Mattie said unhappily.

26

31 Aug 9:21p   Director C:*.*

Finally cornered Wilkie, the pious little weasel. I got him coming out of the schoolhouse, after they broke up for the night. He looks at me kind of funny through his little designer rims, like it was some kind of holy secret. We all *know* it's going to leak—The Tragic Last Moments. Some asshole wants to pay off his brat's orthodontist, he takes a couple big ones from one of the tabloid jerks buzzing around, and read all about it over your Raisin Bran. Boise will have a shitfit all over our heads. Wilkie thinks he won't have to swallow any of it if he keeps his mouth shut like a good little teammate. I got news for you, twerp: It don't work that way.

I didn't ask him about Cat. Not directly. I took him on a wild Indian chase—as it were! I'd already picked up some of it, enough to know she and the Indian fried together up on the south side of the drainage. The Division supe told me. He was up above them on the ridge. BLM guy named Zack Hartwig, *not* in good shape, I might add! Couldn't stop blubbering, he never even met any of them, for Crissake. I took him into the station and gave him one of my Pepsis out of the fridge and told him he ought to see someone. You'd have thought I was giving him the Hope Diamond. Jesus. Anyway, so I'm hanging around the schoolhouse and during one of their breaks, I get ahold of Wilkie's sidekick, Holmes; now there's a guy who likes to hear his own balls clinking. He goes, Well I could tell you a thing or two, but of course—and I go, Of course, I respect you for that, it must be difficult, blah, blah, blah, and he can't resist. He drops enough to let me know something funny went down between Cat and the Indian, but I didn't want to push it. I'm thinking, what, she's balling the Indian when it hits? I got ants in my pants, fire ants, to be specific, I am hurting, but I don't push it. I wait, a hundred years of waiting, finally I nab Wilkie. He gets up on his high horse and gives me a load of his need-to-know bullshit and so I tell him a bunch of the dead Indian's pals up at Deer Lodge are making protest noises and Ned told me to look into it. Like, get with the program, bud.

So he lets the cat out of the bag. Fortunately he doesn't check with Ned. I should say, he let my cat out of the bag, a black velvet bag, blacker than a new burn, an implosion. She rises out of it, a vision in the schoolyard, white, naked as an angel, twisted as rising smoke. People coming and going, headlights slicing the dark, and I can see the smudges of black hair under her arms, the curving corrugated shadows on her ribs, the jut of her hipbone, that taut hollow just inside it, her pussy—her sooty little pussy. She never would let me groom her, the bitch. Not after that first time. She said my tongue was too sloppy. But sometimes she'd let me lay my head on her belly, just above it, and when I breathed her hairs tickled my nose—my reward! I get to hear her shit rumbling!

She deserved what she got. I'm only sorry it wasn't more *prolonged*. Just as I figured, she had the radio, or at least one of them. Wilkie said they had three, the con squad had one, Millville two. So she knew it was coming. She heard it on the radio and hightailed it up onto the side of the drainage. Without responding. That's why I didn't hear her. I had the right frequency. The transmission was okay. Lowry, the squad boss, came in loud and clear, but no one heard a peep from Cat. Wilkie says, all solemn, We'll check out her radio back at the lab. But clearly she was too busy saving her own hide to key in. Wilkie figures she'd passed off her cubees to her rookie girlfriend and was headed back down for the next load. He thinks maybe she saw it coming before the order came to move out. That would have given her the extra seconds. She scrambled up the side, sidestepping the god, and that idiot rookie cow ran up the creekbed. Like trying to run up a chimney. Whoosh, good-bye and so long. But my sweet little Pussy Cat made it up to an old rock slide, and deployed. She must have thought she was home free.

And the Lord God of Justice was pissed! The flames shooting out of his head turned green. Fire roiled in his sacred loins. He burned her while she groaned.

If I don't watch out, I'm going to have to go find my towel! This is what Wilkie found, what he's working with:

Shelter fully deployed, foil burned off (over 500 F), mostly brown adhesive color with some black (under 700 F).

Her hard hat was melted in back, front OK.

Clothes: Heavy char on back of her shirt and right side; yellow on left. Backside of jeans, light char, brown and orange, and back of cotton T-shirt and panties (white!) charred black—so she was getting it on her ass at 470 degrees F. (824 F on her neck!). Extensive burning on skin, he said. Her left side, where she was lying on the ground, was spared and also her pussy. Lower front torso, he said! Very tactful!

So: She was lying, Wilkie said "laying" but I let it go. It hurt, but I let it go! She was *lying* head uphill on her left side under the shelter. The Indian's right hand was touching her back.

Touching? I said, neutral curiosity.

Almost touching, Wilkie corrected. About an inch or two, was his impression.

I said, an inch? He looked at me funny, but I held my ground, didn't say anything.

Then he said the Indian could have been touching her, the inch could have been rigor, the muscles contracting. Said the Indian's shelter was still in its PVC case (like the rookie girl's). His shelter and hard hat were a couple feet below his body. Wilkie estimated ninety percent of the body was charred, only a few scraps of fabric left, which indicates about 900 F. He thinks it was probably a couple thousand degrees at the bottom of the drainage—hell, McCulloch's kid had no feet on him, never mind fabric. That kind of heat, forget it. Even if he had deployed, the shelter would have melted. But up on the side on the drainage, shelter against the rock slide, no fuel to burn, she could have come through. Ergo, what happened?

Wilkie's got two hypotheses:

A. She deploys in the standard way. The Indian makes his own dash for the talus but gets there too late to deploy. He lifts up the edge of her shelter to get in with her, and lets in the flames. She scrunches over to the right side of the shelter. She's lying on her left side, her back to the flames, when the smoke gets her.

Hypothesis B: They were both under the shelter, she on the right side of it, the Indian on the left. Heat and turbulence slam into the left side of the shelter. The Indian rolls up against her to get away from it, pushing her to the right, onto her side, so that the shelter comes up off the Indian, allowing the flames, etc. to get inside the shelter.

I like A better. I would have loved to see her face when the Indian lifts up her shelter to climb in! But in terms of my cover story, the con's red brethren rattling their bars, B works better. She's deploying as the Indian shows up, the two of them get into her shelter, no ugly smidgen of racism here, we're all buddy-buddy. Then the heat hits them, the Indian freaks and kills them both. His fault. Nothing to go on the warpath about. I point this out to Wilkie. The little prick looks at me like I'm some kind of worm!

Says, all pompous, If sharing shelters compromised the safety of firefighter number five (i.e., Cat), this is the first known incident.

I point out that in either scenario, number five's safety was compromised. He likes one over the other?

He goes, I work from the facts, I write up my report. What you people do with it is another matter. Ah, we sleazebags! Shit, what now—

27

Richie Gower winced. "Maybe I made it up," he said despairingly to Agent Chip Zampill. "It could have been a flash off someone's shovel, off one of the saws." He pressed his fingers into his scalp, as if the top of his head were in danger of popping off.

Chip hacked into his fist, hard small coughs that hunched him over, then released him blinking like a man come out of the dark. "Excuse me," he said. He cleared his throat and swallowed. "When you saw the flash, what was your first impression?" Behind Richie's glasses, the misery in his eyes changed to something close to panic. He stood up, still slightly hunched over. "I'll be right back," he said. He reeled around the little folding chair and bolted out of the tent.

Diarrhea, Chip diagnosed. Plus a bad case of survivor's guilt. He let out a philosophical sigh, turned off his tape recorder, and lit up another Marlboro. He had been interviewing all day, eating lunch and supper at his makeshift desk. Now, at almost ten o'clock in the evening, the line of witnesses waiting outside the tent had dwindled. Gower was among the last on his list. So far, he had provided nothing new. Chip looked over his notes.

Richie Gower was twenty-three, originally from Ohio, about to enter his second year of law school in Missoula. He planned to specialize in environmental law. His glasses with their pale plastic rims gave him a nerdy look. Or perhaps it was his indoor pallor: the reddish-blond stubble on his jawline and upper lip showed up clearly against his white skin. Given a summer outdoors, the kid had to be religious about his sunscreen, Chip decided.

Gower belonged to the squad of Millville 'shots who had volunteered to haul water and supplies up the Copper Creek drainage. Of the five of them, he was the only survivor. The squad boss, Wade Lowry, had posted him at the top of the relay. When the order came to move out, Gower was only seventy-five yards below the fire line. Along with four inmates on the detail, he made it to the safety zone in time to deploy his shelter fully. The fifth inmate, a half-breed Crow named Manny Leonard, had died on the side of the drainage next to Cat Carew. Leonard had been serving time on a drug charge. Chip wondered if he had been clean on the fire.

Richie Gower walked carefully back into the tent, his face a shade grayer, but his stance more upright. He lowered himself back into the chair he had left. "Sorry," he apologized. "I've been having, uh, stomach troubles."

"Not surprising," Chip said sympathetically.

Richie shook his head. "This started before. I thought I had some kind of flu. Then they gave us beans and that only made it worse." He looked down at his boots, then met Chip's eyes. "Wade knew."

"Knew what?"

"That I was sick!" Richie burst out angrily. "That's why he put me up top!"

Chip nodded slowly.

Richie's shoulders sagged. "I was pissed that he'd volunteered us. I mean, face it, we'd all just about had it. The only ones who thought it was still a picnic were Jim and Cat. Pami had blisters so big she couldn't get her gloves on—I swear to God, one of them looked like a golf ball! I was shitting my guts out, Wade's knee was acting up—and then he goes and gives me the top. He could have given it to Pami. He could have taken it himself, for Crissake! No one would have bitched. But he didn't. He put me up top. He saved my life, man. He fucking saved my life."

Chip turned the tape back on. "Interview continued. Let's go back to the flash. I'm not clear about the timing. About what time did you finish lunch?"

"About thirteen hundred-thirty. One-thirty. We left the lunch spot maybe ten minutes later, walked back along the line, started down the drainage."

Chip pulled a map of the site out from under a collection of folders. "Can you show me where you waited?"

Richie stood up and leaned over the map on the tabletop. He studied it for a moment, then drew a small circle with the tip of his forefinger. "Somewhere in here, I think."

"And the others strung themselves out down along the drainage."

"Right."

"What did you do while they were climbing down?"

Gower shot him a look of exasperation. "I waited."

"How did you wait?"

"What do you mean, how did I wait? I just sat there and waited."

"You were sitting down?"

Richie flushed. "Look, man, there was nothing spooky going on! The fire was above us, creeping nice and slow down to our line. The wind had picked up, it was blowing pretty good, over fifteen, if I had to guess, but it was blowing upslope. We weren't getting much spotting, nothing we couldn't handle. It wasn't a watch-out situation. Mowatt wouldn't have let us go if it wasn't cool—no matter what Overhead said. He takes care of us, man. Shit, he even got us an extra radio, just to be sure! We were in contact with the line scouts—yeah, I was sitting down! I could have been standing on my head and it wouldn't have been any different."

"What could you see?" Chip inquired mildly.

"Nothing."

Chip waited.

"Sky, a bunch of brush," Richie said. "I couldn't see the others, if that's what you mean. And I couldn't see the road either. The brush was real thick along the creekbed."

"You sitting facing downhill?"

Richie let out a breath. "Yeah."

Chip studied the map. "Facing this way, southwest?"

Richie peered at the map. "I guess so."

"The crews digging line were above and behind you."

"Yes," he said impatiently.

"And where was the flash?"

"Oh." Richie looked disconcerted. "It was in front of me."

Chip waited.

"You mean . . ." He stopped. "It couldn't have been a shovel, we left our shovels up top. Could have been someone's watch, though, one of the guys' below me."

"Try and remember what you thought at the time."

"I thought it was the truck," Richie said slowly. "I thought the truck was leaving, going back to camp. I was sitting there and I caught this flash. Not a quick one. It was kind of slow, like a fish turning over. I stood up, but I couldn't see anything, just the mountains in the distance. I didn't see any smoke—not then. I was thinking that they'd really hoofed it down there—that would have been typical of Cat, plunging down full-tilt, just for the hell of it. Then I thought maybe the truck didn't wait for them to get there. I thought maybe the driver had dumped off all the shit and left."

"What made you think that?"

"I don't know. It just seemed like it should have taken them longer. Even if Cat was playing Wonder Woman. Then, after a while, she got on the radio and said the truck was there, but no driver."

"What time do you think it was when you saw the flash?"

"I don't know," he said crossly. "I was too fucking tired to look at my watch."

"Could it have been the truck arriving?"

"No. The truck was down there, waiting for us, when we left. Mowatt had Cat call and check."

"And that was about one-forty?"

"Something like that."

A short young man in prison denims strolled jauntily into the tent. "Hey," he said to Richie. "How's it goin'?"

Richie didn't answer. He stared at the tabletop, his jaw set.

"Yes?" Chip said severely.

"You Agent Zampill?"

"That's right."

"They said you wanted to see me. Tony Hallihan?" He looked curiously around the vacant tent.

Chip recognized the name. Hallihan was on his list—he was one of the inmates who had survived the blowup. "I'll be with you in a moment. Please wait outside."

Tony Hallihan held up his hands. "Hey. I didn't mean to interrupt or anything like that."

Chip waited.

"No problem," Hallihan assured him. He turned and strolled out.

Richie said bleakly, "Wade shoulda put *them* at the bottom." Chip fished through the papers on his desktop and found Agent Burton's memo on the inmates. Hallihan was in for mitigated homicide. Burton had noted: "Seen talking to Billy Dallas night before fire."

"Did you have any contact with the inmates?" Chip asked Richie.

"Naw. Not really. I heard *him* on the radio." He rolled his eyes toward the entrance flap. "He was bugging Cat about the melons."

"Melons?"

"Cat said they'd sent out a sack of cantaloupes for us."

Chip turned off the tape and gave Richie a card. "Call me if you think of anything else," he said. "Hope you feel better."

"Yeah." Richie stood up. "Thanks," he added lamely.

Chip nodded and lit up another cigarette. "Tell Hallihan he can come in."

"Yeah," Richie said again. He hesitated a moment, then left.

Chip was jotting down a note to himself when Hallihan walked in and, without waiting to be invited, sat down in Richie's chair. Chip let him wait while he took out the tape of Richie Gower's interview, labeled it, and replaced it with a new one. Then he looked up, acknowledged Hallihan with a nod, and asked his permission to tape their conversation.

"Sure," Hallihan said grandly. He eyed Zampill's cigarette. "Mind if I smoke?"

"Go ahead."

Hallihan grinned and shrugged as if embarrassed. "I'm all out."

Chip shook his head. "Sorry. I'm short myself." He turned on the tape, went through the preliminaries. Then he sat back in his chair. "How long you been working fires, Tony?"

"Three—no, four years. Makes a nice change. When I'm not out with the crew, I work in the dairy. We got two hundred and seventy-five cows to milk three times a day."

"Lotta milk."

"You said it." Hallihan shook his head regretfully. "We could turn a nice profit for the taxpayers if they'd let us sell it."

Hallihan was handsome in a greasy sort of way, and Chip could see that he might attract women. If there was a bragging note in his voice, there also was a little-boy-lost look, a vulnerability in his brown eyes. Nonetheless, his presumptive chumminess rubbed Chip the wrong way. Chip asked, "You like working on a crew?"

"Like I said, it's a change. It's hard work." Hallihan nodded solemnly. "You put your life on the line." He let out a stagy sigh. "You never know when your luck's gonna run out. But hey, I'm glad to do it."

"Why?"

Hallihan's eyes went sincere. "Our crew's got a real good reputation. I feel like I'm helping to uphold it." He lowered his voice and leaned forward. "You take the hotshots—now, don't get me wrong. I'm not saying anything bad about the 'shots, not after what happened and all, but for them, it's just a job. For us it's more than that. Being out here makes me feel like I'm more of a contributing member of society. Back in there, I'm a liability." He added piously, "That's what hurts me the most."

Spare us, Chip thought. He took a final drag on his cigarette. There was no ashtray, so he stubbed it out on the leg of his metal chair and dropped the butt in his pocket, along with the others. "What do you recollect about the blowup?" he asked.

"Like I told the guys from Overhead, all the years I been doing this, I never seen anything like the way that fire came on. I don't mind saying I was scared."

"Did you notice anything unusual before the blowup?"

"No, sir. I heard a Huey—sounded like a two-oh-five in my experience. But that's nothing unusual. See, what the helicopters do, is they fill up their buckets down at the river and carry it up the mountain to the fire. That's what they do, back and forth all day, dumping water on hot spots. When the fire blew up on us, I figured it was a chopper's fault." He shook his head in sage disapproval. "Happens all the time. Choppers come in to dump a load on a spot and the wash from their rotors fans it up, gets it off and running. You'd think those pilots would learn."

"It was arson," Chip reminded him.

"Yeah. A real shame."

"You got the order to move out?"

"Yes, sir. I was carrying the handset for our squad."

"Do you recall a communication about melons?"

"Melons?" He frowned and shook his head.

Was he lying? Or merely acting? Hallihan's sincerity had a practiced gloss to it, but it may have been covering up nothing worse than insecurity. "I understand the kitchen sent out some melons with the truck," Chip said.

Hallihan hit his forehead with the heel of his hand. "Right! Cantaloupes." He let out an edgy laugh. "How could I forget!" He downshifted into his confidential voice. "It's the little things that make a difference in this job. We put our lives on the line for society. So I can tell you it means a lot when we feel appreciated."

Chip suppressed an ironical smile; he'd heard an ample share of self-pitying cops making the same speech. He straightened his face. "When the order came to move out—" The question was interrupted by a buzz from his cell phone. He straightened up in his folding chair and plucked the phone out of his pocket. It buzzed again. "Excuse me," he said to Hallihan. He turned off the tape, stood up, and stepped away from the table.

"No problem," Hallihan assured him.

Chip turned his back to the inmate. "Zampill here," he announced impatiently.

"Chip?

He recognized his wife's voice. He had not spoken to her in what, two months now? "Ellen?" he said.

"I'm sorry to bother you. I called your office. They gave me this number."

Chip couldn't remember the last time his wife had called when he'd been out in the field. "Is everything okay?"

She let out a nervous laugh. "Everything's fine."

In the background, he heard a PA system. He couldn't make out the announcement, but the institutional echo was ominously familiar. "Ellen, where are you?" he demanded.

She laughed again. "At the hospital. Jeannie had her baby."

"What—" he broke off. By a small miracle, he stopped himself from saying "What baby?" He felt shaky, as if he had narrowly missed a head-on collision.

"You're a grandfather!" Ellen declared.

"Uh?" he said stupidly. He had known his daughter was pregnant, she had told him just after Ellen moved out. How long ago was that? He said, "Is everything okay?"

"Everything's fine," Ellen said. "Mother and baby are both doing just fine."

"Well, that's fine." Turning, he saw Hallihan looking at him. Hallihan quickly looked away.

His wife asked, "Don't you want to know what it is?"

"Uh, sure. I mean, yes. What is it?"

"A boy, Chip. A *beautiful* baby boy! Seven and a half pounds. They let me hold him—oh, I wish you could see him!" Her voice was bursting with love and pride.

He didn't know what to say.

Ellen went on, "Everything went very quickly. Her water broke early this morning. She was only in labor four hours. The baby didn't waste any time!"

"That's great," he said, injecting enthusiasm into his voice. He wondered if the twerp his daughter had married had been with her. He decided not to ask.

"They said they want to name him after you."

Chip felt stunned. "She doesn't have to do that."

"They want to, Chip. Actually, Jeannie says it was Dean's idea."

"*Dean's* idea?"

"Yes. It seems your son-in-law admires you," she said dryly.

"Ellen, I really can't talk now. I'm in the middle of an interview. I'll have to get back to you."

"You're on that fire. All those kids were killed."

"That's right."

"It was on the news. Terrible."

"Yes. Tell Jeannie—tell her I'm honored."

He waited for his wife to say something, but she didn't. "You doing okay?" he asked vaguely.

"I'm fine. We're all thinking of you, Chip."

"Talk to you later," he said firmly. "I'll call you after I get back home."

"That's okay. You don't have to," she said happily. "I just thought you should know."

He heard a doctor being paged at the other end of the line. "Thanks for calling," he told her.

"You're welcome," she said, a hint of ironic amusement in her voice. "Bye, Chip." She hung up.

The dead air was disconcerting. He folded up the phone and moved back to Hallihan. For a moment he stood frowning down at the papers on the table. Automatically, he fished his Marlboros out of the pocket of his suit jacket. The pack felt light enough to be empty. He tore back the top flap, releasing the scent of tobacco, and saw two cigarettes left. He shook them out in his left hand, crumpled the soft pack in his right. He offered one of the cigarettes to Hallihan.

Surprised, the inmate hesitated, then took it quickly, like a hungry child. " 'Preciate it," he said. He looked it over. "Cowboy cigarettes."

Chip let it go by. He lit up and passed the inmate his lighter. He turned his tape recorder back on. "Tell me about Manny Leonard, the inmate who was killed."

Hallihan made a show of lighting up, taking his time about it, inhaling slowly, exhaling through his nose. As if they were old chums, sitting around with all the time in the world. Chip regretted his moment of generosity.

"Manny?" Hallihan said expansively. "He was new on the crew. A born-again Injun. Don't get me wrong. Like, whatever works. I ain't got nothing against Indians, not like some people." He glanced at Chip for approval.

Chip pulled on his cowboy cigarette.

Hallihan became more businesslike. "He joined one of their groups. Manny was really into all that sh——" He broke off, censoring his word choice. "He was really into it," he amended. "He had this tat done over his heart—a skull wearing a war bonnet."

"A tattoo?"

"Yeah. One of his red brethren designed it. It was supposed to stand for fallen warriors and the strength he could get from his ancestors. It was as big as my hand." Fingers splayed, he covered his left breast pocket with his hand. "The detail was impressive. Cost him a pretty penny." Hallihan blew out a casual stream of smoke. "Guess there's not much left of it now."

"His money?"

Hallihan raised an eyebrow. "I meant the tat."

"Where'd he get the money? Was he doing drugs?"

"I didn't hear anything about that. What he said was, his grandmother sent him the money."

"So what happened? You had the handset. You get the order to move out. Four of you make it. How come he didn't?"

"If I asked myself that once, I asked it a hundred times," Hallihan said sorrowfully.

The kid oughtta be on the soaps, Chip thought. Then it occurred to him: Maybe he'd picked it up from the soaps. Maybe that's what was wrong, why he sounded so canned.

"See, Manny was below me," Hallihan went on. "The other guys on our squad was above me—three of them. Four if you count their guy at the top, the one who was just in here. Never did catch his name."

Chip didn't supply it.

Hallihan shifted in his chair. "Below Manny, there was four of them. The order came over the radio to get out, and when you hear that, you don't sit around twiddling your thumbs, you *move*. I didn't even look behind me. I was scrambling up that slope, yelling at the others to get off their butts." Hallihan held up his hand, tilted it at a sharp angle. "I'm talking steep. We were practically clawing our way up, grabbing on to clumps of grass, rocks, whatever. The footing was real bad. You had rocks flying everywhere, like it was raining rocks. So maybe a rock got him. That happened to one of the Seminoles. Guy made it into his shelter, then bang, a rock lands on his head. Makes you think."

Hallihan sucked on his Marlboro—two quick ones, then a long one. He held the cigarette, Chip noticed, as if it were a joint, with his thumb and the tip of his forefinger close to his mouth. "You didn't alert Leonard," Chip stated.

"No, sir. I figured they would. The 'shots. They was just below him. Didn't make no sense for me to go down to him when they was moving up. That's what I can't figure out, why Manny got caught. I mean, that mother was fast. He'd been some kind of track star before he got in trouble. So you woulda thought he'd've made it. I mean, if they'd bothered to alert him."

He took a final long drag on his cigarette, then crunched it out on the leg of his chair and pocketed the butt, the way he'd seen Chip do it. Lacking a suit jacket, however, he deposited the butt in his work shirt's left breast pocket. There was a muted triumph, a celebration about the gesture. If he had been a car salesman returning a pen to his pocket, Chip would have cursed himself for paying too much.

"Yeah," Hallihan observed philosophically, "you never can tell about people. If it was me in their place, I would have yelled at Manny to get out. It wouldn't make no matter if a guy was a con. It wouldn't matter what he was." He paused and met Chip's eyes. " 'Course," he added, "I don't like to think it might've been a rock off my boot."

The admission made Chip think, for the first time, that perhaps there was hope for Hallihan after all. "Did you know Billy Dallas?" he asked.

Hallihan frowned thoughtfully, then shook his head. "Don't recall that name."

"He was the trusty who drove the supply truck. One of the camp crew."

Hallihan gave another shake of his head. "Don't believe I know him."

Chip looked at the array of papers on the tabletop, then looked back at Hallihan. "One of my agents says you were seen talking to Dallas in the kitchen area the night before the blowup."

"Could be," Hallihan said easily. "We were helping those

guys out with the cleanup. We didn't go on shift till the morning. Like I said, we got a reputation to uphold. Lot of times when we're off shift and we aren't busy eating or sleeping, we'll just help out the camp crew."

"One last question: Did you notice any kind of flash before the blowup?"

"You mean, like an explosion? No, sir, I didn't see anything like that."

Chip turned the tape off. "Okay. That's it for now. Thanks."

Hallihan stood up. "Glad to oblige," he said. "I'm just glad to help out, however I can. Give me a call if you need anything else. You know where to find me." He grinned.

Chip gave him a curt nod.

"Can I ask you a question?"

"You can ask."

"You gonna find out what happened to Manny?"

"The Forest Service has a team working on it. I imagine their report will be a matter of public record."

"It'll have the autopsies?"

"I don't know about that."

"I just want to know what happened to him," Hallihan said stubbornly. When Chip didn't respond, his face went blank. He turned and strolled out of the tent.

Chip made a note to have an agent interview the inmates' correctional officers. Did Manny Leonard really have a grandmother who sent him money? Or had he—and who knows who else—been dealing? Had the kitchen sent something beside melons up the mountain? More important, if drugs were going down, had the blowup been part of it?

Chip shelved the questions. His information was still too thin; hypothesizing at this point would only waste time. He picked up the phone and dialed Ned Voyle's cell phone. Voyle answered immediately. "I'd like to talk with your helicopter pilot, the one who spotted the smoke," Chip said. "ASAP."

28

Mattie backed her Jeep out of the Hotsprings Hotel parking lot, then stopped out in the middle of the main drag, unable to decide which way to go. The encounter with her family, first Harriet, then Jack, left her feeling darkly wounded and disoriented, as if she had been sucked into a vortex that had stripped away her adult life—and Jimmy with it. There were things she needed to do for him, fire people she wanted to talk to, documents to collect, but they were all a blur, a surface chop above a dark, watery hole. "I feel as if I'm drowning in my family," she told Spence. "I don't know which way is up." A car drove around them, blinking its headlights.

"Go left," he decided. "We can regroup at my place. It's just a couple miles out of town. There's a kitchenette. I can rustle up some of my emergency rations."

"Okay." But she made no move to turn.

"You want me to drive?"

"I'm okay." She took her foot off the brake, started the turn, then braked suddenly, pitching him forward in his seat. "Sorry. Just remembered. We need to stop by the schoolhouse. Ivan Wilkie said I could claim Jimmy's packsack there."

Half an hour later, with her son's pack in the backseat, she turned off the Folly River Road onto a dirt driveway marked by an aluminum mailbox. Spence's landlady lived in a two-story farmhouse set back behind a sage-dotted rise. His quarters, a vinyl-sided box with a pop-out bay window, had been added on in back. A pristine-looking concrete path, wide enough for a wheelchair, sloped gently up to an outside entrance. Spence dug a key out of his pocket. "She told me she added it for her mother," he informed Mattie. "Then the mother died and she went into the B&B business. She's big on roses," he warned as he opened the door, stepped inside, and flicked on an overhead light.

Mattie followed carrying Jimmy's packsack. "My goodness," she exclaimed. There were roses everywhere: red roses climbing the trellis-patterned wallpaper, large pink roses splashed across the drawn chintz curtains, a dense pattern of crimson and purple roses woven into the spread of a queen-sized brass bed, maroon cabbage roses hooked into a scatter rug. There were silk tea roses in a florist's green glass vase on a coffee table, crewel roses on linen pillows, and in the air, an assertive potpourri of dried roses that merged with the acrid smell wafting off Jimmy's packsack.

She put the pack down inside the door. She unlaced her boots, left them beside the pack, and padded over in her wool socks to a kitchenette/sitting area. With the exception of the flooring (vinyl with utilitarian gray speckles) and the appliances (a large black TV, a small black microwave), the only furnishings in the room that were not rose-covered were a pink plaid love seat with a ruffled skirt and a small rocking chair upholstered in pink velvet. The frame of the rocker looked old. A family piece passed down the line, Mattie speculated. She ran a finger over the dark carved wood. "Rosewood, do you suppose?" she asked Spence.

"You doubt it?" Stepping on the backs of his running shoes, he walked out of them, leaving them by the door. Without them, she noticed, his limp was more pronounced.

"I told her she should list the place as 'A Bed of Roses,' " Spence said. "She allowed as to how I was not the first to suggest it." He opened a louvered cupboard over the microwave and took out two mugs. From his suitcase on the bed, he fished out a packet of instant soup. She saw that he had a hole in the heel of his sock, his left sock, a beige argyle pattern.

She remembered that in the first months of her marriage, she had actually darned the holes in Eddie's socks—a skill her mother had taught both her and Harriet. After he left, however, there had been no time for such antique economies and, like everyone else, she ended up tossing her own worn-out socks—and Jimmy's—in the trash. What would it have been like to be happily married? To have the leisure for small wifely chores, for mending and baking and dusting? The question triggered a hot squirt of new fury: Where the hell was Eddie? He had not even bothered to call. Jimmy was lying dead in the Missoula morgue and he couldn't be bothered to call! Betrayal burned in her heart, a stinging, white-hot pain.

"Chicken noodle okay?" Spence asked.

"Do I have a choice?" She heard herself; she sounded amazingly normal.

"No."

She tried a game smile. Beneath it, her anger flowed into her breasts like a hot, bitter poison. She sat down hard in the rocker. It emitted a satisfying groan of protest. The chair was small, fashioned for more delicate spines than hers. She wondered if the landlady's mother had used it. Disregarding its age, she rocked aggressively back and forth. Under the protective bill of her cap, she watched Spence puttering in the room's miniature kitchen. Gradually the rocking brought a small relief, a physical easing, as if her milk had let down for a screaming infant.

Spence put their mugs in the microwave and punched in the time with the assurance of a pro. Clearly he knew how to live out of a suitcase, how to comfort himself in strange rooms. He laid out an impressive collection of airline snacks on the coffee table. "Hors d'oeuvres," he announced. From his computer case, he whisked out a mini bar of a half dozen ponies of gin. "Compliments of Delta. Help yourself."

She declined, kept on rocking. He cracked open two for himself and emptied them into a glass. For the soup, he dug deeper into his bag and came up with packets of soda crackers with Arabic letters on their wrappers. She wondered how long they had been in his suitcase: their corners had crumbled into powder. The soup was bright yellow with pale little noodles floating on top. She steadied the chair, tried a spoonful and found it delicious: hot, salty, safe. She felt exhausted, as if she'd come in out of a winter's storm.

Spence settled down with his mug on the ruffled love seat. He looked incongruously masculine.

"What's your wife like?" Mattie wondered aloud. The rudeness of her own question took her by surprise, but she did not apologize.

Spence crumbled a cracker into his soup. "Enid? Talented. Beautiful. Obsessive about her work."

"How long have you been married?"

"Thirteen years. First time for each of us."

"Children?"

Spence smiled and shook his head a little sadly. "Enid isn't the sort." He looked at Mattie, taking her measure. "Not like you," he said.

"I was always working," Mattie protested, siding with the unknown Enid. "My father was more of a mother to Jimmy than I was."

Spence made an impatient gesture with his hand. "But you cared about your son. You worked for him, not in spite of him. It showed."

Mattie was confused. "Did you know him? I didn't think you'd ever met him."

"I didn't. Your dad showed me the pictures in his wallet."

"Dad has pictures of Jimmy in his wallet?"

"There was one of you and Jimmy. He looked about five, a radiant little boy. You could see that he basked in your love."

Spence's eloquence made her suspicious. "My career—it wasn't all for him," she said tartly. "I had my own ambitions."

"Yes, but Enid's an artist," Spence argued. "Artists are by nature supremely selfish. When it comes right down to it, all she really cares about is herself—and, by extension, her sculptures. She would have made a frightful mother." The declaration was half boast. He took a swallow of soup from his mug, then chased it with gin from his glass.

"What sort of sculptures?"

"When I met her she was working in recycled metal. Huge pieces. She spent half her time in junkyards cutting up rusty chassis. It was all she could afford. Then she married me. I keep her in marble." He gave an ironic shrug. "A good career move for her. I'm not the sort of man women fall wildly in love with."

Could it be true? Mattie asked herself. "What sort are you?"

"The sort who picks up the pieces afterward."

"After what?"

"After the demon lover disappears."

There was no self-pity in his voice. He was making a statement of fact. She pondered it for moment. She had never known Gerry Spencer, the frightened boy she had saved. One moment they had been screaming at each other over the roar of the fire, the next she was fighting him in the shelter. When she had visited him in the hospital, he had been unconscious. Yet now that she thought about it, he had a boy-next-door quality about him. Gerald Spencer, writer, student of war, world traveler had a core of niceness that made her feel safe. She imagined he had been the sort of boy of whom mothers approved: clean-cut, sincere, well-mannered.

"Eddie was the demon-lover sort," she mused. She renewed her rocking. "It wasn't so much that he broke my heart into pieces. It was more than that, something more fundamental. I'm not sure what."

"He was your soul," Spence said, as if pointing out the obvious.

"He was a shit." She stopped rocking, took another swallow of soup and brought the conversation back onto firmer turf. "He remarried. A number of times. After he stopped jumping, he got fat. Not really fat. But he lost all his shine. Now he sells real estate. He looks—just ordinary."

"Enid keeps herself thin. A dubious virtue, I've always felt."

Mattie studied him. "You're still in love with her."

"Hmm," he acknowledged.

Was that good or bad? Mattie was uncertain. They lapsed into silence. Mattie finished her soup and stood up. The rocker squeaked lightly. She put her cup in the shoe-box-sized sink next to the microwave, then walked to the door, picked up Jimmy's pack, and looked around for a place to open it. The coffee table was occupied by Spence's stockinged feet and the bouquet of silk roses. She took the pack over to the bed and swung it up onto the coverlet. A bed of roses, she thought. A snatch of her dream came back to her: the crude carts bearing the dead and their possessions. Had they been decked with garlands of roses? She gave herself a shake.

Although the pack had been found inside the safety zone, the heat of the fire had scorched the back of it and deformed the plastic buckles. The front side, however, had come through unscathed. The pack, she decided, must have been lying front side down, its pocket against the ground. She opened the pocket and pulled out two geodetic survey maps. The one on top had been folded to the quadrant that encompassed Section C. Had Jimmy consulted it before he went down the drainage? Was it the last thing he had touched? She set the maps aside and pulled out a fat, dog-eared paperback. There was no artwork on the faded pink cover, only black letters. *Zen and the Art of Motorcycle Maintenance*. She opened it. The pages were yellow and brittle at the edges and some of the sections had come unglued. Passages were underlined, some in ballpoint, some in pencil. By Jimmy? Or by a previous owner?

"To some extent the romantic condemnation of rationality

stems from the very effectiveness of rationality in uplifting men from primitive condition." She read the sentence twice but the words meant nothing. Jimmy had read this? She flipped to the front and found an inscription in green ink on the flyleaf: "For Jimmy—for your own quest! Love, Heather."

What quest? Who was Heather? She set the book aside with the maps and went back to the pocket. She fished out an instamatic camera, fusees, a file, a roll of exposed film, a tin of Skoal—*Jimmy*? She would have been less surprised by a joint of marijuana. She shook the tin, opened it up, but it was, in fact, tobacco. Feeling slightly guilty, she dug into his pack again. She found car keys, a tablespoon from the kitchen drawer at home, a roll of filament tape, double-A headlamp batteries, an army-surplus compass. She weighed the compass in her hand. It was a heavy-duty one, heavier than she would have chosen. But he had always liked to know his direction, Jimmy had.

She thought about Jack's disbelief that Jimmy had been found faceup. Ivan Wilkie hypothesized that he had been running uphill at the time, that a wave of superheated gases rolling before the fire had knocked him over backward. She had not disputed the reconstruction. But now in the shelter of Spence's "Bed of Roses" she realized there was something off-base about the scenario. Yes, as she had argued to her father, the footing in the creekbed was rotten. Nonetheless, she felt sure Jim would have seen the fire coming. One of the commandments of his training was: "Look up, look down, look around."

Or had he been zoned out? Had fatigue made him sloppy? As a commander, she knew it happened with frightening regularity. The real miracle was that so many firefighters escaped the consequences. Still, she agreed with her father: running up the drainage seemed an unlikely choice. The Carew girl must have seen it coming. She ran toward the safety of the talus up on the south side of the drainage. If Jimmy was running away from the fire, why not up the side like Carew? She touched his Skoal can, the worn paperback. How much did she know about Jim?

She replaced the items in the pocket, stood the pack up, and tugged open the main compartment. Suddenly, unexpectedly, she inhaled the essence of her son: a pungent reek of ashes, resinous smoke, and male sweat. She caught the faint chemical tang of his deodorant, of chain-saw exhaust. She smelled his rotten socks, his dirty hair, his sour breath. It was as if he had wafted out of the bag, an invisible but entirely real presence. She could feel him slipping away, dissolving into the scent of a stranger's dried roses. Her knees buckled beneath her. The room was spinning black at the edges. Silently she sank down, fighting nausea, hanging on to the bedspread.

She felt someone holding her under her arms, easing her onto the floor. "It's all right." She heard Spence's voice. She could see nothing. He took off her cap, put a pillow under her head. The pillowcase felt cool. She heard him moving about the room. She felt herself sinking into blackness.

There was a loud crack and a blast of ammonia hit her like a slap. She groaned, tried to raise herself up, and threw up her soup. Kneeling beside her, Spence held her head. Vomit splashed on her socks, on her pant legs, on the landlady's clean pillow. She began to cry. She felt her bowels loosening.

Spence helped her to the bathroom, shut the door, and waited until he heard the flush. Then he walked her back to the bed, helped her undress, and eased her between the covers. She shivered and cried. He doubled the spread over her, found an extra blanket, wiped her face. She slid into a dreamless sleep. She surfaced to the distant strains of harp music—an ancient, vaguely familiar melody in a minor key. She opened her eyes. The light in the room was dim. She saw that Spence had draped a red bandanna over the bedside lamp. Spence himself lay beside her on top of the covers, eyes closed, breathing regularly. He had taken off his jacket and rolled back the sleeves of his shirt like a white-collar husband about to do the dishes. She closed her eyes again and listened. Somewhere beyond the sound of Spence's breathing, the faraway stream of music continued. She imagined green pastures, lichen-covered stone walls, a gray sea, women in black. Cool tears ran out of the corners of her eyes, pooled in her ears.

The next time she woke, Spence was reading. He brought her a glass of water. "What time is it?" she asked.

"Just after midnight."

She took several swallows from the glass, then put it down on the bedside table and sank back into her pillow. "I thought I heard music."

He indicated the wall behind the bed. "Our landlady. Practicing her dulcimer."

"I imagined it was a harp. A Celtic harp."

"Could be. I'm not up on New Age music. I'm a Bach man myself. I hope it didn't bother you. Are you feeling any better?" His eyes were bloodshot and anxious.

She remembered the mess she had made. "Oh, Spence," she apologized. "I'm so sorry." She reached out and touched his face, a light caress.

"I am too." He took her hand away from his face and gave it a sympathetic squeeze. Below the rolled white shirtsleeves, his forearms looked muscular and golden in the lamplight. She felt a sudden swell of lust, anger, and determination. She kissed him fully on the mouth.

He held her like a gentleman, returning the kiss, but with more politeness than passion. "Are you sure you, uh—?" He left the question dangling.

"Yes. Please." Then it occurred to her. "Unless you don't want to?"

He smiled. "Want to what?" he teased, now permitting his hand to stroke her bare back.

She felt her skin tingling under his touch. "What about Enid?" she asked, giving him an out.

He kept on stroking. "Unfortunately, Enid doesn't care what I do in that department."

Oh dear, Mattie thought.

On her right shoulder blade, the tip of his finger worried an old dime-sized scar. "What's this?"

"What?"

He turned her around, examined his find. "Looks like an exit wound."

What was he talking about? She felt his finger traveling down her backbone.

"And here." He stopped midway down her spine. "What are these? Three little blotches all in row. Like tooth marks."

Suddenly she remembered, made the connection—such an odd twist of fate! She laughed. "Those are from *your* fire."

"What?"

"When first we met," she said lightly. "I was wearing a holy medal—a gold one my mother had given me when I was little. It had Jesus on one side and Mary on the other. My sister and I each had one. We used to wear them around our necks on these thin little gold chains. They were supposed to keep us safe. But my chain kept breaking and my mother got tired of fixing it. She said I was too much of a tomboy." Mattie smiled wryly. "Then, after she died, I found it with her things and started wearing it again—on a piece of string. It must have slipped around under my shirt because when we were in the shelter, it melted onto my back. Same thing with my bra—those aren't tooth marks. They're the metal fasteners on my bra."

"I had no idea," Spence said in a shocked tone of voice.

"For heaven's sake, you got the worst of it." She twisted her back away from him, turned to face him.

With the reverence of a penitent, he bowed his head and kissed first one breast, then the next.

They made love. Mattie felt as if she were making love to two of him at the same time: Spence the nurse, with his muscular arms, his knowing fingers, his tenderness; and Gerry, the skinny, anxious boy who had bucked under her half a lifetime ago. The force of his ardor was almost alarming, and when he entered her she worried, for a fleeting second, that she might become pregnant. Afterward, it struck her as an odd worry. Spence had been wearing a sheath, and two months before, she had started birth-control pills to regulate her cycle. Was it simply a matter of wishful thinking? Had some deep atavistic urge to replace her lost child bobbed up on the warm, dark waves of her pleasure? or was it something else—not a symptom of grief, but a kind of a priori *knowing?* There were women who boasted that they knew the precise moment of conception. Mattie had always been skeptical of such talk. (By what route could an egg communicate with the brain?) But as she lay companionably next to Spence, basking in the afterglow of his astonishing vigor, she could not help but wonder: What if he actually had impregnated her?

29

01 Sept 1:28a   Directory C:*.*

Cat's mother was here at the base tonight. She drove up in a taxi, if you can believe it, all the way from Pocatello. The Widow Carew. Works as a secretary for a real estate agency there, someone said. Cat never mentioned her.

I keep thinking about what Wilkie said about the timing. I asked him how long Cat had. He kept going on about the delamination of foil and the burn patterns being consistent with flames coming in underneath the shelter, then finally got around to it: a matter of seconds. As in one or two after flames entered the shelter. Not thirty or forty. So the heat hit her like a train, blew her from here to kingdom come before she knew what was happening. Which is really too bad. I would have liked her to know it was me. I didn't think of it at the time. I was consumed. I was the instrument, the instrument of the god; the future didn't exist yet, only the sordid little burn of her betrayal. But now it's irritating. I would have liked her to appreciate the magnitude of what she did. When the Indian lifted the flap, I would have liked her to see my face, to gasp in recognition, if only for half a second, at the face of Justice! I keep thinking there must have been a way—obviously not the radio—but some way to let her know what was coming down. She wouldn't have believed me. She would have laughed. I can see her laughing—chin up, exposing her throat—like, I dare you to slit it, go ahead. Some people duck their heads when they laugh, curl forward protectively, but she always tossed her head back and you were never sure if she was laughing at you or what. So she wouldn't have believed me. Not when I told her. But—when it happened, when the Indian lifted up the side of her shelter, it would have clicked in her fucking little brain; she would have *known* it was me if only I'd said something.

McCulloch still hanging around bugging everyone. We're trying to wind it up, containment announced last shift, demobe's a zoo and the bitch won't go home, goes around whining in everybody's ear, like we all haven't been bending over backward for her. She was bugging my guys for something, whatever the fuck it was, and I told her she'd have to wait and she looks at me like I crapped birdshit on her head. She takes off her cap, pulls back her hair like she's wiping off the birdshit, hand wipes back, hair sprongs up—the way the sun was hitting it, it looked like fire rippling out her skull! What with the cap on night and day, you don't notice the color; talk about flaming redheads! I forgot whatever the hell it was she wanted! The cap goes back on, she's looking at me through her shades. Doesn't move a muscle, neck a column of ivory, as it were. I have to admit, her skin's not bad for her age, still got all her juices, or eating horsepiss pills, not that they worked any kind of miracle on Margaret. You have to wonder, what would it be like with a redhead.

30

In his youth, before he became a homicide detective, Chip Zampill had volunteered for local brush fires but he had never seen a fire camp on the scale of the Justice. The array of amenities disconcerted him. In addition to his fancy white tent and its electronic hookups, there was the caterer's salad-bar wagon (complete with regulation plastic sneeze guard), the body-sized paper towels dispensed from rollers in the shower trailers, the Laundromat with rows of washing machines churning on flatbed transports. There were trucks that recycled gray water and mobile solar panels that heated it. He felt as if he had landed in an invisible giant's play yard, a maze strewn with gargantuan toys and gadgets. It hardly matched his notion of a fire camp—any more than cappuccino was his idea of a cup of coffee. But he was not complaining. The yellow coffee drum in his white tent held the plain black stuff which had been regularly and cheerfully renewed by pretty little kitchen girls wearing red aprons over their jeans.

After their first twelve hours at the Meander, Zampill and his two underlings had changed out of jacket-and-tie into coveralls. At two in the morning, Chip picked up one of the disposable sleeping bags the camper manager had left for them, took it outside the tent, and unrolled it on a patch of ground. It was white and not much thicker than the disposable diapers his father had worn at the end. Without bothering to unstrap the 9-mm he wore in the pancake holster under his coveralls, he took a short turn in the bag. He was vertical again at four. He lit up a cigarette and ran his battery-powered electric razor over his jaw, but his nap, instead of bouncing him back, left him feeling slow and dull.

The younger men, he could not help but notice, seemed unimpaired. At midnight, Burton had crashed briefly in one of the white bags, but the righteous Orr had worked straight through, stopping only for his daily jog before breakfast. Chip felt his age was beginning to tell. Hell, he was a *grandfather* now. He thought of Ellen, of the vibrancy he'd heard in her voice. Was it simply delight at the baby? Or was she seeing someone? Not that she hadn't every right to see whomever the hell she wanted. She was still an attractive woman. She certainly didn't look old enough to be a grandmother. He remembered his own grandmother, a stout, querulous old woman with wattles at her chin and a critical eye. Ellen had kept her figure, stayed active. She took aerobics, played tennis with her friends. Last winter, after the separation, she had gone cross-country skiing for the first time. She was admirable. Depressingly admirable. Chip sighed and broke into a cough. He hacked into a wadded tissue, inspected the phlegm, saw no fleck of blood. He lit another cigarette.

Twenty-four hours had passed since their arrival and they had made no progress in the investigation. At 5 A.M., Chip had wandered over to the briefing tent. Under the electric lights, the lords of fire were relaxed and jocular. A guy in a white cowboy hat stood up and proclaimed the Justice officially contained; there were appreciative whistles and cheers. A guy wearing wire-rims and a pony tail made a bunch of announcements. Mop-up and land-rehab crews—whatever they were—were being shipped in, the hotshots and helitack crews were being shipped out. Wire-rims requested that crews traveling by commercial airlines shower and change into clean clothes before boarding—there had been complaints from the airlines. A number cruncher nonchalantly projected the cost of the fire in millions of dollars. How would he figure, Chip wondered, the cost of five human lives?

Meanwhile, the sheriff's men and the state troopers were still looking for Billy Dallas, the missing trusty. They had combed the Folly River Valley with police helicopters and canine search parties. They had patrolled the area's campgrounds and four-wheel-drive trails, checked farmers' outbuildings and weekenders' cabins, but found no trace of the fugitive. Agent Orr, who still rankled at not having been given charge of the manhunt, exuded an annoying smugness at their failure. More than once Chip had to remind himself that that was Orr's problem, not his. Maybe they'd break the case, maybe they wouldn't, but in Chip's experience, the sure key to botching it was to try and please everyone.

Their own homework had turned up no evidence that the fire had been set to cover up a drug deal or avenge a deal gone bad. A small quantity of marijuana had passed between the catering staff and several of the clean-up trusties, but by all accounts Billy Dallas, in anticipation of his parole hearing, had not been involved. Further interviews turned up no connection between Dallas and any of the Deer Lodge crew or the Millville crew—no grudges, no obvious motive for homicide. According to the latents people from Missoula, the tire tracks on the wagon road belonged to the burned pickup Dallas had been driving; the technicians found no sign of a second vehicle that might have driven Dallas away from the scene.

Chip's hopes had soared briefly when a tourist had come forward with video footage shot along the Folly River Road just forty minutes before the blowup. The tape showed the fire distantly, billows of smoke on the ridges above the river, and included a pan of the Copper Creek drainage. But the footage proved of interest only to the Forest Service's fire-behavior specialists. As for the owner of the video, a retired prosthetics manufacturer from Boston, both he and his wife (she had been driving their Lincoln so he could film) were certain they had seen no one else on the road—no one on foot, no other cars.

No, they had not gotten out of the car. "Dad" (as his wife called him) had shot the film through the Lincoln's open window.

Yes, they were both right-handed.

No, neither of them had thrown a match out the window. They were offended by the suggestion. "We're not even smokers," the wife had protested in a shocked voice. She cast a disgusted glance at the overflowing Cinzano ashtray on Chip's gray metal desk.

In an attempt to locate other potential witnesses, Agent Burton had spent several futile hours in Plans with the Resource Unit leader and the Documentation Unit leader trying to find a list of incident vehicles or aircraft in the vicinity of Copper Creek on the afternoon of the blowup. But to the intense frustration of all, the transportation records for that shift had disappeared. After no hard copy could be found, a technician tried to pull the information up on the computer, but the computer kept sending up FILE NOT FOUND and WRONG PATH messages. Pretty soon a swarm of blurry-eyed men were glued to the screen. The puzzle energized them. Agent Burton, who considered himself computer-literate, heard words he knew, but found himself unable to extract any meaning from them. "Could someone have erased it?" he wondered aloud.

No one bothered to answer. He repeated the question.

"It's in here somewhere," promised the unit leader. He promised to print it out and send it over as soon as they found it.

By mid-morning, the tent was hot. The detectives tied back its flaps, rolled up the sleeves of their coveralls, and switched from coffee to iced tea. Chip's table faced a side flap. A fan blew at his back. Burton and Orr were nonsmokers, and after failing to convince their superior that, like the offices they had left, the tent was a "smoke-free work environment," they had moved his table, strategically angling it for maximum ventilation. Chip sat with his back to them, blowing dragonlike clouds of smoke out of the tent toward the satellite dish on the roof of the Incident's Communications trailer. Across the top of a yellow lined pad, he doodled with the names of the five dead firefighters: Carew, Gustavisson, Lowry, Sterling—the four hotshots—and Leonard from the inmate squad. He crossed out "Sterling" and wrote "McCulloch." Then he underlined each name. He drew boxes around them. Five little coffins, he thought morosely. He added "Dallas" at the bottom of the page and circled the trusty's name.

Chip had taken to calling Billy Dallas "the Idiot" on the assumption that Billy boy had set the fire himself, most probably out of sheer stupidity. Since the blowup had originated out on the road and not at the end of the wagon track, the Idiot had left his post by the pickup. Had he been waiting for someone? Or was it simply a meaningless stroll, something as dumb as checking out the fishies in the river? In all probability, the Idiot had lit up a smoke and dropped the match. Matches. The investigators found seven, but not the book. So it had taken the Idiot a bunch of tries to light his cigarette. There had been a stiff breeze blowing out of the west. The grass caught, the Idiot ran, five kids died.

If the Idiot hadn't dropped the match himself, perhaps he had seen who did. In any case, the direction of the investigation moved from him (probable cause) up to the victims (deadly effect). But if Dallas didn't oblige them and show up, the next step was to start all over again, this time reversing the direction and probing into the lives of the victims on the chance of finding a cause there. If nothing suspicious turned up, if nothing in their lives offered a clue to the arson, then there was nothing left for them to do but close up shop and go home.

The prospect of interviewing so many bereaved families and friends—the monumental amount of legwork, the incalculable weight of their anguish and sorrow, and probably all for nothing—was disheartening. Beneath the prickle of caffeine, Chip felt the sluggish tug of a weariness that went beyond simple fatigue. Was this what people so solemnly referred to as "burnout"? If so, it felt more like a swamp than a fizzle. He thought of a bumper sticker Ellen had put in his Christmas stocking one year: "I'd rather go fishing." He'd avoided putting it on his car. The anxious hint behind the gag had rankled. But now he was assaulted by the vision of his fly rod in its slender aluminum tube. He knew exactly where it was—propped up with his waders in the left-hand corner of the closet in Jennie's old room. He had not touched it for two, three years. Taking a little time off didn't seem like such a bad idea.

He took a phone call from the governor's office, pacified an aide with the usual bromides. ("To divulge any details at this time would jeopardize the investigation . . .") He adjusted the holster at his crotch, wished he'd remembered to toss a shoulder holster in his bag, then turned back to the names on his yellow pad. For lack of a brilliant insight, he retraced the boxes in a firm hand. Grimly, he lit another Marlboro and sent up a prayer with its smoke: Give us a break.

He was hunting through the papers on his table for a misplaced phone number when he heard Agent Orr greet someone. A certain smarminess in the detective's voice made Chip swivel around. Orr was leaning back in his own chair eyeballing a short Hispanic woman in a Forest Service uniform. Chip blinked. The woman's breasts were wondrously large for her size. Beneath her tailored shirt, they looked as firm and formidable as a pair of torpedoes. Lordy, Chip thought in awe. He felt his humor suddenly improve.

"I need to speak with Agent Zampill," the woman insisted to Orr. She didn't speak with an accent so much as a lilt.

Orr shook his head ruefully. "Guess it ain't my lucky day. Over there." He angled his thumb toward Chip, grinned at her.

The woman did not return his smile. She approached

Chip's worktable. He ground out his cigarette, dislodging butts from the ashtray in the process. He swept the butts off his files onto the ground, stood up, sucked in his stomach, eased the holster under his coveralls with his thumb. "Chip Zampill," he said, meeting her eyes.

"Celia DeJesus."

He made a mental note of the pronunciation. Day-HAYzooz. Her manner was solemn, her posture unyielding, her breasts strictly under control. Nonetheless, despite her rigid armature—or perhaps because of it—she projected a confident, Latin femininity. Her glossy black hair fell in thick curls onto the shoulder of her uniform shirt. Small gold studs in her earlobes caught the morning light. Dark-red liner traced the curve of her lips, black liner and dusky smudges of shadow deepened her brown eyes. Her makeup was peach-colored but the skin on her neck was olive. Chip guessed she was in her early thirties. Without makeup she could probably pass as a teenager.

She thrust a manila mailer at him. "Mattie passed this on to me. I thought you should know about it."

He took the mailer, turned it faceup. It was addressed to "M. MCCULLOCH" in crude block letters. He opened it and slid out the contents: a page torn from a magazine, a color close-up of a woman's crotch. A white woman's crotch. The pubic hair was red. So were her fingernails. They displayed most of a wrinkled pink clitoris. The vagina had been torn away. No, not torn. Burned. Someone had held a match to the lower edge of the page.

Chip looked at Celia. "Mattie gave this to you?"

"I'm the Human Resource officer."

"Give me a hint."

"My job is to deal with sexual harassment, any kind of minority discrimination, violations of civil rights." She rapped out the words in a sharp staccato.

Chip looked back at the photograph. The focus was soft, the coppery pubic hair fluffy, arty glints of light bounced off the red fingernails. Nothing hard-core. To the left of the burned-out bite between the thighs, the sender had pasted a message, each word cut from printed text: "1 Thousand words."

He took a ballpoint from his shirt pocket and initialed and dated both the picture and its envelope. From a cardboard carton by his desk, he fished out a gallon-sized Ziploc bag. He slipped the picture into it and sealed it with yellow evidence tape. The manila mailer he packaged and sealed in a white plastic garbage bag.

Celia watched with interest. "You are going to check for fingerprints?"

"Yes, ma'am. It would help to know who handled it. You and Mrs. McCulloch. Anyone else?"

"Not that I know of. You will have to ask Mattie."

There was a prickle of irritation in her voice. Chip nodded, sat back in his chair.

"She brushed it off," Celia said disapprovingly. "Like it was some kind of prank."

He nodded again, then barked, "Orr!"

Orr trotted over. Chip showed him the picture and watched his reaction. He noted with approval that while the agent might be a righteous pain in the ass, he at least knew how to keep his face straight.

Orr read the pasted-on message. "One picture's worth a thousand words?"

"Evidently."

"Sparkling wit."

Chip turned to Celia DeJesus. "You get a lot of 'pranks' like this?"

"I get complaints about pornographic material. And, yes, usually the material is masquerading as a joke. Of course, there is always a sadistic impulse behind this kind of joke. The intent is to embarrass, to punish, to humiliate the recipient. But what I see isn't—damaged. Not burned. I mean, every one knows her son's burned to death!"

"What about the other pictures?"

"Here? A few have turned up on our web page, yes. But they were generic, they were not directed to Mattie." She looked the two men over. "Sometimes it is difficult to differentiate between sexual harassment and hazing," she lectured. "Hazing is a form of testing, a way of bonding. Male ceremonies of initiation tend to be more cruel, more physically violent than female initiation ceremonies. So in a fire camp, there are often confrontations between male and female cultures, but this incident has nothing to do with any kind of initiatory testing."

Chip pictured her in front of a blackboard. Empowerment 101. He said to Orr, "Ms. DeJesus believes the picture is a threat."

"Exactly," Celia confirmed. "I have seen pictures that are more degrading to women in general: women drinking out of toilets, women with animals—"

Chip stopped her with a listless gesture.

She took a breath. "This one is a threat," she insisted primly.

"Mrs. McCulloch was new to the Command team," Orr stated. "Initiations can get out of hand."

"That would mean someone on the Command team sent it," Celia snapped back. "Initiations are conducted by peers, not by the lower ranks. Mattie had already been relieved as IC when this showed up. This is no collegial test. It is a personal threat."

The men said nothing.

"Whoever sent it could have picked a blonde, a brunette!" she burst out. "Look at it! The pubic hair is red."

"So?" Chip said severely. He did not feel entirely comfortable discussing the color of pubic hair with Ms. DeJesus.

Celia drew herself up. "Ms. McCulloch's a natural redhead. You can't get that color with a dye."

Chip remembered his glimpse of her hair and felt annoyed. Why had he not made the connection?

"It could be coincidence," Orr said. "On the other hand, it could be our guy."

Chip put both the picture and its manila mailer into a large paper bag and handed it to Orr. "Get this up to the lab in Missoula," he ordered. "See if he left us a print. Have them check it against the partials on the matches."

"He?" Celia said sharply.

Orr looked at her. "You think a woman sent it?"

"I don't know who sent it," Celia retorted. "A man, a woman, it could be either."

"Yes, ma'am," Orr said.

She caught the doubt in his voice and scowled at him with feminist disapproval. "You think a woman would not have sent it?"

"If the person who sent it is our arsonist, no. FBI profiles show something over ninety percent of convicted arsonists are male. Young white males."

"Yeah, and they all liked to set cats on fire when they were kids," Chip growled. "It's a bunch of bullshit. FBI profiles never caught anyone." He had no patience with the current vogue for profiles. It was all smoke and mirrors. Fire was a weapon, plain and simple. Men used it, women used it. Last year he'd had a case in Billings, a housewife who took out eight life insurance policies on her husband, poured gasoline over him, and set him on fire. He looked at Orr. "What are you waiting for? Get going. Drive it up there, tell them I told you to wait for it."

"Yes, sir." Agent Orr bustled off.

Celia, however, made no move to leave.

Chip took a breath. "It hadn't occurred to me to think a woman might have sent it," he confessed. "You're thinking a woman here at the Incident?" He wondered if Mattie was a lesbian.

Celia hesitated. "If it was a woman," she mused, "I think it would be a younger woman. My age or younger. Not older."

Chip waited.

"Back in the seventies," she explained, "when women were just beginning to break onto fire crews, there was a lot of hostility, a lot of resentment. My job hadn't even been invented. There was no such thing as 'politically correct.' The women were on their own. They had to put up with abuse from the men—and some of it was more than verbal. If the women didn't accept it, they lost their jobs. I heard stories about crews burning female teammates in effigy. Imagine what that would be like, to see your so-called brothers burning an effigy with your name on it!"

Clearly the notion distressed her. Chip nodded sympathetically, though privately he couldn't see that it was all that big a deal. Maybe he needed more sensitivity classes. He wondered what Ellen would say about burning effigies.

"But that was twenty, twenty-five years ago," Celia was saying. "Women like Mattie, the women who stuck it out, they don't talk about it. If they do, the younger ones just stare at them. They don't understand. They take it for granted that they belong. Many crews are half female." She paused for breath. "My point is, I don't think a woman of McCulloch's generation would send a message like that. Not after all they had been through."

"How about an older man?"

Celia winced and shook her head. "I wouldn't like to say that. There is a saying: 'Some men change, some men never will.' Many of the older men in this business, the ones who opposed putting women on the fire line, changed. Now they are more supportive of women than some of the younger men. But like I told you, this, this thing that came to Mattie, goes beyond sexism, beyond initiation. Sick minds come in all ages."

He stood up. "I appreciate you bringing this to our attention. We need all the help we can get. If you think of something else, if something new comes up, please let me know." He gave her his card. "Even if you think it's unimportant, give me a call. Let me be the one to decide whether it's important.

Don't worry about bothering me. That's what I'm here for. Day and night." It was a routine request, one that he always made of any witness he interviewed, but this time he meant it more than usual.

Some men change, some never will. As he sat back down in his desk chair, Chip Zampill wondered how Celia would categorize him: As a man who could change? Or one who never would? Which was he? He realized, with a vague sense of surprise, that he wanted her good opinion. He wondered what Ellen would make of her.

The phone on his table rang. He picked it up. It was Ned Voyle, the IC. As Chip listened, he felt an electric charge run up his spine, jolting away his sluggishness. He picked up his pencil, jotted a name and number down on his yellow pad. He hung up, stared for a second at the boxed names across the top of the pad: Carew, Gustavisson, Lowry, McCulloch, and Leonard. Then, firmly, he circled Jim McCulloch's box. He thought of Mattie, tall, brave-shouldered, stoically calm. He compressed his lips. The poor woman.

He stood up and scanned the area outside the tent. Men and women on Forest Service business crossed brown patches of grass or stood talking under the pines, but Chip saw no sign of Agent Burton. He picked up the phone to have him paged.

31

01 Sept 11:07a   Directory C:*.*

Our Human Resource slut informs us that she has set up a black-bordered web site for the Great Outpouring, over a thousand hits in the first twelve hours, like we're supposed to genuflect. So I check it out, scroll through this endless pap, a worldwide *throb* of virtual sorrow, as if any of them even knew who any of them were! No one knew Cat like me, no one *knew* what she really was, and now they're talking like she's some kind of patron saint, they're actually posting notes TO her! There was one going on about how their dog had died, I kid you not, then you've got the usual share of assholes climbing up on the ye olde conspiracy wagon; Greenpeace did it to get sympathy, Exxon did it to get mineral rights, the Forest Service did it to sell off the salvage timber! Even the porn posted is laughable, at least compared to the stuff boys over in Finance used to pull up. They had this ongoing game, who can find the worst picture in ten minutes, and I have to admit a couple of the winners got me thinking about new possibilities, a couple fiery refinements, as it were—seems so obvious now I can't think why I hadn't thought of it before. Too bad Cat's not around to try them on! Anyway, now the Finance gang has gone righteous, they dele all stray genitalia off the sympathy page, afraid Our Mother of Sorrows will log on and get an eyeful. Well, they needn't worry, she's savvier than she looks. I heard she didn't turn a hair at my little missive, barely looked at it, and after all the trouble I had to go to finding a red one. You have to wonder what she likes, what she's into. Maybe when all this dies down, after the memorial service, well, it's something to think about; even if she's game, there's no point in rushing anything and there's still the funerals to come, the families apparently want to do their own thing as well, which makes you wonder why we bother. Our show's set for this afternoon, complete with brass band and fly-overs, hey, spare no hard-earned tax dollars! Speaking of which, the almighty dick is asking for satellite pictures, trying to find out if one was passing overhead at the time of the blowup. Now that's something that never occurred to me! Everyone's buzzing about the amazing lenses floating around up there, how the Russians are cooperating; but even if by some freak of fate and technology they do come up with my license plate, it won't do any good, they can't prove it was me in the vehicle; I took care of that right afterward.

32

Jack McCulloch woke up at 6 A.M. in his cabin at the Hotsprings Hotel. He was still fully clothed and the overhead light was still on. He felt so rotten that when he got up to take a leak, he had to sit down on the toilet and then he was able to release no more than a few drops. He drank two glasses of water, chewed up a handful of Tums, swallowed four extra-strength Tylenol with another glass of water, and went back to bed. At ten o'clock, his daughter Harriet knocked on his door, rousing him from an unpleasant doze. "Dad? Dad, are you all right?"

He staggered to the door. Harriet looked him over with a hard eye. "The service is scheduled for this afternoon at three," she informed him. "They're going to send a bus over for us. You need to be presentable by two." She stepped into the room and gave him a tall Styrofoam cup of coffee and a sugared doughnut in a napkin.

He took them without speaking.

Briskly she stepped over to the window, a small rectangle flanked by white cotton curtains. She yanked up the slatted blind. "That's four hours from now, Dad."

He narrowed his eyes, focused on her.

"Okay, okay, I'm going." She retreated.

He deposited the coffee and the doughnut on the dresser next to the glass that Gerald Spencer had removed from his hand last night. He squinted at the glass. There was still a good inch of bourbon left in it. He lowered the blind that Harriet had so fiercely raised. Then, in guilty concession to his daughter, he adjusted the slats, permitting thin strips of daylight into the room. He tried the bathroom again. This time his plumbing cooperated. He drank two more glasses of water and chased them with the leftover bourbon. (No point in letting perfectly good whisky go to waste.) He thought about a shower. Instead he gently lay back down on the bed, keeping one foot on the floor as an anchor.

Just before noon he was wakened again, this time by the sharp ring of the telephone beside his bed. The telephone was a low-end reproduction of the kind of phone Jean Harlow might have used in a bedroom scene. Out of this white, gold-trimmed machine, an eager-beaver male voice identified himself as Agent somebody or other with "the investigation." Jack didn't catch the name. The agent apologized for intruding "at a time like this," but they were hoping Jack would help them out.

"Sure," Jack croaked. He cleared his throat.

"We'd like you to answer a few questions about your grandson, if you don't mind."

He swung his legs over the side of the bed and sat up. "Shoot," he said.

"Mr. McCulloch, was Jim ever involved with drugs in any way?"

The question stunned Jack. "Drugs?"

"Did he ever experiment with marijuana, cocaine?"

"Not in my house!" Jack bristled. He heard silence at the other end of the line. "Not that I knew of," Jack said firmly.

"We're just trying to eliminate possibilities," soothed the agent. "Jim had no problem with substance abuse—that you know of?"

Jack remembered the reek of Indian incense wafting out from under Jim's locked bedroom door, the Visine bottles that kept turning up in odd places around the house—on the bookshelf above the stereo, in the pantry with the cereal—and the appalling surprise of the tiny bronze pipe he'd found one day rummaging through Jimmy's sock drawer looking for his own missing socks. When confronted, Jimmy had sworn up and down that the pipe was not his, swore he had no idea how it got there. Jack had not believed him. Nor had Mattie. But they never caught him. In any case, that was years ago, before he'd gone off to college. Jack cleared his throat, waking up yet another notch. "Jimmy was a good kid," he said.

"Would you say that growing up he was troubled by his parents' divorce?"

"No."

The man waited. Thin bars of sunlight from the window blind slanted across the varnished pine floor. "It was just the way things were," Jack said defensively. "It wasn't like they split up when he was nine, ten. The bum ran out on my daughter when Jim was a baby. He grew up with it."

"I see. How did he do in school?"

Jack hesitated. "Average," he lied. What was the guy after?

"Just a few more questions, Mr. McCulloch. We appreciate your assistance. Did he have any learning disabilities?"

"Nothing that a good smack on the behind couldn't fix."

"What about pets? Did you have a dog, a cat?"

Jack blinked. "No cats. Two dogs. Retrievers." He searched his memory. "Hamsters, tropical fish."

"Did you have any kind of problem with them?"

"The goddamn fish never lasted, I can tell you that."

"What about the hamsters, the dogs?"

"What do you mean?"

"Did he treat them well?"

"Like any kid," Jack said impatiently. "You had to beat him over the head to get him to feed them. What's going on here?"

"We're just trying to get some background, Mr. McCulloch. Did Jim ever have a problem with enuresis?"

"With what?"

"Did he wet his bed?"

Jack felt his blood turn to ice. The top of his scalp prickled. In one motion he slammed down the phone and stood up. "Jesus fucking Christ," he roared to the polished walls. The exertion left him feeling faint. He steadied himself on the dresser, then lowered himself back onto the bed.

33

Just before noon on Sunday, September 1, while Jack McCulloch was talking on the phone in his cabin, Mattie and Spence met in the hotel's lobby and took stools at the empty end of the bar. Mattie, who had spent the morning up at the Meander Campground trying to unearth new clues, ordered a diet cola and club sandwich. Spence ordered a martini with olives. They were served by the hotel's co-owner, a cheerful woman with a cascade of gray hair flowing from a purple plastic clip. She mixed Spence's martini and expertly poured it into a stemmed glass that looked large enough for three drinks. Spence felt he deserved it: he had spent the morning crammed into a phone booth at the back of Sophia's general store. He raised the glass to Mattie. "Cheers," he said ironically. He took a careful sip.

Mattie looked at her soda. The prospect of lifting it up to match his toast seemed too large an effort. She found it impossible to believe that in a few hours she would be attending a memorial service for Jimmy. The proprietor disappeared into the kitchen. "So what did you find out?" she asked Spence.

He replaced the glass on the bar. "Basically, that Rusty Stanislaw is an odious human being." Stanislaw was the waspish little man who, the night before, had cornered Celia over Pami Gustavisson's insurance.

"Surprise, surprise."

"He's got a horse ranch somewhere up near Shelby. By all

accounts, Pami virtually ran the place for him, and apparently on slave's wages, so he was not happy when she decided to try her hand at fighting wildfire. Last April, just before she left, he got her to take out a quarter-million-dollar life-insurance policy. The agent who wrote it up for them is an old chum from Great Falls who also writes the Stanislaws's health insurance. Rusty neglected to mention that Pami was going off to fight fires. The deal was, Rusty would make the payments, and if anything happened to Pami, he and his wife would collect. According to the agent, Pami had no objections to naming the Stanislaws as beneficiaries since she had no blood relatives and she supposedly felt an obligation toward the Stanislaws, especially Mrs. Stanislaw, who has MS and is confined to a wheelchair.

"But here's the rub: The Stanislaws's medical coverage had been dropped in March, just a few weeks before he persuaded Pami to sign on the dotted line. It was the fourth time he'd been dropped, thanks to Mrs. Stanislaw's progressively deteriorating condition. She requires round-the-clock attention, a good measure of which Pami provided pro bono, according to one of her friends. Rusty, however, was determined to keep his wife at home and had already mortgaged their ranch to the hilt to pay for her care."

Mattie sat up, interested. She felt her brain working again, making connections.

"The unfortunate woman would probably be better off in a nursing home," Spence went on. "Pami confided to her friend that Rusty was abusive toward his wife."

"Physically?"

"Is punishing her for soiling her bed by making her wait to have it changed physical abuse or mental?"

"He's our torch?" she demanded, jumping ahead.

He shook his head, took another sip of his martini. "He had a quarter-million-dollar motive. However, as it happens, on Friday, the day of the blowup, he was home all day. The wife's caretaker vouches for him. She comes in at nine in the morning, attends to Mrs. Stanislaw, fixes her lunch and usually leaves around one in the afternoon, after she's cleaned up the kitchen. On Fridays, he's supposed to pay her, but he had missed the previous week, so she was hanging around, waiting for her check. Finally, at two-thirty, she marched out to the corrals and confronted him. He came back to the house with her and wrote it out for her. Of course it bounced."

"You talked to her."

"At length."

"The Copper Creek fire was started around two. You're saying that at two-thirty, Rusty Stanislaw was at home with his wife and the caretaker?"

"Right. Over two hundred miles away. There's no way he could have dropped a match at Copper Creek."

"He could have hired someone," she objected.

"Believe me, Mattie, the man's tighter than a tick. He had me pay for his breakfast, then pinched every last packet of sugar on the table—and all the cream to boot. You heard him last night, how he wasn't going to pay for Pami's funeral. Never mind the fact that he's hoping to get a quarter-million out of her demise. I can't believe he'd pay someone else several thousands dollars when he could have done it himself for nothing."

She was reluctant to let it go. "I think you should tell Zampill."

"Why? He's not going to thank me for snooping around, especially since Stanislaw's a dead end. Besides, I don't want to get sued for slander—and don't think that little turd wouldn't jump at the chance. I'm certainly not about to put the family fortune within his reach. Enid would divorce me if her supply of Italian marble dried up."

Was he serious? She felt an acute pang of disappointment. For a moment, she almost hated him.

"Mattie, at the time of the blowup, there were two thousand firefighters in the immediate area, all with access to radio information on Pami's whereabouts and movements. If the fire was set to kill her, any one of them had more opportunity than Rusty Stanislaw."

She stared at her soda. "I suppose you're right," she said politely.

He leaned closer, lowered his voice. "I promise you, we'll find out who did this." Despite herself, she was stirred by the passion in his voice. She remembered the bandanna-covered lamp beside their bed, remembered the way he had felt inside her. She felt confused, as if a rosy sexual fog had permeated the crevices of her brain. Where did the pleasures of sex end and the pain of loss begin? She could discern no line between them. They spiraled together through her being, at once descending and ascending, a labyrinth without direction. She felt suddenly dizzy. She reached out and steadied herself on the bar. Her hand, pale on the darkly varnished wood, looked like a stranger's.

"You all right?" Spence worried.

"I think so."

Her sandwich arrived, along with a knife and fork tightly swaddled in a green paper napkin. As ordered, the basil mayonnaise was on the side, in a little stainless-steel cup. Darkly crisp edges of bacon and pretty green ruffles of lettuce poked out of golden triangles of toast. Her mouth began to water. None of my apetites seem to be suffering, she thought grimly. "I'll split it with you," she offered Spence.

But before either of them could take a bite, Harriet hailed them from across the lobby. Trailing two other women, she joined them at the bar and eyed her sister's club sandwich. "That looks good."

Mattie did not offer her a bite. She recognized one of the women with her sister: Greta Lowry, Wade Lowry's widow. Mattie had met her at the pool the night before. Greta and Harriet were wearing identical white T-shirts with their jeans. They might have passed for mother and daughter, Mattie thought. Harriet stretched out the front of her T-shirt to display a rectangular picture. "What do you think?" she asked Mattie.

The picture was bordered in deepest black. Inside the mournful frame, five firefighters walked into a peach-colored fire. Or was it a sunset?

"I didn't know whether you'd want one or not," Harriet fretted.

Mattie stared in disbelief at the image on her sister's T-shirt. Five victims. Four marching shoulder to shoulder, one off to the side and a step behind. Was that supposed to be the Indian? The man on the prison crew? She felt a surge of outrage. She wanted to grab the cotton neckband in both hands and rip the image down the middle. A souvenir of Jimmy's death! Harrie had no idea what had happened on that mountain! Not even an inkling! How could she be so, so—

She heard Spence and Harriet making introductions. "This is Cat Carew's mother," Harriet said.

Mattie wrenched her attention off the T-shirt and onto a woman in her early fifties wearing a caftan of gauzy cotton hand-screened with clouds in lavender, lilac, and pink. She appeared to have just come out of the spa: her face was flushed, her wet cherry-tinted hair was pulled back into a stubby ponytail fastened with a Navajo silver barrette. On her fingers she wore a dozen silver rings.

"Please call me Don," the woman said. Her voice was as soft and floaty as her caftan, though beneath the gauzy drapery, her body looked substantial enough, a chunky black spandex block.

"Don?" Spence repeated.

She smiled, met his eyes. "Actually, it's Don Star. But on this plane, most people just call me Don." She pulled out a business card and gave it to him.

Spence read it and passed it on to Mattie. It said:

DAWNSTAR
Psychic, Crystal Healer
Channeling, Tarot Readings, Medicine Wheels
By appointment

The address was an apartment complex in Idaho Falls. Mattie pocketed the card and gave Dawn Carew one of her own.

"I'm so glad to meet you," oohed the psychic. "Really, I think it's just so wonderful the way everything has unfolded!" She laughed with childlike delight. "Like my taxi driver. I really had no idea how I was going to get here, but Joseph was very firm with me. 'Call a taxi,' he said. So I did, and the nicest man appeared and said he was just getting off work and would be glad to drive me himself—all the way at no charge! He said he was just happy to help out, that he knew what it was like, his own daughter passed over thirteen years ago. She was only five at the time, but Joseph was able to recognize her and make the contact. The poor man was so grateful. 'You were sent to me,' he told me."

She beamed at Mattie. "This is such an adventure! I have no idea how I'm going to get back, but like I used to tell Cat when she was a little girl, 'Darling, we must *trust.*' " Her eyes focused on the top of Mattie's head, as if an insect were hovering over her hair. "You must learn to trust, Mattie," she said sadly. The rebuke of a disappointed mother.

"Me?"

"I can see your heart is troubled." She lifted a hand, made a slight caress in the air, describing the curve of a troubled aura. She shook her head. "You must be patient. I know it is hard to wait, but believe me, it's for the best. It's too soon to contact them now, it's not safe yet." She gave Mattie a sympathetic smile. "These sudden passages are tricky, but Joseph will bring them through. 'Mother, do not weep.' That's what he said. And just think of all he went through, the dear man. No, I have every confidence in him. Soon they will bloom into the light. Soon they will know the most blissful peace." She sighed in envy. "Well," she said, briskly changing gears, "I don't want to intrude. I know sisters need to talk. Come along, sweetie," she said to Greta, "we must nourish *our* poor bodies!"

Harriet said to Mattie, "The woman's insane."

Spence said to Mattie, "A discerning eye, your sister."

Mattie said in bewilderment, "Joseph?"

"Chief Joseph. Her spirit guide," Harriet explained.

"*The* Chief Joseph?"

"One and the same."

Spence took a sip of his martini. "One would have thought he'd have gotten a better break in the Happy Hunting Grounds."

Mattie frowned. "What do you mean?"

"After the Trail of Tears, the guy is assigned to a lunatic white woman?"

"I've got to go do something with my hair before the memorial service," Harriet announced. "Will you check on Dad?" she asked Mattie. "Make sure that he's ambulatory? I poked my head in there earlier and almost had it bit off." She cast a look of longing at Mattie's sandwich. Leave, Mattie thought.

But Harriet kept hovering. "By the way, have you heard from Eddie?"

"Eddie?"

Harriet glanced at Spence. "Your husband," she said to Mattie. "Is he coming?"

"My ex-husband. I have no idea if he's coming. I haven't spoken to him." A thought occurred to her. "Did you?"

Harriet shook her head.

A hideous thought occurred: Had Eddie and his new fourth wife been notified? Surely Celia DeJesus had called him, just as she had called the rest of the parents. Hadn't she? What if Celia had misunderstood? Mattie had volunteered to take charge of notifying her own family. What if Celia thought that meant Eddie, too? In a rush of panic, she forgot the T-shirt, forgot her anger at Harriet. Did Eddie even know about Jimmy? "Excuse me," she said to Spence and Harriet. "I've got to make a call."

The pay phone in the lobby was occupied. She hurried out to her car to use the radio. Ten sweaty minutes later she got through to Celia DeJesus at the Command base. To her enormous relief, she learned that yes, Celia had notified Eddie and that he planned to attend.

"Is your pager working?" Celia asked. "I've been trying to raise you."

"I turned it off."

"I need to talk to you. Something's come up."

"Yes?"

"Not on the radio. I need to see you before the memorial service."

Mattie thought of her sandwich waiting on the bar. "I copy. I'll get out there early," she promised Celia.

34

01 Sept 1:40p   Directory C:*.*

Her ashes keep dancing back. I've got these weird black flecks in the corners of my vision, sort of like holes in the skin of the universe—probably just stress. I keep going back to that time we had under the eaves in her bedroom, the circle of candles flickering on the floor, the smell of beeswax like in a church, and cutting drafts of cold when she threw open the window. She was standing naked in front of it, broad daylight, and I gave it to her from behind, her nipples cold as ice. January. Yes, because Margaret flew east for her dad's funeral. I said I couldn't go. Second week in January, talk about free fall. At night the candles made the walls and ceiling move like water. I told her about Mother. Her eyes were half-mast, like a priestess in a trance. She lay back on the mattress, opened her legs. She said, Show me. Show me what she made you do. Do it. Do it.

35

The Forest Service's memorial was scheduled for three o'clock at the bottom of the Copper Creek drainage where the five firefighters had died. The matchsticklike tangle of wind-snapped lodgepole pines had been bulldozed into piles to provide parking and a cluster of funeral-parlor tents had been set up to shelter the families and visiting dignitaries from a hazy sun. Out in front of the tents, a warlike array of media cameras faced a makeshift podium with swags of red-white-and-blue bunting. Behind it, five white poles had been raised to fly five American flags which fluttered lightly at half-mast against the blackened backdrop of the drainage. At distant intervals on the slope, small white crosses marked the sites where the victims had fallen. A slow, irregular procession of mourners climbed the network of baked red paths to leave flowers or kneel in ashes beside the crosses.

As she had promised Celia, Mattie arrived almost an hour early, leaving Spence to drive Jack and Harriet in his rental. She found Brian on the podium, his staff trailing behind him as he moved between the chairs, straightening the rows, issuing last-minute orders, answering a flurry of questions. "Brian," she interrupted. "Have you seen Celia?"

"Sorry." He gave her shoulder a sympathetic squeeze, but his eyes were preoccupied. "Try Mike," he suggested.

She spotted Mike's white cowboy hat under the tents. He

was standing with Frank Cicero and a slight, wiry woman in a pretty print dress. Neither chief had seen Celia.

"Have you met my wife, Annie?" Frank said stiffly.

Mattie shook hands. Annie Cicero had smooth olive skin, an arched nose, and soft hazel eyes. "You doing okay?" she asked.

"So far."

"The worst of it must be not knowing."

What was she talking about? The men looked away, embarrassed.

There was a commotion in the parking area. A pair of deputies were helping a woman in a prison jumpsuit out of the back of a patrol car. She had a chain around her waist with a loop that linked the steel cuffs on her wrists her ankle. Long black hair fell down her back. "Who's that?" Mattie asked.

"Angela Leonard," Mike answered. "The Leonard kid's mother."

Mattie blinked. "What'd she do?"

"Murdered her sister. Stabbed her through the heart in an alcoholic blackout."

Mattie let out a breath. "Speaking of sisters, I'd better go find mine," she said with grim humor. "Nice to meet you," she told Annie. She turned to Mike. "Is Peggy here?"

Mike looked at her, and for a moment Mattie wondered if she'd gotten the name wrong. It was Peggy, wasn't it? Blonde, chunky, wise-mouthed—Peggy?

Then Mike said brusquely, "She couldn't make it. She's been staying with her mother."

"Give her my best."

"I'll do that."

She felt that he wouldn't. Were the Robucks having problems? She hoped not.

The gathering grew. Children ran loose around the tents and a brass high school band from Butte struck up a dirgelike march. The music was lugubrious and occasionally off-key, but the instruments gleamed in the soft white sunlight and the solemn sweetness of the treble notes loosened the dense heaviness around her heart. She felt hot tears well up in her eyes. Oh, Jimmy, she grieved.

Colors blurred—the red-white-and-blue of the flags, the yellows and reds of the late-summer bouquets left on the blackened pitch, the Crayola assortment of team T-shirts and helmets. She imagined Jimmy looking down from the white hazy sky and seeing them, a gathering of his friends and comrades-in-arms, a fire-family affair, casual and brave. Her tears brimmed over, tickled wetly as they threaded their way down her cheeks. She reached under her dark glasses and wiped them across her cheekbones.

What would she and Jack do for Jimmy's funeral back in Missoula? Would her father insist on a requiem mass? She doubted Jimmy had been inside a church since her mother's funeral. That had been held at Saint Francis Xavier's on Pine Street. Although she herself was scarcely a regular, the brownish light inside the church, together with its late-Victorian murals, had always struck her as oppressive. The thought of Jimmy lying in a polished coffin in the nave hit her like a thud of earth. If only it could have been me! A slow bubble of despair rose within her, broke at the back of her throat, a small choking sound.

Keep it together! she ordered. Where was Spence?

She found him with Harriet and Jack under one of the tents. He met her eyes over her sister's head and the intensity in them sent an edgy thrill through her. Their bed of roses. She tried to shut the door on it.

"Dad," she greeted. Her father was red-eyed, straight-backed in the same suit he'd worn to his wife's funeral, and dangerously silent. Experienced in his ways, she ignored him.

She turned to her sister for a ritual embrace. Harriet was wearing a beige summer dress trimmed with black, and black patent-leather heels. Her suburban look, the way her pretty shoes and stockings were dusted with ash, suddenly made Mattie feel protective, grateful for her sister's presence.

"Mattie," Spence was saying. "I think I spotted an old Agence France buddy. If you don't need me . . ."

She looked at him, confused.

"From Vietnam," he said significantly.

"Sure. No problem." Vietnam? What the hell did that have to do with anything? She wanted him to enfold her in his arms.

"Be back in a sec," he assured her.

Harriet leaned in. "Did you see Eddie?"

"No. He's here?"

"Behind you. To the left. Don't look now, he's looking right at us. His new young thing is wearing a veil."

"Excuse me?"

"Like Jackie Kennedy wore. Deepest black, head to toe. She never even *knew* Jimmy!" Harriet hissed angrily.

Mattie turned and saw her ex-husband and his new wife walking toward them. He had lost weight since the last time she'd seen him and some of his old handsomeness had returned. She left the tent to meet him away from Harriet and Jack. "Hello, Eddie," she said. They pecked at each other's cheeks. Like a pair of old hens, she thought.

"You're looking good," Eddie said.

"So are you."

"This is Melinda," he said, putting a proprietary arm around her waist.

Under the black scrim of her veil, which fell from a tiara of black straw, Melinda looked impossibly young, closer to Jimmy's age than Eddie's. Mattie was not particularly surprised to see that Eddie's latest trophy was a redhead. Auburn under her veil and luxuriant enough for a shampoo commercial. She remembered Eddie's long-ago delight in her own flaming tresses and sighed inwardly. At least her name isn't Matilda, she consoled herself. Against all odds, Eddy's second wife had also been a Matilda. "Tilly," she had called herself.

"I'm so . . ." Melinda squeaked wetly under her veil. Her shoulders began to shake.

Eddie squeezed her closer. "She's terribly upset by all this," he informed Mattie. His tone was gravely accusatory, as if his ex-wife were to blame for Melinda's maidenly distress. He loosened his grip on her waist, comforted her with strokes on her behind.

Looking away, Mattie spotted one of Brian's aides leading Smokey the Bear toward her. Smokey? she thought irritably. What was he doing here? A small crowd of excited children danced around him, calling out his name. In the hearts of American schoolchildren, Smokey is second only to Santa Claus, but Mattie was not one of the millions of his fans. The bear's phenomenal success in instilling a fear of wildfire in the public mind made it almost impossible for her to shake loose funding for the extensive kind of prescribed burns that would reduce the incidence of superfires—fires like the Justice.

"Oh, look," groaned Melinda, "Smokey's wearing a black armband!" Her veil quivered. A loud sob escaped.

Eddie glared at Mattie. "Maybe a glass of water. Is there any water here?"

"Try the ambulances," she suggested. Was Smokey's black armband a local improvisation or an official statement? The bear lumbered toward her, turning from side to side with each step, scanning his surroundings through an opening under the bear's mouth. He waved in her direction. His entourage of entranced children tugged at his denim pants, clung to arms. His escort, a young man in fire clothes whom Mattie didn't recognize, tried to clear his path. Adults gathered to watch. Restlessly, Smokey shifted from side to side like a bear about to charge. A small Indian boy tugged on Smokey's arm. "Are you one of Smokey's friends?" Smokey asked in a friendly basso rumble. "What do you do if you find a match?"

"Throw it in the toilet!" yelled one excited child.

Smokey gave his big, shaggy head a slow shake.

"Give it to an adult!" called another child.

"Ve-erry good," praised the bear. "If you find a match, give it to an adult."

Mattie wondered who had drawn the short straw and ended up inside the suit. Years before, she had done her own turn as Smokey and she had almost suffocated under all the fur and foam padding. It had been hard to see out, hard to make oneself heard. This Smokey, however, appeared to be equipped with some kind of state-of-the-art voice amplifier. The costume looked brand-new, its brown fur was still fluffy, still had a synthetic glint. Whoever was wearing it was shorter than most Smokeys. His clean dungarees had been rolled up into cuffs that sagged onto his furry feet.

Smokey's escort trotted over to her with a message. "Mattie? Smokey wants to see you."

"Sorry," she said. "I'm really not up to it."

A boy jumped on Smokey's back, almost toppling him. "Uh-oh," said the escort. He ran back to his charge, plucked the boy off his back, steadied the staggering bear. Clumsily, Smokey patted a few heads. "What does Smokey say?" he asked in his deep masculine voice.

"Only you can prevent forest fires!" his fans chorused jubilantly. A small girl burst into tears. Mattie saw Ivan Wilkie wade in and pluck her out of the fray.

Smokey waved at her, beckoning her over. Mattie waved back but stood her ground.

"Mattie!" the bear growled. "I need you."

"Mattie, Mattie!" chanted the children.

Whoever the asshole is, he's going to *pay*, Mattie thought savagely. She walked over to him. "Hello, Smokey," she greeted.

He latched on to her arm. "We need to talk."

In a steely sotto voce, she ordered, "Remove your paws from my arm."

"We need to talk," he repeated.

"Another time, Smokey."

"NOW!" he roared, startling the onlookers into stunned silence. He released his hold on Mattie's arm, shifted back into friendly-and-firm. "Okay, kids," he intoned in a dignified manner. "Smokey has some work to do. Smokey has some important business with this firefighter here. But my friend TJ—" he gave his escort a kingly clap on the shoulder "—TJ has a special coloring book for each and every one of you."

Mattie led the bear out of earshot. "What is going on here?" she demanded angrily.

"I'm sorry, I tried to page you. Did you turn your pager on?"

The bear's words tumbled out. He sounded like a truck rolling down the interstate. "Who *are* you?" Mattie burst out.

"Mattie, it's me, Celia."

"Celia?"

"Yes!" exclaimed the bear in his basso. "And there's something I must—"

"Celia DeJesus?"

"Yes, yes, it is me in here!"

"This is ridiculous! You're not Celia. You don't sound anything *like* Celia. You're not even a *woman*!"

"You must believe me. Please, Mattie. I'm talking into a machine. It lowers your voice." The bear's brown eyes looked sorrowful.

A trick of light, Mattie thought. The bear's eyes, after all, were only glass.

"Listen to me," Smokey pleaded. "I am sorry to tell you this. But you need to know. It's about your son."

"Jimmy?"

"Yes. The autopsy reports came in. They asked me to tell you. The body they thought was Jim's?"

"Yes?"

"It wasn't."

"Excuse me?"

"It wasn't Jim. It was the trusty, Billy Dallas. The man driving the pickup. They think he ran up the drainage—you know, trying to escape the fire."

"Celia?" Mattie asked in bewilderment.

"I am very sorry, Mattie," Smokey growled softly. "Your son is missing."

36

Missing. Under the funeral awning, Mattie sat in her folding chair with her boots planted apart on the ground, hands resting on the tops of her thighs, back and neck as straight as a carved pharaoh's. Governor Bob Crispin was delivering his eulogy in flamboyant oratorical gusts and the mourners under the tent shifted in their seats like boughs in an unsteady wind, but Mattie and her family sat motionless, eyes unseeing. Missing. She had managed to break the news to them, and to Eddie as well, before the service began. By the time she got to Eddie, the governor's helicopter was descending, roaring over their heads, and she had had to shout it in his ear. "It was not Jimmy's body," she had bellowed. "He's missing!"

Eddie had said nothing.

Melinda, the new wife, held on to her veil with both hands and leaned into them. "But what does that mean?" she had yelled.

"I don't know," Mattie shouted back.

Now the McCulloch family was sitting in their chairs listening to Governor Bob tell a story about hunting elk in "these beautiful mountains." His voice trembled with emotion and several times he stopped—agonizing hiatuses that transfixed his listeners, stopped their communal breath like a paralyzing sting. The governor wiped his eyes with his knuckles. Mattie suspected he was the sort of man who cried at the movies. She was having a hard time making sense of his speech. "I held the still heart of the elk in my hand," Governor Crispin stated. Was he making some sort of personal confession? He seemed to be comparing "the heart of the warrior" (his own heart or the elk's?) to the "hearts of these heroic young men and women."

Were they heroic? Wade Lowry, certainly. He had deployed his shelter, apparently with the intention of getting Pami Gustavisson into it. At the cost of his own life, Wade Lowry had remained with the rookie. Never mind that the fire's wind had blown it out of his hands; the heat in that area had been too intense for survival even inside a shelter. The flashy fuels along the creek—the cheatgrass and fescue and head-high brush fed by spring runoff, then parched by summer sun—had exploded and roared up the drainage like a chimney fire. Ivan Wilkie had said the foil on Wade Lowry's shelter had delaminated and melted, indicating temperatures up to 1600 degrees Fahrenheit.

Clearly Wade's decision, his turning toward Pami had been heroic. Or perhaps "reaction" was a better word than "decision." How conscious had his choice been? No matter, the reaction of Hallihan, the inmate squad leader, had been exactly the opposite: to get out. Like Wade below him, Hallihan had had a radio. He had heard the warning. But he had not attempted to warn his teammate, Manny Leonard, below him; Hallihan had fled up to the top in time to deploy his shelter in the safety zone.

And what about the others who had died? Manny Leonard had run up the east side of the drainage. He had tried to enter the Carew girl's shelter and ended up killing them both. As for Carew, she had been carrying a handset, too. Had she heard the warning? If so, had she tried to warn Jimmy and the trusty? Or had fear obliterated their existence? Mattie was not about to lay blame on any of them, but she saw nothing heroic about trying to save one's own life.

"... five heroic men and women who gave their lives in service to this beautiful mountain ..." the governor went on.

Had Jimmy died for the Frontier Mountains? More to the point, was he dead? She tried to ignore the hope, thin as a blade of green grass. Jimmy could not have survived the blowup. Sixteen hundred degrees Fahrenheit, she reminded herself, chanting it over and over like a mantra. Sixteen hundred degrees. Jimmy would have had no more of a chance of surviving than the convict whose body had been mistaken for his.

In a small, cerebral way, the mistake was a relief, like lifting a rug and finding the lost pieces of a jigsaw puzzle. There was the satisfaction of snapping them into place, of plugging up some of the holes in the picture. The misidentification explained why, for example, the body of firefighter number one, the body closest to the pickup, had been found without a shelter, without a helmet. Billy Dallas had been a driver, not a firefighter. He carried none of the groundpounders' required gear. The mistake also explained why the keys had been left in the truck's ignition. Billy Dallas had not walked out and hitched a ride, as Agent Chip Zampill had theorized. He had run from a fire whose advance through the woods had been hidden by the knob behind the staging area. Perhaps he had been napping while he waited with the 'shots' supplies. By the time the wall of multiplying fires was visible from the pickup, it was too late. Dallas was trapped. The wind was toppling flaming trees across the wagon track. He could not drive out, so he had bolted up the creekbed in a hail of burning pine cones and twigs. When grasses ignited, the fire took off after him, accelerating, according to preliminary estimates, from 120 feet per minute at the edge of the woods, to 600 feet per minute as it roared up the drainage. Hot gases roiling uphill ahead of the flames had overtaken him, whooshed over his head and swept up the front of his body, knocking him backward, burning the oxygen out of his lungs.

Now she could admit to herself what her father had voiced—albeit drunkenly—last night: Jimmy would have been found facedown. In a crisis, when rationality disintegrates, training kicks in, especially physical drills. As a member of a Type-I team, Jimmy was required to practice deploying his shelter until he could get in it in twenty seconds. If there had been no time to deploy fully, he would have been found facedown on the ground with the shelter over his head. And if the wind had torn it out of his hands, at least the shelter's plastic case, along with Jimmy's helmet and the remains of the water bottle on his web belt, would have been found near his body.

So where was he? Where did he fall?

She looked at the white crosses up on the blackened pitch, saw the scene flatten into a photograph on a cardboard jigsaw puzzle. Ivan Wilkie had filled in the pieces around the bottom cross, but higher up, there were large, jagged gaps. How far could Jimmy have run? How could the searchers have missed his body? Could he be lying unconscious out there, burned and barely breathing?

She thought of her dream, of the medieval-like procession of garlanded carts and the way Jimmy had been bandaged in a fetal knees-to-chin position. His dark hair had shone with health. Was the dream a message—the sort of message Mrs. Carew claimed to receive? Was Jimmy trying to let her know he was still alive?

Get a grip, she told herself angrily. Dawn Carew was pathetic, worse than pathetic. Mattie perceived that, under the swirling pastel clouds of her flakiness, she was a manipulator: at best a shrewd opportunist, at worst a predator who thrives on other people's catastrophes. The woman actually seemed to be enjoying her loss.

Mattie turned back to her dream, back to her insight that she had always been trying to "straighten out" Jimmy. But when it came right down to it, it wasn't so much Jimmy she had tried to straighten, as his path. Despite his love of compasses, he lacked personal direction. During high school he seemed to drift through life in large, lazy swirls, like Mrs. Carew's clouds. Now in his sophomore year at the university, he seemed to zig and zag, brilliantly aglow with enthusiasms that lasted scarcely any longer than a burst of lightning. He bounced from course to course, profligately dropping them, ignoring the requirements of his major and "auditing" courses like Elementary Greek for all of two weeks.

"I didn't have the luxury of changing my mind," she had objected.

"Ma," he had argued, "don't you want me to get the most for your money?" He had been serious—not flip—and his high sense of purpose had encouraged her. Still, she worried. When he had committed to the Millville 'shots for a second season, she had been relieved.

Of course, in real life, as in her dream, it was too late to direct him, to straighten him out. He was nineteen years old. She could withhold her money, withhold her approval, or keep on supporting him—whatever she did, she was left standing by an open window, watching him pass. The window in her dream had been small, with panes of wavy glass set in its mullions. An old window in a bare room. There had been no rugs, no furniture.

She felt a surge of sorrow, tamped it back down. Determinedly she plowed through the dream as if she were climbing out its open window. Never mind what it meant. Dead or alive, she knew Jimmy was out there. The whole business had been going on too long. The entrapment had occurred forty-eight hours ago. Neither the Forest Service's Emergency Investigation Team nor the state's homicide agents had given her any answers. It was time to find out what had happened to her son.

A woman on the platform was singing "Amazing Grace." Behind Mattie, someone was sobbing. She glanced at her father. His attention was focused on his hands in his lap. As was his habit when he was planning or plotting, he was absentmindedly pushing back the cuticle of one thumb with the nail of the other. Good, she thought, reassured that however sick last night's binge had left him, he was still functioning. She needed all the help she could get. Harriet would be all right and she knew she could count on Spence. What about Eddie? she wondered. By the time the brass band played Taps, she had formulated her plan of attack.

The search began just before five o'clock that afternoon as the tents and PA system were being dismantled. Brian, Mattie discovered, had issued a press release on the autopsy findings just before the service. The news spread quickly through the local grapevine and she had no trouble mobilizing volunteers to look for Jimmy's body. Ivan Wilkie and several of his EIT colleagues joined the hunt, as did Ned Voyle and a large off-shift contingent from Overhead. Teams of demobilized 'shots, waiting out the mandatory eight-hour rest period before departure to new assignments, volunteered along with the now officially debriefed Millville crew. Despite the grimness of the task, the bereaved 'shots were relieved by the prospect of "doing something to help."

They were joined by a delegation of men from the Circle Seven. The nudists had left both their weapons and their pants at home. They wore hiking boots, cowboy hats or baseball caps, and shirts that flapped carelessly around their naked loins. (Several removed their shirts as the search progressed, and the following year a *Billings Gazette* photographer's shot of a nudist walking in a search line of Nomex-clad grunts won first prize, professional category, in *Parade* magazine's annual "My Country, 'Tis of Thee" photo contest.)

Since law enforcement had already mounted two searches for Billy Dallas, both of which had covered more or less the same ground, Mattie decided not to waste time duplicating their efforts. Both the sheriff's search and Agent Burton's had started at the pickup and moved back up over the knob toward the Folly River, sweeping the burn on both sides of the wagon track. As Ivan Wilkie had discovered, in a burned landscape it was easy enough to "read" a charred body as a piece of tree, but the sheriff's party had included professional trackers and their dogs. If human remains had been in the area, the dogs would have picked up the scent. Furthermore, Agent Burton and the Evidence team from the lab in Missoula had gone over the terrain with the proverbial fine-toothed comb looking for footprints, dropped cigarette butts, or any other items that might point the way to Dallas's whereabouts. Since Ivan Wilkie had already covered the area along the creekbed where the bodies had been found, Mattie drew her starting lines above Ivan Wilkie's grid.

Mattie asked Mike Robuck to coordinate the search on the west slope of the drainage. She took charge of the effort on the opposite slope. Harriet and Eddie and his new wife went back to the hotel, changed into jeans and, along with Spence and Brian, joined her team. She found a handset for Jack and stationed him at the bottom of the creek, where, grid by grid, he recorded their progress on a map spread out on the hood of her Jeep.

The white haze of the afternoon thickened and bunched into nicotine-stained clouds. A lemony light slid over blackened snags, casting shadows on stone and ash. Although she found relief in the simple physical effort of maintaining the slow but steady pace of the search line moving up the slope, Mattie found it hard to concentrate on the ground around her. She kept looking up and down the line, waiting for someone to stop, waiting for someone to call out, for the line to halt, crumple and regather around—whatever it might be. She felt torn between twin dreads: finding Jim and not finding him. Which was worse? The stark fact of his death or merciless incertitude?

Despite the careful pace, she found she was sweating. Puffs of a rotten-onion stink came from her shirt. Her mouth tasted like ashes. Each time she saw a new shape in the blackened stubble, her heart jumped. Was that a branch—or an arm? A stone or a dropped canteen? She had the nightmarish feeling that her eyes were not seeing, that she had missed a vital clue. She felt the impulse to turn around and retrace her steps but was reluctant to break ranks, to leave a gap in the grim moving line. She picked out Spence, three people down, walking next to Eddie, both men totally absorbed in their respective patches of ground. Would Spence have been a better father than Eddie? Would Spence, given his career as a chronicler of wars, have been any more present?

She felt the breeze shift, caught the moldlike smell of retardant. The air was cooling, drifting down the drainage, shifting ash over the flowers piled around the crosses below. Jack raised her on the radio. "Agent Zampill's down here. Wants to talk to you."

She kept on moving, placing one ash-powdered boot firmly in front of the other. "Put him on."

But it was Jack who came back on. "He says he'll catch you after you finish."

Mattie scanned the drainage. The setting sun cast a rich ocher light over the top of the slopes, but the terrain along the creek was already in deep shadow.

Mike, over on the opposite slope, keyed in. "We're going to have to call it off pretty soon. The Air Ops charts put time of sunset at nineteen hundred fifty-one."

Mattie looked at her watch. It said seven-thirty. "Give me five more minutes." She kept her voice level. Inside, she felt a mounting panic. She knew she had to give the volunteers time to put off the slopes. They could not continue the search in the dark. The risk of injury was too great. A fall on this pitch could blow out a knee, break an ankle—or a neck. At the same time, she was gripped by the irrational fear that Jimmy might be alive and in need of immediate help. Please, she prayed, uncertain for what she was praying. *Please.*

But when the searchers descended, there was still no clue as to what had happened to Jimmy. What next? she wondered dully. What do we do now? Try again at dawn?

Frank Cicero drove in a load of prepackaged ice-cream cones and stood at the back of the truck, wreathed in smoke from dry ice, passing them out himself to the returned searchers. The civilians in the crowd took them politely. To them, the cones were merely ice cream—low-end ice cream at that. But to firefighters forbidden cold beer, ice cream in any form was the next-best thing. It was cold, sweet, and rare. In pulling a hundred cones out of dry ice, Frank Cicero had accomplished a miracle of wilderness logistics. Like a successful magician, he beamed with pleasure at his own trick.

Jack McCulloch refused the ice cream. His back was bothering him, he complained to his daughters. Defiantly, he added that he wanted a drink. Eddie offered to drop him and Harriet off at the hotel.

"You need a lift?" Eddie asked Mattie.

"I've got a vehicle." She glanced at her Jeep. Spence was waiting for her beside it. He had put on his jacket, a pale flag in the encroaching blue darkness.

"You staying at the hotel?" she asked Eddie.

"What's the point?" he asked bitterly.

Mattie felt like hitting him.

"Nice to meet you." Melinda extended her hand.

Mattie shook it automatically.

"We'll head on back to Billings, pick up a bite to eat on the way," Eddie informed her. "Keep us posted."

"Right," Mattie said. Beyond Eddie, she saw Agent Chip Zampill observing the family conference. She turned to her father. "I better go see what Zampill wants." An odd expression on her father's face made her ask, "You all right?"

"Jim-dandy."

The expression shocked them all. Jack blinked but did not apologize. "Come on, Daddy," Harriet said, her voice unsteady.

Jack growled, "For Chrissake, I'll be right there." Harriet and Eddie and Melinda retreated toward the parking area. Jack waited until they were out of earshot, then said to Mattie, "Some detective called me this morning. Didn't get his name." He told her about the call.

"He wanted to know if Jimmy *wet his bed?*"

"That's what I said," Jack snapped.

Mattie turned and saw Chip Zampill watching them. "This morning?" she asked her father. "Why didn't you tell me!"

"The blithering idiot woke me up. I went back to sleep and forgot about it. It didn't come back to me till after your friend Zampill came up to me, said he wanted to talk to you. Anyway, it made me think maybe they were going to try and pin the fire on Jim."

Mattie stared at her father. His eyes were hard, his mouth a tight, pained line. He was serious.

Finally she said, "Well, they're not going to."

She moved on to Zampill. He wanted to talk back at the Meander, so she and Spence followed the detective back to the command post. She dropped Spence off in the food area and met Zampill in his white tent. The flaps were down against the night, but Mattie was wearing only underwear beneath her Nomex and the metal chair Zampill offered her felt cold. A bare bulb hung overhead on an orange cord; glaring light bounced off the white vinyl-coated walls. Mattie was reminded of a butcher's white-tiled walk-in. She shivered as Zampill readied his tape recorder, droned her name, the date and time into it.

She took the initiative. "You know about Jimmy," she said.

"Yes."

"Did you call my father this morning?"

"Agent Orr talked to your father on the phone at noon."

"Whenever. We didn't know if it was you or the sheriff. My father was half asleep. Did you tape that conversation?"

On the other side of the table, Zampill leaned back in his chair, folded his arms across his chest. "No."

Mattie leaned back in her own chair, felt cold metal against her back, leaned forward again. She indicated the tape recorder in front of her. "Is this an interrogation?"

Chip Zampill's deadpan mask cracked at the corner of his mouth. He raised a humorous grizzled eyebrow. "If it is, I'm in the hot seat."

Mattie didn't smile.

He sat forward, hands on the table, as if ready to do business. "Mattie, you are a witness, not a suspect. We don't interrogate witnesses. We interview them. This is an interview."

"Is my son a suspect?"

"Have you heard from him?" Chip asked. His tone was mild, as if he were inquiring about someone away on vacation, but the question jolted Mattie.

"No," she said. She let out a nervous snort.

"What?"

She shook her head. "Nothing. It's just—I mean, have you met Cat Carew's mother?"

He had.

"She claims she's psychic. She talks about 'hearing' from the dead. For a second, I thought that's what you meant."

He shot her a sympathetic half-smile, then got back to business. "To answer your question: If Jim turns up alive, obviously we will want to talk to him."

But he had not answered her question. Was Jim a suspect? Had her father guessed correctly? "What is it you want to know?" she asked the detective.

Zampill pondered the question.

Impatient, Mattie burst out, "My son did *not* wet his bed! He did *not* kill small animals. He was perfectly *normal!*"

Zampill nodded and plodded on. "Did he like to set fires?"

The question exasperated her. "Every firefighter likes to set fires! That's the fun part. Fire is power. It's a tool. That's why we pack in fusees and drip torches along with chain saws and Pulaskis. You've heard about fighting fire with fire? Well, that's what I do, set prescribed fires. It's my job. I'm a burn-management specialist."

"I meant, when your son was a little boy. Did he set fires?"

"No," Mattie said stonily.

"I understand you used to take him out with you—on prescribed burns."

Where did he did dig *that* up? "I took him with me once. One time. My sitter was sick. I had to go check on a burn and

Dad was away. It was the middle of the night and I couldn't find anyone to take him. He stayed in my vehicle the whole time. There was no danger, the conditions were perfect, it was all under control. But it was against regulations. Someone reported me. I almost lost my job over it."

"How old was he?"

"Seven."

"Was that around the same time he got caught playing with a fusee in a neighbor's garage?"

Mattie felt a cold chill creeping up her spine. Whom had he been talking to? The neighbor had moved away years ago. She remembered the horror of the episode, the terror of what might have been: the garage exploding into flames, with Jimmy and his playmates trapped inside. The others had named Jimmy as the instigator and perhaps he had been. Perhaps he had boasted about his mother's fusees, the way another child might boast about his father's gun. He had admitted stealing the fusee out of her pack and had taken his punishment stoically. But one of the other mothers would not leave it alone. She had gone to the principal at Jimmy's school and alerted them to Jimmy's "deviant behavior." Had Zampill pulled Jimmy's school records? Did they still exist?

"That was in first grade," she said. "The principal insisted that Jimmy see a psychologist. So we took him to be tested. He came out *normal.*" In Mattie's opinion, it was the hysterical mother who needed help.

"He had no reading problems?"

"He was a slow reader," Mattie admitted cautiously. Which is why the book in his pack had surprised her: its dense, philosophical prose seemed an unlikely choice.

"What about his adolescence?"

"What about it?"

Chip shrugged. "How did he do in school?"

"He was an athlete. He was not academically inclined," Mattie said with dignity. She anticipated the next question: *An athlete who smoked marijuana?*

But Zampill surprised her. "Was he interested in pornography?"

Mattie stared at him.

"Did you ever find magazines in his room?"

"You mean dirty magazines under his mattress? No, I did not. He cleaned his own room. It was a household rule. Everyone cleaned their own room. Chip, what are you getting at?"

"I'm trying to find connections. Connections between the events. Two days ago, someone set a fire that killed five people. Yesterday, someone sent you a burned picture."

Mattie frowned. "Picture?"

"A crotch shot."

"Yes. I gave it to our Human Resource specialist." What did that have to do with anything? Why had Celia passed it on to Zampill?

Chip said, "I sent it up to Missoula for fingerprints. Shortly afterward, I learned that your son is missing. I'm wondering if he might have been the one who sent it."

"That picture?"

"Yes."

"You think Jimmy sent it to me? To his mother?"

Chip watched her with tired eyes.

"That is *sick*," she protested, her voice shaking. She stood up. "That is *really* sick!"

"Yes," he agreed. He coughed into his fist.

"Interview concluded," he droned into the tape recorder. "Nine-oh-five P.M." He turned off the tape and stood up. "Please report any contact from your son," he said. His voice wavered from the effort of suppressing another cough, but beneath the wobble, his warning was as steady as an anchor.

37

01 Sept 9:18p Directory C:*.*

Jesus, it really is amazing when you think about it objectively: Every time McCulloch turns around she makes my job harder! We get back from the great search and Ned goes, You okay?

I can see he thinks I'm teetering, that he's going to stow it away, a little ammo for Evaluation time. But I got him. Instead of brushing it off like he expects, I go belly-up, produce a secret sorrow for him! I tell him the sad tale of Margaret leaving, a sort of mid-life spasm, I say, like I'm embarrassed. I tell him I'm hoping for a reconciliation, so I don't want everyone to know, but he knows how it is, what with everything else on top of it, those poor kids—and now McCulloch's boy missing—I really pulled out the old violin! of course it worked, my CONfidence! He gets all gruff and paternal and there's no way he's going to go negative on me on paper. It's not like I haven't been doing my job, the prick, posturing around now that he's finally got Kingman's seat.

I have to admit, the business with the missing kid was a heart-stopper. No wonder I've got ashes in my peripheral vision! Bingo, all of a sudden I'm thinking could he have seen me? could he have been up there somewhere on the pitch and seen me dropping the match? Could he have seen the car? But it's okay, I know it's okay. Take my little valentine to our Incidental Cunt; I had no idea how my flash of singed pink was going to fit into the grand scheme of

Justice, but it did, *seamlessly*! It puts the finishing touch on her CLOUD, sicko son, sicko mom. If the shoe fits, ha-ha.

Christ. This is the first chance I've had to sit down since the fucking memorial service. I could use a drink—or three! I need to unwind, to catch my breath, to tune into the great design. A little weed would help too, a burnt offering, sacrificial smoke. Cat wasn't the sacrifice. I'm the sacrifice! Everything that lives burns. Cat's dead. It's the living who burn. We burn with the energy of the sun, burn our food into fuel, burn out. Moses saw that in the burning bush (as it were!)—yes! the bush as a living connection between heaven and earth. Cat knew that. She knew she was my connection. And then she defiled it. And the fire of justice, pure and true, consumed her. I just have to stay with it, stay relaxed but alert. I'll deal with the ashes later, see a neurologist if I have to; it could be some kind of nervous symptom, pressure on the optic nerve, all the stress. Blinking doesn't help, but when I focus on the distances, they sort of contract a little, the spots, the little tears shrink a little.

So: a lesson there. Stay focused on the distance, the Big Picture. God is NOT in the details! Nobody's perfect, you make slips. At the service yesterday, La Carew floats over to me and goes on with all this shit about Cat dying a happy hero and I go, Yes, she was a lovely person, in the same vein. I mean I'm picking it up from the mother, her brainless hum, and she looks at me sharp—honest to God, it was like Cat looking at me!—she gives me this look and says, You knew her, then? By reputation, I go, without missing a beat. But I can still see Cat looking at me! Shit like that. It's a dangerous time. You can't blink.

38

Back in their rosy B&B, Mattie and Spence lay stretched out on the top of the bed, side by side, arms folded across their chests. Like a long-married couple who had kicked off their shoes and turned on the TV in a strange motel room, they were still in their clothes, Mattie in dusty fire clothes, Spence in his shirt sleeves—jacket on the back of the chair. The remote lay between them on the rose-covered spread. On the late news, the Copper Creek fatalities were still the top story, but the actual footage of that afternoon's memorial service was cursory, only a few long pans of the gathering, no close-ups of weeping faces, no sound bites of the governor's speech. The anchor devoted a full minute to the disappearance of Jim McCulloch and promised an "in-depth analysis of the tragedy" on the "Dean Dowell Show" immediately after the news.

After the weather, sports, and commercials for Preparation H, Slim Fast, Toyota, and Coca-Cola, Dean Dowell's famous head appeared against a backdrop of city lights. An aging man with boyishly thick brown hair, Dowell welcomed a psychologist "who will join us via satellite from an affiliate studio in Richmond, Virginia. Dr. Louis Galloway is a consultant for the Behaviorial Sciences Unit at the FBI Academy in Quantico, Virginia."

"Good evening, Dean," said the psychologist from a giant-sized screen. He was younger than Dean by some, but had less hair. He wore a dirty-looking Irish fisherman's sweater, as if he'd just come indoors from some manly exertion. Mattie thought he looked more like a horse trainer than a psychologist.

"Dr. Galloway," said Dean, "will you please fill our viewers in on the profile of the so-called 'fire buff' arsonist?"

Dr. Galloway cleared his throat importantly. "First, I should point out that our sample population in this category are volunteer and would-be firefighters. The young man in question, Jim McCulloch, is a paid professional. However, there are interesting cross-correspondences."

Mattie and Spence both sat up in horror as the expert psychologist described Jimmy as fitting the profile of "an inadequate, attention-seeking male who craves the heroic activities of firefighting."

"Regarding the rearing environment," Dr. Galloway went on, "several fire setters in our sample were sons of firefighters or police officers and felt they could not measure up to the father. They had strong ties, however, to the mother."

"In this case," the famous anchor interrupted smoothly, "both parents were firefighters, but the mother was the dominant figure. The father left the marriage early. Would this have encouraged young Jim's sense of inferiority?"

"Possibly." Galloway nodded gravely. "I should point out that the personality of the solitary fire setter manifests more neurotic characteristics and individual psychopathology than those who engage in group fire-setting."

"*Group* fire-setting?" Spence sputtered. "What the hell is that?"

"Shh." Mattie turned up the volume.

"Our sample," Dr. Galloway explained, "showed that delinquent behavior during adolescence was common. In adulthood, we found the need to join fraternal organizations and, of course, a great need for social drinking."

"Thank you, Doctor," Dean Dowell intoned.

"My pleasure," said the doctor.

"Assholes!" Mattie declared angrily. She stabbed at the remote. The TV went blank. Ignoring Spence's consternation, she put on her boots, washed her face, and brought her briefcase in from the Jeep. She moved methodically, deliberately, husbanding the fury within her, trimming its wick to a slow, steady burn. She took out her calculator and spread her maps and her notes out on the coffee table.

For the next two hours she juggled all the information she had collected on the blowup: Ivan Wilkie's measurements and estimates, the reports from fire-behavior and weather specialists, testimony from witnesses on the ridge, transcripts of the radio transmissions, and the charts of her own search that afternoon. She worked equations for rates of feet per second for the fire's spread and for walking, power-hiking, and sprinting on various degrees of slope. She marked coordinates on her map and measured distances. And became increasingly agitated. If Jimmy had been at the bottom of the drainage, his body should have been found within the parameters already searched. Had he been incinerated to ash? Or had he reached the bottom of the drainage with the Carew girl and, for some inexplicable reason, kept on going out toward the road?

She retrieved Jimmy's map from his pack and opened it up, hoping for a clue, a penciled X to mark the spot—the spot of what? But the map was pristine, carefully folded to show the quadrant of the Copper Creek drainage. In sheer frustration, she emptied the pack: Jim's headlamp, his compass, earplugs, flagging, a signal mirror, lip balm, fusees, a lighter, a flattened roll of toilet paper, a small can of fruit cup, a ballpoint, a fireline handbook, the battered paperback copy of *Zen and the Art,* a disposable camera. Again, the acrid smell of the fire permeated the room. She began to cry. She let Spence undress her, lead her from her maps on the coffee table to the bathroom toilet, from sink to bed. Sobbing, she clutched at him as he steered her along. She moved in jerks and lurches, as clumsy as a child dancing on her father's shoes. Then she slept, dreamlessly and chastely between rose-patterned sheets.

As had frequently been the case during the past year, she woke at 4 A.M.—a sharp waking her gynecologist attributed to a natural ebb of estrogen. Spence, who had not yet adjusted to Montana time (at his apartment in New York he rose every morning at six to write), was also awake. They turned to each other in the dark and made slow, dolorous love. She felt herself opening around his hardness and, not surprisingly given the room's decor, the image of a rose came to mind. A skewered rose. It excited her. "Oh my God," she cried in abandon.

Afterward, as they lay together in the dark, the maps she had been staring at all day appeared on the screen of her mind. She saw the perimeters she had drawn in bright pink marker over the black elevation lines of her Xeroxed fire maps. She saw Jimmy's map, pale green with cinnamon-brown elevation lines. A broken black line indicated the wagon track. A small black dot on the west side of the drainage marked an adit.

She started. "An adit," she said out loud.

"Hm?" Spence murmured into the top of her head.

"An adit," she repeated. "The entrance to a mine. Sorry," she apologized as she disentangled herself from his limbs. "I've got to check something." She turned on the bedside lamp, got out of bed, and retrieved the actual maps. She spread them out on the bed and put on her half-frames and leaned over them, her nipples grazing the paper. "Look," she said. Using one forefinger to hold a spot on Jimmy's map, she tapped a spot on her map with the other. "You can see it on his map, but not on ours. On ours, it's blotched." She showed Spence a small blank spot the size of a thumbprint.

Spence put on his glasses. "Looks like the glass on your copier was dirty."

She straightened up. "But they must have searched there. Law enforcement was all over that area. They must have looked inside the mine." She shivered and climbed back under the covers and the maps.

Spence drew a finger down the drainage. "Copper Creek. A copper mine, presumably."

"Could they *not* have looked inside?" Mattie wondered out loud.

"You think he might have run into the mine?"

She told Spence about how Ranger Edward Pulaski had saved his men during the Great Fire of 1910. "Jimmy loved that story when he was a little boy. He made Dad tell it to him over and over."

She rechecked Jimmy's map, consulted her own. "The adit's up here." She showed Spence. "Up on this slope above the wagon track. Dallas drove right by when he brought in the supplies. Jimmy might have known the mine was there, but he would have had to run back into the fire to get to the entrance. And it wasn't like he didn't have a shelter. He would have been thinking about deploying his shelter, not the mine. He should have run with Carew and Leonard, up toward the talus. The slope is less steep, more open, there's less chance of getting hit by a snag."

"What if—" Spence mused, then broke off.

"What?"

"Suppose he was hanging out at the pickup, scarfing down melons with the trusty when he realized what was happening. What if Jimmy tried to lead Dallas to safety, like what's-his-name, his idol?"

"Pulaski." Mattie shook her head. "This isn't 1910. Jimmy would have deployed, gotten Dallas in his shelter with him."

"Not if Dallas looked at it and thought, No way. Not if he panicked and ran." He searched her eyes. "The way I tried to, if you remember."

"Then we would have found Jimmy *and* his shelter near the pickup," Mattie argued.

Reluctantly, she folded up her maps. She slid back down between the covers and lay staring at the ceiling. "I wonder which maps the sheriff's people used—theirs or ours."

"It doesn't make any difference," Spence said, smoothing

back a wayward curl of her hair. He was tempted to blow on it. Against the white pillowcase, it looked as if it might ignite.

"But it does!" she protested. "You couldn't see the adit on ours."

"It doesn't make any difference."

"And why not?"

"Because in either case, you need to see it for yourself."

She thought about it a long moment. "You're right," she conceded. She swung her legs out of the bed and stood up. "Come on," she said. "The sun will be up in less than an hour. Do you want the first shower?"

"Where are we going?"

She looked surprised. "To have a look at that mine."

39

Gerald Spencer, chronicler of wars, was no stranger to the sight of mothers searching through ashes for the remains of their sons. The rubble was usually more urban—piles of shattered concrete sprouting reinforcing wire instead of charred timber—and the women usually wore scarves wrapped around their heads and noses, not a molded orange helmet, but he felt the same sense of inadequacy as he hiked after Mattie up to the abandoned adit above the Copper Creek wagon track. It was not only her sturdiness, her numb determination that made him feel deficient. It was also his own difficulty in finding words to describe the devastation of the blowup. Leave aside her personal anguish. The physical scene of the tragedy was challenging enough. The pre-dawn twilight and the small craters left by uprooted trees suggested the word "moonscape"—which he immediately rejected as hackneyed and ridiculously inaccurate. There were no trees on the moon. "Ground zero" connoted explosive force, but a man-made impact, not the convective whirl of a fire storm. "Wasteland"? "Hades"? In fact, the ruined landscape felt eerily familiar, as if he were walking through an epic poem, a text studied long ago at wooden desks with inkwells. Tree trunks, bare of limbs, lay scattered across one another like—like what? Felled troops on a Homeric battlefield? The conceit pleased him. He toyed with it—then his censor snatched it away: For heaven's sake, the bodies in this catastrophe are not *trees*!

He followed her up the side of the drainage. She moved like an athlete in her fire clothes, setting a brisk pace, stepping lightly over and around the fallen trees. Spence counted himself in good shape (thanks to his workouts at his club back in New York) but he broke into a sweat keeping up with her, and the acrid morning air felt cold on his neck. He had a disconcerting sense of reversal: usually it was Enid lagging behind—when she bothered to accompany him on one of his rambles. Furthermore, although he and Mattie were moving uphill toward a dawning sky, the puffs of fine gray ash around their ankles made him feel as if they were sinking into a fog-strewn Underworld. Up was down. Even the lone brittle pines capriciously left standing had the reversed look of a photographic negative: brown bark had been burned black, dark needles were scorched brown.

"Snags," Mattie called the upright dead trees. She gave them a wide berth, instructed Spence to do the same. "They may look stable," she warned, "but you can't tell by looking. The roots may be burned away. They can coming crashing down on top of you at any moment—there's no warning. It's a major hazard for mop-up crews. 'Snag' is the gender-free term," she added with dry humor. "Old-timers call them 'widow-makers.' "

Snag, widow-maker, he repeated to himself, as if he were memorizing Latin vocabulary. Her humor reassured him. He had been reluctant to leave their bed of roses, but the excursion seemed to agree with her. He consoled himself for missed sleep with hopes for his new book. Since the blowup, random snatches of conversation, details, perspectives had been percolating furiously, like coffee over too high a flame. He had not yet discovered his purpose, not yet found a story in the bitter brew, but now that he was up and out of his warm bed, he felt a selfish little thrill of anticipation. The scene was a keeper: the mother hunting for her son in the cold light of dawn. If she found him, so much the better, a contemporary pietà, a virgin in a hard hat kneeling over the incinerated remains. For despite the full wanton pleasure she took in their lovemaking, he saw her as a virgin—not the victim-virgin with a lily clutched to her breast, but a warrior-virgin hefting a shield, a woman of power at once vulnerable and untouchable.

He inspected the charred log in his path (it was definitely a log) and stepped over it. Wherever her search for Jimmy took him, whatever role it would play in his book, he had no idea. The end wasn't important. What mattered was the process. He was *on,* working again, *alive.* Like the golden bird rising from its proverbial ashes, he was once again unfolding his wings.

A year and half before, in the gray of a Manhattan February, Spence had lunched with his literary agent, an elegant younger man whom success had made vain. During the course of the meal (stiff white tablecloth, heavy silverplate, a single stem of freesia in a cut-glass vase), Spence had complained about his writerly doldrums. He was tired of bleeding over wars no one read about. It was wearing him out. The agent, who regarded Spence as a charity case to begin with, had little interest in his client's personal problems. He poured himself another glass of excellent Merlot (Spence, being the supplicant, was paying) and somewhat impatiently suggested that a more popular approach to warfare would stand a better chance in the current marketplace. Thus, in a desultory fashion, Spence had conceived of a book about fire as a weapon. More out of habit than any sort of enthusiasm, he had started a notebook, clipped articles, browsed through library stacks, talked long-distance on the phone to former colleagues-in-battle, but he had gotten nowhere with his proposal, never mind a chapter outline.

Then, at the beginning of August, his researches had led him to the Justice—and serendipitously to Mattie, who had sparked his interest, fanned interest into inspiration. Then the blowup. He stopped to catch his breath, hand on uphill knee, leaning into the slope, and saw in his mind's eye a double helix superimposed over the blasted hillside: the shape of life. Was it the shape of his story? The trick was, he knew from experience, not to confuse the two.

Mattie was orienting herself with a compass and Jim's map, but they traversed the slope several times before she stumbled over a remnant of iron track on which the mine's cars had carried ore down to the wagon road below. The log beam over the mine's entrance had long ago collapsed, and the resultant fall of dirt and rocks had left only a crawl hole in the side of the hill. A slide of downed trees from above further obscured the entrance.

Mattie stood there studying it, saying nothing.

"Not exactly a landmark, is it?" Spence observed.

"He never would have found it," she said flatly. "Not with all the smoke. Not in a crown fire." She nudged a blackened trunk with her boot.

"Crown fire?"

"That's what it was, a running crown fire. It started in the grass along the highway, then hit the woods, leaped up into crowns of the trees and ran." She took a breath. "You were right. I needed to see this. There's no way he could have found it. Doesn't look like it was ever much of an operation."

"Well," Spence countered, "there was enough in there to warrant a tramway. They were getting something out of it."

"Copper?"

"Probably. At the end of the last century, there was a big demand for it. The country was going electric. Edison had invented the lightbulb, Morse the telegraph, Bell the telephone. Copper was king. But the market was monopolized by a bunch of copper barons in Boston who controlled the oldest, and richest, deposits in the country. Their mines were in Michigan. Then out here in Montana, the Anaconda Company discovered copper in their derelict silver mines and entered the game. East met West in a price war, the price of copper plummeted, and small players, like Thomas Foley of Folly River fame, went bust."

Mattie looked at him. "How do you know all this?"

"I read it on the back of the menu at the Hotsprings Hotel. I wonder if this one was his. The Gander Mine, it was called. As in 'What's sauce for the goose is sauce for the gander.' "

She shook her head, amused, but her eyes were distant and sad.

"As it happens," he prattled on in an attempt to divert her, "my own inheritance is derived from Michigan copper."

"Really?"

"Hmm," he assured her. "My 'mother lode,' Enid calls it—from my mother's side, you see. My father loved her money—and treated her very badly. Suffice it to say that when I finished school, I escaped to Oregon and the peripatetic life of a reporter."

"But you ended up back in the East."

"My father died. I went home to tidy up and met Enid. And there we are," he added lamely. He felt embarrassed, as if he'd said too much.

But she was interested. "What about your mother?"

"Oh, she's hanging in there. Eighty-eight years old and still sharp as a tack. Of course, she's got nurses round the clock, that sort of thing. Enid manages it all beautifully. They're quite close, Enid and my mother. Actually, when you get down to it, I'm rather superfluous."

Mattie smiled. "I'm sure you do yourself an injustice."

"Would it were so." He walked over to inspect the entrance. "Do you want to go in? Have a look?"

She hesitated. "Might as well," she decided. "As long as we're here. If you don't mind."

"No, no," he assured her, but the prospect of crawling back into the bowels of the hill, even for the sake of his book, made him cringe inwardly. Mattie, on the other hand, clearly wanted to plunge in.

She took out a pair of headlamps from her pack and handed him one. He put it on and scrambled after her over the rocks blocking the entrance. The tunnel was low, hand-dug, its crumbly walls and ceiling reinforced with timbers—ax-hewn from what Spence saw by the rays of his headlamp. The tracks were still in place in the dirt floor, which was strewn with piles of rusted-out cans, brown beer bottles, and flattened wads of toilet paper. The only smell was cold smoke. A whir of wings swooped past his ear. He swung violently aside, bumped hard into the tunnel wall, loosening a shower of fine dirt onto his head and shoulders. Mattie's headlamp spun around, slicing the darkness like a laser.

"It's all right," Spence said, more firmly than he felt. "It was just a bat." He brushed off his linen jacket, wondered if there was a dry cleaner this side of Butte.

"Yuk." She shuddered.

"You want to keep going?"

"Just a short way."

Ducking over, he followed her into the blackness ahead. The tunnel sloped down, shutting out all memory of daylight. Sixty, seventy feet in, a small mountain of fallen dirt and rocks blocked the passage. The ceiling had caved in. The pile of collapsed earth was dry and ocher-colored.

"When do you think this happened?" Mattie wondered. "Could it be recent?"

She can't think he's behind it, Spence thought in alarm. "Hard to say."

"There's air coming through. Can you feel it? Through the top." She shone her light into the gap of blackness across the top of the barrier. Then the ray of light slid down to her boots. With her heel, she took several quick swipes at the dirt. "It looks the same. What's on top and what's underneath. Not that that means anything. There's no weather in here. It could have happened fifty years ago." She paused. "Or yesterday." She flashed her light back into the gap.

Spence's heart fell. "Do you want me to go get a shovel?" he offered. "You must have one in your Jeep."

Her light jiggled as she shook her head. "There's no way he's back in there." She sniffed the air. "Besides, if he was, we'd smell him, wouldn't we?" She sniffed again.

"I would think so. But, as you say, there's no weather. It's cool and dry—" He stopped short, balking at the prospect of speculating on the rate of decomposition of her son's body.

"Jimmy!" she called. The suddenness of it made Spence jump.

"JimEEEEEEEE!" Her son's name echoed in the velvety blackness. Somewhere behind them a rock fell. "JimEEEEEEEEEEE!" she bayed.

"Mattie?" he worried.

She held up her hand to still him, and stood listening to the blackness for what seemed to Spence like half an eternity. Then slowly she lowered her hand but made no move to leave. "You don't think he could be here?" she wondered. Her voice was quiet but Spence could hear the anguish in it. He took a step closer. As she turned toward him, the rays of their headlamps crossed like swords in the dark. "Do you?" she pleaded.

He took a breath. "No," he said.

"Oh God," she said. He caught a flash of tears brimming in her eyes but could find no word of comfort. It was as if the blackness between them had solidified, hardened around them into coal, petrifying her in loss and despair and him in his own inadequacy, forever four feet away. He could not even lift an arm, a finger.

She broke the spell. "I guess we better get out of here," she said. "Before it caves in on us."

Back out in the burn, a pink sun rose over the ridge above them, bathing the blackened drainage in rosy light. Spence felt giddy with relief. Tunnels gave him the creeps. Being buried alive, his mouth packed with dirt—he had seen corpses that way, victims excavated from genocidal graves—it was not the way he would choose to go. "I don't know about you," he said to Mattie, "but I could use a cup of hot coffee." The bar in the lobby of the Hotsprings Hotel served morning coffee in thick, white mugs. Spence imagined a shot of cognac on the side.

But Mattie was not tempted by the notion of coffee. She seemed to have rallied, to have found another plan. "If you don't mind, I'd like to work our way over to the rock slide where they found Leonard and Carew. I keep thinking that's the direction Jim would have run, toward the talus. We can hike down to the Jeep from there. Maybe with the sun low behind us, we might—" She broke off, as if her hope might evaporate in the telling.

"Right."

Slowly, they picked their way across the side of the drainage, aiming at the two white crosses still in the shadow of the ridge above them. They spread out, taking parallel paths, and Spence tried to keep his attention focused, but Mattie was as slow as a sleepwalker. Never mind coffee, he thought irritably. He should have brought along a couple of ponies of cognac—he thought he had a few Lufthansa Martells in his suitcase collection.

For the tenth time (so to speak, for he had lost the actual count) Mattie stopped to turn a slow, full circle. Inch by inch, she scanned the entire drainage from a new vantage. She was standing on a mound on the slope above him and the light had turned golden, giving her the painterly look of a booted hero poised above new land. But her slow-motion turning was hardly rapacious; her movement had a dreamy quality, as if she had discovered a private ritual.

Abruptly, she stopped mid-circle. She cocked her head, looked up, looked sharply around.

"What?" he called. "What is it?"

She did not answer. Like a robin listening for worms, she turned her head without moving her body. He climbed up to her. She clutched at his arm. "Do you hear it?" she demanded. Under the brim of her helmet, her eyes were wide, rolling as she cocked her head.

He listened, heard nothing, only the wind on the high ridges. His heart sank. She's losing it, he thought. "Mattie—" he said uncomfortably. Then he heard it, a low snoring that made the hair stand up on the back of his neck. An animal? It sounded uncannily human. There it was again, slightly bubbly on the inhale, a long groan on the exhale. He felt her fingers biting into the bone of his arm. Where was it coming from?

She let go of him. "Jim!" she cried. She plunged off her hillock, crashing through knee-high skeletons of burned sage and churning up a storm of gray ash. At the base of the mound, she waded into a tangle of charred brush and fell on all fours. "Jimmy!" she barked at the ground.

Spence heard a strange, hollow echo.

Then he saw it, the hole. About six feet across and camouflaged by a litter of fire-blown debris. "My God," he muttered. The boy had fallen down an old mine shaft. The mound on which she had been standing was excavated soil.

She tore the headlamp from her helmet and turned the light down the hole. Twenty feet down, there was a flash of silver foil. The foil moved.

"He's *alive*." She looked at Spence, her eyes wild with hope, then dove back over the hole. "*Jimmy!*" she called down.

"Ma?" A feeble croak.

Spence saw Mattie kneeling at the rim of the hole, head tilted back, eyes squeezed closed, hands lifted in an excruciating gesture of joy. Her rigid fingers trembled with contained emotion. He felt suddenly faint.

"Jimmy." This time her voice was commanding, sharp as a slap. "Jimmy, hang on. We're going to get you out. Just hang on." Fumbling, she yanked her radio from her chest harness and keyed in the Meander base. "McCulloch calling Incident Command. In need of assistance. We have located my son."

Her voice was unbearably calm. The flat serenity with which she related logistical particulars made Spence want to weep. And it was at that moment that he realized he had fallen in love.

It took all day to raise Jim McCulloch from the bottom of the shaft. Safety Officer Grant Sonderdank, together with the Incident's medical officer and several EMTs were the first responders. Chip Zampill arrived on the scene. The sheriff's department was notified and the local search-and-rescue team showed up to help out. The media picked up the commotion on the scanner and arrived in force with sound booms and television cameras. Brian Flaherty arrived to keep them at bay. Celia DeJesus arrived with Jack McCulloch and Harriet under her wing. She escorted them through the crowd of workers to the rim of the shaft, where they knelt and called down encouragements.

"We love you, Jimmy!" Harriet sobbed. "We love you!"

"Keep yer pecker up, boy!" Jack shouted.

Mattie held on to Celia and wept silent tears of relief and joy. She saw Spence beaming at her across the hole. Suddenly self-conscious, she smiled back through her tears, then burst into embarrassed laughter.

In the first hour, rescuers lowered down blankets and water. Jim was conscious but sounded frail. He complained of pain in his right ankle and left shoulder. The search-and-rescue team rushed a coffin-shaped wire basket up the slope, then spent the next hour studying the shaft and debating methods of anchoring ropes. Someone tried and failed to drive a truck with a come-along up to the shaft. Someone else called the telephone company for a winch. A party equipped with chain saws went hunting for timbers to build a tripod over the hole. A contingent of recreational climbers arrived with ropes and harnesses, pulleys and ascenders.

Frustrated by the delays, Mattie snatched up a webbed harness and announced, "I'm going down to him."

But one of the climbers, a slight, gaunt-looking young man

with a blond ponytail, happened to be an EMT. Mattie yielded to his expertise. Quickly and with breath-taking agility, he rappelled down the crumbling side of the shaft. He called for splints, for tape, for another light, for the basket. It took him over an hour to maneuver Jim into it, then there was another wait while they set the tripod's timbers and rigged the ropes.

"Ma?" Jim called.

Mattie knelt over the hole. "Sweetheart, I'm right here."

"What happened to the others?"

She let a beat too many go by. "Jimmy, let's focus on getting you out of there."

She listened, waited, but he made no protest. She sat back on her heels, saw Chip Zampill taking it in.

Spence found it hard to take his eyes off her. While the faces moving around her were tense, preoccupied by the mechanics of the rescue, Mattie's expression was opaque, as smooth and unyielding as polished marble. The pinched lines in her face were gone. She talked to Zampill, to the rescuers, to her family. She was polite, self-contained, luminous.

He felt as if they all were being rescued, pulled up out of the hole, redeemed by her confidence, her stubborn physical energy. The sensation of being saved, the sheer luxuriousness of it, was a novel one for Spence. Mattie had once saved his life, but at the time he had scarcely been conscious, and later his own behavior had shamed him. In the intervening years, he had become a rescuer of damsels in distress. He had rescued his wife Enid from poverty and artistic despair. During the course of his travels he had rescued an assortment of other women from war, famine, and rape. The business of saving them, of course, was a self-serving habit: it made him feel worthy of their love, of his own fortune and its attendant privileges. But now, as Mattie and her army of rescuers worked to raise up her son, for the first time Spence had the heady sensation of being saved. It was like melting into a warm bath. How seductive! No wonder Christianity had caught on—the Buddhists had a path, the Jews had the law, but Christians had a *Saviour*!

During a lull, Mattie brought him a cold can of a sports drink. "You want to keep your fluids up," she instructed.

"You sound like one of my mother's nurses," he complained. But the drink tasted like nectar. He felt shy, virginal. As he stood beside her, he was assaulted by a fantasy of moving to Montana, writing with a view of mountains from his cabin window. "Mattie," he declared happily, "I must tell you—"

"Mattie!" someone called. "We're ready!"

Half an hour later, Jimmy McCulloch surfaced headfirst from the shaft. His body was encaged in a wire basket, swaddled in blankets and crisscrossed with straps. For a moment, he hung under the tripod like a victim of medieval torture. His face was black with soot and sunken in with dehydration, but he was grinning. A cheer went up from the crowd. The onlookers applauded and hugged each other. Spence found he could not speak. He blinked and felt tears roll out of his right eye. He wiped them away and was surprised to see that his hand came away clean. For some reason, he had imagined his own face to be as black as Jimmy McCulloch's.

Part III

THE SACRIFICE

40

Jimmy was borne down the slope by a huddle of rescuers, then loaded into a small green-and-white helicopter. There was no room for Mattie. It clattered up into the sallow haze of the afternoon sky, hovered a moment, and languidly nosed north toward Missoula. Don't let it crash, she prayed.

"Mattie." It was Brian. "I tried to break loose a chopper for you, but Mike said no way." His tone was sincere, apologetic, as if trying to appease a celebrity.

"It's not like I'm on the team," she reminded him dryly. Then, seeing the worry in his eyes, she softened. "Thanks, Brian. I appreciate it, but we've got all the vehicles here. We need to get them back."

He gave her an appraising look. "Drive carefully."

"Right."

"Let me know if there's anything I can do."

"Great. Thanks," she added distractedly. She hurried off to her Jeep.

Three hours, two Diet Cokes, and a hundred and eighty miles later, she walked into the emergency room of Saint Patrick's hospital in Missoula. Jim had been examined and X-rayed and was already in the operating room having his ankle set and pinned. In addition to second-degree burns on his ears and minor burns across his upper back, he had sustained a compound fracture of his left tibia just above the ankle and a broken collarbone.

Spence arrived. He had checked out of their B&B and packed her gear into his rental. Jack and Harriet, who had returned to Sophia to pick up their bags, arrived soon after. Reporters began showing up. Mattie and Jack gave interviews in the waiting room. The doctor appeared in surgical greens: Jim was as strong as an ox, he declared cheerfully. The surgery had "gone without a hitch." Jim would be back on his feet—or at least, back on one foot—in a week or so. The doctor chuckled at his little joke. Relieved, they chuckled along.

They left the doctor to the reporters and went out for Chinese food. Afterward, Jack and Harriet took Spence back to the house. Mattie spent the night in the hospital, on a reclining chair in her son's room. "It's not really necessary," the floor nurse said. She looked no older than Jimmy. "Of course, if you'd feel more comfortable being with him . . ."

Jimmy slept loudly and heavily, his ankle elevated in its cast, his right arm in a sling across his chest. He scarcely woke when nurses came in to check his pulse, his temperature, the IV in his left arm. He had been wearing his hard hat backward, so the back of his neck had been protected from the heat, but his ears had burned and they were swollen, large and blistered.

In the gray light of early morning he woke and asked again about his teammates. Mattie told him what she knew about the fatalities: how the fire had been set near the road with a match; how Wade Lowry and Pami Gustavisson and Cat Carew had died along with Billy Dallas, the driver of the pickup, and an Indian inmate named Manny Leonard. He listened without expression, his eyes fixed somewhere above the sheet over his knees. When she had finished, he closed his eyes and went back to sleep.

She felt irked. She had refrained from bombarding him with questions about his ordeal. He would have to give official statements soon enough. She was prepared to get his story in pieces, detail by detail, layer by layer. She might not know the whole of his ordeal for weeks—if then. But she had expected that he would have at least a few questions about his friends.

As if he were a stranger, she studied his knobby length under the sheets. He was taller by some than Eddie—Eddie, who had the compact build of a gymnast. Sallow adult toes poked out of Jim's cast—when was the last time she had considered her son's toes? And then there was the growth of beard on his slack jaw. The blackness of it was startling, like a pirate's. It pointed up his underground pallor, his starved cheeks.

Was it really all over? she wondered.

A brown woman in a blue cotton shower cap brought breakfast on a salmon-colored plastic tray: a box of cereal, a carton of milk, grapefruit sections in a little beige dish, scrambled eggs and wilted toast under a beige lid. Mattie cranked up her son and adjusted his pillows, taking care to avoid touching his burned ears. She unwrapped the utensils from the paper napkin, set them by his left hand. "You want some help?"

"I can manage."

But his hand made no move toward the tray. She noticed the Band-Aid covering the tip of his forefinger. The finger was orange with disinfectant. "What happened there?"

"A rat got me."

"There were rats down there?"

He blinked himself more awake, made an effort for her. "I think it was a rat. Probably a pack rat, but I never really saw it. It chomped down on me and I freaked. I could hear it scurrying around but I couldn't see anything. I thought it had fallen in with me—you know, fleeing the fire. There was this excavated area at the bottom of the shaft, like a crawl space. I thought they'd dug down, taken out some samples. I thought I was trapped in the bottom of a dry hole with this sucker. But I couldn't find him." He let his head drop back into the pillows. "So I figured he had a way out, that I was in a section of collapsed tunnel. It must have been an old air shaft. It filled up with smoke and I couldn't breathe. I thought that was it. Next thing I remember it was pitch-black and I could feel the air moving through." He closed his eyes. "I kept wishing I had my headlamp."

She waited. He was dozing off. "Jim."

He opened them.

"Can I feed you?"

"No."

She waited for him to pick up his fork, start eating. But he made no move. "We found the adit," she told him, if only to keep him awake. "Did you hear me yelling for you?"

He frowned. "Maybe. I thought it was a dream. You sort of lose track after a while."

"We went back in as far as we could. Maybe we got closer than we thought."

His eyelids dropped. But he *had* to eat! His breathing deepened. She could not stand it. She stood up. "Jim," she said sharply. "I'm going to get some breakfast. You want me to bring you something back?"

He focused.

"Do you want something from the cafeteria?"

"No."

"How about a doughnut? Or some cold OJ? Do you think you could eat a banana?"

"Ma."

"You have to eat." She paused. "Okay. I'm going."

Chip Zampill arrived at the hospital early, while Mattie was in the cafeteria eating nonfat yogurt and trying to read the *Missoulian* with her coffee. Chip had spent the night at a Days Inn out by the airport. He had eight hours of sleep, a breakfast special of steak-and-eggs under his belt, and the smoke of only two cigarettes in his lungs—although from the way the girls at the nurses' station sniffed at him, you'd think he'd stepped on a turd. He grinned at them. He was feeling pretty good. He considered waiting till lunch for his next smoke.

He found Jim McCulloch dozing uneasily over his breakfast tray. Good-looking kid, he noted. Took after the father. Not that there was anything wrong with Mattie's looks. But from what he had seen of Eddie Sterling at the memorial service, twenty years younger he could have stood in for Tom Cruise.

Chip introduced himself, showing his shield and his tape recorder.

"I thought maybe you were the doctor," Jim complained. "Whatever they're giving me is wearing off."

"I can come back later, if you're not up to it now."

"It's okay."

"Glad to have you back in the land of the living."

"Me too." His face was haggard, his eyes bleak.

Chip got down to business. "What would help us out right now," he said, "is an account of your movements—starting when you left the lunch spot."

"Okay."

"Hang on a sec." He turned on the tape recorder, droned the date, time, and Jim's name into it, then set it down beside the breakfast tray. "You had lunch up on the ridge?" he prompted.

"Yeah. In the safety zone. Then Wade, that's our squad leader, volunteered us to go bump up some water." He shrugged, then winced. "Cat took the lead. She had one handset. Then me, then Pami and Wade. He had the other set. Wade put Richie at the top and the inmates in between them. I was supposed to make the contact with the driver—Wade was kind of old-fashioned that way."

Out in the corridor, a cart loudly rattled by. "What way?" Chip turned up the volume on his tape recorder.

"Like trying to protect the women. It used to bug Cat. I figured no way she's going to let me go ahead of her, but I wasn't going to make an issue out of it, she could take care of herself, and anyway, it was between her and Wade, not her and me. I was the low guy on the totem pole—next to Pami. Anyway, we get down there, and she stops below Pami, tells me to go on ahead, which surprised me a little, but then you could never tell about Cat. She was not exactly what you'd call predictable."

He stopped, reached awkwardly across his tray for the water glass on the bedside table.

"Here." Chip handed it to him, then looked at the tray. "You done here?"

"Yeah."

Chip removed the tray, put it on the floor outside the door, and closed the door.

Jim took a short, discouraged pull on his water. "It was part of her image: the free spirit. She used to get on my case, kept telling me I should be more spontaneous—whatever that means." He looked up. "It's hard to believe they're gone."

"Hm." Chip waited a couple of beats, a respectful pause for the dead, then resumed. "So you made the contact with the trusty?"

Jim took a breath. "I went down to the pickup and there was no one there. I hollered, but there was no answer. So I picked up a couple cubees and carried them up to Cat. I told her the stuff was all there, including a sack of melons, but no driver. She took the water and started up to Pami, and I went back down for the next load."

He closed his eyes.

Chip gave him a minute. Then he said, "Jim?"

"Yeah?"

"You want to finish this later?"

"No. I had this funny feeling that something wasn't right. I wasn't sure, but something about the air seemed funny. It was blowing pretty good up the drainage, into my face as I started back down, but at the same time, I could feel it blowing on the back of my neck. I thought, that's weird. But it felt pretty good, I mean I'd worked up a decent sweat, so I just kept on going. Maybe if I'd gone back up to Cat, said something, she'd have called Wade. Maybe they'd all have made it."

The door to the room opened. Mattie poked her head in, then followed with a Styrofoam cup of coffee and her newspaper. She saw Zampill's tape recorder turning on the empty tray table. "Don't let me interrupt," she said. She moved to the window, gazed out it, declaring herself a nonparticipant. Zampill turned back to Jim. "You went down to the truck a second time?"

"Yes. Still no driver. I left the melons and the MREs, picked up two more cubees and started hiking up, and suddenly the wind got hot and there were embers blowing by me. I turned around and saw trees torching on the top of the knob, then all of a sudden it was a wall of flames going up fifty, a hundred feet. It started to roll down into the drainage, and I saw this guy coming out of the trees. I dropped the water and yelled at him to come with me. I took my shelter out of its case to use as a heat shield and starting running across the slope. It happened so fast. One minute I'm thinking about melons, then the next minute the woods are exploding. We'd talked about escape routes earlier and I'd studied the map. I knew the old mine adit was behind me. It was closer than the talus, but there was no way I could get to it, so I ran for the rock slide. The heat was intense. I could feel my ears burning. I didn't think I was going to make it. Then I saw this hole in the ground and jumped in."

Mattie willed herself to keep looking out the window.

Zampill asked, "Dallas didn't follow you?"

"Dallas?"

"The driver."

Jimmy was quiet for a long time. Mattie looked around. But he had not dozed off. "I'm not even sure he heard me yelling at him," he said. "It was pretty loud."

Zampill nodded. "Did you see any of the others?"

"After the blowup?"

"Yes."

"I saw someone deploying up by the rock slide. It was hard to see with all the dust and ash blowing around, but I saw the silver foil. I didn't know who it was. Mom says it was Cat. The Indian tried to get in her shelter?"

"That's what they think," Zampill confirmed. "Let me go back to the trusty, to the driver of the supply truck. Did you see him after you yelled at him to follow you?

Jim closed his eyes. "No."

"Just a couple more questions."

He lifted his left hand: a dull invitation to go ahead.

"You yelled at the driver to follow you, then you took out your shelter and ran up the east side of the drainage—is that right?"

Jim nodded.

"For the tape," Zampill said.

"That's right."

"Did you look back to see if the driver was behind you?"

"I told you, he wasn't."

"But you looked back."

"Yes."

"And what did you see?" Zampill persisted.

Jim shifted uncomfortably under the covers and winced. "The woods going up," he said irritably.

Mattie made a move to intervene, but Zampill ignored it. "Jim," he pressed on. "What about before the blowup? Did you notice anything unusual?"

"Just what I told you about the wind."

"What about another vehicle?"

Jim frowned. "At the staging area? No, just the pickup."

"Did you go out to the road at any time?"

"No."

Zampill turned off the recorder, pocketed it. "Thanks, Jim. Hope you're feeling better soon." He put his card on Jim's tray table. "If you think of anything else, let me know." The words came out automatically, like a prayer that had lost its meaning.

"Are you going to get the guy who started it?" Jim challenged.

Zampill summoned up his energy. "I'm sure going to try."

Mattie cornered him out in the corridor. "Is my son still a suspect?" she demanded. She had not liked Zampill's last question about the road.

He wrinkled up his forehead, rubbed the back of his neck. "Mattie," he said and she saw the regret in his brown eyes. "No one can corroborate his story. Dallas, the Carew girl, Wade Lowry—they're all dead."

In the room behind them, a loud voice asked, "Mr. Terrell, have you had a bowel movement today?"

They moved toward the elevator. Mattie asked, "How hard are you going to try?"

"Excuse me?"

"You told Jim you were going to try to find the person who set the fire."

He saw the accusation in her eyes and suddenly felt grimy. Wearily, he shifted into a confidential mode. "Let me be frank. This case has had top priority. We've been working round the clock on it, giving it our best shot. But at this point, we've done just about all we can. There's nothing more to go on. You come up with something, any kind of lead at all, and I'll run it down myself." He punctuated the declaration with a nod. "Stay in touch." He walked off to the elevator.

Out on the sidewalk in front of the visitor's entrance, he stopped to light up a cigarette. It was a sunny morning, the sky above the buildings across the street was a clear Montana blue and the strips of hospital lawn looked cool and green, but his earlier, upbeat mood had dissipated. He felt the weight of too many unsolved cases, too many years of not enough time, too many dead people—this last lot, none of them yet thirty. How hard would he try?

He shook his head, sucked on his cigarette. His last slender hope for the case had died with the lab report from Latents: the anonymous crotch shot had yielded only smudged partials. They had no witnesses except the Gower kid who thought—but wasn't sure—that he had seen the flash of a windshield. The Incident staff still had not found the missing transport records for the shift when the fire was started. Scratch the veneer of military efficiency and the Incident was as sloppy as the next bureaucracy. It was possible, at least theoretically, that they might discover a new witness—if the records surfaced. But given the general eagerness to cooperate with the investigation, Chip guessed that by this time, any firefighter with information would have come forward—unless, of course, it was one of the Justice people who had dropped the match. If that was the case, the haystack narrowed down to about two thousand men and women.

Impatiently, he took another drag on his Marlboro. He watched a woman come out the hospital's glass doors onto the sidewalk. She took a pack of cigarettes from her purse and lit up. She saw him watching, flashed him a conspiratorial smile. A nice enough looking woman, about his own age, in her summer dress.

No, he thought. Ignoring the woman, he crushed out his cigarette in the sand pail beside the door and went inside. He located a pay phone, took out his credit card, and found Ellen's number in his pocket calendar. She had given it to him and he had written it down and never used it. He hesitated, then dialed. She was probably at Jeannie's, helping out with the baby. He would just leave a quick message on her machine. Tell her he was headed back to Helena. Wanted to see the baby. Something like that.

But she picked up. "Oh," he said, unnerved. "I didn't think you'd be home."

"Chip."

"I thought you'd be with Jeannie."

"Oh, she's doing fine. Dean's home with her. He's taking the week off."

At some cost, he pushed his dislike for his son-in-law aside. "That's nice."

"He is a bit hard to take at times," Ellen admitted.

Encouraged, Chip asked, "How's the baby?"

"He's fine. How are you? I saw they found the boy."

"Yeah. I was just talking to him. I'm in Missoula."

"That's what they said, they were taking him to Saint Pat's. He's okay?"

"Yeah." It came out angrily.

She did not respond right away. "You think he did it?"

After a long moment he answered, "No. I don't think so." Until she asked, he had not been sure.

"Terrible," she clucked, but the direction of her sympathy was unclear to him.

"I was wondering . . . you want to go to Italy?"

"Do I want to go to Italy?" she asked in amazement.

"I was thinking about it, thought maybe you'd like to come along."

There was a long, careful silence. Then she said, "Maybe we should try lunch first?"

He tried not to sound disappointed. "Fine."

"Tomorrow?"

"I'll call you." He could feel her armor clinking shut. "I'll call you tonight," he promised. He hung up. How many times had he promised?

41

03 Sept 09:54p   Directory C:*.*

Still stuck at the Justice. There was talk about mobilizing a short team under Ned to work a fire up on the highline, but no such luck. The EIT nixed it, said they weren't ready to release us! Shit, it took the assholes two days just to decide in what order to interview people and then they started quibbling over the interview matrix! We'll be here till Kingdom Come. Zampill & Co gone. Ned passed off to the local forest two days ago. Everybody antsy, nothing better to do than sit around playing Quake—except Frank. Turns out he's a solitaire addict. Switched to a real deck after his doctor told him he was going blind staring at the screen. One click of the mouse, a new game. Fifty games at a stretch without blinking. Forget your eyes, Cicero, I tell him, it's your brain you should be worrying about.

Enough to drive you nuts, all those fucking beeps. I had to get out of there. Besides, you never know when some lazy butt's going to look over your shoulder now that everyone's got the time to mind everyone's business. So here I sit in the can running my batteries down, toking on my last joint. Walked damn near a quarter mile to the farthest ones and and wouldn't you know, someone else had the same idea, you could smell it walking by!

I wonder if that's what it could be, some kind of eye strain like Frank had. They're still there, my black spots. I can't tell if they're there all the time and I forget about them, ignore them, or if they come and go. I'll have to get it checked out. If they keep us here, I can take another run up to Missoula. Saw the boy this afternoon, still in the hospital. Flew up with the EIT guys, Wilkie and the fire-behavior guy, and the union rep and me. The EIT guys were all hovering around his bed, all reverential, like they were hanging on to the dying words of a holy saint, but what with his shelter keeping in his body heat and the water he had left in his canteen, he could have lasted another day, easy.

I bought him a bunch of flowers, a get-well from Overhead, I told him, but he scarcely looked at them. Forty bucks and the brat can't be bothered. This on top of the untold thousands we had to shell out for his rescue. It really is too bad he didn't croak. On the other hand, if he'd bought it at the bottom of the shaft, I never would have known what happened to him, there would always be that uncertainty: Where is he, what did he see, would he turn up someday out of the blue? I never would have known. This way I can take care of it. It's hard to tell what he did see. I couldn't very well grill him with all the guys there, but he saw something, I know he saw something. I was standing back against the wall, giving the guys the space, and they were going over it, piece by piece, and I'm going so far so good, and then they finally get him up on the side of the drainage where he's got a shot of the road. I checked it out as soon as we got back, turns out you *can* see the road from up there. You can't see where I dropped the match, the knob is in the way, but on the east bank of the creek, you've got a shot of the highway, so it might just be possible that he saw me, not that he could pick me out of a lineup or anything, not at that distance and with all the smoke and everything, but he could have seen the vehicle, seen where I stopped and got out.

He was telling how he was running across the pitch, the dragon on his ass, then he stops, like he's remembered something. They wait, not saying anything, just waiting.

The kid goes, The detective, the one who was here this morning, he wanted to know if I saw the trusty, if I looked back.

They're all ears.

I didn't see him. But I did look back, he says.

Then he looks past them, like they don't exist, and looks right at me—or maybe through me; shit, I don't know, but he's staring at me with this odd look on his face, like he sees me and he doesn't see me. So I stand there, arms crossed, not moving, not even blinking, like I'm out in the woods suddenly face to face with a young bear.

You looked back, someone reminds him.

Yeah, he says.

You wear glasses, Jim? someone else said, the fire-behavior guy, I think.

He shakes his head, no. Well, I already knew that, I'd checked that out too, he's 20/20, not that it matters. You've got poor visibility, heightened emotional state, he's hardly a reliable star witness, not that it's going to come to that, but you think they would have checked it out.

So the fire-behavior guy tries to pin him down on flame lengths. Then he's down the hole, but they don't want to know about that, like they don't want to intrude on his precious ordeal, and I'm standing there thinking did he see me or not. The union guy starts massaging his ego and Wilkie the idiot's running around trying to find out what the hospital did with his Nomex—we must preserve the relics at all cost—and the nurse comes in to give the kid his dope. Wilkie's still off relic-hunting, and the others go off for coffee and I tell them I'll meet them in the cafeteria, I've got to use the head. So I duck into the men's and give them five minutes and go back in. It's perfect. He's out of it, snoring like a jackhammer, the corridor's empty, and he's not hooked up to anything that will bring them running if he goes flat-line. So I shut the door, look around for an extra pillow and of course there isn't one, it's worse than the fucking Twilight Motel! Anyway, I decide to use the one he's using, I can stick it back under his head afterward, and I'm just about to pull it out when the door opens. It's McCulloch and her almighty Author!

They come in and we whisper back and forth and she strokes his forehead and the Author moves me out into the corridor. The hero needs his rest—it was sickening! Obviously she spoils him rotten. Mother never let me get away with anything. No excuses. when she said time to play big boy, that was it. If I messed up, whack, she let me have it. Cat said it taught me to be an attentive lover! something to be said for early conditioning.

What I'm thinking is a new, improved ring of fire. The only problem is my pussycat is gone. In a two-second puff of superheated smoke, lungs first. Should have been cunt first. Shades of what might have been. It's like I'm raking the ashes, looking for a coal, and when I find it, shit, it burns me up. Well a new magic ring   definitely   but in good time first the boy

42

On Wednesday morning, after a stay of less than forty-eight hours, Jim McCulloch was discharged from Saint Patrick's hospital in Missoula. Mattie arrived with Spence and Jack to bring him home. She brought along a pair of Jim's sweatpants to pull over his cast and a shirt to button over his sling. He allowed Jack and Spence to help him dress, but even with their help, the effort exhausted him. As they waited for the nurse to come with the official word of dismissal, he dozed on the bed in his clothes. Mattie worried that the doctor was sending him home too early. But Jack was restless. He paced back and forth in the little room, kept peering out into the corridor for the nurse. "The sooner we get you out of here, the sooner you'll mend," he growled to his grandson.

Jim opened his eyes. "Huh?"

"Nothing. Go back to sleep," Mattie instructed.

He blinked himself awake. "What's the holdup?"

"I don't know." She reached out and felt his brow. "You okay? How do you feel?"

"For God's sake, leave the boy alone," Jack snapped. "He's fine!"

Jim shot his mother a look of amusement. "Pops knows best."

"You betcha," Jack assured them. "We get you home, get a couple decent meals into you, you'll be good as new." He looked his grandson over and nodded. "I can tell you one thing. You're a darned sight better off than Ranger Pulaski was when they pulled him out of his hole."

Jim blinked with interest. "I thought he went right back to work."

Jack shook his head. "His lungs were scorched, his hands were burned, and his eyes were damaged. I don't recollect exactly what the problem was. Some kind of smoke damage, maybe. Whatever it was, when he came to, he couldn't see. They had to lead him out. He was virtually blind. He never did fully recover."

Jim frowned. "How did his hands get burned?"

"He was standing guard at the mouth of the mine, trying to keep his men inside, when the fire swept over them and his horse's tail caught on fire. He beat it out with his hands."

"They had horses in there with them?"

"Two of them. Ranger Pulaski had ridden in to warn his men on one and had packed a bunch of supplies for them on the other. The men were hungry, so they cooked themselves up a big dinner. Finally Pulaski got them to move out. One of the older guys, a guy with rheumatism, was having trouble keeping up, so Pulaski put him on his own horse, took the reins, and led the way on foot."

"You never told me that," Jim accused, as if Jack had betrayed the old story. "You never said he went blind. Or that he had horses."

"Did the horses survive?" Spence asked.

"The smoke got 'em." Jack growled.

No one said anything. Jack shook his head. "That wasn't the worst of it. On top of all Ed Pulaski suffered, the government refused to give him his due." Once again he stuck his head out into the corridor. "Where the devil did that nurse get to?"

"So what happened?" Jim insisted. "What happened to Pulaski after the fire?"

"Well," Jack began, "he spent a couple weeks in the hospital. Like I said, he was more than half blind, which worried him a good deal, but he didn't have the money for the eye operation he needed. Congress had passed a law saying injured firefighters should be reimbursed for time missed from the job, but the catch was, he'd accumulated all this sick leave. He was forty years old and he'd scarcely been sick a day in his life. So he used his sick leave to recuperate and the pencil pushers figured he wasn't losing any pay, so he never got reimbursed.

"Then, a couple years later, Congress appropriated some money to compensate firefighters for injuries from dangerous work, but someone left Pulaski's name off the list, so he missed out there, too.

"Finally his friends got together and nominated him for a Carnegie Hero Medal. It came with a thousand-dollar award, but he didn't get that either. The Carnegie judges said all he'd done was nothing more than was necessary to save his own life—which of course, was bullshit. If that's all he had in mind, he never would have left his dinner table to ride out to warn his crew at Placer Creek. He knew the fire was headed toward Wallace—that's where he lived, just over the border in Wallace, Idaho. He could have stayed home and taken care of Mrs. Pulaski and their little girl. Instead, he rode out to Placer to warn his crew. And when it started looking bad, he could have saved himself on his horse, but he refused to forsake his men.

"So some of the survivors wrote letters to the Carnegie people saying that Ranger Pulaski had staked his own life to save theirs, but nothing came of it. He never did pass the goddamn hero test. Meanwhile, he still needed money for his eye operation—"

"Wait a minute," Mattie interrupted. "What happened to Mrs. Pulaski?"

"Oh, she knew how to take care of herself. A train came in to evacuate the women and children, but she refused to get on it. She wasn't about to leave without her husband. By all accounts, it was a mob scene, everyone scrambling to get on the train with their suitcases and their possessions all bundled up in sheets and blankets. The mayor had to order the twenty-fifth Infantry to throw able-bodied men off the cars, and even then, when the train pulled out of the station, there were drunks clinging to the roof of the cars and hanging on to the sides of the engine. But Mrs. Pulaski took her little girl and walked out of town and waited out the fire on a barren tailings flat. That night, the fire ripped through the east side of Wallace, destroying the railroad station, a hotel, a couple breweries, and something like a hundred and fifty homes, burned them right to the ground. Two men died. One trying to rescue his pet parrot from his burning house. The other fella died in the hotel fire. Anyway, in the morning, Mrs. Pulaski walked home and found her house was still standing. The fire had jumped that part of town." Jack shook his head. "She waited all day for news of her husband, then, around three o'clock in the afternoon, she saw three men coming up the road. The big one in the middle had his eyes bandaged and was being led by the other two. And that was Ed Pulaski."

Jack stopped and looked Jim over. "He'd lost six of his men, but others had it worse. At Selzer Creek, twenty-eight men were burned beyond recognition. I think it was eighteen lost at Big Creek. In the Coeur d'Alene forest alone, seventy-two firefighters died." Jack's tone was scolding, as if he were warning Jim not to make too much of a fuss about a mere five deaths.

Mattie bridled. "It's not a numbers contest, Dad."

Jack's eyes flashed with annoyance. "What?"

Mattie compressed her lips.

"You going to let me tell this?"

She glanced at Spence.

"So what happened to Pulaski?" Jim intervened from the bed.

Jack snorted at his daughter and turned back to Jim. "Like I was trying to tell, he needed the money to get his eyes fixed. So he started fiddling around in his shop and after a bit he came up with a new firefighting tool. He took it to his supervisors, presented it to them at a meeting. Well, they didn't think much of it. But Pulaski went home and kept tinkering with it, fooling around with the balance and so forth, and when he got it the way he wanted, he wrote to the U.S. Patent Office. They sent him all the papers to fill out, but he hadn't counted on there being a patent fee. He didn't have the money for it, so that was that. He dropped the idea of taking out a patent. That would have been around 1913, 1914, about the same time he'd been put up for the hero award.

"Meanwhile, men out on the line started using his tool and finding it pretty handy. By the time Pulaski died in 1931, it was so popular that the forest inspector for the region, a fella called C. K. McHarg, began thinking about having it manufactured as standard equipment. So McHarg wrote to the U.S. Patent Office, saying he wanted to patent it and assign the royalties to Pulaski's widow. The money 'would assist Mrs. Pulaski very materially' was how he put it, so you figure her husband hadn't left her with much of anything. Finally McHarg gets a long memo back saying it's too late for a patent. Turns out if an invention has been in use for over two years without a patent, the inventor loses the right to it. The best the U.S. Patent Office could do was give the tool his name."

Jack McCulloch scratched the back of his neck. "I don't think he would have cared much one way or the other about having his name on it. He wasn't a man who made a lot of himself. What he took pride in was the skill of his hands, making something rough into something useful. The only reason he let his friends go after the hero medal was he needed the money for his operation."

"Did he ever get it?" Spence wondered.

"I think he did. I don't know how. It wasn't in the file."

"What file?" Mattie asked.

"They've still got his file at Region One headquarters. It's all in there, all the correspondence."

A metallic clatter interrupted. A nurse rolled a wheelchair into the room. "So you're going to leave us, Jim?" she teased.

On Thursday, September 5, the day after Jim was released from the hospital, the McCulloch family attended Wade Lowry's funeral. The service was held at ten in the morning at the newly erected Community Hope Baptist church out by the public golf course. Neither Wade nor Greta Lowry belonged to the church—in fact, they had no religious affiliation—but Greta was set on a church. Her first choice had been the historic Episcopal church downtown, but the pastor there would neither donate nor rent out the premises, so she settled for the Baptists, a compromise that made no one happy. Wade's crewmates had wanted to hold a joint service in the town of Millville for all three of their lost crewmates, and Wade's parents had wanted a small private service out at the family ranch in Potomac, where three generations of Lowrys were buried in a cottonwood grove. Arguments over the arrangements left all parties tense, but Greta was unyielding. She was determined to "do it right" for her husband.

The church itself, with its low fieldstone facade, metal mansard roof, and skinny aluminum spire, had all the charm of a suburban branch bank. Greta consoled herself with its practical aspects: it was handicapped-accessible and its parking lot could accommodate the school buses full of her husband's fellow teachers and former students. It took over an hour for the mourners to sign in, one at a time, in the little white satin guest book posted in the dim brown vestibule.

Inside the church, contemporary stained-glass windows cast amber and purple oblongs over the mourners' heads and shoulders. Wade's crewmates wore their red T-shirts tucked into clean Nomex jeans. Six of them bore his coffin down the aisle on their shoulders. Behind the casket, the rest marched single file. Richie Gower pushed Jim in his wheelchair. (Jim's shoulder injury kept him from using crutches—the doctor promised a walking cast in a few weeks.) Greta Lowry, in a black sundress and black sunglasses, followed the 'shots. In her arms, she carried the squirming two-year old Wade Junior, whom she had dressed in a red T-shirt "just like Daddy's." When a bearded guitarist stepped forward to a microphone and sang Vince Gill's "Go Rest High on That Mountain," small pockets of grief erupted in the congregation; several teenaged girls were overcome and had to be assisted outside into the sunlight.

Mattie wept behind her aviator shades. Through the blur of tears, she kept her eyes on the back of her son's head. Jim's wheelchair was parked off to one side of Wade Lowry's polished cherry-wood coffin. For whom am I crying? she wondered. The living or the dead?

She accepted a tissue from Harriet, who was sitting beside her. Along with Jack and Spence, Harriet's husband Stan was in their pew. He had left his law practice and flown in from Seattle expecting to attend Jim's funeral. One of the 'shots (to Mattie's disconcertment, his name vanished from her head) had ushered them up front and seated them just behind the pews reserved for the Lowry family.

The Lowrys had all squeezed into the first pew, leaving the two behind them empty and giving Mattie an unobstructed view. Wade's parents, John and Ruth, sat stoically as their grandchild climbed over their laps, peeked out between their shoulders, hid under the seat. Greta's head and shoulders bobbed and shivered.

In a sweet, twangy tenor, the guitarist sang of a troubled life, of being "no stranger to the rain." Greta emitted a loud groan. Frightened, her son began to cry. Ruth Lowry comforted the child. A young man in a pale blue sports coat comforted Greta.

"Go rest high on that mountain," came the refrain. The song was a killer. Mattie pulled another tissue from Harriet's packet, blew her nose, and watched the man's hand on Greta's bare back.

There was something possessive about the way it traveled up and down the sobbing woman's tanned spine. Mattie doubted he was her brother.

On the way out, she whispered to Harriet, "Who was that with Greta?"

Harriet's lips tightened. "A colleague, I think."

Since the burial (at the family ranch) was private, Greta received people outside the church. The line was long and patient. Friends of the deceased respectfully made room for Jim in his wheelchair and Richie Gower, who was pushing it. Mattie and the rest of the family were waved into line behind them. A clump of Mattie's former teammates, Ned, Mike, Brian, came over to shake Jim's hand. Mattie almost didn't recognize them in their dark suits.

The line inched forward. When they finally reached Greta, Mattie saw that the man in the pale-blue sports coat was beside her, his hand still on her back. On seeing Harriet, Greta threw herself into her arms and began sobbing anew. While Harriet held her, Mattie looked around for Ruth and John Lowry and spotted them waiting by the hearse, surrounded by a small clump of their own friends.

"I should say something to the parents," she murmured to Spence, and she crossed a manicured triangle of lawn to present her condolences.

"I'm so sorry," she said to John Lowry. "I just want you to know—" The confusion on his face made her break off. Thinking that perhaps he did not recognize her out of fire clothes (she was wearing her good navy blue silk suit), she smiled sympathetically and said, "Mattie McCulloch."

Lowry's face hardened. "I know who you are." Abruptly he turned and strode away.

Startled, Mattie scanned the faces around her.

"You!" It was Ruth Lowry. Her eyes were furious. "How

dare you!" she shrieked. "How dare you come here! *Your* son is alive! You killed Wade! Isn't that enough for you?" She thrust an accusatory finger at Mattie's nose. "You killed my son!"

Her words rang out with booming clarity. Mattie felt as if she had been deafened by an iron bell. The world suddenly went silent. No hum of conversation, no whoosh of passing traffic, only the ringing echo: *You killed my son!*

"You are not going to get away with this," Ruth Lowry hissed. "You are going to pay! We are going to make you pay!"

In her left ear, Mattie heard her brother-in-law Stan. "Do not say a word," he instructed in his lawyer's voice.

In her right ear, she heard Spence. "Time to go."

She saw a fan of photographers moving toward them across the green grass. She took a last look at the quivering Ruth Lowry and allowed Spence and her brother-in-law, one at each elbow, to escort her across the parking lot to her Jeep.

Back at home, they sat out on the porch waiting for Jack and Stan to come back with the pizzas they had ordered by phone for lunch. Richie Gower and a crewmate named Sean Koska had driven Jim home and accepted Mattie's invitation to join them. As they helped Jim out of his wheelchair into a chaise, Spence offered to mix up a pitcher of martinis. "I think we all could use a little something after *that*."

"We've still got another one to go," Mattie objected. A service for Pami Gustavisson and Cat Carew was to be held in Millville later that afternoon.

"All the more reason," Spence said. But there were no takers. He retreated to the kitchen and came back with a gin on the rocks.

Mattie brought a pillow out from the living room for Jim. "You're supposed to keep it elevated," she reprimanded him. She bent over and stuffed the pillow under his leg.

Jim looked at her. "You okay?"

She shrugged. "That was pretty bad."

"Those people. They behaved abominably," Harriet declared.

Mattie looked down at her navy blue pumps, eased them off her feet. "I can't really blame them. I was the IC. Their son's dead. I come marching up—"

Harriet interrupted. "There's more to it than that."

"What do you mean?"

Harriet glanced at Jim and his two friends. "I mean it's not just you," she reassured her sister. She hesitated. "It's complicated. The Lowrys are barely speaking to Greta."

The caution in her voice made Mattie sit up. "On account of the wrangle over the church?"

"No." Harriet glanced pointedly at Jim.

Jim caught the look. "What?" he demanded.

She shook her head. "Greta told me in confidence. She was very upset. She's carrying around a lot of guilt."

"I'm glad to hear it," Richie Gower cracked.

The porch was suddenly quiet.

"She was going out on him," Jim stated. "Everyone knew about it."

"I didn't know about it," Sean objected. He looked shocked.

"You're no one, Koska," Richie intoned.

Spence put his drink down on the little glass table next to Mattie's chaise. "Greta Lowry was having an affair?" he asked Jim.

"That's what Wade told me. He said they'd gone to counseling about it."

"The guy in the church?" Sean demanded. "The one who was all over her?"

"You can see how it might have tipped the Lowrys over the edge," Harriet observed to Mattie.

"She was humping *him?*" Sean persisted.

"What difference does it make?" Jim asked wearily. "I mean, now."

"None, I hope," Spence answered. "Do you know lover boy's name?"

Jim shook his head. "All Wade said was, a teacher friend. A shop teacher."

Spence looked at Mattie. "I think we need to do a little homework here."

43

The day after the two funerals of his three crewmates, Jimmy woke up in a strange bed with a thumping hangover. His headache and nausea were slivered with the pain of his fractures, his collarbone and his tibia. Judging by the light on the pine boughs outside his window, it was close to noon. He realized he was home—not in his own room upstairs, but in the guest room on the ground floor. His grandfather had added it on to the house when Grandma Kate (whom Jimmy did not remember) became ill.

Jim had no recollection of how he had gotten home, but he did remember where he had been—at the wake for Cat and Pami at Culligan's Café—and he remembered, with increasing discomfort, his mother standing in their driveway in the dark in her nightgown, letting loose at whoever had driven him home. TJ? Sean? Not Richie, he was certain of that.

The service for the girls had been held in the Millville Fire Station. Afterward the crew had loaded him and Mrs. Carew into someone's van and they had all driven up into the mountains to scatter the girls' ashes—"to the four winds," as Mrs. Carew kept saying, but in fact the wind had died. They stood along the side of the road with the setting sun behind them and passed the plastic boxes up and down the line like popcorn at the movies. They had begun shyly, with reverent handfuls, but there was a surprising amount of the remains, and pretty soon they were all—even Mrs. Carew—"casting" vigorous fistfuls which, disappointingly, did not float away on the evening air, but fell like sand. Before long, the ground below the guardrail was white with a confetti of bone ash and chips. To Jimmy, whose seat in the wheelchair gave him a closer perspective of the weeds and rocks, the ceremony seemed more like a littering than a laying-to-rest. His crewmates' remains felt chalky under his fingernails, and after each helping from the boxes, he had to repress the urge to wipe his hand on his jeans. At the end, no one knew what to do with the empty boxes. Toss them in the dumpster? Recycle them? They ended up in the trunk of someone's car.

The party afterward at Culligan's had been good. A real wake. There had been lots of stories, some of which were new to Jimmy and which set off bright little dings of illumination and recognition. He felt an intimacy with the dead girls that he had not felt when they were alive. It was easy to imagine them present, the next shoulder over, listening and smiling with approval as the rest of them laughed and cried and hugged each other and danced and fell down. Toward the end, Richie had picked a fight. When an onlooker had yelled, "It should have been you, you shit!" Richie had broken down and sobbed. Then Mrs. Carew, who was pretty far gone herself, made him lie down on the dance floor and everyone had had to touch his third eye and say, "You are forgiven," and in the middle of it all, Richie started snoring.

Although the crush of friends in Culligan's had been reassuring, Jim felt alien, no longer one of the crowd. The smells of alcohol and varnished wood, the soft light from the beer signs, the collection of billed caps strung like a lei over the backbar, all belonged to another life. It was awkward partying in a wheelchair—all the more so because, on account of his shoulder, he could not maneuver himself through the crowd but had to rely on his teammates to wheel him around. People bumped into him, slopped beer on him, talked over his head. At some point he had taken a couple of the painkillers the doctor had given him—he had had to ask someone to open the childproof vial for him. He remembered laying his head down on one of the tables, feeling the vibrations of the music through the tabletop, and the cool vinyl under his cheek.

The bedroom door opened and Jack came in carrying a glass brimming with something pink and violently fizzy. He put it down on the bedside table. "A little pick-me-up," he said.

Jimmy squinted suspiciously at the elixir. It looked like the work of a mad Disney alchemist. "What is it?"

"It's good for what ails you, that's what it is."

When in doubt, delay. Jim propped himself up and groaned. "I gotta pee first."

His grandfather passed him the coffee can he'd been using as a urinal. When he was done, Jack took the can but insisted, "Now drink up."

Jim winced, took a tentative sip of the explosive liquid. It tasted salty, bitter and minty, thick on the tongue despite the prickles of its fizz. "What'd you put in here?"

Jack listed half a dozen over-the-counter nostrums.

"Jesus. You're gonna kill me."

"No, sir. You think I don't know what I'm talking about? It'll make you feel better."

Jim took three swallows and burped loudly. "Excuse me. How's Mom?"

"Your chauffeur took down the mailbox. She told me she took his car keys. He spent the night—what was left of it—on the porch."

"Who was it?"

"What do you mean, who was it?"

"I mean, who drove me home?"

Jack raised an eyebrow. "I never saw the who of it. He was gone when I came downstairs this morning. But I'm sure your mother will be pleased to fill you in on the details." He went into the bathroom, emptied the can, and returned. "You may want to lay low for a while longer," he advised. He scowled at the sizzling pink medicine. "Go on. Bottoms up."

Not wanting to alienate his ally, Jim drank the dose with a sense of doom. He sank back into his pillow and closed his eyes. What's a little more puke? he thought listlessly. Down in the hole, after he had passed out from all the smoke, he had dreamed he was lying with his face in a pool of cold fruit cocktail—a soothing, blissful dream. When he had come to, he found he was lying in his own vomit.

Now, he burped again and found, to his surprise, that he felt marginally better. Like the slow sweep of a heavy wing, his hangover lifted a few notches and he slipped into a minty pink doze.

At five o'clock his grandfather transferred him from bed to the chaise on the porch. Harriet and Stan had flown back to Seattle earlier that afternoon. "They said to say good-bye. They didn't want to wake you," Jack told him.

His mother brought him a bowl of chicken noodle soup on a tray covered with a linen mat. There was a linen napkin to match and a little plate of carefully overlapped Saltines. "Thanks, Mom," he said humbly, but she refused to meet his eyes. He took a breath. "I'm sorry about last night."

She said nothing. With a slight shock, he saw there were tears in her eyes. "Ma?"

"I can't believe you were so stupid!" she burst out. "You could have been killed! You come back from the dead and first thing you do is go out and pull a stunt like that—why didn't you call? I would have come and picked you up."

"I passed out."

"Do you think you're immune to death? Do you really think you're impervious?"

A spark of mischief surfaced through Jim's guilt. "As a matter of fact . . ."

"It's not funny, Jim."

"Sorry."

Mattie struggled to let it go. She sat down in a cushioned

chair, stared at the porch's sisal rug, and saw again the blackened, contracted limbs of the body she had believed was his.

"You want something?" Jack offered. "A soda?"

She looked up, surprised by his solicitousness. "Maybe when Spence gets here." She turned back to her son. "I'm putting him in your room. Now that Harriet and Stan are gone, there's no point having him staying in a motel."

Jim swallowed a spoonful of soup. "So what's going on with him?"

Mattie was aware that her father had paused in the doorway. "He's been very supportive."

"Is it serious?" Jim persisted.

"He's a married man," Jack said dismissively.

"That's not what I asked," Jimmy retorted.

"Spence is my friend," Mattie told her son. "A true friend. He's trying to help me find out who set the fire." She hesitated, then took the plunge. "You should know that you're under suspicion."

"Me?"

The sight of his pale, shocked face constricted her heart. "No one can confirm your movements."

"But that's ridiculous! If I set it, how did I end up in that hole? I would have run in the opposite direction, not into the blowup!"

"All I'm telling you is what I got out of Chip Zampill—the agent who took your statement in the hospital. It's not over. Zampill hasn't closed the investigation, but he's putting it on the back burner. He says he doesn't have the resources to take the circumstantial route, to start checking out the lives of the victims, see if anyone had a motive for murder." She stopped. "Do you know of anyone who would want you dead?"

"Moi?"

"I'm serious."

"Me too."

"You have no enemies? You're not in any kind of trouble?"

"*No.*" He looked at his mother with curiosity. "What kind of trouble?"

"Girl trouble. Drug trouble. I don't know what kind of trouble!" She ducked her head in frustration, pressed her fingers into her scalp as if to hold it down.

From the doorway, Jack said, "If you are, we need to know." His voice was steady, firm.

"I'm not in any kind of trouble. Okay?" Jim flushed angrily. "What about you, Ma?" he countered. "You've got more enemies than I do. What about all the people who'd like to see you fall off the fire ladder?"

Jack growled, "Eat your soup before it gets cold." He let the screen door bang behind him as he exited to get his drink. Mattie ran a thoughtful finger along the faded piping on the cushion of her chair. The fabric was almost ten years old, the chintz peonies now almost invisible. It was time to get the cushions recovered. Or buy new ones. Perhaps new ones would be cheaper. A European cabana-type stripe, maybe. She had seen some in one of the catalogs.

"I can't believe the police are dropping out!" Jimmy protested to his mother. "It's only been—what, a week?"

"A week today," Mattie confirmed.

"One fucking week!"

She glanced in the direction of the screen door. Her father didn't tolerate language in the house. "I'm not going to let it go," she promised. "And you're right. It could have been anyone. Someone in the system. Someone in the camp. A psychopathic tourist, a paid torch—I don't know! We have to start someplace. The most obvious place is the victims."

Through the screens, late rays of coppery sunlight bathed the tops of the pines that sheltered the house. Mattie breathed in the scent of dust and dry pine needles and recounted what Spence had discovered about Pami's employer, Rusty Stanislaw. "He made no bones about wanting her insurance money," she informed her son. "He was home at the time, so there's motive but no opportunity. Same with Greta Lowry."

"Greta?"

"Wade's death may have saved her a divorce, but both she and her boyfriend were at school when the fire blew up."

Jimmy shook his head like a dog shaking off water. "I thought school didn't start until after Labor Day."

"Teacher's workday. We checked it out yesterday, went to the school, talked to the teachers. This morning Spence drove down to Deer Lodge to talk to the warden about Manny Leonard and Billy Dallas. He should be back pretty soon. I've got a meat loaf in the oven."

A memory tugged at Jim, something someone had said about Cat last night at Culligan's bar. Was it Howard, her housemate? He had stayed in a booth, hesitant to mingle, like a second-class guest.

"You want some more?" Mattie asked, indicating his bowl.

"Not right now."

"Maybe you'd like some meat loaf later on, with us?"

"Sure," he conceded absently. Then, as she lifted the soup tray, the memory came flooding back. "*Mom.*"

The tray stopped in midair. "What?"

"I just remembered. Something Cat's housemate told me last night. It's probably nothing, but . . ."

"What?"

"Howard—that's her housemate—told me someone was hassling her. He said she'd been involved with this guy. Then she brushed him off but he wouldn't leave her alone. He said it had gotten ugly."

"How do you mean, ugly? Did he threaten her?"

"No. She threatened *him*. You know what she was like."

"Actually, I don't." Mattie was not even sure what Catherine Carew looked like.

"Well—she was wild. She would try anything once. Anything."

"Anything."

Jim looked embarrassed. "All I know is what this guy Howard said."

"And what was that?"

"That she was into some kinky stuff with this guy."

Mattie looked out at the coppery pines. "You mean, sexually."

"Yes."

"Like what? Whips and chains?"

"I don't know, Mom! He didn't go into it. It was beside the point!"

"And what was the point? I'm sorry if I'm being dim."

"The point was, she could take care of herself."

44

Howard Tweed and Cat Carew had shared a converted carriage house behind a substantial Victorian on a tree-lined street near the university. The little rental had a cottagey charm, enhanced by weedy-looking dooryard beds of black-eyed Susans, yarrow, and daylilies, but the owner had cut corners on the insulation, so the heat bill in winter was higher than Cat, who was already in residence when Howard answered her to-share ad, had led him to believe. Next time, he resolved, before he rented a place, he would ask to see the bills. After a year of thermostat wars (she turning it up, he turning it down) he submitted an ultimatum for the coming winter: either he would find a new place to live or she would pay seventy-point-three percent of their heat bill for December, January, and February.

"October, November, March, and April we go fifty-fifty," he proposed, showing her his calculations.

To his relief—for he really had not wanted to move—she had agreed without argument. "No problem," she said airily, waving away his figures.

"You agree?"

She had laughed at his surprise, a deep throaty laugh. "Hey, Howie, I'm not about to start sweating the small stuff!" She had not needed to add, "Like you." Howard was majoring in accounting at the business school. He did not mind Cat's teasing; the reverse, he felt it added dash to his life, as if he had acquired a zany older sister along with his share of the house.

Each had a garretlike bedroom upstairs—formerly quarters for the groom and stableboy. The downstairs, where the horses had been stabled, they shared. The old stalls had been knocked out long before to make a two-car garage. Then the garage had been converted into a combination living room/kitchen with exposed brick walls. The space was barely large enough for the massive secondhand sofa that faced the TV. Cat said she had moved it in by herself, which seemed an impossible feat—she was half his size—but after getting to know her, Howard did not doubt it.

When Jimmy called Howard early Saturday morning to ask if he would talk to his mother and a reporter friend about Cat, Howard was flattered and curious. He had not met any of Cat's crewmates before the wake at Culligan's, but he had liked Jim—he seemed less full of himself than some—and he had heard that Mrs. McCulloch was under professional attack on account of the entrapment. "To talk privately," Jim said.

"No problem," he said, and no sooner were the words out of his mouth than he realized it was Cat's expression. He also realized that it was a problem: Mrs. Carew was staying in Cat's room, packing up her things. He did not want to talk about Cat in front of her. "Better make it after lunch," he suggested. Mrs. Carew would be gone by then. Two of Cat's friends from the bakery where she had worked last winter had volunteered to drive Mrs. Carew and her daughter's things back to Pocatello.

At the wake, Howard had found Dawn Carew amazing: an exotic like her daughter, but softer, plumper, at once childlike and maternal, dancing to her own music. He had been moved by her openness, her willingness to "celebrate" Cat's life in a seedy roadside café. He could not imagine his own mother celebrating his life, even at her country club.

But next day, Mrs. Carew (he found himself reluctant to call her Dawn) had been more subdued, less generous. She had gone through the house inch by inch, with greedy eyes and grasping fingers. "Is this hers? What about this? And this?" Howard realized he was going to have to buy a new TV, even though he had paid to have Cat's repaired. Mrs. Carew took the coffeemaker, dishes, pots, flatware, the vacuum. He lied about the sofa. "It came with the house," he told her. And when he asked for a photo Cat had taken and framed—a black-and-white Ansel Adams–type shot of bear grass on a mountainside—Mrs. Carew lifted it off the wall and said sadly, "Ah, yes. It's a lovely one. You have a good eye, Howard." She pressed the photo to her bosom and promised, "I'll see that you get a copy." But he knew he never would, just as he knew she would never reimburse him for the fifty-three-minute phone call she had made to Hawaii to "a dear old family friend." She had even packed (in one of the cardboard cartons he had spent half the afternoon running around town to find for her) a little tin of herb tea that had exactly two bags left in it.

That night he heard her crying through the wall. At first the sound had shocked him. Then, as he lay in bed listening, he had the feeling it was a summons. That she wanted him to get up, knock on her door, ask if she was okay. But he had not. Instead, he had pulled his pillow over his head.

Although Howard expected Mrs. Carew to be gone by noon, Cat's bakery friends were late with their borrowed van, so when Mattie and Spence arrived, the moving had only just begun and Mrs. Carew was still very much present. To Howard's embarrassment, she seemed to assume that Mattie and Spence had shown up to help. "Oh, how good of you!" she exclaimed. Gamely, they joined in. Spence assisted Howard and the two bakers in maneuvering Cat's queen-sized mattress down the little stairway, while Mattie dismantled the wire shelving in Cat's closet.

When the van was finally loaded, Howard was surprised, after all the wrangling, to see how little space his dead housemate's possessions took up. There was the TV wrapped in her red-and-white quilt, the box of kitchen things, a box of papers and books, a couple of cartons of clothes and shoes. Stacked beside the bare mattress, they looked paltry.

DawnStar Carew hugged everyone good-bye. "You're a sweetheart," she told Mattie. "Now I don't want you to worry. As I told you, our Joseph is an experienced hand in this sort of situation. As soon as anything comes through, I'll let you know."

"About what?"

"About your son."

"Oh." Mattie was confused, but wasn't sure she wanted to press further. She smiled politely. "Thank you."

But Dawn was quick on the uptake. "Oh, I'm sorry! How stupid of me! Your Jim's still with us, isn't he?"

"Um, yes."

"Well, it can't be helped." She gave Mattie a sympathetic squeeze. "We all have our crosses to bear . . . Howard." She embraced him, then turned to the others. "Howard has taken such wonderful care of me. He spent all yesterday afternoon running around finding boxes for me. I feel as if I've gained a son!"

"Glad to help out," Howard said.

She cocked her head as if listening to someone else, then held up a hand. "Wait!" She scrambled into the van and a moment later came back with Cat's photograph of bear grass. She showed it around. "Cat took it," she told them. She smiled a brave, wistful smile. "Wildflowers by my wildflower. We want you to have it, Howard. To remember her by."

We? Howard wondered.

Inside, the house was quiet. There were clean rectangles on the walls where posters had been removed and dust balls along the baseboard where the TV trolley had stood. Mattie felt the house settling into a new, tentative emptiness. She watched Howard lay the framed photograph down on the kitchen counter. He was a large youth, with a big Anglo-

Saxon nose and a straight, prim mouth. His expression was thoughtful as he gazed at the picture of bear grass. With thumb and forefingers of both hands, he aligned the bottom edge of the frame with the edge of the counter.

"Would you prefer us to come back another time?" Mattie asked.

"No." He removed his fingers from the frame.

They sat down in the living area, Mattie and Spence on the enormous sofa, Howard in his own canvas sling chair. Mattie explained her mission. "Basically," she concluded, "we'd like to rule out murder. Do you know if anyone had any reason to kill your housemate?"

"To kill her? No."

"Or do her harm. Jim said she was harassed by a man whom she'd stopped seeing."

"Oh, him. Well, he called a lot at first, but she wouldn't talk to him. Then he started calling at five o'clock in the morning, waking me up and not saying anything, but I knew it was him."

"When was this?" Mattie inquired.

"Oh, January, February? Sometime after Christmas break. It was weird, because he knew she was working at the bakery, that she wouldn't be home. It was like he wanted to know who was in the house while she was gone. I wondered if he was stalking her. I complained to the telephone company about it, but they weren't any help, so I told Cat. I thought she ought to go the police, report it, but she wasn't worried. She said she'd take care of it herself."

"Did she?"

"Yeah. She said she'd talked to him and it was cool. The calls stopped. I forgot about it. Then the first week of June, he called again. I remember because exams were over and I was working on a paper I had to make up. It was her day off. He called later than usual, around seven o'clock. I knew it was him. It sounded like he was on a car phone. Anyway, this time he asked for her. I told him she was asleep, and could I take a message, and he told me to wake her up, it was an emergency. So I told him to hang on and went and woke her up. She was furious. She let him have it, told him she'd splash his name all over the newspaper if he ever called again." Howard raised an admiring eyebrow. "And it worked. He never called back—at least as far I as know."

"Do you know what his name was?" Mattie asked.

Howard shook his head. "It made me wonder if he was somebody, him not wanting his name in the paper. Or maybe he just didn't want his wife to find out. But I don't even know if he was married. I thought it was none of my business." He moved restlessly in his chair. His eyes were worried.

"What did he look like?" Spence asked. "How old was he?"

"I never saw him. That was the good thing about Cat and me in this place. It's real small, but our schedules worked out. She was usually gone all night—bartending out at Culligan's or working in the bakery—so I had the place to myself to study or whatever. During the day, when she slept, I had classes or would work in the library. Some weeks we scarcely bumped into each other." Howard stood up. Two strides took him to the kitchen counter. He leaned back against it, ran a finger along the frame of Cat's photograph.

"One time I came home in the middle of the day to get something—a book I thought I had in my carrel at the library—and decided I might as well have some lunch as long as I was home and while I was fixing it, I realized she, uh, had company."

"Did you see who it was?" Spence asked.

"No, I just heard them." He raised his eyes up to the kitchen ceiling. "I sucked up my ramen and left. I never saw him."

Keeping her voice even, Mattie said, "Jim understood that they were involved in some kind of kinky sex?"

Howard shifted his weight from one large sneaker to the other. "When I complained about the phone calls, Cat told me that he was a weirdo and that she'd tried to heal him with some kind of yoga sex. 'High sex,' she called it. Something about moving energies around the body. I didn't get what she was talking about and I really didn't want to get into it with her."

Mattie nodded sympathetically.

He shrugged. "That one time I came home?"

"Yes?"

"It sounded just—normal."

"Did she say why she broke it off?" Spence asked.

"Not really. I assumed she got bored."

"Did she have a lover after him?" Mattie wondered.

"Not that I knew of."

"What about his first name?" Spence persisted. "She must have called him something when she talked about him."

"My pervert."

"What?"

"That's how she referred to him. 'My pervert.' She used to try and shock me, so I was never sure how much she said was for effect. She liked to keep people off balance." He picked up the framed photograph on the counter, put it down again. He looked from Mattie to Spence. "I thought her sex life was none of my business." He ran his hand over his face, as if trying to wipe away doubt. "She said he liked to play games with fire."

Mattie and Spence stared at him.

"I thought she was just bragging!" he burst out. "You know, like telling me how hot she was. What was I supposed to do?"

45

Sunday night, after what he described to Mattie as a twenty-four-hour "pub crawl" through Missoula's bars and cafés, Spence met a young woman in the parking lot of a downtown motel. As she had informed him over the phone, she was driving a black Honda civic. She got out of her car wearing a black leather bustier with ankle-zip jeans and golden high-heeled sandals. In the mercury-vapor light, the exposed bulges of her breasts had a lavender tinge. She climbed into the passenger seat of Spence's rental. "Hi, there," she said. Her smile was more edgy than sensual. At the corners of her blunt nose and between the plucked arcs of her eyebrows, ranges of pimples cracked her heavy makeup, but her teeth looked healthy, straight and milk-fed American. "How you doing, hon?" she asked.

"Fine, thanks," he said. "I was hoping you could help me out." He handed her a fifty.

She looked at it. "I'm going to need a lot more than that. For a specialty."

"And for information?"

She gave him an appraising look. "What kind of information?"

"About people who play fire games."

"Information." She cocked her head. "You mean you just want to talk?"

"Right."

She checked her watch. "Ten minutes," she stipulated. Her eyes were bored. Almost regretfully, she took the bill, tucked it down into her bustier, then arched her back, dutifully proffering the bulges of her lavender-tinted breasts. "So you're into fire games. Tell me how you like to play."

"Uh, it's not me."

"Hey, sweetie, don't be shy," she encouraged in a voice that was warmer, more humorous than her shrewd eyes. He explained what he wanted. She chewed on the side of her thumb as she listened. Her painted fingernails were as long and curving as a mandarin accountant's. In the light through the car window, they gleamed navy blue. He noticed she had a miniature crescent on the nail of her forefinger—silver moon, a silver claw?

"Huh," she said when he finished. "You're a writer? What do you write?"

"Books, mostly. Nothing you've ever heard of."

"Try me."

He shook his head. "You wouldn't know them."

"What, you think I only read the Marquis de Sade?" The name rolled off her tongue with an expert French accent.

"No, no," he assured her. "Of course not." Where had she picked up her French?

"You got a problem with Sade?" she demanded.

"No, it's not that. As a matter of fact, I have a problem with my publisher. The reason it's unlikely you would know my books is the runs are so tiny they go out of print after my aged mother does her Christmas shopping."

The girl frowned, uncomprehending, and moved back to the Marquis. "You should read him if you're into fire games," she recommended. "There's this really far-out scene where this woman roasts her own daughter. She's got the little girl in the fireplace and these servants doing all sorts of stuff to her while she's getting it off on watching the kid burn up!"

Could it be satire? Spence wondered. He had never read Sade. Had the Copper Creek arsonist stayed to watch? He directed his informant back to the entrapment.

"Yeah, I saw it all on TV." She shook her head. "You really know what's-her-name? The one whose son fell down the shaft?"

"Mattie McCulloch. She's an old friend."

"I saw them pulling him out. She must be pretty happy."

"Well, of course. But—"

"You know," the girl went on, "it's the families I feel sorry for. No matter how bad it was for those guys who got caught, it was only once. It's over for them. For the families, it keeps on going. It would be real hard to get it out of your head, what it was like for your loved one before he passed. Even if it was only a couple seconds—a couple seconds can take a very long time," she observed, as if speaking from grim experience.

"Mattie was in command. She feels responsible to the families."

"I can see that." Absently, she ran a fingertip back and forth over the little map of bumps beside her nostril. "I saw tonight where the fire was contained. Some police spokesman said the investigation was still 'ongoing.' Like I said to my boyfriend, you know what that means. Forget it."

"We'd rather not."

"Yeah. Well, I don't know that it'll help any, but you could try talking to Loreen. She got burned in July by some psycho. I mean, literally. Got her nose broke in the bargain."

The next morning, when Spence told Mattie what he had learned, she insisted on accompanying him to interview Loreen. Given Mattie's immediate celebrity, and the fact that when fame knocks, however lightly, locked doors tend to open, he agreed. So Mattie donned her Forest Service uniform, and after spending the morning—Monday morning—at her office in Fort Missoula, she met Spence and Loreen at the merry-go-round in a newly constructed pocket park above the Clark Fork. The bright blare of circus music suggested a crowd, but in fact, the only rider was a small solemn-faced Indian girl strapped to a white charger bedecked with ribbons and roses. Spence and Loreen stood with the child's grandmother watching her fly round and round.

The prostitute was fat, blonde, and probably not out of her teens. The rims of her ears were studded with multiple earrings, but she wore no makeup. Her skin was a sunburned pink which, together with her white-blond eyebrows and lashes, gave her an albino look. She was wearing a loose smocklike top in a floral print, white nylon slacks, and white athletic shoes.

The venue was her choice. From the merry-go-round, a paved walkway followed the course of the river and she was trying to lose weight by exercising during her lunch hour. She had already lost eighteen pounds, she told them. "Only seven more and I'm halfway to my goal." Her goal was fifty pounds by Christmas—which, given her size, seemed reasonable enough. She must have weighed close to two hundred pounds, Mattie estimated.

"It's really helped my back as well, all this walking," Loreen said happily. "I don't mind telling you, lifting clients is murder on your back."

Mattie blinked behind her sunglasses.

"Loreen works in a nursing home," Spence supplied.

"Assisted-living center," Loreen corrected.

"They're lucky to have you," Spence declared gallantly.

"I don't know about that."

There was an awkward silence. They moved aside for a jogger. When he was out of earshot, Loreen said to Mattie, "So you want to know about the guy who burned me?"

"Please."

"Broke my nose, too. Said I wasn't doing it right, but I had the feeling he was making it up as he went along—" She broke off and looked at them. "What exactly do you want to know?"

"Who he was. Did you get his name?" Mattie asked.

She shook her head.

"Do you remember what he looked like, Loreen? Can you describe him?"

She looked uncomfortable. "Well, tall, but not too tall. Maybe medium tall?"

"As tall as me?" Spence asked.

She frowned. "He had his shoes off. He was taller than me, I know that."

"What about his build?"

"I'd say average."

Mattie nodded. "How old, do you think?"

"Hard to tell. He was older, I could tell that. His hair felt thin on top—though some of the younger ones suffer hair loss. But I'm pretty sure he was older. It took him a real long time to get it up."

"What color was his hair?"

"Brownish? It was kinda dim in the room. He had a mustache, I know that. An old-fashioned one."

"How do you mean, old-fashioned?"

"It was skinny, like in one of those old pirate movies."

Spence asked, "Did you notice any scars, birthmarks?"

"He was circumcised," she offered helpfully.

They walked past a pair of lovers lying together on the grass under a tree. A medium tall, out-of-shape middle-aged man, Mattie thought discouragely. With a skinny, maybe brown, mustache.

"On the TV?" Loreen said to Mattie.

"Yes?"

"They called you the boss of fire bosses."

" 'Fire boss' is the old term. My title was Incident Commander."

"Yeah, that's what they said. They were explaining the system, how it was like the military and all that. So I don't know if this means anything, but he kept telling me he was a fire boss. Like I was supposed to be impressed. At the time, I figured it was just part of his fun and games. Then I heard it on TV. Fire boss. It made me wonder."

Mattie felt her heart skip a beat. "You think he was in the Command system?"

"Well, it made me wonder. I kept watching the TV, thinking maybe I'd see him, maybe he was one of the generals or whatever. But after a while, everyone started looking familiar. I mean, they keep showing the same stuff over and over."

"What if I showed you some pictures?" Mattie pressed.

"I could try." Her voice was dubious.

"We'd appreciate any help you can give us."

She stopped and looked from one to the other. "I got his license plate."

They stared.

"Insurance," she explained. "A girlfriend taught me that. Always memorize the john's plates. She's dead now." Her eyes were sad and wise. She dug into the pocket of her flimsy white pants, pulled out a pink message slip. "You think he was the one who set the fire?"

Mattie nodded at the slip in the girl's hand. "That should help us find out."

Like a poker player protecting her hand, she pressed the pink slip against her floral bosom. "No cops. I don't want to lose my job."

Mattie looked at Spence.

"No cops," Loreen insisted urgently. "It's not just my job. I don't want that creep coming after me."

"Understandably," Spence said.

"Loreen," Mattie said, "the only way we're going to get this guy is to work with the cops. You know that. If we all work together, you will not get hurt! I promise!"

Her face closed.

"Please," Mattie begged. "You've got to trust us!"

Loreen kept on walking, saying nothing. Mattie and Spence stayed with her. Finally she stopped in the middle of the path and thrust the slip at Mattie.

Mattie took it like a gift check, without unfolding it. She inserted it into her breast pocket and secured the flap. "Thank you. I promise you, Loreen, he won't hurt you again!"

"I hope not," Loreen said glumly.

Mattie took out a business card, scribbled a number on the back, and gave it to the girl. "Here's my home number. I want you to call me anytime. I mean it. Anytime. We're going to get this guy!"

Loreen looked at the card, looked at Mattie. "You're much prettier than on TV."

Mattie gave her a firm hug, kissed her plump, scrubbed cheek, and wondered what it would have been like to have a daughter.

46

After leaving Loreen, Mattie called Chip Zampill in Helena on her car phone. On the back of his card, he had written the private number of a direct line to his desk, but to her disappointment, a machine answered. She left a message saying she had a new lead, then punched in the number on the front of the card. A secretary answered and informed her that Agent Zampill would be out of the office until tomorrow morning. "Is it an emergency?" the secretary inquired. Mattie hesitated. "No," she decided with some reluctance. "But if he checks in, please tell him I called." She hung up and let out an impatient blast of air. "What now?" she asked Spence.

"I think we need more information on the fire bosses at the Justice," he answered thoughtfully.

"That's a lot of bosses. You're talking team leaders all the way up to section chiefs."

"Let's start at the top."

She looked at him. "Ned?"

"Why not?"

Mattie looked Ned Voyle over in her mind's eye. "I don't know. He's no Boy Scout, but it's hard to imagine that he would . . ." She did not finish her sentence.

"Hard to imagine anyone would, but someone did. What do you know about your teammates outside the Justice? How many of the Command team live in the Missoula area, for example?"

Mattie frowned. "Ned Voyle. Mike and Peggy Robuck. I imagine Brian does too—he works downtown at the Forest Service's Regional Headquarters. The others I'm not sure. I think Grant lives somewhere down the Bitterroot Valley, maybe around Hamilton?"

"Let's have lunch," Spence suggested. "Then we'll go see Brian. He's the one to start with."

"Why?"

"He's in public relations, isn't he?"

"What has that got to do with Loreen?" she demanded anxiously.

"Nothing. But he should be able to give us some basic facts about who's who on the team."

They ate lunch at a storefront bar near the courthouse. The pressed-tin ceiling was painted brown, the walls were tan, and the worn plush armchairs in the lounge area had faded into various shades of nicotine.

"Perfect," Spence approved. "Not a fern in sight." He ordered a martini.

Mattie wondered to herself what was wrong with ferns. The dim sepia atmosphere of the place struck her as quasi-derelict. Spence seemed to enjoy the leisurely service, but it made her restless. When she shifted in her elephantine brown chair, its cushions exhaled the breath of old cigars. She asked for the bill before Spence could ask for a second cup of coffee and hurried him over to the Forest Service's Regional Headquarters, a classical Federal-style stone building four blocks away on Pine Street. They found Brian in his office. He was obviously surprised to see them.

Out of fire clothes, he looked more imposing—his crisply pressed shirt and well-tailored gabardine trousers conferred a bureaucratic stature that the democratic Nomex did not, but his manner was genial and he greeted Mattie like a long-lost friend. So I'm still in the club? she wondered cynically. She reintroduced Spence.

"Right, right," Brian said as the two men shook hands. "How's your book coming along? Uses of fire in war, isn't it?"

"Well, that's the direction I was headed. Now I'm thinking of doing something on the fatalities."

"You and everyone's mother. Last couple days, we've had a regular swarm of authors." He dropped two big names.

Spence, who knew both people in person and respected neither, swallowed the bile of jealousy. "Huh," he said, as if to convey a collegial interest. Then he made his request. "Mattie thought you might be able to give me some background on the Command team. Job descriptions, group history, old clips, photos. She's sketched out the Command system for me, but I'd like something more personal. How long the Justice team has been together, which fires you've worked. Ideally, I'd like to interview each of the major players at the Justice."

"To what end?"

"I'm just following my nose at this point. You know what it's like with a book."

Brian gave him a wary smile.

"My feeling is," Spence went on in a confidential tone, "that everyone's focused on the victims. I like to explore the Command team's path as well, see where and how it intersects with the victims."

Brian looked thoughtful. "Let me go through the files, see what I can put together for you. As for interviews, I can't speak for the others—that's up to each of them. But I can give you their numbers and I'll be glad to talk with you myself. Why don't you give me a couple hours, then drop back here around four?"

"Great," Spence said warmly. "If my publisher buys it, I'll put you in my acknowledgments!"

"Just doing my job," he objected modestly, but Mattie could see that the offer pleased him.

"How's Jim doing?" he asked her.

"Pretty well. Thanks."

"Couldn't be easy for him, having to keep going over it, not only for the EIT, but the cops as well."

"Actually he doesn't seem to mind that," Mattie said.

"Oh?"

"He said it's helped him get a handle on what happened. He was pretty disoriented at first. It seems to be coming back to him in bits and pieces."

Brian waited for more, his eyes sympathetic, but Mattie was ready to move on. "We'll see you later, then," she told him.

Out on the street, the September afternoon was warm and soft. Yellow leaves lay on the sidewalk like kindergarten cutouts, and the sky was bright blue above the Victorian cornices of the Higgins Avenue storefronts. She remembered shopping with Jimmy for school, remembered the smells of new pencils, new sneakers, and peanut butter in his lunch box. A Ninja Turtle lunch box. It seemed like no time at all. She thought of all the work waiting for her on her desk. "If I'm going to keep my job, I should probably check in at my office," she said with some reluctance.

Spence nodded. "I might get more out of him without you there." There was a slight question in his voice, as if he were asking permission.

She smiled. "You don't want me," she teased.

He cocked an eyebrow at her.

She laughed. The impatience that had been needling her since their conversation with Loreen suddenly vanished into soft, autumnal air. She felt unreasonably happy.

Later that afternoon, Spence snapped a new tape and new batteries into his tape recorder and went back to Brian's office. As it happened, he was not there. According to his assistant, who apologized profusely, he had been called to a last-minute meeting. He had, however, left Spencer a list of phone numbers, both work and home, of the Command team who had worked the Justice Peak Fire. He had also left a pile of folders filled with press clippings and Forest Service newsletters.

Leafing through the folders at a desk provided by the assistant, Spence formulated an initial plan of attack. He would put together a list of every fire the Justice Overhead team had fought over the last two or three years, compare it to a list of the fires the Millville crew had fought in the same period, and see if and when the Command team intersected with Cat Carew. Not that an overlap would prove anything—Cat could have met her "fire boss" anywhere—but given the swamp of information in the folders, it would at least offer a solid first step.

At the same time, he found it hard to wrench his thoughts away from Mattie: the smooth strength in her legs as they had walked to Brian's office together, the way her stubborn hair had blazed in the sunlight, her slow smile. Was the warmth in her eyes really for him? For him alone? or was it simply a social skill, a trick of charm? He groaned inwardly. He recognized his symptoms as classic: the dire sinkings and surges in his belly, the exquisite flutters and thumps of his heart, the obsessive loop of his thoughts—unmistakably he had fallen in love. But the diagnosis offered no balm. What about Mattie? Was there anything more in her heart for him than fondness? What did she think of him? He wanted to lay the arsonist at her feet, bound neck to ankles, a gift for her to open with the sword of Justice. Lovingly he played with an assortment of execution scenarios, found the ferocious violence of them extremely satisfying, then shook himself back to reality. At the very least, he resolved, he would lay his book at her feet. He might not be able to give her blood or justice, but he could offer a bouquet of answers. He imagined the dedication, "To Mattie." He faltered. What next? Something sparse, profound, something irresistible—of course. Determinedly, he attacked the pile of clippings.

In the second folder, as he picked up a back issue of a regional newsletter, a photo on the front page leaped out at him. It was a group shot of the Type 1 chiefs who had commanded a project fire in the Garnet Range three years before. Owen Kingman had been IC and many of the men at Justice Peak had worked with him on the Garnet team. They had posed together, Nomex sleeves rolled up, arms draped across one another's shoulders, comradely grins under their billed caps. The photo was full-page, large enough so their faces were clearly visible. Two of the men sported mustaches.

Spence felt a galvanizing shiver of discovery. He sat up in his chair. Carefully, he matched the names in the caption to the faces in the photo. He matched them a second time, left to right, front row to back. Then he folded the newsletter in half, slipped it in his notebook with Brian's list of phone numbers, and left.

47

08 Sept 10:17p   Directory C:*.*

Finally back home, heroes trailing clouds of tragedy. EIT didn't let us go till yesterday, the idiots. So it was back and forth, back and forth between the fire camp and Missoula, first to see my Leftover in the hospital then Thursday macho man Robuck ferried a bunch of us up for the for the funerals—two in one day you have to wonder why we bothered with the memorial service. The Lowry kid had a casket, the silver handles would have done a Renaissance pope proud. The relatives wanted a casket so a casket they got, top-of-the-line, compliments of USFS and *this* taxpayer, thank you very much. Ridiculous. It's not like they could have had a viewing or anything. As for Cat, she and her pal went back into the furnace! We got a two-fer out of the funeral home. So there were two "urns" (read plastic boxes!) up front for the service and two humongous arrangements of red roses so no one could say we cheaped out. We didn't stick around for the scatterings, flew right back to camp.

Now it's back to the old grind, all heroes back to their cubicles, please! Everyone at the office very respectful, but there's always that letdown coming off a fire, that ache of exile, as if we'd all been banished from paradise. Some guys tie one on, others do laundry. I do both. I get a nice buzz on, I'm down in the laundry, the fucking washing machine's actually working, I'm on my second load—darks. I did whites first put them in the drier then the drier dings and I take out the things and there's my little towel—my souvenir! I like the idea of hanging it back up in the guest john. But it's real linen, it needs to be ironed if it's going to look right. I figure, how hard could it be? But the iron, even on steam, doesn't get it stiff and smooth—looking like it's supposed to be, it still looks sort of floppy, so I stick it under the faucet, wet it down and go over it again with the iron dry at the Cotton/Linen setting, and I can see it's going to work. Only problem, the towel's real wet, so I have to keep going over it. To tell the truth, it feels pretty good, the repetition, and I'm thinking about guests drying their hands on it, and *not knowing*! I'm standing there ironing, going over it and I realize I'm halfway to a hard-on. I'm thinking hey it's like Proust's madeleine, only the magic of touch instead of taste; all I need is a touch of the towel to bring it all back, the fire in the loins and so forth—then the phone rings. it's Margaret which is annoying enough, but she hums and hahs and I finally go, Margaret, you didn't call to find out how I am and she comes back with, Actually I was wondering how the McCulloch boy was.

I'm thinking what the fuck is going on here, so I tell her I hear he's doing as well as can be expected under the circumstances. I'm thinking she just wants the inside dope, something to one-up her do-gooding pals, but at the same time I've got this feeling something weird's going on, so I keep chatting her up and she lets it drop, this writer stopped by earlier this evening.

Oh I go. What's his name?

Gerald Spencer, she says. He was nice, she says. I hope it was okay to talk to him?

So I go, What's it got to do with me, you talk to whomever you want.

She says, He just wanted a little background on the Command team, the kind of stress you guys are under, how you deal with it—yadda yadda.

Did you tell him about my little problem, Margaret, I ask her.

Oh no, of course not, she goes.

But she's lying. I can tell. That's why she called me up, she's got the guilts. Don't worry about it, I tell her. What else did he want to know about me?

Nothing, she says.

Nothing?

Nothing. Stuff like when you shaved off your mustache.

My mustache? Like we're talking *weirdness here*. It doesn't make sense. I hang up then I remember my towel, it's smoking! Margaret's fucking ruined it! There's this big brown iron mark on it, right above the monogram. Christ! I start freaking out, pour lemon-scented Clorox all over it, Tide, some kind of blue shit, hot water, cold water, I'm scrubbing like fury and end up sticking my middle finger through it, I'm giving myself the finger, and it's like someone else's, it could have been a chicken bone sticking through.

I think, whoa, hang on here, bud, what's coming down? Then it hits me. Like I walked into a freezer. All of a sudden I turn cold. I'm scared. Like the Finger of God's warning me off Jimmy boy. Margaret's phone call was a warning, the towel burning was a warning.

So I go, okay and I give it a little space, visit the concept a little, and I start crying, I'm crying into the tide and it smells so clean, and then bang, sharp as Mommie Dearest's slap, I can hear her, clear as day, You stupid little shit, can't you ever get anything right. I'm fucking five years old and I can't get her off, she's heaving away on the bed like a beached whale, and I'm drowning in despair, O God, the despair of it—

And I stop and think, You are really being stupid, boyo. You're just running scared, it's your own fear talking, not God giving me the finger! Stay rational, you just need to clean up, a little soap and water, good as new.

So I go over the alternatives and I realize it has to be. There's simply no acceptable alternative. Sober up and get him gone.

The business with the towel is not a warning, I'm not going to get my wee-wee OR my immortal soul incinerated, thank you very much. The trick is to do it right this time.

48

The following morning, Agent Chip Zampill returned Mattie's call at work. Carefully keeping the flourish out of her voice, Mattie produced the license number of the man who had burned Loreen's pubic hair and broken her nose.

To her satisfaction, Zampill sounded impressed. "Good job," he praised. "Shouldn't take long to trace. I'll give you a call if it pans out."

"Why wouldn't it?"

"The john might not have any connection to the Justice."

Mattie hung up. She looked down at the galleys on her desk—a paper on fire in needle-leaf forests. The editor of a forestry journal had asked her to review it. She picked up her pencil, then put it down and called Spence.

"We're only guessing that Loreen's john and Cat's pervert are one and the same," she told him.

"Yes, but I think they are." His voice was hard, but there was a bright edge of excitement in it too. "I'll meet you back at the house after work. There's someone I want to talk to."

He was on to something, she was sure of it. "Who?"

"Loreen."

She felt frustrated, a captive at her desk. "I won't be home till late," she half-wailed. "I've got a goddamn meeting." She lowered her voice. "I miss you!"

By the time she got home at ten, both Jack and Jimmy had

gone to bed and Spence was at the kitchen table working on his laptop. They embraced, long and hard and without speaking, as if they had been separated by an ocean.

She pulled back, a rush of words spilled out of her. "I thought the thing would never end, people were going on and on, there was no way I could just up and leave—" Seeing his face, she broke off. "Yes?"

"Chip Zampill called. The license plate. It belongs to Brian Flaherty."

"What?"

"Loreen's john was Brian Flaherty."

"Brian?" It seemed impossible. Of all the men on the team, he was the most genial, the safest— "Are you sure?"

"Yes," he answered grimly.

"You mean the PR guy, the guy we went to see yesterday?"

"One and the same. Your Information officer at the Justice. When Loreen said her john had a mustache, I thought of Grant Sonderdank, the Safety guy. When I was going through the folder Brian had left for me, I found a team picture. Brian had one too. So I went to see his wife."

"You did? You didn't tell me that last night!" she protested.

"I wasn't sure. Not till this afternoon, when I went back to Loreen and showed her the picture. Zampill's call confirms it."

She shook her head, confused. Brian Flaherty was Cat's "pervert"? Images from the Justice flashed back: Brian outside the briefing tent, energetic in his fire clothes, welcoming her aboard the team; Brian with Grant in the chalet's office listening to Spence tell his entrapment story; Brian shepherding her through the press conference after the blowup, his consideration, his sympathy. She felt a sudden wave of nausea. "He killed those kids?"

"All we know is he was at the Twilite Motel with Loreen in July. Zampill's coming over to Missoula tomorrow to have a chat with him. Do you know his wife? Margaret, her name is."

"No," Mattie said. She sat down. "Go on."

"A bit dumpy-looking, but pretty. Maternal marshmallow. Sweet little voice, lives in a basement apartment in a new townhouse. She took the family photographs and the silver. Said she didn't want anything else."

He picked up the notebook beside his laptop, flipped several pages, and began reciting from his notes. "The youngest daughter lives with her, the two older ones—a boy and girl—are off at college. Margaret says she doesn't need much for herself, she's just glad to be on her own. She said they'd had a very difficult winter. She said that they'd never really had a satisfying sex life. And listen to this! She said he had a problem with impotence, even at the beginning of the marriage. It had gotten worse in the last few years, but he refused to talk to his doctor. Drank heavily, ridiculed the idea of a therapist." He closed the notebook. "She told me the only thing that worked was fellatio, and sometimes that was iffy."

"She told you *that?*"

He shrugged. "People will tell you most anything about their sex lives—if you just ask. What offends is questions about money. On that account she was vague, but I'd guess she's precariously close to the poverty line. I had the impression she didn't want to rock the boat for fear he'd cut the kids' tuition off."

"What about girlfriends?"

"She says she suspected, but never found out who. She has nothing to link him to Cat."

"Phone bills."

He shook his head. "All local calls."

"What about his fire games?"

Spence brightened marginally. "I asked Loreen about that when I showed her the group picture. She picked him out, by the way. Pointed to him right off." He took a breath. "She told me what they did. She said she hadn't wanted to go into it with you there, but he had this ritual—"

"Please." Mattie raised a hand to stop him. Visions of Brian Flaherty's sex games were the last thing she needed dancing in her head. "What I wondered is, could Margaret testify that he was into fire? Sexually, I mean."

"She had no idea what I was talking about. I also asked if he ever hit her. The idea shocked her. She said he'd been a good husband. Blames herself a lot for the breakup. Thinks she should have been more patient with 'his little problem.'"

"God," Mattie said. "It's so awful." She looked up at Spence from her chair, felt tears swimming in her eyes.

"Yes. It is," he agreed.

49

09 Sept 2:17p   Directory C:*.*

iiiiiiiiiiiiiiiiiiiiiiii IIIII can not beliiiiiiiiiiiiiieve iiiiiiit—somethii
iiiiiiiiiiii
iiiiiiiiiiiiiiiiiiiiiiiiiiiiiiiiiiiiiiiiii
thank God for Small favors, in this case a little flake of potato chip under the i. The last thing I need is to have my laptop go on the blink. What I need is to get it down, to work through it. It's hard to believe (as I started to say!) that she turned up after all this time. The Whore, a new card in the deck! I'd completely forgotten about her. Chesterton calls coincidence a spiritual pun but in this case I feel like I'm missing it. I should call up the old biddy Carew, get her to lay out the tarot for me, give me a reading!

In any case there's nothing they can do about it, nothing. I just need to figure it out. I reeeeeeeeeeeeeeead
shit

Was I eating potato chips last night?

THE WHORE. I'm sure it's McCulloch's doing, she and her writer pal. Last night he was snooping around Margaret, first thing this morning Zampill shows up at my office, I haven't even finished my coffee. He's got another cop with him, one I haven't seen before. To ask a few more questions, they said.

So I say, Shoot, and Zampill goes into a Miranda drill.

What's going on, I ask them, and of course they don't say squat. I've got a pile of shit a mile high on my desk and at the same time

I'm wondering what they've got, has the kid talked, so I say, Look, I don't have time to play games, and Zampill nods and pulls out his cards: the whore, my license plate.

I think it was at that point I realized that McCulloch has to go too, both of them, the witch-bitch and her pussy-licking little nit. The nit gets his, she's going to be a royal pain in the ass about it no matter how careful I am. I don't know why I didn't see it before! Clarity, like growth, seems to come in increments.

It shook me up a bit, Zampill's pulling it out of his ass like that, but now I can hear things clicking, falling into place, like I finally got the right combination and the safe is unlocked. All I need is to pull open the door, a simple matter of following through.

I tell Zampill, Clearly there's a mistake. I shake my head. Jesus, that's terrible, what's next? The poor girl. What's her name?

He just looks at me.

She must have got the number wrong, I say. Maybe she's dyslexic. Which was a mistake. Look, I go. I don't mean to be flip. But you come in here and accuse me of setting some unfortunate girl's private parts on fire—I let them have it but they don't back off.

He wants to know when I shaved off my mustache. I'm going WHAT but I humor him. Last spring sometime, I say. I got tired of putting shoeblack on it, I say.

Does he crack a smile?

Noooh. The two of them look at each other. Then the other one, the younger one says, Where were you at the time of the Copper Creek blowup?

I look at him as if he's crazy. At the Meander, I say.

No one remembers seeing you after lunch, he says.

Jesus fucking Christ! I can't believe it! They've been going around behind my back, grilling the team about where the fuck I was after lunch! I tell them to get the hell out, from now on if they've got any questions they can talk to my attorney.

Well, it's not even worth calling the asshole, not the way he bills, you can hear his meter dinging every fifth word. It's just that fat little whore's word versus mine. They're not buying mine but so what, it's not like I put the room on my Visa, like the cunt's going to give me bonus mileage points! As for where I was after lunch on the fatal day, for all anyone knows I was in the can shitting my guts out. There's no connection. Goes to show how desperate they are, Zampill's got nothing and knows it, you could see it on their faces, Jesus, McCulloch should give them cop-face lessons!

so they go. now here I am staring at my new card, Whore-cum-burned-snatch. I can't even remember if I cum-ed!

Just went back over this whole file, found her in July. I have to say, it's pretty compelling reading, not just the whore, I found all sorts of stuff I'd forgotten, a lot of important insights, my connection to the fabric of the universe and so on. I'm going, hey, I'm a pretty insightful kind of guy! Seriously, when you think of all the crap that's written in the guise of self-help, it made me think I should give it a try, turn these notes into something that might actually *help* someone, something to think about.

09 Sept 09.02p   Directory C:*.*

can't see the forest for the trees?
Answer: burn them.
A koan of my own!
wheelchair might be tricky   the script I know by heart!

50

On Wednesday, September 11, Mattie ate lunch at her desk: a ham-and-low-fat-cheese sandwich on whole-wheat bread, a Baggie full of baby carrots. In an attempt to reclaim her working self, she turned to her pet project, a long-term study of how wildfire changed vegetation in plots she had measured out in her district. She pulled out her latest field notes and began plugging degrees of heat and flame lengths, amounts of duff consumed and degrees of scorch into her computer. Usually, she took a mindless pleasure in the work: watching the slow buildup of numbers and the emerging patterns was like trying to read a river's hidden currents. But now she found herself staring blankly at the numbers on the screen; images of the blowup, the funerals, kept bombarding her. She felt the need to reconfigure her command at the Justice, to review each step of each day through the lens of last night's revelations about Brian Flaherty. Snatches of conversation with him took on new, hideously disturbing meanings; how much had she let him influence her decision-making? Would she have done anything differently?

Then there was the question of Spence. *He's a true friend*, she had told her father. What did that mean? How much longer would Spence stay? The thought of him leaving, flying back to New York, made her feel suddenly bereft. She wondered if Enid was beautiful. She imagined heavy, dark hair, dramatic Arthurian jewelry. She was, after all, an artist, a sculptor whose talent Spence not only seemed to admire, but to revere. Did she truly see him only as a convenience? Or was his confession simply a pose? Spence was a writer, he had a creative life of his own. Likely enough, Enid nurtured and supported his explorations as much as he respected hers. It was Enid, after all, who took care of his mother. And in the end, when it came right down to it, were not all lasting marriages intricate balances of convenience?

Sitting alone in front of her computer screen, Mattie felt like the Little Match Girl standing out in the cold gazing through an upper-story window at a private feast. She saw a golden supper, a sparkling couple, artists both of them, flushed with the heady wine of creativity. From the pavement below the window, her own abilities seemed dull and utilitarian. She had climbed the fire ladder, but the rungs under her feet had a thin, aluminum ring.

The phone rang, a raucous caw that made her jump. She picked it up, hoping it was Spence, and heard a loud crackle of static. "Hello?" she called over the interference.

"McCulloch?" A male voice.

"Yes?" She waited. "Hello? Who is it?"

"Brian Flaherty."

Brian. The walls of her office seemed to heave. "We've got a bad connection," she said, trying to keep her voice natural.

"I've got Jim."

"What do you mean, you've got Jim?"

"Well, I don't want to be melodramatic. Let's just say I borrowed him." Despite the fuzzy line, Mattie caught a sleazy coyness in his voice.

"What is going on?" she snapped. "What do you want with him?"

"I just want to talk to you. Privately."

"So what has Jim got to do with anything?"

"That remains to be seen," he said jovially. "If you bring anyone with you—and I mean *anyone*—your boy's going up in smoke."

Mattie opened her mouth. No words came out.

"McCulloch. You there?"

She took a breath. "Yes."

"I'm serious. This time he gets burned all the way through, not just singed."

"Let me talk to him."

"You don't believe me?"

"I said, let me talk to him."

She heard an odd muffled commotion at the other end of the line, then a coughing, choking sound. "Ma? Don't come! Don't do what he—"

She realized in horror that it *was* Jimmy. "Jim?" she barked into the receiver. "Jimmy?"

"Convinced?" Brian asked.

"Brian, for God's sake!" she pleaded through a burst of static. "Brian? Brian, you're breaking up!"

"Wait."

She strained to hear. Whatever he was doing, it was taking a long time. How had he gotten Jim? Had Brian gone to the house? Jack was supposed to have taken Jim out to the university to talk to his dean about his classes. Was Jack okay? What about Spence? Spence never would have let Brian near Jim.

"Brian!" she called frantically into the phone. "Brian, where are you!" But he did not answer. Where was he? How could she possibly find them?

"McCulloch?" Brian said into her ear. The line was suddenly clear. "Where are you?" she demanded. "Are you on a radio?"

"Cell phone. One of the great conveniences of modern crime. We're out at the old Parvis Feed Mill. Out Orange, across the railroad tracks. I don't want to see anyone with you. None of your pals. No cops. Nobody. I'll keep an eye out for you. A bird's eye," he smirked.

"What?"

"There's a convenient little cupola up here on the roof. Full of old machinery and pigeon shit, but worth the climb! Great view of the Bitterroot. Plus, you can see all the way up and down the street, into the alleys, into the Dumpsters. Three hundred and sixty degrees. A sniper's wet dream—as it were! I'll be on the lookout for you. If I see *anyone* else, I mean *anyone,* your Jimbo gets to play Joan of Arc. I've got a nice little stage all set up downstairs. A theater-in-the-round, you might say!"

Mattie's mouth was dry. She swallowed. "Don't do anything till I get there!"

"Still giving orders."

"Brian. I'll do whatever you say. We can work this out."

"I'm sure we can. Come alone."

"I copy."

"Thatta girl. Be a good little soldier."

She slammed down the receiver, then picked it up to call home and stopped. She slowed her own breath and felt a deliberate calm take over, the practiced response of years on the fire line. In the canvas briefcase she had taken with her to Justice, she found the camp's Xeroxed phone directory. Under the command listings, she found the numbers of Brian's cell phone and his pager. She tore out the page, fished out Zampill's card, and was about to punch in his number, when caution stopped her. If Brian called her extension to check on her and found the line busy, it might set him off.

Help me, she prayed as she ran downstairs, out of the building to her Jeep. Help us. Out in the parking lot, she pulled out her cell phone and called home. The machine answered. Her heart sank. Were Spence and her father lying dead on the floor?

"Dad, Spence," she told the machine. "If you're there, pick up. Brian Flaherty's kidnapped Jim. This is not a joke. He's holding him at Parvis Feed. Call Agent Zampill, but *don't come* or he'll kill Jim." She read Zampill's numbers into the phone. "Don't come!" she repeated.

From her toolbox in the back of the Jeep, she hefted a ham-mer, then settled on a screwdriver, a heavy-duty one with a long steel shaft. She slipped it into the side pocket of her khakis and saw that the plastic grip protruded. She shoved the shaft down, slitting the bottom of the pocket, then took a step. The steel poked awkwardly against her thigh but her pants were baggy enough to hide it. It was better than nothing.

She called Chip Zampill on the drive to the feed mill, and after several tries got patched through to his office in Helena. A secretary informed her that he was in Missoula for the day.

She took a deep breath. "I'm in Missoula. This is an *emergency*."

"Yes, ma'am. I'll transfer you to one of the detectives."

Mattie felt like throwing the phone out the window. "No," she instructed. "Give me his pager number."

She drove out of Fort Missoula, picked up Reservoir Road. It was an overcast day, gray and cool. The familiar drive enhanced her sense of unreality, but she did not dismiss Brian's threat as deranged rhetoric. She saw clearly that if he had in fact murdered Cat Carew and the others, he would not hesitate to kill her son—however deranged the reason for it. Moreover, she did not believe that he "just wanted to talk" to her. Why bother to kidnap Jim if all he wanted was to talk to her? Her fears were compounded by the venue Brian had chosen. There were ways to deal with volatile human beings. But the explosive mixture of grain dust and air in an old elevator could not be cajoled or captured.

Zampill was not answering his page. She got the secretary again on the line who, in turn, connected her to a detective she had not met. He informed her that Chip Zampill was supposed to be at the state forensics lab that afternoon. Mattie described the situation as she crossed the Orange Street Bridge. The detective's voice was matter-of-fact, his questions practical—a response which gave her hope. She gave him Brian's cell-phone number. "He says he can see everything from the roof of the elevator. I'm going to get him down."

"Wait for backup," the agent instructed.

"He said he'd kill Jim if he saw anyone!"

"I understand. I'm going to call the lab, raise Chip, get you help. *Don't go in alone.*"

"I copy."

"Mrs. McCulloch, if you go in there, you're giving him what he wants. You'll be giving him even more bargaining power."

"I copy," she repeated. She took a breath. "It might be a good idea to have the fire department on standby," she suggested.

The feed mill loomed against the pale gray sky like a ruined tenement towering above an abandoned slum of shacks and lean-tos. Sheet-metal siding, rusty and warped, sheathed the sides of the elevator, the roofs of the sheds around its base. Four stories up, faded red letters read "Parvis FEEDS." Telephone wires strung on gibbetlike poles ran under the windows at the top of the tower. The poles followed railroad tracks out into the distance beyond the tower where lead-colored clouds banked over empty brown hills.

Mattie bumped over a siding and parked beside a delivery van sitting on rusted axles. Through the windshield of her Jeep, she peered up at the cupola on the roof on the elevator. There was a small window on each side, but the glass had been broken out, leaving square black holes. Was he watching from them?

If you go in there, you'll give him even more bargaining power, the detective had warned. He was assuming the police could strike some sort of bargain for Jim's life. But could you bargain with a firebug? The detective had not heard Brian on the phone—the casualness of his voice, the sickening hint of anticipatory glee. The exchange had revolted and terrified her. Every instinct told her that Brian Flaherty was beyond negotiation, but how reliable were her instincts? How reliable was an unknown detective?

She felt the awkwardness of the screwdriver against her leg. Her body felt like lead. She sat in the Jeep. She waited one minute, two minutes. What was she waiting for? For Zampill to come to her rescue? For the whole thing to go away? Jim's choked voice kept looping through her head: *Ma. Don't come!* She timed another minute, centered herself with breathing, and got out of the Jeep.

She stood beside the open door and yelled up to the cupola at the top of the elevator. "Brian!"

No answer. She reached into the Jeep, gave a blast of the horn. Several pigeons flew off the rusting roof. She waited some more, then shut the Jeep's door and walked toward a nailed-up door at the base of the elevator.

"Stay there," Brian called down.

She saw no movement in the cupola. "Where's my son?"

"I said, stay there."

Five interminable minutes later (what if the police drove up, sirens wailing?) a door opened in a shed built against the wall of the elevator. Brian stepped out into the sunlight. His face was flushed. In a lemon-colored polo shirt and pale blue slacks, he looked as if he should have had a golf club in his hand instead of a handgun. Mattie found the outfit surreal. Then she remembered her first glimpse of him at the Justice: As she drove up to the chalet, he had been practicing his swing under the cottonwoods.

Inside the shed, it was black and stifling. It took her eyes several moments to adjust, but even before she saw the rotting dropcloths and stacks of paint cans along the walls, the stink of turpentine struck dread into her heart. As she stumbled through the shed, Brian's revolver poking her in the back, the idea of being trapped in a structure fire scared her far more than any wildlands fire.

Brian pushed her through a boarded-up office. Broken wooden file drawers, knee-deep piles of paperwork on the floor, every surface covered with the fine beige talc of grain dust. The dust, combustible as gunpowder, was even thicker in the next room—evidently a sack room. Burlap bags lay strewn across the rough plank floor; a bag-stitcher hung from the ceiling on an frayed electric cord. She tried to force herself to concentrate on the layout, to memorize the sequence of rooms. At the same time, she knew with certainty that if fire broke out, they would not make it out the way they had come in.

They turned a corner, went down a ramp, turned another corner. Daylight from small high windows filtered down into a large processing area. Dust-coated cobwebs hung like rags from massive overhead beams. Columns of pipes ran up one wall, a hulking boiler took up a corner. In an opening between the rafters, a pair of six-foot-long steel rollers were suspended over a troughlike vat in the center of the room. The chamber smelled of moldy grain, iodine, mice droppings—and something else. Machine oil?

"This way."

The note of pride in his voice sent a chill of horror down her spine. She followed him around the vat, ducked under a collapsed conveyor belt. Were they headed back toward the sack room? The machine-oil smell became stronger.

She saw the wheelchair first, parked beside a short flight of steps, empty. She almost cried out. She followed Brian up the steps onto a concrete loading platform and saw Jim. He was sitting on a bed of straw bales built around one of the posts that supported the floor above. His legs stuck straight out in front of him, his new cast cleanly white in the gloom. A bandage of duct tape covered his mouth. Repeated loops of yellow nylon line bound his upper body to the post. But he was moving, straining against his bounds. He was alive. For a moment Mattie felt faint with relief.

She steadied herself. On the floor near the bed of bales lay a gym bag and a pair of dark blue cans. Two five-gallon cans sat neatly side by side. What she had been smelling was not machine oil. It was kerosene. She saw that Jimmy's sweatpants were soaked with it. So, presumably, were the bales of straw beneath him. His lean face was pale. Above the duct tape across his mouth, his eyes were black holes of fear and humiliation.

She surveyed the length of the platform, looking for possible avenues of escape. Along the front of the platform, a silver thread of daylight shone along the bottom of sliding metal doors. They were in a loading bay, she realized. Just beyond the doors lay fresh air—oxygen that would feed any fire certainly, but the proximity of the outside world reassured her. Had Brian brought in the straw bales through these doors? She saw bolts along the top and bottom, but in the dimness could not make out if they were set. At the far end of the platform, partially screened by a brick partition, there was a stairway going up to a loft, but the stairs offered less hope of exit than the doors. Sections of the loft's floor were missing. Directly above Jim, the rafters were entirely exposed. If his stagelike straw bed was set on fire, the gaping hole in the ceiling would serve as a chimney. Brian's placement of the bales, she realized, was no accident. If he was mad, it was a madness with a precise method. She noticed that he had swept the concrete floor; by one of the posts, there was a small, tidy pile of dust and straw. A push broom leaned against the post.

This can't be happening, she thought. It's all some kind of terrible mistake. Then she saw the candles, a circle of them on the floor around the bales of reeking straw. Fat beeswax candles, the expensive kind sold in upscale catalogs. One of them was lit. All it would take was a kick to ignite the bales under Jim.

Brian watched her take in the scene with satisfaction. "All the world's a stage," he quoted, "and all the men and women merely players." He indicated the candles with his gun. "Your footlights, madam." He smiled. Maintaining kicking range of the lit candle, he deposited his gun in his gym bag, pulled a Bic out of his slacks' pocket. "Here. Light the others."

She stared at him in disbelief.

"Help me out and no one will get hurt," he promised.

"I do what you want and then what? You let us go?" Mattie's voice was incredulous.

"Exeunt the players, stage right. There's a door over there." He nodded in the direction of the stairs.

"Where?"

"Just behind that partition. I left it unlocked. We exit. The building goes up. Think of it as a community service. You have to admit, the place is a terrible eyesore."

Was there actually a door at the bottom of the stairs? Mattie felt a surge of hope. "What do you want?"

"One thing at a time. First you light the candles."

"First you untie my son." Somewhere above them, on another floor, there was a commotion of wings. They all looked up into the darkness above the open rafters, watched a silent cloud of dust shifting down. "Please!" she begged. "At least untie him from the post. Look at him. He's not going anywhere. If something happens, we need to be able to get him out of here quickly."

Brian considered Jim, then shot Mattie a cagey little smile. To her surprise, he agreed. "All right. You do it." He flicked his Bic, met her eyes, then blew out the flame.

Without taking her eyes off the lighter, she moved around the bales.

"Go ahead," he invited.

She knelt on the bales behind Jimmy. The kerosene-soaked straw felt cold under her bare knees. Praying that the screwdriver in her shorts did not show, she examined the cords. Brian had used two of them. She worked loose the knots that lashed Jim to the column and he slumped forward with a groan, his arms still trussed to his chest by the second cord. She steadied him with a hand on his good shoulder.

Brian seemed to approve. "Tell you what. You stay right there. *I'll* light the candles." Mattie remembered Loreen's observation: the prostitute had guessed that Brian had been making things up as he went along. But this time, Mattie didn't think so. The change seemed less like an improvisation than a correction to an existing script.

She watched him move slowly around the bales lighting candles. Suddenly she felt tired. What difference does it make, she thought. One candle or a dozen? She observed with detachment that Brian's movements had a priestly gravity. He might have been genuflecting at the Stations of the Cross. She knelt next to Jim, listened to his breathing, but avoided his eyes. The look in them was more than she could bear. Another flurry of wings, and a dull thump on the ceiling above, made them both jump. Zampill? Mattie wondered, scarcely daring to hope.

Brian, however, did not look up from his candles. When he had finished, he stood at the foot of the bed—or was it an altar? In the soft-flickering glow of the candles on the floor, his face looked young, boyishly so, and vulnerable. For a moment, Mattie could see what his wife had loved in him. But when he spoke, his voice was surly.

"Take off your clothes," he ordered.

He wants to screw me in front of Jim? She was more astonished than frightened: This whole rigmarole, just to get it up?

A muffled ringing came from the gym bag on the floor. Brian frowned. The ringing continued. Mattie felt a wild stab of hope. Were the police outside? Brian walked to his gym bag by the blue cans, pulled his cell phone, flipped it open. He listened for a moment, then snapped it shut. "Must be the wrong number," he announced, unconcerned. He dropped the phone back into the bag, returned to his altar. "Okay. Take off your clothes."

Through the duct tape over his mouth, Jim let out a muffled bellow. In one nimble motion, Brian stepped over a candle and struck the boy in the face. His head made a sickening thump against the heavy timber of the post. "*Stop!*" Mattie screamed, lunging between them. "Stop! I'll do it!" She saw Brian lower his fist, a smear of blood on his knuckles. A bright trickle dripped out of Jim's nose. He kept making noises through the tape, high-pitched, staccato *no*'s. Mattie ignored him, scrambled to her feet. She peeled off her shirt, pulling it over her head without unbuttoning it, dropping it behind her, then added her bra. She pulled down her khakis and her underpants together, bunching the fabric around the screwdriver, tugging the legs over her sneakers, determined not to give them up. If there was any hope of escape, it wasn't barefoot. With the side of her foot, she pushed the bundle up against Jim's cast.

Brian's eyes were on her crotch. "Talk about flaming redheads!" The remark was easy, jocular, reminiscent of the way he had been at the Justice, but the eagerness in his breath made her skin crawl.

She waited for him to approach, to step up onto the bed of bales, but he stayed put, turning his Bic over and over in his hand. "Okay. Here's your first line. 'Time for you to be a big boy, my darling.' " The voice coming out of him was a rich, shockingly feminine contralto.

It stopped Mattie's breath, stopped Jim's muffled protest.

In his own voice Brian instructed, "Say it."

Warily, Mattie said, "Time for you to be a big boy, my darling."

He flushed angrily. "Not to me! To him!"

She turned and looked down at Jim. "Time for you to be a big boy, darling," she repeated woodenly.

"*My* darling," he corrected.

"My darling."

"Now the whole thing!"

She looked back at Jim, saw something unreadable in his eyes, and spoke to his knees. "Time for you to be a big boy, my darling."

Brian visibly relaxed. "Now Jim. You say, 'Yes, Mama.' That's all you have to say. I'm going to take the tape off you, and when she gives you your cue, you say, 'Yes, Mama.' "

Jim made no response.

Mattie said quickly, "He'll do it, Brian."

"Got him by the short hair—as it were!" He walked over to Jim, put one knee on the bale, and tested the edge of the duct tape across Jim's mouth. "Ready?"

Jim was stony. He said nothing.

Brian ripped off the tape. Tears streamed out of Jim's eyes. He worked his mouth. "Fuck you," he said hoarsely to Brian. Brian hit him again.

"Brian! We'll do it. We'll do whatever you say." She grabbed Jim's pinioned arm, dug her fingers into his biceps. "Say it," she ordered Jim.

"Yes, Mama." There was contempt in his voice, hatred in his eyes—not for Brian. For her. Mattie felt her heart harden. She had felt his hatred before, during the battles of his adolescence. She had cried with the pain of it, raged at night into the privacy of her pillow, but she had stood firm. She would not indulge his anger now.

Brian raised an eyebrow. "Very good," he approved, as if Jim's delivery had exceeded his expectation. He returned to his director's post at the foot of the bed of bales.

She gave Jim's arm a final, smaller squeeze and released him. "It's going to be all right," she muttered under her breath. He snorted, turned his head from her. She stood up, stepped forward to face Brian.

"Listen to Mama," Brian told Jim. "Just do what she tells you and let nature take its course!" He chuckled. Mattie's stomach tightened. She could see that he had an erection.

"Okay," he said cheerfully. "Take his pants off."

The request stunned her. "What?"

"Take his pants off. Then we can get started."

"You mean," she said slowly, "you want him to—participate?"

"For Chrissake, Mom, he wants you to fuck me!"

She looked at her son, at his kerosene-soaked sweats. Wouldn't he be better off without them if the bales caught fire?

Brian mocked, "For someone who's supposed to be the wonder girl of the Forest Service, you're not real quick on the uptake."

She was aware of Jim watching her. She was also aware that she was standing naked and alone. She realized that she could not rely on Zampill's intervention. She was responsible for saving her son's life and her own. If they all burned up in the attempt, then at least she would have rid the world of a monster. For there was no question in her mind. Sane or insane, Brian Flaherty was a monster. "No," she decided.

Brian frowned. "What do you mean, no?"

"We're not playing." She heard the finality in her own voice, sensed rather than saw a wave of relief in her son.

Brian flicked the lighter in his hand. A flame sprang up from his fist. "Are you sure? Better to fuck than burn. To paraphrase Saint Paul."

She said nothing.

"You said you'd do it!"

"I changed my mind."

"Bitch," he snarled. "Burn in hell." He lowered his fist to the bale.

"Wait!"

He stopped, looked up, smiled. "Wait?"

"You've got the wrong game, Brian." She knelt in front of him. "You need to be in it. Like you did with Cat." She heard herself, heard the coquettish tone in her voice, and felt sick.

"What would *you* know about it?" he said contemptuously.

She floundered for a moment. "Fire is the gift of the gods," she improvised, giving the statement a solemn authority.

He narrowed his eyes, released his thumb from the lighter. The flame died. "Go on."

"It was stolen from the gods. By—" She drew a blank.

"Prometheus, you ignorant cunt!"

"Help me, Brian," she pleaded. "I'll do anything you want. Teach me. Come up here and teach me." Ignoring Jim, she moved backward on her knees to make room on the bales. "Let me take your pants off, Brian. You need to be free." She gave his bulging crotch an appreciative smile. "Let me free you." She groped along the side of Jim's cast, feeling for her pants, for her screwdriver. She wished it were a knife.

Brian hesitated.

She ran her free hand around her breasts, down her belly, along the inside of her thigh. She felt the blessing of adrenaline rush through her body. Get him in your mouth. Chomp down. Strike up through the ribs.

51

Chip Zampill parked two blocks from the feed mill and approached the elevator on foot via an alley between the collapsing sheds. He waited five minutes for the backup he had requested, then went in alone. It took him twenty minutes to work his way from a side entrance up to the loft above the loading platform where Brian was holding Mattie and Jim. The loft was dark, an obstacle course of giant-sized gear wheels and broken floorboards. Twice, the movement of pigeons in the upper stories jerked his heart to a stop, froze his body mid-step. In the dust-laden dark, his eyes itched and teared. He felt an asthmatic tightness in his chest. I'm too old for this, he thought more than once. Nonetheless, by silently placing his feet on the joists and coordinating his wheezing breath with surprisingly graceful shifts of weight, he managed to get into position without giving himself away. Now he was lying at the edge of a section of missing floorboards, gun warming in his hand, trying to get a bead on Brian Flaherty.

He looked down into the sort of soft, golden glow depicted in Nativity paintings. The manger, however, was soaked with kerosene, the Titian-haired Virgin was naked, and the Child a grown man bound, not in swaddling clothes, but in nylon clothesline. Flaherty remained at the periphery of the scene. Once, to remove the tape from Jim's mouth, he came in the line of fire, but Chip held back, afraid of hitting Jim or his mother.

Dispassionately, he followed the dialogue. The content neither surprised nor disgusted him; like an actor preoccupied with his own entrance, the lines were important only for his cue. "Let me take your pants off, Brian." Mattie's voice was warm and reassuring. She's got guts, Chip thought. He watched her moving backward on the straw, making room for Brian. Good girl.

He heard the thump of a dropped shoe, the jingle of change in a trousers pocket. Now Mattie was kneeling below him. He saw the top of her head, her breasts, the tops of her thighs. He saw her right hand slip off her thigh, slide to the shorts she had taken off and pushed against her son's leg. Then Brian climbed up onto the straw bales. Naked and erect below his lemon-colored polo shirt, he stood over Mattie. Chip glanced at Jim. His face was calm, his eyes on his mother's hand fumbling in the crumpled shorts. What is she doing?

He saw her left hand reach out and stroke Brian's calf, a light, soothing touch. Brian shifted his weight onto his right foot, took a step closer to her.

Suddenly Chip was not too old. His itching eyes sharpened, his breathing cleared. There were only two things in the universe: the sight on the barrel of his revolver and a lemon-colored shirt. Chip calculated the trajectory and aimed two inches below the collar placket. Any lower was to risk Mattie's head. One more step, he urged Brian.

At that moment, a floorboard groaned over by the steps leading up to the platform. Chip saw Brian nimbly hop off the straw bales, over the lit candles. He retrieved his Glock from his gym bag. In the shadow below the platform, Chip caught a movement. His backup? What the hell did he think he was doing? Whoever it was moved with stealthy grace. His pale jacket seemed to float in the dark.

Taking advantage of the distraction, Jim started edging himself to the edge of the bales. "Mom!" he hissed at Mattie. "Get the candles!"

But Brian waved them both back onto the stage with his

gun. His face had paled, but his voice was controlled. "Come out where I can see you or I'll kill them both right now." He took a step sideways, out of Chip's line of sight.

Chip pushed himself up off his stomach for a new angle. The plank under his left kneecap let out a sharp, dry crack. A shifting of dust floated down onto Mattie's and Jim's heads.

Brian glanced up, puzzled by the noise of movement overhead, then focused on the man coming up the steps at the far end of the concrete platform. Gerald Spencer emerged from the dark, hands raised, eyes steady and alert, his rumpled jacket a white flag of surrender.

"Spence!" Mattie cried.

"Put your gun down," Brian said angrily. "*Now.*"

Slowly Spence lowered his arms.

Chip swore and scrambled to his feet. Gun in one hand, radio in the other, he ran across the planks to the stairway that went down to the loading platform.

Mattie saw Brian swing his gun around, raise it unwaveringly toward Spence. "No!" she barked. She leaped off the bales, screwdriver in hand. Like a wolf jumping for the kill, she sprang at Brian from the side, thrusting both herself and her screwdriver upward, aiming for the throat. She felt the steel shaft slide in, bump off something. She heard several shots, was dimly aware of Jim hopping away from the bales. She felt the heat of Brian's body, the force in it. His arm was pushing against her neck, choking her. She kept pushing, jiggling the screwdriver in his throat. Brian staggered backward and she fell with him. She felt warm candle wax on her ankles. With a great whooshing sound, the straw stage ignited. She let go of the screwdriver and rolled away from Brian, away from the flames.

As if in slow motion, she saw him raise himself to his knees, then onto his feet. His groin was dripping blood. He staggered forward a step, raised his gun, and fired. Why doesn't he die? she wondered. She stayed low, under the smoke, sliding away from the heat on her belly. Over the noise of the fire, she heard

Jim shouting, heard more shooting, saw Brian fall back into fire. The next thing she knew someone caught her under the arms and dragged her out into the sweet, bright air of daylight.

"Jimmy, Jimmy!" she croaked. She heaved herself over onto her knees, breaking loose from her rescuer's grip. "My son's in there! I have to get—"

"He's out!" someone called into her ear over the roar of the fire. "We've got him!"

"He's out?"

"Get back, get them out of here," she heard someone else yelling. Blindly, she felt herself being moved backward, away from the heat. A blanket was wrapped around her. Frantically, she whipped it away. "Jimmy's safe?" she demanded. She choked on the words. Racked by coughing, she doubled over.

"Your son's okay, Mattie."

The voice sounded familiar. Zampill? She heard the wail of approaching sirens, again felt the blanket on her shoulders, felt her feet stumble along with whoever was hustling her away. Down concrete steps, down off the loading deck, over railroad tracks. She straightened up, twisted back toward the elevator, saw black smoke streaming out its corrugated seams. "No, wait, wait!" she cried. "Spence. Spence was in there, too!"

"We've got him," Chip Zampill said. His voice was flat.

Something was wrong. She focused on the detective's face. He looked haggard, older than she had thought.

"Move it, move it," someone was shouting at them. Men in black helmets were pulling a hose from a chartreuse-colored engine.

"I want to see them," she said to Zampill. "Where are they?" Suddenly she started shivering. She clenched her teeth to stop their chattering. She remembered shivering uncontrollably on the delivery table after Jimmy was born.

Zampill steered her through a gathering crowd to a patrol car. The rear passenger door was open. Jimmy was in the backseat, reeking of kerosene, his cast poking out the door. "Ma," he said.

She stared at him. The blood from his nose had dried, a rusty smear across his mouth and chin. But there was no sign of any other blood. "You okay?"

"Yeah."

"You didn't get hit?"

"No."

She turned to the detective. "Where's Spence?"

Chip Zampill's face was grave. "We've called an ambulance. It should be here any minute."

"But he's okay?"

"He took one in the chest."

"He did? When?"

"After you jumped Flaherty. You jumped, and Spencer hit him in the groin, same time. Flaherty got one off before he went down."

She remembered Brian falling backward into the flames. "Spence shot Brian twice?"

"That was me, the second hit."

"I kept jiggling the goddamn screwdriver! He wouldn't go down!"

"Happens that way sometimes."

She shuddered, looked back at the burning feed mill. White arcs of water from fire hoses hit the roofs of the sheds around the base of the elevator. At the top, atomic-sized clouds of smoke boiled out of the cupola's empty windows. "Did they get Brian out?"

"No," Chip said brusquely.

"But Spence, he's going to be okay, isn't he?"

"It looks pretty serious."

She saw the sorrow and the pity in his eyes. But he can't die! she wanted to scream. It's only just started.

She turned on Jimmy. "How did Brian get you?" she demanded. "Why did you let him get you?"

Jim bridled. "Jesus, Ma, do you think I'd have gone with

him if I knew?" He drew a breath. "Granddad was out somewhere. I picked up the phone. He told me who he was, said that Richie—Richie Gower, one of the crew?"

"Yes?"

"Flaherty said that Richie had had some kind of breakdown. That he was in the hospital and that his shrink thought maybe if I talked to him, it would help. So I told Flaherty, sure. I ended up here." He added dully, "He told me if I didn't do exactly what he said, he'd kill you. Mom, I'm sorry—" He broke off. She saw the pain in his dark eyes.

Mattie felt her own eyes fill. "Oh, sweetheart—" She steadied herself. "It was not your fault," she declared fiercely. She looked to Chip for confirmation.

"Flaherty was bad news," he pronounced.

Mattie felt a new attack of the shivers coming on. She snugged her blanket more tightly around herself. "Where's Spence? I want to see him." She looked at Jimmy. "You okay?"

"Go ahead."

She hesitated.

"I'm fine. Except for my ankle. I guess you could say I got active on it too soon."

52

Gerald Spencer died in the ambulance on the way to the hospital. He was attended by a stately black woman with a lilting Caribbean accent, a silent white youth with flowing golden hair, and Mattie, still naked under her rough, olive-drab blanket. Although the ride was only a matter of blocks, to Mattie it seemed a very long time. Despite the flashing lights and the insistent wail of the siren, she felt they were processing slowly and solemnly through the streets, as if floating on a barge down some unknown river. Moreover, despite the apparatus of life support—the tubes, the electrodes, the oxygen mask—there was an aura of fatality in the ambulance. They were moving inexorably toward the mouth of a tunnel. As Mattie listened to Spence's ragged breathing, the hundred things she thought she wanted to say no longer seemed important. She mirrored his breathing with her own, held his hand. It felt cold and heavy. His fingernails were blue.

On the other side of the gurney, the black woman felt for his pulse. Under his plastic mask, Spence mumbled something. The woman lifted the mask and leaned close. Mattie caught the scent of ripe apples. "Are you in pain?" the woman asked.

Without opening his eyes, Spence announced dreamily, "You have the hands of a queen."

She replaced the mask. Her brown eyes met Mattie's across Spence's chest. She smiled the smile of an indulgent mother.

Spence's last words were a compliment to a stranger. He had no words for Mattie, no reassurance or request. But the moment before he died, he opened his blue eyes wide and looked at her, an intensely lucid gaze that affirmed every corner of her being. It gave her a jolt. He knows me, knows me all the way through, she realized. She felt bathed in his love.

53

In the first week of October, a month after the Justice Peak Fire was contained, snow fell over the mountains of western Montana. Down in the Frontiers, it fell silently on the white crosses in Copper Creek, forming soft lozenges along the arms, raising pillows around their bases, then burying them until spring.

Up at Flathead Lake, snow blanketed the roof of a waterfront cabin. That morning Ivan Wilkie and other members of the investigation team had signed the final report of their findings on the Copper Creek fatalities. By the late afternoon, Ivan and his wife Elizabeth were soaking in the hot tub on the cabin's deck. Through clouds of steam, they watched the snow dropping into the still, dark waters of the lake. Their children were at Liz's mother's. Inside, the wood box was full and a bottle of Taittinger waited in the refrigerator. "What if we get snowed in?" Liz worried.

Ivan smiled. "What if?"

In Missoula, the snow covered the piles of blackened timbers and sheets of corrugated metal on the site of the old Purvis Feed Mill. At Cat Carew's cottage, which her former housemate Harold Tweed now shared with an environmental biology student, the dry stalks in the tangled dooryard garden bloomed again with snowy flowers. Five blocks away, small whirlwinds of snow blew across the university's quadrangle, swirling around the emblematic bronze grizzly and giving Jimmy McCulloch, who had progressed to crutches, a fair excuse for cutting his afternoon class, Introductory Soils.

By the time Mattie arrived home from work, it was dark and the snow was already six inches deep. She deposited the groceries for dinner on the kitchen counter. In the mail she found a postcard from her sister Harriet. The Roman Colosseum against a glossy blue sky. Harriet and her husband were spending ten days in Italy. Harriet wrote:

> Hi. Here's where the lions ate the holy martyrs. Great weather, sunny and dry. I'm thinking about going to nursing school! Guess who we bumped into in the Piazza Navona? Your detective and wife—her name's Ellen. Nice. Four of us had a glass of vino—I mean 1 each!
>
> Love to all,
> Harrie & Stan

The postcard, and for some reason the falling snow, made Mattie miss Spence. She found she no longer missed him throughout the stretch of each day, a dull, constant, debilitating ache, but in acute clumps: when driving a sweep of open highway in her Jeep, turning a page at her desk, kneeling on a wet forest floor. Missing him was like exploring empty pockets: by the shape of each one, she tried to imagine what it might have held. She wished she had something real of his to touch. A pen. Even one of his mini bottles of gin.

She cleared the kitchen counter of mail and put away the groceries. To her surprise, Jack had invited Dr. Doris for dinner. Doris, she corrected herself, though it sounded naked without the "Doctor."

"Is this a date?" she had asked her father.

"She's young enough to be my daughter!" he had blustered.

"Younger than this daughter, if I had to guess."

"I just invited her over to try some real Irish stew."

As if there were such a thing as fake Irish stew. So Mattie brought home the lamb and the potatoes and the carrots and an expensive round loaf of peasant bread to boost the everyday stew into guest fare. Jack made the stew, fortifying himself with beer and fretting that "Doris" might not make it on account of the snow.

"All the more stew for us chickens," Jimmy teased.

Mattie shot her son a warning look. Whatever the chiropractor was doing to or with her father, it was an improvement.

But Dr. Doris was not deterred by the snow. She arrived in a spiffy little pickup with a blade affixed to the front and neatly plowed the length of their driveway. She came into the house, apple-cheeked and bearing a bottle of Australian red.

They ate in the kitchen, Mattie and Jim, Jack and Dr. Doris. Doris. Looking soft and pretty in a lilac mohair sweater. Mattie noticed that when she smiled at Jack, it was with genuine affection. Perhaps, Mattie speculated, Doris was older than she looked. Idly, Mattie fingered her uneaten bread, plucked and rolled a small piece of it into a pellet. What would it be like to have another woman in the family? If her father married Doris and produced a child, she, Mattie, would end up playing grandmother to her own half-sibling.

With a pang, she remembered her fantasy of becoming pregnant in the bed of roses she had shared with Spence. For that's all it had been, a fantasy. The day after the fire at the feed mill, the day after Spence had died in the ambulance, she had unexpectedly gotten her period. She had bled normally, but had been unable to shake the thought that it was Spence's blood she was losing, not her own, that Spence's life was somehow ebbing out of her.

"You're off your feed," her father accused.

She looked up from her pellet of bread.

Jack nodded at her plate. "You've scarcely touched it."

"It's very good, Dad. As usual."

"Too much salt?" Jack worried. He looked around the table.

"Not for me," Doris reassured him. She looked at Mattie curiously.

Mattie, who had not visited Dr. Doris's office since before the fire, felt obliged to justify her lack of appetite. "I was thinking about Spence."

"Your writer friend?" Doris asked.

"Hmm."

Jack drained his wineglass. "What about him?"

She smiled wistfully. "Wishing it had ended better, I guess."

Jack snorted. "One miracle ain't enough for you?" With the grand gesture of an impresario, he swept a hand toward Jimmy. "Resurrected from an early grave."

"Pops," Jimmy objected.

Mattie found she could not speak. A clot of tears swelled in her throat. Avoiding eyes, she picked up her plate in one hand and Jimmy's in the other and carried them to the sink. She scraped hers into the garbage, then rinsed them both under the tap, holding each one under the water a bit longer than necessary. She loaded them into the dishwasher. Straightening up, she asked Doris, "Would you care for some coffee?" It came out stilted, colder than she had intended.

Doris, however, responded easily. "Oh. That would be nice. Let me help you." She stood up, reached for Jack's plate.

"Sit down, both of you," he ordered, holding his plate down with both hands. "I haven't finished yet."

"It's all gone, Dad," Mattie said, relieved to find her normal voice. "Jim ate enough for three."

Jack reached for the wine bottle, refilled his glass, and in a gallant sweep, lifted it to both Doris and his daughter. "To the fairer sex," he toasted.

Jimmy shot his mother an ironic look.

But Mattie recognized the toast as a peace offering—however awkwardly wrapped. "Thanks, Dad," she acknowledged. She sat down at the table, gave Doris a complicit, female smile.

Doris said kindly, "I'm sorry about your friend."

"Thank you." She felt a rush of gratitude to Doris. How much had Jack told her?

"I saw in the papers that his widow is a famous artist," Doris went on.

"A sculptress," Jack said.

"Sculptor," Mattie corrected. "I never met her. Just talked to her on the phone—afterward. She said she might fly out in the spring."

"Were there children?" Doris wondered.

"No kids," Mattie said.

Jack studied the tablecloth, then looked up, his face sober. "He had one."

Mattie blinked. "Spence?"

"A son. The mother was Vietnamese. They were lost during the war. He told me he'd spent a fortune trying to find them, but no luck. He had no idea whether they were alive or dead. It bothered him."

"When did he tell you this?"

"When we were down there at the hotel."

She felt a small pang of jealousy.

"He was in love with you," Jack stated flatly.

She looked up in surprise.

"It was clear as daylight. And I'll tell you something else. It was the first time since that bum you married walked out on you that you even looked at someone else."

"Oh, Dad, that's not true!"

"I'm not talking about *dates*."

She saw Jimmy's face, alert with interest. But was it true? Had her heart really been so tightly wrapped all those years? Was that Spence's gift to her—a loosening of the old bonds? Somehow it didn't seem entirely right. She wanted to think of what had happened between them as something larger than a corrective treatment. She felt as if he had left her with a ball of light. Sometimes it was small and compact, a painful searing in the vicinity of her heart. Sometimes it expanded, a delicate luminousness throughout her entire being. Whatever its name, it was there, inescapable as air.

She thought back to the first conversation she had had with him—her first night at the Justice. They had sat together in the lamplight of the chalet's living quarters and he had spoken of the time, so many years ago, when she had rescued him. How presumptuous she had been to dismiss what he had called "her gift"! She had imagined that he was laboring under a false sense of obligation to her. But if her own ball of light was any indication, being saved was not a burden. It was a freedom.

"We need to make a toast," Jack announced. "You, too." He frowned at Mattie, who had been drinking water. She brought another wineglass from the cupboard. Ceremoniously he distributed the last of the wine among them. She was aware of the snow falling outside in the dark, of the snugness of their kitchen, of the jewel-dark wine.

"To Spence." Jack McCullough lifted his glass and cleared his throat. "The good that he did lives on. It was not interred with his bones." He paused, looked at the faces around him, and gave an emphatic nod. "And that's the truth of it."

They clinked their glasses, one on one, and drank to the man who was Gerald Spencer.

HANDBOOK OF BUSINESS FORMULAS AND CONTROLS

Books by Spencer A. Tucker

SUCCESSFUL MANAGERIAL CONTROL BY RATIO-ANALYSIS
McGraw-Hill Book Company, New York, 1961.

COST-ESTIMATING AND PRICING WITH MACHINE-HOUR RATES
Prentice-Hall, Inc., Englewood Cliffs, N.J., 1962.

THE BREAK-EVEN SYSTEM: A TOOL FOR PROFIT PLANNING
Prentice-Hall, Inc., Englewood Cliffs, N.J., 1963.

PRICING FOR HIGHER PROFIT: CRITERIA, METHODS, APPLICATIONS
McGraw-Hill Book Company, New York, 1966.

THE COMPLETE MACHINE-HOUR RATE SYSTEM FOR COST-ESTIMATING & PRICING
Prentice-Hall, Inc., Englewood Cliffs, N.J., 1975.

CREATIVE PRICING FOR THE PRINTING & ALLIED INDUSTRIES
North American Publ. Co., Philadelphia, 1975.

HANDBOOK OF BUSINESS FORMULAS AND CONTROLS
McGraw-Hill Book Company, New York, 1979.

Respective Foreign Translations

JAPANESE TRANSLATION OF "Successful Managerial Control by Ratio Analysis"
Charles F. Tuttle Co., Tokyo, 1964.

CONTROL DE GESTION (METODO DE LOS RATIOS)
Editorial Hispano Europea, Barcelona, 1968.

L'EVALUATION DES COUTS ET LA DETERMINATION DES PRIX PAR LA METHODE THM
Enterprise Modern D'Edition, Paris, 1965.

BREAK-EVEN-ANALYSE: DIE PRAKTISCHE METHODE DER GEWINN-PLANUNG
Verlag Moderne Industrie, Munich, 1966.

EL SISTEMA DEL EQUILIBRIO: INSTRUMENTO PARA LA PLANIFACACION DE LAS UTILIDADES
Herrero Hermanos Sucs, Mexico City, 1966.

WINST EN WINSTPLANNING
Samson Uitgeverij BV., Alphen Aan Den Rijn, Holland, 1968.

POLITICA DE PRECIOS
Ediciones Deusto, Bilbao, Spain, 1971.

GERMAN TRANSLATION OF "Successful Managerial Control by Ratio Analysis"
Verband Fur Arbeitstudien REFA F.V., Darmstadt, Germany, 1966.

HANDBOOK OF BUSINESS FORMULAS AND CONTROLS

SPENCER A. TUCKER, Ph.D., P.E.
President, MARTIN & TUCKER, INC., Management Consultants
and
Managing Director, PROFIT PLANNING & MANAGEMENT INSTITUTE

McGRAW-HILL BOOK COMPANY

New York St. Louis San Francisco Auckland
Bogotá Düsseldorf Johannesburg London Madrid Mexico
Montreal New Delhi Panama Paris São Paulo
Singapore Sydney Tokyo Toronto

Library of Congress Cataloging in Publication Data
Tucker, Spencer A
Handbook of business formulas and controls.
Includes index.
1. Business mathematics. 2. Corporate
planning—Mathematical models. 3. Decision-
making—Mathematical models. 4. Costs, Industrial
—Mathematical models. I. Title.
HF5691.T83 658.1'55 78-26737
ISBN 0-07-065421-2

1234567890 MUBP 7865432109

The editors for this book were W. Hodson Mogan and Joseph Williams,
the designer was Bill Frost (Dimensions), and the production supervisor was
Thomas G. Kowalczyk. It was set in Palatino by Monotype
Composition Company, Inc.

Printed by Murray Printing Company and bound by the Book Press.

For my grandsons,
Adam, Eric, and David

CONTENTS

ABOUT THE AUTHOR

President of Martin & Tucker, Inc., Management Consultants, the author has in 36 years of professional practice served more than 460 companies in the United States, Canada, Mexico, Western Europe, and the Orient in profit planning, cost estimating and pricing, evaluation of the firm, production methods and work standards.

As Managing Director of the Profit Planning & Management Institute, he has personally conducted 97 workshop sessions for top and middle management. More than 4,700 executives have been trained in his profit-planning concepts, tools, and techniques.

To recognize profit planning as a profession, paralleling recognition of professional competence and integrity in other disciplines, in 1977 Dr. Tucker developed the Certification Program by which qualified candidates can receive the professional designation CPP (Certified Profit Planner). The written examination is administered by the Board of Certification of Profit Planning & Management Institute, composed of 28 outstanding business leaders in the United States and Canada, executives of major trade associations, professional consultants, and eminent people from academic life.

The author of seven books and more than 300 articles in

professional journals and trade magazines, Dr. Tucker is a Registered Professional Engineer in New York, thirteen other states, and two Canadian provinces. He is the only non-accountant to be awarded the Lybrand Gold Medal from the National Association of Accountants, the highest award of the accounting profession. A second singular honor is being the only U.S. recipient of a grant from the Ottawa government to improve profitability in Canadian converting industries. Dr. Tucker is also the first nominee for the first National Medal of Science (Management) to be awarded by the President on the recommendation of the National Academy of Sciences. His textbooks have been translated into five languages and adopted by many colleges and universities throughout the world.

Dr. Tucker, who holds graduate degrees in industrial engineering and business administration, was awarded an honorary Ph.D. to recognize the original contributions made through his professional practice.

FOREWORDS

Active participants and interested observers of today's business scene will quickly recognize the contributions made by Tucker in this book. More importantly, the businessman, whether his particular expertise is marketing, production, or finance, now has at his fingertrips a compilation of practical day-to-day illustrated business problems together with logical, easily understood solutions—if you will, both a reference source and a checklist.

For all of us confronted with cost/profit problems and opportunities, a considerable amount of valuable time is consumed determining the relevant data required and the manner in which they should be evaluated or pretested. The complex variables of the business world certainly increase the need for timely rational and concise data. Direct costing is the major building block which fulfills this requirement.

Beginning with Chapter One, where Tucker states that "In order to make any kind of economic decision, the direct or out-of-pocket costs must be known," through to the final chapter on Integrated Control Ratios, this book allows the businessman to make better use of the most critical of his assets, namely his own time and that of his key management. This work, once and for all, should bury the type of computerized management information which misleads management by giving an aura of authenticity.

Professional business skills, whether applied by a full-time staff or by outside consultants, is usually beyond the economic means of the small businessman. This does not diminish the need for these skills. Therefore, this book becomes necessary as an effective aid to his decision making.

Loan officers of lending institutions will find the chapters on financial management and their control ratios an excellent checklist in assessing the meaningfulness of the financial indices that form a part of all loan instruments.

The significance of sales mix, production mix, asset mix, and the mix between liabilities and net worth, and how to measure and model the impact of these changes on the enterprise, is spelled out in clear, concise terms.

For members of Boards of Directors, who today play an increasingly important role in charting the well-being of the company, this book is mandatory.

F. S. K. WILLIAMS, CA, CPP
Financial Consultant
Toronto

Spencer Tucker has brought together an outstanding compilation of quantitatively expressed meaningful business relationships for the first time in a single text. He presents for each functional area of management a series of formulas and ratios, thereby providing a system of informational controls essential for the successful operation of a business in today's dynamic, complex, and competitive industrial environment.

Both managers and business academicians will find this text a source of invaluable techniques for decision making, management controls, and performance measurement for both the overall company or division, as well as the functional areas of marketing, finance, managerial accounting, production, and purchasing.

With the advent and rapid growth of data-base management information systems, Spencer Tucker's basic and advanced control ratios (Chapters 7 to 17) could readily be programmed and integrated into management information and control software. Then sales, production, and other timely output data could be developed within the computer system with appropriate managerial reports generated. Using Tucker's ratios, these output reports could show current status, comparison of current to past performance or comparison to target.

The text also provides an excellent framework for the kinds of integrative material required for business policy courses at the senior and MBA levels in colleges of business and schools of management. Such courses could easily be designed to integrate the entire business curriculum by utilizing the text's formulas and control ratios as the basis for demonstrating managerial decision-making criteria at various levels of the organization.

SAMUEL S. STEPHENSON, DR. ENG. SC.
Professor and Director of MBA Program
College of Business & Public Administration
Florida Atlantic University
Boca Raton, Florida

As one of Spencer Tucker's disciples it is no hardship to write a foreword to this his latest and probably his most important work to date. It used to be said that management is the art of making irrevocable decisions on the basis of inadequate information. Today, with emphasis on a total systems approach, management is less an art than a science; and Spencer Tucker leaves no room for inadequacy in the determination of data required to assess correctly the financial impact of various courses of action that may be taken by operating managers.

What Spence recognized a long time ago was essentially that fixed or period costs, whether pure, or present as a component of mixed costs, were being treated quite arbitrarily in the cost recovery process by many accounting practitioners and that cost information, produced "in accordance with generally accepted accounting principles," more often than not obscured the rational behavior of direct cost components and contributed to faulty decision making (sometimes with catastrophic effect) when such data were used by decision makers to determine the correctness of one course of action over another.

The human side of enterprise and the impact of corporate decisions on the quality of life are attracting more and more attention, but profits are still the measure of business well-being and their optimization the major raison d'etre of corporate existence.

While this work may not add to the plethora of descriptive literature on management theory, it represents a *real breakthrough* for the normative prescriber who needs to choose between alternatives. The choice between maximizing the return on total capital employed or the percentage return on stockholders' equity may involve non-economic variables to be sure, but the financial effects of either decision may be determined quickly and with validity by judicious use of this handbook. Similarly, the rationalization of product lines, ranking of multiproduct profitability, determination of facility hourly contribution to period cost recovery, make or buy decisions, and a host of other questions at the heart of the management process are grappled with by managers daily. What has been needed is a reference work that would enable managers to get at the answers quickly and with the assurance that the cost data involved in the equations being used behave rationally and consistently throughout their solution.

For the practicing manager who understands the dynamics of cost behavior and real profit, and for the business student groping with the concept of direct, period and mixed costs, contribution pools and accelerated period cost recovery, the intelligent use of the "tools" supplied by Spencer Tucker in *Handbook of Business Formulas and Controls* can be of incalculable importance to his or her decision-making capability.

During my years as Dean of Business, working with students and faculty in the development of curriculum for business courses involving financial analyses, the availability of such a work as this would have added significantly to the teaching/learning process.

This book, while long overdue, must be hailed as the super nova in the firmament of current publications written for the business constituency.

GAVIN CLARK
Consultant, Center for
Executive Management,
Seneca College, Toronto

Dr. Tucker's handbook will certainly be put to good use by our corporate staff to improve their management expertise. It is my intention to see that all of our management decision makers keep a copy in their office for ready reference. Besides looking up specific formulas and particular examples for problems at hand, I know the handbook will also be extremely useful in stimulating rational decision making.

There are many many occasions in our business problem-solving activities when we do not realize an analytical technique for our particular problem has been developed. I know from my own personal experience, in leafing through the prepublication draft, that I saw a number of techniques of which I was not previously aware.

Certainly, since the end of World War II, the managing of a business enterprise has become much more of a science and less of an art. Although I personally feel that management will always contain some degree of art, it is also true that in today's competitive environment scientific tools and rational decision making are essential to the success of every business. In fact, I know of no business today which can operate successfully within an environment of a totally subjective decision-making process.

For many years now there have been numerous handbooks of engineering formulas. As every engineer knows, these books are highly useful because they have summarized under one cover a number of disciplines which are normally found in separate texts. This is also true of Dr. Tucker's handbook. Here, under one cover, are numerous formulas, along with techniques and applications, that would only be available if we had a number of separate texts. It is also equally true that Dr. Tucker, in his own inimitable style, has developed *many useful formulas that are not found in any existing text.* In fact, my own association with Dr. Tucker has shown him to be a very insightful person who has developed a number of formulas and approaches to solving business problems that cut through the maze of folklore and get to the very heart of the problem. He is the sort of man who studies the problem exhaustively and is not comfortable in putting down the solution until he has thoroughly explored all of its ramifications.

Another advantage of the book, and a very important point, is the illustrative applications. A formula by itself is of absolutely no use unless it can be applied. The illustrations and applications show how to do this. Many handbooks of engineering formulas and other scientific information miss this point completely and such a handbook is only of use to those who are thoroughly familiar with the subject. Dr. Tucker understands this point extremely well and has not made the same error in his book.

I am sure that our company and others who use this handbook will want to refer from time to time to some of the more comprehensive texts on the particular application. But I can think of no better place to start than referring to this handbook first.

RALPH JINDRICH
President
Chicago Rivet & Machine Co.
Bellwood, Ill.

Dr. Tucker's latest book is a handbook of formulas covering a wide area of controls. The reader will find numerous formulas in three basic areas, including *manufacturing, financial, and sales management*. In addition, the handbook contains both simple and complex formulas within each area, and terms for the formulas are well-defined. One can find many uses for these formulas. For example, there are formulas for capital investment decisions, both of a simple nature and those involving exceeding manufacturing capacity.

Other formulas in the handbook would be particularly helpful for computer solution work in the areas of operational research. In the marketing area there are formulas for pricing involving incremental costing and profit calculations. I particularly like the variety of formulas and parameters that allow a composite evaluation of salesmen, sales territories, etc.

While not all of the formulas may be applicable or useful in a particular situation, the handbook contains a variety of such extent that many will be useful to the typical manager or executive.

Dr. Tucker's latest book is another step forward in controlling business results in ways other than by the traditional income statement and balance sheets.

JAMES M. BAKER
President
Albert Ramond and Associates, Inc.
Management Consultants

One of the greatest disappointments of the accounting student on entering the professional world is the discovery that there is no cost accounting system that looks like anything he studied from the textbooks. The following pages are a textbook that will bridge that credibility gap and, indeed, will have continuing value.

Assuming the reader has more than a passing acquaintance

with the fundamentals of cost of management accounting, and is a businessman, here at last is a compendium, even a manual, of the formulas and ratios that can be used by the business manager without an interpreter, by the financial managers as a handbook, and by the student to polish off his understanding of financial controls. Given that there is a system of cost accounting and reporting, management will benefit from emphasis on the control information that the system can make available. Here is the source of widest range of those control questions that have wanted to be asked and here are the references to provide these simple control indicators.

Business can be very complicated, and notwithstanding that mathematical techniques have been hailed in many quarters as a simple solution to a number of management problems, control data is as important to the business manager as the instruments are to an airplane pilot. Managing a business without the proper control information is flying blind. The simplest accounting records have the ingredients for a broadened function of analysis, interpretation and planning. This book, properly called a handbook, has the formulas and ratios to broaden that basic information.

K. W. SIMPSON, C.A.
Partner
Price Waterhouse & Co.
Montreal

A prime responsibility of all managers is improved performance of activities. When projecting and developing improvements, a manager needs two kinds of data: One set tells how effective performance was yesterday compared to a base; the other projects what would occur tomorrow under varying given conditions. In planning actions, a manager usually can choose from several possibilities to optimize and gain the greatest advantage in given circumstances.

Managers often make spot decisions by hunch or with

meager data. Many times superficially arrived at decisions may appear valid on the surface, yet when examined by sharp criteria pertinent to the situation, these decisions may be faulty. Managers should use measurements appropriate to the situation which will clearly demonstrate the advantage of one approach over another.

In this unique volume, Spencer Tucker has put together logical and rational means to breathe life and meaning into simple raw data and to provide measures which can support practically every decision a manager must make, whether in sales, production, purchasing, utilization of capital and resources, and many other areas. Some managers may want to develop their own special indices for specific situations that require sharp analysis. For example, company managers usually accept the supposition that increased sales volume is a desired goal. However, the questions raised are: At what price? What does the product mix do to the plant's capacity? What are the effects of tight delivery schedules on plant productivity and costs? Can engineering and purchasing support the increased sales? Does the company have the resources to finance the increased volume? Can the plant facilities economically produce the volume? There are numerous others. Summing up these questions is the underlying and ever important question: What is the overall effect on bottom line profits?

Critically important in decision making is the ability to discern trends, up and down, good and bad. Spotted early enough, a trend can signal the need for changes to head off a catastrophe or reap a windfall. Historical data in reports almost always tells too little of what is occurring because each piece of data is not shown related to others in a way that clearly shows trends. More pertinent to decisions regarding tomorrow, yesterday's data may not reflect tomorrow's conditions. With increased use of computers, even small companies have ample data on various aspects of company operations.

Tucker's unique approaches recognize that examining individual operations or aspects of a business may show that the activity is getting better. However, when several of the data are integrated, it may well happen that the composite shows a worsening trend which could cause serious difficulties if not recognized sufficiently early. Tucker shows managers how to integrate several controls by his tertiary ratios.

Tucker's approach to creating live ratios and indices will greatly reduce a manager's need to pour through mountains of computer print-outs. A handful of well designed ratios plotted with past events and along a projected future path will clearly indicate areas and functions that require remedial attention. This approach to decision making is the essence of simplicity, yet solidly based on sound logic and reasoning.

MITCHELL FEIN
Professional Engineer

ACKNOWLEDGMENTS

The creative task of writing a handbook requires intense concentration—and the author must be concerned about perspective, emphasis, and clarity. He needs a professional individual who can objectively aid him in the continuous process of self questioning.

Fortunately, my valued associate and good friend, Tom Lennon—who has extensive management consulting experience—somehow found the time and motivation to review the manuscript.

His analytical, disciplined mind provided many suggestions which have improved the quality of the finished book—and for that I am sincerely appreciative.

I thank also my number one son, Michael M. Tucker, for his talents and conscientiousness, and for finding and correcting critical errors in logic, formula constructions, and computations.

SPENCER A. TUCKER
Little Neck, N.Y.

EXHIBITS

HANDBOOK OF BUSINESS FORMULAS AND CONTROLS

SECTION ONE

BUSINESS FORMULAS

PREFACE TO SECTION ONE

This section is intended for use by those in the business enterprise who must evaluate the interrelationships between various operating and financial factors in order to make practical business decisions, and to make profit planning more effective.

Formulas are given to cover the areas of pricing, marketing, investments, make-or-buy, selection among alternate facilities or methods, scarce-factor product evaluations, break-even system applied to alternative courses of action in all economic areas, and the time value of money and economic choices.

Chapter 1 emphasizes and illustrates the need for a rational *direct-cost* measurement system vis-à-vis a conventional full-cost absorption system. The *contribution* concept is also presented and discussed, and provides the groundwork for the problem-solving concepts in the remaining chapters in Section I.

Each formula is presented first in its basic form and then illustrated by means of problems and solutions. The "problems" are numbered as *applications* with a title given, if appropriate, to make it easy for the reader to locate the type of decision he or she is interested in. Following the formula presentation in the first part of the chapters, typical, practical business problems are stated and solved, with procedural steps used to arrive at the solution.

In this section 127 formulas and equations are given, together with 592 problems and solutions.

CHAPTER ONE

INTRODUCTION TO BUSINESS FORMULAS

The underlying requirement for an economic decision is rational costs. These decisions should lead to better profit and a healthier capital structure. Cost must be the basis for profit management. The question is, "What kind of cost?" This is where the trouble starts! In cost estimating, pricing, profit planning, justifying capital expenditures, testing proposed alternative actions, etc., cost is the crucial factor. If the costs used are muddled, arbitrary, guessed at, or indefensible, management can wind up making wrong decisions. Thus, traditional cost data used for a make-or-buy decision might tell management to "make" when it should "buy," and vice versa.

Not being multiprofessionals, managers are often dependent on cost practitioners who are spoon-feeding them information. For example, events which may confuse managers can lead to questions about the year-end results (as an example):

> *How come* we generated more sales this year than last and wound up with less profit on the bottom line?
>
> *How come* we operated our equipment more hours this year and showed less profit than last year?

> *How come* we consumed more materials and labor than last year, produced more physical units of production, and came away with less profit?

Cost should have a definite, unchanging definition so that it means the same thing to all people who talk about it. Yet, depending on the training, methods, and experience of the cost person, the company can be victimized by a personal technique favored by the analyst. Therefore, decisions in areas of profit determination are subjective and a function prejudiced in favor of the specific method being employed.

COST CONSISTENCY

If different individuals were employed in the company, each of whom learned profit measurement in different schools or through different experiences, each could produce a *different* number. And each would argue persuasively in its defense. Which cost is right? Who will make that determination? Would it not be risky to make go-no-go decisions before knowing the correct and defensible number?

Cost then is not cost in the sense that everyone is talking about the same number! Under this unpredictable environment, costs don't stand still—and they should if we are referring to the same company, same product, etc. *Costs shouldn't change simply because an analyst is replaced!*

Wholesale dilution of company profits, growth, and longevity could be destroyed by the accident of *who* developed the cost data, *who* is doing the profit analyses, *who* is doing the pricing, *where* and *how* they learned their methods, and *where* and *how* they received their experiences.

RITES ARE WRONG

Cost determination and problem solving abounds with procedures and rituals resembling primitive tribal rites. The activity resembles the practice of sorcery and witchcraft, where the witch doctor dances around the tribal fire and divines magic numbers from which decisions are made. To produce consistent profits, this magical number must always be the correct and only one.

The ritualizing seems to require another "professional": the sorcerer. He or she does the planning in this tribal profit environment, and predicts grandiosely what will happen in the future, regarding facilities, customers, product mix, and a forecast of future sales revenue. And mind you, the sorcerer seems to be able to do this even though the customers' plans are not definite, nonexistent, shaky, or casual.

What happens to the company which has built its plans on these factors and then stands by while its profits do not come to fruition? Unfortunately, witchcraft methods don't work; the evil spirits of tradition, rigidity, and unrealistic academic methods are not exorcised, and they dominate the firm's profit structure. Such practices mislead; worse yet, they engender a false sense of security. Instead of getting the maximum profit potential from every transaction and time period (regardless of a particular current economic condition), the drive for an adequate return on the company's total capital employed degenerates into a strange set of business practices, viz., keeping facilities busy, keeping material usage high, paying sales commissions on loss work (not apparent to the manufacturer), etc. When the first two are used as panaceas for profit, it leads inevitably to the year-end "how come" questions.

Ironically, the supporting paperwork underlying witchcraft methods is gigantic. Worse yet, when these data are reduced to computer printouts, there develops an unwarranted degree of credibility which seems to obviate the need to question the bases of the magical assumptions. After all, in addition to professional accountants and estimators, don't we have systems and procedures experts, programmers, and software analysts? Too often this entire effort is an abdication of the managerial task and boils down to *automating the confusion*, i.e., organizing neatly what is arbitrary, traditional, and obscuring.

PITFALLS OF TRADITIONAL COSTS

In an unbelievably complex business, where very few factors are predictable, and where an almost infinite number of interweaving variables is faced, there cannot be any place for arbitrary, unrealistic systems (no matter how quick and convenient). Competition and survival demand clear, unclouded, unqualified, provable, rational data—logically developed, easily traceable, securely understood, and simple to implement. Anything less leads to insecurity, or a rejection of any method. Thereafter, decision making takes place by instinct, impulse, and emotion.

Traditional or conventional cost methods are those generally developed and used by accountants who are removed from day-to-day competitive turbulence in particular, and from the vagaries of the market generally. Their major concern, for example, is to make sure that the imputed product cost covers *all* costs. All or total unit product costs are termed "full" costs—commonly known as "absorption" costs.

If the accountant sees activity or volume dropping, he or she will want to increase the unit cost, so that all costs are "covered." This means trying to make customers partners with you in your profit planning. Obviously, it makes no sense at all to increase prices when business is bad or when you're losing business to competitors. Nor is it good business to lower prices when business is good and you're taking business away from competitors. Obviously, this approach loses business when it's needed the most and can generate lots of profitless volume when business is good.

How are "full" costs arrived at? This is an area for arbitrariness because it contains many costs which were forced to become identified with products. "Full" cost is an attempt to charge to a product every cost incurred regardless of its behavior. In this approach, direct labor and its related fringe benefits are clear-cut and are handled without problems. But what about factory supervision, office rent, administrative salaries, etc., which cannot be directly identified with a product the way direct labor can? Here is the heart of the problem! For in order to get the "full" costs, the accountant is forced to take costs which are not specifically incurred by that product and convert them into directly and tangibly related costs. The ways this procedure takes place are myriad and arbitrary. Each approach yields a different cost. They are also misleading when used for internal decisions and most crucially cause profit problems at the pricing point. For example, to include a manager's salary in a product cost sheet, there are several options open to the cost developer, among which the most prevalent are?

1. Dump it into the existing "overhead" pot and then relate it to direct-labor dollars as a percentage. This is spreading overhead with a bulldozer—filling the holes and leveling the peaks—so that every dollar of direct labor carries the same amount of overhead expense. Granted this method is convenient, but it is also deadly because it buries the specific costs and makes pricing an exercise in faith and chance.
2. Charge it to a facility and include it in the hourly overhead rate. This carries the pitfalls previously demonstrated; i.e., the greater the activity, the less the unit cost, and vice versa.

To demonstrate the first method:

	Product A Inexpensive	Product B Expensive
Direct labor cost—all operations	$10	$ 4
Overhead cost applied as 150% of direct labor cost	15	6
Total of direct labor and overhead costs	$25	$10

Assuming the same material cost for both products, the markup process used to arrive at a selling price could price the company out of the markets for Product A and seriously underprice Product B. In this method, pricing is approached as an internal arithmetic exercise without any reference to the market or competitive price levels. This could have the effect of keeping expensive facilities very busy generating high profitless activity ("How come, etc?"), with inexpensive equipment perhaps sitting idle. Ironically, if annual machine activity is used as the compass for profit direction, then frequently this could lead to the unprofitable acquisition of additional expensive facilities.

If one cost is applied on the basis of another, then logic would dictate that there be a cause-and-effect relationship between them as there would be between direct-labor cost and fringe benefits. But where are the cause-and-effect factors between machinery depreciation, administrative salaries, building rental, etc., *and direct labor*? In the foregoing example,

Product A is penalized with a heavy overhead charge simply because the direct-labor cost is high—and Product A is run on a less-expensive facility. Product B, on the other hand, gets the benefit of a much lower overhead charge due to the accident of low direct-labor cost—*not because the overhead is really lower.* Neither makes good business sense.

In the second case, various allocation formulas are used to develop an annual "full" cost of a facility and then divided by some kind of annual hours (e.g., expected, maximum, same as last year, last year + 10%, practical, and probable competitor's). As an example, the cost person allocates a portion of all annual costs to a machine, which total $120,000. The hourly cost rates are directly affected by someone's guess about the hours (the sorcerer), as follows:

Annual Hours Projected (Hoped for)	Hourly Cost Rate
2,000	$60
3,000	40
4,000	30
5,000	24
6,000	20

We can't go much higher than 6,000 hours since that is just about maximum on a three-shift basis. If we could, we would approach a point where the maximum activity approaches minimum cost. (And just as silly in this concept, zero activity would give infinite cost! Quite a way to run a business!) Returning to the tabulation of activity vs. hourly cost rate, suppose a sales forecast shows that the machine is expected to run only 3,000 hours in the coming year. According to the numbers game, this should call for a $40 rate. But then the sales department says that $40 is not a salable rate and pushes management into lowering the number. (Has it ever gone the other way?) The rationale is usually, "We've got to be more competitive!" (But not more profitable?) Obviously, the way to be more competitive in this exercise is to raise the projected hours. Why then bother about costs in the first place?

It is no wonder then that managements question drops in profit in the face of high machine activity, large sales increases, etc. Nevertheless, they persist in using these indices as panaceas for profit. Ironically also, the magic formula keeps expensive facilities very busy, running up to and beyond capacity and requiring unjustified investments in additional high-priced equipment. Then when management uses the same activity-volume approach to profit, and the new facilities begin to lag in activity, management cuts prices to attract the sought-for volume. When this practice is followed, *all members of an industry suffer and nobody wins, as prices are driven down to the point where few can realize an adequate return on their investments.* For example, the hourly *direct* cost of operating a machine is $22. (These are all the costs directly traceable to and identified with operating this machine, viz., direct labor, fringe benefits, electricity, etc.) If management decided to sell the use of this machine for $16 per hour because of "full"-cost information they received which told them that it "cost" less than $16, what's the effect on profit? Simple. Each hour sold at $16 generates a cash loss of $6 per hour. And the busier this machine is, the faster losses are accumulated. The proof is elementary: you take in $16 from the market and pay out of your pocket, without any ifs, ands, or buts, $22 to make the part on that machine. The one reason we call direct costs out-of-pocket, or o.o.p., costs is to dramatize where the cost money is coming from. So if you are advised by a friend that "More volume does it!!," your answer should be: "Does it??" (And he's no friend!)

If cost does not stand still in the face of all of the arbitrary cost formulas prevalently used (for a variety of decisions), what cost figure should be used to determine the expected profit? Shouldn't management know how much economic benefit a product or a decision is expected to contribute before they agree to a price or select one path from among several alternatives? Shouldn't management be sure of this measurement without having to be placed in the position of selecting from a variety of cost figures?

RATIONAL COST

Let's take a simple example of a man operating a retail store. He sells only one item, for which he pays his supplier 8¢ each, and his only other expense is the rent, which costs $1,000 per year.

The rent is obviously a fixed or period cost which does not change with ups or downs in sales volume. In this sense, the fixed cost is incurred with the passage of time (hence, period cost), whereas the 8¢ unit product cost is incurred with the sale of each item. Thus the 8¢ is a directly related cost which the man must take out of his pocket to support the sales of each item. If the current, "going," or competitive selling price for the item is 10¢ each, how much profit per unit will this man make if he agrees to meet the price? Of course, the problem would be a lot easier if there were no period costs involved. In that case, the profit measurement is simple:

Selling price	= $.10
Direct cost	= .08
Profit	= $.02

But he does have period cost, and so now the problem is how to reflect some of that $1,000 rent into the cost of the item, so that he can use the resulting cost in price evaluations. The typical solution is *allocation* and *unitization*. In this type of situation, the allocation used is generally volume; i.e., how many items are expected to be sold in the coming period. While this is an exercise in foretelling the future, it is nonetheless practiced almost universally in industry.

Let's see how. The man forecasts an annual volume of 100,000 items. This would produce the following profit measurement at a 10¢ price?

Unit selling price	= $.10
Unit direct cost	= .08
Unitized period costs: $1,000/100,000	= .01
"Full" cost	= .09
"Profit"	= $.01

Of course, that "profit" per unit will happen only if the man sells 100,000 units in the year. But how does he know this in advance? If he sold less, his year-end profit would no longer be 100,000 times 1¢, or $1,000, but would be in relation to the unrealized volume. Suppose another man operating that business was not so optimistic and projected an annual volume at 25,000 units. In that case, the unitized period costs would be 4¢, the "full" costs 12¢, and the "loss" per unit 2¢. Obviously, then, the measurement of profit and the price decision is made a function of guessing the future—surely a weak basis for running a business.

The way to evaluate the economic benefit of price is to compare the cash inflows with the cash outflows without trying to force a period cost into becoming a direct cost, as per the above tabulation. In this approach, we are comparing two completely rational, tangible, objective, traceable quantities, viz., the money received from the sale which goes into the man's pocket and the money spent for the product which he pays out of his pocket. Logic dictates that the difference between these two quantities is just as rational a figure. But we can't call this "profit" because there has not been any consideration given to the rent (fixed) cost.

CONTRIBUTION

When each item is sold at 10¢, the man has two cents left over with which to pay his rent. Obviously, he needs to sell enough of these two-cent pieces to accumulate the $1,000. Whenever that occurs, he has reached the point of no-profit–no-loss, or break-even. As the volume exceeds this break-even volume, he starts to earn a profit. Thus, profit measurement is a function of *time* and cumulative sales. If you think profit can be measured by the order or product, you must be prepared to defend the way you allocated or unitized period costs. Each different allocation method must produce a different "full" cost and therefore a different "profit" on the same transaction. Which is right? And are you willing to bet your company's profit structure on any one arbitrary method?

When the direct costs are subtracted from the selling price, the difference is an amount of money *contributed* towards the payment of period costs. When the amount of gross *contribution* equals the period costs, the company breaks even, the period costs are fully paid, and any additional contribution is considered real profit (without quotes).

Besides the contribution figure (always measured in dollars) there is another vital tool in pricing and profit planning. This is the ratio of contribution to sales obtained by dividing the contribution by the revenue figure, viz., $.02/$.10 = 20%. Thus the rate of contribution in the sales dollar is 20%. Because of convenience, we use that rate as a decimal, viz., .20, and call it the PV (profit-volume ratio). Thus the sale of the item has a *characteristic* PV of .20.

The PV assesses the contributing power of the sales dollar and thus of the product, product line, machine, customer, territory, end-use category, etc. But the use of sales revenue need no longer be the panacea for profit or the directional benchmark.

PRODUCT-LINE "PROFIT"

Management also wishes to assess profit in various ways (by product line, division, etc.). To make this evaluation, they require costs which are specifically identified with each profit segment. Given the data in Exhibit 1-1, management is faced with the illogical task of *allocating* annual costs to each one of the product lines shown so that they can *calculate* the profit of each. To make this allocation of the total annual costs of $5,400,000, they have to select a factor by which these costs can be imputed to each line. Their choices are many; they can allocate the annual costs to each line by using: annual facility hours; sales revenue; piece volume; weight of material; direct-labor dollars; direct-labor hours; forecasted units of production; etc. It should be clearly understood that for each allocation factor used, a different "profit" is imputed to each product line. The answer to the question of which method is correct is academic. What's crucial is that such an analysis can mislead management as it can show the loser to be the winner and vice versa.

CONTROL OF PRODUCT MIX

When a company doesn't have rational costs, it's perfectly possible (and usually probable) for them to make *less* profit on *more* sales. And hopefully vice versa (but usually accidentally). The

EXHIBIT 1-1 A MAJOR STUMBLING BLOCK IN PROFIT PLANNING
(How to allocate costs for profit determinations?)

THE GOAL: What annual profit is earned in each of the following folding-carton product lines?

Data	Annual Total	Product Lines: Food	Cosmetics	Garment
Sales	$6,000,000	$2,000,000	$2,000,000	$2,000,000
Costs	5,400,00	?	?	?
Profit	600,000	?	?	?

THE PROBLEM: What method should be used to *allocate* costs to product lines for profit measurement?

	Food	Cosmetics	Garment
A. *Annual machine-hour method?*			
Allocated costs	$1,600,000	$2,800,000	$1,000,000
"PROFIT"	400,000	(800,000)	1,000,000
B. *Annual tons consumed method?*			
Allocated costs	1,800,000	600,000	3,000,000
"PROFIT"	200,000	1,400,000	(1,000,000)
C. *Annual revenue generated method?*			
Allocated costs	1,800,000	1,800,000	1,800,000
"PROFIT"	200,000	200,000	200,000
D. *Annual pieces produced method?*			
Allocated costs	2,300,000	2,400,000	700,000
"PROFIT"	(300,000)	(400,000)	1,300,000

following are examples of profit results vs. sales in the same company:

CASE A

Product line 1:	$2 million sales @ PV of .15	=	Contrib. $300,000
Product line 2:	$2 million sales @ PV of .20	=	Contrib. $400,000
Product line 3:	$ .5 million sales @ PV of .30	=	Contrib. $150,000
Totals	$4.5 million sales		Contrib. $850,000
		Less:	Period costs $700,000
			Profit $150,000

CASE B

Product line 2:	$1 million sales @ PV of .20	= Contrib.	$200,000
Product line 3:	$2 million sales @ PV of .30	= Contrib.	$600,000
Product line 4:	$ .5 million sales @ PV of .40	= Contrib.	$200,000
Totals	$3.5 million sales	Contrib.	$1,000,000
		Less: Period costs	$ 700,000
		Profit	$ 300,000

Here we see that in the same company it is possible to generate more profit on less sales, i.e., twice as much profit on sales of $1 million less. How? By separating work according to product classification, identifying each by its characteristic PV, and then making sure that sales representatives sell contribution (within the limits of machine capacity and other scarce factors) instead of selling revenue for its own sake. Of course, it is desirable to support a sales compensation plan by paying commissions on order contribution instead of on order revenue. Otherwise, the direct cost system and contribution goals become weakened when sales representatives are rewarded for generating sales revenue dollars, which makes the profit goals self-defeating.

Just as important, especially where the company is operating at or near the limits of capacity, the drop in unprofitable volume liberates *additional machine time* and involves the company in *less working capital* (as shown by the two previous cases), which they can then devote to more profitable work. In Case A, product line 1 generates a high revenue with a low PV and uses up critical facility time and working capital. In Case B, after the company has rational cost data, it can safely drop product line 1 and instead develop and promote product line 4, which their antiquated, arbitrary cost system told them was not profitable.

DIRECT COSTS ESSENTIAL

In order to make any kind of economic decision, the direct, or out-of-pocket, costs must be known. These data are also used in developing characteristic product-line PV's as well as the cumulative PV characteristics of other segments of the business, such as by customer, end-use category, territory, sales representative, critical facility, or division. Such data provide marketing intelligence which cannot be obtained in any other manner.[1] Direct costs are required to make any kind of economic decision required in the firm, as will be demonstrated in the business formulas starting in the following chapters.

DIRECT-COST SEPARATION

Costs which change with volume, or are incurred with the manufacture of the product, or are identified directly with a facility, a transaction, or a decision, are called *direct costs.* Period costs are those which are incurred with the passage of time and do not have direct identifiability characteristics. A good test of whether a cost is direct or period is whether or not that cost is discontinuable if the action is not taken. If it is, that cost should be considered direct.

Thus, direct labor, materials, and freight out are all direct costs. Building rent, machine depreciation, and the president's salary are all period costs. So far, it seems like the classification of the two cost categories is going to be easy. So far that is true if we refer only to those costs which are either wholly direct or wholly period in behavior. But many accounts include expenses which are *mixed,* i.e., which contain elements of both direct and period, like electricity. This cost has a "demand" component

[1] See Spencer A. Tucker, *Pricing for Higher Profit: Criteria, Methods, Operations,* New York: McGraw-Hill, 1966.

which is considered a fixed (period) element (rated in kilowatts). The "energy" portion, which changes with activity (rated in kilowatthours), should be treated as a direct cost.

But when separations are not performed and period and direct costs are scrambled together, it is impossible to relate volume to costs, and profit planning as well as other decisions are weakened. Sometimes the direct-cost approach is used partially, as shown in the following example.

A manufacturer is estimating the cost of a part which is to be produced on one machine. It is cost-estimating this job under the conditions that the facility is expected to operate 3,000 hours in the coming year. It has a proper separation of direct and period costs. The annual period costs are $30,000 and the unit direct cost is $10. The cost sheet is prepared as follows:

Unit direct cost	= $10
Unitized period cost: ($30,000/3,000 hours)	= $10
"Full" cost	= $20
Markup of 10%	= $ 2
Target selling price (TSP)	= $22

Now let's assume that the company has to estimate and price this job in a period of economic softening, or when more competitors have entered the market. The company believes that now it will only be able to run the facility 1,000 hours in the next 12 months. Substantially, though, the direct costs will remain approximately the same. The data are:

Unit direct cost	= $10
Unitized period cost: $30,000/1,000 hours	= $30
"Full" cost	= $40
Markup of 10%	= $ 4
TSP	= $44

Here is a situation frequently encountered in companies

which say they are "on direct costs" but don't understand its markings. This usually happens when non-marketing-oriented people run the pricing function: the direct costs create an opportunity which is then eroded because it is used in a traditional manner. As previously alluded to, this places management in the unbusinesslike position of raising prices in bad times and lowering them in good times. Pricing can't be done in a vacuum, separated from the real facts of life: the competitive marketplace. In the case of good and bad times, the formula-ized price separates the manufacturer from having to know prevailing market prices as follows:

	Good Times	Bad Times
Unit direct cost	$10	$10
"Full" cost	$20	$40
TSP	$22	$44
Market price	$25	$22
Contribution	$15	$12

In good times, if the order was sold at the target price, it would have deprived the diecaster of an additional $3 of contribution. And in bad times, if the manager rejected a price *$18 below his "full" cost,* he would have deprived himself of $12 of contribution *at a time he needed it the most!*

COST BEHAVIOR

Some costs, like electricity, will always have direct-cost and period-cost components. The proportions of the two will vary, depending on the specifics of manufacture. But, there are other costs which one company will consider period, another direct, and another mixed. And that is the way it should be. Simply because a cost is classified as period in one company is no reason for another company to automatically adopt that classification. These differences usually occur with mixed costs.

COMPARISON: TRADITIONAL VS. RATIONAL

ESTIMATING WITH "FULL" COSTS

Production Center	Required Std. Hrs. per 1,000	"Full" Hourly Cost[2]	"Full" Production Cost per 1,000
A	20.00	$45.70	$914.00
B	12.50	8.80	110.00
C	14.75	16.10	237.48
D	13.50	16.10	217.35

Total "full" production cost per 1,000	= $1,478.83
Material and other order-related costs	= 2,891.17
Estimated tool maintenance	= 430.00
"Full" costs per 1,000	= $4,800.00
Markup: 10%	= 480.00
Target selling price per 1,000	= $5,280.00

When the sales representative quotes this target selling price to a prospect (or existing customer), he or she is told that the "going," competitive, or prevalent market price for this part is $4,400 or *$400 below* the *manufacturer's "full" cost.* The tendency would be to reject the order at the offered price in the belief that *all costs won't be "covered."* Without having the direct costs of that inquiry, the producer has two options open:

1. Turn down the order.
2. Accept the order at the $4,400 price, using any of the following rationales:
   a. We need the business.
   b. We must keep our equipment busy.

[2] See Spencer A. Tucker, *The Complete Machine—Hour Rate System for Cost-Estimating and Pricing*, Englewood Cliffs, N.J.: Prentice-Hall, 1975.

c. The order is so big that somehow we'll make money on it.
d. If my competitor can do it, so can I.

ESTIMATING WITH DIRECT COSTS

If direct costs were available, the manufacturer would be able to measure the *contribution* it could generate by booking the order. The following is the same estimate with only the direct facility costs included in hourly cost, the annual period costs having been previously separated:

Production Center	Required Std. Hrs. per 1,000	Direct Hourly Cost	Direct Production Cost per 1,000
A	20.000	$18.80	$ 376.00
B	12.500	6.20	77.50
C	14.750	9.60	141.60
D	13.500	9.60	129.60

Total direct production costs per 1,000	=	$ 724.70
Material and other order-related costs	=	2,891.17
Estimated tool maintenance	=	430.00
Direct costs per 1,000	=	$4,045.87
Competitive selling price per 1,000	=	$4,400.00
Potential contribution	=	$ 354.13
PV of transaction, if booked	=	.08

Now the company has a basis for making a rational decision. If its facilities are not fully loaded, taking this work would generate a contribution not otherwise available. If different work competing for the same use of facility hours can produce a higher contribution, the company would turn down the job, and vice versa. There are other considerations, of course, and these are treated in the author's pricing book. The use of marked-up "full" costs have led manufacturers into inadvertently turning down good business and winding up only with the orders where price levels were accidentally at or above their "full" costs. This has made the business operation a customer-formula-dominated one instead of profit-directed.

TELL IT LIKE IT IS

The rules to follow in making economic decisions are:

1. *Tell costs like they are!* Then you will be measuring contribution as it really is.
2. If you want to make some concession in price, etc., *do it at the contribution* level. In that way, you'll be making a decision without distorting the direct costs.
3. Do not try to compensate for market conditions, competition, changes in activity, etc., in your costs. Do it in the contribution and this will give you the desired change in price.
4. Keep costs pure, purified, and updated, and accurate contribution will follow. Use ground zero for measuring height. If you use something else and it keeps changing, you can never measure the altitude.

FORMULAS

A formula is a convenient way of marshalling all factors into one expression to enable rapid and consistent solution, either for comparative purposes, as in the case of choosing among alternatives, or for the purpose of arriving at absolute value, as in setting a target selling price.

It is worth repeating that while values are inserted in formulas in order to obtain solutions, those solutions will be valueless and highly misleading if questionable and arbitrary data are used.

In the following chapters, business formulas are presented covering the principal decision areas of the firm. These formulas require, together with other rational data, the availability of well-engineered direct costs. Practical examples which demonstrate the use of the formulas and solutions to all problems are provided. Data and values for substitution of values come from various schedules and exhibits included in each chapter.

CHAPTER TWO

BASIC PROFIT-PLANNING FORMULAS

This chapter provides formulas which illustrate and measure the relationships between the amounts on the basic Annual Profit Plan (such as profit, contribution, direct costs, and fixed costs) and the characteristics of the break-even point.

Part A presents the formulas with simple calculations.
Part B provides illustrative applications of the formulas in a variety of company situations.
Part C is a glossary of formulas and description of terms.

PART A: FORMULAS

Since there are relationships between the basic data, each element can be expressed in a variety of ways (formulas) relating to other elements. In actual application, the formula can then be selected which requires known or most easily calculated data.

All sample calculations are based on the following sample company data:

BASIC ANNUAL PROFIT PLAN

Annual sales revenue	$1,000,000
Annual direct costs	800,000
Annual period (fixed) costs	100,000
Annual pre-tax profit	100,000
Annual (gross) contribution	200,000
Annual (composite) PV	.20
Annual break-even sales point	500,000

SALES REVENUE

Formulas

$$S = C + DC \quad (2\text{-}1)$$
$$S = DC/(1 - PV) \quad (2\text{-}2)$$
$$S = C/PV \quad (2\text{-}3)$$
$$S = (P + FC)/PV \quad (2\text{-}4)$$
$$S = P + TC \quad (2\text{-}5)$$

Calculations

$$S = \$200{,}000 + \$800{,}000 = \$1{,}000{,}000 \quad (2\text{-}1)$$
$$S = \$800{,}000/(1 - .20) = \$800{,}000/.80 = \$1{,}000{,}000 \quad (2\text{-}2)$$
$$S = \$200{,}000/.20 = \$1{,}000{,}000 \quad (2\text{-}3)$$
$$S = (\$100{,}000 + \$100{,}000)/.20 = \$1{,}000{,}000 \quad (2\text{-}4)$$
$$S = \$100{,}000 + \$900{,}000 = \$1{,}000{,}000 \quad (2\text{-}5)$$

PROFIT

Formulas

$$P = S - (FC + DC) \quad (2\text{-}6)$$
$$P = (S \times PV) - FC \quad (2\text{-}7)$$
$$P = (S - BE) \times PV \quad (2\text{-}8)$$
$$P = C - FC \quad (2\text{-}9)$$

Calculations

$$P = \$1{,}000{,}000 - (\$100{,}000 + \$800{,}000) \quad (2\text{-}6)$$
$$= \$1{,}000{,}000 - \$900{,}000$$
$$= \$100{,}000$$
$$P = (\$1{,}000{,}000 \times .20) - \$100{,}000 \quad (2\text{-}7)$$
$$= \$200{,}000 - \$100{,}000$$
$$= \$100{,}000$$
$$P = (\$1{,}000{,}000 - \$500{,}000) \times .20 \quad (2\text{-}8)$$
$$= \$500{,}000 \times .20$$
$$= \$100{,}000$$
$$P = \$200{,}000 - \$100{,}000 \quad (2\text{-}9)$$
$$= \$100{,}000$$

CONTRIBUTION

Formulas

$$C = S - DC \quad (2\text{-}10)$$
$$C = FC + P \quad (2\text{-}11)$$
$$C = S \times PV \quad (2\text{-}12)$$

Calculations

$$C = \$1{,}000{,}000 - \$800{,}000 \quad (2\text{-}10)$$
$$= \$200{,}000$$
$$C = \$100{,}000 + \$100{,}000 \quad (2\text{-}11)$$
$$= \$200{,}000$$
$$C = \$1{,}000{,}000 \times .20 \quad (2\text{-}12)$$
$$= \$200{,}000$$

PV

Formulas

$$PV = C/S \quad (2\text{-}13)$$
$$PV = 1 - (DC/S) \quad (2\text{-}14)$$
$$PV = (P + FC)/S \quad (2\text{-}15)$$

Calculations

$$PV = \$200{,}000/\$1{,}000{,}000 \quad (2\text{-}13)$$
$$= .20$$

$$PV = 1 - (\$800{,}000/\$1{,}000{,}000) \quad (2\text{-}14)$$
$$= 1 - .80$$
$$= .20$$
$$PV = (\$100{,}000 + \$100{,}000)/\$1{,}000{,}000 \quad (2\text{-}15)$$
$$= .20$$

TOTAL COSTS

Formula

$$TC = DC + FC \quad (2\text{-}16)$$

Calculation

$$TC = \$800{,}000 + \$100{,}000 \quad (2\text{-}16)$$
$$= \$900{,}000$$

DIRECT COST

Formulas

$$DC = TC - FC \quad (2\text{-}17)$$
$$DC = S \times (1 - PV) \quad (2\text{-}18)$$

Calculations

$$DC = \$900{,}000 - \$100{,}000 \quad (2\text{-}17)$$
$$= \$800{,}000$$
$$DC = \$1{,}000{,}000 \times (1 - .20) \quad (2\text{-}18)$$
$$= \$1{,}000{,}000 \times .80$$
$$= \$800{,}000$$

PERIOD (FIXED) COST

Formulas

$$FC = TC - DC \quad (2\text{-}19)$$
$$FC = S - (DC + P) \quad (2\text{-}20)$$

Calculations

$$FC = \$900{,}000 - \$800{,}000 \quad (2\text{-}19)$$
$$= \$100{,}000$$
$$FC = \$1{,}000{,}000 - (\$800{,}000 + \$100{,}000) \quad (2\text{-}20)$$
$$= \$100{,}000$$

BREAK-EVEN SALES

Formulas

BE = FC/PV (2-21)
BE = S − (P/PV) (2-22)
BE occurs, when C = FC
BE occurs, when TC = S

Calculations

BE = \$100,000/.20 (2-21)
= \$500,000
BE = \$1,000,000 − (\$100,000/.20) (2-22)
= \$1,000,000 − \$500,000
= \$500,000
BE: S × PV = FC
\$500,000 × .20 = \$100,000
\$100,000 = \$100,000
BE: DC + FC = S
(\$500,000 × .80) + \$100,000 = \$500,000
\$500,000 = \$500,000

PART B: APPLICATIONS

Application 1: PERIOD COSTS INCREASE

Compute the (*a*) PV, (*b*) break-even sales point, and (*c*) profit if period costs rise by \$50,000 in the basic annual profit plan.

SOLUTIONS

(*a*) PV = C/S (2-13)
= \$200,000/\$1,000,000
= .20 (unchanged)
(*b*) BE = FC/PV (2-21)
= \$150,000/.20
= \$750,000
(*c*) P = C − FC (2-9)
= \$200,000 − \$150,000
= \$50,000

Application 2: DIRECT COSTS DECREASE

Compute the (*a*) PV, (*b*) break-even sales point, and (*c*) profit if direct costs decrease by $50,000 in the basic annual profit plan.

SOLUTIONS

(*a*) PV = C/S
= $250,000/$1,000,000
= .25

(*b*) BE = FC/PV
= $100,000/.25
= $400,000

(*c*) P = C − FC
= $250,000 − $100,000
= $150,000

Application 3: PROFITS AT DIFFERENT COST LEVELS

At an annual sales level of $1 million, (*a*) over what range are the sales profitable and at (*b*) what profit rate? (*c*) What are the annual profits? (*d*) What conclusions can be drawn? (Use data of Applications 1 and 2.)

SOLUTIONS

Using the data of Application 1:

(*a*) Profitable sales are those over the break-even sales level of $750,000, or $1,000,000 − $750,000 = $250,000.

(*b*) The rate of profit is equal to the PV above the break-even point.

(*c*) Profit over the break-even point:
P = PS × PV (2-23)
= $250,000 × .20
= $50,000

Using the data of Application 2:

(*a*) Over the break-even level of $400,000, or $600,000

(*b*) .25

(*c*) P = \$600,000 × .25
= \$150,000

(*d*) A change in period (fixed) costs changes only the break-even point, but not the PV.

(*e*) A change in direct costs only changes both the break-even point and the PV.

(*f*) The lower the break-even point, the earlier profits are generated, and vice versa.

(*g*) The higher the PV, the greater the profit rate over the break-even point, and vice versa.

Application 4: PROFITS FROM EXPANSION

Management is considering modernizing their equipment, which would increase period costs to \$200,000 and reduce direct costs to \$600,000, in the basic annual profit plan. Compute (*a*) BE and (*b*) P of this proposal. (*c*) What conclusions can be drawn?

SOLUTIONS

(*a*) PV = C/S
= \$400,000/\$1,000,000
= .40
BE = FC/PV
= \$200,000/.40
= \$500,000 (unchanged)

(*b*) P = C − FC
= \$400,000 − \$200,000
= \$200,000 (doubled)

(*c*) A decrease in direct costs can offset an increase in period costs to result in an unchanged break-even point. The reverse is also true.
Two companies (or two divisions, product lines, etc.) can have the same break-even point, with all other economic characteristics being completely different.
Since the break-even points remain the same, doubling the value of the PV results in doubling of the profit.

Application 5: PROFITS AT DIFFERENT SALES LEVEL

Make the same calculations and observations regarding the cost data of Application 4, but under the conditions where annual sales in each case are only $600,000. (Proposed vs. basic plan)

SOLUTIONS

(*a*) $C = S \times PV$ (2-12)
$= \$600{,}000 \times .40$
$= \$240{,}000$ (proposed)
$P = C - FC$
$= \$240{,}000 - \$200{,}000$
$= \$40{,}000$ (proposed)

(*b*) $C = \$600{,}000 \times .20$
$= \$120{,}000$ (basic)
$P = \$120{,}000 - \$100{,}000$
$= \$20{,}000$ (basic)

Since the lower annual sales level is above the unchanged break-even point, annual profit will still maintain a 2:1 relationship between the proposed and the basic profit plans.

Application 6: TESTING A PROPOSED SALES EXPANSION OF 80%

Management wishes to test the future effects of developing a program for increasing sales 80% over the basic profit plan. To support this expansion, they would have to acquire additional production machinery, warehouse facilities, and talent. They project that a doubling of annual profit will result according to the following estimates (assume no changes in price and product mix):

Sales	$1,800,000
Direct costs	$1,200,000
Period costs	$ 400,000
Pre-tax profit	$ 200,000

QUESTIONS AND SOLUTIONS

(*a*) What is the annual or composite PV of this proposal?

C = S − DC (2-10)
= $1,800,000 − $1,200,000
= $600,000

PV = C/S
= $600,000/$1,800,000
= .333

(*b*) What would the annual contribution be for annual sales of $1,500,000?

C = $1,500,000 × .333
= $500,000

(*c*) Why doesn't the PV change when the annual sales level changes?

Answer: In this type of economic environment the direct costs will change in direct proportion to the change in sales, leaving the ratio of contribution to sales unchanged.

Application 7: WHAT IF SALES EXPAND TO ONLY 30%?

Before putting the above program into effect, management wishes to test what profit would result if sales increased to only $1.3 million. Compute the profit two different ways. To solve this problem, formula (2-23) is used.

SOLUTION 1

(*a*) BE = FC/PV
= $400,000/.333
= $1,200,000

P = PS × PV (2-23)
= ($1,300,000 − $1,200,000) × .333
= $100,000 × .333
= $33,333

SOLUTION 2

$$\begin{aligned} P &= C - FC \\ &= (\$1{,}300{,}000 \times .333) - \$400{,}000 \\ &= \$433{,}333 - \$400{,}000 \\ &= \$33{,}333 \end{aligned}$$

Comment: In most cases, the first method is the more cumbersome of the two. The second method is more direct and does not require a BE calculation.

Application 8: WHAT PROFIT IF NO SALES INCREASE?

In testing the same program, management wishes to know what would happen to profits if sales failed to develop more than $1,000,000. (Note: in a real-life implementation of the proposal, one could not readopt the basic plan once the expansional steps were made.) Compute the profit both ways as above.

SOLUTION 1

$$\begin{aligned} BE &= \$1{,}200{,}000 \\ P &= (-\$200{,}000) \times .333 \\ &= \$66{,}667 \text{ loss} \end{aligned}$$

SOLUTION 2

$$\begin{aligned} P &= (\$1{,}000{,}000 \times .333) - \$400{,}000 \\ &= \$333{,}333 - \$400{,}000 \\ &= \$66{,}667 \text{ loss} \end{aligned}$$

Application 9: EFFECT OF PRICE DECREASE ON PROFIT

In the same program proposal, management now wants to test the effect of price level on profit, assuming that the 80% volume increase could be attained but with an overall 15% unit price reduction. Perform four profit computations.

SOLUTION 1

$$\begin{aligned} \text{New annual revenue} &= 85\% \times \$1{,}800{,}000 \\ &= \$1{,}530{,}000 \end{aligned}$$

C = \$1,530,000 − \$1,200,000
  = \$330,000
P = \$330,000 − \$400,000
  = (\$70,000) loss

Comment: PV and BE do not have to be calculated. Solutions 2 to 4 are detailed methods of calculating profit.

SOLUTION 2

PV = \$330,000/\$1,530,000
  = .2156862
BE = \$400,000/.215682
  = \$1,854,582
P = (\$1,530,000 − \$1,854,582) × .2156862
  = (−\$324,582) × .2156862
  = \$70,008 (loss)

SOLUTION 3

P = (\$1,530,000 × .2156862) − \$400,000
  = \$330,000 − \$400,000
  = \$70,000 (loss)

Comment: All formulas reflect a basic logic, exemplified as follows:

SOLUTION 4

Planned profit of original proposal	= \$200,000
Loss of revenue due to price	= \$270,000
Net effect	= (\$70,000) loss

Application 10: INCREASING THE PV TO OFFSET HIGHER COSTS

Management is entertaining a proposal to enlarge its productive capacity, which would add \$75,000 to present period costs. What would the PV have to be to justify this added cost, while maintaining the same profit of \$100,000?

SOLUTION

PV = (P + FC)/S (2-15)
  = (\$100,000 + \$175,000)/\$1,000,000
  = .275

Application 11: WHAT INCREASE IN SALES TO OFFSET PERIOD COST INCREASE?

If management cannot increase its PV to this new level because of an inability to reduce costs and/or increase prices, what level of sales volume is required to pay for the $75,000 increase?

SOLUTION

$$S = (P + FC)/PV \qquad (2\text{-}4)$$
$$= (\$100{,}000 + \$175{,}000)/.20$$
$$= \$1{,}375{,}000$$

Appication 12: EFFECT OF PRICE INCREASE ON PROFIT

Management is able to effect a 10% price increase. Calculate P.

SOLUTION

A non-volume increase in price will generate additional profits in the same amount: profit increase = $100,000; total profit = $200,000. Checking this by formulas:

$$P = C - FC$$
$$= \$300{,}000 - \$100{,}000$$
$$= \$200{,}000$$
$$P = (S \times PV) - FC$$
$$= (\$1{,}100{,}000 \times .27273) - \$100{,}000$$
$$= \$300{,}000 - \$100{,}000$$
$$= \$200{,}000$$

Application 13: NEW PROFIT WITH REDUCTION IN DIRECT COSTS

Management is able to effect a 10% reduction in direct costs. Calculate P.

SOLUTIONS

$$P = C - FC$$
$$= \$280{,}000 - \$100{,}000$$
$$= \$180{,}000$$

$$
\begin{aligned}
P &= (S \times PV) - FC \\
&= (\$1{,}000{,}000 \times .28) - \$100{,}000 \\
&= \$280{,}000 - \$100{,}000 \\
&= \$180{,}000
\end{aligned}
$$

Application 14: NEW PROFIT WITH REDUCTION IN DIRECT COSTS AND INCREASE IN PRICE

Management is able to increase prices by 10% and at the same time reduce direct costs by $50,000. Calculate P.

SOLUTIONS

$$
\begin{aligned}
PV &= C/S \\
&= \$350{,}000/\$1{,}100{,}000 \\
&= .3182 \\
P &= (\$1{,}100{,}000 \times .3182) - \$100{,}000 \\
&= \$350{,}000 - \$100{,}000 \\
&= \$250{,}000 \\
P &= C - FC \\
&= \$350{,}000 - \$100{,}000 \\
&= \$250{,}000
\end{aligned}
$$

Application 15: FINDING A PERIOD COST MAXIMUM

Under the conditions stated for the previous problem, what is the maximum amount of period costs management can incur without generating a loss?

SOLUTION

This is another way of asking the amount of period costs required to break even, since BE occurs, when C = FC. The company will break even when period costs do not exceed the contribution of $350,000, thus they can increase by $250,000 to a total of $350,000. And BE occurs, when C of $350,000 = FC of $350,000, and

$$
\begin{aligned}
P &= C - FC \\
&= \$350{,}000 - \$350{,}000 = 0
\end{aligned}
$$

Application 16: NEW PV REQUIRED TO OFFSET COST OF ADDITIONAL FACILITIES

The company is considering purchasing high-speed equipment in order to reduce its direct costs and increase its PV. If the added fixed costs are expected to be $150,000 and annual sales are planned for $1,400,000, with a profit of $150,000, what PV must result?

SOLUTION

P = S − (FC − DC) (2-6)
With terms rearranged,
DC = S − P − FC
= $1,400,000 − $150,000 − $250,000
= $1,000,000
C = S − DC (2-10)
= $1,400,000 − $1,000,000
= $400,000
PV = C/S
= $400,000/$1,400,000
= .2857

Application 17: WHAT MINIMUM SALES INCREASE TO OFFSET HIGHER PERIOD COSTS?

The company improves its manufacturing productivity and lowers its percentage of material waste, thus reducing its direct costs and generating an annual PV of .25. If the company adds $125,000 to its period costs by installing better production devices and a quality control effort, what minimum increase in annual sales must be generated without decreasing its planned profit of $150,000?

SOLUTION

BE = FC/PV
= $125,000/.25
= $500,000
Proof:
P = (S × PV) − FC
= ($1,500,000 × .25) − $225,000
= $375,000 − $225,000
= $150,000

Application 18: SEGMENTAL PROFIT

A company (any company) is operating profitably and is offered a piece of business with a volume of \$400,000 carrying a PV of .30. Calculate the profit of this segment.

SOLUTION

$$C = S \times PV \qquad (2\text{-}12)$$
$$= \$400{,}000 \times .30$$
$$= \$120{,}000$$

Since the company is profitable, it is operating above its break-even point, and additional contribution is all profit. Thus, Incremental C = Incremental P.

Application 19: PROFIT OF A SALES OFFICE

If this same company has to open a district sales office with an annual period cost of \$100,000 to support this incremental business, how would the profit of this segment be affected?

SOLUTION

$$\text{Incremental P} = \text{Incremental C} - \text{Incremental FC}$$
$$= \$120{,}000 - \$100{,}000$$
$$= \$20{,}000$$

Application 20: BREAKING EVEN ON AN EXECUTIVE SALARY

The company is considering the employment of a marketing manager at an annual salary of \$50,000. What minimum annual sales increase must be generated so that the company will break even on this additional expense if its annual PV is .20?

SOLUTION

$$BE = FC/PV$$
$$= \$50{,}000/.20$$
$$= \$250{,}000$$

Proof:

$$P = (\$1{,}250{,}000 \times .20) - \$150{,}000$$
$$= \$100{,}000 \quad \text{(unchanged)}$$

Application 21: PROFIT WITH A MIX OF PV'S

A company's total sales revenue consists of a mixture of \$2 million of volume carrying a PV of .25 and a \$4 million segment with a PV of .15. The company's annual period costs are \$500,000. Calculate (*a*) P and (*b*) BE.

SOLUTION

(*a*) P = C − FC
= (\$2,000,000 × .25) + (\$4,000,000 × .15) − \$500,000
= (\$500,000 + \$600,000) − \$500,000
= \$600,000

(*b*) PV = \$1,100,000/\$6,000,000
= .183333
BE = \$500,000/.18333
= \$2,727,272

Application 22: ADDITIONAL PROFIT FROM SALES INCREMENT

In the data of the previous problem, how much additional profit will be generated for each sales increment of \$1 million? To solve this problem, formula (2-24) is used.

SOLUTION

IP = IS × PV (2-24)
= \$1 million × .18333
= \$183,333

Application 23: PRODUCT-LINE SELLING PRICE AT A TARGET PV

Find the selling price of product line A to yield a PV of .42 to the company. Its direct costs are \$116,000.

SOLUTION

S = DC/(1 − PV) (2-2)
= \$116,000/(1 − .42)

= \$116,000/.58
= \$200,000

Proof:

C = \$200,000 − \$116,000
= \$84,000
PV = \$84,000/\$200,000
= .42

Application 24: FINDING THE SALES-PROFIT EQUALIZING POINT

A company with present sales of \$1,000,000 incurs period costs of \$200,000, a composite PV of .35, and a pre-tax profit of \$150,000. It is considering the acquisition of faster equipment to reduce direct costs and improve the PV to at least .40. This move would raise period costs to \$300,000 and would cut profits to \$100,000. To what level would sales have to be increased to yield the same profit in both situations? (i.e., find the sales-profit equalizing point.) (To solve this problem, formula (2-25) must be used.)

SOLUTION

Sep = iFC/iPV (2-25)
= \$100,000/.05
= \$2,000,000

Proof:

Present structure: P = (S × PV) − FC
= (\$2,000,000 × .35) − \$200,000
= \$700,000 − \$200,000
= \$500,000

Proposed improvement: P = (\$2,000,000 × .40) − \$300,000
= \$800,000 − \$300,000
= \$500,000

PART C: GLOSSARY OF FORMULAS AND TERMS FOR PERIOD MEASUREMENTS

FORMULAS

(2-1)	S	= C + DC	(2-14)	PV	= 1 − (DC/S)
(2-2)	S	= DC/(1 − PV)	(2-15)	PV	= (P + FC)/S
(2-3)	S	= C/PV	(2-16)	TC	= DC + FC
(2-4)	S	= (P + FC)/PV	(2-17)	DC	= TC − FC
(2-5)	S	= P + TC	(2-18)	DC	= S × (1 − PV)
(2-6)	P	= S − (FC + DC)	(2-19)	FC	= TC − DC
(2-7)	P	= (S × PV) − FC	(2-20)	FC	= S − (DC + P)
(2-8)	P	= (S − BE) × PV	(2-21)	BE	= FC/PV
(2-9)	P	= C − FC	(2-22)	BE	= S − (P/PV)
(2-10)	C	= S − DC	(2-23)	P	= PS × PV
(2-11)	C	= FC + P	(2-24)	IP	= IS × PV
(2-12)	C	= S × PV	(2-25)	Sep	= iFC/iPV
(2-13)	PV	= C/S	(2-26)	DC	= S − C

TERMS

C = period of gross contribution
DC = direct cost
FC = period (fixed) cost
BE = break-even sales point
PV = % of contribution to sales revenue (profit-volume ratio)
P = period profit
PS = range of profitable sales
TC = total costs
S = period sales revenue
IP = incremental profit
IS = incremental sales volume
Sep = sales-profit equalizing point
iPV = increase in PV
iFC = incremental FC

CHAPTER THREE

UNIT AND INCREMENTAL PROFIT-PLANNING FORMULAS

The formulas in this chapter deal with unit and segmental measurements (per product, per order, per facility-hour, etc.) and measure the effects of incremental changes in variable profit-planning data. Applications and solutions are given for each situation or problem.

Period (fixed) costs are not unitized, for the reasons given in Chapter 1. Period costs are used only where they are separable and identifiable with the event under measurement, and in no case arbitrarily allocated.

Part A presents the formulas and applications of a business segment and unit selling prices.
Part B gives the profit formulas of a business segment and applications.
Part C presents formulas for determining the contribution of a business segment or unit and solves a variety of problem applications.
Part D discusses PV formulas and applications.
Part E gives formulas and applications for using break-even in making unit decisions.

Part F is a glossary of formulas for unit and segmental measurements.

Part G is a glossary of terms used in the formulas.

PART A: SALES AND UNIT SELLING PRICES

Formulas (2-1) through (2-5) from Chapter 1 can be applied to unit and segmental measurements also.

FORMULAS

$$SP = uC + uDC \quad (3\text{-}1)$$
$$SP = uDC/(1 - PV) \quad (3\text{-}2)$$
$$SP = uC/PV \quad (3\text{-}3)$$
$$St = Sa + Sb + \cdots + Sn \quad (3\text{-}4)$$
$$uTSP = uDC/(1 - \text{target } PV) \quad (3\text{-}5)$$

Application 1: FIND TARGET PRICE WITH TARGET PV

A product has a direct cost of $12 each and a PV of .40 is targeted. Find (*a*) the target selling price of each unit, (*b*) the unit profit, and (*c*) the change in PV for sales quantities of 1,000 and 10,000 units.

SOLUTION

(*a*) $TSP = \$12/(1 - .40) \quad (3\text{-}5)$
$= \$12/.60$
$= \$20$

(*b*) Unit profit is not determinable because of the wide variety of arbitrary factors for allocating period costs, each of which would yield a different "profit." Period costs are identified only with the passage of time.

(*c*) For 1,000 units: $S = 1{,}000 \times \$20 = \$20{,}000$

For 10,000 units: $S = 10{,}000 \times \$20 = \$200{,}000$

For 1,000 units: $DC = 1{,}000 \times \$12 = \$12{,}000$

For 10,000 units: $DC = 10{,}000 \times \$12 = \$120{,}000$

For 1,000 units: $C = \$20{,}000 - \$12{,}000$
$= \$8{,}000$
For 10,000 units: $C = \$200{,}000 - \$120{,}000$
$= \$80{,}000$
For 1,000 units: $PV = \$8{,}000/\$20{,}000$ (2-13)
$= .40$
For 10,000 units: $PV = \$80{,}000/\$200{,}000$
$= .40$

Comment: Where there is no change in unit direct costs and unit selling prices, there is no change in PV. Volume changes only the amount of contribution generated.

Application 2: BASIC PRODUCT MIX IN TOTAL SALES

The product mix (sales mixture) of a company consists of $1 million of product line ABC, $4 million of product line DEF, and $2 million of product line XYZ. Compute the total sales revenue.

SOLUTION

$$St = Sa + Sb + \cdots + Sn \quad (3\text{-}4)$$
$$= \$1{,}000{,}000 + \$4{,}000{,}000 + \$2{,}000{,}000$$
$$= \$7{,}000{,}000$$

PART B: PROFIT OF A BUSINESS SEGMENT

FORMULAS

$$iP = iS - (iFC + iDC) \quad (3\text{-}8)$$
$$iP = (iS \times PV) - iFC \quad (3\text{-}9)$$
$$iP = iC - iFC \quad (3\text{-}10)$$

Application 3: CALCULATE DIVISIONAL PROFIT

Calculate the divisional profit, before corporate allocation, where divisional sales are $6,000,000, identifiable direct costs are $3,500,000, and period costs specifically incurred at the division are $1,500,000.

SOLUTION

$$iP = iS - (iFC + iDC) \quad (3\text{-}8)$$
$$= \$6{,}000{,}000 - (\$1{,}500{,}000 + \$3{,}500{,}000)$$
$$= \$1{,}000{,}000$$

Application 4: CALCULATE SEGMENTAL PROFIT

The same company adds a segment of sales volume amounting to $1,200,000, carrying a PV of .22 with no increase in period costs. What is the added profit?

SOLUTION

$$iP = (iS \times PV) - FC \quad (3\text{-}9)$$
$$= (\$1{,}200{,}000 \times .22) - 0$$
$$= \$264{,}000$$

Application 5: PROFITS OF NEW PRODUCT LINE

The company adds a new product line which generates $2,000,000 in sales, requires direct costs of $800,000, and incurs an additional period cost to support this line of $600,000. What are the profits of the new product line?

SOLUTION

$$iP = iC - iFC \quad (3\text{-}10)$$
$$= \$1{,}200{,}000 - \$600{,}000$$
$$= \$600{,}000$$

Application 6: TOTAL DIVISIONAL PROFITS

What are the total divisional profits?

SOLUTION 1

$$P = S - (FC + DC) \quad (2\text{-}6)$$
$$= (\$6{,}000{,}000 + \$2{,}000{,}000) - [(\$1{,}500{,}000 + \$600{,}000) + (\$3{,}500{,}000 + \$800{,}000)]$$
$$= \$8{,}000{,}000 - \$6{,}400{,}000$$
$$= \$1{,}600{,}000$$

SOLUTION 2

$$P = \$1{,}600{,}000 + \$264{,}000$$
$$= \$1{,}864{,}000$$

PART C: CONTRIBUTION OF A BUSINESS SEGMENT OR UNIT

FORMULAS

$$uC = SP - uDC \quad (3\text{-}11)$$
$$uC = SP \times PV \quad (3\text{-}12)$$
$$iC = iS - iDC \quad (3\text{-}13)$$
$$cC = (Sa \times PVa) + (Sb \times PVb) + \cdots + (Sn \times PVn) \quad (3\text{-}14)$$
$$ugCa = Sa \times PVa \quad (3\text{-}15)$$
$$cC = ugCa + ugCb + \cdots + ugCn \quad (3\text{-}16)$$
$$cC = (uCa \times a \text{ units}) + (uCb \times b \text{ units}) + \cdots + (uCn \times n \text{ units}) \quad (3\text{-}24)$$

Application 7: CALCULATE THE UNIT CONTRIBUTION

An item sells for \$5, for which the direct costs are \$3. Calculate the unit contribution two different ways.

SOLUTIONS

$$uC = SP - uDC \quad (3\text{-}11)$$
$$= \$5 - \$3$$
$$= \$2$$
$$uC = SP \times PV \quad (3\text{-}12)$$
$$= \$5 \times .40$$
$$= \$2$$

Application 8: COMPUTE COMPOSITE CONTRIBUTION OF PRODUCT LINES

Data on a company's sales mixture shows 3 product lines as follows: \$7,250,000 for A; \$4,300,000 for B; and \$2,800,000 for C. The respective characteristic PV's are .22, .38, and .51. Compute the composite contribution of the mixture.

SOLUTION

$$cC = (Sa \times PVa) + (Sb \times PVb) + \cdots + (Sn \times PVn) \quad (3\text{-}14)$$
$$= (\$7{,}250{,}000 \times .22) + (\$4{,}300{,}000 \times .38) + (\$2{,}800{,}000 \times .51)$$
$$= \$1{,}595{,}000 + \$1{,}634{,}000 + \$1{,}428{,}000$$
$$= \$4{,}657{,}000$$

Application 9: PROFITS OF COMPOSITE MIX

If period costs of the previous company are $2,100,000, compute the profit.

SOLUTION

$$P = C - FC \quad (2\text{-}9)$$
$$= \$4{,}657{,}000 - \$2{,}100{,}000$$
$$= \$2{,}557{,}000$$

Application 10: COMPOSITE CONTRIBUTION OF PRODUCT MIX

The product mix of Company A is as follows: 10,000 a's; 15,000 b's; and 23,000 c's. The unit contributions, respectively, are: $22.36, $18.42, and $12.78. Compute the composite contribution.

SOLUTION

$$cC = (uCa \times a \text{ units}) + (uCb \times b \text{ units}) + \cdots + (uCn \times n \text{ units}) \quad (3\text{-}24)$$
$$= (\$22.36 \times 10{,}000) + (\$18.42 \times 15{,}000) + (\$12.78 \times 23{,}000)$$
$$= \$223{,}600 + \$276{,}300 + \$293{,}940$$
$$= \$793{,}840$$

Application 11: PROFIT OF A PRODUCT MIX

If the period costs of Company A are $430,000, compute the profit.

SOLUTION

$$P = C - FC \tag{2-9}$$
$$= \$793,840 - \$430,000$$
$$= \$363,840$$

Application 12: COMPUTE DC, PV, AND BE

If annual sales of Company A are $2 million, compute the (*a*) annual direct costs, (*b*) composite PV, and (*c*) annual break-even point.

SOLUTIONS

(*a*) $DC = S - C$ (2-26)
$= \$2,000,000 - \$793,840$
$= \$1,206,160$

(*b*) $PV = C/S$ (2-13)
$= \$793,840/\$2,000,000$
$= .39692$

(*c*) $BE = FC/PV$ (2-21)
$= \$430,000/.39692$
$= \$1,083,342$

Application 13: NEW PROFITS FROM UNIT SALES INCREASES

If Company A doubles the unit sales of its three products and sales rise to $4 million, what are the (*a*) new profits and (*b*) composite PV?

SOLUTION

(*a*) New P = Original P + Added C
= $363,840 + $793,840
= $1,157,680

(*b*) New PV = [$793,840 + ($793,840)]/$4,000,000
= .39692

PART D: PV

FORMULAS

$$PV = uC/SP \quad (3\text{-}17)$$
$$PV = iC/iS \quad (3\text{-}18)$$
$$PV = 1 - (uDC/SP) \quad (3\text{-}19)$$
$$cPV = (\%Sa \times PVa) + (\%Sb \times PVb) + \cdots + (\%Sn \times PVn) \quad (3\text{-}20)$$
$$BE = FC/cPV \quad (3\text{-}21)$$

Application 14: COMPUTE PV OF PRODUCT LINE

Company B adds a $4 million product line for which the direct costs are $3.2 million. Compute the PV of this added line.

SOLUTION

$$iC = iS - iDC \quad (3\text{-}13)$$
$$= \$800{,}000$$
$$PV = iC/iS \quad (3\text{-}18)$$
$$= \$800{,}000/\$4{,}000{,}000$$
$$= .20$$

Application 15: COMPUTE CHANGE IN ANNUAL PV

After adding the new product line, Company B's total sales are $20 million. Its previous PV was .15. Compute the changed PV for the new total sales.

SOLUTION

$$\text{Former } C = \$16 \text{ million} \times .15$$
$$= \$2{,}400{,}000$$
$$\text{New } C = \$2{,}400{,}000 + \$800{,}000$$
$$= \$3{,}200{,}000$$
$$= \$3{,}200{,}000/\$20{,}000{,}000$$
$$= .16$$

Application 16: COMPUTE PV OF PRODUCT MIX

DATA

Product Line	Characteristic PV	% of Total Planned Sales
A	.30	20
B	.20	30
C	.10	50

Annual period costs = $500,000

Compute the break-even point.

SOLUTION

$$\begin{aligned} cPV &= (\%Sa \times PVa) + (\%Sb \times PVb) + \cdots \\ &\quad + (\%Sn \times PVn) \qquad (3\text{-}20) \\ &= (.20 \times .30) + (.30 \times .20) + (.50 \times .10) \\ &= .06 + .06 + .05 \\ &= .17 \\ BE &= FC/cPV \qquad (3\text{-}21) \\ &= \$500{,}000/.17 \\ &= \$2{,}941{,}176 \end{aligned}$$

Application 17: CHANGE IN BE WITH CHANGE IN PRODUCT MIX

In the above company, management decides to pay incentive compensation to its sales representatives based on contribution generated instead of a commission on sales revenue. As a direct result of this action, the emphasis is placed on PV and, with PV's remaining the same, the respective percentages by product line change to 50, 30, and 20. Calculate the new break-even point.

SOLUTION

$$\begin{aligned} cPV &= (.50 \times .30) + (.30 \times .20) + (.20 \times .10) \\ &= .23 \\ BE &= \$500{,}000/.23 \\ &= \$2{,}173{,}913 \end{aligned}$$

Application 18: PROFITS FOR TWO CONDITIONS OF PRODUCT MIX

(*a*) Compute the profit at an annual sales level of $4 million for both conditions of product mix. (*b*) Explain the difference.

SOLUTION

(*a*) *Original:* P = (S × PV) − FC (2-7)
= ($4,000,000 × .17) − $500,000
= $180,000
Changed: P = ($4,000,000 × .23) − $500,000
= $420,000

(*b*) A decrease in the PV of .06 reduces the contribution in the total revenue by $4 million × .06, or $240,000

Application 19: NEW SALES TO EQUALIZE PROFIT

To equal the profit of the changed mix, compute the level of sales required at the original mix.

SOLUTION

S = (P + FC)/PV (2-4)
= ($420,000 + $500,000)/.17
= $920,000/.17
= $5,411,765

Application 20: PROPOSAL TO ADD FACILITIES WITH CHANGED MIX

The company is now entertaining a proposal to install a a quality-control department at an annual period cost of $60,000, with the expectation that unit direct costs will be reduced. They project that waste and reject costs will drop, thereby increasing the three characteristic PV's to .34, .23, and .12, respectively. Compute the new profit for this proposal at the changed volume mix.

SOLUTION

cPV = (.50 × .34) + (.30 × .23) + (.20 × .12) (3-20)
= .170 + .069 + .024
= .263

P = ($4,000,000 × .263) − $560,000
= $492,000

Proof:
Increase in cPV = .033 × $4,000,000 = $132,000
Increase in FC = $60,000
Increase in P = $132,000 − $60,000
= $72,000

Application 21: PLANNING A SECOND SHIFT FOR RISE IN PV

In addition to the previous proposal, the above company extends its planning to include *making* some of items previously *purchased.* Because of the attractiveness of their product lines (in terms of improved PV), it is considering the addition of a second shift. The revised data are:

Product Line	PV	% of Total Sales
A	.41	70
B	.26	20
C	.16	10
Period costs rise to $700,000		

Calculate P at $6,000,000 in sales.

SOLUTION

cPV = (.7 × .41) + (.2 × .26) + (.1 × .16)
= .355
P = ($6,000,000 × .355) − $700,000
= $1,430,000

Application 22: FAILURE TO GET OPTIMISTIC SALES PROJECTION

The company fails to book the optimistic increase in sales and the level remains at $4 million. Compute (*a*) PV and (*b*) profit.

SOLUTION

PV = no change
P = ($4,000,000 × .355) − $700,000
= $720,000

Application 23: MODELING SEVERAL PROFIT PLANS

To complete the modeling of various profit plans, the company wishes to test what the consequences would be of an overall price decrease in its markets at the $4 million level. Calculate the profit if this softening amounts to 15%.

SOLUTION

$$\begin{aligned}\text{Loss of profit} &= \$4{,}000{,}000 \times .15\\ &= \$600{,}000\\ \text{New profit} &= \$720{,}000 - \$600{,}000\\ &= \$120{,}000\end{aligned}$$

Application 24: INCREASE IN SALES TO COMPENSATION FOR DROP IN PV

For the data of the previous problem calculate (*a*) the new composite PV and (*b*) the level of sales required to restore the profit of $720,000 (Application 22).

SOLUTION

(*a*)
$$\begin{aligned}S &= \$4{,}000{,}000 \times .85\\ &= \$3{,}400{,}000\\ DC &= \$4{,}000{,}000 \times (1 - .355) && (2\text{-}18)\\ &= \$2{,}580{,}000\\ C &= \$3{,}400{,}000 - \$2{,}580{,}000\\ &= \$820{,}000\\ PV &= \$820{,}000/\$3{,}400{,}000\\ &= .2412\end{aligned}$$

(*b*)
$$\begin{aligned}S &= (P + FC)/PV && (2\text{-}4)\\ &= (\$720{,}000 + \$700{,}000)/.2412\\ &= \$5{,}887{,}231\end{aligned}$$

Application 25: MODEL PROFIT PLAN FOR TESTING PROPOSALS

A manufacturer has modeled a profit plan for the purpose of testing the effects of future proposals. Data are:

Product Line	Characteristic PV	Expected % of Total Sales
X	.20	60
Y	.25	20
Z	.35	20
Annual period costs = $350,000		

Compute the (*a*) annual PV, (*b*) contribution, and (*c*) profit at a $2 million sales level.

SOLUTION

(*a*) $cPV = (.6 \times .20) + (.2 \times .25) + (.2 \times .35)$ (3-20)
$= .24$

(*b*) $cC = S \times cPV$ (3-25)
$= \$2{,}000{,}000 \times .24$
$= \$480{,}000$

(*c*) $P = \$480{,}000 - \$350{,}000$
$= \$130{,}000$

Application 26: TESTING EFFECTS OF PRODUCTION IMPROVEMENTS

The company now wishes to test the effects of improving its machinery mix, which would involve capital outlays with accompanying increases in period costs. A proposed changed profit-planning model shows:

Product Line	Characteristic PV	Expected % of Total Sales
X	.22	30
Y	.27	20
Z	.42	50

What maximum increase in annual period costs can be tolerated without the incurrence of losses at the $2 million sales level?

SOLUTION

$$\begin{aligned}
\text{New cPV} &= (.3 \times .22) + (.2 \times .27) + (.5 \times .42) \\
&= .33 \\
\text{New cC} &= \$2{,}000{,}000 \times .33 \\
&= \$660{,}000
\end{aligned}$$

If BE occurs when C = FC, and original FC = $350,000, then the increase in FC to BE = $660,000 − $350,000

Application 27: ADDITIONAL SALES TO OFFSET HIGHER PERIOD COSTS

At these higher period costs, what level of sales must be generated to produce an annual profit of $200,000?

SOLUTION

$$\begin{aligned}
C &= FC + P && \text{(2-11)} \\
&= \$660{,}000 + \$200{,}000 \\
&= \$860{,}000 \\
S &= C/PV && \text{(2-3)} \\
&= \$860{,}000/.33 \\
&= \$2{,}606{,}060
\end{aligned}$$

Application 28: TESTING EFFECTS OF MARKET PRICE SOFTENING

The company tests its downside exposure by testing the effects of a price softening of 10% in their markets. (*a*) What would be the annual profits at the same sales level? (*b*) Under these conditions, what level of sales would be required to generate a profit of $200,000?

SOLUTION

$$\begin{aligned}
(a)\quad \text{New P} &= \text{former P} - \text{drop in revenue} \\
&= \$200{,}000 - (10\% \times \$2{,}606{,}060) \\
&= \$200{,}000 - \$260{,}606 \\
&= (\$60{,}606)\ \text{loss} \\
(b)\quad \text{New C} &= \$860{,}000 - \$260{,}606 \\
&= \$599{,}394 \\
\text{New S} &= \$2{,}606{,}060 - \$260{,}606 \\
&= \$2{,}345{,}454
\end{aligned}$$

New PV = \$599,394/\$2,345,454
= .25555

Required sales to generate a P of \$200,000:

S = (P + FC)/PV (2-4)
= (\$200,000 + \$660,000)/.25555
= \$3,365,218

Comment: In this specific company, an overall price decrease of 10% requires a 168% in sales to generate the same profit.

PART E: BREAK EVEN FOR UNIT DECISIONS

FORMULAS

BEu = FC/uC (3-26)
BEu = cDC/uC (3-27)
Qep = increase in cDC/increase in uC (3-28)
Qep = increase in cDC/decrease in uDC (3-29)
P = (sold units − BEu) × uC (3-30)

Application 29: BREAK-EVEN MANIPULATIONS

A product sells for \$10 each. Its direct cost is \$8 each. If the only other cost of this enterprise is an annual period cost of \$100,000: (*a*) what volume of units is required to be sold annually to break even; (*b*) what is the break-even sales volume; (*c*) what is the profit for 60,000 sold units; (*d*) what are the profits at a sales volume of \$800,000?

SOLUTION

(*a*) BEu = FC/uC (3-26)
= \$100,000/\$2
= 50,000 units

(*b*) PV = \$2/\$10
= .20

BE = FC/PV
= \$100,000/.20
= \$500,000

Proof:

50,000 units × \$10 each = \$500,000

(*c*) P = (sold units − BEu) × uC (3-30)
= (60,000 − 50,000) × \$2
= \$20,000

(*b*) P = (\$800,000 − \$500,000) × .20 (2-8)
= \$60,000

Application 30: FINDING QUANTITY-EQUALIZING POINT WITH BE

A company can manufacture a product using either of two methods, both of which will produce the identical quality. Method A is a conventional process where the direct cost for setup is \$10 with a running cost of \$6 per thousand. Method B is faster but requires a setup cost of \$30. Its running cost is \$2 per thousand. Obviously, the company would want to use the faster method when the quantity to be run is large, and vice versa for the slower process. Calculate at what run quantity the processing on either method will produce the same direct cost. (This quantity-equalizing point will then provide management with a tool for scheduling a run based on its quantity.)

SOLUTION

It is important to keep in mind for both period and unit profit-planning measurements that *a change in direct cost is equal but opposite to a change in contribution.* Thus a decrease in direct cost of \$1,000 is equal to an increase in contribution and vice versa. And, an increase in unit direct cost is equal to a decrease in unit contribution and vice versa.

Qep = increase in cDC/increase in uC (3-28)
= (\$30 − \$10)/(\$6 − \$2) per 1,000
= \$20/\$4 per 1,000
= 5,000 units

Comment: The logic is that there is a specific quantity at which the costs of both methods are the same. Therefore, the run quantity which will equalize the costs of both methods is that quantity times the increase in unit contribution which will be exactly sufficient to pay for the increase in setup costs.

Proof:

Method A Cost for 5,000 units = \$10 + (5 × \$6)
= \$40

Method B Cost for 5,000 units = \$30 + (5 × \$2)
= \$40

Thus if the company processes a run of 3,000 units on Method B instead of on A, it would lose \$8 of contribution. And if it schedules a run of 7,000 units on A instead of B, it would lose \$22.

Application 31: QUANTITY-EQUALIZATION

Methods C and D are available to a company both of which will produce a product unit of exact quality. Calculate the quantity-equalizing point from the following data:

Method	Speed	Setup Time	MHRdc
C	1,000/hour	1 hour	\$22
D	4,000/hour	8 hours	\$48

SOLUTION

Setup cost for Method C = (1 × \$22)
= \$22

Setup cost for Method D = (8 × \$48)
= \$384

Hours per 1,000 for Method C = 1

Hours per 1,000 Method D = .25

Run cost per 1,000 for Method C = 1 × \$22
= \$22

Run cost per 1,000 for Method D = .25 × \$48
= \$12

Then, Qep = (\$384 − \$22)/(\$22 − \$12) per 1,000 (3-28)
= \$362/\$10 per 1,000
= 36,200 product units

Application 32: SELECTING THE MORE ECONOMICAL PRODUCTION PROCESS

A commercial printing company processes work of one to four colors. To produce this work, it uses one-, two-, and four-color presses, as required. At times, the plant runs four-color jobs on a four-color press and at other times runs four-color work on a two-color press by passing the job through twice. This latter procedure requires two makereadies (setups) and two run operations. The estimating department wants to develop a policy which it can use in determining what procedure would be the more economical for four-color work, depending on the size of the job to be printed. It is obvious to the estimators that for very small jobs, they would schedule two "passes" through the two-color press, and for very large jobs, it would be more economical to process such jobs once through the four-color press. To assure the minimum direct-cost for jobs, the estimators wish to know the quantity of sheets at which running on either method would produce the same cost. The following data are available:

Method	Speed	Makeready Hrs.	MR MHRdc	Run MHRdc	No. of Passes
two-color	1800/hour	4 per pass	$23	$23	2
four-color	3600/hour	11	$51	$58	1

SOLUTION

Qep = increase in MR costs/decrease in run costs per 1,000
= [(11 × $51) − (8 × $23)]/($25.56 − $16.11) per 1,000
= $377/$9.45 per 1,000
= 39,894 sheets

Application 33: PROVING THE BE METHOD

In the above problem, an order requiring approximately 40,000 "impressions" could be run on either press at the same direct cost, assuming that each is available when needed. To prove the point, calculate the "conversion" cost for a run of 18,000 impressions on both presses; 72,000 on both facilities, and for the Qep of 39,894.

SOLUTION

18,000 on two-color = \$184 + (10 × \$23 × 2
= \$644
18,000 on four-color = \$561 + (5 × \$58)
= \$851 (higher cost; quantity below Qep)
72,000 on two-color = \$184 + (40 × \$23) × 2
= \$2,024 (higher cost; quantity above Qep)
72,000 on four-color = \$561 + (20 × \$58)
= \$1,721
39,894 on two-color = \$184 + (\$22.163333 × \$23) × 2
= \$1,203.51 (same cost)
39,894 on four-color = \$561 + (11.081666 × \$58)
= \$1,203.74 (same cost)

Application 34: BE QUANTITY AND PROFIT FROM EQUIPMENT ACQUISITION

A manufacturer buys and consumes 800,000 parts annually, which it uses in making one of its products. Its purchase cost is \$.33 each. The manufacturer is considering the acquisition of facilities which would enable it to produce this part at an internal direct cost of \$.29 each. If such facilities are acquired, the additional period cost that it would have to incur would be \$11,200. Without considering the cost of capital or the incremental return on such capital; compute (*a*) at what quantity the manufacturer would break even on this acquisition, and (*b*) what profits, if any, will be generated at the annual consumption rate.

SOLUTION

(*a*) BEu = FC/uC (3-26)
= \$11,200/(\$.33 − \$.29)
= \$11,200/\$.04
= 280,000 part units

(*b*) iP = iC − iFC (3-10)
= (800,000 × $.04) − $11,200
= $32,000 − $11,200
= $20,800
iP = (Su − BEu) × uC (3-30)
= (800,000 − 280,000) × $.04
= 52,000 × $.04
= $20,800

PART F: GLOSSARY OF FORMULAS FOR UNIT MEASUREMENTS

(3-1) SP = uC + uDC
(3-2) SP = uDC/(1 − PV)
(3-3) SP = uC/PV
(3-4) St = Sa + Sb + ··· + Sn
(3-5) uTSP = uDC/(1 − Target PV)
(3-6) uTSP = (Target CPH × hours) + uDC
(3-7) uTSP = (Conversion DC × MUa) + (Mt × MUb)
(3-8) iP = iS − (iFC + iDC)
(3-9) iP = (iS × PV) − iFC
(3-10) iP = iC − iFC
(3-11) uC = SP − uDC
(3-12) uC = SP × PV
(3-13) iC = iS − iDC
(3-14) cC = (Sa × PVa) + (Sb × PVb) + ··· + (Sn × PVn)
(3-15) ugCa = Sa × PVa
(3-16) cC = ugCa + ugCb + ··· + ugCn
(3-17) PV = uC/SP
(3-18) PV = iC/iS
(3-19) PV = 1 − (uDC/SP)
(3-20) cPV = (%Sa × PVa) + (%Sb × PVb) + ··· + (%Sn × PVn)
(3-21) BE = FC/cPV
(3-22) CPH = ugC/hours
(3-23) iVC = Incremental cash + receivables + inventory
(3-24) cC = (uCa × a units) + (uCb × b units) + ··· + (uCn × n units)
(3-25) cC = S × cPV
(3-26) BEu = FC/uC
(3-27) BEu = cDC/uC

(3-28) Qep = increase in cDC/increase in uC
(3-29) Qep = increase in cDC/decrease in uDC
(3-30) iP = (Su − BEu) × uC

PART G: GLOSSARY OF TERMS FOR UNIT MEASUREMENTS

iP = incremental profit; segmental profit
iS = incremental sales
iFC = incremental period costs; separable period costs directly identified with a product line, division, etc.
iDC = incremental direct costs; direct costs specifically identified with a product line, etc.
iC = incremental contribution
uC = unit contribution
uDC = unit direct costs
ugC = unit gross contribution (or a product, product-line, order, etc.)
SP = unit selling price (of a product, order, facility-hour, etc.)
CPH = gross contribution per facility-hour
CPX = gross contribution per scarce factor unit X
MUa = markup percentage applied to cost a
St = total revenue of the sales of product lines a to n
S = sales revenue of product line a
cFC = nonseparable common period costs
cPV = composite PV (for the period)
%Sa = percentage of the total sales revenue generated by product line a
PVa = characteristic PV of product line a
cC = composite contribution
iVC = incremental variable capital (current assets)
uTSP = unit target selling price
BEu = break-even point measured in units
Qep = quantity-equalizing (or crossover) point measured in units
cDC = one-time direct costs, as in a machine set up cost for processing
MHRdc = direct-cost machine-hour rate
Su = sales volume measured in units
Mt = material cost

CHAPTER FOUR

FORMULAS FOR OPERATING DECISIONS

The formulas, problems, and solutions given in this chapter deal with both unit and incremental decisions. Period costs are treated as incremental and/or in total for the time period under measurement. Problems in this chapter cover typical business transactional and operating decisions. The formulas used are variations and expansions of those from the previous two chapters, plus additional ones given at the end of this chapter. The glossary of formulas and terms are listed on page 88.

Application 1: MANUFACTURER'S REP. OR SALESPERSON

A manufacturer is considering expanding the sales effort in his markets either by using a manufacturer's representative or by adding a salesperson to his payroll. Data for these alternatives follow:

	Presently	With Mfrs. Rep.	With Salesperson
Annual sales	$3,000,000	$3,600,000	$3,600,000
Direct costs	1,600,000	1,980,000	1,920,000
Period costs	1,100,000	1,100,000	1,116,000
Pre-tax profit	$300,000	$520,000	$564,000

Since the additional sales of $600,000 has not come to fruition, management would like to know the sales equalizing point of both alternatives.

SOLUTION

PV, rep. = iC/iS (3-18)
= ($600,000 − $380,000)/$600,000
= .367

PV, salesperson = ($600,000 − $320,000)/$600,000
= .467

Sep = iFC/iPV (2-25)
= $16,000/(.467 − .367)
= $16,000/.10
= $160,000

Application 2: PRICE VARIANCES AND WAGE INCREASE IMPACT ON PROFIT

A company projects a basic profit plan as follows:

	Per Unit	Per Year
Planned unit volume		100,000
Sales revenue	$10.00	$1,000,000
Direct costs:		
Direct material	2.80	280,000
Direct labor	2.00	200,000
Direct overhead	2.20	220,000
Total direct costs	7.00	700,000
Contribution	3.00	300,000
PV	.30	.30
Period costs		290,000
Pre-tax profit		$10,000

(*a*) How would profits change if prices were increased 10% and volume of units decreased by 10% and 30%?

(*b*) If prices are reduced 10%, how much additional sales and units are required to produce the same profit in the basic profit plan?

(*c*) In the event of a 10% wage increase, how much will prices have to be increased to keep the PV at .30? By how much will prices have to be increased to maintain the original profit at the 100,000-unit level, irrespective of the change in PV?

SOLUTION

(*a*) P = ($4 × 90,000) − $290,000
= $70,000

(*b*) uC = $3 − $1
= $2

To maintain the same profit, the contribution must remain the same: therefore, new units required equals $300,000/$2, or 150,000 (a 50% increase).

(*c*) New Sales = 150,000 × $9
= $1,350,000 (a 35% increase)

New DC = $7 + (.10 × $2)
= $7.20

New SP = $7.20/(1 − .30) (3-2)
= $10.29

New S = DC + FC + P
= $290,000 + ($7.20 × 100,000) + $10,000
= $1,020,000

New SP = $1,020,000/100,000
= $10.20

or: New SP = Original SP + additional C to offset additional DC
= $10.00 + $.20
= $10.20

Application 3: BREAKING EVEN ON PRODUCT-LINE PROMOTIONAL EXPENSES

A manufacturer with three product lines wishes to spend $50,000 of fixed promotional costs for each product line in an effort to expand the sales of each. By what amount of additional sales must each line generate to offset these incremental costs? The data follow:

	A	B	C
Annual sales	$2,000,000	$1,000,000	$1,000,000
Direct costs	1,700,000	500,000	700,000
Contribution	300,000	500,000	300,000
PV	.15	.50	.30

SOLUTION

iS of A = iFC/PV
= $50,000/.15
= $333,333
iS of B = $100,000
iS of C = $166,667

Application 4: ALTERNATE METHODS OF MACHINERY EXPANSION

A company is considering two alternate methods of expansion to support an expected sales increase. One involves a group of high-speed separate machines. The second calls for automated in-line equipment. At what sales point will both alternatives earn the same profit according to the following data?

	Present	High Speed	In-Line
Sales	$6,000,000	$8,000,000	$8,000,000
Direct costs	4,000,000	3,000,000	2,000,000
Period costs	1,000,000	2,500,000	4,000,000
Contribution	2,000,000	5,000,000	6,000,000
PV	.333	.625	.750
Pre-tax profit	1,000,000	2,500,000	2,000,000

SOLUTION

Sep = iFC/iPV (2-25)
= ($4,000,000 − $2,500,000)/(.750 − .625)
= $1,500,000/.125
= $12,000,000

Application 5: COMPARING ALTERNATE PROFITS

Compare the profits of both alternatives at sales of $10 and $20 million.

SOLUTION

$$
\begin{aligned}
\text{P, high speed at \$10 million} &= (\$10{,}000{,}000 \times .625) \\
&\quad - \$2{,}500{,}000 \\
&= \$3{,}750{,}000 \quad \text{(higher)} \\
\text{P, in-line at \$10 million} &= (\$10{,}000{,}000 \times .75) \\
&\quad - \$4{,}000{,}000 \\
&= \$3{,}500{,}000 \\
\text{P, high speed at \$20 million} &= (\$20{,}000{,}000 \times .625) \\
&\quad - \$2{,}500{,}000 \\
&= \$10{,}000{,}000 \\
\text{P, in-line at \$20 million} &= (\$20{,}000{,}000 \times .75) \\
&\quad - \$4{,}000{,}000 \\
&= \$11{,}000{,}000 \quad \text{(higher)}
\end{aligned}
$$

Application 6: WHAT MAXIMUM PERIOD COSTS TO GENERATE TARGET RETURN ON CAPITAL EMPLOYED?

An analysis of a company's two product lines show the following data:

	X	Y
Sales	$3,000,000	$5,000,000
PV	.40	.30

If its total capital employed is $10 million, to what maximum level must period costs be held in order to provide a 15% pre-tax return on the TCE?

SOLUTION

$$
\begin{aligned}
\text{Annual C} &= (\$3{,}000{,}000 \times .40) + (\$5{,}000{,}000 \times .30) \\
&= \$2{,}700{,}000
\end{aligned}
$$

$$
\begin{aligned}
\text{RTCE} &= \text{TCE} \times \%\ \text{Return} \qquad (4\text{-}2) \\
&= \$10 \text{ million} \times .15 \\
&= \$1{,}500{,}000
\end{aligned}
$$

Max. FC = $2,700,000 − $1,500,000
= $1,200,000

Application 7: ADDITIONAL PRODUCT-LINE SALES TO OBTAIN RTCE

The directors of the above company adopt a policy calling for a minimum 17% pre-tax return on TCE. Capacity limitations restrict total sales to $8 million. By how much would sales of product line X have to rise to fulfill this objective.

SOLUTION

New RTCE = $10,000,000 × .17
= $1,700,000, a $200,000 increase
iS of X = $200,000/(.40 − .30)
= $2 million
S of X = $2 million + $3 million
= $5 million
S of Y must be decreased to $3 million.
New RTCE = New C − FC
= ($5 million of X × .40) + ($3 million of Y × .30) − $1.2 million
= ($2 million + $.9 million) − $1.2 million
= $1,700,000

Application 8: ECONOMIC COMPARISON—SECOND SHIFT, ADDED EQUIPMENT OR OVERTIME

A profit structure shows the following data:

Total sales	$5,100,000
Direct cost	3,300,000
Contribution	1,800,000
PV	.353
Period costs	1,200,000
Pre-tax profit	600,000

The above represents full capacity for one-shift operation. Thirty percent more business is available to the company which requires additional capacity. It can obtain this increase in three different ways: with a second shift; by adding production equipment; or by using existing equipment and labor on overtime. The profit structures for the three alternatives now are (000's omitted):

	Second Shift	Add Equipment	Overtime
Total sales	$6,630	$6,630	$6,630
Direct costs	4,450	4,290	4,590
Contribution	2,180	2,340	2,040
PV	.329	.353	.308
Period costs	1,400	1,700	1,200
Pre-tax profit	780	640	840

While the overtime is most profitable at the $6,630,000 sales level, it generates the lowest PV. On the other hand, adding equipment, while producing the least profit at this sales level, results in the highest PV. The second-shift alternative is in the middle for both profit and PV.

(*a*) At what sales level will it be more profitable to eliminate the overtime and switch over to a second shift?

SOLUTION

$$\begin{aligned} \text{Sep} &= (\$1{,}400 - \$1{,}200)/(.329 - .308) \qquad (2\text{-}25)\\ &= \$9{,}523{,}810 \end{aligned}$$

(*b*) If a second shift has been installed, what must sales be to justify eliminating the shift in favor of additional facilities?

SOLUTION

$$\begin{aligned} \text{Sep} &= (\$1{,}700 - \$1{,}400)/(.353 - .329)\\ &= \$12{,}500{,}000 \end{aligned}$$

(*c*) If a second shift cannot be organized because of the lack of qualified workers, at what sales point will it pay to switch from overtime directly to additional facilities?

SOLUTION

$$\begin{aligned} \text{Sep} &= (\$1{,}700 - \$1{,}200)/(.353 - .308)\\ &= \$11{,}111{,}111 \end{aligned}$$

Application 9: LOWERING PRICE AT INCREASED VOLUME TO MAINTAIN THE SAME TRCE

The selling price of a company's product is $100 each. Its planned annual sales volume is 60,000 units. A quantity of 10,000 additional units is offered, which would require an additional investment in manufacturing facilities of $400,000, which would add $200,000 annually in period costs. At what unit SP would the additional quantity have to be priced to maintain the present 10% RTCE? The data are:

Present sales revenue ($100 × 60,000)	$6,000,000
Direct costs	3,000,000
Period costs	2,500,000
Pre-tax profit	500,000
Variable capital (60% of DC)	1,800,000
Fixed capital	3,200,000

SOLUTION

New TCE required = (60% × $3,500,000) + $3,600,000
= $5,700,000
RTCE = $570,000

iS = iFC + iDC + iP
= $200,000 + $500,000 + $70,000
= $770,000

SP = $770,000/10,000
= $77

Application 10: INCREASE IN PRODUCTIVITY REQUIRED TO JUSTIFY FASTER MACHINE

The manufacturing manager is telling top management that small increases in labor productivity would be required to justify buying a faster machine. The proposed equipment would add $2 million to period costs. What increase in productivity would be required at the same profit based on the following company data before the proposal?

Sales		$20 million
Direct labor	$4 million	
Direct materials	$6 million	
Direct overhead	$4 million	
Total direct costs		$14 million
Contribution		$ 6 million
Period costs		$ 4 million
Pre-tax profit		$ 2 million

SOLUTION

To maintain the same profit, contribution would have to increase by $2 million to offset (pay for) the additional period costs. Therefore, the total direct costs must be reduced by $2 million. As this reduction is being expected from direct labor:

Increase in productivity = original direct-labor cost/new direct-labor cost
= $4 million/$2 million
= 2, or twice the original productivity

Application 11: MINIMUM QUANTITY REQUIRED TO SWITCH PRODUCTION MACHINES

The production of parts can be done on two different machines of the same basic type. Each machine produces a different number of parts per cycle, and operates at different speeds, costs, etc. Given the following data, find the minimum quantity at which the company should switch from A to B.

	Machine A 4 parts/cycle	Machine B 10 parts/cycle
Speed in cycles per hour	1,250	1,000
Output per hour	5,000	10,000
Part plugs	4	10
Plug cost each	$100	$80
Setup time in hours	3	7
Setup MHRdc	$42	$57
Run MHRdc	$49	$72

SOLUTION

Qep = increase in cDC/decrease in uDC (3-29)
= (setup cost B − setup cost A)/(run cost A − run cost B)

$$= \frac{[(10 \times \$80) + (7 \times \$57)] - [(4 \times \$100) + (3 \times \$42)]}{(\$49/5{,}000) - (\$72/10{,}000)}$$

= \$673/\$.0026
= 258,846 parts

The next group of formulas and problems deals with the use of product, order, and/or job estimates and price evaluations. Data are provided from a model die casting cost estimate, shown in Exhibit 4-1.

Application 12: PROPOSED CONCESSION TO CUSTOMER ON PRICE

The customer wants to pay a price of \$275 per 100. Your decision?

SOLUTION

No. This would generate a cash loss per 100 of \$281.14 − \$275 = \$6.14, called "negative contribution," or a total cash loss of \$337.64.

Application 13: PROPOSED CONCESSION TO CUSTOMER ON QUANTITY

The customer offers to double the quantity of her order at the \$275 price. What then?

SOLUTION

No sale!

New DC = (2 × \$15,462.64) − one prep cost of \$113.95
= \$30,811.33
Cost for 11,000 order = (\$275 × 110) − \$30,811.33
= (\$561.33) negative contribution, cash loss

Comment: In job shop manufacturing using common or

EXHIBIT 4-1

Customer: White & Co. Ordered Qty: 5,000 Metal: Alum.

Piece weight: 2.136 lbs.[1] Exp. Waste: 4% Overrun: 10%

PLANNED QUANTITY: 5,500 EST. QUANTITY: 5,720

Conversion

Production Center	Standard Hours per 100	Standard Hours Allowed	OOP MHR		Direct Conversion Cost
Prep:					
* Setup diecast-800T	—	4.00	$24.79		$ 99.16
* Setup trim press	—	.50	16.27		8.14
* Setup straighter	—	.50	13.29		6.65
				SUB	$113.95
Run:					
Diecast-800T	1.25	71.50	24.79		1,772.49
First inspect.	.625	35.75	10.36		370.37
File	2.50	143.00	13.29		1,900.47
Trim press	.625	35.75	16.27		581.65
Straighten	2.50	143.00	13.29		1,900.47
Final inspect.	.333	18.33**	9.82		180.00
Pack	1.000	55.00**	9.82		540.10
				SUB	$7,245.55
TOTAL DIRECT CONVERSION COST				=	$7,359.50

DOC's:

Metal: 2.136 # @ $.62 /# 5,720 pieces	=	$ 7,575.11
Packaging: 275 @ $.50 ea.	=	137.50
Die Maintenance: 1 hour @ $26.59	=	26.59
Freight out: 117.4 cwt. @ $3.10/cwt.	=	363.94
TOTAL DIRECT ORDER COST***	=	$15,462.64
Per 100	=	$281.14

[1] Piece weight shown includes net casting weight plus individually allocated metal loss.

* Includes dismount time.

** For *planned* quantity.

*** Before commissions.

joint facilities, frequent setups of machines are required. Where preparatory costs are a small portion of total conversion costs, as in Exhibit 4-1, the effect of order quantity is negligible.

Application 14: CONTRIBUTION AND PV OF PROPOSED CONCESSION

The prevalent, or "going," market price for this job is \$310 per 100. Find (*a*) the contribution per 100, (*b*) the gross contribution of the order, and the (*c*) PV of the inquiry.

SOLUTION

(*a*) C = \$310 − \$281.14 per 100
= \$28.86 per 100
PV = \$28.86/\$310
= .093
(*b*) C = \$17,050 − \$15,462.64
= \$1,587.36
(*c*) PV = \$1,587.36/\$17,050
= .093

BASIC QUESTION: ***How is the decision made whether to accept or reject the price?***

1. How *not* to make it:
   a. If my competitor can take it at that price, so can I.
   b. If \$310 is the "going" price, I must accept it to stay in business.
   c. I have to take it to keep my expensive facilities busy.
   d. I don't know what to do since I can't tell how much of my fixed (period) expenses are "covered."
2. Is the \$310 really a prevalent price or the result of price cutting? If I haven't forced the price down in order to get the job, and the prospective customer has not gone on a "fishing expedition" to set one diecaster against the other, in order to drive down the price levels, I have *to approach my decision in the following manner:*

a. How loaded are my major facilities—the die-caster principally?
b. What is the characteristic PV of presently booked business scheduled to run on my facilities?
c. Is this job better or worse?
d. If facilities are loaded and this job is worse, I don't want it on economic grounds. (However, there may be strategic reasons for booking it.)
e. If facilities are not loaded, and this job has a PV below what I've been getting, then this job will provide me with contribution not otherwise available.
f. So I'll take the job *providing* it is not so large that it will displace more profitable work in the near future.

Application 15: SELLING PRICE BASED ON TARGET PV

If the company has been getting a PV of .22 for this class of work, what selling price per 100 would have to be targeted?

SOLUTION

$$\begin{aligned} TSP &= uDC/(1 - \text{target PV}) \qquad (3\text{-}5) \\ &= \$281.14/(1 - .22) \\ &= \$281.14/.78 \\ &= \$360.44 \text{ per } 100 \end{aligned}$$

Application 16: INCREASE IN SP TO PROVIDE FOR SALES COMMISSION

How would this price have to be increased to provide for a 7% sales commission?

SOLUTION

Handle the commission as if it were part of the PV (.22 + .07):

$$\begin{aligned} TSP &= \$281.14/(1 - .29) \\ &= \$395.97 \text{ per } 100 \end{aligned}$$

The next group of problems relate to the data given in Exhibit 4-2.

EXHIBIT 4-2

Customer: Brown Co. Ordered Qty: 1,500 Metal: Alum.

Piece weight: .26 lbs.[1] Exp. Waste: 11% Overrun: 10%

PLANNED QUANTITY: 1,650 EST. QUANTITY: 1,832

Conversion

Production Center	Standard Hours per 100	Standard Hours Allowed	OOP MHR		Direct Conversion Cost
Prep:					
* Setup diecaster-500T	—	2.00	$23.11		$ 46.22
* Setup trim press	—	.50	15.47		7.74
* Setup tumbler	—	.50	15.69		7.85
				SUB	$ 61.81
Run:					
Diecast-500T	1.111	20.36	23.11		470.52
First inspect	.556	10.19	10.36		105.57
Trim press	.250	4.58	15.47		70.85
Tumbler-vibrator	.100	1.83	15.69		28.71
Final inspect + Pack	.125	2.06**	9.82		20.23
				SUB	$695.88
TOTAL DIRECT CONVERSION COST				=	$757.69

DOC's:		
Metal: .26# @ $.52/# × 1,832 pieces	=	$247.69
Packaging: 8 @ $.50 ea.	=	4.00
Die Maintenance: 1.5 hours @ $26.59	=	39.89
Freight out: 4.3 cwt. @ $4.60/cwt.	=	19.78
TOTAL DIRECT ORDER COST***	=	$1,069.05
Per 100	=	$64.79

[1] Piece weight shown includes net casting weight plus individually allocated metal loss.

* Includes dismount time.

** For *planned* quantity.

*** Before commissions.

Application 17: TARGETING CONTRIBUTION FOR HIGHER RETURN ON FACILITY CAPITAL

If the company decided that a PV of .22 was equitable for the previous job, is it also acceptable for this one? (Note that the part to be cast is smaller and made on a 500-ton machine instead of on an 800-ton facility.)

SOLUTION

The economic objective of the diecaster should be the generating of an acceptable return on invested capital with equipment representing the fixed and inescapable portion of TCE. In the previous job, conversion cost is 47.6% of total direct cost. In this job, it's 70.88%. That means that more contribution per sales dollar (higher PV) is necessary to reflect a higher investment and to give the same return that was provided by a .22 PV in the previous job.

Application 18: TSP FOR TARGET PV

What is the TSP for this job at a PV of .33?

SOLUTION

TSP = \$64.79/.67
= \$96.70 per 100

Application 19: CUSTOMER CONCESSION; ABSORB SPECIAL COSTS

The customer rejects the \$96.70 TSP and instead offers to pay \$85 per 100, providing the diecaster is also willing to absorb the cost of a special fixture costing \$400. Calculate the gross contribution of this proposal.

SOLUTION

C = (\$85 × 16.50) − \$1,069.05 − \$400
= (\$66.55) negative contribution, cash loss

Application 20: HIGHER QUANTITY TO OFFSET SPECIAL COSTS

A customer asks that her proposal be reconsidered, suggesting that she may be willing to order a higher quantity. How would this suggestion be evaluated?

SOLUTION

Find the minimum order quantity that would fully pay for the $400 device.

BEu = cDC/uC (3-27)
= $400/($85 − $64.79)
= $400/$20.21 per 100
= 1,979 pieces

Application 21: WHAT CONTRIBUTION AND PV AT A SPECIFIC QUANTITY

Since an order for 1,979 pieces would generate a gross contribution of zero, what would be the (*a*) gross contribution and (*b*) PV for an order of 2,200 pieces?

SOLUTION

(*a*) C = (2,200 − 1,979) × $20.21 per 100
= $44.66
(*b*) PV = $44.66/$1,870
= .0239

APPLICATION 22: QUANTITY REQUIRED FOR TARGET PV

What quantity would be required for a PV of .18 on the transaction?

SOLUTION

Expanding on S = DC/(1 − PV) (2-2)
we would have:
Total sales revenue = total DC/(1 − desired PV)
Total sales revenue = $85 per 100 × unknown number of units Q

By rearranging terms and expanding direct costs by separating DC and cDC, we would have:

$$Q = \frac{\text{cDC} + \text{additional cDC}}{\text{SP} \times (1 - \text{PV}) - \text{run cost per unit}} \qquad (4\text{-}3)$$

$$= \frac{\$61.81 + \$400}{[\$85 \times (1 - .18] - \$61.04}$$

$$= \frac{\$461.81}{(\$85 \times .82) - \$61.04}$$

$$= \frac{\$461.81}{\$8.66}$$

$$= 5{,}333 \text{ pieces}$$

The next group of problems refer to Exhibit 4-3.

Application 23: EFFECT ON CONTRIBUTION WITH 8% PRICE INCREASE

The market price for this job is \$30 per 100. At 1,000 pieces, the contribution is \$2.48 per 100; PV is .083. Because of the relatively high usage of the casting machine, and considering also the contribution level of other work which can run on this facility, management decides that the \$30 price is inequitable. The diecaster counterproposes a price 8% higher, or \$32.40 per 100. What would be the effect on contribution?

SOLUTION

$$C = S - DC$$
$$= \$32.40 - \$27.52$$
$$= \$4.88, \text{ almost double the original contribution}$$

Comment: In this job, an 8% price increase practically doubles the contribution and all other economic measurements, to be presented later. Not all sales structures, product lines, unit estimates, etc., behave in the same manner.

EXHIBIT 4-3

Customer: Std. Product Metal: Zinc Piece weight: .122 lbs.[1]

Exp. Waste: 6% Planned Qty. 1,000 Est. Qty. 1,060

Conversion

Production Center	Standard Hours per 100	Standard Hours Allowed	OOP MHR	Direct Conversion Cost
Prep:				
* Setup Diecast (NOTE A)	—	.1	$19.22	$ 1.922
* Setup Trim Press " "	—	.01	11.40	.114
Run:				
Diecast-200T	.833	8.33	19.22	160.10
Trim Press	.060	.64	11.40	7.30
Tumble	.040	.42	14.30	6.01
Pack	.400	4.00**	7.27	29.08
TOTAL DIRECT CONVERSION COST				= $204.53

DOC's:		
Metal: .122# @ $.41/# × 1,060 pieces	=	$ 53.02
Packaging: 10 @ $.40 ea.	=	4.00
Die Maintenance: .75 hours @ $18.17	=	13.63
TOTAL DIRECT STANDARD COST***	=	$275.18
Per 100	=	$ 27.52

[1] Piece weight shown includes net casting weight plus individually allocated metal loss.

* Includes dismount time.

** For *planned* quantity.

*** Before commissions.

NOTE A:

Apportioned to 1,000-piece planned quantity. Balance similarly distributed to other standard products.

Application 24: CONTRIBUTION BELOW "FULL" COST

Because of habit and a bit of skepticism, the diecaster is maintaining the old, traditional "full"-cost system and running it parallel with the new direct-cost system until he feels secure about the latter. "Full" costs on this job are computed to be $35 per 100, and he has marked it up 15% to a selling price of $36.75. His salesperson brings him the customer's willingness to pay $32.40, but he turns it down using the rationale that the price is $2.60 per 100 below his "full" costs and therefore would not be "covering" his fixed (period) costs. How much contribution does that decision cost the diecaster on a 10,000-piece order?

SOLUTION

C = 10,000 × $4.88 per 100
= $488, perhaps at a slow time when he needs it the most!

Application 25: NEW SP WITH NO CHANGE IN Q AND PV

The customer wants a concession on price based on higher ordered quantities. He is willing to pay $30 per 100 for a 5,000-piece order and would entertain ordering twice that amount in return for a lower unit price. Calculate the new unit SP at the 10,000-piece quantity, holding the PV the same.

SOLUTION

At 5,000, PV = $132.26/$1,500
= .088
At 10,000, New DC = (10 × $275.18) − (9 × $2.04)
= $2,733.44
At 10,000, S = $2,733.44/.912
= $2,997.19
SP = $29.97 per 100 (a 3¢ per 100 reduction!)

Comment: Evaluate the real effect of hypnotic pricing "buzz" words, such as "high volume" and "triple quantities." Often small price concessions are made because of the allure of higher revenue, etc., without realizing that such reductions can wipe out contribution.

Application 26: GROSS CONTRIBUTION PER FACILITY-HOUR (CPH)

A manufacturer produces several types of products on the same major facility at different times. This major equipment carries a high invested capital value and is used as a "joint" or "common" facility. One way of measuring how profitable such a facility is used is to relate the contribution generated by the product to the number of hours that facility is used in producing the item. Two different products A and B are run at different times on such a machine, each generating $1,000 of contribution. A requires 10 hours of machine time to produce the order, and B needs 50. Compute the contribution per hour for each.

SOLUTION

CPH = ugC/hours (3-22)
For A, CPH = $1,000/10
= $100
For B, CPH = $1,000/50
= $20

Comment: If a maximum of 2,000 annual hours were available for this facility, then A-type products would yield an annual contribution of $200,000, and the B-type $40,000. These results would obtain regardless of differences in PV. As an example of two transactions:

	A	B
iS	$8,000	$5,000
iDC	7,000	4,000
iC	1,000	1,000
PV	.125	.200

Application 27: CPH BY PRODUCT LINE ON ONE FACILITY

A job shop converts 3 types of product units. Their CPH's on one major facility are: \$30, \$50, and \$70, with a maximum annual availability of 3,000 hours. If each product will make equal use of the machine, compute the annual contribution from this mix.

SOLUTION

$$\begin{aligned} iC &= \text{CPH} \times \text{hours} \qquad (4\text{-}4) \\ &= (\$30 \times 1{,}000) + (\$50 \times 1{,}000) + (\$70 \times 1{,}000) \\ &= \$30{,}000 + \$50{,}000 + \$70{,}000 \\ &= \$150{,}000 \end{aligned}$$

Application 28: COMPUTE CONTRIBUTION FROM ANNUAL MIX OF FACILITIES

The conclusion to be drawn from the previous problem is that a company can have an infinite number of different annual contributions from the same 3,000 hours. Compute annual contribution from the following usage mix, respectively, related to the previous problem: 10%, 20%, 70%.

SOLUTION

$$\begin{aligned} iC &= (\$30 \times 300) + (\$50 \times 600) + (\$70 \times 2{,}100) \\ &= \$186{,}000 \end{aligned}$$

The next group of problems refer to the following condensed cost-estimating data:

Item and Quantity: 60 million sq. in. laminated foil and paper pouch stock

Production Center	Direct Conversion Cost
Prep:	
Extruder-laminator	\$ 49.86
8-color gravure press	156.90
Total prep.	\$ 206.76

Run:	
Extruder-laminator	$ 232.68
8-color gravure press	183.05
Slitter-rewinder	166.60
Wrap and palletize	36.80
Total run	$ 619.13
Total direct conversion cost	$ 825.89
Direct materials cost	$5,610.10
Total Direct Order Cost	$6,435.99
Cost per 1,000 sq. in.	.107

Application 29: WHAT PV AT A TSP?

Find the PV of this estimate if it is booked at a SP of $.152 per 1000 sq. in.

SOLUTION

PV = uC/uSP
= $.045/$.152
= .296

Application 30: WHAT MINIMUM ORDER QUANTITY TO BREAK EVEN ON SPECIAL COST?

The customer is considering switching her business to you from a competitor, providing she doesn't have to repay for etching the gravure cylinders which are in the possession of the competitor. The cost that this converter would have to pay, in order to book this business, is $375 per cylinder, or a total of $3,000. (*a*) Find the minimum order quantity required to insure against generating a cash loss. (*b*) What is the contribution at this new quantity?

SOLUTION

(*a*) BEu = cDC/uC (3-27)
= $3,000/$.045
= 66.67 million

(*b*) C = Q × uC (4-5)
= 66.67 million × $.045
= $3,000

Application 31: GROSS CONTRIBUTION WITH SPECIAL COST ABSORBED

What is the gross contribution at a quantity of 100 million square inches with the converter paying for the $3,000?

SOLUTION

Run + materials cost per 1,000
= ($619.13 + $5,610.10)/60 million
= $.10382

Run and materials for 100 million = $10,382.05
Add one preparatory cost = $206.76
Add cylinder etching cost = $3,000.00
C = S − DC
= (100 million × $.152/1,000 − $13,588.81
= $1,611.19

Application 32: SP TO YIELD A TARGET PV WITH SPECIAL COST ABSORBED

Find the SP per 1,000 sq. in. at the original estimated quantity of 60 million, to yield a PV of .296 with the converter paying for the $3,000 etching cost.

SOLUTION

Total DC at 60 million = $6,435.99 + $3,000
Total DC per 1,000 = $9,435.99
SP = DC/(1 − PV) = $.15727
= $.15727/.704
= $.2234/1,000 sq. in.

Comment: The offsetting price increase caused by the additional $3,000 DC is 47%.

Application 33: CPH OF BOTTLENECK FACILITY

The expensive bottleneck facility in this flexible packaging converting operation is the eight-color gravure press.

Calculate the CPH if the gross contribution is all being referred to this facility. Makeready requires 6 hours and the run time for the 60 million quantity is 7 hours, with a unit SP of \$.2234 per 1,000 sq. in.

SOLUTION

C = S − DC
= (60 million × \$.2234) − \$9,435.99
= \$13,404 − \$9,435.99
= \$3,968.01
CPH = \$3,968.01/(6 + 7)
= \$305.23

Application 34: CPH AT ORIGINAL SP

What would the CPH be at the original SP of \$.152 per 1,000 sq. in.?

SOLUTION

CPH = (\$9,120 − \$9,435.99)/13
= − (\$315.99)/13
= − (\$24.31) negative contribution

Application 35: CONSEQUENCE OF KEEPING FACILITY "BUSY"

What would be the economic consequences of using this facility under these CPH conditions?

SOLUTION

The more this press is run, the more cash losses are created. It would be preferable if the press was idle as each hour generates a direct, traceable cash loss of \$23.31.

Application 36: CONTRIBUTION OF LONG-TERM CONTRACT

In another company, management is attracted by large volume and high sales revenue and is considering a proposal from a major user of their product. Their initial contact stems from a current estimate for 2,000 pieces.

The condensed cost estimate follows:

Operation	Direct Conversion	Standard Hours
Prep. 1 machine	$ 136.78	5
Run 1 machine	2,484.60	20
Total conversion cost	2,621.38	
Direct material cost	4,180.00	
Total Direct Order Cost	$6,801.38	
Cost each	$3.40	
Market SP each	$3.90	
Critical facility hours		25
CPH		$40

The customer now suggests that she would place an order for her annual requirements of 200,000 pieces—to the exclusion of any other supplier—if the SP is $3.60. Neglecting freight costs, find the (*a*) net contribution of the contract, (*b*) the PV, and the (*c*) CPH, if the cost of short-term capital used for 3 months to finance the direct costs is 10% annually.

SOLUTION

(*a*)
$$\text{Total DC} = \underset{[\$136.78}{\underline{\text{Prep.}}} + \underset{(100 \times \$2{,}484.60)}{\underline{\text{Run}}} + \underset{(100 \times \$4{,}180)]}{\underline{\text{Material}}} \times \underset{(10\%/4 + 1)}{\underline{\text{Interest}}}$$

$$= (\$136.78 + \$248{,}460 + \$418{,}000) \times 1.025$$
$$= (\$666{,}596.78) \times 1.025$$
$$= \$683{,}261.69$$

$$S = \$3.60 \times 200{,}000$$
$$= \$720{,}000$$
$$C = \$720{,}000 - \$683{,}261.69$$
$$= \$36{,}738.31$$

(*b*)
$$PV = \$36{,}738.31/\$720{,}000$$
$$= .051$$

(*c*)
$$CPH = \$36{,}738.31/[(20 \times 100) + 5] \text{ hours}$$
$$= \$36{,}738.31/2{,}005 \text{ hours}$$
$$= \$18.32 \text{ per hour}$$

Application 37: LOST CONTRIBUTION OPPORTUNITY

To agree to the above contract, management would have to use up one shift on this machine at a CPH lower than what they could get on other work. If their mix of current transactions yields a composite CPH of $38.82, calculate the lost contribution.

SOLUTION

Lost contribution = ($38.82 − $18.32) × 2,005 hours
= $20.50 × 2,005 hours
= $41,102.50

Application 38: SHORT-TERM FINANCING COST

If management takes this contract, how much is their short-term financing costs?

SOLUTION

3-month financing cost = $666,596.78 − 683,261.69
= $16,664.91

Application 39: TSP FOR CURRENT CPH

Calculate the target unit SP if management wishes to reflect their current CPH of $38.82 under the conditions of Application 36.

SOLUTION

TSP = (required facility hours × target CPH) + DC (4-7)
= (2,005 × $38.82) + $683,261.69
= $77,834.10 + $683,261.69
= $761,095.79
Unit SP = $761,095.79/200,000
= $3.81

Application 40: PRICING FOR TARGET CPH

A company uses two machine centers in producing a part. Calculate (*a*) the TSP per unit and the (*b*) PV of the transaction for a quantity of 5,000, if the processing requires 44 hours on Machine X and 18 hours on Machine Y. The target CPH's, respectively, are \$62 and \$28, and the DC are estimated to be \$2,148.

SOLUTION

(*a*) $\text{TSP} = [(44 \times \$62) + (18 \times \$28) + \$2{,}148]$ (4-7)

$= \$5{,}380$

$\text{Unit SP} = \$5{,}380/5{,}000$

$= \$1{,}076$

(*b*) $\text{PV} = \$3{,}232/\$5{,}380$

$= .60$

Application 41: MAKE OR BUY?

A company has a contractual production schedule which calls for making 1,000 parts per month on one of its machines for one 3,000-hour shift. It has an alternate choice of purchasing finished parts from an outside supplier. They have prepared make-or-buy data according to the following monthly analysis:

Per 1,000	Make	Buy
Direct material cost	\$10,000	
Direct conversion cost	7,000	
Period conversion cost	5,000	
Total direct cost	17,000	\$20,000
"Full" conversion cost	22,000	

Should the company make or buy?

SOLUTION

Buying will be selected if the company uses "full" costs in making this determination. The decision should be made by comparing differences in cash outflows, because if either alternative is selected, the total *period* costs of the company will remain unchanged. The period conversion cost of \$5,000 is an arbitrarily allocated cost and it cannot be defended for reasons previously given.

By making, the company reduces its monthly direct cost by \$20,000 – \$17,000, or \$3,000. This provides an additional \$36,000 of annual contribution.

Application 42: RETURN ON VARIABLE CAPITAL, RE: MAKE OR BUY

As in most business decisions, a gain in one area requires an additional support in another, as follows: (applies to Application 41)

Changes in Annual Variable Capital	Make	Buy
Cash and accounts receivable	\$ 73,000	\$ 79,000
Inventory	410,000	260,000
Total annual variable capital	\$483,000	\$339,000

This shows that in order to gain from the additional \$36,000 of annual contribution, the company must employ an additional amount of variable capital (current assets). Should it make or buy?

SOLUTION

$$\begin{aligned} RCE &= iC/iCE \qquad (4\text{-}8) \\ &= \$36{,}000/(\$483{,}000 - \$339{,}000) \\ &= \$36{,}000/\$144{,}000 \\ &= 25\% \end{aligned}$$

Once the percentage return has been found, the decision now revolves around the attractiveness of the return. If no company policy is established, alternatives which may be competing for the use of the same capital have to be examined.

Application 43: DISPLACING MORE CONTRIBUTING ORDERS

The company decides to proceed with the "make" because it likes the 25% return and doesn't have any other work to schedule for that machine. However, suppose that this contractual work is displacing other more contributing work which averages $46 of CPH. Under those circumstances, should the company make or buy?

SOLUTION

Contract CPH = $36,000/2,000 hours
= $18
Lost C from "make" = gain from "buy" − loss from "buy"
= C from alternate use − additional DC
= ($46 × 2,000) − $36,000
= $56,000
The company should "buy."

GLOSSARY OF FORMULAS AND TERMS

FORMULAS

(4-1) TCE = variable capital (current assets) + present market value of fixed assets
(4-2) TRCE = TCE × % return (=P)
(4-3) Q = (cDC + additional cDC)/(SP × [1 + PV] − run cost per unit)
(4-4) iC = CPH × hours
(4-5) C = Q × uC
(4-6) iC = (Su − BEu) × uC
(4-7) uTSP = (required hours Machine a × TCPHa) + ··· + (required hours Machine n × TCPHn) + DC
(4-8) RCE = iC/iCE

TERMS

TCE = Total capital employed
TRCE = Target return on total capital employed
RCE = Return on capital employed (per unit, project, etc.)
CE = Capital employed
Q = Quantity of units
TCPH = Target CPH
TCPHa = TCPH of facility a
uTSP = Target selling price of the order, product, transaction, etc.

CHAPTER FIVE

ADVANCED PROFIT-PLANNING FORMULAS

This chapter deals with problems, solutions, and formulas for evaluating deeper elements of the profit plan. An important part of this chapter is identifying the sources of contribution and their supportive segments of capital. Product costs are separated into these segments for purposes of equitable markup and measurements, and for determining the contribution of individual manufacturing facilities. A glossary of formulas and terms are listed on pages 111 to 113.

The first set of problems is based on data provided in Exhibit 5-1.

Application 1: PLANNED AND BREAK-EVEN PV OF ANNUAL PROFIT PLAN

Compute the planned PV and break-even PV of the profit plan.

SOLUTION

PV = $2,045,000/$6,422,000
 = .3184

The break-even point is reached when C = FC; therefore,

PV = $645,000/$6,422,000
 = .1004

EXHIBIT 5-1 PROFIT PLAN

Total Capital Employed = $3,500,000
Target return = 40% = 1,400,000 (pre-tax)

Planned Sales Revenue			$6,422,000	
Projected Direct Costs:				
Material	2,094,000			
Conversion	2,283,000			
Total		4,377,000		
Planned Annual Contribution			2,045,000	(Planned PV = .3184)
Less: Period (Fixed) Costs			645,000	(BE PV = .1004)
Pre-tax Profit			1,400,000	

Separate markups of cost to obtain annual selling prices:

A. *On Annual Material Cost:*

= (Target return %/annual turnover of material investment) + 1.0
= (40%/4) + 1.00
= 110%, or 1.10

SP of material	= $2,094,000 × 1.10
	= $2,303,400
Material contribution	= $209,400
Conversion contribution	= ($2,045,000 − $209,400)
	= $1,835,600

B. *On Annual Conversion Cost:*

SP of Conversion	= sales revenue − SP of material
	= $6,422,000 − $2,303,400
	= $4,118,600
or: SP of conversion	= conversion cost + conversion contribution
	= $2,283,000 + $1,835,600
	= $4,118,600
Markup on conversion cost	= SP of conversion/conversion cost
	= $4,118,600/$2,283,000
	= 1.804

Application 2: TWO SOURCES OF CONTRIBUTION

Show that the two sources of contribution are equal to the total planned contribution.

SOLUTION

$$\begin{aligned}
MTS &= Mt \times muMT && (5\text{-}30)\\
&= \$2{,}094{,}000 \times 1.10\\
&= \$2{,}303{,}400\\
MtC &= MtS - Mt && (5\text{-}29)\\
&= \$2{,}303{,}400 - \$2{,}094{,}000\\
&= \$209{,}400\\
CnS &= Cn \times muCn && (5\text{-}20)\\
&= \$2{,}283{,}000 \times 1.804\\
&= \$4{,}118{,}600\\
CnC &= CnS - Cn && (5\text{-}5)\\
&= \$4{,}118{,}600 - \$2{,}283{,}000\\
&= \$1{,}835{,}600\\
C &= CnC + MtC && (5\text{-}12)\\
&= \$1{,}835{,}600 + \$209{,}400\\
&= \$2{,}045{,}000
\end{aligned}$$

Application 3: SP OF MATERIAL FOR RTCE

A company's annual investment in material turns over six times. Calculate the material SP of a transaction if the material cost is $1,800 and the desired return on capital is 15%.

SOLUTION

$$\begin{aligned}
muMt &= (RTCE\ \%/\text{material turnover}) + 1.00 && (5\text{-}23)\\
&= (15\%/6) + 1.00\\
&= 1.025\\
MtS &= \$1{,}800 \times 1.025 && (5\ .21)\\
&= \$1{,}845
\end{aligned}$$

Application 4: COMPUTE MARKUP ON CONVERSION COST AND CALCULATE CONVERSION PV

In another company's annual profit plan, the RTCE is 20% and the annual material selling price is $2 million. If annual planned sales are \$6 million and annual conversion costs are \$1.5 million, compute (*a*) the markup on conversion costs, (*b*) the annual conversion sales revenue, (*c*) the CnPV, and (*d*) the CnC.

SOLUTION

(*a*) muCn = \$4 million/\$1.5 (5-24)
= 2.6667
(*b*) CnS = \$6 million − \$2 million (5-8)
= \$4 million
(*c*) CnPV = \$2.5 million/\$4 million (5-13)
= .625
(*d*) CnC = \$4 million − \$1.5 million (5-5)
= \$2.5 million

Application 5: ANNUAL PLANNED CONTRIBUTION OF PROFIT PLAN AND GPV

If this company's annual material investment turnover is 4 times, calculate (*a*) the annual planned contribution of its profit plan, and (*b*) the GPV.

SOLUTION

(*a*) Each turn must be marked up by (20%/4) + 1.00 = 1.05
Mt = \$2,000,000/1.05
= \$1,904,762
MtC = MtS − Mt (5-29)
= \$2,000,000 − \$1,904,762
= \$95,238
C = CnC + MtC
= \$2,500,000 + \$95,238
= \$2,595,238
(*b*) GPV = C/S (5-15)
= \$2,595,238/\$6,000,000
= .4325

Application 6: TSP OF PRODUCT UNIT

The company has estimated the conversion cost of \$1,473 per unit and a material cost of \$681 per unit for a product line. Calculate the target selling price of a product unit which will provide the company with its desired 20% RTCE.

SOLUTION

$$\begin{aligned} uTSP &= (Cn \times muCn) + (Mt \times muMt) \qquad (5\text{-}19) \\ &= (\$1{,}473 \times 2.6667) + (\$681 \times 1.05) \\ &= \$3{,}928 + \$715 \\ &= \$4{,}643 \end{aligned}$$

Application 7: uTSP OF TWO PRODUCTS

Condensed data from two product cost sheets show the following:

	Product A	Product B
Direct materials cost/unit	$10.00	$ 5.00
Direct conversion cost/unit	2.00	7.00
Total direct cost	$12.00	$12.00

(*a*) Calculate the uTSP of each product if the markups from the company's profit plan show a 10% markup on materials cost and 79% markup on conversion cost. Show also the (*b*) uC and (*c*) GPV of each.

SOLUTION

	A		B	
MtS:	$10 × 1.10 =	$11.00	$5.00 × 1.10 =	$ 5.50
CnS:	2 × 1.79 =	3.58	7.00 × 1.79 =	12.53
(*a*) uTSP:		$14.58		$18.03
DC:		12.00		12.00
(*b*) uC:		2.58		6.03
(*c*) GPV:		.177		.334

Application 8: SEPARATE MARKUPS ON MATERIAL AND CONVERSION COSTS

Selling prices which are targeted on obtaining a desired rate of return on a company's capital (as above) have no market intelligence since they use only one company's data, which cannot reflect competitive influences or market demand. Such TSP's are useful solely as an internal financial tool by measuring variances between such target prices and market prices, thus evaluating the extent to which the company's pricing is achieving its targeted capital return. Suppose that the market readily accepts the TSP for A but rejects the price B as being one dollar too high. If the company accepts a $17.03 price for B, the uC of B is still almost twice as high as A. Under this circumstance, which product is providing the company with a higher rate of return on the capital invested in each and why?

SOLUTION

Product A has the higher rate of return because both markups were consistently applied to both products which are derived from the same capital plan. Each dollar of materials cost has to be sold at $1.10, and each dollar of conversion cost has to be sold at $1.79 in order to satisfy the return goal. The difference between the two markups is a function of the amount and nature of the capital used, the risk element, and the length of time such capital is to be employed.

The investment in material is a current one turning back to the company in a rapid cash-to-cash cycle. If material is not purchased for the product, there is no material investment.

On the other hand, the investment in machinery (fixed assets), by which the conversion operation takes place, has a much longer cycle depending on its useful life. If a product is not made, the capital investment in the machine continues as a risk against possible future profitable use.

So while Product A has twice the material cost, Product B has 2½ times the conversion cost. For this reason, B requires a uC of $6.03 to provide a capital return equal to what a uC of $2.58 generates for A.

Application 9: CALCULATE CONVERSION PV

Compute the CnPV of both products at the respective uTSP's.

SOLUTION

CnPV of A = \$1.58/\$3.58
= .4413
CnPV of B = \$5.53/\$12.53
= .4413

Application 10: WHY USE CnPV?

What is the purpose of developing CnPV data? Isn't the GPV good enough?

SOLUTION

The gross PV of a transaction is a *velocity* figure. It shows the speed with which the sales revenue dollar is generating contribution and should not be used as a sole guide to pricing. As we saw, a lower PV product could be providing the company with a greater return than one of higher PV.

The CnPV is derived from removing the distorting effect of raw materials (someone else's) from the measurement of relative profitability. The CnPV is a contribution measurement of the use of fixed capital machinery without the influence of contribution developed from selling raw materials.

Application 11: CPH AND CnPH

The following data of two products show the same uDC, uSP, and uC. Product X requires 8 major facility hours and Y needs 40. Calculate for each product the (*a*) GPV, (*b*) CnPV, (*c*) CPH and (*d*) CnCPH.

	X			Y		
	uDC	uSP	uC	uDC	uSP	uC
Mt	\$5,000	\$5,500	\$ 500	\$1,000	\$1,100	\$ 100
Cn	1,000	1,900	900	5,000	6,300	1,300
Totals	\$6,000	\$7,400	\$1,400	\$6,000	\$7,400	\$1,400

SOLUTION

(*a*)	GPV for X = .189	GPV for Y = .189
(*b*)	CnPV for X = .474	CnPV for Y = .206
(*c*)	CPH for X = $175.00	CPH for Y = $35.00
(*d*)	CnCPH for X = $112.50	CnCPH for Y = $32.50

Comment: Even though both have the same GPV, it's the CnPV and CnCPH that show the real differences in facility "profitability."

Application 12: CnPH AND CnPV

Why develop CPH and CnPH data? Isn't the PV or CnPV enough of a measurement?

SOLUTION

A high contribution rate in the revenue dollar is desirable if there are enough facility hours to manufacture the products represented by that revenue. However, when the sole criterion for pricing and price acceptances are based on PV, there is the danger of running out of facility time before achieving the RTCE. The booking of business must consider the extent to which facility time will be used. This *scarce factor* approach is crucial in profit planning and is critical when the company is operating near or at their maximum practical capacity.

Application 13: COMPARATIVE CPH'S

Referring to the data of Application 7, both products are to be made on the same facility and the company is near its limits of machine capacity. They have a choice of accepting an order of 10,000 units of A which uses 300 hours or 14,000 units of B requiring 1,200 hours. Which will generate an inflow of more dollars of contribution per unit of time?

SOLUTION

uC of A = $2.58 × 10,000
= $25,800

uC of B $= \$6.03 \times 14{,}000$
$= \$84{,}420$
CPH of A $= \$25{,}800/300$ hours
$= \$86.00$
CPH of B $= \$84{,}420/1{,}200$ hours
$= \$70.35$

Application 14: SCARCE FACTOR PRICE EVALUATION

(*a*) Which orders should be booked if machine time is not a limiting factor? (*b*) Which orders should be booked if only 300 hours can be spared?

SOLUTION

(*a*) If there is no time limit, book both orders.
(*b*) With a 300-hour limitation, A should be booked. If the 300 hours are given to B, even if the customer would accept one-fourth of his original order, the company would generate a contribution of $21,105 instead of the $25,800 available for A.

Application 15: SCARCE FACTOR PRICE TARGETING

Calculate the TSP of a quantity of parts manufactured on two machines requiring 110 and 80 hours of processing. The respective CnCPH's are $52 and $147. Conversion costs are $9,240 and materials cost $4,150. The RTCE is 25% and the material markup is 12%. Find also the (*b*) GPV and (*c*) CnPV.

SOLUTION

(*a*) The basic formula, S = C + DC, expands into:

$$\text{uTSP} = (\text{CnCPHa} \times \text{a hours}) + (\text{CnCPHb} \times \text{b hours}) + \text{Cn} + \text{MtS} \quad (5\text{-}33)$$
$$= (\$52 \times 110) + (\$147 \times 80) + \$9{,}240 + (1.12 \times \$4{,}150)$$
$$= \$17{,}480 + \$9{,}240 + \$4{,}648$$
$$= \$31{,}368$$

(*b*) GPV $= \$17{,}978/\$31{,}368$
$= .5731$

(*c*) CnPV = \$17,480/(\$17,480 + \$9,240) (5-13)
= .6542

Application 16: MARKET INTELLIGENT PRICING

A company has developed a system of market intelligence by sorting out similar classes of work sold to a specific market and accumulating contribution data. One of its product lines has a characteristic CnPV of .61 and an inquiry for quotation is received which has an estimated conversion cost of \$12.37 each and a standard material selling price of \$3.68 per unit. What would be the selling price of the part which is compatible with other part prices in that product line?

SOLUTION

uTSP = Cn/(1 − CnPV) + MtS (5-32)
= \$12.37/(1 − .61) + \$3.68
= \$12.37/.39 + \$3.68
= \$35.40

Application 17: LEVEL MARKUP ON DIRECT CONVERSION COST

Exhibit 5-1 shows that each dollar of direct conversion cost is targeted to be sold at \$1.804 regardless of the nature of the operation or facility at which such conversion cost is incurred. (*a*) Is this equitable? (*b*) How is such a deficiency overcome?

SOLUTION

(*a*) No, because it does not differentiate for the various investment values of such facilities. By using this *level* markup, \$100 of conversion cost incurred at a machine worth \$10,000 would be targeted to sell at the same price as \$100 of conversion cost spent at a facility valued at \$100,000, making both uTSP's \$180.40.

(*b*) This limitation is remedied by a method of developing specific target conversion CPH's which respects the present market values and usages of each production center in the company. When these TCn-CPH's are then added to their respective MHR's, the result is a hourly target conversion selling price for each production center. Hence,

uCnS = CnCPHa + MHRa (5-11)

Exhibit 5-2 is a constructional worksheet showing how individual TCnCPH's are developed.

Exhibit 5-3 is a schedule of production centers for the company shown in Exhibit 5-1, listing the TCnCPH, MHRdc, and the uCnS. Note that if the level markup was used, each MHR would be increased to the CnS by the same amount.

Application 18: LEVEL AND DIFFERENTIAL MARKUPS

What are the comparative effects of cost estimating a product and then using the level and differential markup approaches?

SOLUTION

Using the level markup, a product requiring long usage of expensive capital equipment in its operational sequence would yield a disproportionately lower target selling price than one using inexpensive facilities in its manufacturing sequence for the same time.

By the use of differential markups, the target selling prices would be in proportion to the use and investment of fixed capital, thus providing management with a better financial control tool in policing its target return on total capital employed.

Application 19: DIFFERENTIAL MARKUPS ON MATERIALS

Is there also a differential markup approach that could be used for materials cost?

ANSWER

Yes. As shown earlier, a basis for the materials markup was the annual turnover of materials investment as related to the overall target return % on TCE.

EXHIBIT 5-2 WORKSHEET FOR BASIC DIFFERENTIAL MARKUP (TARGET CONVERSION CONTRIBUTION PER HOUR BY FACILITY) TO OBTAIN TCnCPH AND uCnS BY INDIVIDUAL MACHINE

Production Center	No. of Units	Total Present Market Value[a] for Center	(A) Basic[b] CnCPH/ Unit	(B) Annual Assigned Hours[a]	Basic[c] Annual Contrib. (A × B)	(D) Target (Convers.) C.P.H. (A × C)	(E) OOP[d] MHR[d]	uCnS (TSP/hr) (D + E)	Target Annual Convers. Contrib.	Convers. PV[e]
A	1	$20,000	$2.00	1,000	$2,000	$12.50	$9.20	$21.70	$12,500	.576
B	3	30,000	1.00	1,500	1,500	6.25	6.60	12.85	9,375	.486
C	2	15,000	.75	2,000	1,500	4.69	7.30	11.99	9,375	.391
D	1	30,000	3.00	1,000	3,000	18.75	8.05	26.80	18,750	.700
Annual Contribution Totals					$8,000				$50,000	

$$\text{Target Factor} = \frac{\text{Target Conversion Contribution}^{f}}{\text{Basic Annual Contribution}} = \frac{\$50{,}000^{g}}{\$\ 8{,}000} = 6.25\ (C)$$

Comment: This technique produces TCnCPH's which are in direct proportion to respective PMV's per unit. Thus, the basic CnCPH's of $2.00 and $1.00 and the target CnCPH's of $12.50 and $6.25 are in direct proportion to the unit PMV's of $20,000 and $10,000 for Centers A and B, respectively, unaffected by the respective OOP MHR's.

Notes:

[a] From MHR's Converting Facilities Classification Sheet (CFCS).
[b] PMV per unit factored down by 10,000 for ease of handling.
[c] Trial amount.
[d] From MHR's Expense Assignment Worksheet (EAW).
[e] PV of conversion contribution only, without the distorting inclusion of materials cost and direct-order charges.
[f] From an Annual Profit Plan, assume $50,000.
[g] From the Profit Plan.

EXHIBIT 5-3. DERIVATION OF TCnCPH AND uCnS (BASED ON SUMMARY PROFIT PLAN OF EXHIBIT 5-1)

Production Center	Basic CnCPH/ Unit*	Annual Assigned Hours	Basic Annual Contrib.	Per Unit TCnCPH	M.H.R. OOP	M.H.R. uCnS
Adj. die cutters	$ .380	5,570	$ 2,117	$ 1.86	$11.72	$13.58
Solid die cutters	.270	16,425	4,435	1.33	9.42	10.75
PHP die cutters	3.000	5,780	17,340	14.75	10.78	25.53
Guillotines	2.050	3,870	7,934	10.08	10.84	20.92
Printers: P2	.045	4,925	222	.22	9.16	9.38
Printers: 18Q	1.100	10,740	11,814	5.41	7.41	12.82
Printers: 18M	1.410	18,920	26,677	6.93	7.41	14.34
Printers: S4	.450	815	367	2.21	11.16	13.37
Printers: 20F	2.100	5,440	11,424	10.32	11.54	21.86
Printers: 10E	3.000	3,750	11,250	14.75	12.12	26.87
Small jets	.600	1,810	1,086	2.95	12.43	15.38
Large jets	.700	1,100	770	3.44	12.68	16.12
Offset jets	1.800	2,040	3,672	8.85	12.79	21.64
Multi- #1250	.650	1,875	1,219	3.20	16.10	19.30
Mgd Printer	.700	3,680	2,576	3.44	18.13	21.57
Heidelberg-LP	.230	240	55	1.13	10.96	12.09
SO folders	1.100	14,870	16,357	5.41	10.86	16.27
LO folders	2.400	13,660	32,784	11.80	11.15	22.95
MO folders	4.400	3,895	17,138	21.63	13.38	35.01
Bindery equipt.	.105	9,950	1,045	.52	5.98	6.50
Auto clasp	.650	510	332	3.20	9.10	12.30
Auto Str. & Butt.	.850	510	434	4.18	6.11	10.29
Patch	.750	465	349	3.69	7.88	11.57
Insert. mach.	.540	1,270	686	2.65	4.06	6.71
Hand fold	.040	3,875	155	.20	3.71	3.91
WR-STD folders	1.400	18,770	26,278	6.88	10.53	17.41
WRW folders	2.000	38,110	76,220	9.83	12.87	22.70
RW folders	4.500	7,560	34,020	22.12	14.42	36.54
Mark IV folders	8.000	8,000	64,000	39.32	14.85	54.17
Window punch	.125	5,335	667	.61	7.88	8.49
			$373,423			

$$\text{Target Factor} = \frac{\$1{,}835{,}600^{**}}{\$\ 373{,}423} = 4.9156$$

* Obtained by dividing unit PMV by 10,000.

** From Profit Plan of Exhibit 5-1.

There are also other factors besides investment turnover which should affect the markup, viz., scarcity of materials; exotic nature of the materials required; deterioration of the materials; specially engineered, nonstandard materials; etc.

Application 20: ECONOMIC ORDER MEASUREMENTS

Data for the following cost estimate is taken from Exhibit 5-3:

Production Center	Standard Hours	MHRdc	uCnS	Cn	uTSP
Prep	8	$14.85	$54.17	$ 118.80	$ 433.36
Run	40	9.42	10.75	376.80	430.00
Run	126	14.85	54.17	1,871.10	6,825.42
			Totals	$2,366.70	$7,688.78

Compute the (*a*) GPV and (*b*) CnPV, if the processing of this work is done on customer supplied material. Calculate the (*c*) CnC and (*d*) CnPV of the third facility. Compute the (*e*) TSP and (*f*) CnPV of the transaction, if the level markup of 1.804 is used. (*g*) Calculate the difference in the two TSP's.

SOLUTION

(*a*), (*b*), (*f*) GPV = CnPV = CnC/CnS (5-13)
= ($7,688.78 − $2,366.70)/$7,688.78
= $5,322.08/$7,688.78
= .6922

(*c*) CnC = CnS − Cn (5-5)
= $6,825.42 − $1,871.10
= $4,954.32

(*d*) CnPV = $4,954.32/$6,825.42
= .7259

(*e*) CnS = Cn × muCn (5-20)
= $2,366.70 × 1.804
= $4,269.53

(*g*) Difference = $7,688.78 − $4,269.53
= $3,419.25 (amount understated by using level markup)

Application 21: TSP COMPARISON: LEVEL VS. DIFFERENTIAL MARKUPS

Calculate for the following estimate, the difference between the two TSP's:

Production Center	Standard Hours	MHRdc	uCnS	Cn	uTSP
Prep	2	$ 5.98	$ 6.50	$ 11.96	$ 13.00
Run	348	3.71	3.91	1,291.08	1,360.68
Run	18	16.10	19.30	289.80	347.40
Run	212	5.98	6.50	1,267.76	1,378.00
			Totals	$2,860.60	$3,099.08

SOLUTION

CnS = $2,860.60 × 1.804
= $5,160.52

$5,160.52 − $3,099.08 = $2,061.44 (amount overstated by using level markup)

Application 22: CALCULATING LIST PRICES

A manufacturer wishes to issue a price list for its various products which will return a desired rate of capital return. She can accomplish this task by either a markup on a product's total direct cost or on its conversion costs separately from materials cost. If the direct cost is $145 per unit, consisting of a Cn of $95 and Mt of $50, calculate the two list prices when the desired GPV is .44, the target CnPV is .63, and the muMt is 1.08.

SOLUTION

$$
\begin{aligned}
SP &= uDC/(1 - PV) && (3\text{-}2)\\
&= \$145/(1 - .44)\\
&= \$258.93\\
CnS &= Cn/(1 - CnPV) && (5\text{-}10)\\
&= \$95/(1 - .63)\\
&= \$256.76\\
MtS &= \$50 \times 1.08\\
&= \$54\\
SP &= \$256.76 + \$54\\
&= \$310.76
\end{aligned}
$$

Application 23: NEW GPV TO EQUALIZE PRICES

What would the GPV of the previous problem have to be to equal the SP of $310.76?

SOLUTION

$$
\begin{aligned}
PV &= 1 - (uDC/SP) && (3\text{-}19)\\
&= 1 - (\$145/\$310.76)\\
&= 1 - .4666\\
&= .5334
\end{aligned}
$$

Application 24: LIST PRICES GENERATED BY COMPUTER

Another manufacturer is preparing a price list for its products to be generated and updated by computer. Unit DC data, consisting of machine-hour rates and standard production hours (for the range of order quantities) are fed in, and the computer performs all of the extensions and holds these in memory banks. Since a group of products is sold to different markets, the manufacturer wants to reflect different characteristic GPV's in its list prices. It plans to do this by feeding into its computer a characteristic markup factor representing the desired PV of the specific market. The computer will then print out the set of list prices. How should the manufacturer do this?

SOLUTION

$$muDC = 1/(1 - PV) \qquad (5\text{-}34)$$

Application 25: PUBLISHED LIST PRICES

In the above company, list prices are published based on various quantities for a specific product. The uDC per 1,000 for Product A are \$12.30 for an order quantity of 1,000 units; \$9.60 for 10,000 units; and \$7.90 for 25,000 units. Compute the list prices for each if the target PV is .20.

SOLUTION

$$\begin{aligned} muDC &= 1/(1 - .20) \\ &= 1/.80 \\ &= 1.25 \end{aligned}$$

$$\begin{aligned} \text{SP per 1,000 for 1,000-unit order} &= \$12.30 \times 1.25 \\ &= \$15.375 \\ \text{SP per 1,000 for 10,000-unit order} &= \$9.60 \times 1.25 \\ &= \$12.00 \\ \text{SP per 1,000 for 25,000-unit order} &= \$7.90 \times 1.25 \\ &= \$9.875 \end{aligned}$$

Application 26: LINEAR PROGRAMMING

For reasons of market strategy and product-line enrichment, a company makes two products on a common facility, instead of using the machine capacity solely for one. Each product is manufactured at its own rate of speed, requires a characteristic level of variable capital support, and generates a specific unit contribution. Considering these variables, the company wishes to find the specific quantity of each product which will generate maximum period contribution.

SOLUTION

To find the optimum combination of the two product quantities, the simplex method of the linear programming technique can be used, as demonstrated in the following application.

Application 27: MAXIMIZING CONTRIBUTION FROM JOINT PRODUCTS ON COMMON FACILITY

Find the optimum quantity (*N*) per month for each of product a and b which will maximize monthly contribution. Total variable capital is limited to $110,000 per month. The specific data for each product are:

	Product a		Product b
uDC	$ 11		$ 8
uSP	$ 17		$ 15
Maximum monthly sales potential in units	10,000		8,000
Maximum capacity of common facility	14,000	*or*	10,000
uC	$ 6		$ 7

SOLUTION

State the production constraints imposed by potential unit sales and available capital, viz.:

Sales: Na ≤ 10,000 and Nb ≤ 8,000
Capital: $11Na + $8Nb ≤ $110,000 (1)

State the production constraints imposed by machine capacity, viz.,

Na/14,000 = no. of months required to produce N units of a
Nb/10,000 = no. of months required to produce N units of b

Then, (Na/14,000) + (Nb/10,000) ≤ 1 (1 month)
and,

10Na + 14 Nb ≤ 140,000 (2)

Solving Equations I and II simultaneously gives the optimum quantities of each product which will maximize contributions as follows:
Eq. (1): $11Na + $8Nb = $110,000
Na = $10,000 − .7273Nb

Substituting Na in Eq. (2),

$$10(10{,}000 - .7273Nb) + 14Nb = 140{,}000$$
$$Nb = 5{,}946 \text{ units per month}$$[1]

Substituting value of Nb in Eq. (1),

$$\$11Na + \$8(5{,}946) = \$110{,}000$$
$$Na = 5{,}676 \text{ units per month}$$[1]

$$\text{Max. monthly } C = (\$6 \times 5{,}676) + (\$7 \times 5{,}946) = \$75{,}678$$

Application 28: GPV OF PRODUCT COMBINATION

Find the GPV of the monthly product combination.

SOLUTION

$$S = (\$17 \times 5{,}676) + (\$15 \times 5{,}946) = \$185{,}682$$
$$PV = \$75{,}678/\$185{,}682 = .4076$$

Application 29: ECONOMIC LOT QUANTITY

A company is interested in finding its minimum-cost order quantity (economic-lot size) to manufacture an item. Its setup cost is $20, required usage of the item is 30,000 per year, and the inventory holding cost is $.10 each per year.

SOLUTION

$$mcoQ = \sqrt{\frac{2 \times cDC \times Q}{hDC}} \qquad (5\text{-}37)$$

$$= \sqrt{\frac{(2 \times \$20 \times 30{,}000)}{\$.10}}$$

$$= \sqrt{\frac{\$1{,}200{,}000}{\$.10}}$$

$$= \sqrt{12{,}000{,}000}$$

$$= 3{,}464 \text{ pieces per lot}$$

[1] No other combination of product quantities will generate a higher contribution per month for the stated sales, capital and production constraints.

Application 30: MINIMUM COST OF ECONOMIC LOT QUANTITY

What is the minimum cost of this lot in the above application, if the uDC of the item is $.50 each?

SOLUTION

$$\text{tDC} = \frac{(\text{cDC} \times Q)}{\text{mcoQ}} + \frac{(\text{hDC} \times \text{mcoQ})}{2} + (\text{uDC} \times Q) \quad (5\text{-}38)$$

$$= \frac{(\$20 \times 30{,}000)}{3{,}464} + \frac{(\$.10 \times 3{,}464)}{2} + (\$.50 \times 30{,}000)$$

$$= \$15{,}346.41$$

Application 31: FINDING THE LOWEST COST QUANTITY

A manufacturer has a contract to produce one of its parts at an annual quantity of 260,000. Required delivery to its customer calls for 5,000 parts per week. Setting up to produce 5,000 for 52 times a year would be costly. Alternatively, to produce the entire contract with a single setup would generate a large inventory holding cost. Find the run quantity which would result in the lowest cost of fulfilling this annual contract if setup cost is $130 each and the unit inventory holding cost is 3 cents per year.

SOLUTION

$$\text{mcoQ} = \sqrt{\frac{(2 \times \text{cDC} \times Q)}{\text{hDC}}} \quad (5\text{-}37)$$

$$= \sqrt{\frac{(2 \times \$130 \times 260{,}000)}{\$.03}}$$

$$= \sqrt{\frac{\$67{,}600{,}000}{\$.03}}$$

$$= \sqrt{2{,}253{,}333{,}333}$$

$$= 47{,}469 \text{ parts per run}$$

If 47,469 parts are to be processed for each setup, there will be 260,000/47,469 = 5.48 batches per year, or setup and run every 9.5 weeks.

Application 31: MINIMUM-COST ORDER QUANTITY

Besides manufacturing its own parts, the above company also buys parts and sells them under its own brand name. Its purchase costs are $20 per order, and its holding costs consists of two elements: (1) all inventory holding costs, except interest on the capital tied up in inventory, of $.01 per unit, and (2) the interest rate of 10%. Find the minimum-cost order quantity, if annual part usage is 120,000 and uDC is $.18.

SOLUTION

The basic mcoQ formula must now be modified as follows:

$$\text{mcoQ} = \sqrt{\frac{(2 \times \text{cDC} \times \text{Q})}{[\text{hDC} + (\text{i} \times \text{uDC})]}} \qquad (5\text{-}39)$$

$$= \sqrt{\frac{(2 \times \$20 \times 120{,}000}{[\$.01 + (.10 \times \$.18)]}}$$

$$= \sqrt{\frac{\$4{,}800{,}000}{\$.028}}$$

$$= \sqrt{171{,}428{,}570}$$

$$= 13{,}093$$

Application 32: NEW MINIMUM-COST QUANTITY AT MAXIMUM CAPACITY

As in most manufacturing companies, a time lapse exists between the start of delivery and the completion of the entire order. This causes variations in inventory levels because of procurement lead time, which would raise the minimum-cost order quantity. Find the new mcoQ of Application 31 if the maximum capacity of parts for this company is 1,600 per day.

SOLUTION

This requires a further expansion of the basic mcoQ formula:

$$\text{mcoQ} = \sqrt{\frac{(2 \times \text{cDC} \times \text{Q})}{\text{hDC} \times [1 - (\text{Q}/260 \times \text{dpr})]}} \qquad (5\text{-}40)$$

$$= \sqrt{\frac{(2 \times \$130 \times 260{,}000)}{\$.03 \times \left(1 - \dfrac{260{,}000}{260 \times 1{,}600}\right)}}$$

$$= \sqrt{\frac{\$67{,}600{,}000}{\$.03 \times (1 - .625)}}$$

$$= \sqrt{\frac{\$67{,}600{,}000}{.01125}}$$

$$= 77{,}518 \text{ lot size}$$

Application 33: uTSP BASED ON TRTCE

A company wishes to price one of its products to return a certain rate on the total capital employed in manufacturing the product. Neglecting competitive market prices, calculate the unit target selling price given the following data:

iFC = \$100,000	TRCE = 25%
uDC = \$.40	FCE = \$50,000
Q = 500,000	VCE = 30% of sales

SOLUTION

$$\text{SP} = \frac{[\text{iFC} + (\text{uDC} \times \text{Q}) + (\text{TRCE} \times \text{FCE})[/\text{Q}}{[1 - (\text{TRCE} \times \text{VCE})]} \qquad (5\text{-}41)$$

$$= \frac{[\$100{,}000 + (\$.40 \times 500{,}000) + (.25 \times \$50{,}000)]/500{,}000}{[1 - (.25 \times .30)]}$$

$$= \frac{(\$100{,}000 + \$200{,}000 + \$12{,}500)/500{,}000}{.925}$$

$$= \frac{\$.625}{.925}$$

$$= \$.67567$$

GLOSSARY OF FORMULAS AND TERMS

FORMULAS

(5-1) Cn = (direct labor, fringe benefits, and other charges directly associated with labor manning at production centers) + (direct overhead costs traceable to, and specifically identifiable with, production centers) + (other direct overhead costs not traceable to, and not incurred specifically by, production center or order transaction).

(5-2) $Cn = CnS - CnC$

(5-3) $Cn = CnS \times (1 - CnPV)$

(5-4) $CnC = C - MtC$

(5-5) $CnC = CnS - Cn$

(5-6) $CnC = CnS \times CnPV$

(5-7) $CnC = (a \text{ hours} \times TCnCPHa) + \cdots + (n \text{ hours} \times TCnCPHn)$

(5-8) $CnS = S - MtS$

(5-9) $CnS = CnC + Cn$

(5-10) $CnS = Cn/(1 - CnPV)$

(5-11) $uCnS = CnCPHa + MHRa$

(5-12) $C = CnC + Mtc$

(5-13) $CnPV = CnC/CnS$

(5-14) $CnPV = (Cn/CnS) - 1$

(5-15) $GPV = C/S$

(5-16) $GPV = (CnC + MtC)/(CnS + MtS)$

(5-17) $uTSP = CnS + MtS$

(5-18) $uTSP = CnC + Cn + MtS$

(5-19) $uTSP = (Cn \times muCn) + (Mt \times muMt)$

(5-20) $CnS = Cn \times muCn$

(5-21) $MtS = Mt \times muMt$

(5-22) $MtS = Mt + MtC$

(5-23) $muMt = (RTCE\ \%/\text{material turnover}) + 1.00$

(5-24) $muCn = CnS/Cn$

(5-25) $MtPV = MtC/MtS$

(5-26) $CnCPHa = uCnS - MHRa$

(5-27) $TCnCPH = \text{annual } uCnS/\text{planned annual facility hours}$

(5-28) $RTCE = (CnC + MtC) - FC\ (= P)$

(5-29) $MtC = MtS - Mt$

(5-30) $MtS = Mt \times muMt$

(5-31) $CnCPH = CnC/hours$

(5-32) $uTSP = Cn/(1 - CnPV) + MtS$

(5-33) $uTSP = (CnCPHa \times a\ hours) + \cdots + (CnCPHn \times n\ hours) + Cn + MtS$

(5-34) $muDC = 1/(1 - PV)$

(5-35) $muCn = 1/(1 - CPV)$

(5-36) $TRVCE = net\ c/IVCE$

(5-37) $$mcoQ = \sqrt{\frac{(2 \times cDC \times Q)}{hDC}}$$

(5-38) $$tDC = \frac{(cDC \times Q)}{mcoQ} + \frac{(hDC \times mcoQ)}{2} + (uDC \times Q)$$

(5-39) $$mcoQ = \sqrt{\frac{(2 \times cDC \times Q)}{[hDC + (i \times uDC)]}}$$

(5-40) $$mcoQ = \sqrt{\frac{(2 \times cDC \times Q)}{hDC \times [1 - (Q/260 \times dpr)]}}$$

(5-41) $$SP = \frac{[iFC + (uDC \times Q) + (TRCE \times FCE)]/Q}{[1 - (TRCE \times VCE)]}$$

TERMS

Cn = direct conversion cost
CnS = selling price of conversion (conversion revenue)
CnC = conversion contribution
CnPV = conversion PV
uCnS = selling price of facility-hours
muCn = markup on conversion cost
CnCPH = conversion CPH
CnCPHa = conversion CPH of facility a
TCnCPH = target CnCPH
TCnCPHa = target CnCPHa
TRCE = target return on total capital employed
Mt = material cost (in the broader sense, all direct-order charges)
MtS = selling price of materials (materials revenue)

MtC = material contribution
MtPV = material PV
muMT = markup on material cost
GPV = gross PV of the period or unit
uTSP = target SP of a unit
Net C = product-line contribution less specific (not common) identifiable period costs
TRVCE = target return on variable capital employed in product line
IVCE = variable capital specifically identified by product line
FCE = fixed capital employed
VCE = variable capital employed expressed as a percentage of sales volume
dpr = daily production rate
mcoQ = minimum-cost order quantity, economic-lot size
hDC = inventory holding cost per year
i = interest rate
tDC = total direct cost

CHAPTER SIX

ECONOMIC CHOICE, TIME, AND MONEY FORMULAS

This chapter deals with problems, solutions, and formulas for evaluating and justifying projects involving the use of capital and for comparing economic choices. Most of these problems consider the time value of money and readers are referred to the end of this chapter (pages 132 to 145) for investment tables which provide worked-out factors required in the various formulas given. The glossary of formulas and terms are listed on pages 130 to 132.

Application 1: RETURN ON INCREMENTAL INVESTMENT

Referring to Application 34 of Chapter 3, if the capital cost of the facilities needed to make the part in house is \$280,000, compute the return on this incremental investment.

SOLUTION

$$
\begin{aligned}
RCE &= P/TCE \qquad (6\text{-}1)\\
&= \$20{,}800/\$280{,}000\\
&= 7.43\%
\end{aligned}
$$

Application 2: CALCULATE CONTRIBUTION PER POUND TO OBTAIN DESIRED RTCE

In the above company, what would the contribution per pound have to be to provide a return of 20% on the additional TCE?

SOLUTION

$$uC = \frac{(TCE \times TCE) + FC}{Q} \quad (6\text{-}2)$$

$$= \frac{(\$280{,}000 \times .20) + \$11{,}200}{800{,}000 \text{ pounds}}$$

$$= \$.084 \text{ per pound}$$

Application 3: ANNUAL USAGE TO GENERATE TRTCE

A plastic converter presently buys converted stock at $.70 per pound. If he purchased an adhesive-laminator to make the stock in-house, his uDC would be $.50 per pound; incremental FC, $11,000 per year; incremental variable capital, $80,000; and additional fixed capital, $100,000. Calculate: (*a*) annual consumption to break even; (*b*) RTCE for an annual usage of 100,000 pounds; (*c*) annual usage to provide a 15% return on TCE.

SOLUTION

(*a*) $BEu = FC/uC$ (3-26)

$= \$11{,}000/(\$.70 - \$.50)$

$= 55{,}000$ pounds

(*b*) $RCE = [(100{,}000 - 55{,}000) \times \$.20]/ \$180{,}000$ (6-1)

$= 5\%$

(*c*) $$Q = \frac{FC + (FCE \times RCE)}{uC - (uVC \times RCE)} \quad (6\text{-}3)$$

$$= \frac{\$11{,}000 + (\$100{,}000 \times .15)}{\$.20 - (\$.80 \times .15)}$$

$= 325{,}000$ pounds

Application 4: SIMPLE INTEREST

A manufacturer borrows $25,000 at 8% simple interest per annum. What payment must be made to pay off this obligation at the end of 6 years?

SOLUTION

$$\begin{aligned} s &= p \times [1 + (n \times i)] \qquad (6\text{-}4) \\ &= \$25{,}000 \times [1 + (6 \times .08)] \\ &= \$37{,}000 \end{aligned}$$

Application 5: PROVIDING A SINGLE DEPOSIT FOR A FUTURE PERFORMANCE INCENTIVE

Management deposits $50,000 in a performance incentive for its key employees. The fund earns interest at 8% per year and is compounded quarterly. What will be the value of the fund at the end of 5 years?

SOLUTION

Since there are 4 interest periods, $i = 8\%/4 = 2\%$. In five years, there will be 5 × 4, or 20 interest periods. Use the *spca* factor, viz., *future worth of a present sum*, from the compound-interest table, where $i = 2\%$ and $n = 20$, and find the factor 1.486.

$$\begin{aligned} s &= p \times \text{spca} \qquad (6\text{-}5) \\ &= \$50{,}000 \times 1.486 \\ &= \$74{,}300 \end{aligned}$$

Application 6: PRESENT WORTH OF A FUTURE SUM

At the beginning of a year, a company deposited a sum of money in a reserve fund that earned interest at the rate of 7% per year. Exactly 10 years later the value of this fund was $78,693.68. What was the amount of the original deposit?

SOLUTION

Use the *sppw* factor, viz., *present worth of a future sum*, where $i = 7\%$ and $n = 10$, and find the factor .5083.

$$\begin{aligned} p &= s \times \text{sppw} \qquad (6\text{-}6) \\ &= \$78{,}693.68 \times .5083 \\ &= \$40{,}000 \end{aligned}$$

Application 7: PROVIDING FOR FUTURE EXPANSION

A manufacturer made deposits of $100,000 at the end of each of four years to provide for future expansion. The fund earns annual interest at the rate of 5%. What was the value of the fund at the time of the fourth deposit?

SOLUTION

Use the *usca* factor, viz., *future worth of a uniform series,* where $i = 5\%$ and $n = 4$, and find the factor 4.310.

s = r × usca (6-7)
= \$100,000 × 4.310
= \$431,000

Application 8: PROVIDING FOR THE PURCHASE OF A NEW FACILITY

A company borrows $150,000 to finance the purchase of a new facility and is obligated to repay the debt at the end of 6 years at 10% interest. To accumulate this sum, the company plans to make five equal annual payments in a fund earning interest at the rate of 4%. If the first deposit to the fund is made one year after getting the loan, what is the amount of the annual deposit required?

SOLUTION

Use the *spca* factor, where $i = 10\%$ and $n = 6$, and find the factor 1.772.

s = p × spca (6-5)
= \$150,000 × 1.772
= \$265,800 (sum to be paid at expiration of loan)

Use the *sfp* factor, *uniform series worth of a future sum or sinking fund factor,* where $i = 4\%$ and $n = 6$, and find the factor .15076.

r = s × sfp (6-8)
= \$265,800 × .15076
= \$40,072 (annual deposit corresponding to the future value)

Application 9: ANNUAL VS. LUMP-SUM PAYMENTS

The engineering department of a manufacturing company has invented a device to improve production operations and has received patent rights. Management decides to offer the rights to non-competing companies in its industry. Two companies are bidding for the patent rights: Brown Manufacturing Co. offers an annuity of 15 annual payments of $20,000 each, the first payment to be made 1 year after the sale of the patent. Green Industries, Inc. offers to make an immediate lump-sum payment of $200,000. If the selling company believes that it can invest its capital at 10%, which offer should be accepted?

SOLUTION

Use the *uspw* factor, *present worth of a uniform series,* where $i = 10\%$ and $n = 15$, and find the factor 7.606.

p = r × uspw (6-9)
= $20,000 × 7.606
= $152,120 (present worth of the annuity)

Green Industries' offer is better by $47,880 ($200,000 − $152,120).

Application 10: DEMAND ACCOUNT VS. INTEREST-BEARING FUND FOR IMPROVING OPERATIONS

At the beginning of the calendar year, a company had accumulated $122,500 in a demand account to be used for improving production operations. Management now wishes to establish an interest-bearing fund which will pay an 8% interest rate, compounded quarterly, into which it will make quarterly deposits (starting April 1) for 4 years. Calculate the amount of the quarterly payment.

SOLUTION

Use the *cr* factor, *uniform series worth of a present sum,* where $i = 2\%$ and $n = 16$, and find the factor .07365.

r = p × cr (6-10)
= $122,500 × .07365
= $9,022.13

Application 11: SELECTING THE BETTER OF TWO ALTERNATIVES FOR INVESTED CAPITAL

A company is considering the building of a new warehouse and must choose between two methods of construction. The data are:

	A	B
First cost	$100,000	$45,000
Salvage value	$18,000	$5,000
Life, years (*n*)	45	20
Annual maintenance cost	$1,500	$4,200
Annual taxes per $100	$1.50	$1.50
Annual insurance per $1,000	$3	$8

If this company earns 8% on its invested capital, which method of construction is the better alternative?

SOLUTION

aoc of A = $3,300
aoc of B = $5,235
Use the *cr* factor.

ac of A = [(p − sa) × cr] + (sa × i) + aoc (6-11)
= [($100,000 − $18,000) × .08259] + ($18,000 × .08) + $3,300
= $11,512

ac of B = [($45,000 − $5,000) × .10185] + ($5,000 × .08) + $5,235
= $9,709

Since the annual cost of the B method of construction is lower, it is the better economic choice.

Application 12: WHICH DESIGN PLAN IS MORE ECONOMICAL?

Two design plans are being considered by management for the construction of a balcony to house additional office space in their present building. Information on the two design plans follows:

	Plan X	Plan Y
Construction cost	$60,000	$90,000
Annual maintenance cost	$6,000	$3,500
Life, years (*n*)	15	30
Salvage value	0	0

Which design plan is the more economical if a 6% interest rate is used?

SOLUTION

Use the *cr* factor

ac of X = (p × cr) + aoc (6-12)
= ($60,000 × .10296) + $6,000
= $12,178

ac of Y = ($90,000 × .07265) + $3,500
= $10,038.50

Plan Y is the more economical.

Application 13: ECONOMIC CHOICE BETWEEN TWO CAPITAL PROPOSALS

Sometimes the life of a particular proposal can't be estimated, especially if the plan involves a new concept or newly introduced materials. In the previous problem, determine the more economical investment if the life of Plan Y is not known.

SOLUTION

1. Equate the annual costs of both plans and solve for the unknown cr.
2. $12,178 = ($90,000 × cr) + $3,500
   cr = .09642
3. Interpolating the cr factor in the 6% compound interest table gives the life as 16.7 years.
4. Since 16.7 years exceeds the life of Plan X, it is the more economical.

Application 14: SELLING TO OUTSIDERS FACILITY TIME OF PROPOSED ADDITIONAL MACHINE

A manufacturing company is planning to buy capital equipment to reduce its direct production costs. It estimates that when it is not using this machinery for producing its own products, it can sell the use of the available machine time to others. Is the investment justified if the equipment costs \$100,000 and has a salvage value of \$15,000, a life of 6 years, and an annual maintenance cost of \$2,000? The estimated annual reduction in direct production costs is \$12,000 and the income from outside rental of the equipment is \$4,000 per year. Ordinarily, the manufacturer is able to earn 10% on its investments.

SOLUTION

ac of new equipment = [(p − sa) × cr] + (sa × i)
+ aoc (6-11)
= [(\$100,000 − \$15,000)
× .22961] + (\$15,000 × .10)
+ \$2,000
= \$23,017

ac of not purchasing
new equipment = additional labor cost
+ lost rental income
= \$12,000 + \$4,000
= \$16,000

Investment is not justified because of the \$7,017 lower annual cost of not purchasing the equipment, viz., \$23,017 − \$16,000 = \$7,017.

Application 15: CHOICE BETWEEN PURCHASING ONE MACHINE OR ANOTHER

Management has a choice between purchasing Machine E or Machine F, based on the following data:

	Machine E	Machine F
Acquisition cost	\$40,000	\$90,000
Salvage value	\$4,000	\$10,000
Life, years	10	6
Period operating costs	\$6,000	\$2,000
Unit direct costs, each	\$5.00	\$1.50

If money is worth 8%, what annual unit volume of the product to be manufactured is required to justify the purchase of either machine?

SOLUTION

Let Q equal the number of annual units produced and equate the annual costs (ac) of each machine to find the annual unit quantity which would cost the same for either machine. Use cr factor.

$$\begin{aligned}\text{ac of E} &= [(\$40{,}000 - \$4{,}000) \times .14903] \\ &\quad + (\$4{,}000 \times .08) + (\$6{,}000 \\ &\quad + [\$5 \times Q]) \qquad (6\text{-}11) \\ &= \$5{,}365 + \$320 + \$6{,}000 + \$5Q \\ &= \$11{,}685 + \$5Q \\ \text{ac of F} &= [(\$90{,}000 - \$10{,}000) \times .21632] \\ &\quad + (\$10{,}000 \times .08) + [\$2{,}000 + (\$1.50 \times Q)] \\ &= \$17{,}306 + \$8.00 + \$2{,}000 + \$1.50Q \\ &= \$20{,}106 + \$1.50Q\end{aligned}$$

Equating both annual costs:

$$\$11{,}685 + \$5Q = \$20{,}106 + \$1.50Q$$

$$Q = 2{,}406 \text{ units}$$

If annual volume is expected to be greater than 2,406 units, Machine F is the economical choice and vice versa.

Application 16: BUY OUTSIDE COMPUTER TIME OR PURCHASE OWN COMPUTER?

A company is presently renting 480 annual hours of outside computer time at a charge of $60 per hour. Management is considering the purchase of its own in-house computer for $130,000, plus annual operating, maintenance, and insurance costs of $9,000. It would trade in the computer at the end of 10 years for an estimated $40,000. At an interest rate of 8% on borrowed capital, should the company purchase their own computer or continue to rent?

SOLUTION

$$\begin{aligned}\text{ac} &= (p - sa)/n + [(p - sa) \times i \times (n + 1)/2n] \\ &\quad + (sa \times i) + aoc \qquad (6\text{-}13) \\ &= \$90{,}000/10 + (\$90{,}000 \times .08 \times 11/20) \\ &\quad + (\$40{,}000 \times .08) + \$9{,}000 \\ &= \$25{,}160\end{aligned}$$

ac of renting = \$60 × 480
= \$28,800

It is more economical to own than to rent.

Application 17: WHEN TO REPLACE A FACILITY

A press was installed at a total cost of \$60,000 and used for 5 years. During that time, its trade-in value and operating costs changed as follows:

End of Year	Trade-in Value	Annual Operating Cost
1	\$36,000	\$13,000
2	24,000	15,000
3	18,000	21,000
4	15,000	28,000
5	12,000	40,000

When would it have been most economical to replace this press with an exact replacement, if the cost of money is 8%? Assume that the cost of a new press remained unchanged during this period.

SOLUTION

Calculate the ac of each year using:

$$ac = [(p - sa) \times cr] + (sa \times i) \qquad (6\text{-}14)$$

But first, calculate the sppw of each year = aoc × sppw:

Year 1: \$13,000 × .9259 = \$12,037
Year 2: \$15,000 × .8573 = \$12,860
Year 3: \$21,000 × .7938 = \$16,670
Year 4: \$28,000 × .7350 = \$20,580
Year 5: \$40,000 × .6806 = \$27,224

Calculate p for each year cumulatively:

n		Cumulative p
0		\$ 60,000
1	\$ 60,000 + \$12,037 =	72,037
2	72,037 + 12,860 =	84,897
3	84,897 + 16,670 =	101,567
4	101,567 + 20,580 =	122,147
5	122,147 + 27,224 =	149,371

Use formula in item 1 above to develop ac for each year:

Year 1: ($36,037 × 1.08000) + ($36,000 × .08) = $41,800
Year 2: ($60,897 × .56077) + ($24,000 × .08) = $36,069
Year 3: ($83,567 × .38803) + ($18,000 × .08) = $33,867
Year 4: ($107,147 × .30192) + ($15,000 × .08) = $33,550
Year 5: ($137,371 × .25046) + ($12,000 × .08) = $35,366

Since the lowest ac is $33,550, the press should have been discontinued at the end of the fourth year.

Application 18: WHICH FACILITY TO PURCHASE, BASED ON OPPORTUNITY COST?

A company is considering the purchase of a facility to provide repair services to its production machinery. An average of 15 pieces of machinery require repair each week and the *opportunity cost* of having an equipment breakdown is estimated at $40 for each day of lost production time. Facility A costs $10,000 and can make 20 repairs per week. Facility B costs $40,000 and can make 70 repairs per week. The cost per repair is the same on either facility. Both have lives of 7 years with no salvage value. Management policy calls for a 15% return on this investment. Which facility should be purchased?

SOLUTION

Facility A, r = p × cr (6-10)
= $10,000 × .24036
= $2,404

Facility A, lost production time:
Average per occurrence = 15/[(20 − 15) × 20]
= 15/100
= .15 week
Total per year = 15 × 52 × .15
= 117 weeks

Facility A, time being repaired:
Average per repair = 1/20
= .05 week
Total per year = 15 × 52 × .05
= 39 weeks

Facility A, total waiting
and repair time per year = 117 + 39
= 156 weeks
Facility A, total cost per year = 7 × \$40 × 156
= \$43,680
Facility A, total annual cost = \$2,404 + \$43,680
= \$46,084

Performing the same calculations for Facility B:
r = \$9,614
Average per occurrence = .004 week
Total per year = 3.12 weeks
Average per repair = .014 week
Total per year = 10.9 weeks
Total waiting and repair time per year = 14.02 weeks
Total cost per year = \$3,926
Total annual cost = \$13,540
Facility B is the economic choice.

Application 19: PURCHASE NEW OR USED MACHINE?

Management is considering whether to buy a new or used machine for performing the same operation. The data follow:

	New Machine	Used Machine
Purchase cost	\$100,000	\$40,000
Life, years	8	6
Salvage value	\$15,000	0
Annual operating costs	\$90,000	\$120,000

Since an additional capital sum of \$60,000 is involved, management wants to know what the rate of return would be on this incremental capital.

SOLUTION

Equate the annual costs of both machines and solve for the unknown i portion of the cr.

$$[(\$100,000 - \$15,000) \times \text{cr}] + (\$15,000 \times i) + \$90,000 = (\$40,000 \times \text{cr}) + \$120,000$$

$$\$85,000 \times \text{cr} + (\$15,000 \times i) = \$40,000 \times \text{cr} + (\$30,000)$$

The problem now is to experimentally find an interest rate which when used in the cr factor will produce approximately the same annual costs.
Using an *i* of 30%:

$$\$85{,}000 \times .34192 + (\$15{,}000 \times .30)$$
$$= \$40{,}000 \times .37839 + (\$30{,}000)$$
$$\$33{,}563 = \$45{,}136$$

To get a closer equality, use an *i* of 50%:

$$\$85{,}000 \times .52030 + (\$15{,}000 \times .50)$$
$$= \$40{,}000 \times .54812 + (\$30{,}000)$$
$$\$51{,}726 = \$51{,}925$$

Thus, the rate of return on the additional $60,000 is approximately 50%.

Application 20: FUTURE RESALE VALUE OF NEW MACHINE FOR MINIMUM ANNUAL SAVINGS

A machine which costs $50,000 today has an estimated resale value of $5,000 ten years from now. If the investor wants a 20% return on her money, what must be the minimum pre-tax end-of-the-year annual savings?

SOLUTION

O = annual equivalent disbursements
− annual equivalent receipts (6-15)

$$O = (-p \times cr) + r + (sa \times sfp) \quad (6\text{-}15)$$
$$O = (\$-50{,}000 \times cr) + r + (\$5{,}000 \times sfp)$$
$$r = (\$50{,}000 \times .23852) - (\$5{,}000 \times .03852)$$
$$= \$11{,}733$$

Or, alternatively,

O = present equivalent disbursements
− present equivalent receipts (6-16)

$$O = -p + (sa \times sppw) + (r \times uspw) \quad (6\text{-}16)$$
$$O = \$50{,}000 - (\$5{,}000 \times sppw) + (r \times uspw)$$
$$O = \$50{,}000 - (\$5{,}000 \times .16151) + (r \times 4.1925)$$
$$r = \$11{,}733$$

Application 21: ANNUAL USAGE TO JUSTIFY PURCHASE OF FACILITY

Two 25-horsepower electrical motors are being considered. Data on the analysis follow:

	Motor A	Motor B
Purchase cost	\$1,000	\$750
Efficiency	85%	82%
Annual period cost	\$150	\$115
Electricity cost per horsepower-hour	\$.05	\$.05

How many hours of full-load operation per year are necessary to justify the purchase of Motor A?

SOLUTION

The approach to this problem is to find the number of annual operating hours where total costs of either motor will be the same, i.e., that number of annual hours where TC of A = TC of B.

$$\begin{aligned} TC &= FC + DC \qquad (2\text{-}16) \\ TC \text{ of } A &= \$150 + (25/.85 \times \$.05 \times Q) \\ &= \$150 + \$1.47Q \\ TC \text{ of } B &= \$115 + (25/.82 \times \$.05 \times Q) \\ &= \$115 + \$1.52Q \end{aligned}$$

Equating both total costs:

$$\begin{aligned} \$150 + \$1.47Q &= \$115 + \$1.52Q \\ \$.05Q &= \$35 \\ Q &= 700 \text{ hours/year} \end{aligned}$$

Application 22: WHAT ANNUAL INVESTMENT TO PURCHASE FACILITY IN FUTURE?

A group of production machines cost \$600,000, with an estimated life of 15 years and a salvage value of \$60,000. The treasurer of this company wishes to invest a sum of money each year so that at the end of 15 years the cost of the machines will have been recovered. What annual investment would have to be made in a fund earning 10%?

SOLUTION

$$r = s \times sfp \qquad (6\text{-}8)$$
$$= (\$600{,}000 - \$60{,}000) \times .03147$$
$$= \$16{,}994$$

Application 23: WHAT CAPITAL EXPENSE IS JUSTIFIED FOR ANNUAL SAVINGS?

What expenditure is justified for the installation of a sprinkler system that will save $2,400 per year in insurance premiums if its life is estimated at 30 years and interest costs are 8%?

SOLUTION

$$p = r \times uspw \qquad (6\text{-}9)$$
$$= \$2{,}400 \times 11.258$$
$$= \$27{,}019$$

Application 24: ROYALTY BASIS OR OUTRIGHT PAYMENT FOR PATENT?

A company is presently licensed to produce a part on which the patent has seven more years to run. The company makes 75,000 of these units annually and pays the inventor $1,000 per year plus 5 cents per part. The inventor offers to sell the patent outright for $30,000. If a 10% return is desired on the investment, will it pay for the company to buy the patent?

SOLUTION

It will not pay for the company to buy the patent unless the present worth of the future payments to be made on the patent is greater than the present sum of $30,000 required to purchase it.

Annual payments on the patent

$$= \$1{,}000 + (75{,}000 \times \$.05)$$
$$= \$4{,}750$$

$$p = r \times uspw$$
$$= \$4{,}750 \times 4.868$$
$$= \$23{,}123$$

Since p is less than \$30,000, it will *not* pay to buy the patent.

Application 25: REPAIR OLDER FACILITY OR REPLACE WITH NEW MACHINE?

On the basis of the following data, is it more economical to repair a 10-year-old piece of capital equipment which originally cost \$45,000 or to replace it with a new one? Repairs to the existing equipment will cost \$15,000 and will extend its usefulness for five more years. A new machine will cost \$40,000 and will last for 10 years. Annual costs for repairs and maintenance will be \$2,400 more for the repaired machine than for the proposed new one. Use an interest rate of 8%.

SOLUTION

$$r = p \times cr \qquad (6\text{-}10)$$

$$\begin{aligned} r \text{ of the old} &= (\$15{,}000 \times .25046) + \$2{,}400 \\ &= \$3{,}757 + \$2{,}400 \\ &= \$6{,}157 \\ r \text{ of the new} &= \$40{,}000 \times .14903 \\ &= \$5{,}961 \end{aligned}$$

Since the annual cost of the new machine is less than the total annual costs of the repaired one, the old machine should be replaced.

Application 26: BUILD OWN POWER PLANT OR CONTINUE TO BUY FROM UTILITY COMPANY?

A company uses 1 million kilowatt-hours (kWh) annually in its operations, which it pays for at the rate of 4 cents per kWh. Will it pay the company to build its own power plant to supply this capacity under the following assumptions: first cost, \$130,000; annual operation and maintenance, \$16,000; life, 15 years; salvage value, \$12,000, insurance, 2%; and cost of money, 7%?

SOLUTION

Present ac = 1,000,000 × \$.04
= \$40,000
r = (\$130,000 − \$16,000) × cr of .10979
= \$12,516
ac of company plant = \$12,516 + \$16,000
+ (.02 × \$130,000)
= \$31,116

Since the total annual cost for a company plant is less than the cost of purchased energy, it would pay for the company to install its own plant.

GLOSSARY OF FORMULAS AND TERMS

FORMULAS

(6-1) RCE = P/TCE

(6-2) $uC = \dfrac{(TCE \times RCE) + FC}{Q}$

(6-3) $Q = \dfrac{FC + (FCE \times RCE)}{uC - (uVC \times RCE)}$

(6-4) s = p × [1 + (n × i)]

(6-5) s = p × spca

(6-6) p = s × sppw

(6-7) s = r × usca

(6-8) r = s × sfp

(6-9) p = r × uspw

(6-10) r = p × cr

(6-11) ac = [(p − sa) × cr] + (sa × i) + aoc

(6-12) ac = (p × cr) + aoc

(6-13) ac = (p − sa)/n + [(p − sa) × (n + 1)/2n] + (sa × i) + aoc

(6-14) ac = [(p − sa) × cr] + (sa × i)

(6-15) O = annual equiv. disbursements − annual equiv. receipts

(6-15) O = (−p × cr) + r + (sa × sfp)

(6-15) r = (p × cr) − (sa × sfp)

(6-16) O = present equiv. disbursements − present equiv. receipts

(6-16) O = −p + (sa × sppw) + (r × uspw)
(6-16) r = [p − (sa × sppw)]/uspw

TERMS

RTCE = return on total capital employed
RCE = return on capital employed
TCE = total capital employed
P = profit; RCE
FCE = fixed capital employed
uVC = unit variable capital
p = value of payment at beginning of first interest period
s = value of payment at end of nth interest period
n = life in years
n = number of interest periods
r = sum paid at end of each period for n periods
i = interest rate per period, %
spca = a factor*: future worth of a present sum
sppw = a factor*: present worth of a future sum
usca = a factor*: future worth of a uniform series
sfp = a factor*: sinking fund factor
uspw = a factor*: present worth of a uniform series
cr = a factor*: capital recovery factor
aoc = annual operating cost
ac = annual cost
sa = salvage value

FORMULAS DERIVING VALUES IN INTEREST TABLES

spca	$= (1 + i)^n$	(compound amount factor for a single payment; future worth of a present sum)
sppw	$= \dfrac{1}{(1 + i)^n}$	(present-worth factor for a single payment; present worth of a future sum)
usca	$= \dfrac{(1 + i)^n - 1}{i}$	(compound amount factor for a uniform series; future worth of a uniform series)

* Values for factors are given in standard interest tables according to *n* in years and *i* in percent. Appropriate tables follow the end of this chapter.

FORMULAS DERIVING VALUES IN INTEREST TABLES (*Continued*)

$$\text{sfp} = \frac{i}{(1+i)^n - 1}$$ (sinking-fund factor; uniform series worth of a future sum)

$$\text{uspw} = \frac{(1+i)^n - 1}{i(1+i)^n}$$ (present-worth factor for a uniform series)

$$\text{cr} = \frac{i(1+i)^n}{(1+i)^n - 1}$$ (uniform series worth of a present sum; capital recovery factor)

INTEREST TABLE FOR $i = 2\%$

n	sfp	cr	sppw	uspw	spca	usca
1	1.00000	1.02000	0.9804	0.980	1.020	1.000
2	0.49505	0.51505	0.9612	1.942	1.040	2.020
3	0.32675	0.34675	0.9423	2.884	1.061	3.060
4	0.24262	0.26262	0.9238	3.808	1.082	4.122
5	0.19216	0.21216	0.9057	4.713	1.104	5.204
6	0.15853	0.17853	0.8880	5.601	1.126	6.308
7	0.13451	0.15451	0.8706	6.472	1.149	7.434
8	0.11651	0.13651	0.8535	7.325	1.172	8.583
9	0.10252	0.12252	0.8368	8.162	1.195	9.755
10	0.09133	0.11133	0.8203	8.983	1.219	10.950
11	0.08218	0.10218	0.8043	9.787	1.243	12.169
12	0.07456	0.09456	0.7885	10.575	1.268	13.412
13	0.06812	0.08812	0.7730	11.348	1.294	14.680
14	0.06260	0.08260	0.7579	12.106	1.319	15.974
15	0.05783	0.07783	0.7430	12.849	1.346	17.293
16	0.05365	0.07365	0.7284	13.578	1.373	18.639
17	0.04997	0.06997	0.7142	14.292	1.400	20.012
18	0.04670	0.06670	0.7002	14.992	1.428	21.412
19	0.04378	0.06378	0.6864	15.678	1.457	22.841
20	0.04116	0.06116	0.6730	16.351	1.486	24.297

INTEREST TABLE FOR i = 2% (*Continued*)

n	sfp	cr	sppw	uspw	spca	usca
21	0.03878	0.05878	0.6598	17.011	1.516	25.783
22	0.03663	0.05663	0.6468	17.658	1.546	27.299
23	0.03467	0.05467	0.6342	18.292	1.577	28.845
24	0.03287	0.05287	0.6217	18.914	1.608	30.422
25	0.03122	0.05122	0.6095	19.523	1.641	32.030
26	0.02970	0.04970	0.5976	20.121	1.673	33.671
27	0.02829	0.04829	0.5859	20.707	1.707	35.344
28	0.02699	0.04699	0.5744	21.281	1.741	37.051
29	0.02578	0.04578	0.5631	21.844	1.776	38.792
30	0.02465	0.04465	0.5521	22.396	1.811	40.568
31	0.02360	0.04360	0.5412	22.938	1.848	42.379
32	0.02261	0.04261	0.5306	23.468	1.885	44.227
33	0.02169	0.04169	0.5202	23.989	1.922	46.112
34	0.02082	0.04082	0.5100	24.499	1.961	48.034
35	0.02000	0.04000	0.5000	24.999	2.000	49.994
40	0.01656	0.03656	0.4529	27.355	2.208	60.402
45	0.01391	0.03391	0.4102	29.490	2.438	71.893

INTEREST TABLE FOR i = 4%

n	sfp	cr	sppw	uspw	spca	usca
1	1.00000	1.04000	0.9615	0.962	1.040	1.000
2	0.49020	0.53020	0.9246	1.886	1.082	2.040
3	0.32035	0.36035	0.8890	2.775	1.125	3.122
4	0.23549	0.27549	0.8548	3.630	1.170	4.246
5	0.18463	0.22463	0.8219	4.452	1.217	5.416
6	0.15076	0.19076	0.7903	5.242	1.265	6.633
7	0.12661	0.16661	0.7599	6.002	1.316	7.898
8	0.10853	0.14853	0.7307	6.733	1.369	9.214
9	0.09449	0.13449	0.7026	7.435	1.423	10.583
10	0.08329	0.12329	0.6756	8.111	1.480	12.006

INTEREST TABLE FOR $i = 4\%$ (*Continued*)

n	sfp	cr	sppw	uspw	spca	usca
11	0.07415	0.11415	0.6496	8.760	1.539	13.486
12	0.06655	0.10655	0.6246	9.385	1.601	15.026
13	0.06014	0.10014	0.6006	9.986	1.665	16.627
14	0.05467	0.09467	0.5775	10.563	1.732	18.292
15	0.04994	0.08994	0.5553	11.118	1.801	20.024
16	0.04582	0.08582	0.5339	11.652	1.873	21.825
17	0.04220	0.08220	0.5134	12.166	1.948	23.698
18	0.03899	0.07899	0.4936	12.659	2.026	25.645
19	0.03614	0.07614	0.4746	13.134	2.107	27.671
20	0.03358	0.07358	0.4564	13.590	2.191	29.778
21	0.03128	0.07128	0.4388	14.029	2.279	31.969
22	0.02920	0.06920	0.4220	14.451	2.370	34.248
23	0.02731	0.06731	0.4057	14.857	2.465	36.618
24	0.02559	0.06559	0.3901	15.247	2.563	39.083
25	0.02401	0.06401	0.3751	15.622	2.666	41.646
26	0.02257	0.06257	0.3607	15.983	2.772	44.312
27	0.02124	0.06124	0.3468	16.330	2.883	47.084
28	0.02001	0.06001	0.3335	16.663	2.999	49.968
29	0.01888	0.05888	0.3207	16.984	3.119	52.966
30	0.01783	0.05783	0.3083	17.292	3.243	56.085
31	0.01686	0.05686	0.2965	17.588	3.373	59.328
32	0.01595	0.05595	0.2851	17.874	3.508	62.701
33	0.01510	0.05510	0.2741	18.148	3.648	66.210
34	0.01431	0.05431	0.2636	18.411	3.794	69.858
35	0.01358	0.05358	0.2534	18.665	3.946	73.652
40	0.01052	0.05052	0.2083	19.793	4.801	95.026
45	0.00826	0.04826	15.705	20.720	5.841	121.029

INTEREST TABLE FOR $i = 5\%$

n	sfp	cr	sppw	uspw	spca	usca
1	1.00000	1.05000	0.9524	0.952	1.050	1.000
2	0.48780	0.53780	0.9070	1.859	1.102	2.050
3	0.31721	0.36721	0.8638	2.723	1.158	3.152
4	0.23201	0.28201	0.8227	3.546	1.216	4.310
5	0.18097	0.23097	0.7835	4.329	1.276	5.526
6	0.14702	0.19702	0.7462	5.076	1.340	6.802
7	0.12282	0.17282	0.7107	5.786	1.407	8.142
8	0.10472	0.15472	0.6768	6.463	1.477	9.549
9	0.09069	0.14069	0.6446	7.108	1.551	11.027
10	0.07950	0.12950	0.6139	7.722	1.629	12.578
11	0.07039	0.12039	0.5847	8.306	1.710	14.207
12	0.06283	0.11283	0.5568	8.863	1.796	15.917
13	0.05646	0.10646	0.5303	9.394	1.886	17.713
14	0.05102	0.10102	0.5051	9.899	1.980	19.599
15	0.04634	0.09634	0.4810	10.380	2.079	21.579
16	0.04227	0.09227	0.4581	10.838	2.183	23.657
17	0.03870	0.08870	0.4363	11.274	2.292	25.840
18	0.03555	0.08555	0.4155	11.690	2.407	28.132
19	0.03275	0.08275	0.3957	12.085	2.527	30.539
20	0.03024	0.08024	0.3769	12.462	2.653	33.066
21	0.02800	0.07800	0.3589	12.821	2.786	35.719
22	0.02597	0.07597	0.3418	13.163	2.925	38.505
23	0.02414	0.07414	0.3256	13.489	3.072	41.430
24	0.02247	0.07247	0.3101	13.799	3.225	44.502
25	0.02095	0.07095	0.2953	14.094	3.386	47.727
26	0.01956	0.06956	0.2812	14.375	3.556	51.113
27	0.01829	0.06829	0.2678	14.643	3.733	54.669
28	0.01712	0.06712	0.2551	14.898	3.920	58.403
29	0.01605	0.06605	0.2429	15.141	4.116	62.323
30	0.01505	0.06505	0.2314	15.372	4.322	66.439

INTEREST TABLE FOR $i = 5\%$ (*Continued*)

n	sfp	cr	sppw	uspw	spca	usca
31	0.01413	0.06413	0.2204	15.593	4.538	70.761
32	0.01328	0.06328	0.2099	15.803	4.765	75.299
33	0.01249	0.06249	0.1999	16.003	5.003	80.064
34	0.01176	0.06176	0.1904	16.193	5.253	85.067
35	0.01107	0.06107	0.1813	16.374	5.516	90.320
40	0.00828	0.05828	0.1420	17.159	7.040	120.800
45	0.00626	0.05626	0.1113	17.774	8.985	159.700

INTEREST TABLE FOR $i = 6\%$

n	sfp	cr	sppw	uspw	spca	usca
1	1.00000	1.06000	0.9434	0.943	1.060	1.000
2	0.48544	0.54544	0.8900	1.833	1.124	2.060
3	0.31411	0.37411	0.8396	2.673	1.191	3.184
4	0.22859	0.28859	0.7921	3.465	1.262	4.375
5	0.17740	0.23740	0.7473	4.212	1.338	5.637
6	0.14336	0.20336	0.7050	4.917	1.419	6.975
7	0.11914	0.17914	0.6651	5.582	1.504	8.394
8	0.10104	0.16104	0.6274	6.210	1.594	9.897
9	0.08702	0.14702	0.5919	6.802	1.689	11.491
10	0.07587	0.13587	0.5584	7.360	1.791	13.181
11	0.06679	0.12679	0.5268	7.887	1.898	14.972
12	0.05928	0.11928	0.4970	8.384	2.012	16.870
13	0.05296	0.11296	0.4688	8.853	2.133	18.882
14	0.04758	0.10758	0.4423	9.295	2.261	21.015
15	0.04296	0.10296	0.4173	9.712	2.397	23.276
16	0.03895	0.09895	0.3936	10.106	2.540	25.673
17	0.03544	0.09544	0.3714	10.477	2.693	28.213
18	0.03236	0.09236	0.3503	10.828	2.854	30.906
19	0.02962	0.08962	0.3305	11.158	3.026	33.760
20	0.02718	0.08718	0.3118	11.470	3.207	36.786

INTEREST TABLE FOR $i = 6\%$ (*Continued*)

n	sfp	cr	sppw	uspw	spca	usca
21	0.02500	0.08500	0.2942	11.764	3.400	39.993
22	0.02305	0.08305	0.2775	12.042	3.604	43.392
23	0.02128	0.08128	0.2618	12.303	3.820	46.996
24	0.01968	0.07968	0.2470	12.550	4.049	50.816
25	0.01823	0.07823	0.2330	12.783	4.292	54.865
26	0.01690	0.07690	0.2198	13.003	4.549	59.156
27	0.01570	0.07570	0.2074	13.211	4.822	63.706
28	0.01459	0.07459	0.1956	13.406	5.112	68.528
29	0.01358	0.07358	0.1846	13.591	5.418	73.640
30	0.01265	0.07265	0.1741	13.765	5.743	79.058
31	0.01179	0.07179	0.1643	13.929	6.088	84.802
32	0.01100	0.07100	0.1550	14.084	6.453	90.890
33	0.01027	0.07027	0.1462	14.230	6.841	97.343
34	0.00960	0.06960	0.1379	14.368	7.251	104.184
35	0.00897	0.06897	0.1301	14.498	7.686	111.435
40	0.00646	0.06646	0.0972	15.046	10.286	154.762
45	0.00470	0.06470	0.0727	15.456	13.765	212.744

INTEREST TABLE FOR $i = 7\%$

n	sfp	cr	sppw	uspw	psca	usca
1	1.00000	1.07000	0.9346	0.935	1.070	1.000
2	0.48309	0.55309	0.8734	1.808	1.145	2.070
3	0.31105	0.38105	0.8163	2.624	1.225	3.215
4	0.22523	0.29523	0.7629	3.387	1.311	4.440
5	0.17389	0.24389	0.7130	4.100	1.403	5.751
6	0.13980	0.20980	0.6663	4.767	1.501	7.153
7	0.11555	0.18555	0.6227	5.389	1.606	8.654
8	0.09747	0.16747	0.5820	5.971	1.718	10.260
9	0.08349	0.15349	0.5439	6.515	1.838	11.978
10	0.07238	0.14238	0.5083	7.024	1.967	13.816

INTEREST TABLE FOR i = 7% (*Continued*)

n	sfp	cr	sppw	uspw	psca	usca
11	0.06336	0.13336	0.4751	7.499	2.105	15.784
12	0.05590	0.12590	0.4440	7.943	2.252	17.888
13	0.04965	0.11965	0.4150	8.358	2.410	20.141
14	0.04434	0.11434	0.3878	8.745	2.579	22.550
15	0.03979	0.10979	0.3624	9.108	2.759	25.129
16	0.03586	0.10586	0.3387	9.447	2.952	27.888
17	0.03243	0.10243	0.3166	9.763	3.159	30.840
18	0.02941	0.09941	0.2959	10.059	3.380	33.999
19	0.02675	0.09675	0.2765	10.336	3.617	37.379
20	0.02439	0.09439	0.2584	10.594	3.870	40.995
21	0.02229	0.09229	0.2415	10.836	4.141	44.865
22	0.02041	0.09041	0.2257	11.061	4.430	49.006
23	0.01871	0.08871	0.2109	11.272	4.741	53.436
24	0.01719	0.08719	0.1971	11.469	5.072	58.177
25	0.01581	0.08581	0.1842	11.654	5.427	63.249
26	0.01456	0.08456	0.1722	11.826	5.807	68.676
27	0.01343	0.08343	0.1609	11.987	6.214	74.484
28	0.01239	0.08239	0.1504	12.137	6.649	80.698
29	0.01145	0.08145	0.1406	12.278	7.114	87.347
30	0.01059	0.08059	0.1314	12.409	7.612	94.461
31	0.00980	0.07980	0.1228	12.532	8.145	102.073
32	0.00907	0.07907	0.1147	12.647	8.715	110.218
33	0.00841	0.07841	0.1072	12.754	9.325	118.933
34	0.00780	0.07780	0.1002	12.854	9.978	128.259
35	0.00723	0.07723	0.0937	12.948	10.677	138.237
40	0.00501	0.07501	0.0668	13.332	14.974	199.635
45	0.00350	0.07350	0.0476	13.606	21.002	285.749

INTEREST TABLE FOR $i = 8\%$

n	sfp	cr	sppw	uspw	spca	usca
1	1.00000	1.08000	0.9259	0.926	1.080	1.000
2	0.48077	0.56077	0.8573	1.783	1.166	2.080
3	0.30803	0.38803	0.7938	2.577	1.260	3.246
4	0.22192	0.30192	0.7350	3.312	1.360	4.506
5	0.17046	0.25046	0.6806	3.993	1.469	5.867
6	0.13632	0.21632	0.6302	4.623	1.587	7.336
7	0.11207	0.19207	0.5835	5.206	1.714	8.923
8	0.09401	0.17401	0.5403	5.747	1.851	10.637
9	0.08008	0.16008	0.5002	6.247	1.999	12.488
10	0.06903	0.14903	0.4632	6.710	2.159	14.487
11	0.06008	0.14008	0.4289	7.139	2.332	16.645
12	0.05270	0.13270	0.3971	7.536	2.518	18.977
13	0.04652	0.12652	0.3677	7.904	2.720	21.495
14	0.04130	0.12130	0.3405	8.244	2.937	24.215
15	0.03683	0.11683	0.3152	8.559	3.172	27.152
16	0.03298	0.11298	0.2919	8.851	3.426	30.324
17	0.02963	0.10963	0.2703	9.122	3.700	33.750
18	0.02670	0.10670	0.2502	9.372	3.996	37.450
19	0.02413	0.10413	0.2317	9.604	4.316	41.446
20	0.02185	0.10185	0.2145	9.818	4.661	45.762
21	0.01983	0.09983	0.1987	10.017	5.034	50.423
22	0.01803	0.09803	0.1839	10.201	5.437	55.457
23	0.01642	0.09642	0.1703	10.371	5.871	60.893
24	0.01498	0.09498	0.1577	10.529	6.341	66.765
25	0.01368	0.09368	0.1460	10.675	6.848	73.106
26	0.01251	0.09251	0.1352	10.810	7.386	79.954
27	0.01145	0.09145	0.1252	10.935	7.988	87.351
28	0.01049	0.09049	0.1159	11.051	8.627	95.339
29	0.00962	0.08962	0.1073	11.158	9.317	103.966
30	0.00883	0.08883	0.0994	11.258	10.063	113.283

INTEREST TABLE FOR i = 8% (*Continued*)

n	sfp	cr	sppw	uspw	spca	usca
31	0.00811	0.08811	0.0920	11.350	10.868	123.346
32	0.00745	0.08745	0.0852	11.435	11.737	134.214
33	0.00685	0.08685	0.0789	11.514	12.676	145.951
34	0.00630	0.08630	0.0730	11.587	13.690	158.627
35	0.00580	0.08580	0.0676	11.655	14.785	172.317
40	0.00386	0.08386	0.0460	11.925	21.725	259.057
45	0.00259	0.08259	0.0313	12.108	31.920	386.506

INTEREST TABLE FOR i = 10%

n	sfp	cr	sppw	uspw	spca	usca
1	1.00000	1.10000	0.9091	0.909	1.100	1.000
2	0.47619	0.57619	0.8264	1.736	1.210	2.100
3	0.30211	0.40211	0.7513	2.487	1.331	3.310
4	0.21547	0.31547	0.6830	3.170	1.464	4.641
5	0.16380	0.26380	0.6209	3.791	1.611	6.105
6	0.12961	0.22961	0.5645	4.355	1.772	7.716
7	0.10541	0.20541	0.5132	4.868	1.949	9.487
8	0.08744	0.18744	0.4665	5.335	2.144	11.436
9	0.07364	0.17364	0.4241	5.759	2.358	13.579
10	0.06275	0.16275	0.3855	6.145	2.594	15.937
11	0.05396	0.15395	0.3505	6.495	2.853	18.831
12	0.04676	0.14676	0.3186	6.814	3.138	21.384
13	0.04078	0.14078	0.2897	7.103	3.452	24.523
14	0.03575	0.13575	0.2633	7.367	3.797	27.975
15	0.03147	0.13147	0.2394	7.606	4.177	31.772
16	0.02782	0.12782	0.2176	7.824	4.595	35.950
17	0.02466	0.12466	0.1978	8.022	5.054	40.545
18	0.02193	0.12193	0.1799	8.201	5.560	45.599
19	0.01955	0.11955	0.1635	8.365	6.116	51.159
20	0.01746	0.11746	0.1486	8.514	6.727	57.275

INTEREST TABLE FOR i = 10% (*Continued*)

n	sfp	cr	sppw	uspw	spca	usca
21	0.01562	0.11562	0.1351	8.649	7.400	64.002
22	0.01401	0.11401	0.1228	8.772	8.140	71.403
23	0.01257	0.11257	0.1117	8.883	8.954	79.543
24	0.01130	0.11130	0.1015	8.985	9.850	88.497
25	0.01017	0.11017	0.0923	9.077	10.835	98.347
26	0.00916	0.10916	0.0839	9.161	11.918	109.182
27	0.00826	0.10826	0.0763	9.237	13.110	121.100
28	0.00745	0.10745	0.0693	9.307	14.421	134.210
29	0.00673	0.10673	0.0630	9.370	15.863	148.631
30	0.00608	0.10608	0.0573	9.427	17.449	164.494
31	0.00550	0.10550	0.0521	9.479	19.194	181.943
32	0.00497	0.10497	0.0474	9.526	21.114	201.138
33	0.00450	0.10450	0.0431	9.569	23.225	222.252
34	0.00407	0.10407	0.0391	9.609	25.548	245.477
35	0.00369	0.10369	0.0356	9.644	28.102	271.024
40	0.00226	0.10226	0.0221	9.779	45.259	442.593
45	0.00139	0.10139	0.0137	9.863	72.890	718.905

INTEREST TABLE FOR i = 15%

n	sfp	cr	sppw	uspw	spca	usca
1	1.00000	1.15000	0.8696	0.870	1.150	1.000
2	0.46512	0.61512	0.7561	1.626	1.322	2.150
3	0.28798	0.43798	0.6575	2.283	1.521	3.472
4	0.20027	0.35027	0.5718	2.855	1.749	4.993
5	0.14832	0.29832	0.4972	3.352	2.011	6.742
6	0.11424	0.26424	0.4323	3.784	2.313	8.754
7	0.09036	0.24036	0.3759	4.160	2.660	11.067
8	0.07285	0.22285	0.3269	4.487	3.059	13.727
9	0.05957	0.20957	0.2843	4.772	3.518	16.786
10	0.04925	0.19925	0.2472	5.019	4.046	20.304

INTEREST TABLE FOR i = 15% (*Continued*)

n	sfp	cr	sppw	uspw	spca	usca
11	0.04107	0.19107	0.2149	5.234	4.652	24.349
12	0.03448	0.18448	0.1869	5.421	5.350	29.002
13	0.02911	0.17911	0.1625	5.583	6.153	34.352
14	0.02469	0.17469	0.1413	5.724	7.076	40.505
15	0.02102	0.17102	0.1229	5.847	8.137	47.580
16	0.01795	0.16795	0.1069	5.954	9.358	55.717
17	0.01537	0.16537	0.0929	6.047	10.761	65.075
18	0.01319	0.16319	0.0808	6.128	12.375	75.836
19	0.01134	0.16134	0.0703	6.198	14.232	88.212
20	0.00976	0.15976	0.0611	6.259	16.367	102.444
21	0.00842	0.15842	0.0531	6.312	18.822	118.810
22	0.00727	0.15727	0.0462	6.359	21.645	137.632
23	0.00628	0.15628	0.0402	6.399	24.891	159.276
24	0.00543	0.15543	0.0349	6.434	28.625	184.168
25	0.00470	0.15470	0.0304	6.464	32.919	212.793
26	0.00407	0.15407	0.0264	6.491	37.857	245.712
27	0.00353	0.15353	0.0230	6.514	43.535	283.569
28	0.00306	0.15306	0.0200	6.534	50.066	327.104
29	0.00265	0.15265	0.0174	6.551	57.575	377.170
30	0.00230	0.15230	0.0151	6.566	66.212	434.745
31	0.00200	0.15200	0.0131	6.579	76.144	500.957
32	0.00173	0.15173	0.0114	6.591	87.565	577.100
33	0.00150	0.15150	0.0099	6.600	100.700	664.666
34	0.00131	0.15131	0.0086	6.609	115.805	765.365
35	0.00113	0.15113	0.0075	6.617	133.176	881.170
40	0.00056	0.15056	0.0037	6.642	267.864	1779.090
45	0.00028	0.15028	0.0019	6.654	538.769	3585.128

INTEREST TABLE FOR $i = 30\%$

n	sfp	cr	sppw	uspw	spca	usca
1	1.00000	1.30000	0.7692	0.769	1.300	1.000
2	0.43478	0.73478	0.5917	1.361	1.690	2.300
3	0.25063	0.55063	0.4552	1.816	2.197	3.990
4	0.16163	0.46163	0.3501	2.166	2.856	6.187
5	0.11058	0.41058	0.2693	2.436	3.713	9.043
6	0.07839	0.37839	0.2072	2.643	4.827	12.756
7	0.05687	0.35687	0.1594	2.802	6.275	17.583
8	0.04192	0.34192	0.1226	2.925	8.157	23.858
9	0.03124	0.33124	0.0943	3.019	10.604	32.015
10	0.02346	0.32346	0.0725	3.092	13.786	42.619
11	0.01773	0.31773	0.0558	3.147	17.922	56.405
12	0.01345	0.31345	0.0429	3.190	23.298	74.327
13	0.01024	0.31024	0.0330	3.223	30.288	97.625
14	0.00782	0.30782	0.0254	3.249	39.374	127.913
15	0.00598	0.30598	0.0195	3.268	51.186	167.286
16	0.00458	0.30458	0.0150	3.283	66.542	218.472
17	0.00351	0.30351	0.0116	3.295	86.504	285.014
18	0.00269	0.30269	0.0089	3.304	112.455	371.518
19	0.00207	0.30207	0.0068	3.311	146.192	483.973
20	0.00159	0.30159	0.0053	3.316	190.050	630.165
21	0.00122	0.30122	0.0040	3.320	247.065	820.215
22	0.00094	0.30094	0.0031	3.323	321.184	1067.280
23	0.00072	0.30072	0.0024	3.325	417.539	1388.464
24	0.00055	0.30055	0.0018	3.327	542.801	1806.003
25	0.00043	0.30043	0.0014	3.329	705.641	2348.803
26	0.00033	0.30033	0.0011	3.330	917.333	3054.444
27	0.00025	0.30025	0.0008	3.331	1192.533	3971.778
28	0.00019	0.30019	0.0006	3.331	1550.293	5164.311
29	0.00015	0.30015	0.0005	3.332	2015.381	6714.604
30	0.00011	0.30011	0.0004	3.332	2619.996	8729.985

INTEREST TABLE FOR $i = 20\%$

n	sfp	cr	sppw	uspw	spca	usca
1	1.00000	1.20000	0.8333	0.833	1.200	1.000
2	0.45455	0.65455	0.6944	1.528	1.440	2.200
3	0.27473	0.47473	0.5787	2.106	1.728	3.640
4	0.18629	0.38629	0.4823	2.589	2.074	5.368
5	0.13438	0.33438	0.4019	2.991	2.488	7.442
6	0.10071	0.30071	0.3349	3.326	2.986	9.930
7	0.07742	0.27742	0.2791	3.605	3.583	12.916
8	0.06061	0.26061	0.2326	3.837	4.300	16.499
9	0.04808	0.24808	0.1938	4.031	5.160	20.799
10	0.03852	0.23852	0.1615	4.192	6.192	25.959
11	0.03110	0.23110	0.1346	4.327	7.430	32.150
12	0.02526	0.22526	0.1122	4.439	8.916	39.581
13	0.02062	0.22062	0.0935	4.533	10.699	48.497
14	0.01689	0.21689	0.0779	4.611	12.839	59.196
15	0.01388	0.21388	0.0649	4.675	15.407	72.035
16	0.01144	0.21144	0.0541	4.730	18.488	87.442
17	0.00944	0.20944	0.0451	4.775	22.186	105.931
18	0.00781	0.20781	0.0376	4.812	26.623	128.117
19	0.00646	0.20646	0.0313	4.843	31.948	154.740
20	0.00536	0.20536	0.0261	4.870	38.338	186.688
21	0.00444	0.20444	0.0217	4.891	46.005	225.026
22	0.00369	0.20369	0.0181	4.909	55.206	271.081
23	0.00307	0.20307	0.0151	4.925	66.247	326.237
24	0.00255	0.20255	0.0126	4.937	79.497	392.484
25	0.00212	0.20212	0.0105	4.948	95.396	471.981
26	0.00176	0.20176	0.0087	4.956	114.475	567.377
27	0.00147	0.20147	0.0073	4.964	137.681	681.853
28	0.00122	0.20122	0.0061	4.970	164.845	819.223
29	0.00102	0.20102	0.0051	4.975	197.814	984.068
30	0.00085	0.20085	0.0042	4.979	237.376	1181.882

INTEREST TABLE FOR i = 50%

n	sfp	cr	sppw	uspw	spca	usca
1	1.00000	1.50000	0.6667	0.667	1.500	1.000
2	0.40000	0.90000	0.4444	1.111	2.250	2.500
3	0.21053	0.71053	0.2963	1.407	3.375	4.750
4	0.12308	0.62308	0.1975	1.605	5.062	8.125
5	0.07583	0.57583	0.1317	1.737	7.594	13.188
6	0.04812	0.54812	0.0878	1.824	11.391	20.781
7	0.03108	0.53108	0.0585	1.883	17.086	32.172
8	0.02030	0.52030	0.0390	1.922	25.629	49.258
9	0.01335	0.51335	0.0260	1.948	38.443	74.887
10	0.00882	0.50882	0.0173	1.965	57.665	113.330
11	0.00585	0.50585	0.0116	1.977	86.498	170.995
12	0.00388	0.50388	0.0077	1.985	129.746	257.493
13	0.00258	0.50258	0.0051	1.990	194.620	387.239
14	0.00172	0.50172	0.0034	1.993	291.929	581.859
15	0.00114	0.50114	0.0023	1.995	437.894	873.788
16	0.00076	0.50076	0.0015	1.997	656.841	1311.682
17	0.00051	0.50051	0.0010	1.998	985.261	1968.523
18	0.00034	0.50034	0.0007	1.999	1477.892	2953.784
19	0.00023	0.50023	0.0005	1.999	2216.838	4431.676
20	0.00015	0.50015	0.0003	1.999	3325.257	6648.513

SECTION TWO BUSINESS CONTROLS

PREFACE TO SECTION TWO

This section is intended for use by business managers at any echelon in the manufacturing organization, as well as in business enterprises other than manufacturing, including warehousing, distribution, transportation, wholesaling, and investment banking. Industrial engineers and business administrators will also find it useful for preparing managerial control data for senior and middle management. Cost accountants, budgeting people, and marketing people will also make effective use of the concepts included in this section in preparing penetrating analyses for vital trend information.

The purpose of this section is to explain and demonstrate a technique for developing and using meaningful ratios based on production, sales, and financial data which are available (or can be developed) within a company.

First, the ratios are employed to evaluate facets of the company's profile which are vital to its growth and survival. Then control is provided through planning and corrective decisions based on the interrelationships and behaviors of the ratios.

The technique has proven its effectiveness in hundreds of businesses with sales volumes ranging from $250,000 to $120 million per year. Simple arithmetic is used throughout.

Controls tell management how well the company is doing in comparison to previous periods, and set up targets for remedial managerial action. Presented are 251 specific ratios which typify and diagnose practical situations and conditions encountered in manufacturing. The control technique is based on the following theses:

a. Any event or happening in any area of a company is not unrelated nor isolated from other events. Neither is it absolute in value.
b. Any one event is invariably related to others.
c. Managerial action on isolated, unrelated events is shallow and can be destructive.
d. Maximizing in any one area can cause larger negations elsewhere in the company.

It recognizes that typically, the managing task is complicated by:

e. The widening role of data *subtlety*, the elusive hidden areas, and the insidious creeping changes that constrain a company's ability to grow, compete, and survive.
f. The unending streams of economically *unweighted* data from which are expected balanced decisions.
g. The impairment of judgment resulting from being buried in a morass of data and insecurity as to the objectivity of decisions and actions.
h. A lack of time in which to coordinate, plan, develop, and create.

The proper concept of management control as exemplified in this technique is that:

i. Effective control means an ongoing series of evaluations and decision making.
j. Decision making requires accurate and fast appraisals of the movements and interrelationships of data and events.
k. There is one optimum decision for a given set of circumstances or events.
l. Companies have different characteristic economic personalities, cast from the composites of those who manage them, and each will not respond in the same way to the same set of events or stimuli.
m. Managing must be done by specifics, not averages; and should be done while the events are alive, not after the facts.
n. Managing should prevent the development of hard-to-remove patterns by testing the effects of decisions before implementing them.
o. Management should advertise widely throughout the organization that it is the possessor of effective and dynamic control data.

The objective of control ratios is to predigest and give action priority to the events and data competing for attention so that the manager can act on "first things first," fully confident of their ultimate effect on the company. The term *control* means different things to different people; but what it means to this author is *action designed to be imposed during the useful life of the event rather than after it has ended.*

No brief is held for particular production techniques, marketing methods, or financial structures. The book takes the condition and affairs of the company as they stand and shows how to evaluate and control its activities from the grass-roots level to the board chairperson. It shows how decisions can be tested in advance, how to determine where there is need for managerial action and what it is worth to the company, how to remedy negative conditions, and how to preserve positive patterns.

While the method and rationale for constructing ratios are given, the reader is cautioned against believing that there are *general* ratios which can be applied to all companies. All ratios must be specific, designed and tailored to fit individual company characteristics.

CHAPTER SEVEN

INTRODUCTION TO MANAGEMENT CONTROLS

Industrial competition has steadily moved into the subtler areas of operations, to where the hidden things are important. These areas form the banks of present-day profit. Years ago, one company could successfully compete against another if it had lower base hourly rates or less-expensive sources of materials. Today, though, the competitive battlefields are in the elusive and sometimes hidden areas of operations. Successful profit-making control now comes from constantly unmasking disguised costs or negative events, from policing and guarding against insidious creeping changes, from lighting up a hitherto unknown area of profit potential.

Profit planning requires much more than these efforts. Profit planning for the longer term must include action for growth and survival. It must plan for continuous profits which are made consistent with the financial state of health of the company. The maximization of profits is no guarantee of financial health, and in fact when profits are maximized to the exclusion of other considerations, the company can get into serious difficulty. The drive for high profits has forced many companies to the brink of bankruptcy because of the stretching of the capital structure by the requirements of supporting such drives.

The goal of the manufacturing enterprise should be the continuance of an optimum profit consistent and coexistent with its financial state of health, with due consideration for the firm's growth and longevity.

The one single function charged with accomplishing these objectives is *management.*

No matter how refined and sophisticated the competitive areas; no matter how complex the inner workings of the company; no matter how variable the market; no matter how changeable the technology; a manager must somehow be a modern alchemist. He or she must place all these variable ingredients in a pot and turn them into gold. And management must be able to do this consistently, regardless of the nature of the ingredients. Without the proper tools, the manager is lost and frustrated. Sometimes managers think they have the right tools, but sometime later may find out that they didn't accomplish what was planned, and worse yet, that they caused harm to the company.

GENERATIONS OF EVENTS

Every second in industry, in every square inch of company property, data of some kind are being born out of events, facts, acts, circumstances, and costs. These events have differing significance, move at different speeds, and occur at different intervals. Any event, no matter how small, no matter where it occurs, is felt to some degree in the company's economy, and it is management's job *to manage* with full regard for the total impact of these events.

Some of these acts are transient; some occur regularly; and some are reportable and accumulate in written reports:

Indirect labor: up 6%
84 out of 114 sales department quotations lost
New sales for new products: 2%
Unusable waste: 11%
Production center activity: off 15%
Quotation mortality: 45%
Current ratio: 3.1:1

Customer credits for poor quality: up 12%
Period productivity: 112%
Period billing: $62,500
Average collection period: 64 days
Customer potential obtained: 55%
Fixed assets: 89% of net worth
Average cost of salesperson's contact: $52.17

This is a tiny fraction of the events and data that *exist* and *happen* in any company constantly, regardless of its size. Of course, the above list shows what happened *after* it happened. The manager must know about the elements causing these data *while the events are happening* so that he or she may be able to influence the character of the reported data. The job is really twofold: not only must the manager see the *elements*, or *start* of a trend, before they develop into a full trend; he or she must also take the proper action to correct a negative circumstance after it has been reported.

What does the manager do about the above list of facts, then, assuming for the moment that it includes all the reportable events in the company? Which should be tackled first? Which are negative? Which are positive? Since all events are related onto the other, isn't it fallacious for the manager to act on any of these unless he or she knows in advance the impact of an action on the other areas of the company?

The rise in indirect labor may be positive if it supported effectively, more highly automated operations and greater productivity per man-hour. The rise in period productivity may be negative if it caused an amount of excess costs sufficient to wipe out the potentially higher contribution. The economy of the customers' potential obtained depends on the expenses of obtaining it and effect of the resulting product mix on fixed expense recovery in production.

It is recognized that companies collect all kinds of data indiscriminately. Effective reporting of the events, then, is the first and necessary step in proper managerial control. Acting on these unrelated events is fallacious and dangerous. Each event impacts differently on the company at different times.

IMPACT OF EVENTS

Not only does each event or act have an impact in its own area, it affects some other areas and the company as an organic whole; viz., an event in sales will have an impact in the sales department. It will also have an impact in production, based on what facilities will be used to make the article. The same dollar sales can make widely different use of the equipment based purely on the type of product. The sales act will also affect the financial areas because of the working capital needed to support the production of the sold product. This affects the inventory level and the current-asset and borrowed-capital structure. The same dollar sales can make widely different demands on inventory and capital.

INTERRELATIONSHIP OF EVENTS

Acts and events all happen at once, constantly. Events do not necessarily occur in sequence; they may happen simultaneously. Each causes an effect; each makes something change within the company. There also are facts happening or being born which have an effect though not formally reported. All events are related to other facts or events, and invariably they change with respect to each other.

ONE-FACT MANAGING

An act or event can produce a seemingly positive effect at its home base but can cause a negative event to occur elsewhere. A reduction in the material handlers' labor is positive in itself, but compared with the impact it has elsewhere, the first event may not be so positive. Reducing the materials-handling payroll may cause a piling up of work-in-process, overcommitment in inventory, increase in rejects caused by crowded conditions, etc.

Here is an example of a typical decision beneficial to one area of a company and of the impacts it causes elsewhere. Management, wanting to increase production efficiency, decides to replace an antiquated hand-assembly setup with an automatic assembly line. Preliminary investigation shows that striking improvements will result. Production will have twice the capacity, and direct labor will be reduced 75%. Savings from direct labor alone will pay for the new equipment in 9 months.

Assuming that the company buys the new equipment *on the basis of the above two facts,* let's see what questions will at once arise not only in production but in other areas of the company.

Sales Can new sales be added to absorb the increase in capacity? If not, then the new equipment will remain idle one-half the time and the cost of owning this equipment may rapidly offset the direct labor savings. If new sales are added, will this require additional sales effort and expenses? Where will the sales come from, and what will be the cost of penetrating new markets and territories to obtain them? How will the contact cost be affected? Will this increase the load of sales administration, estimators, quotations?

Capital Can the company's financial structure stand the cost of the new equipment? How will the cost be affected by alternative methods of financing? Will the financing selected to minimize the cost weaken the stockholders' interests? How will their return on their investment be affected? Will this acquisition seriously limit expansional aims of the company; will it interfere with the company's ability to pay its current obligations promptly? At doubled production, how will this affect the company's liquid assets in terms of inventory? Will this seriously affect the working capital position or the level of the net worth? If sales do not double, how will the lack of fixed expense recovery affect the capital structure?

Maintenance Will the new equipment have to be serviced by outside specialists? What are the estimated costs for this service, and how often is it expected to be used? If no outside service is needed, will the company have to train one of its own people? At what cost? If the equipment breaks down, how much will the downtime cost the company per hour?

Tooling and Setup What is the average cost of setting up the new equipment? Will the increased productivity of the equipment offset these costs? If a variable product mix is sold, what is the cost of the setup time for each product or run? How much will the special tooling cost the company, and how often will it have to be changed?

Material Inventory How much additional raw material will have to be carried in inventory? Is there enough space in the plant to store the extra material? What is the cost of this space? Can better use be made of it, or is it limiting another vital production effort?

Indirect Labor Will the indirect labor force have to be increased to support the higher output of the machine? How many materials handlers, shipping clerks, inspectors, billing clerks, estimators, etc., have to be added? Will this installation require additional supervision, or can the existing supervisory crew handle it properly?

Pricing Policies If the double production is obtained, should savings be passed on to customers to encourage the flow of orders by means of marginal pricing? Should the company retain the added earnings to placate its stockholders? Should there be a middle point; where should it be? Should provision be made in pricing to compensate for the effects of inflation for future replacement? If there are no savings the first year, should the customers be charged higher prices to help the company pay its losses?

Profits How much more sales will the company have to make to compensate for its increase in fixed costs while maintaining the same number of profit dollars? What will be the profits if no increase is obtained? How much more sales will be required to balance a specific unit-price reduction and still maintain the same profit? What will the profits be if sales rise only slightly after a price reduction? How much more vulnerable is the company to recessions? Will this acquisition place it in the position of not being able to readily adjust expenses to income?

These are but a few of the areas that are affected immediately by the decision to buy the new equipment, and the questions listed by no means give a complete picture of the other myriad events that will be born. If management carries out its investigations properly, giving economic weight to the areas affected and their interrelationships, and finds a positive answer by appraising the total impact on the company now and in the future, then it has justified its decision.

TRADITIONAL MANAGING

The varieties of management techniques are as numerous as the number of people using them. In some plants, managing may take the form of a daily tour through the plant and a chat with the plant manager, which the latter makes as revealing as he or she wishes. In other plants management relies heavily on traditional accounting and financial reports to say nothing of myriad logs, traditional ratios, performance records, etc.

The profit-and-loss statement is a report of an event after it has happened. For managerial control purposes it is ancient history. Even if profit-and-loss statements are issued frequently, they should not be used as a managerial tool. The figures represent an *averaging of the peaks and valleys* of the economy. They cover over the regular and transient events, the profit leaks and the profit-making opportunities, the variations in product mix, expense recovery, etc.

Proper management calls for the managing of people, in the areas they control, but most importantly, *at the time they are doing it or controlling it.* It is practically impossible to go back to find the profit leaks. Everyone's memory seems to fail under these circumstances. Usually when plant operating data are 24 hours old, they are old. In 48 hours, they turn rancid; in a week, they are ancient history. Even if people can remember, they usually will not make themselves vulnerable to criticism.

Those managers who are aware of the infinite, interweaving events in manufacturing enterprise and know they do not have the tools to cope with them are indeed frustrated. What disturbs them is the feeling that perhaps they did not make the best possible decisions from the facts they had. After all, the decisions and actions that can be taken from one set of data are many. What mature manager doesn't doubt that he is being kept in an ivory tower by self-seeking subordinates being spoon-fed only the information they want him to have?

The manager must feel secure in order to function effectively. Managers who must spend time away from the details of the everday operation in order to propagate the business must traditionally depend on others for information and answers without being able to make any intelligent *verification* of accuracy or honesty of the data. The problem of the busy owner-manager is integrity in the judgment and honesty of those who collect, present, and interpret the facts for him.

THE TOOLS MANAGEMENT NEEDS

Management needs fast and accurate, economically weighted data. When it reads about an act in one of its reports, it must know what that act really means, what its real impact is on the company, what worth is has as a measure or appraiser of a condition. What does gross payroll of $12,000 mean? What does the salesbook entry of $6,000 mean? What does 162 hours of downtime mean? What does 145 contacts for the sales department mean?

The first step in giving meaning to these seemingly unrelated events is by means of ratios. Thus payroll to sales begins to mean something; downtime to direct labor gives some perspective; sales dollars to contacts is also more meaningful than the isolated events or facts.

To be effective, these ratios must be sufficiently detailed so that they evaluate the smallest areas: *direct administrative expense to direct-labor hours* tells the administrative load that each direct hour must carry before a profit can be earned, which is the place to test one of the effects of adding more staff people; *contacts to sales of new product* evaluates the difficulty or ease of selling new products when compared with existing product sales; *inventory to current liabilities* will tell the extent to which (for one thing) the product mix is affecting the capital structure.

The value and computation of any one ratio at any instant is an evaluator of a condition existing up to that point. Thus *direct administrative expense to direct labor* may be high, but it may be less than it was in the previous period. When examined in isolation, the value may look too high and therefore negative; this is the old way. However, considering the changing values from period to period tells whether the condition is improving or worsening. Management should not be concerned with the absolute value of the ratio—just the relative value—since everything is in a state of flux.

The first tool, then, that the manager needs is a set of ratios from all areas of the company by which to observe the positive and negative movements of the company. He or she must have these data frequently at a level suitable to his or her managerial rank in the company. The higher the rank, the less detailed the ratios, and vice versa. When peaks and valleys occur, the manager will know why and what some of the causative elements were. The negatives stand out like a sore thumb, and the manager is not made to wait until they all pile up and show themselves on the profit-and-loss statement.

Regardless of the direction in which a ratio is heading, since it is composed of individual pieces of data, the movement of the ratio will affect other ratios and data. One positive movement can cause a whole flock of movements which are positive, negative, or both. If an action is taken on the basis of the movement of one ratio without first measuring its effect on other critical areas, it is little improvement over one-fact managing.

Once the meaning of the movement and direction of the ratios or the composite indices is known, the manager is more secure in taking actions and making decisions. He or she can counsel or discipline intelligently and objectively, knowing the full economic weight of the subject under discussion, and can feel secure in making decisions because the effects of the decision were tested before making it. Using this technique, the manager knows when to tolerate an excess, when a reduction in a cost is not favorable and positive. He is able to counsel with his key people. He no longer has to wait for the periodic financial and operating statements to tell him what happened—he knows.

In the words of Lincoln, "If we could first know where we are and whither we are tending, we would better judge what to do and how to do it".

CHAPTER EIGHT

DATA FOR CONTROL RATIOS

Events occur in every molecule of a company's geography and during each microsecond of its life. It is management's job to influence the events, to exploit them, or to respond to them. First, however, management must know about them: where they are, when they happened, what their impact and implications are likely to be. Before that can occur, of course, the events—all events—must be reported.

Many meaningful events in the typical firm are recorded, but some are not; and to the extent that they are not, management is guessing when it makes decisions or attempts to evaluate a situation.

UNRELATED DATA

An event is happening—an act, a circumstance, something that has taken place. It is complete, self-contained, and factual: the new clerk added to the office receives *x* dollars per week; *y* dollars of shipments were made last month. This type of data is unweighted; that is, the fact or event does not in itself reveal its economic effect on the company. To make such data meaningful, they must have economic weight and economic perspective.

We refer to unrelated data as *primary* data, i.e., data that cannot in themselves be used to predict or objectively appraise performance, economy, progress, trend, growth, movement, direction, or profitability. However, primary data are used as the basis for making the necessary predictions and evaluations. They are the ingredients from which we can derive *ratios* which give economic meaning to the events and permit objective diagnosis, decision making, and assessments of all areas of a company's economy and activity.

In this book, ratio control is applied to the three major areas of the firm: *production; sales/marketing;* and *finance.*

PRIMARY PRODUCTION SOURCES

The two major sources of primary production data and events are:

1. Those involving factory labor and production equipment.
2. Those involving factory costs and statistics, including all administrative expenses.

FACTORY LABOR AND PRODUCTION EQUIPMENT

Factory labor is one of the most variable elements in the entire manufacturing effort. The performance and economy of labor exert strong influences on the total company. Management must have close control of the labor effort so that it can obtain local economies at the grass-roots operating level. The cumulative effects of such small economies can make an important difference.

With proper primary data, literally thousands of appraisals can be made from which management can take fast, confident action. Not only will these data allow penetrating evaluations at the grass-roots level, but they help management assess the overall productive effort and the extent to which it is harmonious with the activities of sales and with the financial functions. First, however, the basic information must be identified, reported, and analyzed. Then, when it is given economic meaning by means of ratios, it can be evaluated.

Identify and Report Factory Labor To identify and report the actions and costs of human effort, each category of labor must be consistently named and classified.

1. *Direct-productive labor.* Productive labor, a *direct cost,* sometimes referred to as direct labor, is the actual applied effort. It should be reported daily and must be related to the type of work done, product identification, equipment on which it was performed, etc. Not all of a worker's time is productive, as when he or she must wait for materials or wait for a machine to be repaired. Separating the delays between avoidable and unavoidable provides the troubleshooting targets, and these too must be reported in written form.
2. *Support labor.* Sometimes called indirect labor, these are the people who support the direct productive effort, such as materials handlers; and those who service production, such as maintenance people; and those who service the general plant, such as the porters. Daily tickets should be made out for all nonproductive people, except those on permanent assignments, like the porters and sweepers.

Workers' Daily Time and Production Tickets The output and time consumed in work should be identified by the machine used, the job, product or customer's order, and the operation. All delays should be identified, codified as to cause, and reported. In addition to its value in checking order profitability and contributing to the control of overall factory economy, the installation of a production-reporting procedure is a useful *psychological* cost-reduction tool. People perform better when they know that their efforts are being monitored, and supervisors know that such a procedure can yield an indirect appraisal of their effectiveness. (However, if management vacillates or procrastinates on the action it should take, or if it fails to look at the tickets and the workers discover this, then the reporting system will collapse.)

FACTORY AND ADMINISTRATIVE COSTS AND STATISTICS

These primary production data include all events bearing on production, except those facts listed on the factory labor payroll. Such elements as rent, depreciation, and demand electrical costs, are not easily changed. Administrative expenses, on the other hand, tend to remain fixed because of a management idea or concept. And very often their level is too high in relation to their productivity and to their need in the organization. Only when their impact is measured in terms of their drag on production effort, is this recognized.

PRIMARY SALES SOURCES

The amount of sales data that can be collected is almost limitless. And yet it is all grist for the manufacturing mill. Sales data provide the contact and liaison with matters physically external to the business, but prime determinants of its life and growth. In the marketplace, a company competes, observes the pulse and trend of demand, and attempts to reflect these at its home base.

Many small to medium-sized businesses do not tabulate the sales and market information so vital to their operations. Of those that do, many don't interrelate the data to make them meaningful. Not only is this tabulation required to evaluate the effectiveness of the selling effort, it is essential for interrelating the data from other areas, so that balanced decisions result. What's the sense of incurring selling expenses to further penetrate the market if the company is at the point of uneconomical expansion or if the company's capital position will not stand the cost of production equipment to support such penetrations? Why push a product which generates a negative profit contribution?

The typical reports common to most businesses are: the orders received per week or per day; orders booked; and perhaps, backlog figures. The latter assesses a running balance between the manufacturing velocity and the sales booking efforts. Orders received per week or per any period is an unrelated figure and cannot be intelligently used to evaluate the extent of the sales effort, let alone control it. Nor can it be used as a controller of internal economy until it has been related to another facet of the economy. "Backlog" also involves both production speed and sale velocity; it is not a control.

Needed is the type of sales data that will permit objective appraisal of the sales effort as a separate activity (as for the production source) and then later use in developing ratios with primary data from other sources.

Once data are obtained, summarized, and evaluated, many determinations can be made:

1. Are sales representatives productive and implementing the directives of the company?
2. Are they selling to old, existing customers, where they are sure of a warm reception, instead of persisting in getting new accounts, which are not as easy to sell?
3. Is the sales representative directed to that type of activity which will not bottleneck critical facilities?
4. Is the amount of entertainment expenses related to departmental or individual sales representative's productivity and performance?
5. Is the segment in the product-development expense which has been reserved for sales prospecting being exceeded? How is this related to market acceptance for the product?
6. What percentage of total sales by dollars and number of accounts to date is for new business? New products?

   A total dollar sales performance figure hides the productivity of the worker and the department. The accumulation of sales dollars after once booking a customer is not as major an accomplishment as the original booking. Where a sales representative produces an acceptable amount of contribution from many accounts, or where a certain portion of the accounts represents the tough pre-sales effort, his or her record is considered productive.
7. How is the department's time and that of the individual sales representative divided between servicing old customers and getting new ones? (How about the mortality rate of the customers being presently serviced and the effect this will have on the company ten years hence without the presence of new business? How about the increased movement of competition and the effect on acquiring new accounts?)

8. What share of the product and territory market is available to the company? How much has been obtained?
9. What does it cost to obtain the market potential in a given territory, and is it justified in terms of the sales expenses involved?
10. To what extent are selling prices being reduced in order to earn commissions? (Compensation based on contribution will reverse this practice.)

Again here, as in the production sources of events and primary data, the evaluations that can be made, once the above information is available, are almost limitless.

re: SALES QUOTAS

A standard is based on a *possible* performance. This means that management must have some control over what raw work it creates or deposits on which the workers are to perform. Thus, for example, from time-study standards, a worker in a leather tannery is required to dehair so many kips per hour to attain standard. The kips are there, so is the equipment; and management knows that the task is reasonable and measurable. In other instances, management knows that a plant manager can deliver the required output at a waste level below 5%; that an office manager can provide the general office services at ⅛% of the annual sales income; that the controller can financially manage the enterprise at the forecasted level with an average circulating capital level of x dollars and with a standard of z dollars for distress discounts to customers plus interest on emergency bank loans; etc.

But who can measure the caprices of the market and tie a sales representative's performance to it? Isn't that tantamount to putting a farm hand on quota for harvesting vegetables from a produce farm that the management hasn't even seen? A production worker has control over his or her effort and output; the work is there if he or she wants to do it. The sales representative has no control over the sales quota, and doesn't even know if it exists.

The sales or contribution quota, *unlike a standard,* is a hope on management's part that the potential exists. It functions as an intimidating incentive—a wishful target. If the hope is supported by competent market analysis, then management has a guide, not a payoff base.

Effective productivity control over sales representatives takes place when sales management has enough information from all sales, market, and production areas to be able to key a sales representative's efforts to the markets and to the areas of maximum profitability of the company. Therefore the best sales incentive compensation is one directly pegged to the day-to-day economic needs of the company, instead of volume for the sake of an unrealistic quota, rewarding the sales representative for a *contribution* to the economic position of the company. This is a highly measurable criterion, and it works.

PRIMARY FINANCIAL AND CAPITAL SOURCES

There are two principal types and primary financial events:

1. Those relating to period operating performance.
2. Those relating to the financial state of health at any instant.

The first is found in the profit-and-loss (P&L) or income and expense statement. It is also found in the various schedules which are actually part and parcel of the P&L. These include the various overhead expense schedules for manufacturing expenses, selling and administrative expenses, fixed expenses, and the like.

The second is found in the balance sheet and in all its supporting financial schedules, such as liquid and working assets, fixed assets, and current liabilities.

PERIOD PERFORMANCE

The profit-and-loss statement reports how well management has *operated* the business in a past period with the tools furnished to it. Management sold the product, manufactured it, using labor, materials, equipment, and housing facilities, and by managerial talent produced a profit or a loss.

The categories or accounts under which P&L data are listed should be broken down finely enough so that analysis can be made in a consistent way. Thereafter, the same information should be reported for the same category. Overlap and inconsistency only mislead. Thus the lumping together of indirect materials and indirect labor in one expense account defeats the aim of analysis and control. Putting the depreciation of the company automobile in the sales expense account one month and in the administration expense account the next, where no change in use has occurred, defeats the aim of analysis and control.

Exhibit 8-1 shows a recommended format of a profit-and-loss statement. To be effective for control of manufacturing, such a statement should be produced frequently. The accounting procedure must be straightforward enough to permit the regular entry of data and postings to the various accounts. This quite naturally includes data for the balance sheet as well.

The P&L in itself is ineffective as a managerial tool. Its data are unrelated and unweighted. No management can really make an objective decision based on the magnitude of the administrative salaries alone nor on the amount of indirect materials in itself.

Moving averages of expenses or other items on the financial statements are not effective control. The moving average is really a device which makes the wide excursions in individual statements psychologically more attractive to management. The reason is quite simple. The function of a moving average is to smooth out the fluctuations so that some sort of visible trend emerges. This would be fine if the moving average automatically took into consideration the characteristic changes that occurred in the internal economy of a company in the period for which the averages were constructed. These data are also valid for meaningful ratios.

Averages of any description tend to hide the facts. Surely a company experiences peaks and valleys in normal operations, and if all conditions remained the same, then a moving average can be considered as revealing some sort of trend, even though its use is still not effective as a managerial control. But let's say that conditions do not remain the same. Suppose the product-volume mix seriously changed. This could affect the state of

EXHIBIT 8-1 PRIMARY CAPITAL AND FINANCIAL DATA (P&L FORM)

Identifying Letters	Item
ba	Net sales
bb	Direct material cost
bc	Direct labor cost
bd	Total indirect labor cost
be	Nonproductive manufacturing labor cost
bf	Maintenance and repair labor cost
bg	Supervisory labor cost
bh	Total nonlabor manufacturing expenses
bi	Machinery and space costs
bj	Power costs
bk	Total stand-by expenses
bl	Depreciation charges
bm	Insurance expenses
bn	Rent and taxes
bo	Cost of goods sold (factory cost)
bp	*Gross profit*
bq	Total variable G&A expenses
br	Management costs
bs	Services and supplies
bt	Total variable selling expenses
bu	Salaries and commissions
bv	Service and supplies
bw	Contact expenses
bx	Total standby expenses
by	Basic business management costs
bz	Basic sales management costs
ca	Depreciation charges
cb	Insurance expenses
cc	Rent and taxes
cd	Interest on loans
ce	Cost of sales (total cost)
cf	*Net profit*

EXHIBIT 8-1 (*Continued*)

Prime cost	=	bb + bc
Factory cost	=	bo
Total cost	=	ce
Total overhead	=	bd + bh + bk + bq + bt + bx
Factory overhead	=	bd + bh + bk
Conversion cost	=	ce − bb
Fixed charges	=	bk + bx
Variable expenses	=	bb + bc + bd + bh + bq + bt
Cost of owning fixed asset	=	bf + bi + bk
Cost of sales	=	ce

expense recovery, and a surge could occur, either way, which might enter into a moving average figure in much the same way as a so-called normal-period excursion. How would management know? The change in mix might be for the worse, which would show up as a drop on the curve, but management might accept it as a normal expected swing and therefore miss the opportunity for troubleshooting it.

Moving averages make impressive-looking charts and graphs, but dependence on them for managerial control can be costly.

STATE OF HEALTH

The balance sheet pictures the financial state of health of the business at the instant the figures are listed. The balance sheet of the next operating period shows what effect the operating had on the company's financial state of health. In dollar terms, it shows to what extent the financial status has improved or worsened as a result of how operating changed the volume and velocity of the stream of capital flow. Exhibit 8-2 shows a basic balance sheet format.

Both balance sheet and profit-and-loss data must be available. One without the other is of little help in managerial decision making. The comparison of both can be likened to that of a track athlete. The athlete's performance, that is, the length of the dash and the time taken, is to the profit-and-loss statement as the athlete's respiration, blood pressure, and pulse rate after the dash are to the balance sheet. The runner may perform well

EXHIBIT 8-2 PRIMARY CAPITAL AND FINANCIAL DATA (BALANCE SHEET FORM)

Identifying Letters	Item
	ASSETS (*the present location of the capital*)
aa	Current (circulating capital)
aa	Cash
ab	Receivables (accounts, notes)
ac	Inventory
ad	Total current assets
	Fixed (fixed capital)
ae	Machinery
af	Land and buildings
ag	Total fixed assets
ah	TOTAL ASSETS
	LIABILITIES (*the source of the capital*) (*borrowed*)
	Current (short-term borrowed capital)
ai	Payables (account notes, loans)
aj	Total current liabilities
	Noncurrent (long-term borrowed capital)
ak	Payables (mortgages, bonds)
al	Total noncurrent fixed liabilities
am	TOTAL LIABILITIES
	NET WORTH (*the source of the capital*) (*owned*)
an	Issued capital stock
ao	Reserves
ap	Retained earnings
aq	TOTAL NET WORTH
ar	TOTAL LIABILITIES AND NET WORTH

Tangible net worth = aq = (an + ao + ap)
Working capital = ad − aj
Total capital employed = total assets = ah or ar
Funded debt = al

in the race but may drop dead afterward or be seriously limited in future performances.

In the balance sheet, as in the profit-and-loss section, information must be properly divided and consistently reported.

The balance sheet, like the profit-and-loss statement, is inadequate as a managerial tool. What might be a proper state of health for one condition in the company may not be for a changed state a short time later. Fixed assets alone or cash in the bank alone cannot be used to make balanced managerial decisions.

The aim throughout this book is not to make accountants out of managers and executives. Even successful controllers who themselves usually have an early formal accounting training must think as businesspeople and not as auditors or cost engineers. The aim is to take the mystery out of the statements and integrate their information into the stream of managerial action by interrelationships with other data in the company. The goal also is to focus attention on those areas of finance which ordinarily receive only casual attention and an attitude of waiting for the outside auditors to come in, while, in the interim, malignancies develop in the capital structure.

In analogic terms, the purpose is to help you to drive your automobile properly: to keep you to the right, to stop and go on clear signals, to indicate when to change course and how to make the turn, to persuade you to stop when sight or judgment is impaired, to warn you of icy roads at unknown distances, to get you accustomed to the road, and to bring you safely home, relaxed and secure that you can make the entire trip all over again. However, our job is not to teach you the principles of internal-combustion engines or fuel chemistry. Those tools are provided for you. You must learn their characteristics and how best to use them.

CHAPTER NINE

BASIC CONTROL RATIOS FOR PRODUCTION

Management's problems are wider in scope and more complex than they have ever been. This is due largely to the greater effect the hidden items now have on the company economy. Companies competed on the basis of increased mechanization, faster and better product development, and quicker market tapping. Later, companies took a giant step ahead of their competitors with improved operational methods and wage incentives for production workers. Financially wise managers exploited the capital dollar and found better methods of financing; machine-hour rate estimating began to solve the problem of product cost; and management discovered how to use manufacturers' representatives.

ACTING ON PRIMARY DATA

Acting on primary data is fallacious and can have negative impacts on the total economy. Profits in production are hidden in the small areas. Maintenance expenses may appear to be satisfactory, but may be out of proportion to the usage of the machine, to the direct labor effort, and to the value of the equipment. Or these expenses may be in line with the running hours used, but out of line with the tax-reported depreciation expense.

These facts or events in themselves cannot be the managerial targets. Management cannot appraise the economy, movement, or growth of its business by watching the gyrations of the numerous events that are always happening in production. The increases or decreases in the various activity factors cannot be used as a barometer until each has been given economic meaning.

MAKING PRIMARY DATA MEANINGFUL

Primary data in themselves are a report of an event which has no economic meaning. A piece of isolated, unrelated data requires another piece of data to which it can be compared. Management must know the reaction that a piece of primary data causes some place else before it knows anything at all about the real effect of the event. To make events meaningful, each must be compared with the circumstances they affect or by which they are affected. An indirect labor-to-direct labor ratio may be too low for one set of conditions and too high for another. Relationships must be optimized to the conditions immediately obtaining.

ELEMENTARY RATIOS

When primary data are interrelated, they become meaningful to management. This allows management to take action on what they reveal. It is done by constructing ratios between pieces of primary data. Thus one piece is weighted against another for evaluation of effect.

There are two major considerations:

1. The way the ratio is constructed for the area it is to evaluate.
2. The narrowness or broadness of the ratio, that is, the limitations of the ratio.

Ratio Constructions The number of angular degrees through which the *steering wheel* turns is no measure of the miles traveled by an automobile. Nor would the weight gain of a person be evaluated directly by the pounds of food eaten. Obviously, not all people eat food of the same caloric content, and not all people burn calories at the same rate.

Each ratio should be developed for a specific purpose, for a particular area, and the desirable movement of each ratio should be known in advance; that is, whether up or down is the positive direction. Ratios should not be expected to move linearly: double the running time of the equipment does not necessarily mean double the maintenance expenses. Some ratios move faster than others as they ascend the scale: downtime may increase directly with setup time, but the supervisory expenses to direct labor may decrease with increased activity because of the semivariable nature of the supervisory loading. Ratios do not have absolute value; they are proportions and have only relative values. It is this value which is watched from period to period. Primary data are absolute, and we have seen that these data have no value unless they are related to something else. In the ratios, the primary data lose their identity and are evaluated by effect, not magnitude.

Ratio Limitations An elementary ratio is a comparison of one piece of primary data with another. As such, any two pieces of primary data, no matter how small (as long as they are relevant), can be made into an elementary ratio. This ratio can evaluate an activity, an area, or an effort. However, a two-fact ratio evaluates with a specific qualification, but does produce a desired effect at the grass-roots level.

For example, work productivity is the ratio of earned hours to clock hours on incentive work. However, if the people were on incentive work for a tiny portion of the week, a high productivity does not figure prominently as a causative factor in the factory economy. Obviously, before productivity means anything, a factor has to be added for the proportion of the available work hours on which this productivity was obtained. A ratio of indirect labor to direct labor, showing the level of support required by the productive workers, is significant only for policing the expense trends or the directives of line management. It may not be a fair appraiser of a facet of the production economy because its positive movement may be opposite to what is positive for the entire production economy. For example, it is positive for this ratio to decrease. This shows that there is less indirect labor being spent to support the direct labor effort. However, when it goes down, it might cause bottlenecks in production, or there may not be enough service for direct productive workers and output might go down. On rising, this ratio might enhance the productive efforts, accelerate the work-in-process, and so improve the overall factory economy.

Therefore, other factors have to be added to this ratio to give it greater economic meaning, such as total labor to plant output. Elementary ratios, however, can be used for specific and limited purposes.

At any rate, unless elementary ratios are well defined and their purpose well conceived, they can be misleading.

As we said before, when a piece of primary data is born, it causes reactive data elsewhere, but not necessarily in one place. An elementary ratio has the qualification of a *particular place* where it has effect. Direct labor to downtime is a direct-labor elementary ratio affecting downtime; direct labor to maintenance expense is a direct labor elementary ratio bearing on the maintenance effort; etc.

The direct-labor event may have different effects on waiting time, downtime, and maintenance expense. In some ratios, it is the direct labor that is the causative factor; in others, the direct labor is the recipient of the effect. Waiting time may affect the amount of direct labor applied, but the amount of direct labor applied may impact on the amount of maintenance incurred. Therefore, no one elementary ratio can evaluate a broad area but they can be useful for localized troubleshooting and the uncovering of the generation of trends.

MORE ADVANCED RATIOS

Production events are also related to events *outside* of the production area for lending even more economic weight to their evaluations. Thus we would have direct labor to sales; direct labor to administrative expenses; direct labor to value of customers' returns; etc. These are discussed later in the book.

To get broader, more effective ratios for managerial action, higher-order ratios are required. They combine elementary ratios and separate primary data in a way which gives an evaluation of a larger area. These are called tertiary ratios and are also discussed later.

DATA FOR ELEMENTARY PRODUCTION RATIOS

Before elementary ratios can be developed, it is necessary to have the production events reported in proper form. As indicated in Chapter 8, this is accomplished by daily time and production tickets on which the magnitude and nature of the time spent are detailed. Then the information is collated and summarized on a payroll analysis. This record is an extension of the traditional payroll journal and can be kept separately in memo form if desired. Not only does the listing for each employee show his or her gross pay, deductions, and net pay, it also distributes the gross pay according to the nature, location, direction, and cost of the work the employee performed during the week.

This record shows instantly the *size* of the controllable cost elements, but we still have to go further to appraise their movements and true economic effect. Obviously, many judgments can be formed from just this analysis without further refinement. The payroll analysis obviously has limitations. It indicates how and where the money was spent, but it doesn't show *how well* it was spent. Nor does it show how those expenditures impact on the other areas of the company.

Each industry has criteria for ratio selection. Some ratios are more meaningful to one industry than to another. A radio-assembly plant would not care much about machinery running time or the velocity of fixed expense recovery. The company would probably be more interested in assembly versus wiring time for various products. A foundry might be interested in interoperational ratios like coremaking versus moldmaking. A folding-carton plant might be interested in cut and crease versus stripping.

The elementary ratios have these functions:

1. To evaluate an economic area.
2. To evaluate an activity.
3. To evaluate human performance.
4. To be a part of a more advanced control.

5. To be a cross-check on cost estimating and budgeting.
6. To be the best form of historical data. (If nothing else, events are controlled from soaring by proving to people that under the same circumstances, their past performances were better. This is not done fairly with unrelated primary data.)

Exhibit 9-1 shows the primary data extracted from a payroll analysis. The plant selected is engaged in the manufacture of a line of proprietary consumer products and in addition sells some open capacity time. The plant employs approximately 275 people, including workers in the press room, welding, metal cleaning, metal finishing, screw machines, secondary operations, subassembly, final assembly, materials handling, machine shop, receiving, stores and shipping; sweepers and porters; factory clerical; manufacturing engineering; production manager; plant manager; and staff.

Each of the items appearing in Exhibit 9-1 is given a code number which is used for convenience in constructing the elementary ratios. These code numbers range from 1 to 47.

ELEMENTARY PRODUCTION RATIOS

GROSS PRODUCTIVITY (9-1)

CONSTRUCTION	$\frac{\text{Earned direct hours on standards}}{\text{Direct clock hours on standards}}$
CODES	$\frac{\mathbf{26}}{\mathbf{27}}$
SUBSTITUTE VALUES	$\frac{3{,}340}{2{,}842}$
RATIO VALUE	1.175, or 117.5%
POSITIVE DIRECTION	Up
USE	Appraisal of workers' efforts; equity of production standards; control of premium or subsidy hours; amount of standards coverage; timekeeping problems.

EXHIBIT 9-1 PRIMARY PRODUCTION DATA, FROM PAYROLL ANALYSIS

Item	Code	Dollars	Code	Hours
Total gross paid payroll	1	23,106.00	24	11,714
Total clocked payroll	2	22,057.00	25	11,160
Direct labor:				
On standard: Earned	3	6,156.30	26	3,340
Clock			27	2,842
Off standard: Clock	4	6,643.65	28	3,729
Total direct labor	5	12,799.95	29	6,571
Indirect labor:				
Downtime: Miscellaneous waits	6	1,706.00	30	964
For equipment repairs	7	69.75	31	37
For tool repairs	8	118.40	32	64
Excess direct labor: Jig and die trouble	9	75.70	33	42
Equipment trouble	10	192.50	34	110
Material trouble	11	78.35	35	41
Other: Tool and fixture making	12	1,113.60	36	392
Setup	13	402.30	37	201
Maintenance and repairs	14	782.10	38	322
Salvage, rework, reprocess	15	563.70	39	320
Service	16	1,746.80	40	936
Supervision	17	1,716.00	41	560
Factory engineering	18	1,297.00	42	440
Factory clerical	19	304.00	43	160
Total indirect labor	20	10,166.20	44	4,589
Direct labor subsidy (lost)	21	290.15	45	159
Direct incentive premium (gained)	22	909.15	46	498
Indirect incentive premium	23	139.85	47	56

NET PRODUCTIVITY (9-2)

CONSTRUCTION $$\frac{\text{Clock DL hours on standard} - \text{DL subsidy hours} + \text{direct incentive premium hours}}{\text{Direct clock hours on standard}}$$

CODES $$\frac{\mathbf{27 - 45 + 46}}{\mathbf{27}}$$

SUBSTITUTE VALUES $$\frac{3{,}181}{2{,}842}$$

RATIO VALUE 1.12, or 112%

POSITIVE DIRECTION Up

USE As per Ratio (9-1) after considering paid subsidy hours. The subsidy reduces the economic benefit of higher productivity.

WORK STANDARDS COVERAGE (9-3)

CONSTRUCTION $$\frac{\text{Clock direct hours on standards}}{\text{Total direct-labor clock hours}}$$

CODES $$\frac{\mathbf{27}}{\mathbf{29}}$$

SUBSTITUTE VALUES $$\frac{2{,}842}{6{,}571}$$

RATIO VALUE 0.433, or 43.3%

POSITIVE DIRECTION Up

USE Percentage of total direct labor on measured standards; appraisal of industrial engineering effort; supervisory tendency to remove measurement of "nonstandard" work.

PERFORMANCE INDEX (9-4)

CONSTRUCTION
$$\frac{\text{Clock DL hours on standards} - \text{DL subsidy hours} + \text{direct incentive premium hours}}{\text{Total direct-labor clock hours}}$$

CODES
$$\frac{\mathbf{27 - 45 + 46}}{\mathbf{29}}$$

SUBSTITUTE VALUES
$$\frac{3{,}181}{6{,}571}$$

RATIO VALUE 0.484, or 48.4%

POSITIVE DIRECTION Up

USE Appraises economy of direct labor, considering coverage and application of work standards, and attained productivity.

IMPROVEMENT INDEX (9-5)

CONSTRUCTION
$$\frac{\text{Clock DL on standards} - \text{DL subsidy hours} + \text{direct incentive premium hours}}{\text{Total clock hours}}$$

CODES
$$\frac{\mathbf{27 - 45 + 46}}{\mathbf{25}}$$

SUBSTITUTE VALUES
$$\frac{3{,}181}{11{,}160}$$

RATIO VALUE 0.286, or 28.6%

POSITIVE DIRECTION Up

USE Evaluates the economic balance between net productivity and the total of unmeasured direct-labor and indirect-labor support.

WORKER STANDARDS CONSISTENCY (9-6)

CONSTRUCTION $\dfrac{\text{Direct-labor subsidy hours}}{\text{Direct incentive premium hours}}$

CODES $\dfrac{\mathbf{45}}{\mathbf{46}}$

SUBSTITUTE VALUES $\dfrac{159}{498}$

RATIO VALUE 0.319

POSITIVE DIRECTION Down

USE Compares "lost" hours with "gained" hours. Shows by what quantity of hours the workers failed to earn their task, and relates that to the number of extra paid hours the workers received by exceeding their task.

INDIRECT SUPPORT (9-7)

CONSTRUCTION $\dfrac{\text{Total indirect-labor hours}}{\text{Total DL clock hours + direct incentive premium hours}}$

CODES $\dfrac{\mathbf{44}}{\mathbf{29 + 46}}$

SUBSTITUTE VALUES $\dfrac{4{,}589}{7{,}069}$

RATIO VALUE 0.649

POSITIVE DIRECTION Down

USE Assesses, for budgeting purposes, the utilization of the indirect labor support of productive labor.

INDIRECT USAGE (9-8)

CONSTRUCTION $\frac{\text{Total indirect-labor hours}}{\text{Total paid hours}}$

CODES $\frac{\mathbf{44}}{\mathbf{24}}$

SUBSTITUTE VALUES $\frac{4{,}589}{11{,}714}$

RATIO VALUE 0.391

POSITIVE DIRECTION Down

USE Evaluates what portion of the gross paid hours was spent on indirect labor.

EXCESS COST (9-9)

CONSTRUCTION See Exhibit 9-1.

CODES $\frac{\mathbf{6 + 7 + 8 + 9 + 10 + 11 + 15 + 21}}{\mathbf{5}}$

SUBSTITUTE VALUES $\frac{3{,}094.55}{12{,}799.95}$

RATIO VALUE 0.241

POSITIVE DIRECTION Down

USE A more incisive type of control, this index compares the reducible costs with the productive labor cost.

EXCESS DIRECT-LABOR COST (9-10)

CONSTRUCTION See Exhibit 9-1.

CODES $\frac{\mathbf{9 + 10 + 11}}{\mathbf{5}}$

SUBSTITUTE VALUES $\frac{346.55}{12{,}799{,}95}$

RATIO VALUE 0.027

POSITIVE DIRECTION Down

USE Indicates how much more should be added to the existing direct-labor dollar to budget for direct-labor excesses; and to what extent equipment and material troubles prevent the full application of standards.

SETUP INDEX (9-11)

CONSTRUCTION $\frac{\text{Setup hours}}{\text{Total direct-labor clock hours}}$

CODES $\frac{\mathbf{37}}{\mathbf{29}}$

SUBSTITUTE VALUES $\frac{201}{6{,}571}$

RATIO VALUE 0.0306

POSITIVE DIRECTION Down

USE Shows much setup time is required for each direct-labor hour, applied by department or to groups of similar machines.

MAINTENANCE AND REPAIR INDEX (9-12)

CONSTRUCTION $\frac{\text{Maintenance and repair hours}}{\text{Total direct labor}}$

CODES $\frac{\mathbf{38}}{\mathbf{29}}$

SUBSTITUTE VALUES $\frac{322}{6{,}571}$

RATIO VALUE 0.048

POSITIVE DIRECTION Down

USE Shows how much maintenance and repair time is required for each direct-labor hour; best applied by department or by groups of similar machines.

SETUP EFFECTIVENESS (9-13)

CONSTRUCTION $\frac{\text{Setup hours}}{\text{Earned direct-labor hours}}$

CODES $\frac{\mathbf{37}}{\mathbf{26}}$

SUBSTITUTE VALUES $\frac{201}{3{,}340}$

RATIO VALUE 0.0602

POSITIVE DIRECTION Down

USE Compares setup hours with earned direct-labor hours and assesses the effect that the quality of the setup has on running time and productivity.

PRODUCTIVITY PLANNING (9-14)

CONSTRUCTION $\frac{\text{Direct incentive premium}}{\text{Misc. waiting cost}}$

CODES $\frac{\mathbf{22}}{\mathbf{6}}$

SUBSTITUTE VALUES $\frac{909.15}{1{,}706.00}$

RATIO VALUE 0.533

POSITIVE DIRECTION Up

USE Relates the cost of the direct incentive premium to the cost of miscellaneous waits; compares the impact that waiting time has on the incentive earnings.

INDIRECT SUPPORT COST (9-15)

CODES $\frac{\mathbf{20}}{\mathbf{5}}$

SUBSTITUTE VALUES $\frac{\$10{,}166.20}{\$12{,}799.95}$

RATIO VALUE 0.795

POSITIVE DIRECTION Down

OTHER SUGGESTED RATIOS

The previous 15 elementary production ratios are given for illustrative purposes and should be considered empirical. There are, however, many more which the reader can construct from the same primary data or from data created to highlight a critical area. The following ratios are suggested without usage comment, and left to the creative thinking of the reader:

INDIRECT USAGE COST (9-16)

CODES	$\frac{\mathbf{20}}{\mathbf{1}}$
SUBSTITUTE VALUES	$\frac{10{,}166.20}{23{,}106.00}$
RATIO VALUE	0.446
POSITIVE DIRECTION	Down

DOWNTIME INDEX (9-17)

CODES	$\frac{\mathbf{6 + 7 + 8}}{\mathbf{5}}$
SUBSTITUTE VALUES	$\frac{1{,}894.15}{12{,}799.95}$
RATIO VALUE	0.148
POSITIVE DIRECTION	Down

TOOL AND FIXTURE COST (9-18)

CODES	$\frac{\mathbf{12}}{\mathbf{5}}$
SUBSTITUTE VALUES	$\frac{1{,}113.60}{12{,}799.95}$
RATIO VALUE	0.087
POSITIVE DIRECTION	Varies

SUPERVISORY INDEX (9-19)

CODES	$\frac{41}{29}$
SUBSTITUTE VALUES	$\frac{560}{6{,}571}$
RATIO VALUE	0.0853
POSITIVE DIRECTION	Down

SUPPORT COST (9-20)

CODES	$\frac{16 + 17 + 18 + 19}{5}$
SUBSTITUTE VALUES	$\frac{5{,}063.80}{12{,}799.95}$
RATIO VALUE	0.396
POSITIVE DIRECTION	Down

SERVICE COST (9-21)

CODES	$\frac{16}{5}$
SUBSTITUTE VALUES	$\frac{1{,}746.80}{12{,}799.95}$
RATIO VALUE	0.136
POSITIVE DIRECTION	Down

CRITERIA FOR DEVELOPMENT OF RATIOS

Not all industries react to change in the same way; each has its own special personality. This implies that *evaluation* must be the first step. Determining when and how to develop control ratios should be given weights according to:

1. The absolute magnitude of the money involved in an area.
2. The extent of volatility.
   a. Its movement in relation to events
   b. Its reducibility and controllability
   c. The ease and cost of reporting it
   d. Its function as a clue or indicator to other important areas

THE MANAGEMENT OF THE ELEMENTARY RATIOS

The ratios developed provide managers with an appraisal of various areas. When these ratios are translated into a more condensed form, rapid decision making can be made. These are called *advanced ratios.* Obviously, the level of these advanced ratios is related to the echelon at which they are going to be used.

A plant manager should be interested more in week-to-week movement in the plant's economy. The questions in the mind of the plant manager are: What is the net effect? Have I gone ahead or slipped backward? How well have my subordinate supervisors taken care of the losses so that they don't recur? And have they been made sufficiently aware of where profits are germinating so that those likewise can be recognized and preserved?

Suppose that a new week's figures show a drop in Ratio (9-1). Is it time to charge in and take action? Suppose Ratio (9-4) increased? Wouldn't that be a sign of forward movement? But suppose that with an upturn of Ratio (9-4), Ratio (9-5) decreased, what then? A glance at the construction of the ratios will show that if Ratio (9-4) increased, with a decrease in Ratio (9-5), the offender lay somewhere in the indirect labor category. If both Ratios (9-4) and (9-5) move up, the manager can feel secure that there is a positive current throughout the production force. If these two controls go in different directions, a glance at which other ratios became negative sets the stage for his action.

The manager explains this circumstance to the supervisors concerned and then observes the changes that take place in it in future weeks. Of course, these two ratios do not report on the entire production picture, since the economy of indirect labor or the quality of production has yet to be assessed in relation to the productivity improvements. The integration of additional facets of the production economy is a subject of the next chapter. However, let us continue to explore various specific areas before going on to the next chapter.

Suppose the *support* ratios dropped, giving a sign of forward movement. Is this good or bad? The first thing to check is whether or not what they were supporting suffered. If shipments decreased, maybe the lack of materials handlers or insufficient warehouse workers was the reason why.

And it's still possible for Ratio (9-10) to increase and for Ratio (9-9) to decrease in the same week. If the reverse is true, then the difficulty lies in either excessive downtime, rework, or both.

In general, these ratios show how well the individual acts were performed, how well the money was spent, and to what extent those acts affected other cost areas of the company. These indices showed that a certain portion of the payroll was used productively, wastefully, or for the furtherance of the manufacturing effort. They showed how certain acts caused waste of materials, of time, and of the tools of production. The controls also showed the effect they were having on efforts and expenses outside of the production area.

Regardless of their level, whether controls are the simple ones which define very narrow areas or the more sophisticated ones given in the next section, they are ineffective unless used immediately. And again it must be stressed that just by the act of discussing them with the line people, a positive effect will be obtained.

This is another way of saying that when management has the proper evaluation, the proper answer, and the correct information at its fingertips, and this fact is advertised widely throughout the organization, people will become responsive to managerial direction, will not hide the facts, and will seek guidance.

The targets are then brought into sharper focus, management has the right ammunition, and the aim is unclouded and direct.

The timing of ratio information depends on the nature of the ratio. That is, some ratios will be read weekly, and others may not be significant unless a longer period of time transpires.

CHAPTER TEN

ADVANCED CONTROL RATIOS FOR PRODUCTION

Elementary production ratios are used to pinpoint any area of factory labor, and they are a necessary tool for a supervisory effort closer to the scene of action. While it should be management's desire to see that supervisors police every economy-effecting area in the plant, supervisors should be taught the difference between avoidable costs, excess costs, and supporting expenses. Then supervisory action can be carried on with the motive of economic optimizing rather than arbitrary expense reduction.

To see that this is done, management needs broader, more inclusive ratios. Other factors bearing on the factory economy must then be added to give them further economic meaning.

Facts and events must be related to other facts or circumstances which they control or on which they depend. Then the results can be examined in weighted perspective. Elementary ratios compared one fact with another or with several others, and in this way the facts compared were given economic meaning. The ratios of the previous chapter involved factory labor only, and there was no interrelationship between that labor and some of the other factory costs. Nor was there any attempt to integrate the factory labor economy with the administrative costs or with sales.

Obviously, there are optimum relationships between a factory labor effort of maintaining a machine and the amount of depreciation expense incurred in the ownership of the machine. Similarly, the various components of the factory labor effort, with and without the nonlabor factory expenses, should bear some relationship to the expenses of administering and managing the business. For example, it is useful to observe and ultimately control the amount of "drag" that the direct administrative expense places on the direct productive hour.

Ratios which interrelate factory labor, nonlabor factory expenses, administrative expenses, and such performance data as sales and cost of rejects from customers form, in part, advanced production ratios.

The primary data for these ratios are taken from Exhibits 9-1 and 10-1. This information is based on the records of the company and is easily obtainable. The data shown are for the same plant as described in Chapter 9.

EXHIBIT 10-1 PRIMARY PRODUCTION DATA FROM NONPAYROLL SOURCES

Item	Code	Amount
Manufacturing occupancy	a	72,000 sq. ft.
Shipments	b	$98,400
Machinery repair costs (parts + outside and inside labor)	c	$1,140
Dollar value of waste produced in plant	d	$920
Cost of returns rejected from customers	e	$4,660
Total machinery depreciation in period	f	$1,900
Sales, general, and administrative payroll	g	$4,160
Total direct overhead expenses in period	h	$15,880
Machinery running hours	j	3,050
Fixed expense segment of total overhead	k	$8,060
Maximum economical machinery running hours	l	5,000

ADVANCED PRODUCTION RATIOS

SHIPMENTS-PAYROLL INDEX (10-1)

CONSTRUCTION	$\frac{\text{Shipments}}{\text{Total gross payroll}}$
CODES	$\frac{\mathbf{b}}{\mathbf{1}}$
SUBSTITUTE VALUES	$\frac{\$98{,}400}{\$23{,}106}$
RATIO VALUE	4.27
POSITIVE DIRECTION	Up
USE	Sales return per payroll dollar, unadjusted for product mix; trend index.

DIRECT OVERHEAD EXPENSE PRODUCTIVITY (10-2)

CONSTRUCTION	$\frac{\text{Shipments}}{\text{Total direct overhead expenses}}$
CODES	$\frac{\mathbf{b}}{\mathbf{h}}$
SUBSTITUTE VALUES	$\frac{\$98{,}400}{\$15{,}888}$
RATIO VALUE	6.20
POSITIVE DIRECTION	Up
USE	Return per direct-cost overhead dollar; responds sharply to changes in product mix and prices.

MACHINERY ECONOMY INDEX ______ (10-3)

CONSTRUCTION See Exhibits 9-1 and 10-1.

CODES $\frac{7 + 10 + 14 + c}{f}$

SUBSTITUTE VALUES $\frac{\$2,184.35}{\$1,900.00}$

RATIO VALUE 1.15

POSITIVE DIRECTION Down

USE When the ratio value exceeds 1.00, it's time to think about replacement. Test first in the capital area, to check the effect of the purchase on the company, state of health, and financial flexibility.

PRODUCTIVITY ECONOMY INDEX ______ (10-4)

CONSTRUCTION See Exhibits 9-1 and 10-1.

CODES $\frac{22}{14 + 15 + d}$

SUBSTITUTE VALUES $\frac{\$909.15}{\$2,265.80}$

RATIO VALUE 0.401

POSITIVE DIRECTION Up

USE Evaluates extent to which productivity incentive drives generate excess cost; a check on abuses.

INCENTIVE QUALITY INDEX ______ (10-5)

CONSTRUCTION See Exhibits 9-1 and 10-1.

CODES $\frac{22}{9 + 10 + 11 + 14 + 15 + 21 + 23 + d + e}$

SUBSTITUTE VALUES $\frac{\$909.15}{\$7,702.35}$

RATIO VALUE 0.118

POSITIVE DIRECTION Up

USE Overall economy of an incentive plan, a more inclusive control than Ratio (8-1).

ADMINISTRATIVE USAGE INDEX ________ (10-6)

CONSTRUCTION $\frac{\text{Sales, general, and administrative payroll}}{\text{Total direct labor cost}}$

CODES $\frac{\mathbf{g}}{\mathbf{5}}$

SUBSTITUTE VALUES $\frac{\$4,160}{\$12,799.95}$

RATIO VALUE 0.325

POSITIVE DIRECTION Down

USE Assesses cost of "office" services per dollar of direct labor. Valuable for financial planning and development of *machine-hour rates.*[1]

ADMINISTRATIVE LOAD INDEX ________ (10-7)

CONSTRUCTION $\frac{\text{Sales, general, and administrative payroll}}{\text{Total direct labor hours}}$

CODES $\frac{\mathbf{g}}{\mathbf{29}}$

SUBSTITUTE VALUES $\frac{\$4,160}{\$6,571}$

---

[1] See Spencer A. Tucker, *The Complete Machine Hour Rate System for Cost Estimating and Pricing,* Englewood Cliffs, N.J.: Prentice-Hall, 1975.

RATIO VALUE $0.634

POSITIVE DIRECTION Down

USE Assists in setting manning table levels; different activity projections in flexible budgeting.

PRODUCTIVE LOAD INDEX (10-8)

CONSTRUCTION See Exhibits 9-1 and 10-1.

CODES $\dfrac{\mathbf{g + h + (1 - 5)}}{\mathbf{29}}$

SUBSTITUTE VALUES $\dfrac{\$30{,}346.05}{\$6{,}571}$

RATIO VALUE $4.62

POSITIVE DIRECTION Down

USE Return required per direct-labor hour to cover controllable overhead costs; pretesting expansions.

OVERHEAD RETURN INDEX (10-9)

CONSTRUCTION See Exhibits 9-1 and 10-1.

CODES $\dfrac{\mathbf{b}}{\mathbf{g + h + (1 - 5)}}$

SUBSTITUTE VALUES $\dfrac{\$98{,}400}{\$30{,}346.05}$

RATIO VALUE 3.24

POSITIVE DIRECTION Up

USE Rate of total overhead turnover; shows impact of activity on expense absorption.

PRODUCTIVE EXPENSE INDEX (10-10)

CONSTRUCTION	$\frac{\text{Total direct overhead expenses}}{\text{Total direct-labor hours}}$
CODES	$\frac{\mathbf{h}}{\mathbf{29}}$
SUBSTITUTE VALUES	$\frac{\$15{,}880}{\$6{,}571}$
RATIO VALUE	$2.42
POSITIVE DIRECTION	Down
USE	A policing tool for controlling the overhead portion of direct machine-hour rates; essential for cost separation in a direct-cost profit-and-loss statement.

OTHER ADVANCED RATIOS

In addition to the previous 10 ratios, many others can be constructed to sharpen the manager's investigation and control. As in Chapter 9, additional ratios follow in condensed form:

SHIPMENT-PAYROLL INDEX (10-11)

CODES	$\frac{\mathbf{b}}{\mathbf{25}}$
RATIO VALUE	8.81
POSITIVE DIRECTION	Up

DIRECT HOUR SALES RETURN (10-12)

CODES	$\frac{\mathbf{b}}{\mathbf{29}}$
RATIO VALUE	$14.95
POSITIVE DIRECTION	Up

EXPENSE USAGE (10-13)

CODES $\frac{h}{5}$

RATIO VALUE 1.24

POSITIVE DIRECTION Down

MACHINERY UTILIZATION (10-14)

CODES $\frac{f \times a}{j \times b}$

RATIO VALUE 0.456

POSITIVE DIRECTION Down

HOURLY FACILITY RECOVERY (10-15)

CODES $\frac{h}{j}$

RATIO VALUE \$5.21

POSITIVE DIRECTION Down

MACHINE-HOUR RATE (Direct)[2] (10-15a)

CONSTRUCTION $\frac{[(5 + 20) - 22] + c + h}{j}$

SUBSTITUTE VALUES $\frac{[(\$12{,}799.95 + \$10{,}166.20) - \$909.15] + \$1{,}140 + \$15{,}880}{3{,}050}$

RATIO VALUE \$12.81

POSITIVE DIRECTION Down

[2] In developing *direct* machine-hour rates, only the direct portion of sales, general, and administrative payroll should be included.

NOTE: These data develop an average machine-hour rate plant-wide but should be developed for individual machines or groups of similar machines for maximum effectiveness.

Condensed Evaluations At any managerial echelon, the higher level should have a check on the subordinate levels to evaluate their managerial effectiveness and assess how well they use the managerial tools given to them. By so doing, the upper levels are invariably appraising larger segments of the controllable areas than those normally evaluated by subordinate levels. It is burdensome and impractical for upper management to have to wade through each and every elementary ratio to find out how well a broad economic area is faring.

Overall effects, composed of the pluses and minuses always normal to production activity, should be presented to upper management in condensed form. Once these condensed appraisals reveal an overall negative condition, then the elementary ratios are consulted to pinpoint the offenders. The same is done for positive conditions, as management also polices profit areas and capitalizes on them.

Elementary ratios are combined to form what are called *tertiary ratios*. These condense the effect of activities in several small, but common, areas. Tertiary ratios are composed of elementary ratios and primary data from labor and other sources and from some of the advanced ratios previously given in the first section of this chapter.

TERTIARY PRODUCTION RATIOS

PERFORMANCE—EXCESS QUOTIENT ______________ (10-16)

CONSTRUCTION	$\frac{\text{Ratio (9-4)}}{\text{Ratio (9-9)}}$
SUBSTITUTE VALUES	$\frac{0.484}{0.241}$
RATIO VALUE	2.01
POSITIVE DIRECTION	Up

USE Effect of productivity and wage-incentive earnings on excess costs; to establish optimum productivity levels on relationship to the cost of waste generated.

PERFORMANCE—SERVICE QUOTIENT ____________ (10-17)

CONSTRUCTION $\frac{\text{Ratio (9-4)}}{\text{Ratio (9-21)}}$

SUBSTITUTE VALUES $\frac{0.484}{0.136}$

RATIO VALUE 3.56

POSITIVE DIRECTION Up

USE Evaluates optimum level of support to workers on incentive plans.

MANUFACTURING ECONOMY INDICATOR ________ (10-18)

CONSTRUCTION Ratio (9-4) × Ratio (10-11)

SUBSTITUTE VALUES 0.484 × 8.81

RATIO VALUE 4.26

POSITIVE DIRECTION Up

USE An indicator of economic movement in a period, which combines (without weighting) the effects of performance, shipments, and production payroll.

SUPPORT-ADMINISTRATIVE INDEX ______________ (10-19)

CONSTRUCTION Ratio (9-20) + Ratio (10-6)

SUBSTITUTE VALUES 0.396 + 0.325

RATIO VALUE 0.721

POSITIVE DIRECTION Down

USE Evaluates the non-production salary "drag" on the direct labor.

BILLINGS-EXCESS COST INDICATOR (10-20)

CONSTRUCTION Ratio (10-12) × Ratio (9-9)

SUBSTITUTE VALUES 14.95 × 0.241

RATIO VALUE 3.60

POSITIVE DIRECTION Down

USE Evaluates effect of labor utilization on sales capacity.

OVERHEAD ACTIVITY QUOTIENT (10-21)

CONSTRUCTION $\frac{\text{Ratio (9-20)} + \text{Ratio (10-6)} + \text{Ratio (10-13)}}{j}$

SUBSTITUTE VALUES $\frac{0.396 + 0.325 + 1.24}{3{,}050}$

RATIO VALUE 0.00064

POSITIVE DIRECTION Down

USE Policing overhead cost portion of machine-hour rates, particularly in high fixed-investment industries with volatile product mix.

OTHER TERTIARY RATIOS

The following are additional tertiary controls which managers may find useful:

SERVICE JUSTIFICATION INDEX (10-22)

CONSTRUCTION $\frac{\text{Ratio (9-5)}}{\text{Ratio (9-21)}}$

SUBSTITUTE VALUES $\frac{0.286}{0.136}$

RATIO VALUE 2.10

POSITIVE DIRECTION Up

FIXED RECOVERY RETURN (10-23)

CONSTRUCTION $\frac{\text{Ratio (10-12)} \times j}{(\Sigma 30 - 40) - 36}$

SUBSTITUTE VALUES $\frac{14.95 \times 3{,}050}{3{,}037}$

RATIO VALUE 15.01

POSITIVE DIRECTION Up

EXPENSE PRODUCTIVITY INDEX (10-24)

CONSTRUCTION $\frac{\text{Ratio (9-1)}}{\text{Ratio (10-2)} \times \text{Ratio (9-5)}}$

SUBSTITUTE VALUES $\frac{1.175}{6.20 \times 0.286}$

RATIO VALUE 1.77

POSITIVE DIRECTION Up

PERFORMANCE—OVERHEAD INDEX (10-25)

CONSTRUCTION $\text{Ratio (9-4)} \times \frac{26}{g + h}$

SUBSTITUTE VALUES $0.484 \times \frac{3{,}340}{20{,}040}$

RATIO VALUE .0807

POSITIVE DIRECTION Up

CHAPTER ELEVEN

BASIC CONTROL RATIOS FOR SALES: By Salesperson

In manufacturing, there must be contact between the production effort and those who buy and use the items manufactured. This contacting activity must be of such magnitude and quality as to permit the regular disposal of the finished products manufactured, enabling the manufacturer to make a reasonable profit, to prosper, to grow, and to develop new and better products.

ECONOMIC SELLING

The selling function can be run at various economic levels, like any other manufacturing function. As such, it can be evaluated as a separate entity charged with making a profit from the expenses it incurs.

Here, as in the production area, managing is done typically on a one-fact basis. Sales representatives are evaluated based on the amount of gross sales booked or on some other piece of unrelated data. The sales manager in turn is evaluated at the upper managerial level by the total gross sales booked, expenses incurred, etc. These unweighted data are not a proper measure of what the department *could do* in the way of maximum value to the company.

Selling, to be fully effective, must sell the output of the company in a way that enhances and preserves the profit-making potential created after their manufacture. Sales activity must not only be keyed to the market, but to the most profitable products and to the most profitable production centers.

SALES CONTROL

The basic requirements are:

1. A proper managerial framework must be present by which personnel are responsive to direction.
2. Individual sales activity must be reported at regular intervals.
3. Activity data must be interrelated for proper evaluation.

Is a salesperson a good salesperson because he can sell what he likes, in the areas he likes, to the people he is comfortable with? Or is he good when he is like the professional hunter who kills the game he is paid to kill whether it is day or night, hot or cold, deer or lion?

In the control of sales, we are interested:

1. That sales management have realistic targets which support the company's total needs.
2. That upper management and sales management have the tools for evaluating the sales department's implementation of these targets.
3. That the sales manager have the means for evaluating the performances of the salespeople as to productivity, effectiveness, economy, and responsiveness to the direction of his or her personal management by which the targets are hit.

CONTROL RATIOS

As was shown in the preceding chapters, acting on primary facts and events is fallacious, for we are unable properly to assess their meaning individually. However, when primary data are compared with other facts which they control, influence, or affect, then we have a balanced measure.

A salesperson cannot be judged by the number of contacts he or she makes per week, or even by the number of orders sold, because while the sold contacts may be low, the amount of dollars sold may be high, resulting in high sold dollars per contact, which may or may not be desirable.

Similarly, we should not necessarily accept as positive a high number of contacts per week. This contact activity can result in either a high or low volume of orders. If it is a large number of low-dollar orders, the company is involved in a multitransaction cost which may not be desirable; perhaps the high-contact volume resulting in a small number of high-dollar orders is better.

Taking any of these isolated facts in themselves is not a proper measure of a salesperson's performance or responsiveness to direction. Integrating them is.

Some companies report the number of sales a worker makes, together with the number of quotations he or she gives. Again, this is no measure of the worker. What should be known is the quotation acceptance or mortality. What is the ratio between cumulative sales and cumulative quotations? The degree of lag in both, together with the number of quotations it took to accomplish, considering the expenses incurred in generating them, is a more realistic measure of performance.

REQUIRED PRIMARY DATA

Primary data—the events of the day, the unrelated facts—are the meat of the ratios, and they must be collected in some organized fashion. This should be done weekly for each salesperson to show how many contacts he or she made, what resulted from these contacts, and the nature of the results. A suggested form is shown in the salesperson's activity summary of Exhibit 11-1.

Exhibit 11-1 is a summary of daily contact reports and is tabulated weekly. Several cost items were left out of this tabulation of primary data so that the application of the ratio concept might better emerge. Among these are advertising expenses, sales office, clerical and administrative expenses, and other sales expenses like promotional costs, manuals, and training programs.

EXHIBIT 11-1 SALESPERSON'S WEEKLY SALES ACTIVITY SUMMARY SHEET

Sales Activity Summary

Salesperson ______________________ Territory ______________________ Week ended ____________

Product code	Total contacts / Contact cost			Type of contact and status					Amount sold — Type of account				Amount quoted — Type of account				Expenses				
	No. by phone	No. by letter	No. by visit	Prospects				Existing	New		Existing		New		Existing		Auto. exp.	Mileage	Lodging	Entertainment	
	$	$	$	Dead	Possib.	Hot	Sold		No.	$	No.	$	No.	$	No.	$				Prospect	Customer
Existing products *ab*																					
ac																					
bc																					
cd																					
Total existing products																					
New products *WW*																					
YY																					
ZZ																					
Total new products																					
Total all products																					

THE COST TO CONTACT-SELL

This is one of the most deceptive areas in the entire industrial costing picture. So many selling costs are hidden. One manufacturer was appalled when he learned that the 4% rate on the commission schedule amounted in sales cost closer to 16%. This increase was brought about by identifying the following supportive services with the selling function:

1. The salaries of straight-salaried trainees who dug up qualified leads and who otherwise paved the way for the experienced "closer."
2. The salaries of the sales manager and clerks in the sales office.
3. The sales office and expense, other than salaries.
4. The cost of sales promotion, salaries, and expenses.
5. Advertising costs.
6. Entertainment and traveling expenses not applied against commissions.
7. Sales demonstration kits.
8. Direct-mailing costs.
9. Sales manuals.
10. Training kits and programs.

As if that didn't hurt enough, the contact expense, just the cost of knocking on a prospect's door, was calculated to be over $70 each when all the above cost factors were added. On the average, the number of contacts required to make the sale, plus the sales level of the average sale, pegged the *selling cost* in the sales dollar higher than the *direct-labor cost* in the sales dollar. The ironic part of this story, and unfortunately sometimes typical of management, was that all labored tirelessly and incessantly to reduce the direct-labor cost—a necessary and commendable endeavor—paying little or no attention to the evaluation, control, or reduction of the larger segment of total cost—selling costs.

Just as a selling quota is unrealistic because salespeople have no control over the market, so it is hard to set standards of all types of selling performances. Contacts per week, made in certain territories for certain products to certain types of customers, can be standardized and enforced. But sales expense per sales dollar cannot be considered a standard since the salesperson does not have complete control over it.

The number of important ratios that can be developed from these primary data runs into the hundreds. These ratios are valuable, and they validly mirror certain happenings and conditions. They evaluate performances of one form or another that sales management has to know about before making decisions. Not all ratios are suitable for all companies—perhaps not even for two companies in the same industry. The ratio must take into account the characteristics of the particular company, together with the areas in which it needs control.

CONTACT, PRODUCTIVITY, ACTIVITY

It will be noticed that ratios are constructed by using somewhat similar terms. Some ratios contain dollar figures, and others the number of accounts or orders; some contain both. Both are essential for proper evaluation. For example, a weekly sales dollar figure can be obtained from one or twenty sales orders and from one to twenty selling-contact calls. A singleness of evaluation is misleading, since a satisfactory level of sales dollars produced might come from two old contacts, both of whom placed orders. This might have involved 10% of the salesperson's time and is a matter for the sales manager to control. Similarly, another salesperson may have made a satisfactory number of calls from which there were a respectable amount of orders, but the total of these orders might have been so low as to cause a high internal transaction cost. It may be the immature salesperson's way of obtaining managerial approval.

Contacts are made by a personal visit, by telephone, and by letter. Contact method is a valid type of primary data to include in the ratios. In the composition of the ratios, the latter two contact methods are not considered, in the interests of simplicity, so as not to becloud the concepts.

DATA FOR ELEMENTARY SALES RATIOS

Exhibit 11-2 shows how data are tabulated and code-numbered preparatory to the construction of ratios. The data are for one week's effort of each salesperson in the sales department.

The data involve facts concerning new and existing customers and new and existing products, for sales, quotations, contacts, and expenses. Elementary ratios show the interrelationship of these facts and events so that a man can be more effectively directed and his efforts and results compared with other men in the department.

Ratios are simple to develop and are very meaningful. For example, if it is desired to find out the percentage of new accounts brought in by a particular employee in comparison with the total orders he or she sold, you would simply construct the fraction of *new sold accounts* over *total sold accounts*. Referring to Exhibit 11-2, we see that the code designations listed alongside of the appropriate terms would yield the fraction (8 + 9)/23. For Mrs. Greene, the substituted value would be 4/17, meaning that 23.5% of all the accounts she sold was for brand-new accounts. To see how Mrs. Green stacks up with the others in her department regarding the number of new accounts she sold, a fraction of *new sold accounts* over *departmental total sold accounts* would be developed. This would produce the fraction (using the code numbers and letters) (8 + 9)/w, or 4/45, meaning that of the total number of accounts sold in the department, Mrs. Green was responsible for 8.9%.

As we go deeper into the ratio material, it will be shown how the above type of ratio can be expanded to show the percentage of Mrs. Greene's new sold accounts to the department's total of the *new* accounts sold. It can be varied to show the activities of the new and existing product lines to new customers. And the denominator can be varied, depending on the nature of the desired evaluation. The various segments of expenses can likewise be introduced in considering the economy of those expenditures. And the element of territories constitutes still another factor that can be treated in these ratios.

What Are We Evaluating? Basically we are measuring the above mentioned variations for:

1. Order productivity, which shows effort in terms of orders sold.
2. Sales productivity, which shows effort in terms of dollars sold.

EXHIBIT 11-2 PRIMARY SALES DATA (EMPLOYEE)

Code	Sales Effort	Salesperson				Department Code	Dept. Total
		Jones	Smith	Brown	Greene		
	Customer product activity						
1	Total contacts	*27*	*27*	*56*	*42*	a	*152*
2	To existing customers	27	21	14	29	b	91
3	Sold new products	0	1	4	4	c	9
4	Sold existing products	5	7	4	9	d	25
5	Quoted new products	0	0	1	1	e	2
6	Quoted existing products	7	6	2	7	f	22
7	To new customers	0	6	42	13	g	61
8	Sold new products	0	0	2	1	h	3
9	Sold existing products	0	1	4	3	i	8
10	Quoted new products	0	0	7	1	j	8
11	Quoted existing products	0	0	8	6	k	14
	Volume contact activity						
12	Total amount sold and quoted	*$1,800*	*$4,370*	*$1,925*	*$12,850*	l	*$20,945*
13	To existing customers	1,800	4,270	1,080	9,000	m	16,150
14	Sold new products	0	200	310	1,940	n	2,450
15	Sold existing products	1,050	2,930	460	3,800	o	8,240
16	Quoted new products	0	0	90	900	p	990
17	Quoted existing products	750	1,140	220	2,360	q	4,470

18	To new customers	0	100	845	3,850	r	4,795
19	Sold new products	0	0	100	920	s	1,020
20	Sold existing products	0	100	170	970	t	1,240
21	Quoted new products	0	0	250	90	u	340
22	Quoted existing products	0	0	325	1,870	v	2,195
	Summary activity						
23	Total customers sold	5	9	14	17	w	45
24	Total customers quoted	7	6	18	15	x	46
25	Total amount sold	$1,050	$3,230	$1,040	$7,630	y	$12,950
26	Total amount quoted	750	1,140	885	5,220	z	7,995
27	Total new-product contacts	*0*	*3*	*24*	*10*	aa	*37*
28	To existing customers	0	2	6	7	bb	15
29	To new customers	0	1	18	3	cc	22
30	Total existing-product contacts	*27*	*24*	*32*	*32*	dd	*115*
31	To existing customers	27	19	8	22	ee	76
32	To new customers	0	5	24	10	ff	39
	Expense summary						
33	Total employee expense	*$165.20*	*$224.00*	*$178.60*	*$147.70*	gg	*$715.50*
34	Salary	80.00	80.00	80.00	80.00	hh	320.00
35	Automobile	36.00	72.40	36.00	17.60	ii	162.00
36	Total entertainment	*49.20*	*71.60*	*62.60*	*50.10*	jj	*233.50*
37	New customers	0	50.40	29.90	19.40	kk	99.70
38	Existing customers	49.20	21.20	32.70	30.70	ll	133.80

3. Contact activity, which shows effort in terms of contacts made.
4. Quotation productivity, which shows effort in terms of dollar value of quotations.
5. Quotation activity, which shows effort in terms of quotes resulting from contacts.
6. Quotation attempts, which shows effort in terms of orders quoted.
7. Quotation performance, which shows effort in terms of quotational level in total sales.

There are considerable differences in how one type of elementary sales ratio can be constructed. Often management wants a check on who is selling what to whom. It may wish to check new-product activity, but only as it affects existing customers; or it may wish to keep its eye on the activity of obtaining new accounts by virtue of the sales of its new products. Let's take this latter motive and see how the ratio can be established. The first step is to name the area we are evaluating. Let's take *new-customer, new-product productivity*. Referring to Exhibit 11-2, we find that for sold new products to new customers the coded symbol is 8 and for its respective dollar value it is 19. This gives us two numerators to use in separate ratios; but this is a small part of the task of setting up the proper ratio.

WHAT DO WE WISH TO MEASURE?

Exhibit 11-3 tabulates the number of practical variations for measuring *new-customer, new-product productivity*. Note that all the formulas for each of the twelve variations have either symbol 8 or 19 as the numerator, depending on whether orders sold or dollars sold is desired. And all twelve formulas have twelve different denominators. Obviously, each formula evaluates new-customer, new-product productivity in a different way. Here, briefly, is what each ratio evaluates in relation to this productivity:

Line a: As a percentage of *all* customers sold by the employee, irrespective of the type of product. This evaluates the individual's efforts on behalf of the desired area of productivity in comparison with his *total efforts* without any relation to other employees or to the department. Line *a* does this in terms of orders sold, and line *c* by sales dollars.[2]

Line b: As a percentage of all the customers sold by the department, irrespective of the type of product. This evaluates to what extent the individual's efforts contributed to the total departmental score on behalf of the desired area of productivity. This ratio permits an employee-to-employee comparison. Line *b* does this in terms of orders sold, and line *d* by sales dollars.

Line e: As a percentage of all the *new* customers sold by the employee, regardless of the type of product. This is narrower than line *a* since it compares the desired area of productivity with the employee's total *new* customers sold rather than all the customers he or she sold and is a refinement over line *a*. Line *e* is rated in orders sold, and line *g* by sales dollars.

Line f: As a percentage of all the *new* customers sold by the department, irrespective of the type of product. This is similar but more refined than line *b*, because the base of comparison is the department's total *new* customers rather than the total of all sold by the department. Like line *b*, this ratio is used for employee-to-employee comparison and is rated in orders sold; line *h* measures in sales dollars.

Line g: As a percentage of all the *new-product* accounts sold by the employee, regardless of type of customer. This is like line *e*, except that the efforts are compared against new products instead of new customers. Line *i* appraises in orders sold, line *k* in dollar sales.

Line h: As a percentage of all the *new-product* accounts sold by the department, irrespective of the type of customer sold. This ratio is like line *f*, but constructed to show the comparison against new products instead of new customers. This ratio, like lines *b* and *f*, evaluates employees on a comparative basis and is rated in orders sold; line *l* does it by sales dollars.

Number of Variations Exhibit 11-3 shows variations in formulas for the measurement of productivity only. When inquiry into contacting activity and the various appraisals of quotation effort is desired, the number of formulas is considerable.

---

[2] In a company using the direct-contribution system, sales dollar measurements are not significant and are replaced by sold *contribution dollars*.

EXHIBIT 11-3 BASIC VARIATIONS IN AN ELEMENTARY SALES RATIO
Ratio: ***New-customer, new-product productivity***

To show above productivity as a percent of:	Coded Constructions	Percentage value				
		Salesperson				Dept.
		Jones	Smith	Brown	Greene	
(*a*) Total customers sold per employee	$\frac{8}{23}$	0	0	14.3	5.9	6.7
(*b*) Total customers sold by department	$\frac{8}{w}$	0	0	4.4	2.2	
(*c*) Total dollar sales of each employee	$\frac{19}{25}$	0	0	9.6	12.1	7.9
(*d*) Total department's sales	$\frac{19}{y}$	0	0	0.8	7.1	
(*e*) Total new customers sold per employee	$\frac{8}{8+9}$	0	0	33.3	25.0	27.3

(*f*) Total new customers sold by department	$\frac{8}{h + i}$	0	0	18.2	9.1	
(*g*) Total new-customer dollar sales per employee	$\frac{19}{19 + 20}$	0	0	37.0	48.6	45.1
(*h*) Total department's new-customer dollar sales	$\frac{19}{s + t}$	0	0	4.4	40.7	
(*i*) Total new-product accounts sold per employee	$\frac{8}{3 + 8}$	0	0	33.3	20.0	25.0
(*j*) Total new-product accounts sold by department	$\frac{8}{c + h}$	0	0	16.7	8.3	
(*k*) Total new-product sales of each employee	$\frac{19}{14 + 19}$	0	0	24.4	32.2	29.4
(*l*) Total new-product sales of department	$\frac{19}{n + s}$	0	0	2.9	26.5	

And these formulas would apply to the *one* desired area: *new customer, new product.*

Of course, each area requires its own set of formulas as inquiry is made into different products and different customers, namely, new customer, existing product; existing customer, new product; etc.

For more incisive evaluation, the elements of expenses and territories are added, which calls for ratios to reflect the selling efforts with due consideration for these factors.

Since the ratios which can be developed from the primary data listed in Exhibit 11-2 are practically limitless, space does not permit listing all of them. Instead, ratios typical and representative of most of the variations are listed and discussed. These were constructed for actual use by the author in various companies and situations. They give a valid cross section of the data as applied to the control of the sales department.

Because the ratios are applied to four salespeople, there are four values for the same ratio. Therefore, the format of ratio presentation is different than in previous chapters. Exhibit 11-4 shows a tabulation of 45 elementary *employee-effort* sales ratios, and Exhibit 11-5 gives 15 elementary *employee-comparison* sales ratios. Each exhibit lists the ratio number, name, coded construction, and ratio values. Exhibit 11-6 gives *departmental* values of some of the ratios tabulated in Exhibit 11-4.

ELEMENTARY SALES RATIOS

NEW CUSTOMER AND PRODUCT ORDER PRODUCTIVITY (11-1)

$$\frac{\text{New sold customers for new products}}{\text{Total customers sold}} = \frac{8}{23}$$

USE Shows the number of new customers that new products were sold to in comparison with the total number of all customers sold.

NEW CUSTOMER AND PRODUCT SALES PRODUCTIVITY (11-2)

$$\frac{\text{New customer sales for new products}}{\text{Total amount sold}} = \frac{19}{25}$$

USE Shows what portion of the total sales dollars sold was for new products to new customers; is of interest to the sales manager.

NEW CUSTOMER AND PRODUCT CONTACT ACTIVITY (11-3)

$$\frac{\text{New customers contacted for new products}}{\text{Total contacts made}} = \frac{29}{1}$$

USE Shows the percentage of the total number of contacts that were made to new customers for the purpose of selling them new products.

SALES CONTACT YIELD (11-4)

$$\frac{\text{Amount sold}}{\text{Total contacts made}} = \frac{25}{1}$$

USE Compares the total amount of dollar sales with the number of total contacts made in the same period; gives average sales return per contact.

NEW-CUSTOMER SALES PRODUCTIVITY (11-5)

$$\frac{\text{New customer sales}}{\text{Total amount sold}} = \frac{19 + 20}{25}$$

USE Measures what portion of the total sales was sold to new customers.

EXHIBIT 11-4 ELEMENTARY SALES RATIOS (EMPLOYEE EFFORT)

Ratio No.	Name	Coded Constructions	Ratio Value of Salesperson			
			Jones	Smith	Brown	Greene
(11-1)	New-customer and product-order productivity*	$\frac{8}{23}$	0	0	0.143	0.059
(11-2)	New-customer and product-sales productivity*	$\frac{19}{25}$	0	0	0.096	0.121
(11-3)	New-customer and product-contact activity*	$\frac{29}{1}$	0	0.037	0.321	0.072
(11-4)	Sales-contact yield*	$\frac{25}{1}$	38.9	120	18.6	181
(11-5)	New-customer sales productivity*	$\frac{19 + 20}{25}$	0	0.031	0.26	0.248
(11-6)	New-product sales productivity*	$\frac{14 + 19}{25}$	0	0.062	0.394	0.375
(11-7)	New-accounts direction	$\frac{10 + 11}{1}$	0	0	0.268	0.167
(11-8)	Existing-customer, new-product sales productivity	$\frac{14}{25}$	0	0.062	0.298	0.254
(11-9)	New-customer, existing-product sales productivity	$\frac{20}{25}$	0	0.031	0.163	0.127
(11-10)	Existing-customer, new-product order productivity*	$\frac{3}{23}$	0	0.111	0.285	0.235
(11-11)	Existing-customer, existing-product quotation productivity*	$\frac{17}{26}$	1.0	1.0	0.248	0.452

(11-12)	New-customer, new-product quotation productivity	$\frac{21}{26}$	0	0	0.368	0.358
(11-13)	Quotation activity*	$\frac{24}{1}$	0.26	0.22	0.32	0.36
(11-14)	New-customer order attempts*	$\frac{10 + 11}{24}$	0	0	0.835	0.465
(11-15)	New-customer sales attempts	$\frac{21 + 22}{26}$	0	0	0.65	0.376
(11-16)	Existing-customer order attempts	$\frac{5 + 6}{24}$	1.0	1.0	0.167	0.532
(11-17)	Existing-customer sales attempts	$\frac{16 + 17}{26}$	1.0	1.0	0.35	0.625
(11-18)	Quotation performance*	$\frac{26}{25}$	0.715	0.353	0.85	0.685
(11-19)	New business attempts*	$\frac{21 + 22}{25}$	0	0	0.553	0.257
(11-20)	Contact-order productivity*	$\frac{23 + 24}{1}$	0.445	0.555	0.571	0.761
(11-21)	Total dollar productivity	$\frac{12}{1}$	0.086	0.209	0.092	0.615
(11-22)	Average account sale*	$\frac{25}{23}$	210	359	74	448
(11-23)	Average quotation*	$\frac{26}{24}$	107	190	49	348
(11-24)	Average new-customer quotation	$\frac{21 + 22}{10 + 11}$	0	0	3.83	280

* Described in text.

EXHIBIT 11-4 (*Continued*)

Ratio No.	Name	Coded Constructions	Ratio Value of Salesperson			
			Jones	Smith	Brown	Greene
(11-25)	New-customer trend*	$\frac{19 + 20}{26}$	0	0.088	0.305	0.362
(11-26)	New-customer and product-order performance	$\frac{8}{8 + 9}$	0	0	0.333	0.25
(11-27)	Existing-customer, new-product order performance	$\frac{3}{3 + 4}$	0	0.125	0.500	0.308
(11-28)	New-product contact activity*	$\frac{27}{1}$	0	0.111	0.43	0.238
(11-29)	New-customer contact activity	$\frac{7}{1}$	0	0.222	0.75	0.309
(11-30)	New-product quotation activity*	$\frac{5 + 10}{27}$	0	0	0.333	0.20
(11-31)	New-customer quotation activity	$\frac{10 + 11}{29 + 32}$	0	0	0.357	0.538
(11-32)	New-product attempts*	$\frac{5 + 10}{24}$	0	0	0.445	0.133
(11-33)	New product-quotation attempt balance*	$\frac{10}{5}$	0	0	7	1
(11-34)	New-product contact productivity*	$\frac{3 + 5 + 8 + 10}{1}$	0	0.037	0.25	0.167

(11-35)	New-product dollar productivity	$\frac{16 + 14 + 19 + 21}{25}$	0	0.062	0.721	0.505
(11-36)	Average potential sale*	$\frac{12}{23}$	360	485	137.5	755
(11-37)	Average departmental potential sale*	$\frac{12}{w}$	40	97.2	42.5	285
(11-38)	Productivity-return index*	$\frac{12}{23 + 24}$	150	291	60.1	402
(11-39)	Expense productivity*	$\frac{25}{33}$	6.35	14.4	5.84	51.6
(11-40)	Expense-contact cost*	$\frac{33}{1}$	6.12	8.3	3.19	3.52
(11-41)	Entertainment economy*	$\frac{25}{36}$	21.4	45.1	16.6	152
(11-42)	New-account entertainment economy*	$\frac{19 + 20}{37}$	0	1.98	9.03	97.4
(11-43)	Existing-account entertainment economy	$\frac{14 + 15}{38}$	21.4	148	23.6	187
(11-44)	Expense return trend*	$\frac{12}{33}$	10.9	19.5	10.7	87
(11-45)	New-account order entertainment expense*	$\frac{37}{8 + 9}$	0	50.40	4.99	4.85

* Described in text.

EXHIBIT 11-5 ELEMENTARY SALES RATIOS (EMPLOYEE COMPARISON)

Ratio No.	Ratio Title	Coded Constructions	Ratio Value of Salesperson			
			Jones	Smith	Brown	Greene
(11-46)	Sales productivity*	$\frac{25}{y}$	0.08	0.25	0.08	0.59
(11-47)	Productivity potential index*	$\frac{12}{1}$	0.086	0.209	0.092	0.615
(11-48)	Sales performance*	$\frac{23}{w}$	0.11	0.20	0.31	0.38
(11-49)	Quotation performance*	$\frac{24}{x}$	0.15	0.13	0.39	0.33
(11-50)	New-customer and product-order productivity*	$\frac{8}{w}$	0	0	0.0445	0.0223
(11-51)	New-customer and product-sales productivity	$\frac{20}{y}$	0	0	0.0077	0.071
(11-52)	New-product sales productivity	$\frac{14 + 19}{y}$	0	0.0154	0.0316	0.221

(11-53)	New-product quotation activity	$\frac{5 + 10}{aa}$	0	0	0.216	0.054
(11-54)	New-product dollar productivity	$\frac{14 + 16 + 19 + 21}{n + p + s + u}$	0	0.042	0.156	0.804
(11-55)	Contact order productivity	$\frac{23 + 24}{a}$	0.079	0.099	0.21	0.21
(11-56)	Average account sale	$\frac{25}{w}$	23.2	71.8	23.1	169.5
(11-57)	New-customer trend	$\frac{19 + 20}{z}$	0	0.125	0.0338	0.236
(11-58)	Productivity-return index	$\frac{12}{w + x}$	19.8	48	21.2	141
(11-59)	New-account quotation activity*	$\frac{10 + 11}{a}$	0	0	0.10	0.046
(11-60)	New-customer contact activity*	$\frac{7}{a}$	0	0.039	0.376	0.084

* Described in text.

EXHIBIT 11-6 ELEMENTARY SALES RATIOS (DEPARTMENTAL)

Name	Coded Constructions	Ratio Value Computed for Period
New-customer and product-order productivity	$\frac{h}{w}$	$\frac{3}{45} = 0.067$
New-customer and product-sales productivity	$\frac{s}{y}$	$\frac{1{,}020}{12{,}950} = 0.079$
New-customer and product-contact activity	$\frac{cc}{a}$	$\frac{22}{152} = 0.132$
Sales contact yield	$\frac{y}{a}$	$\frac{12{,}950}{152} = 85.2$
New-customer sales productivity	$\frac{s + t}{y}$	$\frac{2{,}260}{12{,}950} = 0.175$
New-product sales productivity	$\frac{n + s}{y}$	$\frac{3{,}470}{12{,}950} = 0.268$
Existing-customer, new-product order productivity	$\frac{c}{w}$	$\frac{9}{45} = 0.20$
Quotation activity	$\frac{x}{a}$	$\frac{46}{152} = 0.30$
New-customer order attempts	$\frac{j + k}{x}$	$\frac{22}{46} = 0.478$
New business attempts	$\frac{u + v}{y}$	$\frac{2{,}535}{12{,}950} = 0.196$
Average account sale	$\frac{y}{w}$	$\frac{12{,}950}{45} = 288$
New-customer trend	$\frac{s + t}{z}$	$\frac{2{,}260}{7{,}995} = 0.282$
New-product dollar productivity	$\frac{n + p + s + u}{y}$	$\frac{4{,}800}{12{,}950} = 0.371$
Average potential sale	$\frac{l}{w}$	$\frac{20{,}945}{45} = 465$
Productivity return index	$\frac{l}{w + x}$	$\frac{20{,}945}{91} = 230$
Expense productivity	$\frac{y}{w}$	$\frac{12{,}950}{715.50} = 18.1$
Entertainment economy	$\frac{y}{jj}$	$\frac{12{,}950}{233.50} = 55.6$

NEW-PRODUCT SALES PRODUCTIVITY (11-6)

$$\frac{\text{New product sales}}{\text{Total amount sold}} = \frac{14 + 19}{25}$$

USE Measures what portion of the total sales was for new products.

EXISTING-CUSTOMER, NEW-PRODUCT ORDER PRODUCTIVITY (11-10)

$$\frac{\text{Existing customers sold for new products}}{\text{Total customers sold}} = \frac{3}{23}$$

USE Shows what portion of the total orders sold was to existing customers for new products; a variation of basic order productivity, it is varied by the type of customer and type of product.

EXISTING-CUSTOMER AND PRODUCT QUOTATION PRODUCTIVITY (11-11)

$$\frac{\text{Existing-customer quotations for existing product}}{\text{Total amount quoted}} = \frac{17}{26}$$

USE Measures what portion of the total dollar value of quotations was devoted to existing accounts for existing products.

QUOTATION ACTIVITY (11-13)

$$\frac{\text{Number of customers quoted}}{\text{Total contacts made}} = \frac{24}{1}$$

USE Shows what portion of the total number of contacts made resulted in quotations.

NEW-CUSTOMER ORDER ATTEMPTS (11-14)

$$\frac{\text{New customers quoted}}{\text{Total customers quoted}} = \frac{10 + 11}{24}$$

USE Measures what percentage of the total number of quotations was given on behalf of new accounts.

QUOTATION PERFORMANCE (11-18)

$$\frac{\text{Amount quoted}}{\text{Amount sold}} = \frac{26}{25}$$

USE Compares the amounts quoted with the amounts sold; hints at what the total sales *might be*.

NEW BUSINESS ATTEMPTS (11-19)

$$\frac{\text{New customers quotations}}{\text{Total amount sold}} = \frac{21 + 22}{25}$$

USE Compares the amount of the new-account quotations with the total amount of sales.

CONTACT-ORDER PRODUCTIVITY (11-20)

$$\frac{\text{No. of customers sold + no. of customers quoted}}{\text{Total contacts made}} = \frac{23 + 24}{1}$$

USE Shows the percentage of the total gross contacts that resulted in accounts sold and quoted. It evaluates how active the salesperson was, but doesn't show the dollar productivity.

AVERAGE ACCOUNT SALE (11-22)

$$\frac{\text{Total amount sold}}{\text{Total customers sold}} = \frac{25}{23}$$

USE Shows the amount of the average sale.

AVERAGE QUOTATION (11-23)

$$\frac{\text{Amount quoted}}{\text{Total number of customers quoted}} = \frac{26}{24}$$

USE Evaluates the amount of the average quotation; an excellent diagnostic tool when used in conjunction with Ratio (11-22).

NEW CUSTOMER TRENDS (11-25)

$$\frac{\text{New customer sales}}{\text{Total amount quoted}} = \frac{19 + 20}{26}$$

USE Shows the relationship between the new-account sales and the total value of the quotations made. The purpose of this ratio is twofold: it shows the results of the efforts to obtain new business, and it also indicates the balance between the quotations and sales situations.

NEW-PRODUCT CONTACT ACTIVITY (11-28)

$$\frac{\text{New-product contacts}}{\text{Total contacts made}} = \frac{27}{1}$$

USE Assesses what proportion of total contacts was made on behalf of new products; determines overall contact effectiveness by comparing with the sales and quotations produced as a result of contact activity.

NEW-PRODUCT QUOTATION ACTIVITY (11-30)

$$\frac{\text{Number of new-product quotations}}{\text{Total new-product contacts}} = \frac{5 + 10}{27}$$

USE Shows what portion of the contacts that were made on behalf of new products was quoted.

NEW-PRODUCT ATTEMPTS (11-32)

$$\frac{\text{Number of new-product quotations}}{\text{Total number of customers quoted}} = \frac{5 + 10}{24}$$

USE Measures the percentage of total number of quotations given on behalf of new products.

NEW-PRODUCT-QUOTATION ATTEMPT BALANCE (11-33)

$$\frac{\text{New-product quotes to new customers}}{\text{New-product quotes to existing customers}} = \frac{10}{5}$$

USE Evaluates the balancing of the effort between new and existing customers for new-product quotations. The departmental value for this ratio in the period under tabulation is shown to be 4, which means that new products are being quoted to new customers four times more than new products are being quoted to existing customers.

NEW-PRODUCT-CONTACT PRODUCTIVITY (11-34)

$$\frac{\text{New products sold and quoted}}{\text{Total contacts made}} = \frac{3 + 5 + 8 + 10}{1}$$

USE Indicates what portion of the contacts made resulted in both orders and quotations; relates new-product attempts, trends, and productivity by showing the order or quotation transaction per contacts; gives an indication of overall contacting efficiency.

AVERAGE POTENTIAL SALE (11-36)

$$\frac{\text{Amount sold and quoted}}{\text{Total accounts sold}} = \frac{12}{23}$$

USE Compares the total value of the sales and quotations made with the number of accounts sold, giving an average dollar value per sold account.

AVERAGE DEPARTMENTAL POTENTIAL SALE (11-37)

$$\frac{\text{Amount sold and quoted}}{\text{Department total number of accounts sold}} = \frac{12}{\text{W}}$$

USE Same as the one preceding, with the difference that the denominator uses the departmental total number of accounts sold instead of the individual-employee total of accounts sold; shows the total contributory effects of the efforts of four employees.

PRODUCTIVITY RETURN INDEX (11-38)

$$\frac{\text{Amount sold and quoted}}{\text{Total number of accounts sold and quoted}} = \frac{12}{23 + 24}$$

USE Compares the dollar value of the sales and quotations with the number of accounts sold and quoted in order to obtain an average sold-quoted amount per account sold and quoted; composite ratio of the average account sale and the average quotation; a proof-of-the-pudding index for any immediate period being evaluated.

EXPENSE ECONOMY

The ratios listed on Exhibit 11-4 and those described to this point deal with the employee and his or her activity, effectiveness, and personal characteristics and give some indication of his or her responsiveness to sales management's direction as regards different classes of products and customers. We have measured the employee's drives and willingness to sell, quote, or otherwise circulate the company's name and reputation. But we have not as yet measured the *cost* of the employee doing any or all these things.

We have not equated his or her activity to the expenses incurred in selling.

Actually, each of the ratios mentioned so far could accommodate the factor of expenses and so lend economic tempering to an employee's overall performance. And performance must include the cost factor; otherwise, the effort to attain objectives might get prohibitively great. This integration of activity with expenses must be known in order that management might be induced to pursue the optimum economic course.

The level of routine expense incurred by the individual salesperson should have some bearing on, or correlation to, the importance of the contact. This importance is measured in sales levels, desirability of customer, desirability of market and territory, product acceptance and propagation, and the relationship of the product sales to the economic needs of the company.

Management must face quite realistically that the entertainment of customers and prospects can be optimized to the sales levels required. Entertainment expense is an efficient catalytic agent in the buyer-seller arena.

Ratio control alerts the salesperson to the fact that the sales manager is not only keeping a close watch but a careful correlation of his expenses to his performances.

Many companies simply equate sales with expenses and accept the average level of expenses per sales dollar as their yardstick. This is tantamount to managing on the basis of a profit-and-loss statement. Waiting for an average of historical data postpones managerial action until after the facts. Smart management knows that all averages contain peaks and valleys, and it must be prepared to take advantage of a positive opportunity at the time it is occurring and must be alerted to negative conditions when they appear.

The ratios described below deal with the relationship of activity, performance, and productivity to the expense level. They are only a few of the large number that could be developed to fit a specific need. The following text describes some of those listed in Exhibit 11-4.

EXPENSE PRODUCTIVITY ______ (11-39)

$$\frac{\text{Sales}}{\text{Total expenses}} = \frac{25}{33}$$

USE Compare the number of sales which each dollar of expenses can produce, or the number of cents of expenses that each dollar of sales requires; a check on the trend.

EXPENSE-CONTACT COST ______ (11-40)

$$\frac{\text{Total expenses}}{\text{Total contacts made}} = \frac{33}{1}$$

USE A relationship between the total expenses and the total number of contacts made; the average expense cost per gross contact.

ENTERTAINMENT ECONOMY ______ (11-41)

$$\frac{\text{Total sales}}{\text{Total entertainment expenses}} = \frac{25}{36}$$

USE Gives the average number of sales produced from each dollar of entertainment expenses; or, the number of average entertainment cents spent for each dollar of sales.

NEW-ACCOUNT ENTERTAINMENT ECONOMY ____ (11-42)

$$\frac{\text{New-account sales}}{\text{New-account entertainment expense}} = \frac{19 + 20}{37}$$

USE Measures the amount of new customer sales obtained for every dollar of entertainment expense.

EXPENSE RETURN TREND ____ (11-44)

$$\frac{\text{Amount sold and quoted}}{\text{Total expense}} = \frac{12}{33}$$

USE Shows how much sales and quotation dollars were obtained for every dollar of total expenses.

NEW-ACCOUNT ORDER ENTERTAINMENT EXPENSE ____ (11-45)

$$\frac{\text{New-account entertainment expense}}{\text{Total new accounts sold}} = \frac{37}{8 + 9}$$

USE Evaluates the average amount of entertainment expense spent for every new account sold.

SALES PRODUCTIVITY ____ (11-46)

$$\frac{\text{Total sales per employee}}{\text{Departmental total sales}} = \frac{25}{y}$$

USE Shows portion of the total departmental sales sold by each man; can be modified for different product and customers and expenses similar to the man-efforts ratios.

PRODUCTIVITY POTENTIAL INDEX (11-47)

$$\frac{\text{Total sales and quotations per employee}}{\text{Dept. total sales and quotations}} = \frac{12}{1}$$

USE Shows percentage of the department's total of sales plus quotations obtained by each employee; can be expended to provide variances of evaluation for customers and products.

SALES PERFORMANCE (11-48)

$$\frac{\text{Total accounts sold per employee}}{\text{Departmental total accounts sold}} = \frac{23}{w}$$

USE Indicates percentage of the department's total accounts sold brought in by each employee; valuable in showing the salesperson's ability to open a large number of accounts even though they may not be productive immediately.

QUOTATION PERFORMANCE (11-49)

$$\frac{\text{Total accounts quoted per employee}}{\text{Departmental total accounts quoted}} = \frac{24}{x}$$

USE Percentage of the department's total accounts quoted as quoted by each employee.

NEW-CUSTOMER AND PRODUCT-ORDER PRODUCTIVITY (11-50)

$$\frac{\text{New sold customers for new products}}{\text{Departmental total customers sold}} = \frac{8}{w}$$

USE New sold accounts for new products as a percentage of the departmental total.

NEW-ACCOUNT QUOTATION ACTIVITY ______ (11-59)

$$\frac{\text{New accounts quoted}}{\text{Departmental total contacts}} = \frac{10 + 11}{a}$$

USE Assesses what portion of the total of the entire departmental contacts each employee converted into quotes.

NEW-CUSTOMER CONTACT ACTIVITY ______ (11-60)

$$\frac{\text{New accounts contacted}}{\text{Departmental total contacts}} = \frac{7}{a}$$

USE Shows the proportion of the department's total number of accounts contacted that was devoted to new customer contacts.

Again, it is worthwhile mentioning that the element of expenses in total, or in its various categories, can be appended to any of the ratios to give expense effect to the values. This may be helpful in appraising a local situation, but is not necessarily the soundest way to control the trends.

Even if management does not carry these ratios beyond the elementary form, it will still derive a degree of evaluation and control superior to what it gets from consulting unweighted data. This information is easy to prepare and can be kept cumulatively for each employee and by upper management for the department as a whole.

For larger companies, the author especially recommends this procedure as ideally suited for data-processing equipment. In some applications, the author was consulted on systems whereby ratios were created and cumulative records stored on memory systems, and limits set on other ratio values, which triggered management to action when exceeded. Because of all the variations that normally take place in larger corporations, properly designed data processing will provide the rapid decisions in all areas as well, for the total integration of data for company-wide decision making.

The smaller companies can derive great benefits from the simple and advanced ratios for evaluation and control by simple computation.

CHAPTER TWELVE

BASIC CONTROL RATIOS FOR SALES: By Product

The previous chapter dealt with means of analyzing and appraising how effective the individual salespeople were in their contacting activity, the resulting productivity, and the economic levels attained in the performance of those functions.

With these indices sales management could determine the weak and strong points of the employees and thus give management a target for counseling and strengthening. They provided sales management with a balanced evaluation, which could be used as a yardstick to determine whether the men were actually implementing the expressed aims and directives of sales management. Finally, they gave management trend figures so necessary to planning, as well as a check on the effectiveness of the sales management.

PRODUCT EVALUATION

The previous chapter provided guides by which the efforts of the employees could be directed, but it did not, however, show how well the individual products were doing; how much it cost to promote and sell them; which customers and territories responded most favorably to them; etc.

So, while the previous chapter evaluated salesperson performance, this chapter assesses product performance without reference to individual people.

This chapter sets up ratios which show what effect the sales efforts have on the movement of specific products. These show the trends for the acceptance of various products by types of customers, territories, etc., including also the relative selling costs of different products.

INVESTMENT IN PRODUCT

Sales come from quotations and contacts: the more contacts properly made, the more sales must result. Therefore, an investment in a new product must be enhanced and protected by requiring a certain type of selling approach and a certain level of sales effort. In this type of evaluation, we are interested only in the effort put forth by the department on behalf of certain products.

It is obvious that management is more interested in the sales success of a product which costs them $50,000 to develop than in one in which they have invested $1,000 of developmental money. Trends toward these successes rest with the amount of contact effort put forth for these products, and this must be under constant policing. So again, one-fact management is inadequate: the total sales level attained may still not be consonant with the needs of management, and developmental-expense recovery surely is one of those needs.

But in addition to high development cost, there is the prospect of high contact and selling costs. Management would want also to control these expenses. Simple ratios incorporating the elements of expenses would give the needed trend information. In some cases, management decides to write off the developmental expense as a loss and gives up the idea of selling a particular new product when it discovers that the contacting, promotional, and selling expenses are uneconomically high. These can so burden the product's selling price as to price the company out of its markets.

Naturally, there are many more considerations that enter here before a decision like this can be made. A principal factor is the value of the lost contribution caused by the removal of the product. The sales expense element must be watched and optimized before it generates large losses in the gross profit segment of operations.

PRODUCT EXPENSE RECOVERY

Product-activity assessment is by no means confined to new products. Again, in evaluating sales performance on total sales, management may be limiting its sphere of control. In a company making more than one product, there can exist within the *same gross sales level* an infinite sales-product mix and an infinite production utilization-product mix. The sales-product mix refers to the fact that a given gross sales level can be composed of different individual product sales. Where each product has a different profit contribution, the final composite profit contribution in gross sales is a function of this product mix.

The other side of the coin is that the varying sales of each product cause variations in the level of production-equipment utilization, and this in turn varies the amount of fixed-expense recovery made by the company. Thus a given gross sales level can have a wide effect on the amount of fixed-expense recovery gained by the company, because of the nature of the product mix and the magnitude of the sales volume of each product in the mix.

Therefore it is essential that management prepare target data or other data by which it can inform the sales manager of the needs for generating contribution in production. Once the data are available, the sales manager must include as part of managing the effort to obtain a specified product mix. It is accomplished by the use of these same ratios, which show the contact, quotational, and sales productivity *by product.*

PRIMARY DATA REQUIRED

Since ratios will be set up to evaluate product activity rather than employee activity, the data reported and summarized for each employee will now have to be compiled in a different form. Exhibits 12-1 and 12-2 show data rearranged *by product,* but using the same information as employed for the employee-effort ratios in the previous chapter.

EXHIBIT 12-1 WEEKLY PRODUCT SUMMARY ANALYSIS

Product Summary Analysis

Territory ________________________ Week ended ________________

Product	Employee	Contacts			Amount sold				Amount quoted				Expenses			
					Type of account								Auto		Entertain.	
		Total	Prospects	Customers	New		Exist.		New		Exist.		$	Miles	Prosp.	Cust.
					No.	$	No.	$	No.	$	No.	$				
	Jones															
a *b*	Smith															
	Brown															
	Greene															
Total																

a *c*	Jones														
	Smith														
	Brown														
	Greene														
Total															
Total															
Z *Z*	Jones														
	Smith														
	Brown														
	Greene														
Total															

EXHIBIT 12-2 PRIMARY SALES DATA (PRODUCT)

Code	Activity	Product							Department
		ab	*ac*	*bc*	*cd*	*WW*	*YY*	*ZZ*	
58	Total contacts	*36*	*27*	*21*	*31*	*11*	*14*	*12*	*152*
39	To new customers	10	11	9	9	5	8	9	61
40	To existing customers	26	16	12	22	6	6	3	91
41	Total customers sold and quoted	*24*	*18*	*7*	*20*	*11*	*9*	*2*	*91*
42	Sold new customers	2	2	1	3	2	0	1	11
43	Sold existing customers	12	7	1	5	5	4	0	34
44	Quoted new customers	4	5	1	4	3	4	1	22
45	Quoted existing customers	6	4	4	8	1	1	0	24
46	Total amount sold and quoted	*$5,895*	*$4,280*	*$760*	*$5,210*	*$3,070*	*$1,600*	*$130*	*$20,945*
47	Sold new customers	480	360	40	360	980	0	40	2,260
48	Sold existing customers	3,100	2,360	80	2,700	1,080	1,370	0	10,690
49	Quoted new customers	940	685	120	450	110	140	90	2,535
50	Quoted existing customers	1,375	875	520	1,700	900	90	0	5,460
51	Total field cost	*140.10*	*152.20*	*89.80*	*161.60*	*44.20*	*54.80*	*72.80*	*715.50*
52	Total automobile expense	27.20	39.20	32.80	36.00	3.60	4.00	19.20	162.00
53	Total entertainment expense	36.90	51.00	23.00	55.60	18.60	26.80	21.60	233.50
54	For new customers	20.20	4.00	6.50	31.60	12.40	3.40	21.60	99.70
55	For existing customers	16.70	47.00	16.50	24.00	6.20	23.40	0	133.80
56	Total automobile and entertainment	64.10	90.20	55.80	91.60	22.20	30.80	40.80	395.50
57	Salary	76.00	62.00	34.00	70.00	22.00	24.00	32.00	320.00

Exhibit 12-3 is a selection of typical ratios as applied to the seven products, together with the values applying to the products. The list of ratios is by no means limited to what is shown in this exhibit. Hundreds of product ratios can be developed to suit specific needs. The numbering system corresponds to those in the previous chapter. Thus, Ratio (12-39) is the product sales equivalent of the salesperson Ratio (11-39).

CONTACT COSTS

Exhibit 12-4 is a listing of four major cost ratios, their formulas, and their values. Using the same data as originally presented in Chapter 11, it shows that on the average it costs less to sell a new-product order and a new-product dollar than it does an existing-product order and dollar.

PRODUCT-PERFORMANCE SUMMARY

Product ZZ appears to be a poor performer as far as the sales department is concerned. It gets the lowest level of sales per contact; it has the lowest average order value; and it requires the most expenses per sales dollar—all this from the aspect of the isolated sales-function evaluation. However, from the aspect of the benefits that the smallest amount of these sales has for production, all the above sales unfunctionality may be unimportant. In the broad company-wide picture, it might be good business to tolerate the excess sales efforts and costs to achieve a net gain for the company. "Excess" is, after all, a relative, not an absolute, term. What is excess in the isolated situation of sales by comparison with other product scores may be a positive aspect when considered in a larger economic framework.

On the other hand, product *bc* is almost as poor a *sales* performer, but as we shall see later on, the effect of product *bc* on the total economy is almost the reverse of that of product ZZ.

Product *WW*, which is herein receiving *sales* praise, likewise has an entirely different effect on the total economy of the company, as will be shown in a later chapter.

One might ask why we use these ratios at all until we have some further insight into the economy of the other areas of the

EXHIBIT 12-3 ELEMENTARY SALES RATIOS (PRODUCT)

Number of Ratio and Name	Coded Constructions	Ratio Value of Product							Department
		ab	*ac*	*bc*	*cd*	*WW*	*YY*	*ZZ*	
(12-4): sales-contact yield	$\frac{47+48}{58}$	99.5	101	5.7	98.8	187	97	3.3	85.2
(12-22): average account sales	$\frac{47+48}{42+43}$	256	302	60	382	294	342	40	288
(12-29): new customer contact activity	$\frac{39}{58}$	0.278	0.407	0.428	0.29	0.455	0.57	0.75	0.40
(12-39): expense productivity	$\frac{47+48}{51}$	25.6	17.9	1.34	18.9	44.7	25	0.55	18.1
(12-40): expense contact cost	$\frac{51}{58}$	3.9	5.65	4.27	5.21	4.01	3.91	6.06	4.70
(12-41): entertainment economy	$\frac{47+48}{53}$	97	53.4	5.2	55	111	51	1.85	55.6
(12-42): new account entertainment economy	$\frac{47}{54}$	23.8	90	6.15	11.4	79	0	1.85	22.7
(12-43): existing account entertainment	$\frac{48}{55}$	186	50.2	4.85	113	174	58.6	......	79.8
(12-45): new account order entertainment	$\frac{54}{42}$	10.10	2.00	6.50	10.53	6.20	......	21.60	9.05
(12-46): sales productivity	$\frac{47+48}{y}$	0.276	0.21	0.009	0.236	0.159	1.06	0.003	

(12-61): average new account sale	$\frac{47}{42}$	240	180	40	120	490	0	40	206
(12-62): new customer sales productivity	$\frac{47}{y}$	0.037	0.028	0.003	0.028	0.076	......	0.003	
(12-63): average account expense	$\frac{51}{42 + 43}$	10	16.9	44.9	20.2	6.33	13.7	72.8	15.9
(12-64): average order contacts	$\frac{58}{42 + 43}$	2.57	3.0	10.5	3.9	1.57	4.66	12	3.47
(12-65): average order potential contacts	$\frac{58}{41}$	1.5	1.5	3	1.57	1	1.55	6	1.67
(12-66): average new-order contacts	$\frac{39}{42}$	5	5.5	9	3	2.5	......	9	5.55
(12-67): new sales contact yield	$\frac{47}{58}$	13.3	13.3	1.9	11.6	89	......	3.33	14.9
(12-68): entertainment order expense	$\frac{53}{42 + 43}$	2.64	5.66	11.50	6.95	2.66	6.70	21.60	5.20
(12-69): nonsalary expense productivity	$\frac{47 + 48}{56}$	55.8	30.2	2.15	33.4	92.8	45.5	1.0	32.5
(12-70): nonsalary contact cost	$\frac{56}{58}$	1.78	3.32	2.66	2.95	2.05	2.2	3.4	2.6
(12-71): nonsalary order expense	$\frac{47 + 48}{52}$	131.5	6.95	3.66	85.00	572	343	2.08	80
(12-72): automobile expense economy	$\frac{56}{47 + 48}$	0.018	0.033	0.465	0.030	0.011	0.023	1.02	0.0305
(12-73): sales dollar expense	$\frac{51}{47 + 48}$	0.039	0.056	0.748	0.053	0.021	0.04	1.82	0.055

EXHIBIT 12-4 PRODUCT COST RATIOS

Ratio no.	Cost of:	Formula	Ratio value, dollars
PC-1	Selling each new-product order	$= \frac{51(WW \text{ to } ZZ)}{42 + 43(WW \text{ to } ZZ)}$	$= \frac{171.80}{12} = 14.34$
PC-2	Selling each existing-product order	$= \frac{51(ab \text{ to } cd)}{42 + 43(ab \text{ to } ZZ)}$	$= \frac{543.70}{33} = 16.47$
PC-3	Selling each new-product dollar	$= \frac{51(WW \text{ to } ZZ)}{47 + 48(NW \text{ to } ZZ)}$	$= \frac{171.80}{3470} = 0.0495$
PC-4	Selling each existing-product dollar	$= \frac{51(ab \text{ to } cd)}{47 + 48(ab \text{ to } cd)}$	$= \frac{543.70}{9480} = 0.0572$

company. The answer is that the ratios or controls provide us with an objective measure. If sales management is told to push product *ZZ* (irrespective of its poor *sales* economy) because it benefits the company, the indices that reveal the doings of product *ZZ* are watched for movement. Management of the indices does not imply making them all go up or down, but simply going to limits prescribed by self or others for the accomplishment of specific goals. Similarly, as we shall see later, sales management will be told to back off on the activity of product *WW*. The indices are the barometers.

CHAPTER THIRTEEN

ADVANCED CONTROL RATIOS FOR SALES

The previous two chapters in the sales section dealt with the development of elementary ratios for evaluating employee effort and product activity. These ratios showed values for one short period and are useful to the sales manager in localizing difficulties and in checking on the employees' conformity to directives from the sales manager respecting type of product, customer, territory, expense level, and nature. By means of the ratio trends, he or she can appraise the characteristics of the employees, their habits, patience, persistence, motivations for certain types of sales work, drives, etc. However, there are some matters which cannot really be evaluated in a short period. These factors influence the manager's predictions concerning the longer-range performances of his or her employees.

ADVANCED RATIOS: FIRST GROUP

Single-period evaluations of employees based on the elementary ratios cannot possibly appraise expected quotational performance. The immediate-period ratio value gives the amount of quotation per contact but can in no way state what percentage of these quotational dollars will come to fruition. To do this, one would need a crystal ball to see the future or one must necessarily use what the quotational acceptance or mortality has been in the past to modify present-period performance. Therefore, in this first group of advanced ratios, historical quotational information is presented.

Another vital factor is customers' potential and how the employees are functioning with respect to it. Selling can be hit-and-miss, with maximization being the prime motive, or it can be designed to provide the company with the best stability possible. Invariably, this greater stability is accompanied by higher sales or contribution at less effort and expense. The consideration of customers' potential as a sales-evaluation factor rests with the assumption that, in the average company, it is less desirable to sell $5 million per year to 4 customers that buy $4.7 million and 40 customers that buy the other $300,000 than to sell the same $5 million to 44 customers that all buy more or less the same amount, even though the latter costs more in contact expenses.

CUSTOMERS' POTENTIAL

The estimate of potential is not objective since it is based on personal opinion, regardless of how scientific the forms or the questioners who collect the data. In this chapter we are interested in: the potential of the customer, i.e., how much of the company's type of product he or she buys in total; the territorial potential, i.e., the amount of the company's type of product that can be consumed in a given geographic area; the market potential, i.e., the trend or tendency for the public to interest themselves in, and ultimately to buy, the type of product made by the company.

Knowing this potential (the determinants of which are outside the scope of this book), the sales department can then set targets for obtaining as large a share of it as it can economically digest, at minimum acquisition cost, but consistent with the economic needs of its production facilities. The control of sales effort, then, is policing to see that potential is considered together with the other factors being measured.

The first step that must be taken is a measure of the buying potential of each customer. The primary tool in this investigation is the salesperson assigned to the account. From him or her comes some indication of what prospects the customer has for the coming year. The customer may also provide hints as to plans for new drives, new products, a better year than last, penetrating new markets, etc.

An effective way is to elicit from the customer his or her own sales forecast. If not given directly, perhaps it can be obtained by inquiring about what percentage over last year's volume is expected. Then by reference to credit-reporting services, an income-and-expense statement helps arrive at an approximate answer. From that point on, one would have to know the breakdown of the customer's profit-and-loss statement in order to determine that percentage disbursed for the company's product. Once that was obtained, the customer's expected yearly disbursements for the type of product the company makes would not be too difficult to approximate.

The missing link is the cost of material in the customer's sales dollar. Very often trade associations will cooperate by supplying a typical P&L statement for their industry, and this would be a close enough guide. The Federal Trade Commission and the Department of Commerce are also excellent sources for typical expense breakdowns. On occasion the studies issued by the Internal Revenue Service showing corporation income-tax returns will provide the information.

GEOGRAPHIC AND INDUSTRY POTENTIAL

To obtain potential concerning a given territory and to ascertain whether or not it is economically justified to penetrate with a sales force, the trade-association-sponsored market surveys are helpful. Often such studies can be obtained free, on loan, or for a nominal printing charge.

Industry potential is quite another thing. A company may get a share of its market in proportion to its size, ability, location, etc. If its share is out of proportion, then controls should be set up to compare its performance with the industry in general to ensure that it is coming close to the goal. This area of forecasting is probably the most difficult because of the lack of objective factors. Each of the reasons contributing to the deviation of the company from a norm in its industry cannot be given objective weight. Customers' tastes, needs, etc., are always changing; the location factor becomes a fluid variable; competition has a volatile effect; etc. Management can only hope to develop as a goal a realistic level of the industry and then attempt to obtain or exceed their share within economical operating limits.

Many public indices or economic indicators are available, such as national income and product, business sales and inventories, construction, factory payrolls, freight-car loadings, consumer prices, and purchasing power. These are contained in regular government publications.

The first figure necessary is the potential of each customer for the company's type of product; that is, we want to know how much of the company's type of product customers buy per year in total and what percentage of that the company may properly expect to receive. We then want to evaluate and control the sales efforts accordingly.

SELLER-BUYER COMPATIBILITY

Whether these potential studies are made or not, management must determine whether it has the right employee for its customer. Just as a change in the product mix will increase profits within the same sales level, so a rotation of the same number of sales "bodies" between salespeople and accounts can well boost the sales level of the company. In the author's experience, the best-organized sales department, complete with modern tabulating equipment, plenty of sales clerical support, as well as a fine line of products, did not ensure the optimum level of sales or mix of sales.

RECORD CUSTOMER'S DATA

Both the historical quotational data and the figures concerning the customer's potential should be recorded in a form which allows ready and simple access.

The performances of quotational success, together with the acquisition of the customer's potential, are combined with the *cumulative* values of the elementary ratios of Chapter 11 to give the first group of the advanced ratios. The primary data used for these ratios are shown in tabular form in Exhibit 13-1. The ratios constructed from these data are shown for the individual employees and for the department in Exhibit 13-2.

The primary data of Exhibit 13-1 show statistics for the current month: items numbered 61, 63, 64, and 66 to 68 and, for the year to date (6-month period), items 60, 62, 65, and 69 to 74. Item 59 refers to the customer's yearly potential, and item 60 is a percentage of that figure based on the elapsed time in the year. In this case it's 6 months, and therefore 50%.

Some of these factors may need clarification:

Contacts refers to a communication by visit (in this case) irrespective of companies contacted. Two visits in the month to one company is counted as two contacts.

Cumulative sales this year means all the sales booked by the salesperson in the six-month period.

The same is true of quotations.

Companies contacted means the number of *different* companies.

Companies sold and quoted means the number of *different* companies.

Total number of companies sold this year means number of *different* companies.

Thus there can be many contacts or many sold orders and few companies sold. This is evidence of the new-account type of salesperson. Likewise, there can be few sold orders and few companies sold. Obviously, the number of orders sold must always be more than the number of different companies sold.

DATA VARIATIONS

Because of the large number of variables present in sales control, the author is attempting to show a different variance with each table drawn. It must be realized that the same format can be used for the analysis and control "by product" (as in Chapter 12), instead of "by employee," which is shown in the table. Similarly, with the introduction of the "number of *different* companies" variance, the reader will be prompted to make his or her own controls, using that factor, of course, where feasible and necessary.

EXHIBIT 13-1 CUMULATIVE AND MONTHLY PRIMARY SALES DATA (EMPLOYEE)

Code	Item	Salesperson				Code	Depart-ment
		Jones	Smith	Brown	Greene		
59	Customer estimated yearly potential	$280,000	$260,000	$152,000	$264,000	nn	$956,000
60	Customer cumulative potential to this month	140,000	130,000	76,000	132,000	oo	478,000
61	Sales this month	3,700	4,600	3,600	9,100	pp	21,000
62	Cumulative sales this year	24,000	44,000	26,000	102,000	qq	196,000
63	Contacts this month	100	100	200	150	rr	550
64	Quotations this month	4,900	4,900	9,400	9,400	ss	28,600
65	Cumulative quota this year	62,000	62,000	118,000	118,000	tt	360,000
	This month total no. of:						
66	Companies contacted	14	30	30	28	uu	102
67	Companies quoted	12	12	26	16	vv	66
68	Companies sold	7	11	17	15	ww	50
69	Total number of companies sold this year	11	39	22	22	xx	94
70	Total cumulative expenses to this month	*2,910*	*3,810*	*3,480*	*3,230*	yy	*13,430*
71	Salary	2,080	2,080	2,080	2,080		8,320
72	Entertainment	430	1,020	890	760		3,100
73	Auto	400	710	510	390		2,010
74	Cumulative contacts to date	500	800	600	450	zz	2,350

EXHIBIT 13-2 ADVANCED SALES RATIOS (EMPLOYEE)

Ratio No.	Name	Coded Constructions	Ratio Value of Salesperson				Department
			Jones	Smith	Brown	Greene	
(13-1)	Customer potential acquisition*	$\frac{62}{60}$	0.171	0.338	0.342	0.774	0.41
(13-2)	Cumulative contact return*	$\frac{61}{63}$	37	46	18	60.6	38.2
(13-3)	Sold accounts index*	$\frac{69}{xx}$	0.117	0.415	0.234	0.234	
(13-4)	Average monthly company sale*	$\frac{61}{68}$	529	418	212	606	420
(13-5)	Average company sale*	$\frac{62}{69}$	2.18M	1.13M	1.18M	4.65M	2.08M
(13-6)	Expense-potential index*	$\frac{60}{70}$	48.1	34.1	21.8	40.9	35.6
(13-7)	Sales-expense index*	$\frac{62}{70}$	8.25	11.5	7.47	31.6	14.6

(13-8)	Average entertainment economy*	$\frac{62}{72}$	54.8	43.1	29.2	134	63.2
(13-9)	Entertainment-potential economy*	$\frac{60}{72}$	326	127	85.3	174	154
(13-10)	Quotation acceptance*	$\frac{62}{62 + 65}$	0.279	0.415	0.18	0.444	0.354
(13-11)	Quotation mortality*	$\frac{65 - 62}{65}$	0.613	0.29	0.78	0.135	0.456
(13-12)	Expense productivity*	$\frac{65 + 62}{70}$	29.6	27.8	41.4	68.1	41.3
(13-13)	Cumulative contact return	$\frac{62}{74}$	48	55	43.5	227	83.5
(13-14)	Average company contact index	$\frac{74}{69}$	45.5	20.5	27.3	20.4	25
(13-15)	Average monthly company contact index	$\frac{66}{68}$	2	2.73	1.765	1.865	2.04
(13-16)	Average company return	$\frac{68}{66}$	0.5	0.367	0.566	0.535	0.49

* Described in text.

It should be obvious that in an earlier chapter, when reference was made to a new or old customer or to total customers sold, the meaning was *number of orders*. And so an evaluation of salespersons was made in part by the comparison between the number of orders quoted and sold, or contacted and quoted, or contacted and sold, without giving weight to the number of *different* companies sold.

Just as it is important to sell as many contacts as seen, it is important that these orders are not all sold to the same customer. If that were done, we would have only as many different customers as there are salespeople. Obviously, then, an important evaluating factor is the *number of different companies sold* within the structure of the *number of orders sold*. Even if no sales take place, the evaluation of contact activity should always reflect this: There must be a balanced relationship between the number of different companies contacted and the number of contacts made. Too many, in dilettante fashion, is as bad as too little, and probably worse in some cases.

Values for the following ratios, for each employee, are given in Exhibit 13-2.

CUSTOMER POTENTIAL ACQUISITION __________ (13-1)

CONSTRUCTION $\dfrac{\text{Cumulative sales this year}}{\text{Customers' cumulative potential to this month}}$

CODES $\dfrac{\mathbf{62}}{\mathbf{60}}$

USE Reveals a vital fact in judging the progress of each employee and of the department. It uncovers improper assignments of high-potential accounts to low producers.

AVERAGE CONTACT RETURN __________ (13-2)

CONSTRUCTION $\dfrac{\text{Sales this month}}{\text{Contacts this month}}$

CODES $\dfrac{\mathbf{61}}{\mathbf{63}}$

USE Equivalent of Ratio (11-4) on a monthly basis.

CUMULATIVE CONTACT RETURN (13-3)

CONSTRUCTION $\frac{\text{Cumulative sales this year}}{\text{Cumulative contacts to this month}}$

CODES $\frac{62}{74}$

USE Shows the respective performances for a 6-month period and ranks the employees accordingly.

AVERAGE MONTHLY COMPANY SALE (13-4)

CONSTRUCTION $\frac{\text{Sold this month}}{\text{Companies sold this month}}$

CODES $\frac{61}{68}$

USE Evaluates the average amount of sales obtained per different company sold.

AVERAGE COMPANY SALE (13-5)

CONSTRUCTION $\frac{\text{Cumulative sales this year}}{\text{Total number of companies sold this year}}$

CODES $\frac{62}{69}$

USE Assesses growth and future potential of salespersons; basis for rotating accounts; check economy of effort by Ratio (13-6).

EXPENSE-POTENTIAL INDEX (13-6)

CONSTRUCTION $\dfrac{\text{Customers' cumulative potential to this month}}{\text{Cumulative expenses this year}}$

CODES $\dfrac{\mathbf{60}}{\mathbf{70}}$

USE Shows how expenses have been justified by the level of obtainable customers' potential; check Ratio (13-7).

SALES-EXPENSE INDEX (13-7)

CONSTRUCTION $\dfrac{\text{Cumulative sales this year}}{\text{Cumulative expenses this year}}$

CODES $\dfrac{\mathbf{62}}{\mathbf{70}}$

USE Proof-of-the-pudding appraisal; this ratio relates the actual performance for the expenses disbursed.

AVERAGE ENTERTAINMENT ECONOMY (13-8)

CONSTRUCTION $\dfrac{\text{Cumulative sales this year}}{\text{Cumulative entertainment expenses}}$

CODES $\dfrac{\mathbf{62}}{\mathbf{72}}$

USE Relates the sales to date with the entertainment expenses to date; assesses judgment in employing the entertainment privilege as a sales tool, either in excess or insufficiently.

ENTERTAINMENT-POTENTIAL ECONOMY ________ (13-9)

CONSTRUCTION $\frac{\text{Customers' cumulative potential to this month}}{\text{Cumulative entertainment expenses}}$

CODES $\frac{60}{72}$

USE A refinement of Ratio (13-6) which pinpoints the justification of the entertainment segment of expenses; shows what trend the entertainment expenses should take.

It should be a truism that today's quotations are tomorrow's sales. Often a quotation does not become a sale, for many reasons. Among them are failure to get the full specifications from the customer, poor attitude, no follow-up, and delay in submitting estimates or samples. Expenses are incurred on behalf of both sales and quotations, and so a fair way of looking at the level incurred is to match it against the total of sales and quotations. The following ratios are some controls to help out.

QUOTATION ACCEPTANCE ________ (13-10)

CONSTRUCTION $\frac{\text{Cumulative sales this year}}{\text{Cumulative sales and quotations this year}}$

CODES $\frac{62}{62 + 65}$

USE Reciprocal of Ratio (13-11) showing the portion of total dollar activity converted into sales so far this year; both Ratios (13-10) and (13-11) show the effectiveness with which quotations are solicited and accepted.

QUOTATION MORTALITY (13-11)

CONSTRUCTION $$\frac{\text{Cumulative quotations to date} - \text{cumulative sales to date}}{\text{Cumulative quotations to date}}$$

CODES $$\frac{65 - 62}{65}$$

USE Assesses what portion of quotations is converted into sales; how that trend continues during the year.

EXPENSE PRODUCTIVITY (13-12)

CONSTRUCTION $$\frac{\text{Cumulative sales and quotations this year}}{\text{Cumulative expenses this year}}$$

CODES $$\frac{62 + 65}{70}$$

USE Relates the total of sales to date and quotations to date with the cumulative expenses.

TERTIARY RATIOS

A large number of elementary ratios may be constructed to evaluate certain segments of the sales effort. Each can accurately pinpoint a characteristic or a condition. However, there is a need for a more-condensed type of evaluating tool for busy management, to provide it with guides and trends. These condensed tools are devised by combining ratios into third-order, or tertiary-type, ratios, similar to procedure in the advanced control of production.

For example, in the last section it was desired to inquire about the productivity of expenses, to see its economic justification, considering the degree of quotation acceptance salespersons were receiving, the level of expense disbursements, and the amount of activity each salesperson was generating. To include all these factors of sales effort, a tertiary ratio is needed.

In the abovementioned example the tertiary ratio produced an index of expense justification. This evaluation was based on six months' data. Obviously, any final figure is the result of management or some type of overt control. Exhibit 13-3 is a listing of tertiary sales ratios and employee-department values.

TERTIARY SALES RATIOS

SALES, EXPENSES, AND CONTACT EFFECTIVENESS ______ (13-17)

CONSTRUCTION

$$\frac{\text{Cumulative sales per expense dollar}}{\text{Cumulative contacts per company sold}}$$

CODES

$$\frac{\textbf{Ratio (13-7)}}{\textbf{Ratio (13-14)}}$$

USE Integrates the level of sales and the expenses of obtaining those sales with the effectiveness used in obtaining accounts from which the sales developed.

CONTACT-ORDER PRODUCTIVITY TO DEPARTMENT PERFORMANCES ______ (13-18)

CONSTRUCTION

$$\frac{\text{Total accts. sold and quoted}}{\text{Total contacts made}} \times \frac{\text{total sales and quotations}}{\text{dept. total sales and quotations}}$$

CODES **Ratio (11-20) × Ratio (11-21)**

USE Relates the effectiveness of the contact effort, in terms of accounts sold and quoted, to the percentage of the department's total sales and quotation amounts obtained by the employee.

EXHIBIT 13-3 TERTIARY SALES RATIOS (EMPLOYEE)

Ratio No.	Name	Coded Constructions	Ratio Value of Salesperson				Department
			Jones	Smith	Brown	Greene	
(13-17)	Sales, expenses, and contact effectiveness	$\frac{\text{Ratio (13-7)}}{\text{Ratio (13-14)}}$	0.181	0.564	0.273	1.48	0.585
(13-18)	Contact-order productivity to department performance	Ratio (11-20) × Ratio (11-21)	0.0383	0.116	0.0526	0.468	
(13-19)	New account probability	Ratio (11-19) + Ratio (13-10)	0	0	0.0995	0.114	0.0694
(13-20)	New account probability—dollar-weighed	Ratio (11-19) × Ratio (13-10) × $\frac{19 + 20}{s + t}$	0	0	0.012	0.0953	
(13-21)	Index of probability	Ratio (13-1) × Ratio (13-10)	0.0477	0.140	0.0615	0.344	0.145
(13-22)	New sales and account performance	Ratio (11-1) × Ratio (11-2) × $\frac{19}{8}$	0	0	6.85	65.6	18.0
(13-23)	New product sales-contact-account performance	$\frac{\text{Ratio (11-5)} \times (14 + 19)/(3 + 8)}{\text{Ratio (11-27)}}$	0	112	62.5	901	317
(13-24)	New customer sales-contact-account performance	$\frac{\text{Ratio (11-5)}}{\text{Ratio (11-29)} \times 7/(8 + 9}$	0	0.0232	0.0495	0.248	0.0788
(13 .25)	Current trend index	$\frac{\text{Ratio (13-4)}}{\text{Ratio (13-5)}}$	0.243	0.37	0.18	0.13	0.202
(13-26)	Contact-potential performance	Ratio (13-1) × Ratio (13-2)	6.33	15.55	6.15	47	15.65
(13-27)	Account assignment justification	$\frac{62}{00}$ × Ratio (13-2)	1.85	4.24	0.98	12.95	
(13-28)	Expense justification	Ratio (13-6) × Ratio (13-10)	13.4	14.15	3.93	18.15	12.6
(13-29)	Compatibility index	Ratio (13-1) × Ratio (13-5)	0.373	0.382	0.404	3.60	0.853
(13-30)	Over-all performance index	Ratio (13-1) × Ratio (13-10) × Ratio (13-7)	0.393	1.61	0.459	10.9	2.12

NEW ACCOUNT PROBABILITY (13-19)

CONSTRUCTION
$$\frac{\text{New acct. quotations}}{\text{Total sales}} \times \frac{\text{cumulative sales to date}}{\text{cumulative sales and quotations to date}}$$

CODES **Ratio (11-19) × Ratio (13-10)**

USE Indicates the chances that the new-business attempts have in developing into new, booked business; effective as a counseling device.

INDEX OF PROBABILITY (13-21)

CONSTRUCTION
$$\frac{\text{Cumulative sales to date}}{\text{Cumulative customer potentials to date}} \times \frac{\text{cumulative sales to date}}{\text{cumulative customer potentials to date}}$$

CODES **Ratio (13-1) × Ratio (13-10)**

USE Shows how the degree of customers' potential obtained by each employee to date will be affected by the employee's record of quotation acceptance; a long-term evaluator of the employees and the department. It relates sales performance on potential to the amount and successes of obtaining quotation opportunities and then converting them into sales. Low scores are indications that management did not assign account potential in accordance with the expected performances of the employees.

NEW SALES AND ACCOUNT PERFORMANCE ______ (13-22)

CONSTRUCTION

$$\frac{\text{New sold accts. for new prods.}}{\text{Total accts. sold}} \times \frac{\text{new accts. sales for new prods.}}{\text{total sales}} \times \frac{\text{new accts. sales for new prods.}}{\text{new sold accts. for new prods.}}$$

CODES **Ratio (11-1) × Ratio (11-2) ×** $\frac{\mathbf{19}}{\mathbf{8}}$

USE Describes and evaluates the relationship between the new-customer, new-product accounts, and dollars sold as weighted in the total number of accounts and dollars sold. This tertiary ratio gives a balanced evaluation of the employee's efforts to obtain new-product business from new customers, without giving undue weight to either large sales dollars or a great number of accounts sold.

NEW PRODUCT SALES-CONTACT-ACCOUNT ______ (13-23)

CONSTRUCTION

$$\frac{\text{New product sales}}{\text{Total sales}} \times \frac{\text{total contacts}}{\text{new product contacts}} \times \frac{\text{new product sales}}{\text{new product accts. sold}}$$

CODES

$$\frac{\textbf{Ratio (11-6)} \times \textbf{(14 + 19)/(3 + 8)}}{\textbf{Ratio (11-27)}}$$

USE Evaluates the economic meaning of the new-product contact effort by integrating the proportion of the total sales that it represents, with the percentage of the total number of contacts it required to obtain those sales, with the size of the new-product account opened. This tertiary ratio is most valuable for the sales managers as a period evaluator of performance. Upper management is certainly interested in the department equivalent of this ratio since it furnishes an idea of how well the department is being managed.

NEW CUSTOMER SALES-CONTACT-ACCOUNT PERFORMANCE (13-24)

CONSTRUCTION

$$\frac{\text{New customer sales}}{\text{Total sales}} \times \frac{\text{total contacts}}{\text{new customer contacts}} \times \frac{\text{new customer accts. sold}}{\text{new customer contacts}}$$

CODES

$$\frac{\textbf{Ratio (11-5)}}{\textbf{Ratio (11-29)} \times \textbf{7/(8 + 9)}}$$

USE This ratio is of a somewhat different character from the one described above. It evaluates the economic meaning of new-customer sales consistent with the proportion of total contacts necessary to obtain them, and adds emphasis to the number of new accounts opened in proportion to the contacts made solely on their behalf. This type of ratio is for use by the sales manager; its departmental equivalent gives upper management an indication of the weighted direction in which the new-account effort is heading.

CURRENT TREND QUOTIENT (13-25)

CONSTRUCTION

$$\frac{\text{Sales this month}}{\text{Companies sold this month}} \times \frac{\text{total no. companies sold to date}}{\text{cumulative sales to date}}$$

CODES **$\frac{\text{Ratio (13-4)}}{\text{Ratio (13-5)}}$**

USE Relates the average company sales this month with the average company sales to date this year. Evaluates whether the employees and the department are advancing over the previous six months' sales productivity, or lagging. If the ratio value is below 1.00, it shows that present productivity is lagging; if it is above 1.00, it is showing an improvement over the past period.

CONTACT-POTENTIAL PERFORMANCE (13-26)

CONSTRUCTION

$$\frac{\text{Cumulative sales to date}}{\text{Customer cumulative potential to date}} \times \frac{\text{sales this month}}{\text{contacts this month}}$$

CODES **Ratio (13-1) × Ratio (13-2)**

USE Relates what each employee did with his assigned potential so far this year (six months), with his or her contacting effectiveness. This tertiary ratio shows the trend of the speed by which acquisition of customers' potential will be accomplished.

ACCOUNT ASSIGNMENT JUSTIFICATION INDEX (13-27)

CONSTRUCTION $\dfrac{\text{Cumulative sales to date}}{\text{Departmental customer cumulative potential to date}} \times \dfrac{\text{sales this month}}{\text{contacts this month}}$

CODES $\dfrac{\textbf{Ratio (13-2)} \times \textbf{62}}{\textbf{00}}$

USE Relates what percentage of the total departmental customer potential was sold by each employee, to his or her sales-contact productivity for the current month. It shows the validity of the assignment of accounts to each employee and thus rates the judgment of the sales manager.

EXPENSE JUSTIFICATION QUOTIENT (13-28)

CONSTRUCTION $\dfrac{\text{Customer cumulative potential to date}}{\text{Cumulative expenses to date}} \times \dfrac{\text{cumulative sales to date}}{\text{cumulative sales to date} + \text{cumulative quotations to date}}$

CODES **Ratio (13-6) × Ratio (13-10)**

USE Relates the degree of quotation acceptance to the expense level incurred as justified by the potential controlled by the employee.

COMPATIBILITY INDEX (13-29)

CONSTRUCTION

$$\frac{\text{Cumulative sales to date}}{\text{Cust. cumulative potential to date}} \times \frac{\text{cumulative sales to date}}{\text{total no. companies sold to date}}$$

CODES **Ratio (13-1) × Ratio (13-5)**

USE Relates the percentage of the customers' potential actually obtained to the average sale per company sold; the degree of compatibility between the buyer and seller. When the number of accounts sold for the sales made begins to rise, this is an indication that small amounts of sales are coming from each or that a few accounts are supplying the major amounts, the others not being given sufficient attention.

OVERALL PERFORMANCE INDEX (13-30)

CONSTRUCTION

$$\frac{\text{Cumulative sales to date}}{\text{Cust. cumulative potential to date}} \times \frac{\text{cumulative sales to date}}{\text{cumulative sales and quota to date}} \times \frac{\text{cumulative sales to date}}{\text{cumulative expenses to date}}$$

CODES **Ratio (13-1) × Ratio (13-10) × Ratio (13-7)**

USE This ratio is one of many overall ratios by which the major areas of an employee's effort can be evaluated. It is a long-range running appraiser which shows the total effect of his or her performance in obtaining the amount of customer potential represented by the accounts which he or she presently holds and the performance on quotation acceptance, plus the economy by which expenses were incurred.

CHAPTER FOURTEEN

INTRODUCTION TO FINANCIAL MANAGEMENT

The previous chapters dealt with the evaluation and control of the production and sales efforts. As we saw, autonomous decisions made in sales react in the production economy. It is essential that both efforts be measured by the same yardstick so that one standard goal can emerge.

PRODUCTION-SALES IMPACT ON CAPITAL

What has to be considered ultimately is the effect of the production and sales events on the financial affairs of the company. For what might be deemed a wise move for sales and production might be a weakening factor in the financial state of the company.

For example, sales and production might agree on the purchase of a new piece of equipment as being feasible and economical within their joint areas of operation, but this acquisition might involve short- or long-term loans that could place the creditors in the position of having more at stake in the business than the owners.

Actually, there are myriad moves which can validly be made in the sales-production area that can cause both positive and negative effects in the company's financial state of health. When some sales-production decisions are measured in the financial area, their impact may be great enough to reverse a decision. Decisions may enhance the financial state of health by having such positive effect in the financial area that production and sales may search for situations where the improvement in the financial structure is enough to justify a production or sales action.

Similarly to the previous treatment of the elementary control of production and sales, this section will deal first with the elementary evaluation of the capital structure—the financial health of the company. It will then discuss the evaluation of financial management, in the light of the needs of the production and sales efforts, and consistent with the needs to satisfy management's profit motives, as well as owners and creditors' needs. The section will then terminate with advanced evaluation and control of the capital structure.

THE CAPITAL STRUCTURE (BALANCE SHEET)

Profit is the goal and motive of business enterprise; one cannot exist without the other. Profit is an ambiguous work; it means many things, depending on the viewpoint of people. Manufacturing management regards profit as the earnings it makes on sales; the owners view profit as the return it obtains on their investment; those who look at profit more conservatively regard it as the return on the total resources used in the business, that is, on the total assets. The sales manager sees profits tied to volume. No one viewpoint is a panacea for profits.

It is possible, and happens often, that what is considered a meager return on sales is an adequate return on the invested funds. As a matter of fact, some owners (stockholders) object to expanding the profits on sales for fear of an effect on the capital structure which might limit the earnings on their investment. At the same time, a high return on sales is not necessarily a guarantee of an adequate return on investment.

The entire complex picture is further compounded by the inflationary speed with which the purchasing power of the dollar is decreased. This leads to burdens of future replacement, using "softer" dollars, and should force a cold realization of the overstated nature of corporate profits. These profits are chameleonlike and change color with variations in the purchasing value of the dollar.

If the company has a balanced capital architecture, that is, balanced to fit its needs today and then controlled so that it can meet the changed need next month, and if this structure is managed and balanced so that it supports the needs of production-sales consistent with its obligations to others, then the company is in the position of "making hay" out of every event that crosses its path. By "hay" is meant both positive and negative situations. Having control and integration of the total data allows an objective "no" as well as a "yes." Important also is that with the security of these data, executives are freed for wider activities, instead of being shackled by the gnawing doubts of subjective information and the pile of "reports" placed on their desks by, at times, self-seeking subordinates.

The goal of business enterprise should be the continuance of a profit with a continuance of a healthy financial state. The preservation or control of this financial state traditionally has been left to accountants. Yet if company-wide organic decisions are to emerge, there must be a basic understanding of these terms by management.

We are confident that in a short time there will be an appreciation of the meanings of optimizing the current assets in relation to sales; maintenance of proportions between the fixed and circulating capital; velocity of capital flow; state of liquidity; turnover of working capital and net worth; inventory turnover; return on invested capital; alternative choices of financing; etc. All these factors are affected by the bilateral decisions of production and sales.

To understand the capital structure, one must have familiarity with the *balance sheet*. This is a tabulation of the financial state of the company *at one instant*. The moment the balance sheet has been drawn up it is obsoleted by new facts—facts which are always changing, as we shall see later. Exhibit 14-1 presents a simplified and condensed balance sheet. While simplified in form, still it shows the health of the company and will not prevent readers from grasping the concepts and applying them to a specific plant.

Exhibit 14-2 is a graphic representation of the capital archi-

EXHIBIT 14-1 PRIMARY CAPITAL AND FINANCIAL DATA (BALANCE SHEET FORM)

Identifying Letters	Item
	ASSETS (*the present location of the capital*)
aa	Current (circulating capital)
aa	Cash
ab	Receivables (accounts, notes)
ac	Inventory
ad	Total current assets
	Fixed (fixed capital)
ae	Machinery
af	Land and buildings
ag	Total fixed assets
ah	TOTAL ASSETS
	LIABILITIES (*the source of the capital*) (*borrowed*)
	Current (short-term borrowed capital)
ai	Payables (account notes, loans)
aj	Total current liabilities
	Noncurrent (long-term borrowed capital)
ak	Payables (mortgages, bonds)
al	Total noncurrent fixed liabilities
am	TOTAL LIABILITIES
	NET WORTH (*the source of the capital*) (*owned*)
an	Issued capital stock
ao	Reserves
ap	Retained earnings
aq	TOTAL NET WORTH
ar	TOTAL LIABILITIES AND NET WORTH

Tangible net worth = aq = (an + ao + ap)
Working capital = ad − aj
Total capital employed = total assets = ah or ar
Funded debt = al

EXHIBIT 14-2 THE CAPITAL ARCHITECTURE

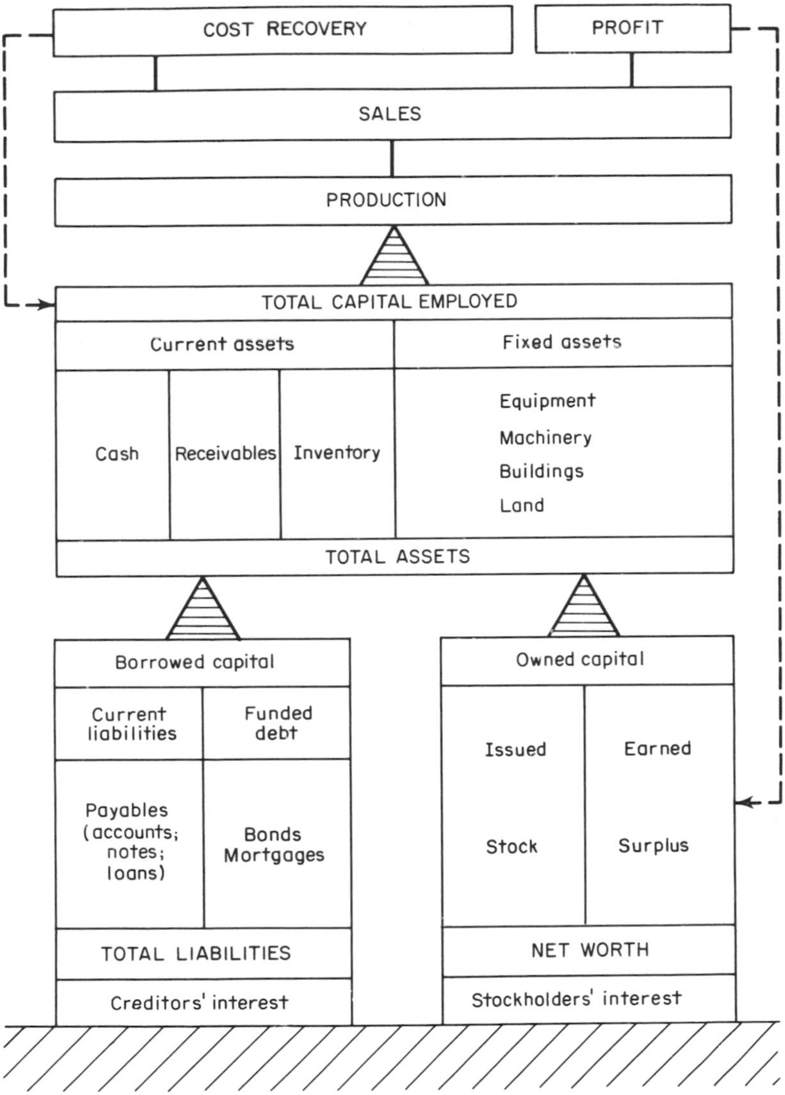

tecture. In essence, the capital, both owned and borrowed, supports the assets (the total capital employed), which in turn are used in manufacturing effort which produces sales. The total of the capital is used to finance the assets; therefore, all the capital employed is equal to all the assets. That is why the total assets are sometimes called the total capital *employed*.

While the total capital is equal to the total assets, the components within both these equal parts can exist in different proportions. Furthermore, these proportions are always in a state of flux. As goods are manufactured in production, the inventory level changes. The accounts receivables change as goods are shipped and invoices collected. The fixed property—the equipment—depreciates each second. The capital also changes: creditors are paid for raw materials, additional purchases made on credit, etc.

The total capital consists of two major parts: the owned capital, which is represented by the shares of stock issued, and the borrowed capital, which the company gets in the form of credit from its suppliers (current) and from bank loans for short periods (current) and that which is obtained on a longer term such as mortgages or bonds (funded) for which the company has pledged a portion of its assets. Borrowed capital, either short- or long-term, is termed liabilities. The owned capital is called the *net worth*. Since the total assets equal the sum of all the capital, it follows, then, that the net worth is equal to the total assets minus the liabilities.

IMPACT OF VARIATIONS IN IDENTICAL CAPITAL LEVELS

It is important for the reader to understand that given the same dollar amount of total assets, the state of health can vary from poor to excellent, depending on the internal proportions of the assets and the proportions between the liabilities and the net worth. For example, a company with total assets of $1 million might have a balance sheet with these proportions:

CASE 1:

Total assets	$1,000,000	Total liabilities	$ 200,000
		Net worth	$ 800,000
	$1,000,000		$1,000,000

Or it might have these proportions:

CASE 2:

Total assets	$1,000,000	Total liabilities	$ 800,000
		Net worth	$ 200,000
	$1,000,000		$1,000,000

Obviously, one of the above two conditions has to be better in a given situation than the other. Both have negative and positive aspects if viewed separately, that is, without the production-sales frame of reference, and without considering the specific industry.

Case 1 shows that the owners "own" the business; that is, the creditors' stake in the business is small compared with the owners' interest. That's a positive aspect. A negative one is that the owners' investment may be too big for the amount of money the company earns; that is, when the profit is compared with the invested capital, it may prove to be lower than what could be obtained from investing in other securities. As this amount grows, a given amount of profits provides a decreasing return on investment.

In Case 2, the creditors have four times the stake in the business of the owners; thus the business invariably is conducted more for the benefit of the creditors than for the benefit of the business. There are other considerations also in this simple proportion. If the company can obtain borrowed capital (loans) at interest rates which are below that which the company earns on the total capital employed, then the larger the proportion of total capital borrowed, the greater the return to the owners or stockholders. Again, an optimum has to be struck between the additional return and the added borrowed capital in relation to the safety of the company.

Let's now vary the assets side of the balance sheet to expand the two foregoing cases into four:

CASE 1A:

Cash	$ 100,000	Current liabilities	$ 200,000
Accounts receivable	600,000	Total liabilities	$ 200,000
Inventory	200,000	Net worth	800,000
Total current assets	$ 900,000		
Fixed assets	100,000		
Total assets	$1,000,000	Total liabilities + net worth	$1,000,000

CASE 1B:

Cash	$ 100,000	Current liabilities	$ 200,000
Accounts receivable	100,000	Total liabilities	$ 200,000
Inventory	100,000	Net worth	800,000
Total current assets	$ 300,000		
Fixed assets	700,000		
Total assets	$1,000,000	Total liabilities + net worth	$1,000,000

CASE 2A:

Cash	$ 100,000	Current liabilities	$ 200,000
Accounts receivable	600,000	Noncurrent liabilities	600,000
Inventory	200,000	Total liabilities	$ 800,000
Total current assets	$ 900,000	Net worth	200,000
Fixed assets	100,000		
Total assets	$1,000,000	Total liabilities + net worth	$1,000,000

CASE 2B:

Cash	$ 100,000	Current liabilities	$ 600,000
Accounts receivable	100,000	Noncurrent liabilities	200,000
Inventory	100,000	Total liabilities	$ 800,000
Total current assets	$ 300,000	Net worth	200,000
Fixed assets	700,000		
Total assets	$1,000,000	Total liabilities + net worth	$1,000,000

Now the problems have been compounded. In addition to the need for finding a balance in the company's financing, as mentioned above, we now have to manage the flow of the capital so that it is in the right place at the right time, i.e., so that it won't cripple operations or won't risk the solvency of the company.

In Case 1A, the division of the fixed and current assets appears sound, unless more equipment is needed in production and the asset tabulation represents an unwarranted frugality. However, in the composition of the current assets, of those assets which are easier to convert into cash if need should arise, two-thirds of them are in accounts receivables. This could be evidence of a poor collection policy or a lack of policing the receivables. As a matter of fact, with a net worth of $800,000 the stockholders' risk is in the hands of the customers; i.e., if the customers do not pay, the effect on the owners' interest is almost in direct proportion.

In Case 1B, the division of the assets leans heavily in favor of the fixed assets in machinery, land, and building—which cannot readily be converted into cash. This lower current asset level lowers the ability of the company to pay its current debts ($200,000) promptly and will make future creditors wary. And when fixed assets are such a large portion of the net worth, it could leave little opportunity for expansion.

In Case 2A, the state of the capital structure with respect to the company's ability to pay its debts promptly is the same as Case 1A, i.e., $900,000 of current assets to $200,000 of current liabilities. However, because of the laxity of collections, the company can be forced to get long-term loans. Obviously, as collections are accelerated, loan interest is saved and the capital structure becomes stronger. Here the creditors' risk is inherent in the worth of the accounts receivable.

In Case 2B, the situation is even worse. There are only 50 cents of current assets for every dollar of current liabilities. This might make mandatory the selling of capital equipment with which to pay current bills if the creditors applied pressure.

Variations like the above four are myriad, even within the same $1,000,000 context. And when the variations of sales levels, earnings, expense recovery, and the like are added, the impacts are considerable and widely different.

GENERATION OF EVENTS

The acts and events which cause changes in the balance sheet or capital structure can be generated from two directions:

1. From the needs in manufacturing: a machine is scrapped, replaced, and repaired; sales are accelerated; etc.
2. From the management of the movement of the funds: a lot of inventory is purchased on speculation; a credit policy is established; loans are made to improve the return on invested capital; etc.

Every act in sales, production, or in any other area of the company will have its effect on the company structure. A decision in sales, even though it has been tested as to its effect on production and found to be positive, *can cause a swing in the proportions of the assets in enough of a negative direction* to invalidate the sales decision. The reverse is also true: An autonomous decision in the financial area for the sake of capital security can have unsound impact on production.

INTEGRATION OF ALL COMPANY DATA

In ultimate total integration we are interested in just how the capital structure changes or would change based on decisions made or to be made elsewhere. We are interested in just how the management of money will support or does support these decisions. In the broadest sense, we want to know how decisions in any one of the three major areas affect the other two so that they can be pretested, so that their effect can be predicted in advance.

Unlike the management of production or sales, the management of money in the business has one important difference. In the management of production or sales the effort is internal and fully controllable, involving people who the company directs. However, in the management of the business funds, if the capital structure is not sound, then the manager finds that "outsiders" over whom he or she has no control begin to figure prominently in the table of organization.

These outsiders are the creditors, principally, who in spite of all the manager's operating and sales efficiency might force him to make decisions which are best for the creditors and poorest for his business. Nonmanaging, nonemployee stockholders are also outside the day-to-day control of management; they very often have a limited viewpoint and an inflexible standard of company growth and efficiency. Often their definitions do not fall within the framework of what management considers to be top effectiveness in manufacturing.

A properly designed and maintained capital structure removes these problems, but it must be policed constantly lest it create problems over which management may not have direct control.

THE OPERATING PERFORMANCE (PROFIT-AND-LOSS STATEMENT)

This is a statement of how well management operated its business in the previous period with the resources listed on the balance sheet. This statement shows the final result of the effectiveness of operating during a period, but it does not show the contributing reasons for the performance.

All net profits are comprised of gross losses and gross profits, and by seeing them both we can remedy the losses and act intelligently on the profits. The gross profits, then, are more properly termed the *profit-making factors* and the gross losses labeled the *profit-losing factors*. Both are *opportunities*.

An income statement shows the subtraction of both the above factors; it does not show how much of each was present. Unless management can see the actual profit-factor recipe, it cannot act. And unless the facts are available in time, the action taken will be wasted. The annual or even quarterly income statement is issued too late *after the facts* for objective action.

However, the income statement is valuable for indicating some important *characteristics* of the company, those best evaluated over a longer period. Among them are the elements of fixed and direct costs incurred in the production of sales. The firm with a large fixed element of expense makes a profit over a narrower range of sales and is vulnerable to lowered price levels

EXHIBIT 14-3 PRIMARY CAPITAL AND FINANCIAL DATA (P&L FORM)

Identifying Letters	Item
ba	Net sales
bb	Direct material cost
bc	Direct labor cost
bd	Total indirect labor cost
be	Nonproductive manufacturing labor cost
bf	Maintenance and repair labor cost
bg	Supervisory labor cost
bh	Total nonlabor manufacturing expenses
bi	Machinery and space costs
bj	Power costs
bk	Total stand-by expenses
bl	Depreciation charges
bm	Insurance expenses
bn	Rent and taxes
bo	Cost of goods sold (factory cost)
bp	*Gross profit*
bq	Total variable G&A expenses
br	Management costs
bs	Services and supplies
bt	Total variable selling expenses
bu	Salaries and commissions
bv	Service and supplies
bw	Contact expenses
bx	Total standby expenses
by	Basic business management costs
bz	Basic sales management costs
ca	Depreciation charges
cb	Insurance expenses
cc	Rent and taxes
cd	Interest on loans
ce	Cost of sales (total cost)
cf	*Net profit*

EXHIBIT 14-3 (*Continued*)

Prime cost	=	bb + bc
Factory cost	=	bo
Total cost	=	ce
Total overhead	=	bd + bh + bk + bq + bt + bx
Factory overhead	=	bd + bh + bk
Conversion cost	=	ce − bb
Fixed charges	=	bk + bx
Variable expenses	=	bb + bc + bd + bh + bq + bt
Cost of owning fixed asset	=	bf + bi + bk
Cost of sales	=	ce

and recessions. Knowing these company traits allows us to make general evaluations.

Exhibit 14-3 is a format of an income statement prevalently used in industry. This profit-and-loss structure is more-or-less conventional, but not the type recommended by the author for internal reporting. A more modern form is the *direct-cost* income statement.[1] Readers who use that form can easily apply the control principles stated herein. Nevertheless, Exhibit 14-3 is generalized enough for widest application.

---

[1] See Spencer A. Tucker, *Pricing for Higher Profit*, New York: McGraw-Hill, 1966 and *The Complete Machine-Hour Rate System for Cost-Estimating and Pricing*, Englewood Cliffs, N.J.: Prentice-Hall, 1971.

CHAPTER FIFTEEN

BASIC CONTROL RATIOS FOR FINANCE

In the previous chapter we noted that the balance sheet and the income statement are composed of various segments. These segments in themselves are meaningless unless contained in some frame of reference. As was done for the production and sales sections of this book, we shall develop ratios which relate one segment with another. Ratios from elements on the balance sheet will be developed, and ratios which relate items in the balance sheet with items in the income statement will also be constructed.

PUBLISHED DATA

Available traditional ratios have been able to assess the level of profits, areas of over- or underinvestment, lack of capital, and trends toward insolvency. These ratios have varied, depending on the type of industry involved. Thus one could expect to find a high proportion of the total assets in equipment for a machine-tool or chemical-processing plant and a low proportion for the radio-assembly plant that uses little fixed assets.

Those ratios are not absolute measures: what's good for one plant may spell disaster for another. The fixed assets to the net worth of a corrugated-container plant at 60% may be considered satisfactory, but apply that to a manufacturer of men's suits and the company is dead. These ratios are indicators only, and rough indicators at that.

Since the ratios are approximate, there is a wide latitude of values within which similar companies operate, and in that range there exists a powerful leverage for increased profits and growth. A few percentage points difference in some ratios holds the clue to perhaps as much or more profit percentage points.

EVENTS VARY RATIO VALUES

We recognize that some of these ratios move faster than others. That means that events in production and sales have varying effects on these ratios. Also, one ratio will have an effect upon another. What remains to be discussed is the significance of these movements, so that proper evaluations can be determined and acted upon.

Some companies used published ratios in order to find out how well they are doing in their industry. In such cases, the ratios are used so that a company can compare its figures with those of competitors and get some measure of self-appraisal.

While this practice has merit, it has elements of inequity too. To appraise a company fairly, the probability of survival has to be integrated with its growth potential and the likely speed of attainment. The traditional financial and operating ratios are concerned with what *is* or what *should be*. In this section we are concerned with *why* they are, and *what causes* them to be. We consider their movements with respect to each other as a key to some other circumstance which can be controlled. Some of the ratios shown will be of the traditional type; others will be new, developed especially for management control.

RATIO MOVEMENTS

This point must be emphasized: the isolated value of a ratio is not given as much importance as its movement from period to period and its interrelation with other ratios. Consider that, like all other matter, the business effort has dimensions, even a fourth dimension. The balance sheet is a report on the state of health of the business at any given moment, and actually it is obsoleted the second it is drawn, because new balance sheet *data*, as yet unwritten, is born to take its place.

The balance sheet, which is a report on the capital structure of the company and the result of financial management, is in a constant state of flux. People cause the facts on the financial statement to *happen* and to *change*. A change in a ratio is the result of the way people acted and affects the capital structure. How the financial function operates to obtain the greatest gain for the company from these effects is the subject of this chapter.

Not all events cause the same volatility of change. Fixed assets in relation to total assets do not change as fast, usually, as the direct labor cost to sales does or the circulating capital changes in relation to sales.

RATIO DATA

Ratios are constructed from balance sheet items and from those items that involve balance sheet and operating data. In the balance sheet grouping, we have those which are a measure of monetary management and those which appraise the structure of capital financing.

It is not the author's purpose to dwell on financial theory. There are many textbooks on that subject for those who are interested in going into further technical details. The primary purpose here is to remove the mystery which seems to enshroud this area and to lay the groundwork for the understanding of the evaluation and control ratios presented later. Essentially, this is a book on control which must integrate all areas if each is to act as part of an organic whole instead of as separate autonomous parts.

APPLICATION OF RATIOS

The typical and traditional financial ratios are effective in getting fast appraisals of the capital status. When ratios involve financial and operating data, trends are seen, especially as regards the productivity of capital and the coordination between the controller, the plant manager, and those who do the purchasing. Sometimes seemingly negative-acting ratio results are desirable from the overall company standpoint if they are more than compensated for elsewhere positively. Perhaps a large inventory is part of a plan to use heretofore unused capacity, the expense recovery from which will more than offset inventory risks.

But ratios are not only used for decision making, they are used for balanced evaluators of conditions. The ratios act as watchdogs. Functioning with valid and balanced judgment, they furnish a device or standard against which decisions can be tested.

The maximum profits to be earned on the total capital employed is the result of the balanced and optimum levels or movements in the areas of pricing keyed to the market; costing for maximum expense recovery; facility utilization; the productivity of the capital structure; and the balancing of sources of investment.

RATIO NOT ABSOLUTE

In the MC concept we are not interested in testing where a particular company ranks against an arbitrary average setup for its industry by various organizations. This does not mean that such standards do not serve a purpose. They do, for purposes of deciding whether or not creditors should sell materials to the company or whether a bank should lend money to a company. For internal control, however, they are not necessarily valid and can be misleading. The author has seen, time after time, situations where the management took pains to keep certain of their ratios within the limits established for their particular industry by impartial organizations and wound up in serious financial difficulty.

For example, a manufacturer always tried to tie her sales and inventory together in a relationship that would be "normal" for her industry. If the industry called for an inventory turnover of 6 (sales/inventory), then as her sales rose, she would permit the level of her inventory to rise in the proportion that always yielded a turnover of 6. What was happening elsewhere in her capital structure was that the amount of capital tied up in inventory was getting too excessive for the net worth of the company, irrespective of its relationship to sales. When this ratio of sales to inventory is not tied to some other factor in the company, like net worth, then the increase in sales can force the company into bankruptcy.

This would seem to indicate that the capital structure cannot be evaluated by the single traditional ratio, but of necessity several must be cast into a composite ratio for a more complete evaluation. However, before such composite ratios can be designed and understood, the elementary type must be constructed and explained. The balance of this chapter is devoted to simple ratios, some of which are of the traditional variety and some of which have been developed to support the aims of control.

ELEMENTARY FINANCIAL RATIOS

Exhibit 15-1 is a tabulation of elementary ratios involving balance sheet and operating data. The formula terms utilize the coded data of Exhibits 14-1 and 14-3. Both the typical and the specially constructed ratios are shown, some of which are described below:

NET-WORTH TURNOVER ____________________ (15-1)

CONSTRUCTION $\frac{\text{Net sales}}{\text{Net worth}}$

CODES $\frac{\textbf{ba}}{\textbf{aq}}$

USE This ratio has different meaning for different classes of interests. From the commercial point of view, it indicates overtrading if it is too large or insufficient volume if too low. From the financial viewpoint, it measures the velocity of the turnover of the invested capital. From the economic angle, it measures the activity of the money which the stockholders have put up as risk. From the investors' standpoint, the higher the ratio, the better the risk.

EXHIBIT 15-1 ELEMENTARY FINANCIAL AND CAPITAL RATIOS

Ratio No.	Ratio Title	Abbreviation	Coded Constructions
(15-1)	Net worth turnover*	NS/NW	ba/aq
(15-2)	Inventory turnover*	NS/INV	ba/ac
(15-3)	Return on invested capital*	NP/NW	cf/aq
(15-4)	Return on total resources*	NP/TCE	cf/ah
(15-5)	Total asset productivity*	NS/TA	ba/ah
(15-6)	Asset balance index*	NP/WC	cf/(ad − aj)
(15-7)	Turnover of working capital*	NS/WC	bb/(ad − aj)
(15-8)	Sales-liability index	TL/NS	am/ba
(15-9)	Collection effectiveness	NS/REC	ba/ab
(15-10)	Net profit	NP/NS	cf/ba
(15-11)	Fixed-asset productivity*	NS/FA	ba/ag
(15-12)	The current ratio*	CA/CL	ad/aj
(15-13)	Inventory-net worth index	INV/NW	ac/aq
(15-14)	Owned capital index*	NW/TCE	aq/ah
(15-15)	Inventory-asset index*	INV/CA	ac/ad
(15-16)	Owned-long-term borrowed capital index	NW/FL	aq/al
(15-17)	Working capital density*	INV/WC	ac/(ad − aj)
(15-18)	Borrowed-owned capital balance*	CL/NW	aj/aq
(15-19)	Fixed capital utilization*	FA/NW	ag/aq
(15-20)	Fixed-asset index	FA/TA	ag/ah
(15-21)	Working capital-funded debt balance	FL/WC	al/(ad − aj)
(15-22)	Lenders' safety factor	FL/FA	al/ag
(15-23)	Owned working capital	WC/CA	(ad − aj)/ad
(15-24)	Borrowed-owned total capital balance*	TL/NW	am/ar
(15-25)	Inventory-capital index*	INV/CL	ac/aj
(15-26)	Inventory-receivables balance*	INV/REC	ac/ab

* Described in text.

Use this ratio to judge whether overtrading or undertrading is present. Overtrading refers to a high level of sales for the capital invested, which invariably requires higher credit to the point where the creditors have more capital at stake than the owners. As the ratio of liabilities to net worth increases, the creditors' margin of safety is reduced and the company may be in serious difficulty, with a drop in earnings or a general trend toward price reduction.

INVENTORY TURNOVER (15-2)

CONSTRUCTION $\frac{\text{Net sales}}{\text{Inventory}}$

CODES $\frac{\textbf{ba}}{\textbf{ac}}$

USE Relates the size of the inventory to the sales; evaluates the existence of obsolescence in inventory. A better test would be one which eliminated the distortion of profits. The ratio would be modified to cost of sales to inventory = ce/ac. The ratio measures the judgment used in the purchase of materials considering the production characteristics of the firm and the need to maintain proportion between the raw materials, work-in-process, and the finished goods. The length of the production cycle and the availability of inventory also figure in this appraisal.

RETURN ON INVESTED CAPITAL (15-3)

CONSTRUCTION $\dfrac{\text{Net profits}}{\text{Tangible net worth}}$

CODES $\dfrac{\textbf{cf}}{\textbf{aq}}$

USE Measures the return on stockholders investment, i.e., the productivity of the owners' invested capital. This ratio shows the success of the business and the effectiveness with which it invested its money compared with probable return from investment in other securities.

RETURN ON TOTAL RESOURCES (15-4)

CONSTRUCTION $\dfrac{\text{Net profits}}{\text{Total capital employed}}$

CODES $\dfrac{\textbf{cb}}{\textbf{ah}}$

USE Shows how many asset dollars are required to produce a dollar's worth of profit. This ratio is helpful in assessing, in general, the profit-asset relationship for different lines of products. In particular, it is most revealing in rating similar plants in a multiplant operation. The ratio expresses the profitability on the use of all the resources of the business and is often mistaken for the return on investment ratio. It measures the effectiveness of management, but is not suitable for investors' evaluation. It shows the return on the total capital employed regardless of its source.

TOTAL ASSET PRODUCTIVITY (15-5)

CONSTRUCTION $\frac{\text{Net sales}}{\text{Total assets}}$

CODES $\frac{\textbf{ba}}{\textbf{ah}}$

USE Provides a general evaluation of how well the resources of the firm are being used. It rates the overall effectiveness of the business and the productivity of its total assets. Useful in observing what happens when it is subdivided into the major elements of fixed assets and inventories in relation to sales.

ASSET BALANCE INDEX (15-6)

CONSTRUCTION $\frac{\text{Net profits}}{\text{Net working capital}}$

CODES $\frac{\textbf{cf}}{\textbf{ad} - \textbf{aj}}$

USE This ratio is valuable for determining certain trends which otherwise are not revealed by other ratios. For example, it is intimately related to net profit to sales. When it is divided by this latter ratio, the result is sales to working capital, ba/(ad − aj); when divided by net profit to net worth, the result is net worth to working capital, aq/(ad − aj). When it climbs, it is an indication that fixed assets are restricting the level of current assets required to carry the large volume of sales. The speed of the climb or rate of change is dependent on the incremental change in fixed assets.

TURNOVER OF WORKING CAPITAL ______ (15-7)

CONSTRUCTION $\dfrac{\text{Net sales}}{\text{Net working capital}}$

CODES $\dfrac{\mathbf{ba}}{\mathbf{ad - aj}}$

USE Measures the effectiveness of the working capital as a confirming health check on the turnover of net worth. While the latter may be acceptable, the presence of a high level of fixed assets may show the working capital to be low, and hence there will be a high value or turnover for this ratio. The ratio net worth to working capital confirms this. In the event of the lack of working capital, additional sums will have to be raised by borrowing rather than ownership because of the large residual magnitude of the owned capital. This would show up as a high ratio or turnover in this ratio.

FIXED-ASSET PRODUCTIVITY ______ (15-11)

CONSTRUCTION $\dfrac{\text{Net sales}}{\text{Fixed assets}}$

CODES $\dfrac{\mathbf{ba}}{\mathbf{ag}}$

USE This ratio indicates the power, virility, and productivity of the equipment and the other capital investments. It is a significant ratio giving an indication of the elasticity of the business, showing how broad or restricted the range is in which sales are made at a profit. If the ratio is high, the standby, or period, expenses are low, the break-even point is low, and there is opportunity for profit to be made over a wider range of sales. As the ratio decreases, it could be an indication of insufficient sales, even with a balanced fixed-asset–net-worth structure; or if the sales level is acceptable, it could be that the level of fixed assets is too high for what the sales effort can reasonably produce and/or too high in comparison with net worth. In the latter case it produces a low elasticity and a consequent lower range of sales over which profits can be earned.

THE CURRENT RATIO (15-12)

CONSTRUCTION $\frac{\text{Current assets}}{\text{Current liabilities}}$

CODES $\frac{\textbf{ad}}{\textbf{aj}}$

USE Appraises the ability of the company to meet its current debts promptly. The ratio is not a particularly accurate barometer because of the varying proportions of cash, accounts receivables, and inventory that comprise the current asset.

OWNED CAPITAL INDEX (15-14)

CONSTRUCTION $\frac{\text{Net worth}}{\text{Total assets}}$

CODES $\frac{\textbf{aq}}{\textbf{ah}}$

USE This ratio shows how much of the business is owned by the stockholders. It is the cornerstone of the capital structure, for it clearly shows the respective interests of the owned and borrowed capital. Therefore, to see what percentage of the business is *not* owned by the owners, the ratio of total liabilities over total assets, am/ah, would apply.

INVENTORY-ASSET INDEX (15-15)

CONSTRUCTION $\frac{\text{Inventory}}{\text{Current assets}}$

CODES $\frac{\textbf{ac}}{\textbf{ad}}$

USE A basic and simple ratio used for measuring the liquidity of the current assets on the theory that the greater the proportion of inventory in the circulating capital, the less the liquidity *level* of that capital.

WORKING-CAPITAL DENSITY (15-17)

CONSTRUCTION $\frac{\text{Inventory}}{\text{Net working capital}}$

CODES $\frac{\textbf{ac}}{\textbf{ad} - \textbf{aj}}$

USE This ratio appraises management's judgment in proportioning its net working capital to the least liquid or densest segment of that capital. Obviously, if it invests too much in inventory, it not only limits the liquidity of the working capital, it may be indicative of poor judgment in balancing stocking and selling.

BORROWED-OWNED CAPITAL BALANCE ________(15-18)

CONSTRUCTION $\frac{\text{Current liabilities}}{\text{Tangible net worth}}$

CODES $\frac{\mathbf{aj}}{\mathbf{aq}}$

USE Shows the proportion between the creditors' working capital in relation to the investment of the owners. Expressed in terms of time, this ratio relates the short-term borrowed capital to the owned capital. It evaluates the protection offered to its creditors by the owners.

FIXED CAPITAL UTILIZATION ________________(15-19)

CONSTRUCTION $\frac{\text{Fixed assets}}{\text{Tangible net worth}}$

CODES $\frac{\mathbf{ag}}{\mathbf{aq}}$

USE Shows the relationship of the owned capital to the investment in productive facilities; measures the utilization of the owned capital in current assets.

BORROWED-OWNED TOTAL CAPITAL BALANCE _(15-24)

CONSTRUCTION $\frac{\text{Total liabilities}}{\text{Tangible net worth}}$

CODES $\frac{\mathbf{am}}{\mathbf{aq}}$

USE Indicates the proportion of the creditors' capital to the total capital; shows the relative interests of the stockholders and the creditors. A ratio value of unity would mean that the creditors supplied $1 for every $1 contributed by the owners.

INVENTORY-CAPITAL INDEX (15-25)

CONSTRUCTION $\dfrac{\text{Inventory}}{\text{Current liabilities}}$

CODES $\dfrac{\textbf{ac}}{\textbf{aj}}$

USE A comparison between obligations which require quick payment and the least liquid of the assets. Since inventory cannot be considered as payment for current debt, this ratio dramatizes the need for an adequate balance among the current assets and also indicates the need for additional working capital that should be supplied by the owners.

INVENTORY-RECEIVABLES BALANCE (15-26)

CONSTRUCTION $\dfrac{\text{Inventory}}{\text{Receivables}}$

CODES $\dfrac{\textbf{ac}}{\textbf{ab}}$

USE Measures the balance between the two least liquid of the current assets.

CHAPTER SIXTEEN

ADVANCED CONTROL RATIOS FOR FINANCE

The previous chapter dealt with the development of simple ratios, what causes their special movements, and how they move with respect to each other. A single ratio evaluates a segment of the capital structure but is unreliable for assessing the structure as a whole. Other factors previously remaining within satisfactory limits begin to go haywire and threaten the foundation of the company.

What should management do about it? How can it get simple, believable data from which to appraise its company? The manager must have the appraisal-making data so that the things he or she wants to do in the company can be reflected in the data. These data should be condensed for convenience so that he or she can quickly grasp the direction in which the company is heading and can extract the factors most responsible.

TERTIARY RATIOS NEEDED

As was done for production and sales, tertiary ratios are developed which integrate various capital effects so that an in-depth appraisal can be made. Tertiary ratios combine the elementary ratios so that a condensed picture of the total movement can be ascertained. Most of the tertiary ratios developed here report on major segments of the capital structure; some assess the total capital improvement or regression; and some evaluate total company performance, including the results of operating.

RATIOS OF COMPOSITE CHARACTERISTICS

Instead of trying to integrate one ratio with all the others, it is possible to relate several of the more important ratios to a larger ratio representing a composite of all the characteristics. This larger ratio is the tertiary ratio. It is easy to construct and calculate *but* it must be designed to support the *needs* and major *characteristics* of the company. Thus the ratio of FA/NW would not be included in a tertiary ratio for a company doing hand assembly of a wide number of items. Obviously, the relationship of inventory, working capital, net worth, and current liabilities would have to be given preference, because these factors would truly affect the overall economy and stability of the company to a greater degree than would the change in fixed assets, which might only consist of factory benches and small hand tools. Keep in mind that the tertiary ratio is assessing the positive or negative *changes* in the structure, not the absolute economic value of assets.

CONSTRUCTION OF TERTIARY RATIOS

Exhibit 16-1 shows a tabulation of various types of tertiary ratio (TR) constructed from the elementary ratios listed in Chapter 15, together with some simple ratios which are obvious and need no special description. Some of these are developed for specific situations, to keep a watchful check on certain conditions; some can be used universally. In general, the ratios deal with the evaluation and control of the state of the capital structure or of financial management; in more specific cases, they report on the structure of the capital together with the results of operating—more like an upper-management tool.

The specific situations for which some of these ratios are developed deal with just when and for what reason the tertiary control is established. If the tertiary controls are installed in a normally healthy and functioning company, then the TR should

EXHIBIT 16-1 TERTIARY FINANCIAL AND CAPITAL RATIOS

Ratio No.	Formula
(16-1)*	$\left(\frac{NP}{NS} + \frac{NP}{NW} + \frac{CA}{TCE}\right) \times \frac{NS}{TCE}$
(16-2)*	$\frac{NS}{INV} \times \frac{WC}{TCE}$
(16-3)*	$\left(\frac{NP}{NS} + \frac{NP}{NW}\right)\frac{CA}{TCE} \times \frac{NS}{TCE}$
(16-4)	$\frac{NP}{TCE} \times CR$
(16-5)*	$\frac{NP}{TCE} \times CR \times \frac{NW}{TL}$
(16-6)*	$\frac{CA}{TCE} \times \frac{NS}{TL}$
(16-7)*	$\frac{NP}{TCE} \times \frac{NS}{CL}$
(16-8)	$\frac{CA}{TCE} \times \frac{NS}{CL}$
(16-9)*	$\frac{NP}{TCE} \times \frac{NS}{TL}$
(16-10)*	$\frac{NP}{NW} \times \frac{NS}{CL}$
(16-11)	$\frac{NP}{TCE} \times \frac{NS}{CA}$
(16-12)*	$\frac{NS}{TCE} \times \frac{CA}{INV} \times \frac{WC}{NW} \times \left(\frac{NP}{NS} + \frac{NP}{NS}\right)$
(16-13)*	$\frac{NP}{NW}\left(\frac{NW}{NW + NS}\right)_a$ or $\frac{NP}{NS}\left(\frac{NS}{NW + NS}\right)_b$
(16-14)*	Ratio $(16\text{-}13)_a \times CR$
(16-15)	$\frac{NP}{NW} \times \frac{TL}{NS}$ or $\frac{NP}{NS} \times \frac{TL}{NW}$

* Described in text.

EXHIBIT 16-1 (*Continued*)

Ratio No.	Formula
(16-16)	$\frac{NW}{TL} + \frac{CA}{TCE} + \frac{TCE}{FA} + \frac{TL}{CL} + \frac{NW}{TCE} + \frac{CA}{INV} + \frac{WC}{TCE}$
(16-17)	$\frac{INV}{CA} \times \frac{CL}{NW}$
(16-18)*	$\frac{NW}{FA + WC}$
(16-19)*	$\frac{CA/CL + CL/NW + NS/INV}{FA/NW + FL/WC + TL/NW + INV/WC}$
(16-20)	$\frac{CA/CL + CL/NW}{FA/NW + FL/WC + TL/NW + INV/WC}$
(16-21)	$\frac{CA/CL \times NP/TL \times NS/INV}{CA/NW(FA/NW + FL/WC)}$
(16-22)*	$\frac{CA/CL \times NP/TL}{CL/NW(FA/NW + FL/WC)}$
(16-23)*	Ratio (15-5) $\times \frac{NS}{INV}$
(16-24)	$\frac{\left[\left(\frac{CA}{TCE} + \frac{NW}{TL}\right)\frac{NP}{NW}\right]\frac{NW}{TCE} + \left[\left(\frac{NS}{NW} + \frac{NS}{AR + INV}\right)\frac{NP}{NS}\right]\frac{TL}{TCE}}{CL/CA + TL/TCE + CL/NS}$
(16-25)*	$\frac{CA/TCE + CA/CL}{FA/TCE + TCE/NW}$
(16-26)*	Ratio (16-25) $\times \frac{CA}{TL} \times \frac{NW}{FA + WC}$
(16-27)*	Ratio (16-25) $\times \frac{CA}{TL} \times \frac{NP}{NS}$
(16-28)*	Ratio (16-25) $\times \frac{CA}{TL} \times \frac{NP}{NW}$
(16-29)*	Ratio (16-26) $\times \frac{NP}{TCE}$
(16-30)*	Ratio (16-25) $\times \frac{NW}{FA + WC}$

* Described in text.

be of the generalized type, but one which reflects some of the major facets of the company's financial and operating personality. In this sense, then, companies select ratios by equating their critical capital characteristics with an important term in the equation.

In other situations, the TR controls could be installed at the development of a very serious condition in the company's life, which could have been prevented had the TR been installed earlier. In this case, TR's are selected which specifically report on the most serious negative factors. Often, several TR's are used simultaneously to report on major areas, together with a more general type which assesses growth and operating performance.

The following is a brief description of some of the ratios shown in Exhibit 16-1.

ADVANCED FINANCIAL RATIOS

(16-1)

CONSTRUCTION $$\left(\frac{NP}{NS} + \frac{NP}{NW} + \frac{CA}{TCE}\right) \times \frac{NS}{TCE}$$

USE Reports on profitability consistent with liquidity and the use of the company's total resources. It is used to show how the effect of the productivity of the total resources on the profits is modified by the magnitude of the circulating capital in the total capital employed. In some situations it shows what effect an increase in inventory will have on the structure without an acceptable increase in sales.

(16-2)

CONSTRUCTION $$\frac{NS}{INV} \times \frac{WC}{TCE}$$

USE Shows the effect of inventory turnover on the working capital position by considering the effect of rising liabilities.

(16-3)

CONSTRUCTION $\left(\frac{NP}{NS} + \frac{NP}{NW}\right)\frac{CA}{TCE} \times \frac{NS}{TCE}$

USE This ratio is similar to Ratio (16-1) but has greater emphasis on the use of the company's total resources. This control is suitable for companies in industries which normally have a high level of fixed assets in total assets. These are industries which sell machine time, such as machine shops, and those in the graphic arts.

(16-5)

CONSTRUCTION $\frac{NP}{TCE} \times CR \times \frac{NW}{TL}$

USE Reports on what Ratio (16-4) does but with the added factor of ownership. It shows whether or not the above ratio grew at the sacrifice of loss of ownership and a consequent increase in the creditors' stake in the business.

(16-6)

CONSTRUCTION $\frac{CA}{TCE} \times \frac{NS}{TL}$

USE It shows the impact on the liabilities of sales increases.

(16-7)

CONSTRUCTION $\frac{NP}{TCE} \times \frac{NS}{CL}$

USE This is widely used, showing how the changes in sales levels affect both the current liabilities and the results from using the total resources.

(16-9)

CONSTRUCTION $\frac{NP}{TCE} \times \frac{NS}{TL}$

USE Shows the effect on the TL caused by sales increases which are justified by the profit increases on the total resources. This ratio is quick to show misleading practices of technical accounting rules about the classifications of the current liabilities.

(16-10)

CONSTRUCTION $\frac{NP}{NW} \times \frac{NS}{CL}$

USE Shows the effect of the degree of liquidity of the CA. As inventory and accounts receivables rise for the same sales level, the ratio will decrease. The poor mixture of the CA may be justified by a sufficient rise in profits.

(16-12)

CONSTRUCTION $\frac{NS}{TCE} \times \frac{CA}{INV} \times \frac{WC}{NW} \times \left(\frac{NP}{NS} + \frac{NP}{NS} \right)$

USE Shows the effect of the inventory turnover on the working capital, consistent with the use of resources and their productivity. It is actually a balancing of inventory, working capital, and the productivity of resources. Another way that this tertiary control can be regarded is as showing the trend of effect that the productivity of the total resources, the mixture of the current assets, and the relationship between the working capital and the net worth have on the operating performance.

(16-13)

CONSTRUCTION $\frac{NP}{NW}\left(\frac{NW}{NW+NS}\right)_a$ or $\frac{NP}{NS}\left(\frac{NS}{NW+NS}\right)_b$

USE This control presents a weighted profit performance between that made on sales and on invested capital.

(16-14)

CONSTRUCTION Ratio (16-13*a*) × CR

USE Makes use of the above ratio and shows the effect of sales-investment profits on the current position. If the NW rises with the same profit, Ratio (16-13*a*) decreases; but when NW rises, TL decreases, and if CL maintains the same proportion in the TL, the CR will rise enough to show a rise in the entire expression. A drop could be an indication of a weakening current position, even at the same level of profits; or maybe increases in sales are not being justified by an improvement in capital structure.

(16-18)

CONSTRUCTION $\frac{NW}{FA + WC}$

USE This is not as much a tertiary ratio as it is a special form of elementary ratio. It is used as a term in other tertiary ratios and is helpful in evaluating the trend of the NW as to its sufficiency in covering the fixed assets and working capital.

(16-19)

CONSTRUCTION $\frac{CA/CL + CL/NW + NS/INV}{FA/NW + FL/WC + TL/NW + INV/WC}$

USE Evaluates the effectiveness of financial management in industries which do not have high inventory turnovers, i.e., foundries, lumber mills, machinery builders, etc. It is useful in most business as an evaluator of the consistency of financial management.

(16-22)

CONSTRUCTION $\frac{CA/CL \times NP/TL}{CL/NW(FA/NW + FL/WC)}$

USE This is another financial type of tertiary ratio, but with the emphasis on the current liabilities.

(16-23)

CONSTRUCTION $\text{Ratio (15-5)} \times \frac{NS}{INV}$

USE This tertiary ratio is of importance in checking on the liabilities position in those industries tending to overtrade. It is considered an integration of the financial structure with the company's capacity and the utilization of its capacity.

(16-25)

CONSTRUCTION $\frac{CA/TCE + CA/CL}{FA/TCE + TCE/NW}$

USE Reports on the *state* of the capital structure without any influence of the operating function. It integrates the state of liquidity with the balancing of the assets and the degree of ownership. It is especially sensitive to deterioration of the structure caused by an unjustified increase in the fixed assets.

(16-26)

CONSTRUCTION $\text{Ratio (16-25)} \times \frac{CA}{TL} \times \frac{NW}{FA + WC}$

USE Sales and operating are likewise not involved in this tertiary control. This ratio reacts somewhat like the preceding one but is especially attuned to the gyrations (particularly as relates to noncurrent liabilities increases) of the financing of the fixed assets and the working capital. It reports on the *management* of the capital structure.

(16-27)

CONSTRUCTION Ratio (16-25) $\times \frac{CA}{TL} \times \frac{NP}{NS}$

USE Shows the effect of profit drives on the liability position. It is helpful in determining whether the drives for profit increase the liabilities to the danger point. Conversely, where liabilities have previously been committed to a high degree, the drop in profits with the same liability level will cause a negative reaction in this control. In a sense, this control shows the *productivity* of the capital structure; that is, the extent that operating and financial management worked together or at cross-purposes.

(16-28)

CONSTRUCTION Ratio (16-25) $\times \frac{CA}{TL} \times \frac{NP}{NW}$

USE Shows a trend toward satisfying the stockholders of the business. Where the manager has a greater desire to placate the stockholders than for earning profits on sales, he or she might unduly expand the borrowed capital, so that a given profit will show a greater return on the invested capital. In so doing, higher interest charges may be incurred which will reduce profits, but possibly not enough to impair the appearance of that profit against invested capital. If the return on the total resources (NP/TCE), however, is equal to or lower than the interest rate paid for borrowed capital, then the impact on the capital structure and on the return on invested capital will be very pronounced.

(16-29)

CONSTRUCTION $\text{Ratio (16-26)} \times \frac{NP}{TCE}$

USE This control introduces to the capital structure the need to make a profit. If Ratio (16-26) decreased, indicating a weakening of the management of the capital structure, there might be a rationale for it if the earnings on the total resources rise sufficiently.

This control, like all the other tertiary ratios, is not a linear one. A given percentage increase in one will not cancel out the effect of the other. Any change in one is bound to be greatly magnified in the other, and so a large improvement in the NP/TCE justified a rather small deterioration in the rest of Ratio (16-26).

(16-30)

CONSTRUCTION $\text{Ratio (16-25)} \times \frac{NW}{FA + WC}$

USE This tertiary ratio reports on the state of the structure as in Ratio (16-25) but slanted toward the ability of the net worth to cover the fixed assets and the working capital. It dramatically calls attention to an unbalancing of the above factors in companies that overtrade and that plan to expand their fixed capital.

EMPIRICAL NATURE OF RATIOS

There are almost an infinite number of tertiary ratios that can be constructed, each designed to serve a specific function. Many will suggest themselves to readers. However, this must be firmly borne in mind: these ratios have no absolute value, but if defined properly, they can pinpoint certain positive or negative qualities; their movements are not necessarily linear, so that the degree of negativeness or positiveness cannot be measured finely. Should a company gradually change its basic personality, product, and way of doing business, a tertiary ratio once selected as being functional may gradually become less useful. Ratios, like the creeping change, must be tested periodically. Generally, however, a well-defined and designed tertiary ratio will remain valid for many years.

CHAPTER SEVENTEEN

INTEGRATED CONTROL RATIOS FOR THE FIRM

The complexities and competitiveness of modern industry require that decisions made by management support and enhance the profit-making abilities of the company, consistent with its state of health. No one really knows the impact of decision making; some try to equate it with the "size" of the decision, assessing it by how many dollars are immediately at stake. The remarkable thing about decisions is that they are powerful levers for influencing the future: the trend, the growth, and ultimately the survival of the company, regardless of its present size.

SUMMARY OF CONTROL CONCEPT

We attempted to show that decision making is not an autonomous procedure, that it must be part of a whole. Yet controls can be established for the production effort with good results, especially if there are no regular means of presenting management with a weighted and balanced evaluation of production economy. Similarly, controls can be set up effectively for the sales activity so that maximum economy is obtained from the employees and the department. In the financial and capital areas, also, controls can be set up. For regardless of anything else, if the production and sales functions, even though working together, cannot be supported by the capital structure, the entire effort is academic. Therefore it is essential that we relate the financial and capital functions to the production and sales efforts. When this is done, we have total company integration, a procedure whereby the effect in any one area can be measured in the other two.

DECISIONS TOTALLY INTEGRATED

Generally, regardless of the particular term used to describe a department's activities any one decision made in production, sales promotion, purchasing, personnel, research and development, etc., can be assigned to production, sales, or capital for purposes of control.

To visualize the effect of decisions in one area as affecting the other two, consider that a decision in production to buy a machine affects the financial position because of the *cost* and *method* of financing it, and this affects the company's capital structure. It also affects the sales area because of the burden on it to obtain sufficient activity to recover the new machine's fixed expenses.

Consider that a decision in the sales area to promote certain products affects the production economy unless the products to be sold are aligned with production's needs for expense recovery. If they are not, the NS/FA might be reduced and/or the inventory under- or overburdened, depending on the product mix sold. The state of the company's vulnerability is changed.

Consider that a decision in the financial area to increase the borrowed portion of the total capital at favorable interest charges so that the return on the investors' capital can be boosted will reduce the current ratio and will cause pressure on the sales to move products of highest dollar value, which might be those of the highest material content. This in turn can negatively or positively affect the cost recovery needs of the production effort, depending on what facilities are involved for these selected products.

No matter where the decisions are made, or their ostensible immediate magnitude, their effect is felt in every molecule of the company's structure. The controls presented in this book will:

1. Give management an objective and weighted evaluation of any facet of its operation.
2. Enable control over any facet of its operation.
3. Give management an objective basis for measuring and pretesting its decisions.

TOTAL INTEGRATION TERTIARY RATIOS

Tertiary ratios for each of the major areas were constructed in Chapters 10, 13, and 16 for production, sales, and capital, respectively. These serve to provide upper management with condensed evaluations within each area.

However, as we saw previously, an event in one area affects events, movements, and economy states throughout the company. Frequently, it is beneficial to management to use control

EXHIBIT 17-1 COMPANY-WIDE TERTIARY RATIOS

Ratio No.	Construction
(17-1)	Ratio (10-23) × Ratio (13-17) × Ratio (16-7)
(17-2)	Ratio (10-25) × Ratio (13-19) × Ratio (16-19)
(17-3)	Ratio (10-16) × Ratio (13-12) × Ratio (16-17)
(17-4)	Ratio (9-5) × Ratio (13-30) × Ratio (16-5)
(17-5)	(AREC/BREC) × (FA/maint., repair, depreciation, and insurance costs.)
(17-6)	(AREC/BREC) × Ratio (16-22)
(17-7)	(AREC/MER) × Ratio (15-11)
(17-8)	(BREC/AREC) × TL
(17-9)	[(INV × MER)/AREC] × Ratio (15-1)
(17-10)	(AREC/BREC) × Ratio (15-4) × Ratio (15-12)
(17-11)	(BREC/AREC) × Ratio (15-1) × Ratio (15-25)
(17-12)	(AREC × TL)/MER
(17-13)	(AREC/BREC × Ratio (15-3)
(17-14)	(AREC/MER) × Ratio (15-2)

indices from which to get a total measure of the impact from one or more events regardless of where they occur in the company. These are called company-wide tertiary ratios and are constructed from data taken from the financial and operating areas. The terms of the ratios are primary data, elementary, advanced, and/or area tertiary ratios in any combination that will produce the desired measurement. And again, this is often an industry criterion.

Exhibit 17-1 lists some typical company-wide tertiary ratios and their constructions.

The following are descriptions and uses of some of these ratios.

COMPANY-WIDE TERTIARY RATIOS

(17-1)

CONSTRUCTION Ratio (10-23) × Ratio (13-17) × Ratio (16-7)

USE Used as a period evaluator of the total company economy. In this expression the profits earned in a previous period are placed in proper perspective: profits reported in the present but earned by previous performance are deserving of a positive evaluation only if the present events are tending toward the production of a profit at some future report date, i.e., simultaneous with the report of a profit, there coexists previous events as yet unconsidered in any profit statement which may influence a future profit positively or negatively. This circumstance is considered in this ratio.

(17-2)

CONSTRUCTION Ratio (10-25) × Ratio (13-19) × Ratio (16-19)

USE Relates the movements of the sales and production efforts to the shifts in the capital structure. Basically, an upward movement is positive and may originate from any of the three major company areas. A tertiary ratio of this type is designed on the assumption that top management is interested in total effect and leaves to the subordinate levels the task of intrafunctional improvement. A positive shift in this ratio is caused by many events, individually, or more commonly by a *combination* of events. These actions can be of various magnitudes and can be either positive or negative. This tertiary ratio gives the total effect on the company.

(17-3)

CONSTRUCTION Ratio (10-16) × Ratio (13-12) × Ratio (16-17)

USE Evaluates the justification for the excessive level of sales expenses in terms of the gains it brings to the company. Management will use this ratio to test in advance the merits of promoting a particular type of product mix.

(17-4)

CONSTRUCTION Ratio (9-5) × Ratio (13-30) × Ratio (16-5)

USE Shows the effect of productivity on the profitability of the company's total resources, consistent with its state of health and the support of sales. If the plant's productivity rises and it is not supported by a suitable effort in sales, the capital position of the company is affected and the value drops. A similar effect is shown when sales effort is being wasted because production cannot support it. This circumstance is felt in the financial areas, and the ratio drops.

Not all negations start in the operating area. For example, if the productive and sales efforts are satisfactory, the condition could be negated if such efforts unbalance the capital structure. Then, even in spite of high sales and shop productivity, this ratio will drop.

TERTIARY RATIOS INVOLVING COST RECOVERY

The state of cost recovery or velocity at any one time, when compared with previous periods and when sales trends are known, represents a fairly complete integration of operating performances; that is, the production-sales efforts and the effect on operating can be measured in terms of expense recovery. The missing link, of course, is the impact that the recovery state attained has on the capital structure, viz., its effect on the inventory levels, the inventory balances, and the trends toward better or poorer states of health, etc.

Acts in any area of the company will affect the state of recovery, its amount, its speed, its change of direction, etc. Conversely, decisions commencing with the needs for improved recovery will likewise impact on other areas. For example, a decision to revise product mix to improve recovery may boost inventory levels; a decision to finance a purchase or add equipment will increase the amount to be recovered. In the first case, the current asset and borrowed capital balance changes; in the second, the velocity of the recovery changes by shifts in equipment usages and an additional burden is placed on the sales effort.

The abbreviations used in the following ratio constructions are:

AREC = actual recovery
BREC = budgeted recovery
MER = maximum economic recovery (before duplication of facilities)

(17-5)

CONSTRUCTION (AREC/BREC) × (FA/maint., repair, depreciation, and insurance costs)

USE Shows the trend of the fixed-asset economy and is useful in predicting future economy for budgeting as well as for testing the probable effects when additional equipment is added.

(17-6)

CONSTRUCTION (AREC/BREC) × Ratio (16-22)

USE The ratio tests revisions of product mix. Obviously, the same sales level can produce varying levels of recovery, depending on the product mix.

(17-11)

CONSTRUCTION (BREC/AREC) × Ratio (15-1) × Ratio (15-25)

USE Appraises the effect of product mix and increased recovery on capital safety.

(17-12)

CONSTRUCTION (AREC × TL)/MER

USE Can the total liabilities stand the effect of using maximum usable capacity?

(17-14)

CONSTRUCTION (AREC/MER) × Ratio (15-2)

USE Shows the effect on inventory of drive for faster expense recovery.

INDEX